KU-048-625

ARCANUM
UNBOUNDED
THE COSMERE COLLECTION

Also by Brandon Sanderson from Gollancz:

*Mistborn*
The Final Empire
The Well of Ascension
The Hero of Ages
The Alloy of Law
Shadows of Self
The Bands of Mourning

*The Stormlight Archive*
The Way of Kings: Part One
The Way of Kings: Part Two
Words of Radiance: Part One
Words of Radiance: Part Two
Oathbringer: Part One
Oathbringer: Part Two

Edgedancer (novella)
Mistborn: Secret History (novella)

*The Reckoners*
Steelheart
Mitosis
Firefight
Calamity

*Legion*
Legion
Legion: Skin Deep
Legion: Lies of the Beholder

Skyward

*Collections*
Legion: The Many Lives of Stephen Leeds
Arcanum Unbounded: The Cosmere Collection
Legion and the Emperor's Soul

Elantris
Warbreaker
Alcatraz
Snapshot (novella)

# ARCANUM UNBOUNDED

## THE COSMERE COLLECTION

BRANDON SANDERSON

GOLLANCZ
LONDON

This edition first published in Great Britain in 2019 by Gollancz.
First published in Great Britain in 2016 by Gollancz
an imprint of the Orion Publishing Group Ltd
Carmelite House, 50 Victoria Embankment
London EC4Y 0DZ

An Hachette UK Company

1 3 5 7 9 10 8 6 4 2



Illustrations by Ben McSweeney and Isaac Stewart



A CIP catalogue record for this book is
available from the British Library.

ISBN (Hardback) 978 1 473 22593 0
ISBN (ebook) 978 1 473 21806 2

Printed in Great Britain by Clays Ltd, Elcograf S.p.A

www.brandonsanderson.com
www.orionbooks.co.uk
www.gollancz.co.uk

*For Nathan Hatfield*
*Who helped the Cosmere come to be.*

# CONTENTS

Acknowledgments 9
Preface 11

THE SELISH SYSTEM 15
The Emperor's Soul 19
The Hope of Elantris 125

THE SCADRIAN SYSTEM 149
The Eleventh Metal 153
Allomancer Jak and the Pits of Eltania, Episodes Twenty-Eight Through Thirty 175
Mistborn: Secret History 197

THE TALDAIN SYSTEM 367
White Sand 371

THE THRENODITE SYSTEM 415
Shadows for Silence in the Forests of Hell 419

THE DROMINAD SYSTEM 475
Sixth of the Dusk 479

THE ROSHARAN SYSTEM 533
Edgedancer 537

# ACKNOWLEDGMENTS

If I were to take the time to individually thank each and every person who helped with all the stories in here, this section might be as long as one of the stories themselves! Instead, I'm going to focus this note on the people who specifically helped put the collection together. (Along with the team that worked on *Edgedancer,* which is the story unique to this collection.)

But I do want to take a moment to give a hearty thanks to those who have worked with me on my short fiction over the years. Early in my career, I would never have dared consider myself a short-fiction writer—but ten years of practice has paid off, and the stories in this collection are the result. (Though do note, I use the word "short" loosely here. Most of these are very long for short fiction.)

A lot of wonderful people have helped me over the years; most of them are the names you'll commonly find at the start of my novels. I'm a lucky man to have had so much encouragement, feedback, and support during my career.

For *Arcanum Unbounded* specifically, Isaac Stewart (my longtime artistic collaborator) is responsible for the beautiful endpapers, the star charts, and most of the symbols you find inside the book. Ben McSweeney did the illustrations for the various stories, Dave Palumbo did the cover art, and Greg Collins was the designer.

Moshe Feder, editor for all of my epic fantasy novels, was the editor on this project—and though he wasn't officially the editor on many of the shorts when they were first published, he has a habit of stepping in and doing revisions for me, unpaid, on any short fiction I write. (Indeed, he gets mad if I don't send them to him, and refuses to invoice me if I try to pay him for them.) So he's done a ton of pro bono work over the years, helping me become a short-fiction writer. He deserves some extra praise for this.

And, as always, the Inciting Peter Ahlstrom was head of my in-house editorial efforts. (Literally in house. He works out of my home.) Peter is responsible for collecting all the comments from various people doing reads, adding his own detailed continuity and editorial notes, and then smoothing everything over once I've taken the hacksaw to stories.

The copyeditor was Terry McGarry. At Tor, thanks go to Tom Doherty, Marco Palmieri, Patti Garcia, Karl Gold, Rafal Gibek, and Robert Davis.

Joshua Bilmes was the agent on this in the United States, and John Berlyne was the agent in the UK. Heaps of thanks go to everyone at their respective agencies.

Our alpha and gamma readers on *Edgedancer* include Alice Arneson, Ben Oldsen, Bob Kluttz, Brandon Cole, Brian T. Hill, Darci Cole, David Behrens, Eric James Stone, Eric Lake, Gary Singer, Ian McNatt, Karen Ahlstrom, Kellyn Neumann, Kristina Kugler, Lyndsey Luther, Mark Lindberg, Matt Wiens, Megan Kanne, Nikki Ramsay, Paige Vest, Ross Newberry, and Trae Cooper.

And, as is traditional, I leave with a hearty thanks to my family: Joel, Dallin, Oliver, and Emily. You guys are awesome!

# PREFACE

The Cosmere has always been full of secrets.

I can trace my grand plan now to several key moments. The first is the emergence of Hoid, who dates back to my teenage years, when I conceived of a man who connected worlds that didn't know about one another. A person in on the secret that nobody else understood. While reading books by other authors, in my mind I inserted this man into the backgrounds, imagining him as the random person described in a crowd—and dreaming of the story behind the story of which he was a part.

The second moment that helped all this come together was reading the later books in the Foundation series by Isaac Asimov. I was awed by how he managed to tie the Robot novels and the Foundation novels together in one grand story. I knew I wanted to create something like this, an epic bigger than an epic. A story that spanned worlds and eras.

The third moment, then, was the first appearance of Hoid in a novel. I inserted him nervously, worried about making everything work. I didn't have my grand plan for the Cosmere at that point, only an inkling of what I wanted to do.

That story was *Elantris.* The next book I wrote, *Dragonsteel,* was never published. (It's not very good.) But in it I devised Hoid's backstory, and the backstory of the entire universe I named the Cosmere. *Elantris* wasn't picked up by a publisher until years after that point—and when it was, I had the grand plan in place. Mistborn, Stormlight, and *Elantris* became the core of it. (And you'll find stories relating to all three in this collection.)

I would guess that most people who read my works don't know that the majority of the books are connected, with a hidden story behind the story. This pleases me. I have often said that I don't want a reader to feel that they need to have my entire body of work memorized in order to enjoy a story. For now, Mistborn is just Mistborn, and Stormlight is just Stormlight. The stories of these worlds are at the forefront.

That isn't to say there aren't hints. Lots of them. I originally intended these cameo hints between the worlds to be much smaller, particularly at first. Many readers, however, grew to love them—and I realized I didn't need to be quite as stingy with the hidden story as I was being.

I still walk a fine line. All of the stories you read are intended to be self-contained, at least within the context of their own world. However, if you do dig deeper, there is much more to learn. More secrets, as Kelsier would say.

This collection takes a step closer to the connected nature of the Cosmere. Each story is prefaced by an annotation from Khriss, the woman who has been writing the Ars Arcanum appendixes at the ends of the novels. You'll also find star maps for each solar system. With things like this, the collection goes further than I've gone before in connecting the worlds. It hints at what is to come eventually: full crossovers in the Cosmere.

The time for that hasn't arrived yet. If all this overwhelms you, know that most of the stories in here can be read independently. A few take place chronologically after published novels—and this is noted at the beginning of those stories, so you know how to avoid spoilers, if you want.

None of the stories in the collection require knowledge of the Cosmere as a whole. The truth is, most of what's going on in the Cosmere hasn't yet been revealed, so you couldn't be expected to be up to date on it all.

That said, I do promise that this collection will provide not just questions, but at long last, some answers.

# ARCANUM UNBOUNDED

## THE COSMERE COLLECTION

# THE SELISH SYSTEM

The Selish System
dwarf planet
comet belt
Ralen / Raa
Ky / Kii
asteroid belt
Oem
Sel / Seol
Donne / Doo

# THE SELISH SYSTEM

CENTRAL to this system is the planet of Sel—home to multiple empires that, uniquely, have remained somewhat ignorant of one another. It is a willful kind of ignorance, with each of the three great domains pretending that the others are mere blips on the map, barely worth notice.

The planet itself facilitates this, as it is larger than most, with its size at around 1.5 cosmere standard, and gravity at 1.2 cosmere standard. Vast continents and sweeping oceans create a diverse landscape, with an extreme amount of variation on this one planet. Here you will find both snow-covered plains and expansive deserts, a fact I would have found remarkable upon my first visit, had I not by then discovered that this was a natural state of many planets in the cosmere.

Sel is notable for being dishardic, one of few planets in the cosmere to attract two separate Shards of Adonalsium: Dominion and Devotion. These Shards were extremely influential in the development of human societies on the planet, and most of their traditions and religions can be traced back to these two. Uniquely, the very languages and alphabets used today across the planet were directly influenced by the two Shards.

I believe that early on, the Shards took an unconcerned approach to humankind—and society was shaped by the slow, steady discovery of the powers that permeated the landscape. This is difficult to determine for certain now, however, as at some point in the distant past, both Devotion and Dominion were destroyed. Their Investiture—their power—was Splintered, their minds ripped away, their souls sent into the Beyond.

I am uncertain whether their power was left to ravage the world untamed for a time, or was immediately contained. This all happened during the days of human prehistory on Sel.

At this point, the bulk of the Investiture that made up the powers of Dominion and Devotion is trapped on the Cognitive Realm. Collectively, these powers—which have a polarized relationship—are called the Dor. Forced together as they are, trapped and bursting to escape, they power the various forms of magic on Sel, which are multitude.

Because the Cognitive Realm has distinct locations (unlike the Spiritual Realm, where most forms of Investiture reside), magic on Sel is very dependent upon physical position. In addition, the rules of perception and intent are greatly magnified on Sel, to the point that language—or similar functions—directly shapes the magic as it is pulled from the Cognitive Realm and put to use.

This overlap between language, location, and magic on the planet has become so integral to the system that subtle changes in one can have profound effects on how the Dor is accessed. Indeed, I believe that the very landscape itself has become Invested to the point that it has a growing self-awareness, in a way unseen on other planets in the cosmere. I do not know how this happened, or what the ramifications will be.

I've begun to wonder if something greater is happening on Sel than we, at the universities of Silverlight, have guessed. Something with origins lost in time. Perhaps the Ire know more, but they are not speaking on the topic, and have repeatedly denied my requests for collaboration.

Brief mention should be given to the entities known as the seons and the skaze, Splinters of self-aware Investiture who have developed humanlike mannerisms. I believe there is a link between them and the puzzle of Sel's nature.

The rest of the system is of little relevance. Though there are a number of other planets, only one exists in a habitable zone—if barely. It is barren, inhospitable, and prone to terrible dust storms. Its proximity to the sun, Mashe, makes it uncomfortably warm, even for one who has spent a good portion of her life on the Dayside of Taldain.

# THE EMPEROR'S SOUL

# PROLOGUE

GAOTONA ran his fingers across the thick canvas, inspecting one of the greatest works of art he had ever seen. Unfortunately, it was a lie.

"The woman is a danger." Hissed voices came from behind him. "What she does is an abomination."

Gaotona tipped the canvas toward the hearth's orange-red light, squinting. In his old age, his eyes weren't what they had once been. *Such precision,* he thought, inspecting the brushstrokes, feeling the layers of thick oils. Exactly like those in the original.

He would never have spotted the mistakes on his own. A blossom slightly out of position. A moon that was just a sliver too low in the sky. It had taken their experts days of detailed inspection to find the errors.

"She is one of the best Forgers alive." The voices belonged to Gaotona's fellow arbiters, the empire's most important bureaucrats. "She has a reputation as wide as the empire. We need to execute her as an example."

"No." Frava, leader of the arbiters, had a sharp, nasal voice. "She is a valuable tool. This woman can save us. We must use her."

*Why?* Gaotona thought again. *Why would someone capable of this artistry, this majesty, turn to forgery? Why not create original paintings? Why not be a true artist?*

*I must understand.*

"Yes," Frava continued, "the woman is a thief, and she practices a horrid art. But I can control her, and with her talents we can fix this mess we have found ourselves in."

The others murmured worried objections. The woman they spoke of, Wan ShaiLu, was more than a simple con artist. So much more. She could change the nature of reality itself. That raised another question. Why would she bother learning to paint? Wasn't ordinary art mundane compared to her mystical talents?

So many questions. Gaotona looked up from his seat beside the hearth. The others stood in a conspiratorial clump around Frava's desk, their long, colorful robes shimmering in the firelight. "I agree with Frava," Gaotona said.

The others glanced at him. Their scowls indicated they cared little for what he said, but their postures told a different tale. Their respect for him was buried deep, but it was remembered.

"Send for the Forger," Gaotona said, rising. "I would hear what she has to say. I suspect she will be more difficult to control than Frava claims, but we have no choice. We either use this woman's skill, or we give up control of the empire."

The murmurs ceased. How many years had it been since Frava and Gaotona had agreed on anything at all, let alone on something so divisive as making use of the Forger?

One by one, the other three arbiters nodded.

"Let it be done," Frava said softly.

# DAY TWO

SHAI pressed her fingernail into one of the stone blocks of her prison cell. The rock gave way slightly. She rubbed the dust between her fingers. Limestone. An odd material for use in a prison wall, but the whole wall wasn't of limestone, merely that single vein within the block.

She smiled. Limestone. That little vein had been easy to miss, but if she was right about it, she had finally identified all forty-four types of rock in the wall of her circular pit of a prison cell. Shai knelt down beside her bunk, using a fork—she'd bent back all of the tines but one—to carve notes into the wood of one bed leg. Without her spectacles, she had to squint as she wrote.

To Forge something, you had to know its past, its nature. She was almost ready. Her pleasure quickly slipped away, however, as she noticed another set of markings on the bed leg, lit by her flickering candle. Those kept track of her days of imprisonment.

*So little time*, she thought. If her count was right, only a day remained before the date set for her public execution.

Deep inside, her nerves were drawn as tight as strings on an instrument. One day. One day remaining to create a soulstamp and escape.

But she had no soulstone, only a crude piece of wood, and her only tool for carving was a fork.

It would be incredibly difficult. That was the point. This cell was meant for one of her kind, built of stones with many different veins of rock in them to make them difficult to Forge. They would come from different quarries and would each have a unique history. Knowing as little as she did, Forging them would be nearly impossible. And even if she did transform the rock, there was probably some other failsafe to stop her.

*Nights!* What a mess she'd gotten herself into.

Notes finished, she found herself looking at her bent fork. She'd begun carving the wooden handle, after prying off the metal portion, as a crude soulstamp. *You're not going to get out this way, Shai,* she told herself. *You need another method.*

She'd waited six days, searching for another way out. Guards to exploit, someone to bribe, a hint about the nature of her cell. So far, nothing had—

Far above, the door to the dungeons opened.

Shai leaped to her feet, tucking the fork handle into her waistband at the small of her back. Had they moved up her execution?

Heavy boots sounded on the steps leading into the dungeon, and she squinted at the newcomers who appeared above her cell. Four were guards, accompanying a man with long features and fingers. A Grand, the race who led the empire. That robe of blue and green indicated a minor functionary who had passed the tests for government service, but not risen high in its ranks.

Shai waited, tense.

The Grand leaned down to look at her through the grate. He paused for just a moment, then waved for the guards to unlock it. "The arbiters wish to interrogate you, Forger."

Shai stood back as they opened her cell's ceiling, then lowered a ladder. She climbed, wary. If *she* were going to take someone to an early execution, she'd have let the prisoner think something else was happening, so she wouldn't resist. However, they didn't lock Shai in manacles as they marched her out of the dungeons.

Judging by their route, they did indeed seem to be taking her toward the arbiters' study. Shai composed herself. A new challenge, then. Dared she hope for an opportunity? She shouldn't have been caught, but she could do nothing about that now. She had been bested, betrayed by the Imperial Fool when she'd assumed she could trust him. He had taken her copy of the Moon Scepter and swapped it for the original, then run off.

Shai's uncle Won had taught her that being bested was a rule of life. No matter how good you were, someone was better. Live by that knowledge, and you would never grow so confident that you became sloppy.

Last time she had lost. This time she would win. She abandoned all sense of frustration at being captured and became the person who could deal with this new chance, whatever it was. She would seize it and thrive.

This time, she played not for riches, but for her life.

The guards were Strikers—or, well, that was the Grand name for them. They had once called themselves Mulla'dil, but their nation had been folded into the empire so long ago that few used the name. Strikers were a tall people with a lean musculature and pale skin. They had hair almost as dark as Shai's, though theirs curled while hers lay straight and long. She tried with some success not to feel dwarfed by them. Her people, the MaiPon, were not known for their stature.

"You," she said to the lead Striker as she walked at the front of the group. "I remember you." Judging by that styled hair, the youthful captain did not often wear a helmet. Strikers were well regarded by the Grands, and their Elevation was not unheard of. This one had a look of eagerness to him. That polished armor, that crisp air. Yes, he fancied himself bound for important things in the future.

"The horse," Shai said. "You threw me over the back of your horse after I was captured. Tall animal, Gurish descent, pure white. Good animal. You know your horseflesh."

The Striker kept his eyes forward, but whispered under his breath, "I'm going to enjoy killing you, woman."

*Lovely,* Shai thought as they entered the Imperial Wing of the palace. The stonework here was marvelous, after the ancient Lamio style, with tall pillars of marble inlaid with reliefs. Those large urns between the pillars had been created to mimic Lamio pottery from long ago.

*Actually,* she reminded herself, *the Heritage Faction still rules, so . . .*

The emperor would be from that faction, as would the council of five arbiters who did much of the actual ruling. Their faction lauded the glory and learning of past cultures, even going so far as to rebuild their wing of the palace as an imitation of an ancient building. Shai suspected that on the bottoms of those "ancient" urns would be soulstamps that had transformed them into perfect imitations of famous pieces.

Yes, the Grands called Shai's powers an abomination, but their only aspect that was technically illegal was creating a Forgery to change a person. Quiet Forgery of objects was allowed, even exploited, in the empire so long as the Forger was carefully controlled. If someone were to turn over one of those urns and remove the stamp on the bottom, the piece would become simple unornamented pottery.

The Strikers led her to a door with gold inlay. As it opened, she managed to catch a glimpse of the red soulstamp on the bottom inside edge, transforming the door into an imitation of some work from the past. The guards ushered her into a homey room with a crackling hearth, deep rugs, and stained wood furnishings. *Fifth-century hunting lodge,* she guessed.

All five arbiters of the Heritage Faction waited inside. Three—two women, one man—sat in tall-backed chairs at the hearth. One other woman occupied the desk just inside the doors: Frava, senior among the arbiters of the Heritage Faction, was probably the most powerful person in the empire other than Emperor Ashravan himself. Her greying hair was woven into a long braid with gold and red ribbons; it draped a robe of matching gold. Shai had long pondered how to rob this woman, as—among her duties—Frava oversaw the Imperial Gallery and had offices adjacent to it.

Frava had obviously been arguing with Gaotona, the elderly male Grand standing beside the desk. He stood up straight and clasped his hands behind his back in a thoughtful pose. Gaotona was eldest of the ruling arbiters. He was said to be the least influential among them, out of favor with the emperor.

Both fell silent as Shai entered. They eyed her as if she were a cat that had just knocked over a fine vase. Shai missed her spectacles, but took care not to squint as she stepped up to face these people; she needed to look as strong as possible.

"Wan ShaiLu," Frava said, reaching to pick up a sheet of paper from the desk. "You have quite the list of crimes credited to your name."

*The way you say that . . .* What game was this woman playing? *She wants something of me,* Shai decided. *That is the only reason to bring me in like this.*

The opportunity began to unfold.

"Impersonating a noblewoman of rank," Frava continued, "breaking into the palace's Imperial Gallery, reForging your soul, and of course the attempted theft of the Moon Scepter. Did you really assume that we would fail to recognize a simple forgery of such an important imperial possession?"

*Apparently,* Shai thought, *you have done just that, assuming that the Fool escaped with the original.* It gave Shai a little thrill of satisfaction to know that her forgery now occupied the Moon Scepter's position of honor in the Imperial Gallery.

"And what of this?" Frava said, waving long fingers for one of the Strikers to bring something from the side of the room. A painting, which the guard placed on the desk. Han ShuXen's masterpiece *Lily of the Spring Pond.*

"We found this in your room at the inn," Frava said, tapping her fingers on the painting. "It is a copy of a painting I myself own, one of the most famous in the empire. We gave it to our assessors, and they judge that your forgery was amateur at best."

Shai met the woman's eyes.

"Tell me why you have created this forgery," Frava said, leaning forward. "You were obviously planning to swap this for the painting in my office by the Imperial Gallery. And yet, you were striving for the *Moon Scepter* itself. Why plan to steal the painting too? Greed?"

"My uncle Won," Shai said, "told me to always have a backup plan. I couldn't be certain the scepter would even be on display."

"Ah . . ." Frava said. She adopted an almost maternal expression, though it was laden with loathing—hidden poorly—and condescension. "You requested arbiter intervention in your execution, as most prisoners do. I decided on a whim to agree to your request because I was curious why you had created this painting." She shook her head. "But child, you can't honestly believe we'd let you free. With sins like this? You are in a monumentally bad predicament, and our mercy can only be extended so far."

Shai glanced toward the other arbiters. The ones seated near the fireplace seemed to be paying no heed, but they did not speak to one another. They were listening. *Something is wrong,* Shai thought. *They're worried.*

Gaotona still stood just to the side. He inspected Shai with eyes that betrayed no emotion.

Frava's manner had the air of one scolding a small child. The lingering end of her comment was intended to make Shai hope for release. Together, that was meant to make her pliable, willing to agree to anything in the hope that she'd be freed.

*An opportunity indeed . . .*

It was time to take control of this conversation.

"You want something from me," Shai said. "I'm ready to discuss my payment."

"Your *payment*?" Frava asked. "Girl, you are to be executed on the morrow! If we did wish something of you, the payment would be your life."

"My life is my own," Shai said. "And it has been for days now."

"Please," Frava said. "You were locked in the Forger's cell, with thirty different kinds of stone in the wall."

"Forty-four kinds, actually."

Gaotona raised an appreciative eyebrow.

*Nights! I'm glad I got that right. . . .*

Shai glanced at Gaotona. "You thought I wouldn't recognize the grindstone, didn't you? Please. I'm a Forger. I learned stone classification during my first year of training. That block was obviously from the Laio quarry."

Frava opened her mouth to speak, a slight smile to her lips.

"Yes, I know about the plates of ralkalest, the unForgeable metal, hidden behind the rock wall of my cell," Shai guessed. "The wall was a puzzle, meant to distract me. You wouldn't *actually* make a cell out of rocks like limestone, just in case a prisoner gave up on Forgery and tried to chip their way free. You built the wall, but secured it with a plate of ralkalest at the back to cut off escape."

Frava snapped her mouth shut.

"The problem with ralkalest," Shai said, "is that it's not a very strong metal. Oh, the grate at the top of my cell was solid enough, and I couldn't have gotten through that. But a thin plate? Really. Have you heard of anthracite?"

Frava frowned.

"It is a rock that burns," Gaotona said.

"You gave me a candle," Shai said, reaching into the small of her back. She tossed her makeshift wooden soulstamp onto the desk. "All I had to do was Forge the wall and persuade the stones that they're anthracite—not a difficult task, once I knew the forty-four types of rock. I could burn them, and they'd melt that plate behind the wall."

Shai pulled over a chair, seating herself before the desk. She leaned back. Behind her, the captain of the Strikers growled softly, but Frava drew her lips to a line and said nothing. Shai let her muscles relax, and she breathed a quiet prayer to the Unknown God.

Nights! It looked like they'd actually bought it. She'd worried they'd know enough of Forgery to see through her lie.

"I was going to escape tonight," Shai said, "but whatever it is you want me to do must be important, as you're willing to involve a miscreant like myself. And so we come to my payment."

"I could still have you executed," Frava said. "Right now. Here."

"But you won't, will you?"

Frava set her jaw.

"I warned you that she would be difficult to manipulate," Gaotona said to Frava. Shai could tell she'd impressed him, but at the same time, his eyes seemed . . . sorrowful? Was that the right emotion? She found this aged man as difficult to read as a book in Svordish.

Frava raised a finger, then swiped it to the side. A servant approached with a small, cloth-wrapped box. Shai's heart leaped upon seeing it.

The man clicked the latches open on the front and raised the top. The case was lined with soft cloth and inset with five depressions made to hold soulstamps. Each cylindrical stone stamp was as long as a finger and as wide as a large man's thumb. The leatherbound notebook set in the case atop them was worn by long use; Shai breathed in a hint of its familiar scent.

They were called Essence Marks, the most powerful kind of soulstamp. Each Essence Mark had to be attuned to a specific individual, and was intended to rewrite their history, personality, and soul for a short time. These five were attuned to Shai.

"Five stamps to rewrite a soul," Frava said. "Each is an abomination, illegal to possess. These Essence Marks were to be destroyed this afternoon. Even if you had escaped, you'd have lost these. How long does it take to create one?"

"Years," Shai whispered.

There were no other copies. Notes and diagrams were too dangerous to leave, even in secret, as such things gave others too much insight to one's soul. She never let these Essence Marks out of her sight, except on the rare occasion they were taken from her.

"You will accept these as payment?" Frava asked, lips turned down, as if discussing a meal of slime and rotted meat.

"Yes."

Frava nodded, and the servant snapped the case closed. "Then let me show you what you are to do."

Shai had never met an emperor before, let alone poked one in the face.

Emperor Ashravan of the Eighty Suns—forty-ninth ruler of the Rose Empire—did not respond as Shai prodded him. He stared ahead blankly, his round cheeks rosy and hale, but his expression completely lifeless.

"What happened?" Shai asked, straightening from beside the emperor's bed. It was in the style of the ancient Lamio people, with a headboard shaped like a phoenix rising toward heaven. She'd seen a sketch of such a headboard in a book; likely the Forgery had been drawn from that source.

"Assassins," Arbiter Gaotona said. He stood on the other side of the bed, alongside two surgeons. Of the Strikers, only their captain—Zu—had been allowed to enter. "The murderers broke in two nights ago, attacking the emperor and his wife. She was slain. The emperor received a crossbow bolt to the head."

"That considered," Shai noted, "he's looking remarkable."

"You are familiar with resealing?" Gaotona asked.

"Vaguely," Shai said. Her people called it Flesh Forgery. Using it, a surgeon of great skill could Forge a body to remove its wounds and scars. It required great specialization. The Forger had to know each and every sinew, each vein and muscle, in order to accurately heal.

Resealing was one of the few branches of Forgery that Shai hadn't studied in depth. Get an ordinary forgery wrong, and you created a work of poor artistic merit. Get a Flesh Forgery wrong, and people died.

"Our resealers are the best in the world," Frava said, walking around the foot of the bed, hands behind her back. "The emperor was attended to quickly following the assassination attempt. The wound to his head was healed, but . . ."

"But his mind was not?" Shai asked, waving her hand in front of the man's face again. "It doesn't sound like they did a very good job at all."

One of the surgeons cleared his throat. The diminutive man had ears like window shutters that had been thrown open wide on a sunny day. "Resealing repairs a body and makes it anew. That, however, is much like rebinding a book with fresh paper following a fire. Yes, it may look exactly the same, and it may be whole all the way through. The words, though . . . the words are gone. We have given the emperor a new brain. It is merely empty."

"Huh," Shai said. "Did you find out who tried to kill him?"

The five arbiters exchanged glances. Yes, they knew.

"We are not certain," Gaotona said.

"Meaning," Shai added, "you know, but you couldn't prove it well enough to make an accusation. One of the other factions in court, then?"

Gaotona sighed. "The Glory Faction."

Shai whistled softly, but it *did* make sense. If the emperor died, there was a good chance that the Glory Faction would win a bid to Elevate his successor. At forty, Emperor Ashravan was young still, by Grand standards. He had been expected to rule another fifty years.

If he were replaced, the five arbiters in this room would lose their positions—which, by imperial politics, would be a huge blow to their status. They'd drop from being the most powerful people in the world to being among the lowest of the empire's eighty factions.

"The assassins did not survive their attack," Frava said. "The Glory Faction does not yet know whether their ploy succeeded. You are going to replace the emperor's soul with . . ." She took a deep breath. "With a Forgery."

*They're crazy,* Shai thought. Forging one's own soul was difficult enough, and you didn't have to rebuild it from the ground up.

The arbiters had no idea what they were asking. But of course they didn't. They hated Forgery, or so they claimed. They walked on imitation floor tiles past copies of ancient vases, they let their surgeons repair a body, but they didn't call any of these things "Forgery" in their own tongue.

The Forgery of the soul, that was what they considered an abomination. Which meant Shai really was their only choice. No one in their own government would be capable of this. She probably wasn't either.

"Can you do it?" Gaotona asked.

*I have no idea,* Shai thought. "Yes," she said.

"It will need to be an exact Forgery," Frava said sternly. "If the Glory Faction has any inkling of what we've done, they will pounce. The emperor must not act erratically."

"I said I could do it," Shai replied. "But it will be difficult. I will need information about Ashravan and his life, everything we can get. Official histories will be a start, but they'll be too sterile. I will need extensive interviews and writings about him from those who knew him best. Servants, friends, family members. Did he have a journal?"

"Yes," Gaotona said.

"Excellent."

"Those documents are sealed," said one of the other arbiters. "He wanted them destroyed . . ."

Everyone in the room looked toward the man. He swallowed, then looked down.

"You shall have everything you request," Frava said.

"I'll need a test subject as well," Shai said. "Someone to test my Forgeries on. A Grand, male, someone who was around the emperor a lot and who knew him. That will let me see if I have the personality right."

Nights! Getting the personality right would be secondary. Getting a stamp that actually took . . . that would be the first step. She wasn't certain she could manage even that much. "And I'll need soulstone, of course."

Frava regarded Shai, arms folded.

"You can't possibly expect me to do this without soulstone," Shai said dryly. "I could carve a stamp out of wood, if I had to, but your goal will be difficult enough as it is. Soulstone. Lots of it."

"Fine," Frava said. "But you will be watched these three months. Closely."

"Three *months*?" Shai said. "I'm planning for this to take at least two years."

"You have a hundred days," Frava said. "Actually, ninety-eight, now."

*Impossible.*

"The official explanation for why the emperor hasn't been seen these last two days," said one of the other arbiters, "is that he's been in mourning for the death of his wife. The Glory Faction will assume we are scrambling to buy time following the emperor's death. Once the hundred days of isolation are finished, they will demand that Ashravan present himself to the court. If he does not, we are finished."

*And so are you,* the woman's tone implied.

"I will need gold for this," Shai said. "Take what you're thinking I'll demand and double it. I will walk out of this country rich."

"Done," Frava said.

*Too easy,* Shai thought. Delightful. They were planning to kill her once this was over.

Well, that gave her ninety-eight days to find a way out. "Get me those records," she said. "I'll need a place to work, plenty of supplies, and my things back." She held up a finger before they could complain. "Not my Essence Marks, but everything else. I'm not going to work for three months in the same clothing I've been wearing while in prison. And, as I consider it, have someone draw me a bath immediately."

# DAY THREE

The next day—bathed, well fed, and well rested for the first time since her capture—Shai received a knock at her door.

They'd given her a room. It was tiny, probably the most drab in the entire palace, and it smelled faintly of mildew. They had still posted guards to watch her all night, of course, and—from her memory of the layout of the vast palace—she was in one of the least frequented wings, one used mostly for storage.

Still, it was better than a cell. Barely.

At the knock, Shai looked up from her inspection of the room's old cedar table. It probably hadn't seen an oiling cloth in longer than Shai had been alive. One of her guards opened the door, letting in the elderly Arbiter Gaotona. He carried a box two handspans wide and a couple of inches deep.

Shai rushed over, drawing a glare from Captain Zu, who stood beside the arbiter. "Keep your distance from His Grace," Zu growled.

"Or what?" Shai asked, taking the box. "You'll stab me?"

"Someday, I will enjoy—"

"Yes, yes," Shai said, walking back to her table and flipping open the box's lid. Inside were eighteen soulstamps, their heads smooth and unetched. She felt a thrill and picked one up, holding it out and inspecting it.

She had her spectacles back now, so no more squinting. She also wore clothing far more fitting than that dingy dress. A flat, red, calf-length skirt and buttoned blouse. The Grands would consider it unfashionable, as among them, ancient-looking robes or wraps were the current style. Shai found those dreary. Under the blouse she wore a tight cotton shirt, and under the skirt she wore leggings. A lady never knew when she might need to ditch her outer layer of clothing to effect a disguise.

"This is good stone," Shai said of the stamp in her fingers. She took out one of her chisels, which had a tip almost as fine as a pinhead, and began to scrape at the rock. It *was* good soulstone. The rock came away easily and precisely. Soulstone was almost as soft as chalk, but did not chip when scraped. You could carve it with high precision, and then set it with a flame and a mark on the top, which would harden it to a strength closer to quartz. The only way to get a better stamp was to carve one from crystal itself, which was incredibly difficult.

For ink, they had provided bright red squid's ink, mixed with a small percentage of wax. Any fresh organic ink would work, though inks from animals were better than inks from plants.

"Did you . . . steal a vase from the hallway outside?" Gaotona asked, frowning toward an object sitting at the side of her small room. She'd snatched one of the vases on the way back from the bath. One of her guards had tried to interfere, but Shai had talked her way past the objection. That guard was now blushing.

"I was curious about the skills of your Forgers," Shai said, setting down her tools and hauling the vase up onto the table. She turned it on its side, showing the bottom and the red seal imprinted into the clay there.

A Forger's seal was easy to spot. It didn't just imprint onto the object's surface, it actually sank *into* the material, creating a depressed pattern of red troughs. The rim of the round seal was red as well, but raised, like an embossing.

You could tell a lot about a person from the way they designed their seals. This one, for example, had a sterile feel to it. No real art, which was a contrast to the minutely detailed and delicate beauty of the vase itself. Shai had heard that the Heritage Faction kept lines of half-trained Forgers working by rote, creating these pieces like rows of men making shoes in a factory.

"Our workers are *not* Forgers," Gaotona said. "We don't use that word. They are Rememberers."

"It's the same thing."

"They don't touch souls," Gaotona said sternly. "Beyond that, what we do is in appreciation of the past, rather than with the aim of fooling or scamming people. Our reminders bring people to a greater understanding of their heritage."

Shai raised an eyebrow. She took her mallet and chisel, then brought them down at an angle on the embossed rim of the vase's seal. The seal resisted—there was a *force* to it, trying to stay in place—but the blow broke through. The rest of the seal popped up, troughs vanishing, the seal becoming simple ink and losing its powers.

The colors of the vase faded immediately, bleeding to plain grey, and its shape warped. A soulstamp didn't just make visual changes, but rewrote an object's history. Without the stamp, the vase was a horrid piece. Whoever had thrown it hadn't cared about the end product. Perhaps they'd known it would be part of a Forgery. Shai shook her head and turned back to her work on the unfinished soulstamp. This wasn't for the emperor—she wasn't nearly ready for that yet—but carving helped her think.

Gaotona gestured for the guards to leave, all but Zu, who remained by his side. "You present a puzzle, Forger," Gaotona said once the other two guards were gone, the door closed. He settled down in one of the two rickety wooden chairs. They—along with the splintery bed, the ancient table, and the trunk with her things—made up the room's entire array of furniture. The single window had a warped frame that let in the breeze, and even the walls had cracks in them.

"A puzzle?" Shai asked, holding up the stamp before her, peering closely at her work. "What kind of puzzle?"

"You are a Forger. Therefore, you cannot be trusted without supervision. You will try to run the moment you think of a practicable escape."

"So leave guards with me," Shai said, carving some more.

"Pardon," Gaotona said, "but I doubt it would take you long to bully, bribe, or blackmail them."

Nearby, Zu stiffened.

"I meant no offense, Captain," Gaotona said. "I have great confidence in your people, but what we have before us is a master trickster, liar, and thief. Your best guards would eventually become clay in her hands."

"Thank you," Shai said.

"It was *not* a compliment. What your type touches, it corrupts. I worried about leaving you alone even for one day under the supervision of mortal eyes. From what I know of you, you could nearly charm the gods themselves."

She continued working.

"I cannot trust in manacles to hold you," Gaotona said softly, "as we are required to give you soulstone so that you can work on our . . . problem. You would turn your manacles to soap, then escape in the night laughing."

That statement, of course, betrayed a complete lack of understanding in how Forgery worked. A Forgery had to be likely—believable—otherwise it wouldn't take. Who would make a chain out of soap? It would be ridiculous.

What she *could* do, however, was discover the chain's origins and composition, then rewrite one or the other. She could Forge the chain's past so that one of the links had been cast incorrectly, which would give her a flaw to exploit. Even if she could not find the chain's exact history, she might be able to escape—an imperfect stamp would not take for long, but she'd only need a few moments to shatter the link with a mallet.

They could make a chain out of ralkalest, the unForgeable metal, but that would only delay her escape. With enough time, and soulstone, she would find a solution. Forging the wall to have a weak crack in it, so she could pull the chain free. Forging the ceiling to have a loose block, which she could let drop and shatter the weak ralkalest links.

She didn't want to do something so extreme if she didn't have to. "I don't see that you need to worry about me," Shai said, still working. "I am intrigued by what we are doing, and I've been promised wealth. That is enough to keep me here. Don't forget, I could have escaped my previous cell at any time."

"Ah yes," Gaotona said. "The cell in which you would have used Forgery to get through the wall. Tell me, out of curiosity, have you studied anthracite? That rock you said you'd turn the wall into? I seem to recall that it is very difficult to make burn."

*This one is more clever than people give him credit for being.*

A candle's flame would have trouble igniting anthracite—on paper, the rock burned at the correct temperature, but getting an entire sample hot enough was very difficult. "I was fully capable of creating a proper kindling environment with some wood from my bunk and a few rocks turned into coal."

"Without a kiln?" Gaotona said, sounding faintly amused. "With no bellows? But that is beside the point. Tell me, how were you planning to *survive* inside a cell where the wall was aflame at over two thousand degrees? Would not that kind of fire suck away all of the breathable air? Ah, but of course. You could have used your bed linens and transformed them into a poor conductor, perhaps glass, and made a shell for yourself to hide in."

Shai continued her carving, uncomfortable. The way he said that . . . Yes, he knew that she could not have done what he described. Most Grands were ignorant about the ways of Forgery, and this man certainly still was, but he *did* know enough to realize she couldn't have escaped as she said. No more than bed linens could become glass.

Beyond that, making the entire wall into another type of rock would have been difficult. She would have had to change too many things—rewritten history so that the quarries for each type of stone were near deposits of anthracite, and so that in each case, a block of the burnable rock was quarried by mistake. That was a huge stretch, an almost impossible one, particularly without specific knowledge of the quarries in question.

Plausibility was key to any forgery, magical or not. People whispered of Forgers turning lead into gold, never realizing that the reverse was far, far easier. Inventing a history for a bar of gold where somewhere along the line, someone had adulterated it with lead . . . well, that was a plausible lie. The reverse would be so unlikely that a stamp to make that transformation would not take for long.

"You impress me, Your Grace," Shai finally said. "You think like a Forger."

Gaotona's expression soured.

"That," she noted, "*was* meant as a compliment."

"I value truth, young woman. Not Forgery." He regarded her with the expression of a disappointed grandfather. "I have seen the work of your hands. That copied painting you did . . . it was *remarkable.* Yet it was accomplished in the name of lies. What great works could you create if you focused on industry and beauty instead of wealth and deception?"

"What I do *is* great art."

"No. You copy other people's great art. What you do is technically marvelous, yet completely lacking in spirit."

She almost slipped in her carving, hands growing tense. How *dare* he? Threatening to execute her was one thing, but insulting her art? He made her sound like . . . like one of those assembly-line Forgers, churning out vase after vase!

She calmed herself with difficulty, then plastered on a smile. Her aunt Sol had once told Shai to smile at the worst insults and snap at the minor ones. That way, no man would know your heart.

"So how *am* I to be kept in line?" she asked. "We have established that I am among the most vile wretches to slither through the halls of this palace. You cannot bind me and you cannot trust your own soldiers to guard me."

"Well," Gaotona said, "whenever possible, I personally will observe your work."

She would have preferred Frava—that one seemed as if she'd be easier to manipulate—but this was workable. "If you wish," Shai said. "Much of it will be boring to one who does not understand Forgery."

"I am not interested in being entertained," Gaotona said, waving one hand to Captain Zu. "Whenever I am here, Captain Zu will guard me. He is the only one of our Strikers to know the extent of the emperor's injury, and only he knows of our plan with you. Other guards will watch you during the rest of the day, and you are *not* to speak to them of your task. There will be no rumors of what we do."

"You don't need to worry about me talking," Shai said, truthfully for once. "The more people who know of a Forgery, the more likely it is to fail." *Besides,* she thought, *if I told the guards, you'd undoubtedly execute them to preserve your secrets.* She didn't like Strikers, but she liked the empire less, and the guards were really just another kind of slave. Shai wasn't in the business of getting people killed for no reason.

"Excellent," Gaotona said. "The second method of insuring your . . . attention to your project waits outside. If you would, good Captain?"

Zu opened the door. A cloaked figure stood with the guards. The figure stepped into the room; his walk was lithe, but somehow unnatural. After Zu closed the door, the figure removed his hood, revealing a face with milky white skin and red eyes.

Shai hissed softly through her teeth. "And you call what *I* do an abomination?"

Gaotona ignored her, standing up from his chair to regard the newcomer. "Tell her."

The newcomer rested long white fingers on her door, inspecting it. "I will place the rune here," he said in an accented voice. "If she leaves this room for any reason, or if she alters the rune or the door, I will know. My pets will come for her."

Shai shivered. She glared at Gaotona. "A Bloodsealer. You invited a *Bloodsealer* into your palace?"

"This one has proven himself an asset recently," Gaotona said. "He is loyal and he is discreet. He is also very effective. There are . . . times when one must accept the aid of darkness in order to contain a greater darkness."

Shai hissed softly again as the Bloodsealer removed something from within his robes. A crude soulstamp created from a bone. His "pets" would also be bone, Forgeries of human life crafted from the skeletons of the dead.

The Bloodsealer looked to her.

Shai backed away. "Surely you don't expect—"

Zu took her by the arms. Nights, but he was strong. She panicked.

Her Essence Marks! She needed her Essence Marks! With those, she could fight, escape, run . . .

Zu cut her along the back of her arm. She barely felt the shallow wound, but she struggled anyway. The Bloodsealer stepped up and inked his horrid tool in Shai's blood. He then turned and pressed the stamp against the center of her door.

When he withdrew his hand, he left a glowing red seal in the wood. It was shaped like an eye. The moment he marked the seal, Shai felt a sharp pain in her arm, where she'd been cut.

Shai gasped, eyes wide. Never had any person *dared* do such a thing to her. Almost better that she had been executed! Almost better that—

*Control yourself,* she told herself forcibly. *Become someone who can deal with this.*

She took a deep breath and let herself become someone else. An imitation of herself who was calm, even in a situation like this. It was a crude forgery, just a trick of the mind, but it worked.

She shook herself free from Zu, then accepted the kerchief Gaotona handed her. She glared at the Bloodsealer as the pain in her arm faded. He smiled at her with lips that were white and faintly translucent, like the skin of a maggot. He nodded to Gaotona before replacing his hood and stepping out of the room, closing the door after.

Shai forced herself to breathe evenly, calming herself. There was no subtlety to what the Bloodsealer did; they didn't traffic in subtlety. Instead of skill or artistry, they used tricks and blood. However, their craft was effective. The man would know if Shai left the room, and he had her fresh blood on his stamp, which was attuned to her. With that, his undead pets would be able to hunt her no matter where she ran.

Gaotona settled back down in his chair. "You know what will happen if you flee?"

Shai glared at Gaotona.

"You now realize how desperate we are," he said softly, lacing his fingers before him. "If you do run, we will give you to the Bloodsealer. Your bones will become his next pet. This promise was all he requested in payment. You may begin your work, Forger. Do it well, and you will escape this fate."

# DAY FIVE

WORK she did.

Shai began digging through accounts of the emperor's life. Few people understood how much Forgery was about study and research. It was an art any man or woman could learn; it required only a steady hand and an eye for detail.

That and a willingness to spend weeks, months, even *years* preparing the ideal soulstamp.

Shai didn't have years. She felt rushed as she read biography after biography, often staying up well into the night taking notes. She did not believe that she could do what they asked of her. Creating a believable Forgery of another man's soul, particularly in such a short time, just wasn't possible. Unfortunately, she had to make a good show of it while she planned her escape.

They didn't let her leave the room. She used a chamber pot when nature called, and for baths she was allowed a tub of warm water and cloths. She was under supervision at all times, even when bathing.

That Bloodsealer came each morning to renew his mark on the door. Each time, the act required a little blood from Shai. Her arms were soon laced with shallow cuts.

All the while, Gaotona visited. The ancient arbiter studied her as she read, watching with those eyes that judged . . . but also did not hate.

As she formulated her plans, she decided one thing: Getting free would probably require manipulating this man in some way.

# DAY TWELVE

SHAI pressed her stamp down on the tabletop.

As always, the stamp sank slightly into the material. A soulstamp left a seal you could feel, regardless of the material. She twisted the stamp a half turn—this did not blur the ink, though she did not know why. One of her mentors had taught that it was because by this point the seal was touching the object's soul and not its physical presence.

When she pulled the stamp back, it left a bright red seal in the wood as if carved there. Transformation spread from the seal in a wave. The table's dull grey splintery cedar became beautiful and well maintained, with a warm patina that reflected the light of the candles sitting across from her.

Shai rested her fingers on the new table; it was now smooth to the touch. The sides and legs were finely carved, inlaid here and there with silver.

Gaotona sat upright, lowering the book he'd been reading. Zu shuffled in discomfort at seeing the Forgery.

"What was that?" Gaotona demanded.

"I was tired of getting splinters," Shai said, settling back in her chair. It creaked. *You are next,* she thought.

Gaotona stood up and walked to the table. He touched it, as if expecting the transformation to be mere illusion. It was not. The fine table now looked horribly out of place in the dingy room. "This is what you've been doing?"

"Carving helps me think."

"You should be focused on your task!" Gaotona said. "This is frivolity. The empire itself is in danger!"

*No,* Shai thought. *Not the empire itself; just your rule of it.* Unfortunately, after eleven days, she still didn't have an angle on Gaotona, not one she could exploit.

"I *am* working on your problem, Gaotona," she said. "What you ask of me is hardly a simple task."

"And changing that table was?"

"Of course it was," Shai said. "All I had to do was rewrite its past so that it was maintained, rather than being allowed to sink into disrepair. That took hardly any work at all."

Gaotona hesitated, then knelt beside the table. "These carvings, this inlay . . . those were not part of the original."

"I might have added a little."

She wasn't certain if the Forgery would take or not. In a few minutes, that seal might evaporate and the table might revert to its previous state. Still, she was fairly certain she'd guessed the table's past well enough. Some of the histories she was reading mentioned what gifts had come from where. This table, she suspected, had come from far-off Svorden as a gift to Emperor Ashravan's predecessor. The strained relationship with Svorden had then led the emperor to lock it away and ignore it.

"I don't recognize this piece," Gaotona said, still looking at the table.

"Why should you?"

"I have studied ancient arts extensively," he said. "This is from the Vivare dynasty?"

"No."

"An imitation of the work of Chamrav?"

"No."

"What then?"

"Nothing," Shai said with exasperation. "It's not imitating anything;

it has become a better version of itself." That was a maxim of good Forgery: Improve slightly on an original, and people would often accept the fake because it *was* superior.

Gaotona stood up, looking troubled. *He's thinking again that my talent is wasted,* Shai thought with annoyance, moving aside a stack of accounts of the emperor's life. Collected at her request, these came from palace servants. She didn't want only the official histories. She needed authenticity, not sterilized recitations.

Gaotona stepped back to his chair. "I do not see how transforming this table could have taken hardly any work, although it clearly must be much simpler than what you have been asked to do. Both seem incredible to me."

"Changing a human soul is far more difficult."

"I can accept that conceptually, but I do not know the specifics. Why is it so?"

She glanced at him. *He wants to know more of what I'm doing,* she thought, *so that he can tell how I'm preparing to escape.* He knew she would be trying, of course. They both would pretend that neither knew that fact.

"All right," she said, standing and walking to the wall of her room. "Let's talk about Forgery. Your cage for me had a wall of forty-four types of stone, mostly as a trap to keep me distracted. I had to figure out the makeup and origin of each block if I wanted to try to escape. Why?"

"So you could create a Forgery of the wall, obviously."

"But why all of them?" she asked. "Why not just change one block or a few? Why not just make a hole big enough to slip into, creating a tunnel for myself?"

"I . . ." He frowned. "I have no idea."

Shai rested her hand against the outer wall of her room. It had been painted, though the paint was coming off in several sections. She could feel the separate stones. "All things exist in three Realms, Gaotona. Physical, Cognitive, Spiritual. The Physical is what we feel, what is before us. The Cognitive is how an object is viewed and how it views itself. The Spiritual Realm contains an object's soul—its essence—as well as the ways it is connected to the things and people around it."

"You must understand," Gaotona said, "I don't subscribe to your pagan superstitions."

"Yes, you worship the sun instead," Shai said, failing to keep the amusement out of her voice. "Or, rather, eighty suns—believing that even though each looks the same, a different sun actually rises each day. Well, you wanted to know how Forgery works, and why the emperor's soul will be so difficult to reproduce. The Realms are important to this."

"Very well."

"Here is the point. The longer an object exists as a whole, and the longer it is *seen* in that state, the stronger its sense of complete identity becomes. That table is made up of various pieces of wood fitted together, but do we think of it that way? No. We see the whole.

"To Forge the table, I must understand it as a whole. The same goes for a wall. That wall has existed long enough to view itself as a single entity. I could, perhaps, have attacked each block separately—they might still be distinct enough—but doing so would be difficult, as the wall wants to act as a whole."

"The wall," Gaotona said flatly, "*wants* to be treated as a whole."

"Yes."

"You imply that the wall has a soul."

"All things do," she said. "Each object sees itself as something. Connection and intent are vital. This is why, Master Arbiter, I can't simply write down a personality for your emperor, stamp him, and be done. Seven reports I've read say his favorite color was green. Do you know why?"

"No," Gaotona said. "Do you?"

"I'm not sure yet," Shai said. "I *think* it was because his brother, who died when Ashravan was six, had always been fond of it. The emperor latched on to it, as it reminds him of his dead sibling. There might be a touch of nationalism to it as well, as he was born in Ukurgi, where the provincial flag is predominantly green."

Gaotona seemed troubled. "You must know something that specific?"

"Nights, yes! And a thousand things just as detailed. I can get some wrong. I *will* get some wrong. Most of them, hopefully, won't matter—they will make his personality a little off, but each person changes day to day in any case. If I get too many wrong, though, the personality won't matter because the stamp won't take. At least, it won't last long enough to do any good. I assume that if your emperor has to be restamped every fifteen minutes, the charade will be impossible to maintain."

"You assume correctly."

Shai sat down with a sigh, looking over her notes.

"You said you could do this," Gaotona said.

"Yes."

"You've done it before, with your own soul."

"I know my own soul," she said. "I know my own history. I know what I can change to get the effect I need—and even getting my own Essence Marks right was difficult. Now I not only have to do this for another person, but the transformation must be far more extensive. And I have ninety days left to do it."

Gaotona nodded slowly.

"Now," she said, "you should tell me what you're doing to keep up the pretense that the emperor is still awake and well."

"We're doing all that needs to be done."

"I'm far from confident that you are. I think you'll find me a fair bit better at deception than most."

"I think that *you* will be surprised," Gaotona said. "We are, after all, politicians."

"All right, fine. But you are sending food, aren't you?"

"Of course," Gaotona said. "Three meals are sent to the emperor's quarters each day. They return to the palace kitchens eaten, though he is, of course, secretly being fed broth. He drinks it when prompted, but stares ahead, as if both deaf and mute."

"And the chamber pot?"

"He has no control over himself," Gaotona said, grimacing. "We keep him in cloth diapers."

"Nights, man! And no one changes a fake chamber pot? Don't you think that's suspicious? Maids will gossip, as will guards at the door. You need to consider these things!"

Gaotona had the decency to blush. "I will see that it happens, though

I don't like the idea of someone else entering his quarters. Too many have a chance to discover what has happened to him."

"Pick someone you trust, then," Shai said. "In fact, make a rule at the emperor's doors. No one enters unless they bear a card with your personal signet. And yes, I know why you are opening your mouth to object. I know exactly how well guarded the emperor's quarters are—that was part of what I studied to break into the gallery. Your security isn't tight enough, as the assassins proved. Do what I suggest. The more layers of security, the better. If what has happened to the emperor gets out, I have no doubt that I'll end up back in that cell waiting for execution."

Gaotona sighed, but nodded. "What else do you suggest?"

# DAY SEVENTEEN

A COOL breeze laden with unfamiliar spices crept through the cracks around Shai's warped window. The low hum of cheers seeped through as well. Outside, the city celebrated. Delbahad, a holiday no one had known about until two years earlier. The Heritage Faction continued to dig up and revive ancient feasts in an effort to sway public opinion back toward them.

It wouldn't help. The empire was not a republic, and the only ones who would have a say in anointing a new emperor would be the arbiters of the various factions. Shai turned her attention away from the celebrations, and continued to read from the emperor's journal.

*I have decided, at long last, to agree to the demands of my faction,* the book read. *I will offer myself for the position of emperor, as Gaotona has so often encouraged. Emperor Yazad grows weak with his disease, and a new choice will be made soon.*

Shai made a notation. Gaotona had encouraged Ashravan to seek the throne. And yet, later in the journal, Ashravan spoke of Gaotona with contempt. Why the change? She finished the notation, then turned to another entry, years later.

Emperor Ashravan's personal journal fascinated her. He had written it with his own hand, and had included instructions for it to be destroyed upon his death. The arbiters had delivered the journal to her reluctantly, and with vociferous justification. He hadn't died. His body still lived. Therefore, it was just fine for them *not* to burn his writings.

They spoke with confidence, but she could see the uncertainty in their eyes. They were easy to read—all but Gaotona, whose inner thoughts continued to elude her. They didn't understand the purpose of this journal. Why write, they wondered, if not for posterity? Why put your thoughts to paper if not for the purpose of having others read them?

*As easy,* she thought, *to ask a Forger why she would get satisfaction from creating a fake and seeing it on display without a single person knowing it was her work—and not that of the original artist—they were revering.*

The journal told her far more about the emperor than the official histories had, and not just because of the contents. The pages of the book were worn and stained from constant turning. Ashravan *had* written this book to be read—by himself.

What memories had Ashravan sought so profoundly that he would read this book over and over and over again? Was he vain, enjoying the thrill of past conquests? Was he, instead, insecure? Did he spend hours searching these words because he wanted to justify his mistakes? Or was there another reason?

The door to her chambers opened. They had stopped knocking. Why would they? They already denied her any semblance of privacy. She was still a captive, just a more important one than before.

Arbiter Frava entered, graceful and long-faced, wearing robes of a soft violet. Her grey braid was spun with gold and violet this time. Captain Zu guarded her. Inwardly, Shai sighed, adjusting her spectacles. She had been anticipating a night of study and planning, uninterrupted now that Gaotona had gone to join the festivities.

"I am told," Frava said, "that you are progressing at an unremarkable pace."

Shai set down the book. "Actually, this is quick. I am nearly ready to begin crafting stamps. As I reminded Arbiter Gaotona earlier today, I do still need a test subject who knew the emperor. The connection between them will allow me to test stamps on him, and they will stick briefly—long enough for me to try out a few things."

"One will be provided," Frava replied, walking along the table with its glistening surface. She ran a finger across it, then stopped at the red seal mark. The arbiter prodded at it. "Such an eyesore. After going to such trouble to make the table more beautiful, why not put the seal on the bottom?"

"I'm proud of my work," Shai said. "Any Forger who sees this can inspect it and see what I've done."

Frava sniffed. "You should not be proud of something like this, little thief. Besides, isn't the point of what you do to *hide* the fact that you've done it?"

"Sometimes," Shai said. "When I imitate a signature or counterfeit a painting, the subterfuge is part of the act. But with Forgery, true Forgery, you cannot hide what you've done. The stamp will always be there, describing exactly what has happened. You might as well be proud of it."

It was the odd conundrum of her life. To be a Forger was not just about soulstamps—it was about the art of mimicry in its entirety. Writing, art, personal signets . . . an apprentice Forger—mentored half in secret by her people—learned all mundane forgery before being taught to use soulstamps.

The stamps were the highest order of their art, but they were the most difficult to hide. Yes, a seal could be placed in an out-of-the-way place on an object, then covered over. Shai had done that very thing on occasion. However, so long as the seal was somewhere to be found, a Forgery could not be perfect.

"Leave us," Frava said to Zu and the guards.

"But—" Zu said, stepping forward.

"I do not like to repeat myself, Captain," Frava said.

Zu growled softly, but bowed in obedience. He gave Shai a glare—that was practically a second occupation for him, these days—and retreated with his men. They shut the door with a click.

The Bloodsealer's stamp still hung there on the door, renewed this morning. The Bloodsealer came at the same time most days. Shai had kept specific notes. On days when he was a little late, his seal started to dim right before he arrived. He always got to her in time to renew it, but perhaps someday . . .

Frava inspected Shai, eyes calculating.

Shai met that gaze with a steady one of her own. "Zu assumes I'm going to do something horrible to you while we're alone."

"Zu is simpleminded," Frava said, "though he is very useful when someone needs to be killed. Hopefully you won't ever have to experience his efficiency firsthand."

"You're not worried?" Shai said. "You are alone in a room with a monster."

"I'm alone in a room with an opportunist," Frava said, strolling to the door and inspecting the seal burning there. "You won't harm me. You're too curious about why I sent the guards away."

*Actually,* Shai thought, *I know precisely why you sent them away. And why you came to me during a time when all of your associate arbiters were guaranteed to be busy at the festival.* She waited for Frava to make the offer.

"Has it occurred to you," Frava said, "how . . . useful to the empire it would be to have an emperor who listened to a voice of wisdom when it spoke to him?"

"Surely Emperor Ashravan already did that."

"On occasion," Frava said. "On other occasions, he could be . . . belligerently foolish. Wouldn't it be amazing if, upon his rebirth, he were found lacking that tendency?"

"I thought you wanted him to act exactly like he used to," Shai said. "As close to the real thing as possible."

"True, true. But you are renowned as one of the greatest Forgers ever to live, and I have it on good authority that you are specifically talented with stamping your own soul. Surely you can replicate dear Ashravan's soul with authenticity, yet also make him inclined to listen to reason . . . when that reason is spoken by specific individuals."

*Nights afire,* Shai thought. *You're willing to just come out and say it, aren't you? You want me to build a back door into the emperor's soul, and you don't even have the decency to feel ashamed about that.*

"I . . . might be able to do such a thing," Shai said, as if considering it for the first time. "It would be difficult. I'd need a reward worth the effort."

"A suitable reward *would* be appropriate," Frava said, turning to her. "I realize you were probably planning to leave the Imperial Seat following your release, but why? This city could be a place of great opportunity to you, with a sympathetic ruler on the throne."

"Be more blunt, Arbiter," Shai said. "I have a long night ahead of me studying while others celebrate. I don't have the mind for word games."

"The city has a thriving clandestine smuggling trade," Frava said. "Keeping track of it has been a hobby of mine. It would serve me to have someone proper running it. I will give it to you, should you do this task for me."

That was always their mistake—assuming they knew why Shai did what she did. Assuming she'd jump at a chance like this, assuming that a smuggler and a Forger were basically the same thing because they both disobeyed someone else's laws.

"That sounds pleasant," Shai said, smiling her most genuine smile—the one that had an edge of overt deceptiveness to it.

Frava smiled deeply in return. "I will leave you to consider," she said, pulling open the door and clapping for the guards to reenter.

Shai sank down into her chair, horrified. Not because of the offer—she'd been expecting one like it for days now—but because she had only now understood the implications. The offer of the smuggling trade was, of course, false. Frava might have been able to deliver such a thing, but she wouldn't. Even assuming that the woman hadn't already been planning to have Shai killed, this offer sealed that eventuality.

There was more to it, though. Far more. *So far as she knows, she just planted in my head the idea of building control into the emperor. She won't trust my Forgery. She'll be expecting me to put in back doors of my own, ones that give* me *and not her complete control over Ashravan.*

What did that mean?

It meant that Frava had another Forger standing by. One, likely, without the talent or the bravado to try Forging someone else's soul—but one who could look over Shai's work and find any back doors she put in. This Forger would be better trusted, and could rewrite Shai's work to put Frava in control.

They might even be able to finish Shai's work, if she got it far enough along first. Shai had intended to use the full hundred days to plan her escape, but now she realized that her sudden extermination could come at any time.

The closer she got to finishing the project, the more likely that grew.

# DAY THIRTY

"THIS is new," Gaotona said, inspecting the stained-glass window.

That had been a particularly pleasing bit of inspiration on Shai's part. Attempts to Forge the window to a better version of itself had repeatedly failed; each time, after five minutes or so, the window had reverted to its cracked, gap-sided self.

Then Shai had found a bit of colored glass rammed into one side of the frame. The window, she realized, had once been a stained-glass piece, like many in the palace. It had been broken, and whatever had shattered the window had also bent the frame, producing those gaps that let in the frigid breeze.

Rather than repairing it as it had been meant to be, someone had put ordinary glass into the window and left it to crack. A stamp from Shai in the bottom right corner had restored the window, rewriting its history so that a caring master craftsman had discovered the fallen window and remade it. That seal had taken immediately. Even after all this time, the window had seen itself as something beautiful.

Or maybe she was just getting romantic again.

"You said you would bring me a test subject today," Shai said, blowing the dust off the end of a freshly carved soulstamp. She engraved a series of quick marks on the back—the side opposite the elaborately carved front. The setting mark finished every soulstamp, indicating no more carving was to come. Shai had always fancied it to look like the shape of MaiPon, her homeland.

Those marks finished, she held the stamp over a flame. This was a property of soulstone; fire hardened it, so it could not be chipped. She didn't need to take this step. The anchoring marks on the top were all it really needed, and she could carve a stamp out of anything, really, so long as the carving was precise. Soulstone was prized, however, because of this hardening process.

Once the entire thing was blackened from the candle's flame—first one end, then the other—she held it up and blew on it strongly. Flakes of char blew free with her breath, revealing the beautiful red and grey marbled stone beneath.

"Yes," Gaotona said. "A test subject. I brought one, as promised." Gaotona crossed the small room toward the door, where Zu stood guard.

Shai leaned back in her chair, which she'd Forged into something far more comfortable a couple of days back, and waited. She had made a bet with herself. Would the subject be one of the emperor's guards? Or would it be some lowly palace functionary, perhaps the man who took notes for Ashravan? Which person would the arbiters force to endure Shai's blasphemy in the name of a supposedly greater good?

Gaotona sat down in the chair by the door.

"Well?" Shai asked.

He raised his hands to the sides. "You may begin."

Shai dropped her feet to the ground, sitting up straight. "You?"

"Yes."

"You're one of the arbiters! One of the most powerful people in the empire!"

"Ah," he said. "I had not noticed. I fit your specifications. I am male, was born in Ashravan's own birthplace, and I knew him very well."

"But . . ." Shai trailed off.

Gaotona leaned forward, clasping his hands. "We debated this for weeks. Other options were offered, but it was determined that we could not in good conscience order one of our people to undergo this blasphemy. The only conclusion was to offer up one of ourselves."

Shai shook herself free of shock. *Frava would have had no trouble ordering someone else to do this,* she thought. *Nor would the others. You must have insisted upon this, Gaotona.*

They considered him a rival; they were probably happy to let him fall to Shai's supposedly horrible, twisted acts. What she planned was perfectly harmless, but there was no way she'd convince a Grand of that. Still, she found herself wishing she could put Gaotona at ease as she pulled her chair up beside him and opened the small box of stamps she had crafted over the past three weeks.

"These stamps will not take," she said, holding up one of them. "That is a Forger's term for a stamp that makes a change that is too unnatural to be stable. I doubt any of these will affect you for longer than a minute—and that's assuming I did them correctly."

Gaotona hesitated, then nodded.

"The human soul is different from that of an object," Shai continued. "A person is constantly growing, changing, shifting. That makes a soulstamp used on a person wear out in a way that doesn't happen with objects. Even in the best of cases, a soulstamp used on a person lasts only a day. My Essence Marks are an example. After about twenty-six hours, they fade away."

"So . . . the emperor?"

"If I do my job well," Shai said, "he will need to be stamped each morning, much as the Bloodsealer stamps my door. I will fashion into the seal, however, the capacity for him to remember, grow, and learn—he won't revert back to the same state each morning, and will be able to build upon the foundation I give him. However, much as a human body wears down and needs sleep, a soulstamp on one of us must be reset. Fortunately, anyone can do the stamping—Ashravan himself should be able to—once the stamp itself is prepared correctly."

She gave Gaotona the stamp she held, letting him inspect it.

"Each of the particular stamps I will use today," she continued, "will change something small about your past or your innate personality. As you are not Ashravan, the changes will not take. However, you two are similar enough in history that the seals should last for a short time, if I've done them well."

"You mean this is a . . . pattern for the emperor's soul?" Gaotona asked, looking over the stamp.

"No. Just a Forgery of a small part of it. I'm not even sure if the final product will work. So far as I know, no one has ever tried something exactly like this before. But there are accounts of people Forging someone else's soul for . . . nefarious purposes. I'm drawing on that knowledge to accomplish this. From what I know, if these seals last for at least a minute on you, they should last far longer on the emperor, as they are attuned to his specific past."

"A small piece of his soul," Gaotona said, handing back the seal. "So these tests . . . you will not use these seals in the final product?"

"No, but I'll take the patterns that work and incorporate them into a greater fabrication. Think of these seals as single characters in a large scroll; once I am done, I'll be able to put them together and tell a story. The story of a man's history and personality. Unfortunately, even if the Forgery takes, there will be small differences. I suggest that you begin spreading rumors that the emperor was wounded. Not terribly, mind you, but imply a good knock to the head. That will explain discrepancies."

"There are already rumors of his death," Gaotona said, "spread by the Glory Faction."

"Well, indicate he was wounded instead."

"But—"

Shai raised the stamp. "Even if I accomplish the impossible—which, mind you, I've done only on rare occasions—the Forgery will not have all of the emperor's memories. It can only contain things I have been able to read about or guess. Ashravan will have had many private conversations that the Forgery will *not* be able to recall. I can imbue him with a keen ability to fake—I have a particular understanding of that sort of thing—but fakery can only take a person so far. Eventually, someone will realize that he has large holes in his memory. Spread the rumors, Gaotona. You're going to need them."

He nodded, then pulled back his sleeve to expose his arm for her to stamp. She raised the stamp, and Gaotona sighed, then squeezed his eyes shut and nodded again.

She pressed it against his skin. As always, when the stamp touched the skin, it felt as if she were pressing it against something rigid—as if his arm had become stone. The stamp *sank in* slightly. That made for a disconcerting sensation when working on a person. She rotated the stamp, then pulled it back, leaving a red seal on Gaotona's arm. She took out her pocket watch, observing the ticking hand.

The seal gave off faint wisps of red smoke; that happened only when living things were stamped. The soul fought against the rewriting. The seal didn't puff away immediately, though. Shai released a held breath. That was a good sign.

She wondered . . . if she were to try something like this on the emperor, would his soul fight against the invasion? Or instead, would it accept the stamp, wishing to have righted what had gone wrong? Much as that window had wanted to be restored to its former beauty. She didn't know.

Gaotona opened his eyes. "Did it . . . work?"

"It took, for now," Shai said.

"I don't feel any different."

"That is the point. If the emperor could *feel* the stamp's effects, he would realize that something was wrong. Now, answer me without thought; speak by instinct only. What is your favorite color?"

"Green," he said immediately.

"Why?"

"Because . . ." He trailed off, cocking his head. "Because it is."

"And your brother?"

"I hardly remember him," Gaotona said with a shrug. "He died when I was very young."

"It is good he did," Shai said. "He would have made a terrible emperor, if he had been chosen in—"

Gaotona stood up. "Don't you dare speak ill of him! I will have you . . ." He stiffened, glancing at Zu, who had reached for his sword in alarm. "I . . . Brother . . . ?"

The seal faded away.

"A minute and five seconds," Shai said. "That one looks good."

Gaotona raised a hand to his head. "I can remember having a brother. But . . . I don't have one, and never have. I can remember idolizing him; I can remember pain when he died. Such *pain* . . ."

"That will fade," Shai said. "The impressions will wash away like the remnants of a bad dream. In an hour, you'll barely be able to recall what it was that upset you." She scribbled some notes. "I think you reacted too strongly to me insulting your brother's memory. Ashravan worshipped his brother, but kept his feelings buried deep out of guilt that perhaps his brother would have made a better emperor than he."

"What? Are you sure?"

"About this?" Shai said. "Yes. I'll have to revise that stamp a little bit, but I think it is mostly right."

Gaotona sat back down, regarding her with ancient eyes that seemed to be trying to pierce her, to dig deep inside. "You know a great deal about people."

"It's one of the early steps of our training," Shai said. "Before we're even allowed to *touch* soulstone."

"Such potential . . ." Gaotona whispered.

Shai forced down an immediate burst of annoyance. How dare he look at her like that, as if she were wasting her life? She loved Forgery. The thrill, a life spent getting ahead by her wits. That was what she *was*. Wasn't it?

She thought of one specific Essence Mark, locked away with the others. It was one Mark she had never used, yet was at the same time the most precious of the five.

"Let's try another," Shai said, ignoring those eyes of Gaotona's. She couldn't afford to grow offended. Aunt Sol had always said that pride would be Shai's greatest danger in life.

"Very well," Gaotona said, "but I am confused at one thing. From what little you've told me of this process, I cannot fathom why these seals even begin to work on me. Don't you need to know a thing's history exactly to make a seal work on it?"

"To make them stick, yes," Shai said. "As I've said, it's about plausibility."

"But this is completely implausible! I don't have a brother."

"Ah. Well, let me see if I can explain," she said, settling back. "I am rewriting your soul to match that of the emperor—just as I rewrote the history of that window to include new stained glass. In both cases, it works because of *familiarity.* The window frame knows what a stained-glass window should look like. It once had stained glass in it. Even though the new window is not the same as the one it once held, the seal works because the general concept of a stained-glass window has been fulfilled.

"You spent a great deal of time around the emperor. Your soul is familiar with his, much as the window frame is familiar with the stained glass. This is why I have to try out the seals on someone like you, and not on myself. When I stamp you, it's like . . . it's like I'm presenting to your soul a piece of something it should know. It only works if the piece is very small, but so long as it is—and so long as the soul considers the piece a familiar part of Ashravan, as I've indicated—the stamp will take for a brief time before being rejected."

Gaotona regarded her with bemusement.

"Sounds like superstitious nonsense to you, I assume?" Shai said.

"It is . . . rather mystical," Gaotona said, spreading his hands before him. "A window frame knowing the 'concept' of a stained-glass window? A soul understanding the concept of another soul?"

"These things exist beyond us," Shai said, preparing another seal. "We think about windows, we know about windows; what is and isn't a window takes on . . . meaning, in the Spiritual Realm. Takes on life, after a fashion. Believe the explanation or do not; I guess it doesn't matter. The fact is that I can try these seals on you, and if they stick for at least a minute, it's a very good indication that I've hit on something.

"Ideally, I'd try this on the emperor himself, but in his state, he would not be able to answer my questions. I need to not only get these to take, but I need to make them work together—and that will require your explanations of what you are feeling so I can nudge the design in the right directions. Now, your arm again, please?"

"Very well." Gaotona composed himself, and Shai pressed another seal against his arm. She locked it with a half turn, but as soon as she pulled the stamp away, the seal vanished in a puff of red.

"Blast," Shai said.

"What happened?" Gaotona said, reaching fingers to his arm. He smeared mundane ink; the seal had vanished so quickly, the ink hadn't even been incorporated into its workings. "What have you done to me this time?"

"Nothing, it appears," Shai said, inspecting the head of the stamp for flaws. She found none. "I had *that* one wrong. Very wrong."

"What was it?"

"The reason Ashravan agreed to become emperor," Shai said. "Nights afire. I was certain I had this one." She shook her head, setting the stamp aside. Ashravan, it appeared, had not stepped up to offer himself as emperor because of a deep-seated desire to prove himself to his family and to escape the distant—but long—shadow of his brother.

"I can tell you why he did it, Forger," Gaotona said.

She eyed him. *This man encouraged Ashravan to step toward the imperial throne,* she thought. Ashravan eventually hated him for it. *I think.*

"All right," she said. "Why?"

"He wanted to change things," Gaotona said. "In the empire."

"He doesn't speak of this in his journal."

"Ashravan was a humble man."

Shai raised an eyebrow. That didn't match the reports she'd been given.

"Oh, he had a temper," Gaotona said. "And if you got him arguing, he would sink his teeth in and hold fast to his point. But the man . . . the man he was . . . Deep down, that was a humble man. You will have to understand this about him."

"I see," she said. *You did it to him too, didn't you?* Shai thought. *That look of disappointment, that implication we should be better people than we are.* Shai wasn't the only one who felt that Gaotona regarded her as if he were a displeased grandfather.

That made her want to dismiss the man as irrelevant. Except . . . he had offered himself to her tests. He thought what she did was horrible, so he insisted on taking the punishment himself, instead of sending another.

*You're genuine, aren't you, old man?* Shai thought as Gaotona sat back, eyes distant as he considered the emperor. She found herself unsettled.

In her business, there were many who laughed at honest men, calling them easy pickings. That was a fallacy. Being honest did not make one naive. A dishonest fool and an honest fool were equally easy to scam; you just went about it in different ways.

However, a man who was honest and clever was always, *always* more difficult to scam than someone who was both dishonest and clever.

Sincerity. It was so difficult, by definition, to fake.

"What are you thinking behind those eyes of yours?" Gaotona asked, leaning forward.

"I was thinking that you must have treated the emperor as you did me, annoying him with constant nagging about what he should accomplish."

Gaotona snorted. "I probably did just that. It does not mean my points are, or were, incorrect. He could have . . . well, he could have become more than he did. Just as you *could* become a marvelous artist."

"I am one."

"A real one."

"I am one."

Gaotona shook his head. "Frava's painting . . . there is something we are missing about it, isn't there? She had the forgery inspected, and the assessors found a few tiny mistakes. I couldn't see them without help—but they are there. Upon reflection, they seem odd to me. The strokes are impeccable, masterly even. The style is a perfect match. If you could manage that, why would you have made such errors as putting the moon too low? It's a subtle mistake, but it occurs to me that you would never have made such an error—not unintentionally, at least."

Shai turned to get another seal.

"The painting they think is the original," Gaotona said, "the one hanging in Frava's office right now . . . It's a fake too, isn't it?"

"Yes," Shai admitted with a sigh. "I swapped the paintings a few days before trying for the scepter; I was investigating palace security.

I sneaked into the gallery, entered Frava's offices, and made the change as a test."

"So the one they assume is fake, *it* must be the original," Gaotona said, smiling. "You painted those mistakes *over* the original to make it seem like it was a replica!"

"Actually, no," Shai said. "Though I have used that trick in the past. They're both fakes. One is simply the obvious fake, planted to be discovered in case something went wrong."

"So the original is still hidden somewhere . . ." Gaotona said, sounding curious. "You sneaked into the palace to investigate security, then you replaced the original painting with a copy. You left a second, slightly worse copy in your room as a false trail. If you were found out while sneaking in—or if you were for some reason sold out by an ally—we would search your room and find the poor copy, and assume that you hadn't yet accomplished your swap. The officers would take the good copy and believe it to be authentic. That way, no one would keep looking for the original."

"More or less."

"That's very clever," Gaotona said. "Why, if you were captured sneaking into the palace trying to steal the scepter, you could confess that you were trying to steal only the painting. A search of your room would turn up the fake, and you'd be charged with attempted theft from an individual, in this case Frava, which is a much lesser crime than trying to steal an imperial relic. You would get ten years of labor instead of a death sentence."

"Unfortunately," Shai said, "I was betrayed at the wrong moment. The Fool arranged for me to be caught after I'd left the gallery with the scepter."

"But what of the original painting? Where did you hide it?" He hesitated. "It's still in the palace, isn't it?"

"After a fashion."

Gaotona looked at her, still smiling.

"I burned it," Shai said.

The smile vanished immediately. "You lie."

"Not this time, old man," Shai said. "The painting wasn't worth the risk to get it out of the gallery. I only pulled that swap to test security.

I got the fake in easily; people aren't searched going in, only coming out. The scepter was my true goal. Stealing the painting was secondary. After I replaced it, I tossed the original into one of the main gallery hearths."

"That's *horrible,*" Gaotona said. "It was an original ShuXen, his greatest masterpiece! He's gone blind, and can no longer paint. Do you realize the cost . . ." He sputtered. "I don't understand. Why, *why* would you do something like that?"

"It doesn't matter. No one will know what I've done. They will keep looking at the fake and be satisfied, so there's no harm done."

"That painting was a priceless work of art!" Gaotona glared at her. "Your swap of it was about pride and nothing else. You didn't care about selling the original. You just wanted your copy hanging in the gallery instead. You destroyed something wonderful so that you could elevate yourself!"

She shrugged. There was more to the story, but the fact was, she *had* burned the painting. She had her reasons.

"We are done for the day," Gaotona said, red-faced. He waved a hand at her, dismissive as he stood up. "I had begun to think . . . Bah!"

He stalked out the door.

# DAY FORTY-TWO

EACH person was a puzzle.

That was how Tao, her first trainer in Forgery, had explained it. A Forger wasn't a simple scam artist or trickster. A Forger was an artist who painted with human perception.

Any grime-covered urchin on the street could scam someone. A Forger sought loftier heights. Common scammers worked by pulling a cloth over someone's eyes, then fleeing before realization hit. A Forger had to create something so perfect, so beautiful, so *real* that its witnesses never questioned.

A person was like a dense forest thicket, overgrown with a twisting mess of vines, weeds, shrubs, saplings, and flowers. No person was one single emotion; no person had only one desire. They had many, and usually those desires conflicted with one another like two rosebushes fighting for the same patch of ground.

Respect the people you lie to, Tao had taught her. Steal from them long enough, and you will begin to understand them.

Shai crafted a book as she worked, a true history of Emperor Ashravan's life. It would become a truer history than those his scribes had written to glorify him, a truer history even than the one written by his own hand. Shai slowly pieced together the puzzle, crawling into the thicket that had been Ashravan's mind.

He *had* been idealistic, as Gaotona said. She saw it now in the cautious worry of his early writings and in the way he had treated his servants. The empire was not a terrible thing. Neither was it a wonderful thing. The empire simply *was.* The people suffered its rule because they were comfortable with its little tyrannies. Corruption was inevitable. You lived with it. It was either that or accept the chaos of the unknown.

Grands were treated with extreme favoritism. Entering government service, the most lucrative and prestigious of occupations, was often more about bribes and connections than it was about skill or aptitude. In addition, some of those who best served the empire—merchants and laborers—were systematically robbed by a hundred hands in their pockets.

Everyone knew these things. Ashravan had wanted to change them. At first.

And then . . . Well, there hadn't been a specific *and then.* Poets would point to a single flaw in Ashravan's nature that had led him to failure, but a person was no more one flaw than they were one passion. If Shai based her Forgery on any single attribute, she would create a mockery, not a man.

But . . . was that the best she could hope for? Perhaps she should try for authenticity in one specific setting, making an emperor who could act properly in court, but could not fool those closest to him. Perhaps that would work well enough, like the stage props from a playhouse. Those served their purpose while the play was going, but failed serious inspection.

That was an achievable goal. Perhaps she should go to the arbiters, explain what was possible, and give them a lesser emperor—a puppet they could use at official functions, then whisk away with explanations that he was growing sickly.

She could do that.

She found that she didn't want to.

That wasn't the challenge. That was the street thief's version of a scam, intended for short-term gain. The Forger's way was to create something enduring.

Deep down, she was thrilled by the challenge. She found that she *wanted* to make Ashravan live. She wanted to try, at least.

Shai lay back on her bed, which by now she had Forged to something more comfortable, with posts and a deep comforter. She kept the curtains drawn. Her guards for the evening played a round of cards at her table.

*Why do you care about making Ashravan live?* Shai thought to herself. *The arbiters will kill you before you can even see if this works. Escape should be your only goal.*

And yet . . . the *emperor* himself. She had chosen to steal the Moon Scepter because it was the most famous piece in the empire. She had wanted one of her works to be on display in the grand Imperial Gallery.

This task she now worked on, however . . . this was something far greater. What Forger had accomplished such a feat? A Forgery, sitting on the Rose Throne *itself*?

*No,* she told herself, more forceful this time. *Don't be lured. Pride, Shai. Don't let the pride drive you.*

She opened her book to the back pages, where she'd hidden her escape plans in a cipher, disguised to look like a dictionary of terms and people.

That Bloodsealer had come in running the other day, as if frightened that he'd be late to reset his seal. His clothing had smelled of strong drink. He was enjoying the palace's hospitality. If she could make him come early one morning, then ensure that he got extra drunk that night . . .

The mountains of the Strikers bordered Dzhamar, where the swamps of the Bloodsealers were located. Their hatred of one another ran deep, perhaps deeper than their loyalty to the empire. Several of the Strikers in particular seemed revolted when the Bloodsealer came. Shai had begun befriending those guards. Jokes in passing. Mentions of a coincidental similarity in her background and theirs. The Strikers weren't supposed to talk to Shai, but weeks had passed without Shai doing anything more than poring through books and chatting with old arbiters. The guards were bored, and boredom made people easy to manipulate.

Shai had access to plenty of soulstone, and she would use it. However, often more elementary methods were of greater use. People always expected a Forger to use seals for everything. Grands told stories of dark witchcraft, of Forgers placing seals on a person's feet while they slept, changing their personalities. Invading them, raping their minds.

The truth was that a soulstamp was often a Forger's last resort. It was too easy to detect. *Not that I wouldn't give my right hand for my Essence Marks right now . . .*

Almost, she was tempted to try carving a new Mark to use in getting away. They'd be expecting that, however, and she would have real trouble performing the hundreds of tests she'd need to do to make one work. Testing on her own arm would be reported by the guards, and testing on Gaotona would never work.

And using an Essence Mark she hadn't tested . . . well, that could go very, very poorly. No, her plans for escape would use soulstamps, but their heart would involve more traditional methods of subterfuge.

# DAY FIFTY-EIGHT

SHAI was ready when Frava next visited.

The woman paused in the doorway, the guards shuffling out without objection as Captain Zu took their place. "You've been busy," Frava noted.

Shai looked up from her research. Frava wasn't referring to her progress, but to the room. Most recently, Shai had improved the floor. It hadn't been difficult. The rock used to build the palace—the quarry, the dates, the stonemasons—all were matters of historic record.

"You like it?" Shai asked. "The marble works well with the hearth, I think."

Frava turned, then blinked. "A *hearth*? Where did you . . . Is this room bigger than it was?"

"The storage room next door wasn't being used," Shai mumbled, turning back to her book. "And the division between these two rooms was recent, constructed only a few years back. I rewrote the construction so that this room was made the larger of the two, and so that a hearth was installed."

Frava seemed stunned. "I wouldn't have thought . . ." The woman looked back to Shai, and her face adopted its usual severe mask. "I find it difficult to believe that you are taking your duty seriously, Forger. You are here to make an emperor, not remodel the palace."

"Carving soulstone relaxes me," Shai said. "As does having a workspace that doesn't remind me of a closet. You will have your emperor's soul in time, Frava."

The arbiter stalked through the room, inspecting the desk. "Then you have begun the emperor's soulstone?"

"I've begun many of them," Shai said. "It will be a complex process. I've tested well over a hundred stamps on Gaotona—"

"*Arbiter* Gaotona."

"—on the old man. Each is only a tiny slice of the puzzle. Once I have all of the pieces working, I'll recarve them in smaller, more delicate etchings. That will allow me to combine about a dozen test stamps into one final stamp."

"But you said you'd tested over a hundred," Frava said, frowning. "You'll only use twelve of those in the end?"

Shai laughed. "Twelve? To Forge an entire *soul*? Hardly. The final stamp, the one you will need to use on the emperor each morning, will be like . . . a linchpin, or the keystone of an arch. It will be the only one that will need to be placed on his skin, but it will connect a lattice of hundreds of other stamps."

Shai reached to the side, taking out her book of notes, including initial sketches of the final stamps. "I'll take these and stamp them onto a metal plate, then link that to the stamp you will place on Ashravan each day. He'll need to keep the plate close at all times."

"He'll need to carry a metal plate with him," Frava said dryly, "*and* he will need to be stamped each day? This will make it difficult for the man to live a normal life, don't you think?"

"Being emperor makes it difficult for any man to live a normal life, I suspect. You will make it work. It's customary for the plate to be designed as a piece of adornment. A large medallion, perhaps, or an upper-arm bracer with square sides. If you look at my own Essence Marks, you'll notice they were done in the same way, and that the box contains a plate for each one." Shai hesitated. "That said, I've never done this exact thing before; no one has. There is a chance . . . and I'd say a fair one . . . that over time, the emperor's brain will absorb the information. Like . . . like if you traced the exact same image on a stack of papers every day for a year, at the end the layers below will contain the image as well. Perhaps after a few years of being stamped, he won't need the treatment any longer."

"I still name it egregious."

"Worse than being dead?" Shai asked.

Frava rested her hand on Shai's book of notes and half-finished sketches. Then she picked it up. "I will have our scribes copy this."

Shai stood up. "I need it."

"I'm sure you do," Frava said. "That is precisely why it should be copied, just in case."

"Copying it will take too long."

"I will have it back to you in a day," Frava said lightly, stepping away. Shai reached for her, and Captain Zu stepped up, sword already half out of its sheath.

Frava turned to him. "Now, now, Captain. That won't be needed. The Forger is protective of her work. That is good. It shows that she is invested."

Shai and Zu locked gazes. *He wants me dead,* Shai thought. *Badly.* She'd figured him out by now. Guarding the palace was his duty, one that Shai had invaded by her theft. Zu hadn't captured her; the Imperial Fool had turned her in. Zu felt insecure because of his failure, and so he wanted to remove Shai in retribution.

Shai eventually broke his gaze. Though it galled her, she needed to take the submissive side of this interaction. "Be careful," she warned Frava. "Do not let them lose even a single page."

"I will protect this as if . . . as if the emperor's life depended on it." Frava found her joke amusing, and she gave Shai a rare smile. "You have considered the other matter we discussed?"

"Yes."

"And?"

"Yes."

Frava's smile deepened. "We will talk again soon."

Frava left with the book, nearly two months' worth of work. Shai knew exactly what the woman was up to. Frava wasn't going to have it copied—she was going to show it to her other Forger and see if it was far enough along for him to finish the job.

If he determined that it was, Shai would be executed, quietly, before the other arbiters could object. Zu would likely do it himself. It could all end here.

# DAY FIFTY-NINE

SHAI slept poorly that night.

She was certain that her preparations had been thorough. And yet now, she had to wait as if with a noose around her neck. It made her anxious. What if she'd misread the situation?

She had made her notations in the book intentionally opaque, each of them a subtle indication of just how *enormous* this project was. The cramped writing, the numerous cross-references, the lists and lists of reminders to herself of things to do . . . Each of these would work together with the thick book as a whole to indicate that her work was mind-breakingly complex.

It was a forgery. One of the most difficult types—a forgery that did not imitate a specific person or object. This was a forgery of *tone.*

*Stay away,* the tone of that book said. *You don't want to try to finish this. You want to let Shai continue to do the hard parts, because the work required to do it yourself would be enormous. And . . . if you fail . . . it will be your head on the line.*

That book was one of the most subtle forgeries she'd ever created. Each word in it was true and yet a lie at the same time. Only a master

Forger might see through it, might notice how hard she was working to illustrate the danger and difficulty of the project.

How skilled was Frava's Forger?

Would Shai be dead before morning?

She didn't sleep. She wanted to and she should have. Waiting out the hours, minutes, and seconds was excruciating. The thought of lying in bed asleep when they came for her . . . that was worse.

Eventually, she got up and retrieved some accounts of Ashravan's life. The guards playing cards at her table gave her a glance. One even nodded with sympathy at her red eyes and tired posture. "Light too bright?" he asked, gesturing at the lamp.

"No," Shai said. "Just a thought in my brain that won't get out."

She spent the night in bed pouring herself into Ashravan's life. Frustrated to be lacking her notes, she got out a fresh sheet and began some new ones she'd add to her book when it returned. If it did.

She felt that she finally understood why Ashravan had abandoned his youthful optimism. At least, she knew the factors that had combined to lead him down that path. Corruption was part of it, but not the main part. Again, lack of self-confidence contributed, but hadn't been the decisive factor.

No, Ashravan's downfall had been life itself. Life in the palace, life as part of an empire that clicked along like a clock. Everything worked. Oh, it didn't work as well as it might. But it *did* work.

Challenging that took effort, and effort was sometimes hard to muster. He had lived a life of leisure. Ashravan hadn't been lazy, but it didn't require laziness to be swept up in the workings of imperial bureaucracy—to tell yourself that next month you'd go and demand that your changes be made. Over time, it had become easier and easier to float along the course of the great river that was the Rose Empire.

In the end, he'd grown indulgent. He'd focused more on the beauty of his palace than on the lives of his subjects. He had allowed the arbiters to handle more and more government functions.

Shai sighed. Even that description of him was too simplistic. It neglected to mention *who* the emperor had been, and who he had become. A chronology of events didn't speak of his temper, his fondness for debate, his eye for beauty, or his habit of writing terrible, *terrible* poetry and then expecting all who served him to tell him how wonderful it was.

It also didn't speak of his arrogance, or his secret wish that he could have been something else. That was why he had gone back over his book again and again. Perhaps he had been looking for that branching point in his life where he had stepped down the wrong path.

He hadn't understood. There was rarely an obvious branching point in a person's life. People changed slowly, over time. You didn't take one step, then find yourself in a completely new location. You first took a little step off a path to avoid some rocks. For a while, you walked alongside the path, but then you wandered out a little way to step on softer soil. Then you stopped paying attention as you drifted farther and farther away. Finally, you found yourself in the wrong city, wondering why the signs on the roadway hadn't led you better.

The door to her room opened.

Shai bolted upright in her bed, nearly dropping her notes. They'd come for her.

But . . . no, it was *morning* already. Light trickled through the stained-glass window, and the guards were standing up and stretching. The one who had opened the door was the Bloodsealer. He looked hungover again, and carried a stack of papers in his hand, as he often did.

*He's early this morning,* Shai thought, checking her pocket watch. *Why early today, when he's late so often?*

The Bloodsealer cut her and stamped the door without a word, causing the pain to burn in Shai's arm. He hurried out of the room, as if off to some appointment. Shai stared after him, then shook her head.

A moment later, the door opened again and Frava entered.

"Oh, you're up," the woman said as the Strikers saluted her. Frava set Shai's book down on the table with a thump. She seemed annoyed. "The scribes are done. Get back to work."

Frava left in a bustle. Shai leaned back in her bed, sighing in relief. Her ruse had worked. That should earn her a few more weeks.

# DAY SEVENTY

"So this symbol," Gaotona said, pointing at one of her sketches of the greater stamps she would soon carve, "is a time notation, indicating a moment specifically . . . seven years ago?"

"Yes," Shai said, dusting off the end of a freshly carved soulstamp. "You learn quickly."

"I am undergoing surgery each day, so to speak," Gaotona said. "It makes me more comfortable to know the kinds of knives being used."

"The changes aren't—"

"Aren't permanent," he said. "Yes, so you keep saying." He stretched out his arm for her to stamp. "However, it makes me wonder. One can cut the body, and it will heal—but do it over and over again in the same spot, and you *will* scar. The soul cannot be so different."

"Except, of course, that it's *completely* different," Shai said, stamping his arm.

He had never quite forgiven her for what she had done in burning ShuXen's masterpiece. She could see it in him, when they interacted. He was no longer just disappointed in her, he was angry at her.

Anger faded with time, and they had a functional working relationship again.

Gaotona cocked his head. "I . . . Now *that* is odd."

"Odd in what way?" Shai asked, watching the seconds pass on her pocket watch.

"I remember encouraging *myself* to become emperor. And . . . and I resent myself. For . . . mother of light, is that really how he regarded me?"

The seal remained in place for fifty-seven seconds. Good enough. "Yes," she said as the seal faded away. "I believe that is exactly how he regarded you." She felt a thrill. *Finally* that seal had worked!

She was getting close now. Close to understanding the emperor, close to having the puzzle come together. Whenever she neared the end of a project—a painting, a large-scale soul Forgery, a sculpture—there came a moment in the process where she could *see* the entire work, even if it was far from finished. When that moment came, in her mind's eye, the work was complete; actually finishing it was almost a formality.

She was nearly there with this project. The emperor's soul spread out before her, with only some few corners still shadowed. She wanted to see it through; she *longed* to find out if she could make him live again. After reading so much about him, after coming to feel as if she knew him so well, she needed to finish.

Surely her escape could wait until then.

"That was it, wasn't it?" Gaotona asked. "That was the stamp that you've tried a dozen times without success, the seal representing why he stood up to become emperor."

"Yes," Shai said.

"His relationship with me," Gaotona said. "You made his decision depend upon his relationship with me, and . . . and the sense of shame he felt when speaking with me."

"Yes."

"And it took."

"Yes."

Gaotona sat back. "Mother of lights . . ." he whispered again.

Shai took the seal and put it with those that she had confirmed as workable.

Over the last few weeks, each of the other arbiters had done as Frava had, coming to Shai and offering her fantastic promises in exchange for giving them ultimate control of the emperor. Only Gaotona had never tried to bribe her. A genuine man, and one in the highest levels of imperial government no less. Remarkable. Using him was going to be far more difficult than she would have liked.

"I must say again," she said, turning to him, "you've impressed me. I don't think many Grands would take the time to study soulstamps. They would eschew what they considered evil without ever trying to understand it. You've changed your mind?"

"No," Gaotona said. "I still think that what you do is, if not evil, then certainly unholy. And yet, who am I to speak? I am depending upon you to preserve us in power by means of this art we so freely call an abomination. Our hunger for power outweighs our conscience."

"True for the others," Shai said, "but that is not your personal motive."

He raised an eyebrow at her.

"You just want Ashravan back," Shai said. "You refuse to accept that you've lost him. You loved him as a son—the youth that you mentored, the emperor you always believed in, even when he didn't believe in himself."

Gaotona looked away, looking decidedly uncomfortable.

"It won't be him," Shai said. "Even if I succeed, it won't *truly* be him. You realize this, of course."

He nodded.

"But then . . . sometimes a clever Forgery is as good as the real thing," Shai said. "You are of the Heritage Faction. You surround yourself with relics that aren't truly relics, paintings that are imitations of ones long lost. I suppose having a fake relic for an emperor won't be so different. And you . . . you just want to know that you've done everything you could. For him."

"How do you do it?" Gaotona asked softly. "I've seen how you speak with the guards, how you learn even the names of the servants. You seem to know their family lives, their passions, what they do in the evenings . . . and yet you spend each day locked in this room. You haven't left it for months. How do you know these things?"

"People," Shai said, rising to fetch another seal, "by nature attempt to exercise power over what is around them. We build walls to shelter us from the wind, roofs to stop the rain. We tame the elements, bend nature to our wills. It makes us feel as if we're in control.

"Except in doing so, we merely replace one influence with another. Instead of the wind affecting us, it is a wall. A *man-made* wall. The fingers of man's influence are all about, touching everything. Man-made rugs, man-made food. Every single thing in the city that we touch, see, feel, *experience* comes as the result of some person's influence.

"We may feel in control, but we never truly are unless we understand people. Controlling our environment is no longer about blocking the wind, it's about knowing why the serving lady was crying last night, or why a particular guard always loses at cards. Or why your employer hired you in the first place."

Gaotona looked back at her as she sat, then held out a seal to him. He hesitantly proffered an arm. "It occurs to me," he said, "that even in our extreme care not to do so, we have underestimated you, woman."

"Good," she said. "You're paying attention." She stamped him. "Now tell me, why exactly do you hate fish?"

# DAY SEVENTY-SIX

I *NEED to do it,* Shai thought as the Bloodsealer cut her arm. *Today. I could go today.*

Hidden in her other sleeve, she carried a slip of paper made to imitate the ones that the Bloodsealer often brought with him on the mornings that he came early.

She'd caught sight of a bit of wax on one of them two days back. They were letters. Realization had dawned. She'd been wrong about this man all along.

"Good news?" she asked him as he inked his stamp with her blood.

The white-lipped man gave her a sneering glance.

"From home," Shai said. "The woman you're writing, back in Dzhamar. She sent you a letter today? Post comes in the mornings here at the palace. They knock at your door, deliver a letter . . ." *And that wakes you up,* she added in her mind. *That's why you come on time those days.* "You must miss her a lot if you can't bear to leave her letter behind in your room."

The man lowered his arm and grabbed Shai by the front of her shirt. "Leave her alone, witch," he hissed. "You . . . you *leave her alone!* None of your trickery or magics!"

He was younger than she had assumed. That was a common mistake with Dzhamarians. Their white hair and skin made them seem ageless to outsiders. Shai should have known better. He was little more than a youth.

She drew her lips to a line. "You talk about *my* trickery and magics while holding in your hands a seal inked with my blood? You're the one threatening to send skeletals to hunt me, friend. All I can do is polish the odd table."

"Just . . . just . . . Ah!" The young man threw his hands up, then stamped the door.

The guards watched with nonchalant amusement and disapproval. Shai's words had been a calculated reminder that she was harmless while the Bloodsealer was the *truly* unnatural one. The guards had spent nearly three months watching her tinker about as a friendly scholar while this man drew her blood and used it for arcane horrors.

*I need to drop the paper,* she thought to herself, lowering her sleeve, meaning to let her forgery slip out as the guards turned away. That would put her plan into motion, her escape . . .

*The real Forgery isn't finished yet. The emperor's soul.*

She hesitated. Foolishly, she hesitated.

The door closed.

The opportunity passed.

Feeling numb, Shai walked to her bed and sat down on its edge, the forged letter still hidden in her sleeve. Why had she hesitated? Were her instincts for self-preservation so weak?

*I can wait a little longer,* she told herself. *Until Ashravan's Essence Mark is done.*

She'd been saying that for days now. Weeks, really. Each day she got closer to the deadline was another chance for Frava to strike. The woman came back with other excuses to take Shai's notes and have them inspected. They were quickly approaching the point where the other Forger wouldn't have to sort through much in order to finish Shai's work.

At least, so he would think. The further she progressed, the more impossible she realized this project was. And the more she longed to make it work anyway.

She got out her book on the emperor's life and soon found herself looking back through his youthful years. The thought of him not living again, of all of her work being merely a sham intended to distract while she planned to escape . . . those thoughts were physically *painful.*

*Nights,* Shai thought at herself. *You've grown fond of him. You're starting to see him like Gaotona does!* She shouldn't feel that way. She'd never met him. Besides, he was a despicable person.

But he hadn't always been. No, in truth, he hadn't ever *truly* become despicable. He had been more complex than that. Every person was. She could understand him, she could see—

"Nights!" she said, standing up and putting the book aside. She needed to clear her mind.

When Gaotona came to the room six hours later, Shai was just pressing a seal against the far wall. The elderly man opened the door and stepped in, then froze as the wall flooded with color.

Vine patterns spiraled out from Shai's stamp like sprays of paint. Green, scarlet, amber. The painting grew like something alive, leaves springing from branches, bunches of fruit exploding in succulent bursts. Thicker and thicker the pattern grew, golden trim breaking out of nothing and running like streams, rimming leaves, reflecting light.

The mural deepened, every inch imbued with an illusion of movement. Curling vines, unexpected thorns peeking from behind branches. Gaotona breathed out in awe and stepped up beside Shai. Behind, Zu stepped in, and the other two guards left and closed the door.

Gaotona reached out and felt the wall, but of course the paint was dry. So far as the wall knew, it had been painted like this years ago. Gaotona knelt down, looking at the two seals Shai had placed at the base of the painting. Only the third one, stamped above, had set off the transformation; the early seals were notes on how the image was to be created. Guidelines, a revision of history, instructions.

"How?" Gaotona asked.

"One of the Strikers guarded Atsuko of JinDo during his visit to the Rose Palace," Shai said. "Atsuko caught a sickness, and was stuck in his bedroom for three weeks. That was just one floor up."

"Your Forgery puts him in this room instead?"

"Yes. That was before the water damage that seeped through the ceiling last year, so it's plausible he'd have been placed here. The wall remembers Atsuko spending days too weak to leave, but having the strength for painting. A little each day, a growing pattern of vines, leaves, and berries. To pass the time."

"This shouldn't be taking," Gaotona said. "This Forgery is tenuous. You've changed too much."

"No," Shai said. "It's on the line . . . that line where the greatest beauty is found." She put the seal away. She barely remembered the last six hours. She had been caught up in the frenzy of creation.

"Still . . ." Gaotona said.

"It will take," Shai said. "If you were the wall, what would you rather be? Dreary and dull, or alive with paint?"

"Walls can't think!"

"That doesn't stop them from caring."

Gaotona shook his head, muttering about superstition. "How long?"

"To create this soulstamp? I've been etching it here and there for the last month or so. It was the last thing I wanted to do for the room."

"The artist was JinDo," he said. "Perhaps, because you are from the same people, it . . . But no! That's thinking like your superstition." Gaotona shook his head, trying to figure out why that painting would have taken, though it had always been obvious to Shai that this one would work.

"The JinDo and my people are *not* the same, by the way," Shai said testily. "We may have been related long ago, but we are completely different from them now." Grands. Just because people had similar features, Grands assumed they were practically identical.

Gaotona looked across her chamber and its fine furniture that had been carved and polished. Its marble floor with silver inlay, the crackling hearth and small chandelier. A fine rug—it had once been a bed quilt with holes in it—covered the floor. The stained-glass window sparkled on the right wall, lighting the beautiful mural.

The only thing that retained its original form was the door, thick but unremarkable. She couldn't Forge that, not with that Bloodseal set into it.

"You realize that you now have the finest chamber in the palace," Gaotona said.

"I doubt that," Shai said with a sniff. "Surely the emperor's are the nicest."

"The largest, yes. Not the nicest." He knelt beside the painting, looking at her seals at the bottom. "You included detailed explanations of how this was painted."

"To create a realistic Forgery," Shai said, "you must have the technical skill you are imitating, at least to an extent."

"So you could have painted this wall yourself."

"I don't have the paints."

"But you *could* have. You could have demanded paints. I'd have given them to you. Instead, you created a Forgery."

"It's what I am," Shai said, growing annoyed at him again.

"It's what you choose to be. If a wall can desire to be a mural, Wan ShaiLu, then *you* could desire to become a great painter."

She slapped her stamp down on the table, then took a few deep breaths.

"You have a temper," Gaotona said. "Like him. Actually, I know exactly how that feels now, because you have given it to me on several occasions. I wonder if this . . . thing you do could be a tool for helping to bring awareness to people. Inscribe your emotions onto a stamp, then let others *feel* what it is to be you . . ."

"Sounds great," Shai said. "If only Forging souls weren't a horrible offense to nature."

"If only."

"If you can read those stamps, you've grown very good indeed," Shai said, pointedly changing the topic. "Almost I think you've been cheating."

"Actually . . ."

Shai perked up, banishing her anger, now that it had passed the initial flare-up. What was this?

Gaotona sheepishly reached into the deep pocket of his robe and withdrew a wooden box. The one where she kept her treasures, the five

Essence Marks. Those revisions of her soul could change her, in times of need, into someone she *could* have been.

Shai took a step forward, but when Gaotona opened the box, he revealed that the stamps weren't inside. "I'm sorry," he said. "But I think giving you these now would be a little . . . foolish on my part. It seems that any one of them could have you free from your captivity in a moment."

"Really only two of them could manage that," Shai said sourly, fingers twitching. Those soulstamps represented over eight years of her life's work. She'd started the first on the day she ended her apprenticeship.

"Hm, yes," Gaotona said. Inside the small box lay sheets of metal inscribed with the separate smaller stamps that made up the blueprints of the revisions to her soul. "This one, I believe?" He held up one of the sheets. "Shaizan. Translated . . . Shai of the Fist? This would make a warrior out of you, if you stamped yourself?"

"Yes," Shai said. So he'd been studying her Essence Marks; that was how he'd grown so good at reading her stamps.

"I understand only one-tenth of what is inscribed here, if that," Gaotona said. "What I find is impressive. Truly, these must have taken years to craft."

"They are . . . precious to me," Shai said, forcing herself to sit down at her desk and not fixate on the plates. If she could escape with those, she could craft a new stamp with ease. It would still take weeks, but most of her work would not be lost. But if those plates were to be destroyed . . .

Gaotona sat down in his customary chair, nonchalantly looking through the plates. From someone else, she would have felt an implied threat. *Look what I hold in my hands; look what I could do to you.* From Gaotona, however, that was not it. He was genuinely curious.

Or was he? As ever, she could not suppress her instincts. As good as she was, someone else could be better. Just as Uncle Won had warned. Could Gaotona have been playing her for a fool all along? She felt strongly she should trust her assessment of Gaotona. But if she was wrong, it could be a disaster.

*It might be anyway,* she thought. *You should have run days ago.*

"Turning yourself into a soldier I understand," Gaotona said, setting aside the plate. "And this one as well. A woodsman and survivalist. That one looks extremely versatile. Impressive. And here we have a scholar. But why? You are already a scholar."

"No woman can know everything," Shai said. "There is only so much time for study. When I stamp myself with that Essence Mark, I can suddenly speak a dozen languages, from Fen to Mulla'dil—even a few from Sycla. I know dozens of different cultures and how to move in them. I know science, mathematics, and the major political factions of the world."

"Ah," Gaotona said.

*Just give them to me,* she thought.

"But what of this?" Gaotona said. "A beggar? Why would you want to be emaciated, and . . . is this showing that most of your hair would fall out, that your skin would become scarred?"

"It changes my appearance," Shai said. "Drastically. That's useful." She didn't mention that in that aspect, she knew the ways of the streets and survival in a city underworld. Her lock-picking skills weren't too shabby when not bearing that seal, but with it, she was incomparable.

With that stamp on her, she could probably manage to climb out the tiny window—that Mark rewrote her past to give her years of experience as a contortionist—and climb the five stories down to freedom.

"I should have realized," Gaotona said. He lifted the final plate. "That just leaves this one, most baffling of all."

Shai said nothing.

"Cooking," he said. "Farm work, sewing. Another alias, I assume. For imitating a simpler person?"

"Yes."

Gaotona nodded, putting the sheet down.

*Honesty. He must see my honesty. It cannot be faked.*

"No," Shai said, sighing.

He looked to her.

"It's . . . my way out," she said. "I'll never use it. It's just there, if I want to."

"Way out?"

"If I ever use that," Shai said, "it will write over my years as a Forger. Everything. I will forget how to make the simplest of stamps; I will forget that I was even apprenticed as a Forger. I will become something normal."

"And you want that?"

"No."

A pause.

"Yes. Maybe. A part of me does."

Honesty. It was so difficult. Sometimes it was the only way.

She dreamed about that simple life, on occasion. In that morbid way that someone standing at the edge of a cliff wonders what it would be like to just jump off. The temptation is there, even if it's ridiculous.

A normal life. No hiding, no lying. She loved what she did. She loved the thrill, the accomplishment, the wonder. But sometimes . . . trapped in a prison cell or running for her life . . . sometimes she dreamed of something else.

"Your aunt and uncle?" he asked. "Uncle Won, Aunt Sol, they are parts of this revision. I've read it in here."

"They're fake," Shai whispered.

"But you quote them all the time."

She squeezed her eyes shut.

"I suspect," Gaotona said, "that a life full of lying makes reality and falsehood intermix. But if you were to use this stamp, surely you would not forget everything. How would you keep the sham from yourself?"

"It would be the greatest Forgery of all," Shai said. "One intended to fool even me. Written into that is the belief that without that stamp, applied every morning, I'll die. It includes a history of illness, of visiting a . . . resealer, as you call them. A healer that works in soulstamps. From them, my false self received a remedy, one I must apply each morning. Aunt Sol and Uncle Won would send me letters; that is part of the charade to fool myself. I've written them already. Hundreds, which—before I use the Essence Mark on myself—I will pay a delivery service good money to send periodically."

"But what if you try to visit them?" Gaotona said. "To investigate your childhood . . ."

"It's all in the plate. I will be afraid of travel. There's truth to that, as I was indeed scared of leaving my village as a youth. Once that Mark is in place, I'll stay away from cities. I'll think the trip to visit my relatives is too dangerous. But it doesn't matter. I'll never use it."

That stamp would end her. She would forget the last twenty years, back to when she was eight and had first begun inquiring about becoming a Forger.

She'd become someone else entirely. None of the other Essence Marks did that; they rewrote some of her past, but left her with a knowledge of who she truly was. Not so with the last one. That one was to be final. It terrified her.

"This is a great deal of work for something you'll never use," Gaotona said.

"Sometimes, that is the way of life."

Gaotona shook his head.

"I was hired to destroy the painting," Shai blurted out.

She wasn't quite certain what drove her to say it. She needed to be honest with Gaotona—that was the only way her plan would work—but he didn't need this piece. Did he?

Gaotona looked up.

"ShuXen hired me to destroy Frava's painting," Shai said. "That's why I burned the masterpiece, rather than sneaking it out of the gallery."

"ShuXen? But . . . he's the original artist! Why would *he* hire you to destroy one of his works?"

"Because he hates the empire," Shai said. "He painted that piece for a woman he loved. Her children gave it to the empire as a gift. ShuXen is old now, blind, barely able to move. He did not want to go to his grave knowing that one of his works was serving to glorify the Rose Empire. He begged me to burn it."

Gaotona seemed dumbfounded. He looked at her, as if trying to pierce through to her soul. Shai didn't know why he needed to bother; this conversation had already stripped her thoroughly bare.

"A master of his caliber is hard to imitate," Shai said, "particularly without the original to work from. If you think about it, you'll realize I needed his help to create those fakes. He gave me access to his studies and concepts; he told me how he'd gone about painting it. He coached me through the brushstrokes."

"Why not just have you return the original to him?" Gaotona asked.

"He's dying," Shai said. "Owning a thing is meaningless to him. That painting was done for a lover. She is gone now, so he felt the painting should be as well."

"A priceless treasure," Gaotona said. "Gone because of foolish pride."

"It was *his* work!"

"Not any longer," Gaotona said. "It belonged to everyone who saw it. You should not have agreed to this. Destroying a work of art like that is *never* right." He hesitated. "But still, I think I can understand. What you did had a nobility to it. Your goal was the Moon Scepter. Exposing yourself to destroy that painting was dangerous."

"ShuXen tutored me in painting as a youth," she said. "I could not deny his request."

Gaotona did not seem to agree, but he did seem to understand. Nights, but Shai felt exposed.

*This is important to do,* she told herself. *And maybe . . .*

But he did not give her the plates back. She hadn't expected him to, not now. Not until their agreement was done—an agreement she was certain she would not live to see the end of, unless she escaped.

They worked through the last group of new stamps. Each one took for at least a minute, as she'd been almost certain they would. She had the vision now, the idea of the final soul as it would be. Once she finished the sixth stamp for the day, Gaotona waited for the next.

"That's it," Shai said.

"All for today?"

"All forever," Shai said, tucking away the last of the stamps.

"You're done?" Gaotona asked, sitting up straight. "Almost a month early! It's—"

"I'm *not* done," Shai said. "Now is the most difficult part. I have to carve those several hundred stamps in tiny detail, melding them together, then create a linchpin stamp. What I've done so far is like getting all of the paints ready, creating the color and figure studies. Now I have to put it all together. The last time I did this, it took the better part of five months."

"And you have only twenty-four days."

"And I have only twenty-four days," Shai said, but felt an immediate stab of guilt. She *had* to run. Soon. She couldn't wait to finish the project.

"Then I will leave you to it," Gaotona said, standing and rolling down his sleeve.

# DAY EIGHTY-FIVE

YES, Shai thought, scrambling along the side of her bed and rifling through her stack of papers there. The table wasn't big enough. She'd pulled her sheets tight and turned the bed into a place to set all of her stacks. *Yes, his first love was from the storybook.* That was why . . . Kurshina's red hair . . . But this would be subconscious. He wouldn't know it. Embedded deeply, then.

How had she missed that? She wasn't nearly as close to being done as she'd thought. There wasn't time!

Shai added what she'd discovered to the seal she was working on, one that combined all of the various parts of Ashravan's romantic inclinations and experiences. She included it all: the embarrassing, the shameful, the glorious. Everything she'd been able to discover, and then a little bit more, calculated risks to fill out the soul. A flirtatious encounter with a woman whose name Ashravan could not recall. Idle fancies. A near affair with a woman now dead.

This was the most difficult part of the soul for Shai to imitate, for it was the most private. Little an emperor did was ever truly secret, but Ashravan had not always been emperor.

She had to extrapolate, lest she leave the soul bare, without passion.

So private, so *powerful.* She felt closest to Ashravan as she teased out these details. Not as a voyeur; by this point, she was a part of him.

She kept two books now. The formal notes of her process said she was horribly behind; that book left out details. The other book was her true one, disguised as useless piles of notes, random and haphazard.

She really was behind, but not so far as her official documentation showed. Hopefully, that subterfuge would earn her a few extra days before Frava struck.

As Shai searched for a specific note, she ran across one of her lists for escape plans. She hesitated. *First, deal with the seal on the door,* the note read in cipher. *Second, silence the guards. Third, recover your Essence Marks, if possible. Fourth, escape the palace. Fifth, escape the city.*

She'd written further notes for the execution of each step. She wasn't ignoring the escape, not completely. She had good plans.

Her frantic attempt to finish the soul, however, drew most of her attention. *One more week,* she told herself. *If I take one more week, I will finish five days before the deadline. Then I can run.*

# DAY NINETY-SEVEN

"Hey," Hurli said, bending down. "What's this?"

Hurli was a brawny Striker who acted dumber than he was. It let him win at cards. He had two children—girls, both under the age of five—but was seeing one of the women guards on the side. Hurli secretly wished he could have been a carpenter like his father. He also would have been horrified if he'd realized how much Shai knew about him.

He held up the sheet of paper he'd found on the ground. The Bloodsealer had just left. It was the morning of the ninety-sixth day of Shai's captivity in the room, and she'd decided to put the plan into motion. She *had* to get out.

The emperor's seal was not yet finished. *Almost.* One more night's work, and she'd have it. Her plan required one more night of waiting anyway.

"Weedfingers must have dropped it," Yil said, walking over. She was the other guard in the room this morning.

"What is it?" Shai asked from the desk.

"Letter," Hurli said with a grunt.

Both guards fell silent as they read. Palace Strikers were all literate. It was required of any imperial civil servant of at least the second reed.

Shai sat quietly, tense, sipping a cup of lemon tea and forcing herself to breathe calmly. She made herself relax even though relaxing was the last thing she wanted to do. Shai knew the letter's contents by heart. She'd written it, after all, then had dropped it covertly behind the Bloodsealer as he'd rushed out moments ago.

*Brother,* the letter read. *I have almost completed my task here, and the wealth I have earned will rival even that of Azalec after his work in the Southern Provinces. The captive I secure is hardly worth the effort, but who am I to question the reasoning of people paying me far too much money?*

*I will return to you shortly. I am proud to say that my other mission here has been a success. I have identified several capable warriors, and have gathered sufficient samples from them. Hair, fingernails, and a few personal effects that will not be missed. I feel confident that we will have our personal guards very soon.*

It went on, the writing covering both the front and the back, so that it didn't look suspicious. Shai had padded it with a lot of talk about the palace, including things that others would assume that Shai didn't know but that the Bloodsealer would.

Shai worried that the letter was too overt. Would the guards find it to be an obvious forgery?

"That KuNuKam," Yil whispered, using a native word of theirs. It roughly translated as a man who had an anus for a mouth. "That imperial KuNuKam!"

Apparently, they believed it really was from him. Subtlety could be lost on soldiers.

"Can I see it?" Shai asked.

Hurli held it out to her. "Is he saying what I think?" the guard asked. "He's been . . . *gathering* things from us?"

"It might not mean the Strikers," Shai said after reading the letter. "He doesn't say."

"Why would he want hair?" Yil asked. "And fingernails?"

"They can do things with pieces of you," Hurli said, then cursed again. "You see what he does each day on the door with Shai's blood."

"I don't know if he could do much with hair or fingernails," Shai said skeptically. "This is just bravado. Blood needs to be fresh, not more than a day old, for it to work in his stamps. He's bragging to his brother."

"He shouldn't be doing things like that," Hurli said.

"I wouldn't worry about it," Shai said.

The other two shared looks. In a few minutes, the guard change occurred. Hurli and Yil left, muttering to one another, the letter shoved in Hurli's pocket. They weren't likely to hurt the Bloodsealer badly. Threaten him, yes.

The Bloodsealer was known to frequent teahouses in the area each evening. Almost she felt sorry for the man. She had deduced that when he got news from home, he was quick and punctual to her door. He sometimes looked excited. When he didn't get news, he drank. This morning, he had looked sad. No news in a while, then.

What happened to him tonight would not make his day any better. Yes, Shai almost felt sorry for him, but then she remembered the seal on the door and the bandage she'd tied on her arm after he'd drawn blood today.

As soon as the guard change was accomplished, Shai took a deep breath, then dug back into her work.

Tonight. Tonight, she would finish.

# DAY NINETY-EIGHT

Shai knelt on the floor amid a pattern of scattered pages, each filled with cramped script or drawings of seals. Behind her, morning opened her eyes, and sunlight seeped through the stained-glass window, spraying the room with crimson, blue, violet.

A single soulstamp, carved from polished stone, rested facedown on a metal plate sitting before her. Soulstone, as a rock, looked not unlike soapstone or another fine-grained stone, but with bits of red mixed in. As if drops of blood had stained it.

Shai blinked tired eyes. Was she really going to try to escape? She'd had . . . what? Four hours of sleep in the last three days combined?

Surely escape could wait. Surely she could rest, just for today.

*Rest,* she thought numbly, *and I will not wake.*

She remained in place, kneeling. That stamp seemed the most beautiful thing she had ever seen.

Her ancestors had worshipped rocks that fell from the sky at night. The souls of broken gods, those chunks had been called. Master craftsmen would carve them to bring out the shape. Once, Shai had found that foolish. Why worship something you yourself created?

Kneeling before her masterpiece, she understood. She felt as if she'd bled everything into that stamp. She had pressed two years' worth of effort into three months, then had topped it off with a night of desperate, frantic carving. During that night, she'd made changes to her notes, to the soul itself. Drastic changes. She still didn't know if they had been provoked by her final, awesome vision of the project as a whole . . . or if those changes had instead been faulty ideas born of fatigue and delusion.

She wouldn't know until the stamp was used.

"Is it . . . is it done?" asked one of her guards. The two of them had moved to the far edge of the room, to sit beside the hearth and give her room on the floor. She vaguely remembered shoving aside the furniture. She'd spent part of the time pulling stacks of paper out from their place beneath the bed, then crawling under to fetch others.

Was it done?

Shai nodded.

"What is it?" the guard asked.

*Nights,* she thought. *That's right. They don't even know.* The common guards left each day during her conversations with Gaotona.

The poor Strikers would probably find themselves assigned to some remote outpost of the empire for the rest of their lives, guarding the passes leading down to the distant Teoish Peninsula or the like. They would be quietly brushed under the rug to keep them from revealing, even accidentally, anything of what had happened here.

"Ask Gaotona if you want to know," Shai said softly. "I am not allowed to say."

Shai reverently picked up the seal, then placed both it and its plate inside a box she had prepared. The stamp nestled in red velvet, the plate—shaped like a large, thin medallion—in an indentation underneath the lid. She closed the lid, then pulled over a second, slightly larger box. Inside lay five seals, carved and prepared for her upcoming escape. If she managed it. Two of them she'd already used.

If she could just sleep for a few hours. Just a few . . .

*No. I can't use the bed anyway.*

Curling up on the floor sounded wonderful, however.

The door began to open. Shai felt a sudden, striking moment of panic.

Was it the Bloodsealer? He was supposed to be stuck in bed, having drunk himself to a stupor after being roughed up by the Strikers!

For a moment, she felt a strange guilty sense of relief. If the Bloodsealer had come, she wouldn't have a chance to escape today. She could sleep. Had Hurli and Yil not thrashed him? Shai had been sure that she'd read them correctly, and . . .

. . . and, in her fatigue, she realized she'd been jumping to conclusions. The door opened all the way, and someone did enter, but it was not the Bloodsealer.

It was Captain Zu.

"Out," he barked at the two guards.

They jumped into motion.

"In fact," Zu said, "you're relieved for the day. I'll watch until the shift changes."

The two saluted and left. Shai felt like a wounded elk being abandoned by the herd. The door clicked closed, and Zu slowly, deliberately, turned to look at her.

"The stamp isn't ready yet," Shai lied. "So you can—"

"It doesn't need to be ready," Zu said, smiling a wide, thick-lipped smile. "I believe I promised you something three months ago, thief. We have an . . . unsettled debt."

The room was dim, her lamp having burned low and morning only just breaking. Shai backed away from him, quickly revising her plans. This *wasn't* how it was supposed to go. She couldn't fight Zu.

Her mouth kept moving, keeping him distracted but also playing a part she devised for herself on the fly. "When Frava finds out you came here," Shai said, "she will be furious."

Zu drew his sword.

"Nights!" Shai said, backing up to her bed. "Zu, you don't need to do this. You *can't* do this. I have work that needs to be done!"

"Another will complete your work," Zu said, leering. "Frava has another Forger. You think you're so clever. You probably have some wonderful escape planned for tomorrow. This time, we're striking first. You didn't anticipate *this,* did you, liar? I'm going to enjoy killing you. Enjoy it so much."

He lunged with the sword, its tip catching her blouse and ripping a line through it at her side. Shai jumped away, shouting for help. She was still playing the part, but it did not require acting. Her heart thumped, panic rising, as she rounded the bed in a scramble, putting it between herself and Zu.

He smiled broadly, then jumped for her, leaping onto the bed.

It promptly collapsed. During the night, while crawling under the bed to get her notes, she had Forged the wood of the frame to have deep flaws, attacked by insects, making it fragile. She'd cut the mattress underneath in wide slashes.

Zu barely had time to shout as the bed broke completely away, crashing into the pit she'd opened in the floor below. The water damage to her room—the mildew she'd smelled when first entering—had been key. By reports, the wooden beams above would have rotted and the ceiling would have fallen in if they hadn't located the leak as quickly as they had. A simple Forgery, very plausible, made it so that the floor *had* fallen in.

Zu crashed into the empty storage room one story down. Shai stood puffing, then peered into the hole. The man lay among the broken remnants of the bed. Some of that had been stuffing and cushioning. He would probably live—she'd been intending this trap for one of the regular guards, of whom she was fond.

*Not exactly how I planned it,* she thought, *but workable.*

Shai rushed to the table and gathered her things. The box of stamps, the emperor's soul, some extra soulstone and ink. And the two books explaining the stamps she had created in deep complexity—the official one, and the true one.

She tossed the official one into the hearth as she passed. Then she stopped in front of the door, counting heartbeats.

She agonized, watching the Bloodsealer's mark as it pulsed. Finally, after a few tormenting minutes, the seal on the door flashed one last time . . . then faded. The Bloodsealer had not returned in time to renew it.

Freedom.

Shai burst out into the hallway, abandoning her home of the last three months, a room now trimmed in gold and silver. The hallway outside had been so near, yet it felt like another country entirely. She pressed the third of her prepared stamps against her buttoned blouse, changing it to match that of the palace servants, with official insignia embroidered on the left breast.

She had little time to make her next move. Soon, either the Bloodsealer would make his way to her room, Zu would wake from his fall, or the guards would arrive for the shift change. Shai wanted to run down the hallway, breaking for the palace stables.

She did not. Running implied one of two things—guilt or an important task. Either would be memorable. Instead, she kept her gait to a swift walk and adopted the expression of one who knew what she was doing, and so should not be interrupted.

She soon entered the better-used sections of the enormous palace. No one stopped her. At a certain carpeted intersection, she stopped herself.

To the right, down a long hallway, lay the entrance to the emperor's chambers. The seal she carried in her right hand, boxed and cushioned, seemed to leap in her fingers. Why hadn't she left it in the room for Gaotona to discover? The arbiters would hunt her less assiduously if they had the seal.

She could just leave it here, in this hallway lined with portraits of ancient rulers and cluttered with Forged urns from ancient eras.

No. She had brought it with her for a reason. She'd prepared tools to get into the emperor's chambers. She'd known all along this was what she would do.

If she left now, she'd never *truly* know if the seal worked. That would be like building a house, then never stepping inside. Like forging a sword, and never giving it a swing. Like crafting a masterpiece of art, then locking it away to never be seen again.

Shai started down the long hallway.

As soon as no one was directly in sight, she turned over one of those horrid urns and broke the seal on the bottom. It transformed back into a blank clay version of itself.

She'd had plenty of time to find out exactly where these urns were crafted and by whom. The fourth of her prepared stamps transformed the urn into a replica of an ornate golden chamber pot. Shai strode down the hallway to the emperor's quarters, then nodded to the guards, chamber pot under her arm.

"I don't recognize you," one guard said. She didn't recognize him either, with that scarred face and squinty look. As she'd expected. The guards set to watching her had been kept separate from the others so they couldn't talk about their duties.

"Oh," Shai said, fumbling, looking abashed. "I am sorry, greater one. I was only assigned this task this morning." She blushed, fishing out of her pocket a small square of thick paper, marked with Gaotona's seal and signature. She had forged both the old-fashioned way. Very convenient, how he'd let her tell him how to maintain security on the emperor's rooms.

She got through without any further difficulty. The next three rooms of the emperor's expansive chambers were empty. Beyond them was a locked door. She had to Forge the wood of that door into some that had been damaged by insects—using the same stamp she'd used on her bed—to get through. It didn't take for long, but a few seconds was enough for her to kick the door open.

Inside, she found the emperor's bedroom. It was the same place she'd been led on that first day when she'd been offered this chance. The room was empty save for him, lying in that bed. He was awake, but stared sightlessly at the ceiling.

The room was still. Quiet. It smelled . . . too clean. Too white. Like a blank canvas.

Shai walked up to the side of the bed. Ashravan didn't look at her. His eyes didn't move. She rested fingers on his shoulder. He had a handsome face, though he was some fifteen years her senior. That was not much for a Grand; they lived longer than most.

His was a strong face, despite his long time abed. Golden hair, a firm chin, a nose that was prominent. So different in features from Shai's people.

"I know your soul," Shai said softly. "I know it better than you ever did."

No alarm yet. Shai continued to expect one any moment, but she knelt down beside the bed anyway. "I wish that I could know you. Not your soul, but *you.* I've read about you; I've seen into your heart. I've rebuilt your soul, as best I could. But that isn't the same. It isn't knowing someone, is it? That's knowing *about* someone."

Was that a cry outside, from a distant part of the palace?

"I don't ask much of you," she said softly. "Just that you live. Just that you *be.* I've done what I can. Let it be enough."

She took a deep breath, then opened the box and took out his Essence Mark. She inked it, then pulled up his shirt, exposing the upper arm.

Shai hesitated, then pressed the stamp down. It hit flesh, and stayed frozen for a moment, as stamps always did. The skin and muscle didn't give way until a second later, when the stamp *sank* a fraction of an inch.

She twisted the stamp, locking it in, and pulled it back. The bright red seal glowed faintly.

Ashravan blinked.

Shai rose and stepped back as he sat up and looked around. Silently, she counted.

"My rooms," Ashravan said. "What happened? There was an attack. I was . . . I was wounded. Oh, mother of lights. Kurshina. She's dead."

His face became a mask of grief, but he covered it a second later. He was emperor. He might have a temper, but so long as he was not enraged, he was good at covering what he felt. He turned to her, and living eyes—eyes that *saw*—focused on her. "Who are you?"

The question twisted her insides, for all the fact that she'd expected it.

"I'm a kind of surgeon," Shai said. "You were wounded badly. I have healed you. However, what I used to do so is considered . . . unsavory by some parts of your culture."

"You're a resealer," he said. "A . . . a Forger?"

"In a way," Shai said. He would believe that because he wanted to. "This was a difficult type of resealing. You will have to be stamped each day, and you must keep that metal plate—the one shaped like a disc in that box—with you at all times. Without these, you die, Ashravan."

"Give it to me," he said, holding his hand out for the stamp.

She hesitated. She wasn't certain why.

"Give it to me," he said, more forceful.

She placed the stamp in his hand.

"Don't tell anyone what has happened here," she said to him. "Neither guards nor servants. Only your arbiters know of what I have done."

The cries outside sounded louder. Ashravan looked toward them. "If no one is to know," he said, "you must go. Leave this place and do not return." He looked down at the seal. "I should probably have you killed for knowing my secret."

That was the selfishness he'd learned during his years in the palace. Yes, she'd gotten that right.

"But you won't," she said.

"I won't."

And there was the mercy, buried deeply.

"Go before I change my mind," he said.

She took one step toward the doorway, then checked her pocket watch—well over a minute. The stamp had taken, at least for the short term. She turned and looked at him.

"What are you waiting for?" he demanded.

"I just wanted one more glimpse," she said.

He frowned.

The shouts grew even louder.

"Go," he said. "Please." He seemed to know what those shouts were about, or at least he could guess.

"Do better this time," Shai said. "Please."

With that, she fled.

She had been tempted, for a time, to write into him a desire to protect her. There would have been no good reason for it, at least in his eyes, and it might have undermined the entire Forgery. Beyond that, she didn't believe that he *could* save her. Until his period of mourning was through, he could not leave his quarters or speak to anyone other than his arbiters. During that time, the arbiters ran the empire.

They practically ran it anyway. No, a hasty revision of Ashravan's soul to protect her would not have worked. Near the last door out, Shai picked up her fake chamber pot. She hefted it, then stumbled through the doors. She gasped audibly at the distant cries.

"Is that about *me*?" Shai cried. "Nights! I didn't mean it! I know I wasn't supposed to see him. I know he's in seclusion, but I opened the wrong door!"

The guards stared at her, then one relaxed. "It isn't you. Find your quarters and stay there."

Shai bobbed a bow and hastened away. Most of the guards didn't know her, and so—

She felt a sharp pain at her side. She gasped. That pain felt like it did each morning, when the Bloodsealer stamped the door.

Panicked, Shai felt at her side. The cut in her blouse—where Zu had slashed her with his sword—had gone all the way through her dark undershirt! When her fingers came back, they had a couple of drops of blood on them. Just a nick, nothing dangerous. In the scramble, she hadn't even noticed she'd been cut.

But the tip of Zu's sword . . . it had her blood on it. Fresh blood. The Bloodsealer had found that and had begun the hunt. That pain meant he was locating her, was attuning his pets to her.

Shai tossed the urn aside and started running.

Staying hidden was no longer a consideration. Remaining unremarkable was pointless. If the Bloodsealer's skeletals reached her, she'd die. That was it. She had to reach a horse soon, then stay ahead of the skeletals for twenty-four hours, until her blood grew stale.

Shai dashed through the hallways. Servants began pointing, others screamed. She almost bowled over a southern ambassador in red priest's armor.

Shai cursed, bolting around the man. The palace exits would be locked down by now. She *knew* that. She'd studied the security. Getting out would be nearly impossible.

*Always have a backup*, Uncle Won said.

She always did.

Shai stopped in the hallway, and determined—as she should have earlier—that running for the exits was pointless. She was in a near panic, with the Bloodsealer on her trail, but she *had* to think clearly.

Backup plan. Hers was a desperate one, but it was all she had. She started running again, skidding around a corner, doubling back the way she'd just come.

*Nights, let me have guessed right about him,* she thought. *If he's secretly a master charlatan beyond my skill, I am doomed. Oh, Unknown God, please. This time, let me be right.*

Heart racing, fatigue forgotten in the moment, she eventually skidded to a stop in the hallway leading to the emperor's rooms.

There she waited. The guards inspected her, frowning, but held their posts at the end of the hallway as they'd been trained. They called to her. It was hard to keep from moving. That Bloodsealer was getting closer and closer with his horrible pets . . .

"Why are you here?" a voice said.

Shai turned as Gaotona stepped into the hallway. He'd come for the emperor first. The others would search for Shai, but Gaotona would come for the emperor, to be certain he was safe.

Shai stepped up to him, anxious. *This,* she thought, *is probably my worst idea ever for a backup plan.*

"It worked," she said softly.

"You tried the stamp?" Gaotona said, taking her arm and glancing at the guards, then pulling her aside well out of earshot. "Of all the hasty, insane, foolish—"

"It *worked,* Gaotona," Shai said.

"Why did you come to him? Why not run while you had the chance?"

"I had to know. I *had* to."

He looked at her, meeting her eyes. Seeing through them, into her soul, as he always did. Nights, but he would have made a wonderful Forger.

"The Bloodsealer has your trail," Gaotona said. "He has summoned those . . . *things* to catch you."

"I know."

Gaotona hesitated for only a moment, then brought out a wooden box from his voluminous pockets. Shai's heart leaped.

He handed it toward her, and she took it with one hand, but he did not let go. "You knew I'd come here," Gaotona said. "You knew I'd have these, and that I'd give them to you. I've been played for a fool."

Shai said nothing.

"How did you do it?" he asked. "I thought I watched you carefully. I was *certain* I had not been manipulated. And yet I ran here, half knowing I'd find you. Knowing you'd need these. I *still* didn't realize until this very moment that you'd probably planned all of this."

"I did manipulate you, Gaotona," she admitted. "But I had to do it in the most difficult way possible."

"Which was?"

"By being genuine," she replied.

"You can't manipulate people by being genuine."

"You can't?" Shai asked. "Is that not how you've made your entire career? Speaking honestly, teaching people what to expect of you, then expecting them to be honest to you in return?"

"It's not the same thing."

"No," she said. "It's not. But it was the best I could manage. Everything I've said to you is true, Gaotona. The painting I destroyed, the secrets about my life and desires . . . Being genuine. It was the only way to get you on my side."

"I'm not on your side." He paused. "But I don't want you killed either, girl. Particularly not by those *things*. Take these. Days! Take them and go, before I change my mind."

"Thank you," she whispered, pulling the box to her breast. She fished in her skirt pocket and brought out a small, thick book. "Keep this safe," she said. "Show it to no one."

He took it hesitantly. "What is it?"

"The truth," she said, then leaned in and kissed him on the cheek. "If I escape, I will change my final Essence Mark. The one I never intend to use . . . I will add to it, and to my memories, a kindly grandfather who saved my life. A man of wisdom and compassion whom I respected very much."

"Go, fool girl," he said. He actually had a tear in his eye. If she hadn't been on the very edge of panic, she'd have felt proud of that. And ashamed of her pride. That was how she was.

"Ashravan lives," she said. "When you think of me, remember that. It *worked*. Nights, it *worked*!"

She left him, dashing down the corridor.

Gaotona listened to the girl go, but did not turn to watch her flee. He stared at that door to the emperor's chambers. Two confused guards, and a passage into . . . what?

The future of the Rose Empire.

*We will be led by someone not truly alive,* Gaotona thought. *The fruits of our foul labors.*

He took a deep breath, then walked past the guards and pushed open the doors to go and look upon the thing he had wrought.

*Just . . . please, let it not be a monster.*

Shai strode down the palace hallway, holding the box of seals. She ripped off her buttoned blouse—revealing the tight, black cotton shirt she wore underneath—and tucked it into her pocket. She left on her skirt and the leggings beneath. It wasn't so different from the clothing she'd trained in.

Servants scattered around her. They knew, just from her posture, to get out of the way. Suddenly, Shai felt more confident than she had in years.

She had her soul back. All of it.

She took out one of her Essence Marks as she walked. She inked it with bold strikes and returned the box of seals to her skirt pocket. Then, she slammed the seal against her right bicep and locked it into place, rewriting her history, her memories, her life experience.

In that fraction of a moment, she remembered both histories. She remembered two years spent locked away, planning, creating the Essence Mark. She remembered a lifetime of being a Forger.

At the same time, she remembered spending the last fifteen years among the Teullu people. They had adopted her and trained her in their martial arts.

Two places at once, two timelines at once.

Then the former faded, and she became Shaizan, the name the Teullu had given her. Her body became leaner, harder. The body of a warrior. She slipped off her spectacles. Her eyes had been healed long ago, and she didn't need those any longer.

Gaining access to the Teullu training had been difficult; they did not like outsiders. She'd nearly been killed by them a dozen different times during her year training. But she had succeeded.

She lost all knowledge of how to create stamps, all sense of scholarly inclination. She was still herself, and she remembered her immediate past—being captured, forced to sit in that cell. She retained knowledge—logically—of what she'd just done with the stamp to her arm, and knew that the life she now remembered was fake.

But she didn't *feel* that it was. As that seal burned on her arm, she became the version of herself that would have existed if she'd been adopted by a harsh warrior culture and lived among them for well over a decade.

She kicked off her shoes. Her hair shortened; a scar stretched from her nose down around her right cheek. She walked like a warrior, prowling instead of striding.

She reached the servants' section of the palace just before the stables, the Imperial Gallery to her left.

A door opened in front of her. Zu, tall and wide-lipped, pushed through. He had a gash on his forehead—blood seeped through the bandage there—and his clothing had been torn by his fall.

He had a tempest in his eyes. He sneered as he saw her. "You've done it now. The Bloodsealer led us right to you. I'm going to enjoy—"

He cut off as Shaizan stepped forward in a blur and smacked the heel of her hand against his wrist, breaking it, knocking the sword from his fingers. She snapped her hand upward, chopping him in the throat. Then she curled her fingers into a fist and placed a tight, short, full-knuckled punch into his chest. Six ribs shattered.

Zu stumbled backward, gasping, eyes wide with absolute shock. His sword clanged to the ground. Shaizan stepped past him, pulling his knife from his belt and whipping it up to cut the tie on his cloak.

Zu toppled to the floor, leaving the cloak in her fingers.

Shai might have said something to him. Shaizan didn't have the patience for witticisms or gibes. A warrior kept moving, like a river. She didn't break stride as she whipped the cloak around and entered the hallway behind Zu.

He gasped for breath. He'd live, but he wouldn't hold a sword again for months.

Movement came from the end of the hallway: white-limbed creatures, too thin to be alive. Shaizan prepared herself with a wide stance, body turned to the side, facing down the hallway, knees slightly bent. It did not matter how many monstrosities the Bloodsealer had; it did not matter if she won or lost.

The challenge mattered. That was all.

There were five, in the shape of men with swords. They scrambled down the hall, bones clattering, eyeless skulls regarding her without expression beyond that of their ever-grinning, pointed teeth. Some bits of the skeletals had been replaced by wooden carvings to fix bones that had broken in battle. Each creature bore a glowing red seal on its forehead; blood was required to give them life.

Even Shaizan had never fought monsters like this before. Stabbing them would be useless. But those bits that had been replaced . . . some were pieces of rib or other bones the skeletals shouldn't need to fight. So if bones were broken or removed, would the creature stop working?

It seemed her best chance. She did not consider further. Shaizan was a creature of instinct. As the things reached her, she whipped Zu's cloak around and tossed it over the head of the first one. It thrashed, striking at the cloak as she engaged the second creature.

She caught its attack on the blade of Zu's dagger, then stepped up so close she could smell its bones, and reached in just below the thing's rib cage. She grabbed the spine and yanked, pulling free a handful of vertebrae, the tip of the sternum cutting her forearm. All of the bones of each skeletal seemed to be sharpened.

It collapsed, bones clattering. She was right. With the pivotal bones removed, the thing could no longer animate. Shaizan tossed the handful of vertebrae aside.

That left four of them. From what little she knew, skeletals did not tire and were relentless. She had to be quick, or they would overwhelm her.

The three behind attacked her; Shaizan ducked away, getting around the first one as it pulled off the cloak. She grabbed its skull by the eye sockets, earning a deep cut in the arm from its sword as she did so. Her blood sprayed against the wall as she yanked the skull free; the rest of the creature's body dropped to the ground in a heap.

*Keep moving. Don't slow.*

If she slowed, she died.

She spun on the other three, using the skull to block one sword strike and the dagger to deflect another. She skirted around the third, and it scored her side.

She could not feel pain. She'd trained herself to ignore it in battle. That was good, because that one would have *hurt.*

She smashed the skull into the head of another skeletal, shattering both. It dropped, and Shaizan spun between the other two. Their backhand strikes clanged against one another. Shaizan's kick sent one of them stumbling back, and she rammed her body against the other, crushing it up against the wall. The bones pushed together, and she got hold of the spine, then yanked free some of the vertebrae.

The creature's bones fell with a racket. Shaizan wavered as she righted herself. Too much blood lost. She was slowing. When had she dropped the dagger? It must have slipped from her fingers as she slammed the creature against the wall.

Focus. One left.

It charged her, a sword in each hand. She heaved herself forward—getting inside its reach before it could swing—and grabbed its forearm bones. She couldn't pull them free, not from that angle. She grunted, keeping the swords at bay. Barely. She was weakening.

It pressed closer. Shaizan growled, blood flowing freely from her arm and side.

She head-butted the thing.

That worked worse in real life than it did in stories. Shaizan's vision dimmed and she slipped to her knees, gasping. The skeletal fell before her, cracked skull rolling free from the force of the blow. Blood dripped down the side of her face. She'd split her forehead, perhaps cracked her own skull.

She fell to her side and fought for consciousness.

Slowly, the darkness retreated.

Shaizan found herself amid scattered bones in an otherwise empty hallway of stone. The only color was that of her blood.

She had won. Another challenge met. She howled a chant of her adopted family, then retrieved her dagger and cut off pieces of her blouse. She used them to bind her wounds. The blood loss was bad. Even a woman with her training would not be meeting any further challenges today. Not if they required strength.

She managed to rise and retrieve Zu's cloak—still immobilized by pain, he watched her with amazed eyes. She gathered all five skulls of the Bloodsealer's pets and tied them in the cloak.

That done, she continued down the hallway, trying to project strength—not the fatigue, dizziness, and pain she actually felt.

*He will be here somewhere. . . .*

She yanked open a storage closet at the end of the hall and found the Bloodsealer on the floor inside, eyes glazed by the shock of having his pets destroyed in rapid succession.

Shaizan grabbed the front of his shirt and hauled him to his feet. The move almost made her pass out again. *Careful.*

The Bloodsealer whimpered.

"Go back to your swamp," Shaizan growled softly. "The one waiting for you doesn't care that you're in the capital, that you're making so much money, that you're doing it all for her. She wants you home. That's why her letters are worded as they are."

Shaizan said that part for Shai, who would feel guilty if she did not.

The man looked at her, confused. "How do you . . . *Ahhrgh!*"

He said the last part as Shaizan rammed her dagger into his leg. He collapsed as she released his shirt.

"That," Shaizan said to him softly, leaning down, "is so that I have some of your blood. Do not hunt me. You saw what I did to your pets.

I will do worse to you. I'm taking the skulls, so you cannot send them for me again. *Go. Back. Home.*"

He nodded weakly. She left him in a heap, cowering and holding his bleeding leg. The arrival of the skeletals had driven everyone else away, including guards. Shaizan stalked toward the stables, then stopped, thinking of something. It wasn't too far off . . .

*You're nearly dead from these wounds,* she told herself. *Don't be a fool.*

She decided to be a fool anyway.

A short time later, Shaizan entered the stables and found only a couple of frightened stable hands there. She chose the most distinctive mount in the stables. So it was that—wearing Zu's cloak and hunkered down on his horse—Shaizan was able to gallop out of the palace gates, and not a man or woman tried to stop her.

"Was she telling the truth, Gaotona?" Ashravan asked, regarding himself in the mirror.

Gaotona looked up from where he sat. *Was she?* he thought to himself. He could never tell with Shai.

Ashravan had insisted upon dressing himself, though he was obviously weak from his long stay in bed. Gaotona sat on a stool nearby, trying to sort through a deluge of emotions.

"Gaotona?" Ashravan asked, turning to him. "I was wounded, as that woman said? You went to a *Forger* to heal me, rather than our trained resealers?"

"Yes, Your Majesty."

*The expressions,* Gaotona thought. *How did she get those right? The way he frowns just before asking a question? The way he cocks his head when not answered immediately. The way he stands, the way he waves his fingers when he's saying something he thinks is particularly important . . .*

"A MaiPon Forger," the emperor said, pulling on his golden coat. "I hardly think *that* was necessary."

"Your wounds were beyond the skill of our resealers."

"I thought nothing was beyond them."

"We did as well."

The emperor regarded the red seal on his arm. His expression tightened. "This will be a manacle, Gaotona. A weight."

"You will suffer it."

Ashravan turned toward him. "I see that the near death of your liege has not made you any more respectful, old man."

"I have been tired lately, Your Majesty."

"You're judging me," Ashravan said, looking back at the mirror. "You always do. Days alight! One day I will rid myself of you. You realize that, don't you? It's only because of past service that I even consider keeping you around."

It was uncanny. This *was* Ashravan; a Forgery so keen, so perfect, that Gaotona would never have guessed the truth if he hadn't already known. He wanted to believe that the emperor's soul had still been there, in his body, and that the seal had simply . . . uncovered it.

That would be a convenient lie to tell himself. Perhaps Gaotona would start believing it eventually. Unfortunately, he had seen the emperor's eyes before, and he knew . . . he *knew* what Shai had done.

"I will go to the other arbiters, Your Majesty," Gaotona said, standing. "They will wish to see you."

"Very well. You are dismissed."

Gaotona walked toward the door.

"Gaotona."

He turned.

"Three months in bed," the emperor said, regarding himself in the mirror, "with no one allowed to see me. The resealers couldn't do anything. They can fix any normal wound. It was something to do with my mind, wasn't it?"

*He wasn't supposed to figure that out,* Gaotona thought. *She said she wasn't going to write it into him.*

But Ashravan had been a clever man. Beneath it all, he had *always* been clever. Shai had restored him, and she couldn't keep him from thinking.

"Yes, Your Majesty," Gaotona said.

Ashravan grunted. "You are fortunate your gambit worked. You could have ruined my ability to think—you could have sold my soul itself. I'm not sure if I should punish you or reward you for taking that risk."

"I assure you, Your Majesty," Gaotona said as he left, "I have given myself both great rewards and great punishments during these last few months."

He left then, letting the emperor stare at himself in the mirror and consider the implications of what had been done.

For better or worse, they had their emperor back.

Or, at least, a copy of him.

# EPILOGUE: DAY ONE HUNDRED AND ONE

"And so I hope," Ashravan said to the assembled arbiters of the eighty factions, "that I have laid to rest certain pernicious rumors. Exaggerations of my illness were, obviously, wishful fancy. We have yet to discover who sent the assassins, but the murder of the empress is *not* something that will go ignored." He looked over the arbiters. "Nor will it go unanswered."

Frava folded her arms, watching the copy with satisfaction, but also displeasure. *What back doors did you put into his mind, little thief?* Frava wondered. *We will find them.*

Nyen was already inspecting copies of the seals. The Forger claimed that he could retroactively decrypt them, though it would take time. Perhaps years. Still, Frava would eventually know how to control the emperor.

Destroying the notes had been clever on the girl's part. Had she guessed, somehow, that Frava wasn't really making copies? Frava shook her head and stepped up beside Gaotona, who sat in their box of the Theater of Address. She sat down beside him, speaking very softly. "They are accepting it."

Gaotona nodded, his eyes on the fake emperor. "There isn't even a whisper of suspicion. What we did . . . it was not only audacious, it would be presumed impossible."

"The girl could put a knife to our throats," Frava said. "The proof of what we did is burned into the emperor's own body. We will need to tread carefully in coming years."

Gaotona nodded, looking distracted. Days afire, how Frava wished she could get him removed from his station. He was the only one of the arbiters who ever took a stand against her. Just before his assassination, Ashravan had been ready to do it at her prompting.

Those meetings had been private. Shai wouldn't have known of them, so the fake would not either. Frava would have to begin the process again, unless she found a way to control this duplicate Ashravan. Both options frustrated her.

"A part of me can't believe that we actually did it," Gaotona said softly as the fake emperor moved on to the next section of his speech, a call for unity.

Frava sniffed. "The plan was sound all along."

"Shai escaped."

"She will be found."

"I doubt it," he said. "We were lucky to catch her that once. Fortunately, I do not believe we have much to worry about from her."

"She'll try to blackmail us," Frava said. *Or she'll try to find a way to control the throne.*

"No," Gaotona said. "No, she is satisfied."

"Satisfied with escaping alive?"

"Satisfied with having placed one of her creations on the throne. Once, she dared to try to fool thousands—but now she has a chance to fool millions. An entire empire. Exposing what she has done would ruin the majesty of it, in her eyes."

Did the old fool really believe that? His naiveness often presented Frava with opportunities; she'd considered letting him keep his station simply for that reason.

The fake emperor continued his speech. Ashravan *had* liked to hear himself speak. The Forger had gotten that right.

"He's using the assassination as a means of bolstering our faction," Gaotona said. "You hear? The implications that we need to unify, pull together, remember our heritage of strength . . . And the rumors, the ones the Glory Faction spread regarding him being killed . . . by mentioning them, he weakens their faction. They gambled on him not returning, and now that he has, they seem foolish."

"True," Frava said. "Did you put him up to that?"

"No," Gaotona said. "He refused to let me counsel him on his speech. This move, though, it feels like something the old Ashravan would have done, the Ashravan from a decade ago."

"The copy isn't perfect, then," Frava said. "We'll have to remember that."

"Yes," Gaotona said. He held something, a small, thick book that Frava didn't recognize.

A rustling came from the back of the box, and a servant of Frava's Symbol entered, passing Arbiters Stivient and Ushnaka. The youthful messenger came to Frava's side, then leaned down.

Frava gave the girl a displeased glance. "What can be so important that you interrupt me here?"

"I'm sorry, Your Grace," the woman whispered. "But you asked me to arrange your palace offices for your afternoon meetings."

"Well?" Frava asked.

"Did you enter the rooms yesterday, my lady?"

"No. With the business of that rogue Bloodsealer, and the emperor's demands, and . . ." Frava's frown deepened. "What is it?"

Shai turned and looked back at the Imperial Seat. The city rolled across a group of seven large hills; a major faction house topped each of the outer six, with the palace dominating the central hill.

The horse at her side looked little like the one she'd taken from the palace. It was missing teeth and walked with its head hanging low, back bowed. Its coat looked as if it hadn't been brushed in ages, and the creature was so underfed, its ribs poked out like the slats on the back of a chair.

Shai had spent the previous days lying low, using her beggar Essence Mark to hide in the Imperial Seat's underground. With that disguise in place, and with one on the horse, she'd escaped the city with ease. She'd removed her Mark once out, however. Thinking like the beggar was . . . uncomfortable.

Shai loosened the horse's saddle, then reached under it and placed a fingernail against the glowing seal there. She snapped the seal's rim with some effort, breaking the Forgery. The horse transformed immediately, back straightening, head rising, sides swelling. It danced uncertainly, head darting back and forth, tugging against the reins. Zu's warhorse was a fine animal, worth more than a small house in some parts of the empire.

Hidden among the supplies on his back was the painting that Shai had stolen, again, from Arbiter Frava's office. A forgery. Shai had never had cause to steal one of her own works before. It felt . . . amusing. She'd left the large frame cut open with a single Reo rune carved in the center on the wall behind. It did not have a very pleasant meaning.

She patted the horse on the neck. All things considered, this wasn't a bad haul. A fine horse and a painting that, though fake, was so realistic that even its owner had thought it was the original.

*He's giving his speech right now,* Shai thought. *I would like to have heard that.*

Her gem, her crowning work, wore the mantle of imperial power. That thrilled her, but the thrill had driven her onward. Even making him live again had not been the cause of her frantic work. No, in the end, she'd pushed herself so hard because she'd wanted to leave a few specific changes embedded within the soul. Perhaps those months of being genuine to Gaotona had changed her.

*Copy an image over and over on a stack of paper,* Shai thought, *and eventually the lower sheets will bear the same image, pressed down. Deep within.*

She turned, taking out the Essence Mark that would transform her into a survivalist and hunter. Frava would anticipate Shai using the roads, so she would instead make her way into the deep center of the nearby Sogdian Forest. Those depths would hide her well. In a few months, she would carefully proceed out of the province and continue on to her next task: tracking down the Imperial Fool, who had betrayed her.

For now, she wanted to be far away from walls, palaces, and courtly lies. Shai hoisted herself into the horse's saddle and bid farewell to both the Imperial Seat and the man who now ruled it.

*Live well, Ashravan,* she thought. *And make me proud.*

Late that night, following the emperor's speech, Gaotona sat by the familiar hearth in his personal study looking at the book that Shai had given him.

And marveling.

The book was a copy of the emperor's soulstamp, in detail, with notes. Everything that Shai had done lay bare to him here.

Frava would not find an exploit to control the emperor, because there wasn't one. The emperor's soul was complete, locked tight, and all his own. That wasn't to say that he was exactly the same as he had been.

*I took some liberties, as you can see,* Shai's notes explained. *I wanted to replicate his soul as precisely as possible. That was the task and the challenge. I did so.*

*Then I took the soul a few steps farther, strengthening some memories, weakening others. I embedded deep within Ashravan triggers that will cause him to react in a specific way to the assassination and his recovery.*

*This isn't changing his soul. This isn't making him a different person. It is merely nudging him toward a certain path, much as a con man on the street will strongly nudge his mark to pick a certain card. It is him. The him that could have been.*

*Who knows? Perhaps it is the him that would have been.*

Gaotona would never have figured it out on his own, of course. His skill was faint in this area. Even if he'd been a master, he suspected he wouldn't have spotted Shai's work here. She explained in the book that her intention had been to be so subtle, so careful, that no one would be able to decipher her changes. One would have to know the emperor with extreme depth to even suspect what had happened.

With the notes, Gaotona could see it. Ashravan's near death would send him into a period of deep introspection. He would seek his journal, reading again and again the accounts of his youthful self. He would see what he had been, and would finally, truly seek to recover it.

Shai indicated the transformation would be slow. Over a period of years, Ashravan would become the man that he'd once seemed destined to be. Tiny inclinations buried deep within the interactions of his seals would nudge him toward excellence instead of indulgence. He would start thinking of his legacy, as opposed to the next feast. He would remember his people, not his dinner appointments. He would finally push the factions for the changes that he, and many before him, had noticed needed to be made.

In short, he would become a fighter. He would take that single—but so hard—step across the line from dreamer to doer. Gaotona could see it, in these pages.

He found himself weeping.

Not for the future or for the emperor. These were the tears of a man who saw before himself a *masterpiece.* True art was more than beauty; it was more than technique. It was not just imitation.

It was boldness, it was contrast, it was subtlety. In this book, Gaotona found a rare work to rival that of the greatest painters, sculptors, and poets of any era.

It was the greatest work of art he had ever witnessed.

Gaotona held that book reverently for most of the night. It was the creation of months of fevered, intense artistic transcendence—forced by external pressure, but released like a breath held until the brink of collapse. Raw, yet polished. Reckless, but calculated.

Awesome, yet unseen.

So it had to remain. If anyone discovered what Shai had done, the emperor would fall. Indeed, the very empire might shake. No one could know that Ashravan's decision to finally become a great leader had been set in motion by words etched into his soul by a blasphemer.

As morning broke, Gaotona slowly—excruciatingly—stood up beside his hearth. He clutched the book, that matchless work of art, and held it out.

Then he dropped it into the flames.

# POSTSCRIPT

In writing classes, I was frequently told, "Write what you know." It's an adage writers often hear, and it left me confused. Write what I know? How do I do that? I'm writing fantasy. I can't know what it's like to use magic—for that matter, I can't know what it's like to be female, but I want to write from a variety of viewpoints.

As I matured in skill, I began to see what this phrase meant. Though in this genre we write about the fantastic, the stories work best when there is solid grounding in our world. Magic works best for me when it aligns with scientific principles. Worldbuilding works best when it draws from sources in our world. Characters work best when they're grounded in solid human emotion and experience.

Being a writer, then, is as much about observation as it is imagination.

I try to let new experiences inspire me. I've been lucky enough in this field that I am able to travel frequently. When I visit a new country, I try to let the culture, people, and experiences there shape themselves into a story.

Once when I visited Taiwan, I was fortunate enough to visit the National Palace Museum, with my editor Sherry Wang and translator Lucie Tuan along to play tour guides. A person can't take in thousands of years of Chinese history in a matter of a few hours, but we did our best. Fortunately, I had some grounding in Asian history and lore already. (I lived for two years in Korea as an LDS missionary, and I then minored in Korean during my university days.)

Seeds of a story started to grow in my mind from this visit. What stood out most to me were the stamps. We sometimes call them "chops" in English, but I've always called them by their Korean name of *tojang.*

In Mandarin, they're called *yìnjiàn.* These intricately carved stone stamps are used as signatures in many different Asian cultures.

During my visit to the museum, I noticed many of the familiar red stamps. Some were, of course, the stamps of the artists—but there were others. One piece of calligraphy was covered in them. Lucie and Sherry explained: Ancient Chinese scholars and nobility, if they liked a work of art, would sometimes stamp it with their stamp too. One emperor in particular loved to do this, and would take beautiful sculptures or pieces of jade—centuries old—and have his stamp and perhaps some lines of his poetry carved into them.

What a fascinating mind-set. Imagine being a king, deciding that you particularly liked Michelangelo's *David,* and so having your signature carved across the chest. That's essentially what this was.

The concept was so striking, I began playing with a stamp magic in my head. Soulstamps, capable of rewriting the nature of an object's existence. I didn't want to stray too close to Soulcasting from the Stormlight world, and so instead I used the inspiration of the museum—of history—to devise a magic that allowed rewriting an object's past.

The story grew from that starting place. As the magic aligned a great deal with a system I'd been developing for Sel, the world where *Elantris* takes place, I set the story there. (I also had based several cultures there on our-world Asian cultures, so it fit wonderfully.)

You can't always write what you know—not exactly what you know. You can, however, write what you see.

# THE HOPE OF ELANTRIS

This story takes place after and contains major spoilers for *Elantris*.

MY lord," Ashe said, hovering in through the window. "Lady Sarene begs your forgiveness. She's going to be a tad late for dinner."

"A tad?" Raoden asked, amused as he sat at the table. "Dinner was supposed to start an hour ago."

Ashe pulsed slightly. "I'm sorry, my lord. But . . . she made me promise to relay a message if you complained. 'Tell him,' she said, 'that I'm pregnant and it's his fault, so that means he has to do what I want.'"

Raoden laughed.

Ashe pulsed again, looking as embarrassed as a seon could, considering he was simply a ball of light.

Raoden sighed, resting his arms on the table of his palace inside Elantris. The walls around him glowed with a very faint light, and no torches or lanterns were necessary. He'd always wondered about the lack of lantern brackets in Elantris. Galladon had once explained that there were plates made to glow when pressed—but they'd both forgotten just how much light had come from the stones themselves.

He looked down at his empty plate. *We once struggled so hard for just a little bit of food,* he thought. *Now it's so commonplace that we can spend an hour dallying before we eat.*

Yet food was plentiful. Raoden himself could turn garbage into fine corn. Nobody in Arelon would ever go hungry again. Still, thinking about such things took his mind back to New Elantris, and the simple peace he'd forged inside the city.

"Ashe," Raoden said, a thought suddenly occurring to him. "I've been meaning to ask you something."

"Of course, Your Majesty."

"Where were you during those last hours before Elantris was restored? I don't remember anything of you for most of the night. In fact, the only time I remember seeing you is when you came to tell me that Sarene had been kidnapped and taken to Teod."

"That's true, Your Majesty," Ashe said.

"So, where were you?"

"It is a long story, Your Majesty," the seon said, floating down beside Raoden's chair. "It began when Lady Sarene sent me ahead to New Elantris, to warn Galladon and Karata that she was sending them a shipment of weapons. That was just before the monks attacked Kae, and I went to New Elantris, completely unaware of what was about to occur. . . ."

Matisse took care of the children.

That was her job, in New Elantris. Everyone had to have a job; that was Spirit's rule. She didn't mind her job—actually, she rather enjoyed it. She'd been doing it for longer than Spirit had been around. Ever since Dashe had found her and taken her back to Karata's palace, Matisse had been watching after the little ones. Spirit's rules just made it official.

Yes, she enjoyed the duty. Most of the time.

"Do we really have to go to bed, Matisse?" Teor asked, giving her his best wide-eyed look. "Can't we stay up, just this once?"

Matisse folded her arms, raising a hairless eyebrow at the little boy. "You had to go to bed yesterday at this time," she noted. "And the day before. And, actually, the day before that. I don't see why you think today should be any different."

"Something's going on," said Tiil, stepping up beside his friend. "The adults are all drawing Aons."

Matisse glanced out the window. The children—the fifty or so of them beneath her care—stayed in an open-windowed building dubbed the Roost because of the intricate carvings of birds on most of its walls. The Roost was located near the center of the city-within-a-city—close to Spirit's own home, the Korathi chapel where he held most of his important meetings. The adults wanted to keep a close watch on the children.

Unfortunately, that meant that the children could also keep a close watch on the adults. Outside the window, flashes of light sparked from hundreds of fingers drawing Aons in the air. It was late—far later than the children should have been up—but it had been particularly difficult to get them to bed this night.

*Tiil is right,* she thought. *Something* is *going on.* However, that was no reason to let him stay up—especially because the longer he stayed awake, the longer it would be before she'd be able to go out and investigate the commotion herself.

"It's nothing," Matisse said, looking back at the children. Though some of them had begun to bed down in their brightly colored sheets, many had perked up and were watching Matisse deal with the two troublemakers.

"Doesn't look like nothing to me," Teor said.

"Well," Matisse said, sighing. "They're writing Aons. If you're that interested, I suppose that we could make an exception and let you stay up . . . assuming you want to practice writing Aons. I'm sure we could fit in another school lesson tonight."

Teor and Tiil both paled. Drawing Aons was what one did in school—something that Spirit had forced them to begin attending again. Matisse smiled slyly to herself as the two boys backed away.

"Oh, come now," she said. "Go get your quills and paper. We could draw Aon Ashe a hundred or so times."

The boys got the hint and slipped back to their respective beds. On the other side of the room, several of the other workers were moving among the children, making certain that they were sleeping. Matisse did likewise.

"Matisse," a voice said. "I can't sleep."

Matisse turned toward where a young girl was sitting up in her bedroll. "How do you know, Riika?" Matisse said, smiling slightly. "We just put you to bed—you haven't tried to sleep yet."

"I know I won't be able to," the little girl said pertly. "Mai always tells me a story before I sleep. If he doesn't, I can't sleep."

Matisse sighed. Riika rarely slept well—especially on nights when she asked for her seon. It had, of course, gone mad when Riika had been taken by the Shaod.

"Lie down, dear," Matisse said soothingly. "See if sleep comes."

"It won't," Riika said, but she did lie down.

Matisse made the rest of her rounds, then walked to the front of the room. She glanced over the huddled forms—many of whom were still shuffling and moving—and acknowledged that she felt their same apprehensiveness. Something was wrong with this night. Lord Spirit had disappeared, and while Galladon told them not to worry, Matisse found it a foreboding sign.

"What *are* they doing out there?" Idotris whispered quietly from beside her.

Matisse glanced outside, where many of the adults were standing around Galladon, drawing the Aons in the night.

"Aons don't work," Idotris said. The teenage boy was, perhaps, two years older than Matisse—not that such things really mattered in Elantris, where everyone's skin was the same blotchy grey, their hair limp or simply gone. The Shaod tended to make ages difficult to determine.

"That's no reason not to practice Aons," Matisse said. "There's a power to them. You can see it."

Indeed, there was a power behind the Aons. Matisse had always been able to feel it—raging behind the lines of light drawn in the air.

Idotris snorted. "Useless," he said, folding his arms.

Matisse smiled. She wasn't certain if Idotris was *always* so grumpy, or if he just tended to be that way when he worked at the Roost. He didn't seem to like the fact that he, as a young teenager, had been relegated to childcare instead of being allowed to join Dashe's soldiers.

"Stay here," she said, wandering out of the Roost toward the open courtyard where the adults were standing.

Idotris just grunted in his usual way, sitting down to make certain none of the children snuck out of the sleeping room, nodding to a few other teenage boys who had finished seeing to their charges.

Matisse wandered through the open streets of New Elantris. The night was crisp, but the cold didn't bother Matisse. That was one of the advantages of being an Elantrian.

She seemed to be one of the few who could see things that way. The others didn't consider being an Elantrian as advantageous, no matter what Lord Spirit said. To Matisse, however, his words made sense. But perhaps that had to do with her situation. On the outside, she'd been a beggar—she'd spent her life being ignored and feeling useless. Yet inside of Elantris she was needed. Important. The children looked up to her, and she didn't have to worry about begging or stealing food.

True, things had been fairly bad before Dashe had found her in a sludge-filled alley. And there were the wounds. Matisse had one on her cheek—a cut she'd gotten soon after entering Elantris. It still burned with the same pain it had the moment she'd gotten it. Yet that was a small price to pay. At Karata's palace, Matisse had found her first real taste of usefulness. That sense of belonging had only grown stronger when Matisse—along with the rest of Karata's band—had moved to New Elantris.

Of course, there was something else she'd gained by getting thrown into Elantris: a father.

Dashe turned, smiling in the lanternlight as he saw her approach. He wasn't her real father, of course. She'd been an orphan even before the Shaod had taken her. And, like Karata, Dashe was sort of a parent to all of the children they'd found and brought to the palace.

Yet Dashe seemed to have a special affection for Matisse. The stern warrior smiled more when Matisse was around, and she was the one he called on when he needed something important done. One day, she'd simply started calling him Father. He'd never objected.

He laid a hand on her shoulder as she joined him at the very edge of the courtyard. In front of them, a hundred or so people moved their arms in near unison. Their fingers left glowing lines in the air behind them—the trails of light that had once produced the magics of AonDor. Galladon stood at the front of the group, calling out instructions in his loose Duladen drawl.

"Never thought I'd see the day when that Dula taught people Aons," Dashe said quietly, his other hand resting on the pommel of his sword.

*He's tense too,* Matisse thought. She looked up. "Be nice, Father. Galladon is a good man."

"He's a good man, perhaps," Dashe said. "But he's no scholar. He messes up the lines more often than not."

Matisse didn't point out that Dashe himself was pretty terrible when it came to drawing Aons. She eyed Dashe, noting the frown on his lips. "You're mad that Spirit hasn't come back yet," she said.

Dashe nodded. "He should be here, with his people, not chasing that woman."

"There might be important things for him to learn outside," Matisse said quietly. "Things to do with other nations and armies."

"The outside doesn't concern us," Dashe said. He could be a stubborn one at times.

Well, most times, actually.

At the front of the crowd, Galladon spoke. "Good," he said. "That's Aon Daa—the Aon for power. Kolo? Now, we have to practice adding the Chasm line. We won't add it to Aon Daa. Don't want to blow holes in our pretty sidewalks now, do we? We'll practice it on Aon Rao instead—that one doesn't seem to do anything important."

Matisse frowned. "What's he talking about, Father?"

Dashe shrugged. "Seems that Spirit believes the Aons might work now, for some reason. We've been drawing them wrong all along, or something like that. I can't see how the scholars who designed them could have missed an entire line for every Aon, though."

Matisse doubted that scholars had ever "designed" the Aons. There was just something too . . . primal about them. They were things of nature. They hadn't been designed—any more than the wind had been designed.

Still, she said nothing. Dashe was a kind and determined man, but he didn't have much of a mind for scholarship. That was fine with Matisse—it had been Dashe's sword, in part, that had saved New Elantris from destruction at the hands of the wildmen. There was no finer warrior in all of New Elantris than her father.

Yet she did watch with curiosity as Galladon talked about the new line. It was a strange one, drawn across the bottom of the Aon.

*And . . . this makes the Aons work?* she thought. It seemed like such a simple fix. Could it be possible?

The sound of a cleared throat came from behind them and they turned, Dashe nearly pulling his sword.

A seon hung in the air there. Not one of the insane ones that floated madly about Elantris, but a sane one glowing with a full light.

"Ashe!" Matisse said happily.

"Lady Matisse." Ashe bobbed in the air.

"I'm no lady!" she said. "You know that."

"The title has always seemed appropriate to me, Lady Matisse," he said. "Lord Dashe. Is Lady Karata nearby?"

"She's in the library," Dashe said, taking his hand off the sword.

*Library?* Matisse thought. *What library?*

"Ah," Ashe said in his deep voice. "Perhaps I can deliver my message to you, then, as Lord Galladon appears to be busy."

"If you wish," Dashe said.

"There is a new shipment coming, my lord," Ashe said quietly. "Lady Sarene wished that you be made aware of it quickly, as it is of an . . . important nature."

"Food?" Matisse asked.

"No, my lady," Ashe said. "Weapons."

Dashe perked up. "Really?"

"Yes, Lord Dashe," the seon said.

"Why would she send those?" Matisse asked, frowning.

"My mistress is worried," Ashe said quietly. "It seems that tensions are growing on the outside. She said . . . well, she wants New Elantris to be prepared, just in case."

"I'll gather some men immediately," Dashe said, "and go collect the weapons."

Ashe bobbed, indicating that he thought this to be a good idea. As her father walked off, Matisse eyed the seon, a thought occurring to her. Maybe . . .

"Ashe, could I borrow you for a moment?" she asked.

"Of course, Lady Matisse," the seon said. "What do you need?"

"Something simple, really," Matisse said. "But it might just help. . . ."

Ashe finished his story, and Matisse smiled to herself, eyeing the sleeping form of the little girl Riika in her bedroll. The child seemed peaceful for the first time in weeks.

Bringing Ashe into the Roost had initially provoked quite a reaction from the children who weren't asleep. Yet as he'd begun to talk, Matisse's instincts had proven correct. The seon's deep, sonorous voice had quieted the children. Ashe had a rhythm about his speech that was wonderfully soothing. Hearing a story from a seon had not only coaxed little Riika to sleep, but the rest of the stragglers as well.

Matisse stood, stretching her legs, then nodded toward the doors outside. Ashe hovered behind her, passing the sullen Idotris at the front doors again. He was tossing pebbles toward a slug that had somehow found its way into New Elantris.

"I'm sorry to take so much of your time, Ashe," Matisse said quietly when they were far enough away not to wake the children.

"Nonsense, Lady Matisse," Ashe said. "Lady Sarene can spare me for a bit. Besides, it is good to tell stories again. It has been some time since my mistress was a child."

"You were Passed to Lady Sarene when she was that young?" Matisse asked, curious.

"At her birth, my lady," Ashe said.

Matisse smiled wistfully.

"You shall have your own seon someday, I should think, Lady Matisse," Ashe said.

Matisse cocked her head. "What makes you say that?"

"Well, there was a time when almost no Elantrian went without a seon. I'm beginning to think that Lord Spirit may just be able to fix this city—after all, he fixed AonDor. If he does, we shall find you a seon of your own. Perhaps one named Ati. That is your own Aon, is it not?"

"Yes," Matisse said. "It means hope."

"A fitting Aon for you, I believe," Ashe said. "Now, if my duties here are finished, perhaps I should—"

"Matisse!" a voice said.

Matisse winced, glancing at the Roost, filled with its sleeping occupants. A light was bobbing in the night, coming down a side street—the source of the yelling.

"Matisse?" the voice demanded again.

"Hush, Mareshe!" Matisse hissed, crossing the street quietly to where the man stood. "The children are sleeping!"

"Oh," Mareshe said, pausing. The haughty Elantrian wore standard New Elantris clothing—bright trousers and shirt—but he had modified his with a couple of sashes that he believed made the costume more "artistic."

"Where's that father of yours?" Mareshe asked.

"Training the people with swords," Matisse said quietly.

"What?" Mareshe asked. "It's the middle of the night!"

Matisse shrugged. "You know Dashe. Once he gets an idea in his head . . ."

"First Galladon wanders off," Mareshe grumbled, "and now Dashe is waving swords in the night. If only Lord Spirit would come back . . ."

"Galladon's gone?" Matisse asked, perking up.

Mareshe nodded. "He disappears like this sometimes. Karata too. They'll never tell me where they've gone. Always so secretive! 'You're in charge, Mareshe,' they say, then go off to have secret conferences without me. Honestly!" With that, the man wandered away, bearing his lantern with him.

*Off somewhere secret,* Matisse thought. *That library Dashe mentioned?* She eyed Ashe, who was still hovering beside her. Perhaps if she coaxed him enough, he'd tell her—

At that moment, the screaming began.

The shouts were so sudden, so unexpected, that Matisse jumped. She spun about, trying to determine the location of the sounds. They seemed to be coming from the front of New Elantris.

"Ashe!" she said.

"I'm already going, Lady Matisse," the seon said, zipping into the air, a glowing speck in the night.

The yells continued. Distant, echoing. Matisse shivered, backing up unconsciously. She heard other things. The ring of metal against metal.

She turned back toward the Roost. Taid, the adult who supervised the Roost, had walked out of the building in his nightgown. Even in the darkness, Matisse could see a look of concern on his face.

"Wait here," he said.

"Don't leave us!" Idotris said, looking around in fright.

"I'll be back." Taid rushed away.

Matisse shared a look with Idotris. The other teenagers who had been on duty watching the kids had already gone to their own homes for the night. Only Idotris and she remained.

"I'm going to go with him," Idotris said, stalking after Taid.

"Oh no you don't," Matisse said, grabbing his arm and pulling him back. In the distance, the yelling continued. She glanced toward the Roost. "Go wake the kids."

"What?" Idotris said indignantly. "After all the work we did to get them to sleep?"

"Do it," Matisse snapped. "Get them up, and have them put their shoes on."

Idotris resisted for a moment, then grumbled something and stalked inside the room. A moment later, she could hear him doing as she asked, rousing the children. Matisse rushed over to a building across the street—one of the supply buildings. Inside, she found two lanterns with oil in them, and some flint and steel.

She paused. *What am I doing?*

*Just being prepared,* she told herself, shivering as the screaming continued. It seemed to be getting closer. She rushed back across the street.

"My lady!" Ashe's voice said. She glanced up to see that the seon was flying back down toward her. His Aon was so dim that she could barely see him.

"My lady," Ashe said urgently. "Soldiers have attacked New Elantris!"

"What?" she asked, shocked.

"They wear red and have the height and dark hair of Fjordells, my lady," Ashe said. "There are hundreds of them. Some of your soldiers are fighting at the front of the city, but there are far too few of them. New Elantris is already overrun! My lady—the soldiers are coming this way, and they're searching through the buildings!"

Matisse stood, dumbfounded. *No. No, it can't happen. Not here. This place is peaceful. Perfect.*

*I escaped the outside world. I found a place where I belonged. It can't come after me.*

"My lady!" Ashe said, sounding terrified. "Those screams . . . the soldiers are attacking the people they find!"

*And they're coming this way.*

Matisse stood, lanterns clutched in numb fingers. This was the end, then. After all, what could she do? Nearly a child herself, a beggar, a girl without family or home. What could she do?

*I take care of the children. It's my job.*

*It's the job Lord Spirit gave me.*

"We have to get them out," Matisse said, sprinting toward the Roost. "They know where to look because we cleaned this section of Elantris. The city is huge—if we get the children out into the dirty part, we can hide them."

"Yes, my lady," Ashe said.

"You go find my father!" Matisse said. "Tell him what we're doing."

With that, she entered the Roost, Ashe hovering away into the night. Inside, Idotris had done as she asked, and the children were groggily putting on their shoes.

"Quickly, children," Matisse said.

"What's going on?" Tiil demanded.

"We've got to go," Matisse said to the young troublemaker. "Tiil, Teor, I'm going to need your help—you and all of the older children, all right? You have to try and help the young ones. Keep them moving, and keep them quiet. All right?"

"Why?" Tiil asked, frowning. "What's going on?"

"It's an emergency," Matisse said. "That's all you need to know."

"Why are *you* in charge?" Teor said, stepping up to his friend, folding his arms.

"You know my father?" Matisse said.

They nodded.

"You know he's a soldier?" Matisse asked.

Again, a nod.

"Well, that makes me a soldier too. It's hereditary. He's a captain, so I'm a captain. And that means I get to tell you what to do. You can be my subcaptains, though, if you promise to do what I say."

The two younger boys paused, then Tiil nodded. "Makes sense," he said.

"Good. Now *move*!"

The boys went to help the younger children. Matisse began to herd them out the front door, into the darkened streets. Many of them, however, had caught on to the terror of the night, and were too scared to budge.

"Matisse!" Idotris hissed, coming closer. "What is going on?"

"Ashe says New Elantris is under attack," Matisse said, kneeling beside her lanterns. "Soldiers are slaughtering everyone."

Idotris grew quiet.

She lit the lanterns, then stood. As she'd expected, the children—even the little ones—gravitated toward the light, and the sense of protection it offered. She handed one lantern to Idotris, and by its glow she could see his terrified face.

"What do we do?" he asked with a shaking voice.

"We run," Matisse said, rushing out of the room.

And the children followed. Rather than be left behind in the dark, they ran after the light, Tiil and Teor helping the smaller ones, Idotris trying to hush those who began to cry. Matisse was worried at bringing light, but it seemed the only way. Indeed, they barely kept the children moving as it was, herding them in the fastest way out of New Elantris—which was the way directly away from the screams, now frightfully close.

That also took them away from the populated sections of New Elantris. Matisse had hoped that they'd run into someone who could help as they moved. Unfortunately, those who weren't out practicing Aons were with her father, practicing with weapons. The only occupied buildings would have been the ones Ashe had indicated were being attacked. Their occupants . . .

*Don't think about that,* Matisse thought as their ragged band of fifty children reached the edges of New Elantris. They were almost free. They could—

A voice suddenly yelled behind them, speaking in a harsh tongue Matisse didn't understand. Matisse spun, looking over the heads of frightened children. The center of New Elantris was glowing faintly. From firelight.

It was burning.

There, framed by the flames of death, was a squad of three men in red uniforms. They carried swords.

*Surely they wouldn't kill children,* Matisse thought, her hand shaking as it held its lantern.

Then she saw the glint in the soldiers' eyes. A dangerous, grim look. They advanced on her group. Yes, they would kill children. Elantrian children, at least.

"Run," Matisse said, her voice quavering. Yet she knew the children could never move faster than these men. "Run! Go and—"

Suddenly, as if out of nowhere, a ball of light zipped from the sky. Ashe moved between the men, spinning around their heads, distracting them. The men cursed, waving their swords about in anger, looking up at the seon.

Which is why they completely missed seeing Dashe charge them.

He took them from the side, coming through a shadowed alleyway in New Elantris. He knocked down one soldier, sword flashing, then spun toward the other two as they cursed, turning away from the seon.

*We need to go!* "Move!" she cried again, urging Idotris and the others to keep going. The children backed away from the sword fight, heading out into the night, following Idotris's light. Matisse stayed near the back, turning with concern toward her father.

He wasn't doing well. He was an excellent warrior, but the soldiers had been joined by two other men, and Dashe's body was weakened by being Elantrian. Matisse stood, holding her lantern in trembling fingers, uncertain what to do. The children were sniffling in the dark behind her, their retreat painfully slow. Dashe fought bravely, his rusty sword replaced by one that Sarene must have sent. He knocked aside blade after blade, but he was getting surrounded.

*I have to do something!* Matisse thought, stepping forward. At that moment, Dashe turned, and she could see cuts on his face and body. The look of dread she saw in his eyes made her freeze up.

"Go," he whispered, his voice lost in the clamor, but his lips moving. "Run!"

One of the soldiers rammed his sword through Dashe's chest.

"No!" Matisse screamed. But that only drew their attention as Dashe collapsed, quivering on the ground. The pain had become too much for him.

The soldiers looked at her, then began to advance. Dashe had taken down more than one of them, but there were three left.

Matisse felt numb.

"Please, my lady!" Ashe floated down beside her, hovering urgently. "You must run!"

*Father is dead. No, worse—he's Hoed.* Matisse shook her head, forcing herself to stay alert. She'd seen tragedy as a beggar. She could keep going. She had to.

These men would find the children. The children were too slow. Unless . . . She looked up at the seon beside her, noting the glowing Aon at his center. It meant "light."

"Ashe," she said urgently as the soldiers approached. "Find Idotris ahead. Tell him to put out his lantern, then lead him and the others to someplace safe!"

"Someplace safe? I don't know if *any* place is safe."

"That library you spoke of," Matisse said, thinking quickly. "Where is it?"

"Straight north from here, my lady," Ashe said. "In a hidden chamber beneath a squat building. It is marked by Aon Rao."

"Galladon and Karata are there," Matisse said. "Take the children to them—Karata will know what to do."

"Yes," Ashe said. "Yes, that sounds good."

"Don't forget about the lantern," Matisse said as he flew away. She turned to face the advancing soldiers. Then, with a shaky finger, she raised a hand and began to draw.

Light burst from the air, following her finger. She forced herself to remain steady, completing the Aon despite her fear. The soldiers paused as they watched her, then one of them said something in a guttural language she assumed was Fjordell. They continued to advance on her.

Matisse finished the Aon—Aon Ashe, the same one inside of her seon friend. But of course the Aon didn't do anything. It just hung there, like they always did. The soldiers approached uncaringly, stepping right up to it.

*This had better work,* Matisse thought, then put her finger in the place that Galladon had demonstrated and drew the final line.

Immediately, the Aon—Aon Ashe—began to glow with a powerful light right in front of the soldiers' faces. They called out as the sudden flash of brilliance shone in their eyes, then cursed, stumbling back. Matisse reached down to grab her lantern and run.

The soldiers yelled after her, then began to follow. And, like the children earlier, they went toward the light—her light. Idotris and the others weren't that far away—she could see their shadows still moving in the night—but the soldiers had been blinded too much to notice the faint movements, and Idotris had put out his light. The only thing for the soldiers to focus on was her lantern.

Matisse led them away into the dark night, clutching her lantern in terrified fingers. She could hear them pursuing behind her as she entered Elantris proper. Sludge and darkness replaced the clean paving stones of New Elantris, and Matisse had to stop moving so quickly, lest she slide and stumble.

She hurried anyway, rounding corners, trying to stay ahead of her pursuers. She felt *so* weak. Running was hard as an Elantrian. She didn't have the strength to go very quickly. Already she was beginning to feel a powerful fatigue inside of her. She couldn't hear any more pursuit. Perhaps . . .

She turned a corner and ran afoul of a pair of soldiers standing in the night. She paused in shock, looking up at the men, recognizing them from before.

*They're trained soldiers,* she thought. *Of course they know how to surround an enemy and cut them off!* She spun to run, but one of the men grabbed her arm, laughing and saying something in Fjordell.

Matisse cried out, dropping the lantern. The soldier stumbled, but held her firm.

*Think!* Matisse told herself. *You only have a moment.* Her feet slipped in the sludge. She paused, then let herself fall, kicking at her captor's leg.

She was counting on one thing: She'd lived in Elantris. She knew how to move in the slime and sludge. These soldiers, however, didn't. Her kick landed true, and the soldier immediately slipped, stumbling into his companion and crashing back to the slimy street as he released Matisse.

She scrambled to her feet, her beautiful bright clothing now stained with Elantris sludge. Her leg flared with a new pain—she'd twisted her ankle. She'd been so careful in the past to keep free of major pains, but this one was stronger than anything she'd gotten before, far stronger than the cut on her cheek. Her leg burned with a pain she could barely believe, and it didn't abate—it remained strong. An Elantrian's wounds would never heal.

Still, she forced herself to limp away. She moved without thinking, only wishing to get away from the soldiers. She heard them cursing, stumbling to their feet. She kept going, hopping slightly. She didn't realize that she had moved in a circle until she saw the glow of New Elantris burning in front of her. She was back where she had begun.

She paused. There he was, Dashe, lying on the paving stones. She rushed to him, not caring anymore about pursuit. Her father lay with the sword still impaling him, and she could hear him whispering.

"Run, Matisse. Run to safety. . . ." The mantra of a Hoed.

Matisse stumbled to her knees. She'd gotten the children to safety. That was enough. There was a noise behind her, and she turned to see a soldier approaching. His companion must have gone a different direction. Yet this man was stained with slime, and she recognized him. He was the one she had kicked.

*My leg hurts so much!* she thought. She turned over, holding to Dashe's immobile body, too tired—and too pained—to move any further.

The soldier grabbed her by the shoulder and pulled her away from her father's corpse. He spun her around, the action bringing other pains to her arms.

"You tell me," he said in a thickly accented voice. "You tell me where other children went."

Matisse struggled in vain. "I don't know!" she said. But she did. Ashe had told her. *Why did I ask him where the library was?* she berated herself. *If I didn't know, I couldn't give them away!*

"You tell," the man said, holding her with one hand, reaching for his belt knife with the other. "You tell, or I hurt you. Bad."

Matisse struggled uselessly. If her Elantrian eyes could have formed tears, she would have been crying. As if to prove his point, the soldier held up his knife before her. Matisse had never felt such terror in her life.

And that was when the ground began to shake.

The eastern sky had begun to glow with the coming of dawn, but that light was overshadowed by a sudden burst of light from around the perimeter of the city. The soldier paused, looking up at the sky.

Suddenly Matisse felt warm.

She didn't realize how much she'd missed feeling warm, how much she'd grown used to the stale coolness of an Elantrian body. But the warmth seemed to flow through her, like someone had injected a hot liquid into her veins. She gasped at the beautiful, amazing feeling.

Something was *right.* Something was wonderfully right.

The soldier turned toward her. He cocked his head, then reached out and rubbed a rough finger across her cheek, where she had been wounded long ago.

"Healed?" he said, confused.

She felt wonderful. She felt . . . her heart!

The man, looking confused, raised his knife again. "You healed," he said, "but I can hurt you again."

Her body felt stronger. Yet she was still just a young girl, and he a trained soldier. She struggled, her mind barely beginning to comprehend that her skin was no longer blotched, but had turned a silvery color. It was happening! As Ashe had predicted! Elantris was returning!

And she was still going to die. It wasn't fair! She screamed in frustration, trying to wiggle free. The irony seemed perfect. The city was being healed, but that couldn't prevent this terrible man from—

"I think you missed something, friend," a voice suddenly said.

The soldier paused.

"If the light healed her," the voice said, "then it healed *me* too."

The soldier cried out in pain, then dropped Matisse, stumbling to the ground. She stepped back, and as the terrible man collapsed, she could finally see who was standing behind: her father, glowing with an inner light, the taint removed from his body. He seemed like a god, silvery and spectacular.

His clothing was ripped where he'd been wounded, but the skin was healed. In his hand he held the very sword that had been impaling him moments before.

She ran to him, crying—she could finally cry again!—and she grabbed him in an embrace.

"Where are the other children, Matisse?" he said urgently.

"I took care of them, Father," she whispered. "Everyone has a job, and that's mine. I take care of the children."

"And what did happen to the children?" Raoden asked.

"I led them to the library," Ashe said. "Galladon and Karata were gone by then—we must have missed them as they ran back to New Elantris. But I hid the children inside, and stayed with them to keep them calm. I was so worried about what was happening inside the city, but those poor things . . ."

"I understand," Raoden said. "And Matisse . . . Dashe's little daughter. I had no idea what she'd gone through." Raoden smiled. He'd given Dashe two seons—ones whose masters had died, and who had found themselves without anyone to serve once they recovered their wits when Elantris was restored—in thanks for his services to New Elantris. Dashe had given one to his daughter.

"Which seon did she end up with?" Raoden asked. "Ati?"

"Actually, no," Ashe said. "I believe it was Aeo."

"Equally appropriate," Raoden said, smiling and standing as the door opened. His wife, Queen Sarene, entered, pregnant belly first.

"I agree," Ashe said, hovering over to Sarene.

Aeo. It meant "bravery."

# POSTSCRIPT

This short story has a rather interesting backstory.

If we flash back to January 2006, we find me having been dating Emily (who would eventually become my wife) for about two months. On one of our dates, Emily told me something amazing. One of her eighth-grade students—a girl named Matisse—had done a book report on *Elantris*. Now, Matisse didn't know that her teacher was dating me. She didn't even know that Emily knew me. It was just a bizarre coincidence.

This report she did was incredible. Instead of a simple write-up, she created a worldbook about Sel; it had sketches and bios of the characters, strips of Elantrian cloth stapled in as examples, and little pouches filled with materials from the book. Emily showed it to me, and it completely blew me away. Back then, I was still very new to being a published writer, and seeing the work that Matisse had put into her report was one of the most striking moments of my early career.

I wanted to do something special as a thank-you for Matisse, who still didn't know that her teacher was dating one of her favorite authors. I decided to write a little companion story to *Elantris*.

In any novel, there are events you decide to leave out for pacing reasons. I knew what was going on inside the city of Elantris when the attack by the Dakhor came. In the back of my mind, I also knew that the children were saved and protected by Dashe and Ashe the seon. I didn't want them to fall like the others; Karata had worked so hard to protect them, and letting the children not have to suffer through the slaughter at New Elantris was my gift to her.

I decided to write a little story to deal with all of this. And because Matisse had inspired me, I decided that I would name a character after her. The Matisse in the story doesn't act like the real Matisse. I didn't know the real Matisse; I'd never met her. Now, though, I've met her a number of times—she comes to my signings on occasion. She even gave us the original *Elantris* book-report book as a wedding gift.

Looking back at this story, I think it might be a tad on the sentimental side. I hope that it doesn't come off as too melodramatic. (Read outside the context of the *Elantris* novel, I think that it might.) But for what the story is, I'm quite pleased with it.

# THE SCADRIAN SYSTEM

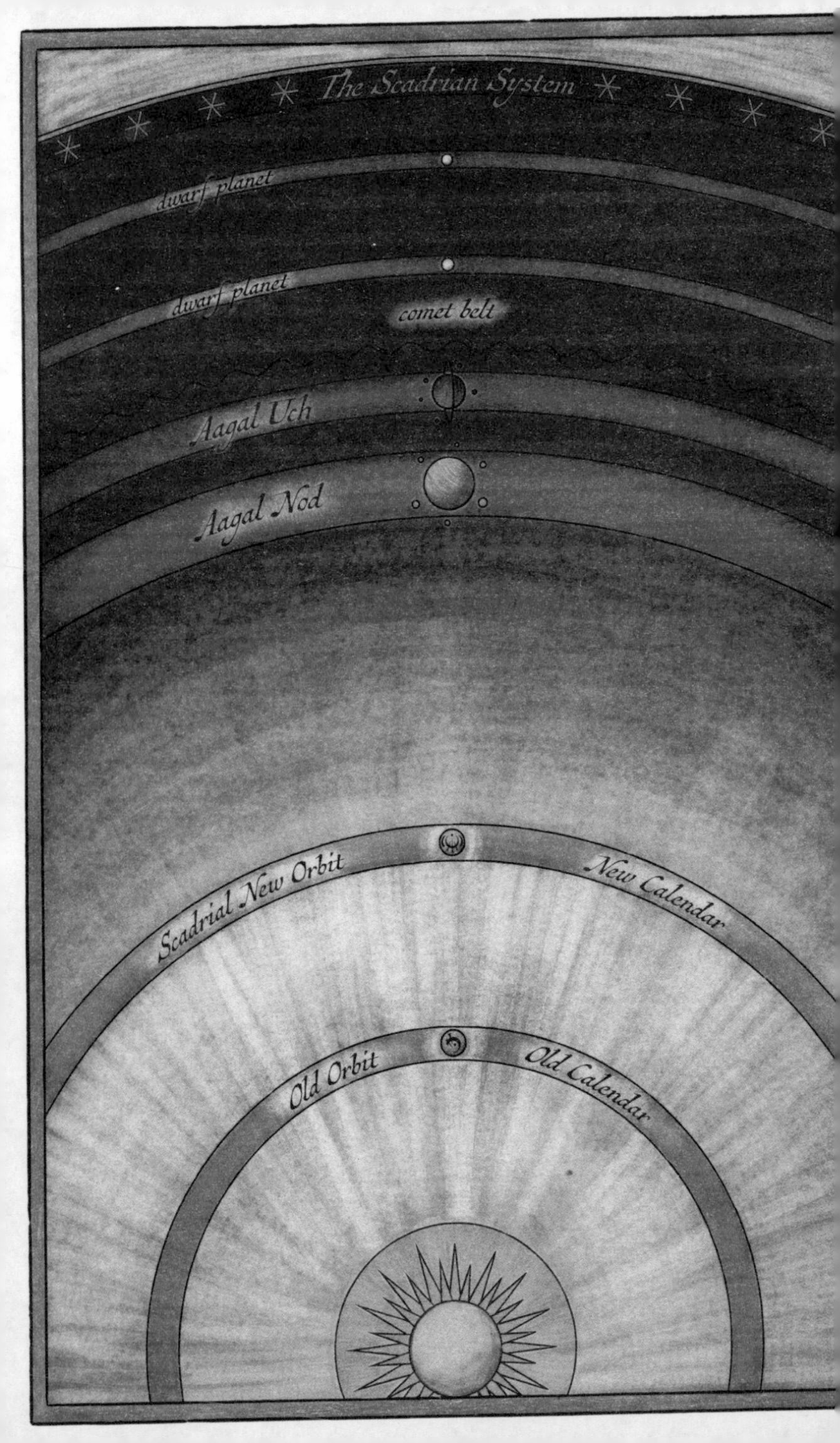
The Scadrian System
dwarf planet
dwarf planet
comet belt
Aagal Uch
Aagal Nod
Scadrial New Orbit
New Calendar
Old Orbit
Old Calendar

# THE SCADRIAN SYSTEM

The inner system here is basically empty, save for the planet Scadrial, which is fortuitous—considering the vast changes the system has undergone because of the influence of its Shards.

The remarkable thing about Scadrial is how well humankind has flourished on it, despite these repeated cataclysms. Surely other planets in the cosmere have seen worse disasters, but on none of them will you find a thriving, technologically advanced society as exists on Scadrial.

Indeed, I am convinced that without the Lord Ruler's oppression of technology on the planet for a thousand years, Scadrial would have eclipsed all others in scientific learning and progress—all on its own, without the interaction between societies we enjoy in Silverlight.

Scadrial, another dishardic planet, is characterized by a host of unique features. It is one of only two places in the cosmere where humankind does not predate the arrival of Shards. Indeed, I am convinced from my studies that the planet itself *did not exist* before its Shards, Ruin and Preservation, arrived in the system. They picked a star with no relevant planets in orbit, specifically choosing this location because it was empty, so they could place there whatever they wished.

Yes, the Shards undoubtedly used humans from Yolen as a model (indeed, both of the Vessels for these Shards were human before their Ascensions) in creating life. Because of this, the flora and fauna on Scadrial are very similar to what you'll find on Yolen. (The non-fain parts, of course.) It is also very similar to Yolen in size and gravitation, both being exactly at 1.0 cosmere standard.

Though the Shards created this planet together, it quickly became the symbol of—and prize in—their conflict. To speak on the personalities of the Vessels themselves is not my field of expertise; better to approach one of my colleagues who specializes in pre-Shattering biography and history, rather than an arcanist. I can say, however, that their conflict is manifested directly in the ways that Investiture is used on Scadrial.

This is a powerful magic, and one where humans themselves have often had access to grand bursts of strength. I would challenge one to identify another planet, save only Roshar, where one can find such strength of Investiture so commonly in the hands of mortals. Periodically throughout Scadrial's history, a man or woman gained access to vast amounts of power, with incredible effects. The most obvious evidence of this is the fact that the star charts Guyn has so kindly provided list *two* orbits for Scadrial. The planet was *literally moved* at various points by individuals wielding immense amounts of Investiture. (As an aside, this has wreaked havoc with trying to understand historical calendars on the planet.)

I have written much about the magics of this planet. Indeed, I could fill entire volumes with my thoughts on Allomancy, Feruchemy, and Hemalurgy. I maintain, however, that the one of these with the largest potential impact on the cosmere is Hemalurgy. Usable by anyone with the right knowledge, this dangerous creation has proven able to warp souls regardless of planet or Investiture, creating false Connections that no Shard designed or intended.

Though the planetary system is rather boring, Scadrial itself has proven intriguing time and time again. This is despite the fact that humans used to live on a relatively small portion of the planet. (A fact that began to change once the extreme environments of the Final Empire were removed.)

From the adaptations (both forced and unforced) of the humans living on her, to the vast transformations of landscape during her different eras, Scadrial remains my favorite planet for scholarly study in the cosmere. The interactions of her magics with natural physics are multitude, varied, and fascinating.

# THE ELEVENTH METAL

This story may be read before the original Mistborn Trilogy.

KELSIER held the small, fluttering piece of paper pinched between two fingers. The wind whipped and tore at the paper, but he held firm. The picture was wrong.

He'd tried at least two dozen times to draw it right, to reproduce the image that she'd always carried. The original had been destroyed, he was certain. He had nothing to remind him of her, nothing to remember her by. So he tried, poorly, to reconstruct the image that she had treasured.

A flower. That was what it had been called. A myth, a story. A dream.

"You need to stop doing that," his companion growled. "I should stop you from drawing those."

"Try," Kelsier said softly, folding the small piece of paper between two fingers, then tucking it into his shirt pocket. He would try again later. The petals needed to be more tear-shaped.

Kelsier regarded Gemmel with a calm gaze, then smiled. That smile felt forced. How could he smile in a world without her?

Kelsier kept smiling. He'd do so until it felt natural. Until that numbness, tied in a knot within him, started to unravel and he began to feel again. If that was possible.

*It is. Please let it be.*

"Drawing those pictures makes you think of the past," Gemmel snapped. The aging man had a ragged grey beard, and the hair on his head was so unkempt, it actually looked *better*-groomed when it was being whipped around by the wind.

"It does," Kelsier said. "I won't forget her."

"She betrayed you. Move on." Gemmel didn't wait to see if Kelsier continued arguing. He moved away; he often stopped in the middle of arguments.

Kelsier didn't squeeze his eyes shut as he wanted to. He didn't scream defiance to the dying day as he wanted to. He shoved aside thoughts of Mare's betrayal. He should never have spoken his concerns to Gemmel.

He had. That was that.

Kelsier broadened his smile. It took effort.

Gemmel glanced back at him. "You look creepy when you do that."

"That's because you've never had a real smile in your life, you old heap of ash," Kelsier said, joining Gemmel by the short wall at the edge of the roof. They looked down on the dreary city of Mantiz, nearly drowning in ash. The people here in the far north of the Western Dominance weren't as good at cleaning it up as people were back in Luthadel.

Kelsier had assumed there would be less ash out here—only one of the ashmounts was nearby, this far out. It *did* seem that the ash fell a little less frequently. But the fact that nobody organized to clean it up meant that it felt like there was far more.

Kelsier curled his hand around the coping of the wall. He'd never liked this part of the Western Dominance. The buildings out here felt . . . melted. No, that was the wrong term. They felt too rounded, with no corners, and they were rarely symmetrical—one side of the building would be higher, or more lumpy.

Still, the ash was familiar. It covered the building here just the same as everywhere, giving everything a uniform cast of black and grey. A layer of it coated streets, clung to the ridges of buildings, made heaps in alleys. Ashmount ash was sootlike, much darker than the ash from a common fire.

"Which one?" Kelsier asked, rotating his gaze among the four massive keeps that broke the city skyline. Mantiz was a large city for this dominance, though—of course—it was nothing like Luthadel. There weren't any other cities like Luthadel. Still, this one was respectable.

"Keep Shezler," Gemmel said, pointing toward a tall, slender building near the center of the city.

Kelsier nodded. "Shezler. I can get in the door easily. I'll need a costume—fine clothing, some jewelry. We need to find a place I can fence a bead of atium—and a tailor who can keep his mouth shut."

Gemmel snorted.

"I've got a Luthadel accent," Kelsier said. "From what I heard on the street earlier, Lord Shezler is absolutely *infatuated* with the Luthadel nobility. He'll fawn over someone who presents himself right; he wants connections to society closer to the capital. I—"

"You aren't thinking like an Allomancer," Gemmel cut him off, his voice gruff.

"I'll use emotional Allomancy," Kelsier said. "Turn him to my—"

Gemmel suddenly roared, spinning on Kelsier, moving too quickly. The ragged man snagged Kelsier by the front of his shirt and shoved him to the ground, looming over him, rattling the roof tiles. "You're Mistborn, not some street Soother working for clips! You want to be taken again? Snatched up by *his* minions, sent back to where you belong? Do you?"

Kelsier glared back at Gemmel as the mists began to grow in the air around them. Sometimes Gemmel seemed more beast than man. He began muttering to himself, speaking as if to a friend Kelsier couldn't see or hear.

Gemmel leaned closer, still muttering, his breath pungent and sharp, his eyes wide and frenzied. This man wasn't completely sane. No. That was a gross understatement. This man had only a fringe of sanity left to him, and even that fringe was beginning to fray.

But he was the only Mistborn who Kelsier knew, and dammit, Kelsier was going to learn from the man. It was either that or start taking lessons from some nobleman.

"Now you listen," Gemmel said, almost pleading. "*Listen* for once. I'm here to teach you how to fight. Not how to talk. You already do that.

We didn't come here so you could saunter in playing nobleman, like you did in the old days. I won't let you talk through this, I *won't.* You're Mistborn. You fight."

"I will use whatever tool I have to."

"You'll fight! Do you want to be weak again, let them take you again?"

Kelsier was silent.

"You want vengeance on them? Don't you?"

"Yes," Kelsier growled. Something massive and dark shifted within him, a beast awakened by Gemmel's prodding. It cut through even the numbness.

"You want to kill, don't you? For what they did to you and yours? For taking her from you? Well, boy?"

"Yes!" Kelsier barked, flaring his metals, shoving Gemmel back.

Memories. A dark hole lined by crystals sharp as razors. Her sobs as she died. His sobs as they broke him. Crumpled him. Ripped him apart.

His screams as he remade himself.

"Yes," he said, coming up onto his feet, pewter burning within him. He forced himself to smile. "Yes, I'll have vengeance, Gemmel. But I'll have it my way."

"And what way is that?"

Kelsier faltered.

It was an unfamiliar experience for him. He'd always had a plan, before. Plans upon plans. Now, without her, without anything . . . The spark was snuffed out, the spark that had always driven him to reach beyond what others thought possible. It had led him from plan to plan, heist to heist, riches to riches.

It was gone now, replaced by that knot of numbness. The only thing he could feel these days was rage, and that rage couldn't guide him.

He didn't know what to do. He hated that. He'd always known what to do. But now . . .

Gemmel snorted. "When I'm done with you, you'll be able to kill a hundred men with a single coin. You'll be able to Pull a man's own sword from his fingers and strike him down with it. You'll be able to crush men within their armor, and you'll be able to cut the air like the mists themselves. You will be a *god.* Waste your time with emotional Allomancy when I'm finished. For now, you kill."

The bearded man loped back to the wall and glared at the keep. Kelsier slowly reined in his anger, rubbing his chest where he'd been forced to the ground. And . . . something odd occurred to him. "How do you know what I was like in the old days, Gemmel?" Kelsier whispered. "Who are you?"

Lamps and limelights were lit in the night, their glow breaking out through windows into the curling mists. Gemmel hunkered beside his wall, whispering to himself again. If he heard Kelsier's question, he ignored it.

"You should still be burning your metals," Gemmel said as Kelsier approached. Kelsier bit off a comment about not wanting to waste them. He'd explained that as a skaa child, he had learned to be very careful with resources. Gemmel had just laughed at that. At the time, Kelsier had assumed the laughter was due to Gemmel's natural erratic nature.

But . . . was it because he knew the truth? That Kelsier *hadn't* grown up a poor skaa on the streets? That he and his brother had lived lives of privilege, their half-breed nature kept secret from society?

He hated the nobility, true. Their balls and parties, their prim self-satisfaction, their superiority. But he couldn't deny, not to himself, that he belonged among them. At least as much as he did among the skaa of the streets.

"Well?" Gemmel said.

Kelsier ignited some of the metals inside him, burning several of the eight metal reserves he had within. He'd heard Allomancers speak of those reserves on occasion, but had never expected to feel them himself. They were like wells of energy he could draw upon.

Burning metals inside of him. How strange it sounded—yet how natural it felt. As natural as breathing in air and drawing strength from it. Each of those eight reserves enhanced him in some way.

"All eight," Gemmel said. "*All* of them." He'd be burning bronze to sense what Kelsier was burning.

Kelsier had only burned the four physical metals. Reluctantly, he burned the others. Gemmel nodded; now that Kelsier was burning copper, all signs of his Allomancy would have vanished to the other man. Copper, what a useful metal—it hid you from other Allomancers, and made you immune to their emotional Allomancy.

Some spoke of copper derogatorily. You couldn't use it to fight; you couldn't change things with it. But Kelsier had always envied his friend Trap, who was a copper Misting. It was a powerful thing to know that your emotions were not the result of outside tampering.

Of course, with copper burning, that meant he had to admit that everything he felt—the pain, the anger, and even the numbness—belonged to him alone.

"Let's go," Gemmel said, leaping out into the night.

The mists were almost fully formed. They came every night, sometimes thick, sometimes light. But always there. The mists moved like hundreds of streams piled atop one another. They shifted and spun, thicker, more *alive* than an ordinary fog.

Kelsier had always loved the mists for reasons he couldn't describe. Marsh claimed it was because everyone else feared them, and Kelsier was too arrogant to do what everyone else did. Of course, Marsh had never seemed to fear them either. The two brothers felt something, an understanding, an awareness. The mists claimed some as their own.

Kelsier jumped down from the low roof, burning pewter to strengthen him so that the landing was solid. Then he followed Gemmel on the hard cobblestones, running on bare feet. Tin burned in his stomach; it made him more aware, made his senses stronger. The mists seemed wetter, their prickling dew cooler on his skin. He could hear rats scurrying in distant alleyways, hounds baying, a man snoring softly in a building nearby. A thousand sounds that would be inaudible to an ordinary person's ears. At times when burning tin, the world seemed a cacophony. He couldn't burn it too strongly, lest the noises grow distracting. Just enough to let him see better; tin made the mists appear more faint to his eyes, though why that should be he did not know.

He trailed Gemmel's shadowed form as they reached the wall around Keep Shezler and placed their backs to it. Atop that wall, guards called to one another in the night.

Gemmel nodded, then dropped a coin. The scrawny, bearded man lurched into the air a second later. He wore a mistcloak—a dark grey cloak that was formed of many tassels from the chest down. Kelsier had asked for one. Gemmel had laughed at him.

Kelsier walked up to the fallen coin. The mists nearby dipped and spun in a pattern like insects moving toward a flame—they always did that around Allomancers who were burning metals. He'd seen it happen to Marsh.

Kelsier knelt beside the coin. To his eyes, a faint blue line—almost like a spider's silk—led from his chest to the coin. In fact, hundreds of tiny lines pointed from his chest to each nearby source of metal. Iron and steel created these lines—one for Pushing, one for Pulling. Gemmel had told him to burn all his metals, but Gemmel often made no sense. There was no reason to burn both steel and iron; the two were opposites.

He extinguished his iron, leaving only the steel. With steel, he could *Push* on any source of metal that was connected to him. The Push was mental, but felt much like shoving against something with his arms.

Kelsier positioned himself above the coin and Pushed on it, as Gemmel had trained him. Since the coin couldn't go downward, Kelsier was instead thrown upward. He popped into the air some fifteen feet, then awkwardly grabbed the coping of the wall above. He grunted, hauling himself up over the edge.

A new group of blue lines sprang up at his chest, thickening. Sources of metal approaching him quickly.

Kelsier cursed, throwing out a hand and Pushing. The coins that had been flying toward him were Pushed back into the night, zipping through the mists. Gemmel walked forward, undoubtedly the source of the coins. He attacked Kelsier sometimes; their first night together, Gemmel had thrown him off a cliff.

Kelsier still couldn't completely decide if the attacks were tests, or if the lunatic was actually trying to murder him.

"No," Gemmel muttered. "No, I *like* him. He almost never complains. The other three complained all the time. This one is strong. No. Not strong enough. No. Not yet. He'll learn." Behind Gemmel was a pair of lumps on the wall top. Dead guards, leaking trails of blood along the stones. The blood was black in the night. The mists seemed . . . afraid of Gemmel, somehow. They didn't spin about him as they did other Allomancers.

That was nonsense. Just his mind playing tricks on him. Kelsier stood up, and didn't mention the attack. It wouldn't do any good. He just had to stay aware and learn as much as he could from this man. Preferably without getting killed in the process.

"You don't need to use your hand to Push," Gemmel grumbled at him. "Wastes time. And you need to learn to keep your pewter burning. You shouldn't have had such a hard time climbing up over the edge of the wall."

"I—"

"*Don't* give me an excuse about saving your metals," Gemmel said, inspecting the keep just ahead. "I've met children of the streets. They don't conserve. If you come at one of them, they'll use everything they have—every scrap of strength, every last trick—to take you down. They know how close to the edge they walk. Pray you never have to face one of those, pretty boy. They'll rip you apart, chew you up, and make new reserves for themselves out of what you leave behind."

"I was going to say," Kelsier said calmly, "that you haven't even told me what we're doing tonight."

"Infiltrating this keep," Gemmel said, eyes narrowing.

"Why?"

"Does it matter?"

"It sure as hell does."

"There's something important in there," Gemmel said. "Something we're going to find."

"Well, that explains everything. Thank you for being so forthcoming. Could you possibly enlighten me on the meaning of life, since you're so great at answering questions all of a sudden?"

"Don't know it," Gemmel said. "I think it's so we can die."

Kelsier suppressed a groan, leaning against the wall. *I said that,* he realized, *fully expecting to get some dry remark in return. Lord Ruler, I miss Dox and the crew.*

Gemmel didn't understand humor, even pathetic attempts at it. *I need to get back,* Kelsier thought. *Back to people who care about living. Back to my friends.*

That thought made him shiver. It had only been three months since the . . . events at the Pits of Hathsin. The cuts on his arms were mostly just scars now. He scratched at them anyway.

Kelsier knew his humor was forced, his smiles more dead than alive. He didn't know why he found it so important to hold off returning to Luthadel, but it was. He had exposed wounds, gaping holes in himself that had yet to heal over. He *had* to stay away. He didn't want them to see him like this. Insecure, a man who huddled in his sleep, reliving horrors still fresh. A man with no plan or vision.

Besides, he needed to learn the things Gemmel was teaching him. He couldn't return to Luthadel until . . . until he was himself again. Or at the very least a scarred version of himself, the wounds closed, the memories quieted.

"Let's be on with it then," Kelsier said.

Gemmel glared at him. The old lunatic didn't like it when Kelsier tried to take control. But . . . well, that was what Kelsier did. Somebody had to.

Keep Shezler was constructed in the unusual architectural style typical of any area of the Western Dominance far from Luthadel. Instead of blocks and peaks, it had an almost organic feel, with four tapering towers up front. He thought that buildings out here must be constructed of stone frames with a kind of hardened mud outside, sculpted and shaped to make all those curves and knobs. The keep, like the rest of the buildings, looked unfinished to Kelsier. "Where?" Kelsier said.

"Up," Gemmel said. "Then down." He jumped from the wall and threw a coin for himself. He Pushed against it, and his weight drove it downward. When it hit the ground, Gemmel launched higher toward the building.

Kelsier leaped and Pushed against his own coin. The two of them bounded across the space between the sculpted wall and the lit keep. Powerful limelights burned behind stained-glass windows; here in the Western Dominance, those windows were often odd shapes, and no two were alike. Had these people no understanding of proper aesthetics?

Closer to the building, Kelsier began to Pull instead of Push—he switched from burning steel to burning iron, then yanked on a blue line leading to a steel window frame. That meant he was Pulled upward, as if he were on a tether. It was tricky; the ground still tugged him downward, and he also still had momentum forward, so when he Pulled he had to be careful not to slam himself into things.

With Pulling, he gained more height. He needed it, as Keep Shezler was tall, as tall as any keep in Luthadel. The two Allomancers bounded up the front facade, grabbing or leaping from the knobs and bits of stonework. Kelsier landed on an outcropping, waved his arms for a moment, then snatched hold of a statue that had been placed there for no reason he could discern. It was covered in bits of glaze of different colors.

Gemmel flew past on the right; the other Mistborn moved with a deft grace. He threw a coin to the side, where it hit an outcropping. Then, by pushing on it, Gemmel nudged himself in just the right direction. He spun, mistcloak streaking the mists, then Pulled himself to a different stained-glass window. He hit and hung there like an insect, fingers grabbing bits of metal and stone.

Powerful limelight shone out through the window, which shattered the light into colors, spraying them across Gemmel as if he too were covered in bits of glaze. He looked up, a smile on his lips. In that light, with the mistcloak hanging beneath him, the mists dancing around him, Gemmel suddenly seemed more regal to Kelsier. Distant from the ragged madman. Something far more grand.

Gemmel leaped out into the mists, then Pulled himself upward. Kelsier watched him go, surprised to find himself envious. *I will learn,* he told himself. *I'll be that good.*

From the start, he'd been drawn to zinc and brass, Allomancy that let him play with people's emotions. It had seemed most similar to what he'd done unaided in the past. But he was a new man, reborn in those dreadful pits. Whatever he had been, it wasn't enough. He needed to become something more.

Kelsier threw himself upward, Pulling his way to the roof of the building. Gemmel kept going up past the roof, flying toward the tips of the four spires that adorned the front of the building. Kelsier dropped his entire bag of coins—the more metal you Pushed off, the faster and higher you could go—and flared his steel. He Pushed with everything he had, sending himself upward like an arrow.

Mists streamed around him. The colorful lights of the stained-glass windows withdrew below. A spire dwindled on either side of him, growing more and more narrow. He shoved off the tin cladding on one of them to nudge himself to the right.

With a final Push of strength he crested the very tip of the spire, which had a knob on top the size of man's head. Kelsier landed on it, flaring his pewter, which improved his physical abilities. That didn't just make him stronger; it made him more dexterous as well. Capable of standing on one foot atop a globe a handspan wide hundreds of feet off the ground. Having performed the maneuver, he stopped and stared at his foot.

"You're growing more confident," Gemmel said. The other man had stopped just shy of the tip of the spire, clinging to it below Kelsier. "That's good."

Then with a quick motion, Gemmel leaped up and swept Kelsier's leg from underneath him. Kelsier cried out, losing control and falling into the mists. Gemmel Pushed against the vials full of metal flakes that Kelsier—like most Allomancers—carried on his belt. That Push shoved Kelsier away from the building and out into the mists.

He plummeted, and lost rational thought for a moment. There was a primal terror to falling. Gemmel had spoken about controlling that, about learning not to fear heights or get disoriented while dropping.

Those lessons fled Kelsier's mind. But he was falling. Fast. Through churning mists, disoriented. It would take only seconds to hit the ground.

Desperate, he Pushed on those vials of metal, hoping he was pointed in the right direction. They ripped from his belt and smashed downward into something. The ground.

There wasn't much metal in them. Barely enough to slow Kelsier. He hit the ground a fraction of a second after Pushing, and the blow knocked the wind from him. His vision flashed.

He lay in a daze as something thumped to the ground beside him. Gemmel. The other man snorted in derision. "Fool."

Kelsier groaned and pushed himself up to his hands and knees. He was alive. And remarkably, nothing seemed broken—though his side and thigh smarted something wicked. He'd have awful bruises. Pewter had kept him alive. The fall, even with the Push at the end, would have broken another man's bones.

Kelsier stumbled to his feet and glared at Gemmel, but made no complaint. This probably *was* the best way to learn. At least it would be the fastest. Rationally, Kelsier would have chosen this—being thrown in, forced to learn as he went. That didn't stop him from hating Gemmel.

"I thought we were going up," Kelsier said.

"Then down."

"Then up again, I assume?" Kelsier asked with a sigh.

"No. Down some more." Gemmel strode across the grounds of the keep, passing ornamental shrubbery that had become dark, mist-shrouded silhouettes in the night. Kelsier hastened up beside Gemmel, wary of another attack.

"It's in the basement," Gemmel muttered. "Basement, of all things. Why a basement?"

"What's in the basement?" Kelsier asked.

"Our goal," Gemmel said. "We had to go up high, so I could look for an entrance. I think there's one out here in the gardens."

"Wait, that actually sounds reasonable," Kelsier said. "You must have hit your head on something."

Gemmel glared at him, then shoved his hand into his pocket and pulled out a handful of coins. Kelsier readied his metals, prepared to fight back. But Gemmel turned his hand to the side and sprayed them across a pair of guards who were jogging up the path to see who was walking through the grounds at night.

The men fell, one of them yelling. Gemmel didn't seem to care that it might reveal the two of them. He stalked on ahead.

Kelsier hesitated for a moment, glancing at the dying men. Employed by the enemy. He tried to feel something for them, but he couldn't. That part of him had been ripped out by the Pits of Hathsin, though a different part was disturbed at how little he felt.

He hurried on after Gemmel, who had found what appeared to be a groundskeeping shed. When he pulled open the door, however, there were no tools, just a dark set of steps leading downward.

"Steel burning?" Gemmel asked. Kelsier nodded.

"Watch for movement," Gemmel said, grabbing a handful of coins from his pouch. Kelsier raised a hand toward the fallen guards and Pulled on the coins Gemmel had used against them, flipping them up toward him. He'd seen Gemmel Pull on things lightly, so that they didn't streak toward him at full strength. Kelsier hadn't mastered that trick yet, and he had to crouch down and let the coins spray over his head into the wall of the shed. He gathered them up, then started down after an impatient Gemmel, who was watching him with displeasure.

"I was unarmed," Kelsier explained. "Left my pouch on top of the building."

"Mistakes like that will end with you dead."

Kelsier didn't reply. It *had* been a mistake. Of course, he'd planned to fetch the coin pouch—and would have, if Gemmel hadn't knocked him off the spire.

The light grew dim, then neared blackness as they continued down the steps. Gemmel didn't produce a torch or lantern, but instead waved at Kelsier to go first. Another test of some sort?

Steel burning within Kelsier let him identify sources of metal by their blue lines. He paused, then dropped the handful of coins to the ground, letting them bounce down the steps. In falling, they let him see where the stairs were, and when they came to a rest that gave him an even better picture.

The blue lines weren't really "seeing," and he still had to walk carefully. However, the coins helped a great deal, and he did see a door latch as it drew near. Behind, he heard Gemmel grunt, and for once it seemed appreciative. "Nice trick with the coins," the man murmured.

Kelsier smiled, approaching the door at the bottom. He felt out for it, grabbing the metal latch. He carefully eased it open.

There was light on the other side. Kelsier crouched—despite what Gemmel might think, he'd done his share of infiltrating and quiet nighttime thefts. He wasn't some new sprout. He had simply learned that survival for a half-breed like him meant either learning to talk or learning to sneak; fighting head-on in most situations would have been foolish.

Of course, not one of the three—fighting, talking, or sneaking—had worked that night. The night he'd been taken, a night when nobody could have betrayed him but her. But why had they taken her too? She couldn't have—

*Stop,* he told himself, padding into the room in a crouch. It was full of long tables crowded with various kinds of smelting apparatus. Not the bulky smithing kind, but the small burners and delicate instruments of a master metallurgist. Lamps burned on the walls, and a large red forge glowed in the corner. Kelsier felt fresh air blow through from somewhere; the other side of the room ended in several corridors.

The room appeared empty. Gemmel entered, and Kelsier reached back to Pull the coins to him again. Some were stained with the blood of the fallen guards. Still in his crouch, he passed a desk full of writing implements and small, cloth-bound books. He glanced at Gemmel, who strode through the room without any attempt at stealth. Gemmel put his hands on his hips, looking around. "So where is he?"

"Who?" Kelsier said.

Gemmel started muttering under his breath, moving through the room, sweeping some of the implements off the tables and sending them crashing to the floor. Kelsier slipped around the perimeter, intent on peeking into the side corridors to see if anyone was coming. He checked the first one, and found that it opened into a long, narrow room. It was occupied.

Kelsier froze, then slowly stood up. There were half a dozen people in the room, both men and women, bound by their arms to the walls. There were no cells, but the poor souls looked as if they'd been beaten within an inch of their lives. They wore only rags, and those were bloodied.

Kelsier shook himself out of his daze, then padded to the first woman in the line. He pulled off her gag. The floor was damp; probably someone had been here recently to toss buckets of water on the prisoners to keep the laboratory from stinking. A gust of wind from the distant end of the hallway that the room eventually opened into brought a breath of fresh air.

The woman grew stiff as soon as he touched her, eyes snapping open and growing wide with terror. "Please, please no . . ." she whispered.

"I won't hurt you," Kelsier said. That numbness inside of him seemed to be . . . changing. "Please. Who are you? What is going on here?"

The woman just stared at him. She winced when Kelsier reached up to untie her bonds, and he hesitated.

He heard a muffled sound. Glancing to the side, he saw a second woman, older and matronly. Her skin had been all but flayed from beatings. Her eyes, however, were not nearly as frantic as those of the younger woman. Kelsier moved over and removed her gag.

"Please," the woman said. "Free us. Or kill us."

"What *is* this place?" Kelsier hissed, working on her arm bonds.

"He's searching for half-breeds," she said. "To test his new metals on."

"New metals?"

"I don't know," the woman said, tears on her cheeks. "I'm just skaa, we all are. I don't know why he picks us. He talks about things. Metals, unknown metals. I don't think he's completely sane. The things he does . . . he says they are to bring out our Allomantic side . . . but my lord, I've no noble blood. I can't . . ."

"Hush," Kelsier said, freeing her. Something was burning through that deep knot of numbness inside of him. Something that was like the anger he felt, but somehow different. It was more. It made him want to weep, yet it was warm.

Freed, the woman stared at her hands, wrists scraped raw from the bindings. Kelsier turned to the other poor captives. Most were awake now. There wasn't hope in their eyes. They just stared ahead, dull.

Yes, he could feel it.

*How can we stand a world like this?* Kelsier thought, moving to help another captive. *Where things like this happen?* The most appalling tragedy was that he knew this sort of horror was common. Skaa were disposable. There was nobody to protect them. Nobody cared.

Not even him. He'd spent most of his life ignoring such acts of brutality. Oh, he'd pretended to fight back. But he'd really just been about enriching himself. All of those plans, all of those heists, all of his grand visions. All about him. Him alone.

He freed another of the captives, a young, dark-haired woman. She looked like Mare. After being freed, she just huddled down on the ground in a ball. Kelsier stood over her, feeling powerless.

*Nobody fights,* he thought. *Nobody thinks they can fight. But they're wrong. We can fight. . . .* I *can fight.*

Gemmel strode into the room. He looked over the skaa and barely seemed to notice them. He was still muttering to himself. He had taken just a few steps into the room when a voice yelled from the laboratory.

*"What is going on here?"*

Kelsier recognized that voice. Oh, he'd never heard it specifically before—but he recognized the arrogance in it, the self-assuredness. The contempt. He found himself rising, brushing past Gemmel, stepping back into the lab.

A man in a fine suit, white shirt buttoned to the neck, stood in the laboratory. His hair was short, after the most current trends, and his suit looked to have been shipped in from Luthadel—it certainly was tailored after the most fashionable styles.

He looked at Kelsier, imperious. And Kelsier found himself smiling. *Really* smiling, for the first time since the Pits. Since the betrayal.

The nobleman sniffed, then raised a hand and tossed a coin at Kelsier. After a brief moment of surprise, Kelsier Pushed on it right as Lord Shezler did. Both were thrown backward, and Shezler's eyes widened in shock.

Kelsier slammed back against the wall. Shezler was Mistborn. No matter. A new kind of anger rose within Kelsier even as he grinned. It burned like a metal, that emotion did. An unknown, glorious metal.

He could fight back. He *would* fight back.

The nobleman yanked on his belt, dropping it—and his metals—from his waist. He whipped a dueling cane from his side and jumped forward, moving too quickly. Kelsier flared his pewter, then his steel, and Pushed on the apparatus on one of the tables, flinging it at Shezler.

The man snarled, raising an arm and Pushing some of it away. Again, the two Pushes—one from Kelsier, one from his foe—struck one another, and they were both slammed backward. Shezler steadied himself against a table, which shook. Glass broke and metal tools clattered to the ground.

"Have you any idea what all of that is worth?" Shezler growled, lowering his arm and advancing.

"Your soul, apparently," Kelsier whispered.

Shezler prowled forward, coming close, then struck with the cane. Kelsier backed away. He felt his pocket jerk, and he Pushed, shoving the coins out of his coat as Shezler Pushed on them. A second later, and they would have cut through Kelsier's stomach—as it was, they ripped out of his pocket, then shot backward toward the wall of the room.

His coat's buttons started to shake, though they only had some metal leaf on them. He pulled off the coat, removing the last bit of metal he was carrying. *Gemmel should have warned me about that!* The leaf had barely registered to his senses, but still he felt a fool. The older man was right; Kelsier wasn't thinking like an Allomancer. He focused too much on appearance and not enough on what might kill him.

Kelsier continued to back away, watching his opponent, determined not to make another mistake. He'd been in street brawls before, but not many. He'd tried to avoid them—brawling had been an old habit of Dockson's. For once, he wished he'd been less refined in that particular area.

He edged along one of the tables, waiting for Gemmel to come in from the side. The man didn't enter. He probably didn't intend to.

*This was all about finding Shezler,* Kelsier realized. *So that I could fight another Mistborn.* There was something important in that. . . . It suddenly made sense.

Kelsier growled, and was surprised to hear the sound coming from him. That glowing anger inside of him wanted vengeance, but also something more. Something greater. Not just revenge against those who had hurt him, but against the entirety of noble society.

In that moment, Shezler—arrogantly striding forward, more concerned for his equipment than the lives of his skaa—became a focus for it all.

Kelsier attacked.

He didn't have a weapon. Gemmel had spoken of glass knives, but had never given one to Kelsier. So, he snatched up a shard of broken glass from the floor, heedless of the cuts on his fingers. Pewter let him ignore pain as he jumped toward Shezler, going for his throat.

He probably shouldn't have won. Shezler was the more accomplished and practiced Allomancer—but it was obvious he was unaccustomed to fighting someone as strong as he was. He battered at Kelsier with the dueling cane. But with pewter Kelsier could ignore that as well, and instead he punched his shard of glass into the man's neck—three times.

In seconds it was over. Kelsier stumbled back, aches beginning to register. Shezler might have broken some of his bones with his battering; the man had pewter too, after all. The nobleman lay in his own blood though, twitching. Pewter could save you from a lot of things, but not a slit throat.

The man choked on his own blood. "No," he hissed. "I can't . . . not me . . . I can't die. . . ."

"Anyone can die," Kelsier whispered, dropping the bloodied shard of glass. "Anyone."

And a thought, a seed of a plan, began to form in his mind.

"That was too quick," Gemmel said.

Kelsier looked up, blood dripping from the tips of his fingers. Shezler croaked a final attempt at breath, then fell still.

"You need to learn Pushes and Pulls," Gemmel said. "Dancing through the air, fighting as a real Mistborn does."

"He was a real Mistborn."

"He was a scholar," Gemmel said, walking forward. He kicked at the corpse. "I picked a weak one first. Won't be so easy next time."

Kelsier walked back into the room with the skaa. He freed them, one by one. He couldn't do much more for them, but he promised that he'd see them safely out of the keep's grounds. Maybe he could get them in touch with the local underground; he'd been in the city long enough to have a few contacts.

Once he had them all freed, he turned to find them looking toward him in a huddled group. Some of the life seemed to have rekindled in their eyes, and more than a few were peeking into the room where

Shezler's corpse lay on the floor. Gemmel was picking through a notebook on one of the tables.

"Who are you?" asked the matronly woman he'd spoken to earlier.

Kelsier shook his head, still looking toward Gemmel. "I'm a man who has lived through things he shouldn't have."

"Those scars . . ."

Kelsier looked down at his arms, sliced with hundreds of tiny scars from the Pits. Removing his coat had exposed them.

"Come on," Kelsier said to the people, resisting the urge to cover up his arms. "Let's get you to safety. Gemmel, what in the Lord Ruler's name are you doing?"

The older man grunted, leafing through a book. Kelsier trotted into the room and glanced at it.

*Theories and suppositions regarding the existence of an Eleventh Metal,* the scrawl on the page read. *Personal notes. Antillius Shezler.*

Gemmel shrugged and dropped the book to the table. Then he carefully and meticulously selected a fork from the fallen tools and other scattered laboratory remains. He smiled and chuckled to himself. "Now *that* is a fork." He shoved it into his pocket.

Kelsier took the book. In moments, he was ushering the wounded skaa away from the keep, where soldiers were prowling the yards, trying to figure out what was happening.

Once they were out into the streets again, Kelsier turned back to the glowing building, which was lit with bright colors and beautiful windows. He listened in the curling mists as the guards' shouting became frantic.

The numbness was gone. He'd found something to replace it. His focus had returned. The spark was back. He'd been thinking too small.

A plan began to bud, a plan he barely dared consider for its audacity. Vengeance. And more.

He turned into the night, into the waiting mists, and went to find someone to make him a mistcloak.

# POSTSCRIPT

This short piece was originally published in the Mistborn Adventure Game pen and paper role-playing game by Crafty Games. When we signed on with Crafty, I promised them a short piece of fiction to go in the book, as a sweetener to fans.

I knew I wanted to do a Kelsier story, and it made sense to do a backstory piece digging into the time when he was training as a Mistborn. Showing Gemmel (whom Kelsier had mentioned in the main series) was important, as it is part of the story of how Ruin manipulated Kelsier into doing what he did in the first volume of the trilogy.

At the same time, I also knew that this story would potentially be read by people who hadn't read the series. Having played many RPGs myself, I know that often one or two people in the group get really excited by a setting and do a campaign there—towing along the rest of the group, who aren't as familiar with it.

One of my goals with this piece, then, was to have something that would act as a little showpiece for the setting—I wanted something the game master could give to his players who were unfamiliar with the books. Something that would get across the tone, explain the magic system quickly, and act as a short introduction.

Because of that, it's a little more expository than the other Mistborn pieces in this collection, which assume that you're already invested in the characters and setting.

# ALLOMANCER JAK AND THE PITS OF ELTANIA

EPISODES TWENTY-EIGHT THROUGH THIRTY

SPECIAL BOUND COLLECTION
OF ALL THREE EPISODES!

EDITED AND ANNOTATED BY HANDERWYM,
JAK'S OWN FAITHFUL TERRIS STEWARD!

This story contains minor spoilers for *The Alloy of Law.*

I BEGIN this week's letter as I awake to a mighty headache.

Truly, dear readers, this pain was incredible—and the effect was a din inside my mind not unlike that of a hundred rifles firing. I groaned and rolled to my knees in the darkened chamber; my face had been resting upon cold rock. My vision shook and took time to recover.

What had happened to me? I remembered my contest with the koloss challenger—a brute sized like a steamrail engine, with strength to match. I had defeated him with a bullet through the eye, had I not? Had I not in so doing maintained the loyalty of the entire koloss clan?*

I climbed to my feet and felt gingerly at the back of my head. There, I found dried blood. Fear not, for the wound was not terrible. Surely I had weathered far worse. This was not nearly as bad as when I had found myself sinking in the ocean, my arms bound, my feet tied to a metal bust of the Survivor as I sank.†

---

* Indeed, this was the outcome of Jak's brave—perhaps foolhardy—plan. See episode twenty-six. At this point, Jak had been "king" of the koloss for three episodes, and had survived the latest of challenges to his authority, getting closer to the secrets they held regarding the Survivor's Treasure.

† See "Allomancer Jak and the Mask of Ages," episode fourteen. There, however, Jak writes that it

The arid air and whistling sound of the wind through broken rock indicated I was still in the Roughs, which was good. These lands of adventure and danger are my natural habitat, and I thrive upon the challenge they provide. If I were to spend too long in the safe and mundane environment of milky Elendel, I fear I would wilt away.

My enclosure was a natural cavern of some sort, with rough stone walls and drooping stalactites on the ceiling. The cavern was shallow, however, and I found that it ended only a few feet back from my initial position. I would not be escaping in that direction, then.*

Cautious of potential gunfire, I edged to the front of the cavern and looked out. As I had guessed from the slight chill to the air, I was elevated. My cavern was on the wall of a small canyon, and the mouth opened only to a steep drop onto a group of rounded rocks far below.

Across from me, atop the ridge on the other side of the canyon, a group of blue figures watched my cavern. The hulking koloss were older ones, their skin stretched and broken, their bodies tattooed and draped with leather created from the skin of the men they had slain and eaten.†

"Why have you stranded me here, dread beasts?" I shouted at them, my voice echoing in the canyon. "And what have you done with the fair Elizandra Dramali? If you have harmed one hair upon her ever-beauteous scalp, you shall know the fury of an Allomancer enraged!"

The savages offered me no reply. They sat around their smoldering fire, and did not even turn in my direction.

Perhaps my situation was not as ideal as I had decided upon my first assessment. The canyon wall outside my cavern was as slick as glass and was as steep as the price of whiskey at Marlie's waystop. I surely could not survive an attempt to climb down, not dizzy as I was from the wound.

---

was a bust of the Lord Mistborn. One wonders if Jak ever stops to read his accounts after their publication. Fortunately for me, he does not seem to.

* One might wonder why Jak felt he needed to escape, as he had not discovered if he was imprisoned, and had not yet tried walking out through the front of the cavern. If you have this concern, might I remind you of the last *eighteen times* Jak awoke with a headache at the beginning of an episode? Each time, he had been captured in some fashion.

† Jak is completely, blissfully unaware of modern scholarship regarding the koloss, which indicates that they rarely (if ever) use actual human skin for their trophies. Indeed, accounts of them eating humans are greatly exaggerated.

But neither could I simply wait. Miss Dramali, my dear Elizandra, might surely be in danger. Curse that woman and her headstrong ways; she should have remained at camp as instructed. I had no idea what might have happened to her, nor to faithful Handerwym.* The koloss would not dare harm him, because of their vow to the Terris people,† but surely he feared for my safety.

I gave little thought to how I had reached this dire location. I needed metal. My system was clean of it; I had burned the last to steady my hands and eyes as I took the perfect shot at the koloss challenger to my throne. Unfortunately, my captors had stolen Glint—brutes though they are, the koloss are wise enough to take the guns from a man, particularly after seeing my skill with my trusty sidearm. They had also taken my vials of metal. Perhaps they wanted to see if those contained whiskey. Some Roughs Allomancers do store their metals in such solutions, but I have always abstained from the process. The mind of a gentleman adventurer needs to retain clarity at all times.‡

Surely the hidden pouch of tin in the heel of my boot would serve me. By misfortune, however, the heel's hidden compartment seemed to have been knocked open during my initial scuffle with the koloss champion. I had lost the pouch! I made a note to myself to speak with Ranette about her heel contraption and its tendency to open unexpectedly.

Disaster! An Allomancer without metal. I was left with only my own wits as a tool. Those—though of no small measure—might not be enough. Who knew what kind of trouble the fair Elizandra might be in at this point?

Determined, I began to feel about the cavern. It was an unlikely chance, but we were in highlands prized precisely because of their keen mining opportunities. Indeed, the Survivor favored me this day, for I located a small glimmering strain of metal along the far wall. Almost

---

* I was actually asleep. It had been a very long day. I'm sure I'd have worried about him if it had crossed my mind to do so. The bed the koloss provided, however, was surprisingly comfortable.

† See episode twenty-five for our discovery of their vow not to harm the Terris, and their explanation for the respect they have paid me during our adventures. It is a matter which I have regarded with some interest.

‡ Didn't he just mention the whiskey he often drinks at the waystop? Perhaps the dens of thieves do not count as a place where a clear mind is required.

invisible, I discovered it only by touch.* In the dim cavern I could not judge the metal's full nature, but I had no other options.

Now, I have found from my infrequent trips to Elendel that I am regarded with a somewhat heroic reputation. I must assure you, good readers, that I am but a humble adventurer, not deserving of an unduly idolized status. That said, while I have never wished for glory,† I do value my reputation. Therefore, if I could remove from your memories the image of this next part of my narrative, I would do so.

However, it has ever been my goal to present to you a sincere and unexpurgated account of my travels in the Roughs. Honesty is my greatest virtue.‡ And so, I offer you the truth of what needed to happen next.

I knelt down and began to lick the wall.

I would not ever wish to look foolish before you, dear readers.§ But in order to survive in the Roughs, a man must be willing to seize opportunity. I did so. With my tongue.

This activity gave me very little tin to burn, but it was enough for a few moments of enhanced senses.¶ I used them to listen with care for some clue as to how I might escape this situation.

I heard two things with my tin-enhanced ears. The first was the tinkling of water. I peeked out of my cavern and saw that the rocks below hid a small stream I had not seen earlier. The other thing I heard was a strange scratching, like that of claws on a branch.

I looked up, hopeful, and there found a crow perched among a sprout of weeds growing from the rocky wall. Could it be?

"Well done!" the crow exclaimed to me in her inhuman voice. "You have found metal even in your prison, Jak. The Survivor is pleased by your ingenuity."

---

* Yes, according to the way he wrote that sentence, he turned invisible for one line. No, he won't let me change it.

† Uh . . .

‡ Technically, this is probably true.

§ Well, it was too late for that after volume one. . . .

¶ I will admit to a healthy skepticism about Jak's wall-licking episode. My research indicates that one is highly unlikely to find pure tin exposed in this way inside of a natural cave formation. Even cassiterite, a tin ore of some relevance, would be unlikely in this area—and that might be too Allomantically impure to produce an effect. But Jak *is* being truthful about having lost his pouch of tin. I found it on the ground of the camp following his second capture, full and unopened.

It *was* her. Lyndip, my spirit guide, sent by the Survivor to me during my most difficult times of trial.* I have long suspected her to be one of the Faceless Immortals,† as the legends speak of them being able to change forms and take the bodies of animals.

"Lyndip!" I exclaimed. "Is Miss Dramali well? The koloss have not harmed her?"

"They have not, bold adventurer," Lyndip said. "But she is captured by them and is being held. You must escape, and quickly, for a dire fate awaits her."

"But how am I to escape!"

"I cannot give you the method," Lyndip said. "I am a guide, but I cannot solve a hero's problems for him. It is not the way of the Survivor, who deems that all men must make their own way."‡

"Very well," I said. "But tell me, guide: Why was I taken captive again? Had I not earned the loyalty of the koloss clan; was I not their king? I defeated the challenger!"

I am certain my frustration shone through, and I hope you do not think less of me—dear reader—to see such harsh words spoken to my spirit guide. However, I was not only concerned for the safety of my dear Elizandra, but was also devastated to lose the loyalty of this tribe of koloss. Savages though they are, they had seemed close to revealing their secrets to me—secrets I was certain would lead me to the symbol of the spearhead, the bloody footprints, and the Survivor's Treasure.

"I do not know for certain," Lyndip said, "but I suspect it was because you used a gun to kill the challenger. Previously, in winning the loyalty of the clan, you did not shoot your rival but frightened him off with the placement of your bullet. Many koloss clans see killing at a distance with guns to be a sign of weakness, not strength."

---

* See episode seven of this narrative for Lyndip's most recent appearance. I will repeat what I said there: I did not see, nor have I ever seen, this supposed talking bird and cannot confirm her existence.

† Never mind that the Faceless Immortals are a mythological feature of the Path, not Survivorism. This theological mixup has never bothered Jak.

‡ I suspect Jak was hallucinating through this entire section, a result of the trauma to his head. Upon doing this edit, I wished several times to be similarly afflicted.

Ruthless beasts—savages indeed.* The gun is the most elegant of weapons, the weapon of a gentleman.

"I *must* escape and rescue the fair Elizandra," I said. "Guide, did you see how I reached this cavern prison? Do the koloss have a secret passage somewhere, and did they bring me up here by that method?"

"I saw, adventuresome one," Lyndip said. "But the truth is not what you will wish to hear. There was no secret passage—instead, you were *thrown* up here by some koloss below."†

"Rust and Ruin!" I exclaimed. Undoubtedly, the beasts—afraid of the powerful weapons I had used—had placed me here to die of starvation, rather than risking the anger of their gods by killing me with their own hands.

I needed a way out, and quickly. I looked out again, and noticed storm clouds in the near distance. This started me thinking. I glanced down at the trickle of water in the canyon floor below. As I had noticed, the sides of this canyon were particularly smooth. As if . . . weathered.

Yes! I spotted distinctive lines on the canyon walls—water lines, from when the river ran bold and deep. My avenue of escape was soon to come! Indeed, the rains dumped on the plains upstream, and water soon surged into the canyon and—propelled by the narrower confines here—the river began to swell.

I waited nervously for the right moment to enter the river, and in my waiting, found time despite my anxiety to pen this letter to you. I sealed it in the special, water-proof pocket of my rugged trousers with the hope that if I should meet my end, it would find its way to you somehow once my body was found.

As rain began to fall on the canyon itself, I could wait no longer. I hurled myself into the risen waters below.‡

---

* I once mentioned to Jak that my people, the Terris, were at one time considered savages—at least according to the records given us by Harmony. He put a hand on my shoulder and said, "It is all right. I am proud to count a savage as my friend." He was so sincere, I dared not explain just how insulting he was being.

† I find this strains plausibility, even for a Jak story. More likely, the koloss lowered him from above.

‡ This marks the conclusion of this episode and the beginning of the next—and no, I don't know how he wrote the last paragraph after sealing the letter in his trousers. Regardless, I doubt you think this is Jak's demise, considering this collected volume contains three episodes of which this is

My readers, I trust this message finds you well. As you may recall, last week's missive ended with a dangerous leap on my part toward a watery doom. I was certain that my time had come, but I am somewhat pleased to say that I have survived. Only "somewhat" because of the revelation that I must soon impart unto you. If you must read on, be warned: The contents of this letter are dreadful, and might produce discomfort—even sickness—in the more frail and youthful among you.

I did leap from my cavern prison into the rising waters of the river. I must severely advise my readers against this kind of activity unless presented with the most dire of circumstances. The waters of a Roughs-style flash flood are dangerous, full of eddies and deadly rocks. If I had been presented with any other option, I surely would have taken it.

The waters churned around me like a stampede. Fortunately, I had experience with surviving waters of this nature.*

The key to swimming in waters such as these is to not fight. One must travel with the current, as a ship allows the sea to pull it. Still, even keeping afloat in such a tempest requires practice, luck, and force of will.

With strength of arm, I managed to steer myself around the most deadly of rocks and survive as the waters of my small tributary merged with the greater waters of the Rancid, the greatest river of the area. Here, the larger amount of water caused slower currents, and I managed with some difficulty to swim to the shore and pull myself free.

Exhausted, still dizzy from my wound, I flopped to the bank of the river. No sooner was I free, however, than a set of strong arms hauled me into the air.

Koloss. I had been captured again.

The beasts hauled me, sopping wet, away from the roaring river. I left

---

only the first. However, many of the weekly broadsheet readers of his letters did indeed worry that this was the end of Jak. Just as they worried at the end of the other three hundred episodes. It often strikes me that I wish I could find these people and discover to whom they sold the contents of their skulls, and for how much. I personally much prefer the audience of the *bound* volumes, such as this one. Their keen regard for my personal annotations proves them to be of a superior taste and intellect.

* See "Allomancer Jak and the Waters of Dread" for several equally implausible instances of Jak swimming strong currents and whitewater rapids. I am left to wonder why these extreme events never happen in my presence.

a trail of water in the dust.* I did not fight against my captors. There were six of them, medium-sized koloss, their blue skin starting to pull tight across their bodies, ripping at the sides of the mouths and around the largest of muscles.

They did not speak to me in their brutal tongue, and I knew I could not defeat six at once. Not without my guns and without metal. I deemed it better to let them drag me where they wished. Perhaps I would be placed back in my cavern prison.

Instead, the koloss carted me toward an incongruous stand of trees, hidden within a small valley of rocks. I had never come to this location before—indeed, the koloss had always steered me away from this area, claiming that it was a wasteland. From whence, then, did come the trees?†

The trees hid a small oasis in the dusty ground, a place where water welled up in a natural spring. I found this curious, as prime watering holes are usually marked on my maps.

They drug me past the trees and around the watering hole, and I saw that it was very deep—so deep that the depths were blue, and I could not make out a bottom. The sides were all of stone. And, with a start, I realized that the pool was shaped vaguely like a spearhead.

Could this be it? The location of the Survivor's Treasure? Had I found it at long last?‡ I looked for the other sign, that of the bloody footprints spoken of in the legends. I did not see them until my wet form was dragged across the stones nearest to the pool.

If you travel long in the Roughs, you will find that water sometimes reveals the true color of stone. This is not so much the case in the city where many of you live, dear readers, as the stones are coated in grime and soot. But here, the land is clean and fresh. The water my body dripped on the stones revealed a pattern in the rock not unlike that of a set of footprints leading into the oasis pool.

---

* I am not sure what happened to the rain that was so instrumental in his escape last episode. He doesn't mention it again.

† An unnecessary "from" is the least of Jak's problems, so I left it. I did manage to snip sixteen superfluous commas from this page. Jak is also under the impression that *koloss* looks better with an exclamation point in the center, and I have yet to ascertain the reason. For my own sanity, I have removed these, though I worry it has come too late.

‡ Yup.

This was it! Though not true footprints, I could see how a weary traveler—reaching this location—might mistake them for such. The invented story of the Survivor himself—bleeding from his spear wound and stopping here to drink—made sense.

The place was accoutred with koloss tattoo designs traced on the rocks and had their leatherwork wrapping some of the tree trunks. This was obviously a holy place for them, which explained both the reason I had never heard of this oasis, and the reason men had vanished in this area. Any who stumbled across this spot were murdered for having witnessed what they should not.

What did it say for my future that they had brought me here?*

There were more koloss here, of course. Some were so ancient that they had burst their skin completely; these sat wrapped in leather to contain the slow seeping of blood from their flesh. If you have never seen a koloss ancient, consider yourself lucky. Their immensity of size is only matched by the strangeness of their features, lacking noses or lips, their eyes bulging from faces of red flesh. Most koloss die of heart attacks before reaching this state. These would continue to grow, even after losing their skin, until that fate claimed them.

In ancient times, ones such as these would be killed. In modern days, however, elderly koloss are revered—or so I had learned, but only through stories.† I suspect that the locations where all tribes keep their elders are as holy as this one.

My guards deposited me before the ancients. I climbed to my knees, wary.

"You have come," said one of the ancients.

"You are not human," another said.

"You have bested our leader and killed all challengers," said the third.

---

* As fanciful as Jak's description of this place sounds, I have seen it myself, and must second his description. The patterns do look like footprints, and the pool appears to have the shape of a spearhead. The koloss do not speak of it to anyone. Incredible as it seems, he actually found the location of the Survivor's Treasure. I take this as proof that Harmony watches over all of us, for only deity could have such a cruel sense of humor as to repeatedly allow a man like Jak to bumble into such remarkable success.

† For this revelation, see episode twenty-five of this narrative.

"What will you do with me?" I demanded, forcing myself to my feet. Sodden and dazed though I was, I would meet my fate head-on.*

"You will be killed," one said.

"It will be according to the will of the daughter of the one who challenged you," said another.

"You must join us," said another.

"Join you?" I demanded. "How?"

"All koloss were once human," said one of the ancients.

I had heard such statements before. And, dear readers, I realize that I disparaged them to you. I considered them silly and fanciful.

It is with a heavy heart that I must tell you that I was wrong. So very wrong. I have since learned the terrible truth. The ancients are right.

Koloss are people.

The process is terrible. To initiate a man into their ranks, they take him and pin him with small spikes of metal. This creates a mystical transformation, during which the man's mind and identity are savagely weakened. In the end, the person becomes as dull and simple as the koloss.

Koloss are not born. Koloss are made. Their barbarity exists inside of all of us. Perhaps this was what dear Handerwym was trying to tell me.†

They said that I had to join them. Was this to be my final end? To live my life as a brute in a distant village, my mind lost?‡

"You spoke of the daughter of the one who challenged me," I said. "Who is this?"

"Me," said a soft, familiar voice.

I turned and found Elizandra Dramali emerging from behind some trees nearby. She no longer wore her dress, and instead was wrapped in leathers that only *just* covered up her most intimate parts. Indeed, a full

---

* Or, in other words, "I couldn't escape immediately, but I wanted to be ready to run screaming like a child as soon as I had the opportunity. So I stood up."

† Well, no. But I'll accept it. Please note that what Jak is saying here is, unfortunately, true. I have seen the process with my own eyes, as have other scholars, and it is widely accepted that this description of the practice is true. I did try to explain this to Jak on several occasions.

‡ Not sure if this is possible. It would be much like dividing by a null set.

description of her figure would be too shocking for my more sensitive readers, and so I will forbear.*

She still wore her spectacles, and her golden hair was pulled back into its customary tail, but her skin . . . her skin was now a shade of blue, such as I had never before seen.

Elizandra, fair Elizandra, was *koloss-blooded.*†

"This can't be!" I exclaimed, staring at my beautiful Elizandra. The woman I had grown to love and cherish above all others. The woman who had somehow hidden her true nature from me all this time.

Elizandra was koloss-blooded.

I wish I did not have to write these words to you, my stalwart readers. But they are true, true as my poor heart bleeds. True as the ink on this page.

"Makeup," Elizandra said, demure eyes downcast. "As you can see, the blue cast to my skin is light, compared to some koloss-blooded. Clever use of powders and gloves have allowed me to hide what I am."

"But your mind!" I said, stepping toward her. "You think and have wit, unlike these beasts!"‡

I moved to reach toward her, but hesitated. Everything I knew about this woman was a lie. She was a monster. Not my fair, wonderful noblewoman, but a creature of the wilds, a murderer and a savage.

"Jak," she said. "I am still me. I was born to koloss, but have not accepted the transformation. My mind is as keen as that of any human. Please, my dear one, see past this skin and look into my heart."§

I could resist no longer. She might have lied, but she was still my

---

* This, of course, did not stop the newspaper editors from including a detailed sketch of this scene in their original printing of the episode.

† The original printing of this story ended the penultimate episode right here, which—I am told—nearly caused riots and prompted a special broadsheet the next day, containing the conclusion of the story. Fortunately, we had sent in all three of these episodes together, in a single pouch. It is a constant source of amazement to me that people are so interested in Jak's raw accounts, rather than waiting for my more sensible, annotated edition. This lack of taste upon the part of the general public is one of the very reasons I left Elendel to travel the Roughs in the first place. It was either that or shoot myself, and my oaths of a steward's pacifism forbid me from shedding blood.

‡ Studies have proven that koloss-blooded individuals are, on average, no less intelligent than ordinary humans—though obviously this is not true for full koloss who have accepted the transformation. Or for most adventurers.

§ I showed this scene to Elizandra, and her response was laughter. Take that as you wish. I would make note, however, that when *I* have spoken to her of this, she has not seemed nearly so ashamed of her heritage, though she did hide it from us all at first.

Elizandra. I stepped into her embrace, and felt her sweet warmth in this time of confusion.

"You are in grave danger, loved one," she whispered into my ear. "They will make you one of them."

"Why?"

"You frightened away their chief," Elizandra whispered. "And ruled the clan despite the challenges we provided. Finally, you killed their greatest champion. My mother."

"The champion was a *woman*?" I asked.

"Of course. Didn't you notice?"

I glanced at the gathered koloss, who wore loincloths, but generally no tops. If there was a way to distinguish the males from the females other than . . . ahem . . . peeking, I did not know it. In fact, I'd rather not have known that some of them were women. My crusty, wind-weathered cheeks did no longer often blush, for the things I've seen would rub your delicate minds raw. But if I'd been capable of a blush, I might have given one at that moment.

"I am sorry, then, for killing her," I said, looking back to Elizandra, who still held me.

"She chose her own course in life," Elizandra said. "And it was one of brutality and murder. I do not mourn her, but I will mourn you, should you be taken into their embrace, dear one. They speak of this being my will, but it is certainly not, though they will not listen to my protests."*

"Why did they lock me away to die in that cavern?" I asked.

"It was a test," Elizandra said. "A final challenge. They would have freed you after three days, if you had not escaped—but as you managed to, you have proven worthy to join their ranks and become their new chief in full. But to do so, you must undergo the transformation! You will lose most of your self, instead becoming one of them, a creature of instinct."†

---

* More laughter here. If you know Zandra, you'd probably realize that any statement that lacks three curses—and a comment about Jak's questionable parentage—cannot truly be attributed to her. But she *does* seem to be fond of him. For some reason.

† For those confused—which includes Jak—this really is the way that one becomes a full koloss. Their children are born with skin that ranges from blue to mottled grey, but not the deep blue of true koloss. These children are generally human, though they have some generous endowments of physical capability. Each child is offered the choice to make the final transformation when they reach

I had to escape, then. This fate would be worse than death—it would be a death of the mind. Though I have gained a great respect for the koloss savages,* I had no intention of ever joining them.

"You steered me here," I realized, looking toward Elizandra. "Ever since we found you in these Roughs, you have been guiding me toward this tribe. You knew of this pool."

"I suspected, from your descriptions of what you sought, this was the location of the treasure," said my fairest one. "But I did not know for certain. I had never been to the holy pool. Jak . . . once they transform you, they plan to do the same to me, against my will. I have resisted this all of my life. I would not let them take my mind as a youth—I will not allow it now!"

"Enough talk!" said one of the elders. "You will be transformed!"

The other koloss began to clap in unison. One of the ancients reached out a trembling, bloody hand, holding in his palm a handful of small spikes.

"No!" I exclaimed. "There is no need! For I am *already* one of you!"

Elizandra's hand tightened on my arm. "What?" she whispered.

"It is the only plan I can think of," I whispered back. Then, more loudly, I proclaimed. "I am koloss!"

"Not possible," said one of the ancients.

"You are not blue," said another.

"You have not the way," said the third.

"I slew your champion!" I declared. "What more proof do you need! Would an ordinary human be strong enough to do this?"

"Gun," said one of the ancients. "It takes not strength to use the gun."

Rust and Ruin! "Well then," I declared, "I will prove it in a final test. For I will bring you the treasure of the Survivor!"

The koloss grew silent. Their clapping stopped.

---

their twelfth year. Those who do not accept the transformation must leave and join human society. By my estimation, many do leave—but just as many ordinary humans, dissatisfied with their lives in the cities, make their way to the koloss tribes and join them, accepting the transformation. From there, no distinguishing is made between those who were originally humans or koloss-blooded.

* Not enough respect to refrain from calling them savages, of course.

"Not possible," said one of the ancients. "Even strongest koloss have failed."

"Then if I succeed, you will know I have told the truth," I said to the beasts.

I was setting myself up for certain death. I wish I could tell you that bravery steered my lips that day, but it was truly just desperation. I spoke of the only thing that occurred to me, the only thing that would let me delay.

If the legends were true, then the treasure was hidden "opposite the sky, raised only by life itself." Opposite the sky must mean at the bottom of the pool—so far down, I could not see it. I would have to dive in and recover the treasure.

"Not possible," said another ancient.

"I will prove it possible!" I declared.

"Jak!" Elizandra said, hand on my arm. "You're a fool!"

"A fool I might be," I said, "but I will not let them take me to be a koloss."

She pulled me to her, suddenly, and kissed me. Very little in life shocks me, dear readers, but that moment achieved the impossible. She had been so cold toward me at times that I was certain my affection would go unrequited.

But this kiss . . . this *kiss*! As deep as the pool beside us, as true as the Survivor's own teachings. As powerful as a bullet in flight, and as incredible as a bull's-eye at three hundred yards. The passion in it warmed me, casting off the chill of my sodden clothing and the fear of a trembling heart.

When she finished, metal flared to life inside of me. Though not an Allomancer, she'd poured some tin dust in her mouth, passing it to me in the kiss!

I pulled back, marveling. "You're amazing," I whispered.

"Well damn, Jak," she whispered back. "You've finally gone and said something smart, for once."*

---

* I believe that this is the only accurate quote from Elizandra in the entire story. She confided in me she threatened to shoot him in the . . . ahem . . . masculine identity if he didn't include it in the official narrative.

The koloss started to clap again. I picked the largest rock I could carry, then—taking a deep breath—leaped into the pool and allowed the rock to pull me downward.

It was deep. Unfathomably deep.*

The darkness soon swallowed me. Dear readers, you must imagine this complete darkness, for I do not believe I can do it justice. To be consumed by the blackness is itself a remarkable experience, but to be in the waters as light flees . . . there is something incredibly horrifying about such an experience. Even my steel nerves gave way to trembling as my descent continued.

A terrible pain struck my ears, though whether this was from my wound, I know not. I dropped for what seemed like forever, until my lungs were burning, my mind growing numb. I nearly let go of my rock.

I could not think. My wound threatened to overwhelm me, and though I could not see, I knew that my vision was growing cloudy. My body was failing me as I plummeted toward unconsciousness. I knew that I would die in these unseen depths.

At that moment, I thought of Elizandra being turned into a koloss, losing the beautiful wit that so charmed me. This thought gave me strength, and I flared my tin.

Flared tin brings clarity of mind, as I have said before. I have never welcomed it as much as I did then; those moments of lucidity forced away the shadow upon my mind.

I felt the coldness of the water, and the pain in my head seemed incredible, but I was *alive.*

I hit the bottom. Not daring to release my rock weight, I felt about me with one hand, frantic. My lungs burned like flared metals. Was it here?

Yes! It was. Something square and unnatural, a box of metal. A strongbox?

I tried to lift it, and managed to make it budge, but it was as heavy as my rock. With dismay, I realized that I could never carry this up to the

---

* And by that he means precisely 18.3 fathoms. I went back and measured.

surface. My body was too weak; swimming with such a weight was more than I could accomplish.

Was I to fail, then? If I reached the surface without the treasure, perhaps they would simply kill me, or perhaps they would make me like them—either way I would be finished.

I worked again to lift the box, but could swim only a few feet. I had no air, no strength. It was useless!

And then, I remembered the poem. Opposite the sky you shall find it, and it shall be raised only by life itself.*

Life itself. What was life down here?

Air.

I fumbled at the sides of the box and found a latch, which released some kind of object. It felt leathery, like a waterskin. I breathed into it, giving up all of the air in my lungs, air which no longer sustained me—but which might still serve me.† Then, I kicked off of the bottom, my metal spent, my air expended.

Eternity.

I burst from the surface of the pool as my vision clouded again. I saw only a moment of light before darkness snatched me back, but soft hands grabbed me and hauled me free of the water before I could sink to my doom. I smelled Elizandra's perfume, and recovered to the sight of her concerned face, cradling my head in her lap. The view of her leather costume from beneath was not particularly proper, but also not unappreciated.

"You fool," she whispered as I rolled over and coughed water from my lungs.

"He has failed!" exclaimed the koloss elders.

At that very moment, something bobbed to the surface of the pool—it appeared to be an inflated bladder of some sort, perhaps from a

---

* Yes, I am aware that he has quoted this poem six different times through the course of this narrative, and has said it a little differently each time. No, he will not allow me to change them and make them consistent.

† Those readers with a knowledge of buoyancy and pressure should probably stop here, as opposed to working out the mathematics of what a single lungful of air could manage under these circumstances.

sheep. I reached into the water and grabbed the strongbox that floated underneath.*

The koloss crowded around as I knelt beside the box and worked at the lock. Elizandra produced the key we had found in Maelstrom's mine, and it fitted† exactly. I turned it with a click, and opened the top.

Inside were spikes.

The koloss shouts first worried me, but they turned out to be shouts of joy. I looked to Elizandra, confused.

"New spikes," she said. "Many of them. With these, the tribe can grow. They were losing the wars with those nearby; my tribe has always been the smallest of those in the area. This will grow them by the dozens. It is a true treasure to them."

I sat back on my heels. I will express some regret to you, dear readers. I travel not for wealth, but for the joy of discovery and the opportunity to share the world with you—but still, this was not the treasure I had hoped to discover. A handful of small spikes? This was what I had searched for months upon months to find? This was the fabled wealth left by the Survivor himself?

"Do not look so morose, dear one," Elizandra said, dumping the spikes for the ancients to take. She pulled back with me as they gathered around. It appeared that the two of us had been forgotten in the excitement. "It seems we have our lives restored to us."

Indeed, the koloss did not stop us as we fled. We quickly left the small oasis valley, making toward the river and—hopefully—the rest of our caravan.‡

I still found myself disappointed. It was then that I noticed something. The box Elizandra carried hadn't tarnished much from what had undoubtedly been over three centuries spent under the waters. I gestured for her to hand it to me, and I buffed at the surface of the lid. Then, I blinked in surprise.

---

* If a bag of air was all that was needed to raise the treasure, one wonders why the grandest of all windbags himself needed the aforementioned sheep's bladder.

† Sigh.

‡ Yes, they forgot about me.

"What?" she asked, stopping in the path.

I grinned. "Pure aluminum, my dear—worth thousands. We have found our treasure after all."

She laughed and favored me with another kiss.

And it is here, my readers, that I must end the account of my travels in the Pits of Eltania. The treasure found, our lives lost—and then recovered—I had fulfilled the dying wish of dear, fallen Mikaff.

It was my grandest adventure yet, and I believe I will rest for a short time before striking out again. I have been hearing of strange lights in the southern skies that can only hide another mystery.

Until then, adventure on!*

---

* And so, we come to the end of another annotated volume. I'm certain that discerning readers of elegance and respectability will appreciate my long-suffering efforts in keeping Jak alive, if only because I suspect these edited accounts provide them with an individual blend of amusement on long winter evenings. I bid you farewell, then. Jak promises further adventure and mystery, but I make a more humble promise. I'm going to try to get him to use proper punctuation in his letters for once in his life. I believe my task to be the more difficult of the two, by far.

Handerwym of Inner Terris
The 17th of Hammondar, 341

# POSTSCRIPT

This is the second of the stories I wrote for Crafty Games, this one to be published in their *Alloy of Law* supplement.

I took a different direction on this story. Since I'd done the first one as more of a showpiece to new readers, I wanted this one to be something deep and interesting for established readers. Revealing how the koloss are made and exist in the second era of Scadrial's sequence seemed the kind of secret that would be intriguing to people.

Many years ago, my brother Jordan came to me wanting to do a radio drama as a podcast. He wanted it to be scripted, written by me—but I just didn't have time. (Writing Excuses was born out of this, though I believe he eventually went to Dan Wells to do some episodes of something more scripted.) He pitched it as the story of an old-time adventurer/explorer. Though I couldn't do the piece, I did spend years thinking about what I might have done, had I had the time.

Allomancer Jak is a direct response to this. The gentleman adventurer, over the top, based off old pulp stories. Writing only that, however, seemed like it wouldn't work. In the Wax and Wayne books, I was already telling stories that were a more authentic evolution of pulp stories, with more solid characterization and less melodrama.

Jak, then, had to be about contrast—a way to highlight the old against the new. Whether he is actually the blowhard that his "faithful steward" implies he is, or whether he's more of a quixotic adventurer with boundless optimism, he is supposed to present a certain level of inauthenticity. A contrast to Wax, in the way that you might contrast the newer incarnations of Batman with the old Adam West Batman. (Note that I love both.)

As an aside, writing Handerwym's annotations was one of the most amusing things I've ever done as a writer.

# MISTBORN: SECRET HISTORY

This novella contains major spoilers for the original Mistborn Trilogy and minor spoilers for *The Bands of Mourning*.

# PART ONE
# EMPIRE

# 1

KELSIER burned the Eleventh Metal.

Nothing changed. He still stood in that Luthadel square, facing down the Lord Ruler. A hushed audience, both skaa and noble, watched at the perimeter. A squeaking wheel turned lazily in the wind, hanging from the side of the overturned prison wagon nearby. An Inquisitor's head had been nailed to the wood of the wagon's bottom, held in place by its own spikes.

Nothing changed, while everything changed. For to Kelsier's eyes, two men now stood before him.

One was the immortal emperor who had dominated for a thousand years: an imposing figure with jet-black hair and a chest stuck through with two spears that he didn't even seem to notice. Next to him stood a man with the same features—but a completely different demeanor. A figure cloaked in thick furs, nose and cheeks flush as if cold. His hair was tangled and windswept, his attitude jovial, smiling.

It was the same man.

*Can I use this?* Kelsier thought, frantic.

Black ash fell lightly between them. The Lord Ruler glanced toward the Inquisitor that Kelsier had killed. "Those are very hard to replace," he said, his voice imperious.

That tone seemed a direct contrast to the man beside him: a vagabond, a mountain man wearing the Lord Ruler's face. *This is what you really are,* Kelsier thought. But that didn't help. It was only further proof that the Eleventh Metal wasn't what Kelsier had once hoped. The metal was no magical solution for ending the Lord Ruler. He would have to rely instead upon his other plan.

And so, Kelsier smiled.

"I killed you once," the Lord Ruler said.

"You tried," Kelsier replied, his heart racing. The other plan, the secret plan. "But you can't kill me, Lord Tyrant. I represent that thing you've never been able to kill, no matter how hard you try. I am hope."

The Lord Ruler snorted. He raised a casual arm.

Kelsier braced himself. He could not fight against someone who was immortal.

Not alive, at least.

*Stand tall. Give them something to remember.*

The Lord Ruler backhanded him. Agony hit Kelsier like a stroke of lightning. In that moment, Kelsier flared the Eleventh Metal, and caught a glimpse of something new.

The Lord Ruler standing in a room—no, a cavern! The Lord Ruler stepped into a glowing pool and the world shifted around him, rocks crumbling, the room twisting, everything *changing.*

The vision vanished.

Kelsier died.

It turned out to be far more painful a process than he had anticipated. Instead of a soft fade to nothingness, he felt an awful *tearing* sensation—as if he were a cloth caught between the jaws of two vicious hounds.

He screamed, desperately trying to hold himself together. His will meant nothing. He was rent, ripped, and hurled into a place of endless shifting mists.

He stumbled to his knees, gasping, aching. He wasn't certain what he knelt upon, as downward seemed to just be more mist. The ground rippled like liquid, and felt soft to his touch.

He knelt there, enduring, feeling the pain slowly fade away. At last he unclenched his jaw and groaned.

He was alive. Kind of.

He managed to look up. That same thick greyness shifted all around him. A nothingness? No, he could see shapes in it, shadows. Hills? And high in the sky, some kind of light. A tiny sun perhaps, as seen through dense grey clouds.

Kelsier breathed in and out, then growled, heaving himself to his feet. "Well," he proclaimed, "*that* was thoroughly awful."

It did seem there was an afterlife, which was a pleasant discovery. Did this mean . . . did this mean Mare was still out there somewhere? He'd always offered platitudes, talking to the others about being with her again someday. But deep down he'd never believed, never really thought . . .

The end was not the end. Kelsier smiled again, this time truly excited. He turned about, and as he inspected his surroundings, the mists seemed to withdraw. No, it felt like Kelsier was *solidifying*, entering this place fully. The withdrawal of the mists was more like a clearing of his own mind.

The mists coalesced into shapes. Those shadows he'd mistaken for hills were buildings, hazy and formed of shifting mists. The ground beneath his feet was also mist, a deep vastness, like he was standing on the surface of the ocean. It was soft to his touch, like cloth, and even a little springy.

Nearby lay the overturned prison wagon, but here it was made of mist. That mist shifted and moved, but the wagon retained its form. It was like the mist was trapped by some unseen force into a specific shape. More strikingly, the wagon's prison bars *glowed* on this side. Complementing them, other white-hot pinpricks of light appeared around him, dotting the landscape. Doorknobs. Window latches. Everything in the living world was reflected here in this place, and while most things were shadowy mist, metal instead appeared as a powerful light.

Some of those lights moved. He frowned, stepping toward one, and only then did he recognize that many of the lights were people. He saw each as an intense white glow radiating out from a human form.

*Metal and souls are the same thing*, he observed. Who would have thought?

As he got his bearings, he recognized what was happening in the living world. Thousands of lights moved, flowing away. The crowd was running from the square. A powerful light, with a tall silhouette, strode in another direction. The Lord Ruler.

Kelsier tried to follow, but stumbled over something at his feet. A misty form slumped on the ground, pierced by a spear. Kelsier's own corpse.

Touching it was like remembering a fond experience. Familiar scents from his youth. His mother's voice. The warmth of lying on a hillside with Mare, looking up at the falling ash.

Those experiences faded and seemed to grow *cold*. One of the lights from the mass of fleeing people—it was hard to make out individuals, with everyone alight—scrambled toward him. At first he thought perhaps this person had seen his spirit. But no, they ran to his corpse and knelt.

Now that she was close, he could make out the details of this figure's features, cut of mist and glowing from deep within.

"Ah, child," Kelsier said. "I'm sorry." He reached out and cupped Vin's face as she wept over him, and found he could feel her. She was solid to his ethereal fingers. She didn't seem able to feel his touch, but he caught a vision of her from the real world, cheeks stained with tears.

His last words to her had been harsh, hadn't they? Perhaps it was a good thing that he and Mare had never had children.

A glowing figure surged from the fleeing masses and grabbed Vin. Was that Ham? Had to be, with that profile. Kelsier stood up and watched them withdraw. He had set plans in motion for them. Perhaps they would hate him for that.

"You let him kill you."

Kelsier spun, surprised to find a person standing beside him. Not a figure made of mist, but a man in strange clothing: a thin wool coat that went down almost to his feet, and beneath it a shirt that laced closed, with a kind of conical skirt. That was tied with a belt that had a bone-handled knife stuck through a loop.

The man was short, with black hair and a prominent nose. Unlike the other people—who were made of light—this man looked normal, like Kelsier. Since Kelsier was dead, did this make the man another ghost?

"Who are you?" Kelsier demanded.

"Oh, I think you know." The man met Kelsier's eyes, and in them Kelsier saw eternity. A cool, calm eternity—the eternity of stones that saw generations pass, or of careless depths that didn't notice the changing of days, for light never reached them anyway.

"Oh, hell," Kelsier said. "There's actually a God?"

"Yes."

Kelsier decked him.

It was a good, clean punch, thrown from the shoulder while he brought his other arm up to block a counterstrike. Dox would be proud.

God didn't dodge. Kelsier's punch took him right across the face, connecting with a satisfying *thud.* The punch tossed God to the ground, though when he looked up he seemed more shocked than pained.

Kelsier stepped forward. "What the hell is wrong with you? You're real, and you're letting *this* happen?" He waved toward the square where—to his horror—he saw lights winking out. The Inquisitors were attacking the crowd.

"I do what I can." The fallen figure seemed to distort for a moment, bits of him expanding, like mists escaping an enclosure. "I do . . . I do what I can. It is in motion, you see. I . . ."

Kelsier recoiled a step, eyes widening as God *came apart,* then pulled back together.

Around him, other souls made the transition. Their bodies stopped glowing, then their souls lurched into this land of mists: stumbling, falling, as if ejected from their bodies. Once they arrived, Kelsier saw them in color. The same man—God—appeared near each of them. There were suddenly over a dozen versions of him, each identical, each speaking to one of the dead.

The version of God near Kelsier stood up and rubbed his jaw. "Nobody has ever done that before."

"What, really?" Kelsier asked.

"No. Souls are usually too disoriented. Some do run, though." He looked to Kelsier.

Kelsier made fists. God stepped back and—amusingly—reached for the knife at his belt.

Well, Kelsier wasn't going to attack him, not again. But he *had* heard the challenge in those words. Would he run? Of course not. Where would he run to?

Nearby, an unfortunate skaa woman lurched into the afterlife, then almost immediately *faded.* Her figure stretched, transforming to a white mist that was pulled toward a distant, dark point. That was how it looked, at least, though the point she stretched toward wasn't a place—not really. It was . . . Beyond. A location that was somehow distant, pointing away from him no matter where he moved.

She stretched, then faded away. Other spirits in the square followed.

Kelsier spun on God. "What's happening?"

"You didn't think *this* was the end, did you?" God asked, waving toward the shadowy world. "This is the in-between step. After death and before . . ."

"Before what?"

"Before the Beyond," God said. "The Somewhere Else. Where souls must go. Where *yours* must go."

"I haven't gone yet."

"It takes longer for Allomancers, but it will happen. It is the natural progress of things, like a stream flowing toward the ocean. I'm here not to make it occur, but to comfort you as you go. I see it as a kind of . . . duty that comes with my position." He rubbed the side of his face and gave Kelsier a glare that said what he thought of his reception.

Nearby, another pair of people faded into the eternities. They seemed to accept it, stepping into the stretching nothingness with relieved, welcoming smiles. Kelsier looked at those departing souls.

"Mare," he whispered.

"She went Beyond. As you will."

Kelsier looked toward that point Beyond, the point toward which all the dead were being drawn. He felt it, faintly, begin to tug on him as well.

*No. Not yet.*

"We need a plan," Kelsier said.

"A plan?" God asked.

"To get me out of this. I might need your help."

"There *is* no way out of this."

"That's a terrible attitude," Kelsier said. "We'll never get anything done if you talk like that."

He looked at his arm, which was—disconcertingly—starting to blur, like ink on a page that had been accidentally brushed before it dried. He felt a *draining.*

He started walking, forcing himself into a stride. He wouldn't just stand there while eternity tried to suck him away.

"It is natural to feel uncertain," God said, falling into step beside him. "Many are anxious. Be at peace. The ones you left behind will find their own way, and you—"

"Yes, great," Kelsier said. "No time for lectures. Talk to me. Has anyone ever resisted being pulled into the Beyond?"

"No." God's form pulsed, unraveling again before coming back together. "I've told you already."

*Damn,* Kelsier thought. *He seems one step from falling apart himself.*

Well, you had to work with what you had. "You've got to have some kind of idea what I could try, Fuzz."

"What did you call me?"

"Fuzz. I've got to call you something."

"You could try 'My Lord,'" Fuzz said with a huff.

"That's a terrible nickname for a crewmember."

"Crewmember . . ."

"I need a team," Kelsier said, still striding through the shadowy version of Luthadel. "And as you can see, my options are limited. I'd rather have Dox, but he's got to go deal with the man who is claiming to be you. Besides, the initiation to this particular team of mine is a killer."

"But—"

Kelsier turned, taking the smaller man by the shoulders. Kelsier's arms were blurring further, drawn away like water being pulled into the current of an invisible stream.

"Look," Kelsier said quietly, urgently, "you said you were here to comfort me. This is how you do it. If you're right, then nothing I do now will matter. So why not humor me? Let me have one last thrill as I face down the ultimate eventuality."

Fuzz sighed. "It would be better if you accepted what is happening."

Kelsier held Fuzz's gaze. Time was running out; he could *feel* himself sliding toward oblivion, a distant point of nothingness, dark and unknowable. Still he held that gaze. If this creature acted anything like the human he resembled, then holding his eyes—with confidence, smiling, self-assured—would work. Fuzz would bend.

"So," Fuzz said. "You're not only the first to punch me, you're also the first to try to *recruit* me. You are a distinctively strange man."

"You don't know my friends. Next to them I'm normal. Ideas please." He started walking up a street, moving just to be moving. Tenements loomed on either side, made of shifting mists. They looked like the ghosts of buildings. Occasionally a wave—a shimmer of light—would pulse through the ground and buildings, causing the mists to writhe and twist.

"I don't know what you expect me to tell you," Fuzz said, hustling up to walk beside him. "Spirits who come to this place are drawn into the Beyond."

"You aren't."

"I'm a god."

*A god. Not just "God." Noted.*

"Well," Kelsier said, "what is it about being a god that makes you immune?"

"Everything."

"I can't help thinking you aren't pulling your weight on this team, Fuzz. Come on. Work with me. You indicated that Allomancers last longer. Feruchemists too?"

"Yes."

"People with power," Kelsier said, pointing toward the distant spires of Kredik Shaw. This was the road the Lord Ruler had taken, heading toward his palace. Though the Lord Ruler's carriage was now distant,

Kelsier could still see his soul glowing up there somewhere. Far brighter than the others.

"What about him?" Kelsier said. "You say that everyone has to bend to death, but obviously that isn't true. He is immortal."

"He's a special case," Fuzz said, perking up. "He has ways of not dying in the first place."

"And if he did die?" Kelsier pressed. "He'd last even longer on this side than I am, right?"

"Oh, indeed," Fuzz said. "He Ascended, if just for a short time. He held enough of the power to expand his soul."

*Got it. Expand my soul.*

"I . . ." God wavered, figure distorting. "I . . ." He cocked his head. "What was I saying?"

"About how the Lord Ruler expanded his soul."

"That was delightful," God said. "It was spectacular to watch! And now he is *Preserved*. I am glad you didn't find a way to destroy him. Everyone else passes, but not him. It's wonderful."

"Wonderful?" Kelsier felt like spitting. "He's a tyrant, Fuzz."

"He's unchanging," God said, defensive. "He's a brilliant specimen. So unique. I don't agree with what he does, but one can empathize with the lamb while admiring the lion, can one not?"

"Why not stop him? If you disagree with what he does, then do something about it!"

"Now, now," God said. "That would be hasty. What would removing him accomplish? It would just raise another leader who is more transient—and cause chaos and even more deaths than the Lord Ruler has caused. Better to have stability. Yes. A constant leader."

Kelsier felt himself stretching further. He'd go soon. It didn't seem his new body could sweat, for if it could have his forehead would certainly be drenched by now.

"Maybe you would enjoy watching another do as he did," Kelsier said. "Expand their soul."

"Impossible. The power at the Well of Ascension won't be gathered and ready for more than a year."

"*What?*" Kelsier said. The *Well of Ascension*?

He dredged through his memories, trying to remember the things Sazed had told him of religion and belief. The scope of it threatened to overwhelm him. He'd been playing at rebellion and thrones—focusing on religion only when he thought it might benefit his plans—and all the while, *this* had been in the background. Ignored and unnoticed.

He felt like a child.

Fuzz kept speaking, oblivious to Kelsier's awakening. "But no, you wouldn't be able to use the Well. I've failed at locking him away. I knew I would; he's stronger. His essence seeps out in natural forms. Solid, liquid, gas. Because of how we created the world. He has plans. But are they deeper than my plans, or have I finally outthought him . . . ?"

Fuzz distorted again. His diatribe made little sense to Kelsier. He felt as if it was important, but it just wasn't *urgent.*

"Power is returning to the Well of Ascension," Kelsier said.

Fuzz hesitated. "Hm. Yes. Um, but it's far, far away. Yes, too far for you to go. Too bad."

God, it turned out, was a terrible liar.

Kelsier seized him, and the little man cringed.

"Tell me," Kelsier said. "Please. I can feel myself stretching away, falling, being pulled. Please."

Fuzz yanked out of his grip. Kelsier's fingers . . . or rather, his soul's fingers . . . weren't working as well any longer.

"No," Fuzz said. "No, it is not right. If you touched it, you might just add to his power. You will go as all others."

*Very well,* Kelsier thought. *A con, then.*

He let himself slump against the wall of a ghostly building. He sighed, settling down in a seated position, back to the wall. "All right."

"See, there!" Fuzz said. "Better. Much better, isn't it?"

"Yes," Kelsier said.

God seemed to relax. With discomfort, Kelsier noticed God was still leaking. Mist slipped away from his body at a few pinprick points. This creature was like a wounded beast, placidly going about its daily life while ignoring the bite marks.

Remaining motionless was hard. Harder than facing down the Lord

Ruler had been. Kelsier wanted to run, to scream, to scramble and move. That sensation of being drawn away was *horrible.*

Somehow he feigned relaxation. "You asked," he said, as if very tired and having trouble forcing it out, "me a question? When you first appeared?"

"Oh!" Fuzz said. "Yes. You let him kill you. I had not expected that."

"You're God. Can't you see the future?"

"To an extent," Fuzz said, animated. "But it is cloudy, so cloudy. Too many possibilities. I did not see this among them, though it was probably there. You must tell me. Why *did* you let him kill you? At the end, you just stood there."

"I couldn't have gotten away," Kelsier said. "Once the Lord Ruler arrived, there was no escaping. I had to confront him."

"You didn't even fight."

"I used the Eleventh Metal."

"Foolishness," God said. He started pacing. "That was Ruin's influence on you. But what was the point? I can't understand why he wanted you to have that useless metal." He perked up. "And that *fight.* You and the Inquisitor. Yes, I've seen many things, but that was unlike any other. Impressive, though I wish you hadn't caused such destruction, Kelsier."

He returned to pacing, but seemed to have more of a spring to his step. Kelsier hadn't expected God to be so . . . human. Excitable, even energetic.

"I saw something," Kelsier said, "as the Lord Ruler killed me. The person as he might once have been. His past? A version of his past? He stood at the Well of Ascension."

"Did you? Hmm. Yes, the metal, flared during the moment of transition. You got a glimpse of the Spiritual Realm, then? His Connection and his past? You were using Ati's essence, unfortunately. One shouldn't trust it, even in a diluted form. Except . . ." He frowned, cocking his head, as if trying to remember something he'd forgotten.

"Another god," Kelsier whispered, closing his eyes. "You said . . . you trapped him?"

"He will break free eventually. It's inevitable. But the prison isn't my last gambit. It can't be."

*Perhaps I* should *just let go,* Kelsier thought, drifting.

"There now," God said. "Farewell, Kelsier. You served *him* more often than you did me, but I can respect your intentions, *and* your remarkable ability to Preserve yourself."

"I saw it," Kelsier whispered. "A cavern high in the mountains. The Well of Ascension . . ."

"Yes," Fuzz said. "That's where I put it."

"But . . ." Kelsier said, stretching, "he moved it. . . ."

"Naturally."

What would the Lord Ruler do, with a source of such power? Hide it far away?

Or keep it very, very close? Near to his fingertips. Hadn't Kelsier seen furs, like the ones he'd seen the Lord Ruler wearing in his vision? He'd seen them in a room, past an Inquisitor. A building within a building, hidden within the depths of the palace.

Kelsier opened his eyes.

Fuzz spun toward him. "What—"

Kelsier heaved himself to his feet and started running. There wasn't much *self* to him left, just a fuzzy blurred image. The feet that he ran upon were distorted smudges, his form a pulled-out, unraveling piece of cloth. He barely found purchase upon the misty ground, and when he stumbled against a building, he *pushed* through it, ignoring the wall as one might a stiff breeze.

"So you *are* a runner," Fuzz said, appearing beside him. "Kelsier, child, this accomplishes nothing. I suppose I should have expected nothing less from you. Frantically butting against your destiny until the last moment."

Kelsier barely heard the words. He focused on the run, on resisting that grip *hauling* him backward, into the nothing. He raced the grip of death itself, its cold fingers closing around him.

Run.

Concentrate.

Struggle to *be.*

The flight reminded him of another time, climbing through a pit, arms bloodied. He would *not be taken*!

The pulsing became his guide, that wave that washed periodically through the shadowy world. He sought its source. He barreled through buildings, crossed thoroughfares, ignoring both metal and the souls of men until he reached the grey mist silhouette of Kredik Shaw, the Hill of a Thousand Spires.

Here, Fuzz seemed to grasp what was going on.

"You zinc-tongued raven," the god said, moving beside him without effort while Kelsier ran with everything he had. "You're not going to reach it in time."

He was running through mists again. Walls, people, buildings faded. Nothing but dark, swirling mists.

But the mists had never been his enemy.

With the thumping of those pulses to guide him, Kelsier strained through the swirling nothingness until a pillar of light exploded before him. It was there! He could see it, burning in the mists. He could almost touch it, almost . . .

He was losing it. Losing himself. He could move no more.

Something seized him.

"Please . . ." Kelsier whispered, falling, sliding away.

*This is not right.* Fuzz's voice.

"You want to see something . . . spectacular?" Kelsier whispered. "Help me live. I'll *show* you . . . *spectacular.*"

Fuzz wavered, and Kelsier could sense the divinity's hesitance. It was followed by a sense of purpose, like a lamp being lit, and laughter.

*Very well. Be Preserved, Kelsier. Survivor.*

Something shoved him forward, and Kelsier merged with the light.

Moments later he blinked awake. He lay in the misty world still, but his body—or, well, his spirit—had re-formed. He lay in a pool of light like liquid metal. He could feel its warmth all around him, invigorating.

He could make out a misty cavern outside the pool; it seemed to be made of natural rock, though he couldn't tell for certain, because it was all mist on this side.

The pulsing surged through him.

"The power," Fuzz said, standing beyond the light. "You are now part of it, Kelsier."

"Yeah," Kelsier said, climbing to his feet, dripping with radiant light. "I can feel it, thrumming through me."

"You are trapped with him," Fuzz said. He seemed shallow, wan, compared to the powerful light that Kelsier stood amid. "I warned you. This is a prison."

Kelsier settled down, breathing in and out. "I'm alive."

"According to a very loose definition of the word."

Kelsier smiled. "It'll do."

# 2

IMMORTALITY proved to be far more frustrating than Kelsier had anticipated.

Of course, he didn't know if he was *truly* immortal or not. He didn't have a heartbeat—which was only unnerving when he noticed it—and didn't need to breathe. But who could say if his soul aged or not in this place?

In the hours following his survival, Kelsier inspected his new home. God was right, it *was* a prison. The pool he was in grew deep at the center point, and was filled with liquid light that seemed a reflection of something more . . . potent on the other side.

Fortunately, though the Well was not wide, only the very center was deeper than he was tall. He could stay around the perimeter and only be in the light up to his waist. It was thin, thinner than water, and easy to move through.

He could also step out of this pool and its attached pillar of light, settling onto the rocky side. Everything in this cavern was made of mist, though the edges of the Well . . . He seemed to see the stone better here, more fully. It appeared to have some actual color to it. As if this place were part spirit, like him.

He could sit on the edge of the Well, legs dangling into the light. But if he tried to walk too far from the Well, misty wisps of that same power trailed him and held him back, like chains. They wouldn't let him get more than a few feet from the pool. He tried straining, pushing, dashing and throwing himself out, but nothing worked. He always pulled up sharply once he got a few feet away.

After several hours of trying to break free, Kelsier slumped on the side of the Well, feeling . . . exhausted? Was that even the right word? He had no body, and felt no traditional signs of tiredness. No headache, no strained muscles. But he *was* fatigued. Worn out like an old banner allowed to flap in the wind through too many rainstorms.

Forced to relax, he took stock of what little he could make out of his surroundings. Fuzz was gone; the god had been distracted by something a short time after Kelsier's Preservation, and had vanished. That left Kelsier with a cavern made of shadows, the glowing pool itself, and some pillars extending through the chamber. At the other end, he saw the glow of bits of metal, though he couldn't figure out what they were.

This was the sum of his existence. Had he just locked himself away in this little prison for eternity? It seemed an ultimate irony to him that he might have managed to cheat death, only to find himself suffering a fate far worse.

What would happen to his mind if he spent a few decades in here? A few *centuries*?

He sat on the rim of the Well, and tried to distract himself by thinking about his friends. He'd trusted in his plans at the moment of his death, but now he saw so many holes in his plot to inspire a rebellion. What if the skaa didn't rise up? What if the stockpiles he'd prepared weren't enough?

Even if that all worked, so much would ride upon the shoulders of some very ill-prepared men. And one remarkable young woman.

Lights drew his attention, and he leaped to his feet, eager for any distraction. A group of figures, outlined as glowing souls, had entered this room in the world of the living. There was something odd about them. Their eyes . . .

Inquisitors.

Kelsier refused to flinch, though by every instinct he dreaded these creatures. He had bested one of their champions. He would fear them no longer. Instead, he paced his confines, trying to discern what the three Inquisitors were lugging toward him. Something large and heavy, but it didn't glow at all.

*A body,* Kelsier realized. *Headless.*

Was this the one he'd killed? Yes, it must be. Another Inquisitor was reverently carrying the dead one's spikes, a whole pile of them, all placed together inside a large jar of liquid. Kelsier squinted at it, taking a single step out of his prison, trying to determine what he was seeing.

"Blood," Fuzz said, suddenly standing nearby. "They store the spikes in blood until they can be used again. In that way, they can prevent the spikes from losing their effectiveness."

"Huh," Kelsier said, stepping to the side as the Inquisitors tossed the body into the Well, then dropped in the head. Both evaporated. "Do they do this often?"

"Each time one of their number dies," Fuzz said. "I doubt they even know what they are doing. Tossing a dead body into that pool is beyond meaningless."

The Inquisitors retreated with the spikes of the fallen. Judging by their slumped forms, the four creatures were exhausted.

"My plan," Kelsier said, looking to Fuzz. "How is it going? My crew should have discovered the warehouse by now. The people of the city . . . did it work? Are the skaa angry?"

"Hmmm?" Fuzz asked.

"The revolution, the plan," Kelsier said, stepping toward him. God shifted backward, getting just beyond where Kelsier would be able to reach, hand going to the knife at his belt. Perhaps that punch earlier had been ill-advised. "Fuzz, listen. You have to go nudge them. We'll never have a better chance of overthrowing him."

"The plan . . ." Fuzz said. He unraveled for a moment, before returning. "Yes, there was a plan. I . . . remember I had a plan. When I was smarter . . ."

"The plan," Kelsier said, "is to get the skaa to revolt. It won't matter how powerful the Lord Ruler is, won't matter if he's immortal, once we toss him in chains and lock him away."

Fuzz nodded, distracted.

"Fuzz?"

He shook, glancing toward Kelsier, and the sides of his head unraveled slowly—like a fraying rug, each thread seeping away and vanishing into nothing. "He's killing me, you know. He wants me gone before the next cycle, though . . . perhaps I can hold out. You hear me, Ruin! I'm not dead yet. Still . . . still here . . ."

*Hell,* Kelsier thought, cold. *God is going insane.*

Fuzz started pacing. "I know you're listening, changing what I write, what I have written. You make our religion all about you. They hardly remember the truth any longer. Subtle as always, you worm."

"Fuzz," Kelsier said. "Could you just go—"

"I needed a sign," Fuzz whispered, stopping near Kelsier. "Something he couldn't change. A sign of the weapon I'd buried. The boiling point of water, I think. Maybe its freezing point? But what if the units change over the years? I needed something that would be remembered always. Something they'll immediately recognize." He leaned in. "Sixteen."

"Six . . . teen?" Kelsier said.

"Sixteen." Fuzz grinned. "Clever, don't you think?"

"Because it means . . ."

"The number of metals," Fuzz said. "In Allomancy."

"There are ten. Eleven, if you count the one I discovered."

"No! No, no, that's stupid. Sixteen. It's the perfect number. They'll see. They have to see." Fuzz started pacing again, and his head returned—mostly—to its earlier state.

Kelsier sat down on the rim of his prison. God's actions were far more erratic than they had been earlier. Had something changed, or—like a human with a mental disease—was God simply better at some times than he was at others?

Fuzz looked up abruptly. He winced, turning his eyes toward the ceiling, as if it were going to collapse on him. He opened his mouth, jaw working, but made no sound.

"What . . ." he finally said. "What have you *done*?"

Kelsier stood up in his prison.

"What have you done?" Fuzz screamed.

Kelsier smiled. "Hope," he said softly. "I have hoped."

"He was perfect," Fuzz said. "He was . . . the only one of you . . . that . . ." He spun suddenly, gazing down the shadowy room beyond Kelsier's prison.

Someone stood at the other end. A tall, commanding figure, not made of light. Familiar clothing, of both white and black, contrasting with itself.

The Lord Ruler. His spirit, at least.

Kelsier stepped up onto the rim of stone around the pool and waited as the Lord Ruler strode toward the light of the Well. He stopped in place when he noticed Kelsier.

"I killed you," the Lord Ruler said. "Twice. Yet you live."

"Yes. We're all aware of how strikingly incompetent you are. I'm glad you're beginning to see it for yourself. That's the first step toward change."

The Lord Ruler sniffed and looked around at the chamber, with its diaphanous walls. His eyes passed over Fuzz, but he didn't give the god much consideration.

Kelsier exulted. She'd done it. She'd actually *done it.* How? What secret had he missed?

"That grin," the Lord Ruler said to Kelsier, "is insufferable. I *did* kill you."

"I returned the favor."

"You *didn't* kill me, Survivor."

"I forged the blade that did."

Fuzz cleared his throat. "It is my duty to be with you as you transition. Don't be worried, or—"

"Be silent," the Lord Ruler said, inspecting Kelsier's prison. "Do you know what you've done, Survivor?"

"I've won."

"You've brought Ruin upon the world. You are a pawn. So proud, like a soldier on the battlefield, confident he controls his own destiny—while ignoring the thousands upon thousands in his rank." He shook his head. "Only a year left. So close. I would have again ransomed this undeserving planet."

"This is just . . ." Fuzz swallowed. "This is an in-between step. After death and before the Somewhere Else. Where souls must go. Where *yours* must go, Rashek."

Rashek? Kelsier looked again at the Lord Ruler. You could not tell a Terrisman by skin tone; that was a mistake many people made. Some Terris were dark, others light. Still, he would have thought . . .

*The room filled with furs. This man, in the cold.*

Idiot. That was what it meant, of course.

"It was all a lie," Kelsier said. "A trick. Your fabled immortality? Your healing? Feruchemy. But how did you become an Allomancer?"

The Lord Ruler stepped right up to the pillar of light that rose from the prison, and the two stared at one another. As they had on that square above when alive.

Then the Lord Ruler stuck his hand into the light.

Kelsier set his jaw and pictured sudden, horrifying images of spending an eternity trapped with the man who had murdered Mare. The Lord Ruler pulled his hand out, however, trailing light like molasses. He turned his hand over, inspecting the glow, which eventually faded.

"So now what?" Kelsier asked. "You remain here?"

"Here?" The Lord Ruler laughed. "With an impotent mouse and a half-blooded rat? Please."

He closed his eyes, and then he stretched toward that point that defied geometry. He faded, then finally vanished.

Kelsier gaped. "He *left*?"

"To the Somewhere Else," Fuzz said, sitting down. "I should not have been so hopeful. Everything passes, nothing is eternal. That is what Ati always claimed. . . ."

"He didn't have to leave," Kelsier said. "He could have remained. Could have survived!"

"I told you, by this point rational people *want* to move on." Fuzz vanished.

Kelsier remained standing there, at the edge of his prison, the glowing pool tossing his shadow across the floor. He stared into the misty room with its columns, waiting for something, though he wasn't certain what. Confirmation, celebration, a change of some sort.

Nothing. Nobody came, not even the Inquisitors. How had the revolution gone? Were the skaa now rulers of society? He would have liked to see the deaths of the noble ranks, treated—in turn—as they had treated their slaves.

He received no confirmation, no sign, of what was happening above. They didn't know about the Well, obviously. All Kelsier could do was settle down.

And wait.

# PART TWO
# WELL

# 1

WHAT Kelsier would have given for a pencil and paper.

Something to write on, some way to pass the time. A means of collecting his thoughts and creating a plan of escape.

As the days passed, he tried scratching notes into the sides of the Well, which proved impossible. He tried unraveling threads from his clothing, then tying knots in them to represent words. Unfortunately, threads vanished soon after he pulled them free, and his shirt and trousers immediately returned to the way they'd looked before. Fuzz, during one of his rare visits, explained that the clothing wasn't real—or rather, it was just an extension of Kelsier's spirit.

For the same reason, he couldn't use his hair or blood to write. He didn't technically have either. It was supremely frustrating, but sometime during his second month of imprisonment he admitted the truth to himself. Writing wasn't all that important. He'd never been able to write while confined to the Pits, but he'd planned all the same. Yes, they had been feverish plans, impossible dreams, but lack of paper hadn't stopped him.

The attempts to write weren't about making plans so much as finding something to do. A quest to soak up his time. It had worked for a few weeks. But in acknowledging the truth, he lost his will to keep trying to find a way to write.

Fortunately, about the time he acknowledged this, he discovered something new about his prison.

Whispering.

Oh, he couldn't *hear* it. But could he "hear" anything? He didn't have ears. He was . . . what had Fuzz said? A Cognitive Shadow? A force of mind, holding his spirit together, preventing it from diffusing. Saze would have had a field day. He loved mystical topics like this.

Regardless, Kelsier *could* sense something. The Well continued to pulse as it had before, sending waves of writhing shock through the walls of his prison and out into the world. Those pulses seemed to be strengthening, a continuous thrumming, like the sense bronze lent one in "hearing" people using Allomancy.

Inside of each pulse was . . . something. Whispers, he called them—though they contained more than just words. They were saturated with sounds, scents, and images.

He saw a book, with ink staining its pages. A group of people sharing a story. Terrismen in robes? Sazed?

The pulses whispered chilling words. *Hero of Ages. The Announcer. Worldbringer.* He recognized those terms from the ancient Terris prophecies mentioned in Alendi's logbook.

Kelsier knew the discomforting truth now. He had *met* a god, which meant there was real depth and reality to faith. Did this mean there was something to that array of religions Saze had kept in his pocket, like playing cards to stack a deck?

*You have brought Ruin upon this world. . . .*

Kelsier settled into the powerful light that was the Well, and found—with practice—that if he submerged himself in the center right before a pulse, he could ride it a short distance. It sent his consciousness traveling out of the Well to catch glimpses of each pulse's destination.

He thought he saw libraries, quiet chambers where distant Terrismen spoke, exchanging stories and memorizing them. He saw madmen huddled in streets, whispering the words the pulses delivered. He saw a Mistborn man, noble, jumping between buildings.

Something other than Kelsier rode with those pulses. Something directing an unseen work, something interested in the lore of the Terris. It took Kelsier an embarrassingly long time to realize he should try another tack. He dunked himself into the center of the pool, surrounded by the too-thin liquid light, and when the next pulse came he pushed himself in the opposite direction—not along with the pulse, but toward its source.

The light thinned, and he looked into someplace new. A dark expanse that was neither the world of the dead nor the world of the living.

In that other place, he found *destruction*.

Decay. Not blackness, for blackness was too complete, too *whole* to represent this thing he sensed in the Beyond. It was a vast force that would gleefully take something as simple as darkness, then rip it apart.

This force was time infinite. It was the winds that weathered, the storms that broke, the timeless waves running slowly, slowly, slowly to a stop as the sun and the planet cooled to nothing.

It was the ultimate end and destiny of all things. And it was angry.

Kelsier pulled back, throwing himself up out of the light, gasping, trembling.

He had met God. But for every Push, there was a Pull. What was the opposite of God?

What he had seen troubled him so much that he almost didn't return. He almost convinced himself to ignore the terrible thing in the darkness. He nearly blocked out the whispers and tried to pretend he had never seen that awesome, vast destroyer.

But of course he couldn't do that. Kelsier had never been able to resist a secret. This thing, even more than meeting Fuzz, proved that Kelsier had been playing all along at a game whose rules far outmatched his understanding.

That both terrified and excited him.

And so, he returned to gaze upon the thing. Again and again he went, struggling to comprehend, though he felt like an ant trying to understand a symphony.

He did this for weeks, right up until the point when the thing *looked* at him.

Before, it hadn't seemed to notice—as one might not notice the spider hiding inside a keyhole. This time though, Kelsier somehow alerted it. The thing churned in an abrupt change of motion, then *flowed* toward Kelsier, its essence surrounding the place from which Kelsier observed. It rotated slowly about itself in a vortex—like an ocean that began turning around one spot. Kelsier couldn't help but feel that an infinite, vast eye was suddenly *squinting* at him.

He fled, splashing, kicking up the liquid light as he backed away into his prison. He was so alarmed that he felt a phantom *heartbeat* thrumming inside of him, his essence acknowledging the proper reaction to shock and trying to replicate it. That stilled as he settled into his customary seat at the side of the pool.

The sight of that thing turning its attention upon him, the sensation of being tiny in the face of something so vast, deeply troubled Kelsier. For all his confidence and plotting, he was basically nothing. His entire life had been an exercise in unintentional bravado.

Months passed. He didn't return to study the thing Beyond; Kelsier instead waited for Fuzz to visit and check in on him, as he did periodically.

When Fuzz finally arrived, he looked even more unraveled than the last time, mists escaping from his shoulders, a small hole in his left cheek exposing a view into his mouth, his clothing growing ragged.

"Fuzz?" Kelsier asked. "I saw something. This . . . Ruin you spoke of. I think I can watch it."

Fuzz just paced back and forth, not even speaking.

"Fuzz? Hey, are you listening?"

Nothing.

"Idiot," Kelsier tried. "Hey, you're a disgrace to deityhood. Are you paying attention?"

Even an insult didn't work. Fuzz just kept pacing.

*Useless,* Kelsier thought as a pulse of power left the Well. He happened to catch a glimpse of Fuzz's eyes as the pulse passed.

And in that moment, Kelsier was reminded why he had named this creature a god in the first place. There was an infinity beyond those eyes, a complement to the one trapped here in this Well. Fuzz was the infinity of a note held perfectly, never wavering. The majesty of a painting, frozen and still, capturing a slice of life from a time gone by. It was the power of many, many moments compressed somehow into one.

Fuzz stopped before him and his cheeks unraveled fully, revealing a skeleton beneath that was also unraveling, eyes glowing with eternity. This creature *was* a divinity; he was just a broken one.

Fuzz left, and Kelsier didn't see him for many months. The stillness and silence of his prison seemed as endless as the creatures he had studied. At one point, he found himself planning how to draw the attention of the destructive one, if only to beg it to end him.

It was when he started talking to himself that he really got worried.

"What have you done?"

"I've saved the world. Freed mankind."

"Gotten revenge."

"The goals can align."

"You are a coward."

"I changed the world!"

"And if you're just a pawn of that thing Beyond? Like the Lord Ruler claimed? Kelsier, what if you have no destiny other than to do as you're told?"

He contained the outburst, recovered himself, but the fragility of his own sanity unnerved him. He hadn't been completely sane in the Pits either. In a moment of stillness—staring at the shifting mists that made up the walls of the cavernous room—he admitted a deeper secret to himself.

He hadn't been completely sane *since* the Pits.

That was one reason why he didn't at first trust his senses when someone spoke to him.

"Now *this* I did not expect."

Kelsier shook himself, then turned with suspicion, worried he was hallucinating. It was possible to see all kinds of things in those shifting mists that made up the walls of the cavern, if you stared at them long enough.

This, however, was not a figure made of mist. It was a man with stark white hair, his face defined by angular features and a sharp nose. He seemed vaguely familiar to Kelsier, but he couldn't place why.

The man sat on the floor, one leg up and his arm resting upon his knee. In his hand he held some kind of stick.

Wait . . . no, he wasn't sitting on the floor, but on an object that somehow seemed to be *floating* upon the mists. The white, loglike object sank halfway into the mists of the floor and rocked like a ship on the water, bobbing in place. The rod in the man's hand was a short oar, and his other leg—the one that wasn't up—rested over the side of the log and vanished into the misty ground, visible only as an obscured silhouette.

"You," the man said to Kelsier, "are very bad at doing as you're supposed to."

"Who are you?" Kelsier asked, stepping to the edge of his prison, eyes narrowed. This was no hallucination. He refused to believe his sanity was that far gone. "A spirit?"

"Alas," the man said, "death has never really suited me. Bad for the complexion, you see." He studied Kelsier, lips raised in a knowing smile.

Kelsier hated him immediately.

"Got stuck there, did you?" the man said. "In Ati's prison . . ." He clicked his tongue. "Fitting recompense, for what you did. Poetic even."

"What I did?"

"Destroying the Pits, O scarred one. That was the only perpendicularity on this planet with any reasonable ease of access. This one is *very* dangerous, growing more so by the minute, and difficult to find. By doing as you did, you basically ended traffic through Scadrial. Upended an entire mercantile ecosystem, which I'll admit was fun to watch."

"Who *are* you?" Kelsier said.

"I?" the man said. "I am a drifter. A miscreant. The flame's last breath, made of smoke at its passing."

"That's . . . needlessly obtuse."

"Well, I'm that too." The man cocked his head. "That mostly, if I'm honest."

"And you claim to *not* be dead?"

"If I were, would I need this?" the Drifter said, knocking his oar against the front of his small loglike vessel. It bobbed at the motion, and for the first time Kelsier was able to make out what it was. Arms he'd missed before, hanging down into the mists, obscured. A head that drooped on its neck. A white robe, masking the shape.

"A corpse," he whispered.

"Oh, Spanky here is just a spirit. It's damnably difficult to get about in this subastral—anyone physical risks slipping through these mists and falling, perhaps forever. So many thoughts pool together here, becoming what you see around you, and you need something finer to travel over it all."

"That's horrible."

"Says the man who built a revolution upon the backs of the dead. At least I only need *one* corpse."

Kelsier folded his arms. This man was wary—though he spoke lightheartedly, he watched Kelsier with care, and held back as if contemplating a method of attack.

*He wants something,* Kelsier guessed. *Something that I have, maybe?* No, he seemed legitimately surprised that Kelsier was there. He had come here, intending to visit the Well. Perhaps he wanted to enter it, access the power? Or did he, perhaps, just want to have a look at the thing Beyond?

"Well, you're obviously resourceful," Kelsier said. "Perhaps you can help me with my predicament."

"Alas," the Drifter said. "Your case is hopeless."

Kelsier felt his heart sink.

"Yes, nothing to be done," the Drifter continued. "You are, indeed, stuck with that face. By manifesting those same features on this side, you show that even your *soul* is resigned to you always looking like one ugly sonofa—"

"Bastard," Kelsier cut in. "You had me for a second."

"Now, that's demonstrably wrong," the Drifter said, pointing. "I believe only one of us in this room is illegitimate, and it isn't me. Unless . . ." He tapped the floating corpse on the head with his oar. "What about you, Spanky?"

The corpse actually mumbled something.

"Happily married parents? Still alive? Really? I'm sorry for their loss." The Drifter looked to Kelsier, smiling innocently. "No bastards on this side. What about yours?"

"The bastard by birth," Kelsier said, "is always better off than the one by choice, Drifter. I'll own up to my nature if you own up to yours."

The Drifter chuckled, eyes alight. "Nice, nice. Tell me, since we're on the topic, which are you? A skaa with noble bearing, or a nobleman with skaa interests? Which half is more *you,* Survivor?"

"Well," Kelsier said dryly, "considering that the relatives of my noble half spent the better part of four decades trying to exterminate me, I'd say I'm more inclined toward the skaa side."

"Aaaah," the Drifter said, leaning forward. "But I didn't ask which you liked more. I asked which you *were.*"

"Is it relevant?"

"It's *interesting,*" the Drifter said. "Which is enough for me." He reached down to the corpse he was using as a boat, then removed something from his pocket. Something that glowed, though Kelsier couldn't tell if it was something naturally radiant, or just something made of metal.

The glow faded as the Drifter administered it to his vessel, then—covering the motion with a cough, as if to hide from Kelsier what he was doing—furtively applied some of the glow to his oar. When he placed the oar back into the mists, it sent the boat scooting closer to the Well.

"*Is* there a way for me to escape this prison?" Kelsier asked.

"How about this?" the Drifter said. "We'll have an insult battle. Winner gets to ask one question, and the other has to answer truthfully. I'll start. What's wet, ugly, and has scars on its arms?"

Kelsier raised an eyebrow. All of this talk was a distraction, as evidenced by Drifter scooting—again—closer to the prison. *He's going to try to jump for the Well,* Kelsier thought. *Leap in, hoping to be fast enough to surprise me.*

"No guess?" Drifter asked. "The answer is basically anyone who spends time with you, Kelsier, as they end up slitting their wrists, hitting themselves in the face, and then drowning themselves to forget the experience. Ha! Okay, your turn."

"I'm going to murder you," Kelsier said softly.

"I— Wait, *what*?"

"If you step inside here," Kelsier said, "I'm going to murder you. I'll slice the tendons on your wrists so your hands can't do anything more than batter at me uselessly as I kneel against your throat and slowly crush the life out of you—all while I remove your fingers one by one. I'll finally let you breathe a single, frantic gasp—but at that moment I'll shove your middle finger between your lips so that you're forced to suck it down as you struggle for air. You'll go out knowing you choked to death on your own rotten flesh."

The Drifter gaped at him, mouth working soundlessly. "I . . ." he finally said. "I don't think you know how to play this game."

Kelsier shrugged.

"Seriously," Drifter said. "You need some help, friend. I know a guy. Tall, bald, wears lots of earrings. Have a chat with him next—"

The Drifter cut off midsentence and leaped for the prison, kicking off the floating corpse and throwing himself at the light.

Kelsier was ready. As Drifter entered the light, Kelsier grabbed the man by one arm and slung him toward the side of the pool. The maneuver worked, and Drifter seemed to be able to touch the walls and floor here in the Well. He slammed against the wall, sending waves of light splashing up.

As Kelsier tried to punch at Drifter's head while he was stumbling, the man caught himself on the side of the pool and kicked backward, knocking Kelsier's legs out from beneath him.

Kelsier splashed in the light, and he tried to burn metals by reflex. Nothing happened, though there was *something* to the light here. Something familiar—

He managed to get to his feet, and caught Drifter lunging for the center, the deepest part. Kelsier snatched the man by the arm, swinging him away. Whatever this man wanted, Kelsier's instincts said that he shouldn't be allowed to have it. Beyond that, the Well was Kelsier's only asset. If he could hold the man back from what he wanted, subdue him, perhaps it would lead to answers.

The Drifter stumbled, then lunged, trying to grab Kelsier.

Kelsier, in turn, pivoted and buried his fist in the man's stomach. The motion gave him a thrill; after sitting for so long, inactive, it was nice to be able to *do* something.

Drifter grunted at the punch. "All right then," he muttered.

Kelsier brought his fists up, checked his footing, then unleashed a series of quick blows at Drifter's face that *should* have dazed him.

When Kelsier pulled back—not wanting to go too far and hurt the man seriously—he found that Drifter was smiling at him.

That didn't seem a good sign.

Somehow, Drifter shook off the hits he'd taken. He jumped forward, dodged Kelsier's attempted punch, then ducked and *slammed* his fist into Kelsier's kidneys.

It *hurt.* Kelsier lacked a body, but apparently his spirit could feel pain. He let out a grunt and brought up his arms to protect his face, stepping backward in the liquid light. The Drifter attacked, relentless, slamming his fists into Kelsier with no care for the damage he might be doing to himself.

*Go to the ground,* Kelsier's instincts told him. He dropped one hand and tried to seize Drifter by the arm, planning to send them both down into the light to grapple.

Unfortunately, the Drifter was a little too quick. He dodged and kicked Kelsier's legs from beneath him again, then grabbed him by the throat, slamming him repeatedly—brutally—against the bottom of the shallower part of the prison, splashing him in light that was too thin to be water, but suffocating nonetheless.

Finally Drifter hauled him up, limp. The man's eyes were glowing. "That was unpleasant," Drifter said, "yet somehow still satisfying. Apparently you already being dead means I can hurt you." As Kelsier tried to grab his arm, Drifter slammed Kelsier down again, then pulled him back up, stunned.

"I'm sorry, Survivor, for the rough treatment," Drifter continued. "But you are *not* supposed to be here. You did what I needed you to, but you're a wild card I'd rather not deal with right now." He paused. "If it's any consolation, you should feel proud. It's been centuries since anyone got the drop on me."

He released Kelsier, letting him slump down and catch himself against the side of the prison, half submerged in the light. He growled, trying to pull himself up after Drifter.

Drifter sighed, then proceeded to *kick* at Kelsier's leg repeatedly, shocking him with the pain of it. He screamed, holding his leg. It should have cracked from the force of those kicks, and though it had not, the pain was overwhelming.

"This is a lesson," Drifter said, though it was difficult to hear the words through the pain. "But not the one you might think it is. You don't have a body, and I don't have the inclination to actually injure your soul. That pain is caused by your mind; it's thinking about what *should* be happening to you, and responding." He hesitated. "I'll refrain from making you choke on a chunk of your own flesh."

He walked toward the middle of the pool. Kelsier watched through eyes quivering with pain as Drifter held his hands out to the sides and closed his eyes. He stepped into the center of the pool, the deep portion, and vanished into the light.

A moment later, a figure climbed back out of the pool. Yet this time, the person was shadowy, glowing with inner light like . . .

Like someone in the world of the living. This pool had let Drifter transition from the world of the dead to the real world. Kelsier gaped, following Drifter with his eyes as the man strode past the pillars in the room, then stopped at the other side. Two tiny sources of metal still glowed fiercely there to Kelsier's eyes.

Drifter selected one. It was small, as he could toss it into the air and catch it again. Kelsier could sense the triumph in that motion.

Kelsier closed his eyes and concentrated. No pain. His leg wasn't actually hurt. *Concentrate.*

He managed to make some of the pain fade. He sat up in the pool, rippling light coming up to his chest. He breathed in and out, though he didn't need the air.

Damn. The first person he'd seen in months had thrashed him, then stolen something from the chamber outside. He didn't know what, or why, or even how the Drifter had managed to slip from one world to the next.

Kelsier crawled to the center of the pool, lowering himself down into the deep portion. He stood, his leg still aching faintly, and put his hands to the sides. He concentrated, trying to . . .

To what? Transition? What would that even do to him?

He didn't care. He was frustrated and humiliated. He needed to prove to himself that he wasn't incapable.

He failed. No amount of concentration, visualization, or straining of muscles made him do what the Drifter had managed. He climbed from the pool, exhausted and chastened, and settled on the side.

He didn't notice Fuzz standing there until the god spoke. "What were you *doing*?"

Kelsier turned. Fuzz visited infrequently these days, but when he did come, he always did it unannounced. If he spoke, he often only raved like a madman.

"Someone was just here," Kelsier said. "A man with white hair. He somehow used this Well to pass from the world of the dead to the world of the living."

"I see," Fuzz said softly. "He dared that, did he? Dangerous, with Ruin straining against his bonds. But if anyone were going to try something so foolhardy, it would be Cephandrius."

"He stole something, I think," Kelsier said. "From the other side of the room. A bit of metal."

"Aaah . . ." Fuzz said softly. "I had thought that when he rejected the rest of us, he would stop interfering. I should know better than to trust an implication from him. Half the time you can't trust his outright promises. . . ."

"Who is he?" Kelsier asked.

"An old friend. And no, before you ask, you can't do as he did and transition between Realms. Your ties to the Physical Realm have been severed. You're a kite with no string connecting it to the ground. You cannot ride the perpendicularity across."

Kelsier sighed. "Then why was he able to come to the world of the dead?"

"It's not the world of the dead. It's the world of the mind. Men—all things, truly—are like a ray of light. The floor is the Physical Realm, where that light pools. The sun is the Spiritual Realm, where it begins. This Realm, the Cognitive Realm, is the space between where that beam stretches."

The metaphor barely made any sense to him. *They all know so much,* Kelsier thought, *and I know so little.*

Still, at least Fuzz was sounding better today. Kelsier smiled toward the god, then froze as Fuzz turned his head.

Fuzz was missing half his face. The entire left side was just gone. Not wounded, and there was no skeleton. The complete half smoked, trailing wisps of mist. Half his lips remained, and he smiled back at Kelsier, as if nothing were wrong.

"He stole a bit of my essence, distilled and pure," Fuzz explained. "It can Invest a human, grant him or her Allomancy."

"Your . . . face, Fuzz . . ."

"Ati thinks to finish me," Fuzz said. "Indeed, his knife was placed long ago. I'm already dead." He smiled again, a gruesome expression, then vanished.

Feeling wrung out, Kelsier slumped alongside the pool, lying on the stones—which actually felt a little like real stone, instead of the fluffy softness of everything else made of mist.

He hated this feeling of ignorance. Everyone else was in on some grand joke, and he was the butt. Kelsier stared up at the ceiling, bathed in the glow of the shimmering Well and its column of light. Eventually, he came to a quiet decision.

He would find the answers.

In the Pits of Hathsin, he had awakened to purpose and had determined to destroy the Lord Ruler. Well, he would awaken again. He stood up and stepped into the light, strengthened. The clash of these gods was important, that thing in the Well dangerous. There was more to all of this than he'd ever known, and because of that he had a reason to live.

Perhaps more importantly, he had a reason to stay sane.

# 2

KELSIER no longer worried about madness or boredom. Each time he grew weary of his imprisonment, he remembered that feeling—that *humiliation*—he'd felt at Drifter's hands. Yes, he was trapped in a space only five or so feet across, but there was *plenty* to do.

First he returned to his study of the thing Beyond. He forced himself to duck beneath the light to face it and meet its inscrutable gaze—he did it until he didn't flinch when it turned its attention on him.

Ruin. A fitting name for that vast sense of erosion, decay, and destruction.

He continued to follow the Well's pulses. These trips gave him cryptic clues to Ruin's motives and plots. He sensed a familiar pattern to the things it changed—for Ruin seemed to be doing what Kelsier himself had done: co-opting a religion. Ruin was manipulating the hearts of the people by changing their lore and books.

That terrified Kelsier. His purpose expanded, as he watched the world through these pulses. He didn't just need to understand, he needed to fight this thing. This horrible force that would end all things, if it could.

He struggled, therefore, with a desperation to understand what he saw. Why did Ruin transform the old Terris prophecies? What was the Drifter—whom Kelsier spotted in very rare pulses—doing up in the Terris Dominance? Who was this mysterious Mistborn to whom Ruin paid so much attention, and was he a threat to Vin?

When he rode the pulses, Kelsier watched for—*craved*—signs of the people he knew and loved. Ruin was keenly interested in Vin, and many of his pulses centered around watching her or the man she loved, that Elend Venture.

The mounting clues worried Kelsier. Armies around Luthadel. A city still in chaos. And—he hated to confront this one—it looked like the Venture boy was *king*. When Kelsier realized this, he was so angry he spent days away from the pulses.

They'd gone and put a *nobleman* in charge.

Yes, Kelsier had saved this man's life. Against his better judgment, he'd rescued the man that Vin loved. Out of love for her, perhaps a twisted paternal sense of duty. The Venture boy hadn't been *too* bad, compared to the rest of his kind. But to give him the throne? It seemed that even Dox was listening to Venture. Kelsier would have expected Breeze to ride whatever wind came his way, but Dockson?

Kelsier fumed, but he could not remain away for long. He hungered for these glimpses of his friends. Though each was only a brief flash—like a single image from eyes blinked open—he clung to them. They were reminders that outside his prison, life continued.

Occasionally he was given a glimpse of someone else. His brother, Marsh.

Marsh *lived*. That was a welcome discovery. Unfortunately, the discovery was tainted. For Marsh was an Inquisitor.

The two of them had never been what one would call familial. They had taken divergent paths in life, but that wasn't the true source of the distance between them—it wasn't even due to Marsh's stern ways butting against Kelsier's glibness, or Marsh's unspoken jealousy for things Kelsier had.

No, the truth was they had been raised knowing that at any point they could be dragged before the Inquisitors and murdered for their half-blooded nature. Each had reacted differently to an entire life spent, essentially, with a death sentence: Marsh with quiet tension and caution, Kelsier with aggressive self-confidence to mask his secrets.

Both had known a single, inescapable truth. If one brother were caught, it meant the other would be exposed as a half-blood and likely killed as well. Perhaps this situation would have brought other siblings together. Kelsier was ashamed to admit that for him and Marsh, it had been a wedge. Each mention of "Stay safe" or "Watch yourself" had been colored by an undercurrent of "Don't screw up, or you'll get me killed." It had been a vast relief when, after their parents' deaths, the two of them had agreed to give up pretense and enter the underground of Luthadel.

At times Kelsier toyed with fantasies of what might have been. Could he and Marsh have integrated fully, becoming part of noble society? Could he have overcome his loathing for them and their culture?

Regardless, he wasn't fond of Marsh. The word "fond" sounded too much of walks in a park or time spent eating pastries. One was fond of a favorite book. No, Kelsier was not *fond* of Marsh. But strangely, he still loved him. He was initially happy to find the man alive, but then perhaps death would have been better than what had been done to him.

It took Kelsier weeks to figure out the reason Ruin was so interested in Marsh. Ruin could *talk* to Marsh. Marsh and other Inquisitors, judging by the glimpses and the sensation he received of words being sent.

How? Why Inquisitors? Kelsier found no answers in the visions he saw, though he did witness an important event.

The thing called Ruin was growing stronger, and it was stalking Vin and Elend. Kelsier saw it clearly in a trip through the pulses. A vision of the boy, Elend Venture, sleeping in his tent. The power of Ruin coalescing, forming a figure, malevolent and dangerous. It waited there until Vin entered, then tried to stab Elend.

As Kelsier lost the pulse, he was left with the image of Vin deflecting the blow and saving Elend. But he was confused. Ruin had waited there specifically until Vin returned.

It hadn't actually wanted to hurt Elend. It had just wanted Vin to see him trying.

Why?

# 3

"It's a plug," Kelsier said.

Fuzz—Preservation, as the god had said he could be called—sat outside the prison. He was still missing half his face, and the rest of him was leaking in larger patches as well.

These days the god spent more time near the Well, for which Kelsier was grateful. He had been practicing how to pull information from the creature.

"Hmmm?" Preservation asked.

"This Well," Kelsier said, gesturing around him. "It's like a plug. You created a prison for Ruin, but even the most solid of burrows must have an entrance. *This* is that entrance, sealed with your own power to keep him out, since you two are opposites."

"That . . ." Preservation said, trailing off.

"That?" Kelsier prompted.

"That's *utterly wrong.*"

*Damn,* Kelsier thought. He'd spent weeks on that theory.

He was starting to feel an urgency. The pulses of the Well were growing more demanding, and Ruin seemed to be growing increasingly eager in its touch upon the world. Recently the light of the Well had started to act differently, condensing somehow, pulling together. Something was happening.

"We are gods, Kelsier," Preservation said with a voice that trailed off, then grew louder, then trailed off again. "We permeate everything. The rocks are me. The people are me. And him. All things persist, but decay. Ruin . . . and Preservation . . ."

"You told me this was your power," Kelsier said, gesturing again at the Well, trying to get the god back on topic. "That it gathers here."

"Yes, and elsewhere," Preservation said. "But yes, here. Like dew collects, my power gathers in that spot. It is natural. A cycle: clouds, rain, river, humidity. You cannot press so much essence into a system without it congealing here and there."

Great. That didn't tell him anything. He pressed further on the topic, but Fuzz grew quiet, so he tried something else. He needed to keep Preservation talking—to prevent the god from slumping into one of his quiet stupors.

"Are you afraid?" Kelsier asked. "If Ruin gets free, are you afraid he will kill you?"

"Ha," Preservation said. "I've told you. He killed me long, long ago."

"I find that hard to believe."

"Why?"

"Because I'm sitting here talking to you."

"And I'm talking to *you.* How alive are you?"

*A good point.*

"Death for one such as me is not like death for one such as you," Preservation said, staring off again. "I was killed long ago, when I made the decision to break our promise. But this power I hold . . . it *persists* and it *remembers.* It wants to be alive itself. I have died, but some of me remains. Enough to know that . . . there *were* plans. . . ."

It was no use trying to pry out what those plans were. He didn't remember whatever this "plan" was that he'd made.

"So it's not a plug," Kelsier said. "Then what is it?"

Preservation didn't reply. He didn't even seem to hear.

"You said to me once before," Kelsier continued, speaking more loudly, "that the power exists to be used. That it *needs* to be used. Why?"

Again no answer. He was going to need to try a different tactic. "I looked at him again. Your opposite."

Preservation stood up straight, turning his haunting, half-finished gaze upon Kelsier. Mentioning Ruin often shocked him out of his stupor.

"He is dangerous," Preservation said. "Stay away. My power protects you. Do not taunt him."

"Why? He's locked up."

"Nothing is eternal, not even time itself," Preservation said. "I didn't imprison him so much as *delay* him."

"And the power?"

"Yes . . ." Preservation said, nodding.

"Yes, what?"

"Yes, he will use that. I see." Preservation started, as if realizing—or maybe just recalling—something important. "My power created his prison. My power can unlock it. But how would he find someone who would do it? Who would hold the powers of creation, then *give them away* . . ."

"Which . . . we don't want them to do," Kelsier said.

"No. It will free him!"

"And last time?" Kelsier asked.

"Last time . . ." Preservation blinked, and seemed to come to himself more. "Yes, last time. The Lord Ruler. I made it work last time. I've put her into the spot to do this, but I can hear her thoughts. . . . He's been working on her. . . . So mixed up . . ."

"Fuzz?" Kelsier asked, uncertain.

"I must stop her. Someone . . ." His eyes unfocused.

"What are you doing?"

"Hush," Fuzz said, voice suddenly more commanding. "I'm trying to stop this."

Kelsier looked around, but there was nobody else here. "Who?"

"Do not assume that the me you see here is the only me," Fuzz said. "I am everywhere."

"But—"

"Hush!"

Kelsier hushed, in part because he was happy to see such strength from the god after so long motionless. After some time, however, he slumped down. "No use," Fuzz mumbled. "His tools are stronger."

"So . . ." Kelsier said, testing to see if he'd be hushed again. "Last time. Rashek used the power, instead of . . . what? Giving it up?"

Fuzz nodded. "Alendi would have done the right thing, as he perceived it. Given the power up—but that would have freed Ruin. 'Giving the power up' is a stand-in for giving the power to him. The powers would interpret that as me releasing him. My power, accepting his touch back into the world, directly."

"Great," Kelsier said. "We need a sacrifice then. Someone to take up the powers of eternity, then use them for whatever he wants instead of giving them away. Well, that is a sacrifice *I'm* perfect to make. How do I do it?"

Preservation regarded him. The creature's earlier strength was no more. He was fading, losing his human attributes. He didn't blink anymore, for example, and didn't make a pretense of breathing in before speaking. He could be utterly motionless, lifeless as an iron rod.

"You," Preservation finally said. "Using *my* power. *You.*"

"You let the Lord Ruler do it."

"He tried to save the world."

"As did I."

"You tried to rescue a boatful of people from a fire by sinking the boat, then claiming, 'At least they didn't burn to death.'" God hesitated. "You're going to punch me again, aren't you?"

"Can't reach you, Fuzz," Kelsier said. "The power. *How do I use it?*"

"You can't," Preservation said. "That power is part of the prison. This is what you did by merging your soul to the Well, Kelsier. You wouldn't be able to hold it anyway. You're not Connected enough to me."

Kelsier settled down to think on this, but before he had time to do much, he noticed an oddity. Were those *figures* in the chamber outside? Yes, they were. Living people, marked by their glowing souls. More Inquisitors come to drop off a dead body? He hadn't seen any of them for ages.

Two people stole into the corridor and approached the Well, passing rows of pillars that showed as illusory mist to Kelsier.

"They're here," Preservation said.

"Who?" Kelsier said, squinting. It was difficult to make out details of faces, with those souls glowing. "Is that . . ."

It was Vin.

"What?" Preservation said, looking toward Kelsier, noting his shock. "You thought I was waiting here for nothing? It happens today. The Well of Ascension is full. The time has arrived."

The other figure was the boy, Elend Venture. Kelsier was surprised to find he wasn't angry at the sight. Yes, the crew should have known better than to put a nobleman in charge, but that wasn't really Elend's fault. He'd always been too oblivious to be dangerous.

Besides, whatever the faults of his parentage, this Venture boy had stayed with Vin.

Kelsier folded his arms, watching Venture kneel beside the pool. "If he touches it, I'm going to slap him."

"He will not," Preservation said. "It's for her. He knows it. I've been preparing her. I tried, at least."

Vin turned, and seemed to be looking at God. Yes, she *could* see him. Was there a way Kelsier could use that?

"You tried?" Kelsier said. "Did you explain what she needs to do? Your opposite has been watching her, interacting with her. I've *seen* him doing it. He tried to kill Elend."

"No," Fuzz said, haunted. "He was imitating me. He looked as I do, to them, and tried to kill the boy. Not because he cares about one death, but because he wanted her to distrust me. To think I am her enemy. But can't she tell the difference? Between his hate and destruction, and my peace. I cannot kill. I've never been able to kill. . . ."

"Talk to her!" Kelsier said. "Tell her what she needs to do, Fuzz!"

"I . . ." Preservation shook his head. "I can't get through to her, can't speak to her. I can hear her mind, Kelsier. His lies are there. She doesn't trust me. She thinks she needs to give it up. I've tried to stop this. I left her clues, and then I tried to make someone else stop her. But . . . I've . . . I've failed . . ."

*Oh, hell,* Kelsier thought. *Need a plan. Quick.*

Vin was going to give up the power. Release the thing. Even without

Preservation's assertions, Kelsier would have known what Vin would do. She was a better person than he had ever been, and she never *had* thought she deserved the rewards she was given. She'd take this power, and she'd assume she had to give it up for the greater good.

But how to change that? If Preservation couldn't speak to her, then what?

Elend stood up and approached Preservation. Yes, the boy could see Preservation too.

"She needs motivation," Kelsier said, an idea clicking in his mind. Ruin had tried to stab Elend, to frighten her.

It was the right idea. He just hadn't gone far enough.

"Stab him," Kelsier said.

"What?" Preservation said, aghast.

Kelsier pushed out of his prison bonds a few steps, approaching Fuzz, who stood just outside. He strained to the absolute limits of his fetters.

"Stab him," Kelsier said. "Use that knife at your belt, Fuzz. They can see you, and you can affect their world. *Stab Elend Venture.* Give her a reason to use the power. She'll want to save him."

"I'm *Preservation,*" he said. "The knife . . . I haven't actually drawn it in millennia. You speak of acting like him, as he pretended I would act! It's horrible!"

"You have to!" Kelsier said.

"I can't . . . I . . ." Fuzz reached to his belt, and his hand shimmered. The knife appeared there. He looked down at it, the blade glistening. "Old friend . . ." he whispered at it.

He looked toward Elend, who nodded. Preservation raised his arm, weapon in hand.

Then stopped.

His half face was a mask of pain. "No . . ." he whispered. "I Preserve . . ."

*He's not going to do it,* Kelsier thought, watching Elend talk to Vin, his posture reassuring. *He can't do it.*

Only one option.

"Sorry, kid," Kelsier said.

Kelsier grabbed Preservation's shimmering arm and *slashed* it across the Venture boy's stomach.

He felt as if he were stabbing his own flesh. Not because of Venture, but because he knew what it would do to Vin. His heart lurched as she rushed to Venture's side, weeping.

Well, he'd saved this boy's life once, so this would make them even. Besides, she would rescue him. She'd *have* to save Elend. She loved him.

Kelsier stepped back, returning to his prison proper, leaving an aghast Preservation to stare at his own hand as he stumbled away from the fallen man.

"Gut wound," Kelsier whispered. "He'll take time to die, Vin. Grab the power. It's *right here.* Use it."

She cradled Venture. Kelsier waited, anxious. If she entered the pool, she'd be able to see Kelsier, wouldn't she? She'd become transcendent, like Preservation. Or would she have to use the power first?

Would that free Kelsier? He had no answers, only an assurance that whatever happened, he could not let that thing Beyond escape. He turned.

And was shocked to find it *there.* He could sense it, pressed against the reality of this world, an infinite darkness. Not just the flimsy imitation of Preservation he'd made before, but the entire vast power. It wasn't in any specific space, but at the same time it was pressed up against reality and watching with a keen interest.

To his horror, Kelsier saw it change, sending forward spines like the spindly legs of a spider. On their end, dangling like a puppet, was a humanoid figure.

*Vin . . .* it whispered. *Vin . . .*

She looked toward the pool, her posture grieved. Then she left Venture and entered the Well, passing Kelsier without seeing him and reaching the deepest point. She sank slowly into the light. At the last moment, she ripped something glowing from her ear and tossed it out—a bit of metal. Her earring?

Once she sank completely, she did not appear on this side. Instead, a storm began. A rising column of light surrounded Kelsier, blocking him from seeing anything but the raw *energy.* Like a sudden tide, an explosion, an instant sunrise. It was all around him, active, *excited.*

*You mustn't do it, child,* Ruin said through his humanlike puppet. How could it speak with such a soothing voice? He could see the force behind it, the destruction, but the face it put on was so kindly. *You know what you must do.*

"Don't listen to it, Vin!" Kelsier screamed, but his voice was lost in the roar of the power. He shouted and railed as the voice conned Vin, warning her that if she took the power she'd destroy the world. Kelsier fought through the light, trying to find her, to seize her and explain.

He failed. He failed *horribly.* He couldn't make himself heard, couldn't touch Vin. Couldn't do anything. Even his impromptu plan of stabbing Elend proved foolish, for she released the power. Weeping, flayed, ripped open, she did the most selfless thing he had ever seen.

And in so doing, she doomed them.

The power became a weapon as she released it. It made a spear in the air and ripped a hole through reality and into the place where Ruin waited.

Ruin rushed through that hole to freedom.

# 4

KELSIER sat on the lip of the now empty Well of Ascension. The light was gone, and with it his prison. He could leave.

He didn't seem to be stretching away and fading. Apparently being part of Preservation's power for a time had expanded Kelsier's soul, letting him linger. Though honestly, he wished he could vanish at this moment.

Vin—glowing and radiant to his eyes—lay beside Elend Venture, clutching him and weeping as his soul pulsed, growing weaker. Kelsier stood up, turning his back toward the sight. For all his cleverness, he'd gone and broken the poor girl's heart.

*I must be the smartest idiot around,* Kelsier thought.

"It was going to happen," Preservation said. "I thought . . . Maybe . . ." From the corner of his eye, Kelsier saw Fuzz approach Vin, then look down at the fallen Venture.

"I can Preserve him," Preservation whispered.

Kelsier spun. Preservation started waving at Vin, and she stumbled to her feet. She followed the god a few feet to something Elend had dropped, a fallen nugget of metal. Where had that come from?

*The Venture boy was carrying it when he entered,* Kelsier thought. That was the last bit of metal from the other side of the room, the twin of the one the Drifter had stolen. Kelsier approached as Vin took the nugget of metal, so tiny, and approached Elend, then put it into his mouth. She washed it down with a vial of metal.

Soul and metal became one. Elend's light strengthened, glowing vibrantly. Kelsier closed his eyes, feeling a thrumming sense of peace.

"That was good work, Fuzz," Kelsier said, opening his eyes and smiling at Preservation as the god stepped over to him. Vin's posture manifested incredible joy. "I'm almost ready to think you're a benevolent god."

"Stabbing him was dangerous, painful," Preservation said. "I cannot condone such recklessness. But perhaps it was right, regardless of how I feel."

"Ruin's free," Kelsier said, looking upward. "That thing has escaped."

"Yes. Fortunately, before I died, I put a plan into motion. I can't remember it, but I'm certain that it was brilliant."

"You know, I've said something similar myself on occasion, after a night of drinking." Kelsier rubbed his chin. "I'm free too."

"Yes."

"This is where you joke that you aren't certain which was more dangerous to release. Me or the other one."

"No," Fuzz said. "I know which is more dangerous."

"Failing marks for effort there, I'm afraid."

"But perhaps . . ." Preservation said. "Perhaps I cannot say which is more *annoying*." He smiled. With his face half melted off and his neck starting to go, it was unnerving. Like a happy bark from a crippled puppy.

Kelsier slapped him on the shoulder. "We'll make a solid crewmember out of you yet, Fuzz. For now, I want to get the *hell* out of this room."

# PART THREE
# SPIRIT

# 1

KELSIER really wanted something to drink. Wasn't that what you did when you got out of prison? Went drinking, enjoyed your freedom by giving it up to a little booze and a terrible headache?

When alive, he'd usually avoided such levity. He liked to control a situation, not let it control him—but he couldn't deny that he thirsted for something to drink, to numb the experience he'd just been through.

That seemed terribly unfair. No body, but he could still be thirsty?

He climbed from the caverns surrounding the Well of Ascension, passing through misty chambers and tunnels. As before, when he touched something he was able to see what it looked like in the real world.

His footing was firm on the inconstant ground; though it was somewhat springy, like cloth, it held his weight unless he stamped hard—which would cause his foot to sink in like it was pushing through thick mud. He could even pass through the walls if he tried, but it was harder than it had been during his initial run, when he'd been dying.

He emerged from the caverns into the basement of Kredik Shaw, the Lord Ruler's palace. It was even easier than usual to get turned about in this place, as everything was misty to his eyes. He touched the things of mist that he passed, so he could picture his surroundings better. A vase, a carpet, a door.

Kelsier eventually stepped out onto the streets of Luthadel a free—if dead—man. For a time he just walked the city, so relieved to be out of that hole that he was able to ignore the sense of dread he felt at Ruin's escape.

He must have wandered an entire day that way, sitting on rooftops, strolling past fountains. Looking over this city dotted with glowing pieces of metal, like lights hovering in the mists at night. He ended up on top of the city wall, observing the koloss who had set up camp outside the town but—somehow—didn't seem to be killing anyone.

He needed to see if there was a way to contact his friends. Unfortunately, without the pulses—those had stopped when Ruin escaped—to guide him, he didn't know where to start looking. He'd lost track of Vin and Elend in his excitement at leaving the caverns, but he remembered some of what he'd seen through the pulses. That gave him a few places to search.

He ultimately found his crew at Keep Venture. It was the day after the disaster at the Well of Ascension, and they appeared to be holding a funeral. Kelsier strolled through the courtyard, passing among the glowing souls of men, each burning like a limelight. Those he brushed gave him an impression of their appearance. Many he recognized: skaa he'd interacted with, encouraged, uplifted during his final months of life. Others were unfamiliar. A disturbing number of soldiers who had once served the Lord Ruler.

He found Vin at the front, sitting on the steps of Keep Venture, huddled and slumped over. Elend was nowhere to be seen, though Ham stood nearby, arms folded. In the courtyard, somebody waved their hands before the group, giving a speech. Was that Demoux? Leading the people in the funeral service? Those were certainly corpses laid out in the courtyard, their souls no longer shining. He couldn't hear what Demoux was saying, but the presentation seemed clear.

Kelsier settled down on the steps beside Vin. He clasped his hands before himself. "So . . . that went well."

Vin, of course, didn't reply.

"I mean," Kelsier continued, "yes, we ended up releasing a world-ending force of destruction and chaos, but at least the Lord Ruler is dead. Mission accomplished. Plus you still have your nobleman boyfriend, so there's that. Don't worry about the scar on his stomach. It'll make him look more rugged. Mists know, the little bookworker could use some toughening up."

She didn't move, but maintained her slumped posture. He rested his arm across her shoulders and was given a glimpse of her as she looked in the real world. Full of color and life, yet somehow . . . weathered. She seemed so much older now, no longer the child he'd found scamming obligators on the streets.

He leaned down beside her. "I'm going to beat this thing, Vin. I *am* going take care of this."

"And how," Preservation said from the courtyard below the steps, "are you going to accomplish *that*?"

Kelsier looked up. Though he was prepared for the sight of Preservation, he still winced to see him as he was—barely even in human shape any longer, more a dissolved bunch of weaving threads of frayed smoke, giving the vague impression of a head, arms, legs.

"He's free," Preservation said. "That's it. Time up. Contract due. He will take what was promised."

"We'll stop him."

"Stop him? He's the force of entropy, a universal constant. You can't *stop* that any more than you can stop time."

Kelsier stood up, leaving Vin and walking down the steps toward Preservation. He wished he could hear what Demoux was saying to this small crowd of glowing souls.

"If he can't be stopped," Kelsier said, "then we'll slow him. You did it before, right? Your grand plan?"

"I . . ." Preservation said. "Yes . . . There was a plan. . . ."

"I'm free now. I can help you put it into motion."

"Free?" Preservation laughed. "No, you've just entered a larger prison. Tied to this Realm, bound to it. There's nothing you can do. Nothing I can do."

"That—"

"He's watching us, you know," Preservation said, looking upward at the sky.

Kelsier followed his gaze reluctantly. The sky—misty and shifting—seemed so distant. It felt as if it had pulled back from the planet, like people in a crowd shying away from a corpse. In that vastness Kelsier saw something dark, thrashing, writhing upon itself. More solid than mist, like an ocean of snakes, obscuring the tiny sun.

He knew that vastness. Ruin was indeed watching.

"He thinks you're insignificant," Preservation said. "I think he finds you amusing—the soul of Ati that is still in there somewhere would laugh at this."

"He has a soul?"

Preservation didn't respond. Kelsier stepped up to him, passing corpses made of mists on the ground.

"If he is alive," Kelsier said, "then he can be killed. No matter how powerful." *You're proof of that, Fuzz. He's killing you.*

Preservation laughed, a harsh, barking noise. "You keep forgetting which of us is a god and which is just a poor dead shadow. Waiting to expire." He waved a mostly unraveled arm, fingers made of spirals of unwound, misty strings. "Listen to them. Doesn't it embarrass you how they talk? The Survivor? Ha! I Preserved them for millennia. What have *you* done for them?"

Kelsier turned toward Demoux. Preservation appeared to have forgotten that Kelsier couldn't hear the speech. Intending to go touch Demoux, to get a view of what he looked like now, Kelsier brushed one of the corpses on the ground.

A young man. A soldier, by the looks of it. He didn't know the boy, but he started to worry. He looked back at where Ham was standing—that figure near him would be Breeze.

What of the others?

He grew cold, then started touching corpses, looking for any he recognized. His motions became more frantic.

"What are you seeking?" Preservation asked.

"How many—" Kelsier swallowed. "How many of these were friends of mine?"

"Some," Preservation said.

"Any members of the crew?"

"No," Preservation said, and Kelsier let out a sigh. "No, they died during the initial break-in, days ago. Dockson. Clubs."

A spear of ice shot through Kelsier. He tried to stand up from beside the corpse he'd been inspecting, but stumbled, trying to force out the words. "No. No, not Dox."

Preservation nodded.

"Wh . . . When did it happen? How?"

Preservation laughed. The sound of madness. He showed little of the kindly, uncertain man who had greeted Kelsier when he'd first entered this place.

"Both were murdered by koloss as the siege broke. Their bodies were burned days ago, Kelsier, while you were trapped."

Kelsier trembled, feeling lost. "I . . ." Kelsier said.

*Dox. I wasn't here for him. I could have seen him again, as he passed. Talked to him. Saved him maybe?*

"He cursed you as he died, Kelsier," Preservation said, voice harsh. "He blamed you for all this."

Kelsier bowed his head. Another lost friend. And Clubs too . . . two good men. He'd lost too many of those in his life, dammit. Far too many.

*I'm sorry, Dox, Clubs. I'm sorry for failing you.*

Kelsier took that anger, that bitterness and shame, and channeled it. He'd found purpose again during his days in prison. He wouldn't lose it now.

He stood and turned to Preservation. The god—shockingly—cringed as if *frightened.* Kelsier seized the god's form, and in a brief moment was given a vision of the grandness beyond. The pervading light of Preservation that permeated all things. The world, the mists, the metals, the very souls of men. This creature was somehow dying, but his power was far from gone.

He also felt Preservation's pain. It was the loss Kelsier had felt at Dox's death, only magnified thousands of times over. Preservation felt every light that went out, felt them and knew them as a person he had loved.

Around the world they were dying at an accelerated pace. Too much ash was falling, and Preservation only anticipated it increasing. Armies of koloss rampaging beyond control. Death, destruction, a world on its last legs.

And . . . to the south . . . what was *that*? People?

Kelsier held Preservation, in awe at this creature's divine agony. Then Kelsier pulled him close, into an embrace.

"I'm so sorry," Kelsier whispered.

"Oh, Senna . . ." Preservation whispered. "I'm losing this place. Losing them all . . ."

"We are going to stop it," Kelsier said, pulling back.

"It can't be stopped. The deal . . ."

"Deals can be broken."

"Not these kinds of deals, Kelsier. I was able to trick Ruin before, lock him away, by fooling him with our agreement. But that wasn't a breach of contract, more leaving a hole in the agreement to be exploited. This time there are no holes."

"Then we go out kicking and screaming," Kelsier said. "You and me, we're a team."

Preservation seemed to *condense,* his form pulling itself together, threads reweaving. "A team. Yes. A crew."

"To do the impossible."

"Defy reality," Preservation whispered. "Everyone always said you were insane."

"And I always acknowledged that they had a point," Kelsier said. "Thing is, while they were correct to question my sanity, they never did have the right reasoning. It's not my ambition that should worry them."

"Then what should?"

Kelsier smiled.

Preservation, in turn, laughed—a sound that had lost its edge, the harshness gone. "I can't help you do . . . whatever it is you think you're doing. Not directly. I don't . . . think well enough anymore. But . . ."

"But?"

Preservation solidified a little further. "But I know where you'll find someone who can."

# 2

KELSIER followed a thread of Preservation, like a glowing tendril of mist, through the city. He made sure to look up periodically, confronting that force in the sky, which had boiled through the mists there and was coming to dominate in every direction.

Kelsier would not back down. He would not let this thing intimidate him again. He'd already killed one god. The second murder was always easier than the first.

The tendril of Preservation led him past shadowy tenements, through a slum that somehow looked even more depressing on this side—all crammed together, the souls of men packed in frightened lumps. His crew had saved this city, but many of the people Kelsier passed didn't seem to know it yet.

Eventually the tendril led him out broken city gates to the north, past rubble and corpses being slowly sorted. Past living armies and that fearsome army of koloss, out beyond the city and a short hike along the river to . . . the lake?

Luthadel was built not far from the lake that bore its name, though most of the city's populace determinedly ignored that fact. Lake Luthadel wasn't the swimming or sport kind of lake, unless you fancied bathing in a soupy sludge that was more ash than it was water—and good luck catching what few fish remained after centuries of residing next to a city full of half-starved skaa. This close to the ashmounts, keeping the river and lake navigable had demanded the full-time attention of an entire class of people, the canal workers, a strange breed of skaa who rarely mixed with those from the city proper.

They would have been horrified to find that here on this side, the lake—and actually the river as well—was inverted somehow. Opposite to the way the mists under his feet had a liquid feel to them, the lake rose into a solid mound, only a few inches high but harder and somehow more substantial than the ground he'd become used to walking upon.

In fact, the lake was like a low island rising from the sea of mists. What was solid and what was fluid seemed somehow reversed in this place. Kelsier stepped up to the island's edge, the ribbon of Preservation's essence curling past him and leading onto the island, like a mythical string showing the way home from the grand maze of Ishathon.

Kelsier stuffed his hands in his trouser pockets and kicked at the ground of the island. It was some type of dark, smoky stone.

"What?" Preservation whispered.

Kelsier jumped, then glanced at the line of light. "You . . . in there, Fuzz?"

"I'm everywhere," Preservation said, his voice soft, frail. He sounded exhausted. "Why have you stopped?"

"This is different."

"Yes, it congeals here," Preservation said. "It has to do with the way men think, and where they are likely to pass. Somewhat to do with that, at least."

"But what is it?" Kelsier said, stepping up onto the island.

Preservation said nothing further, and so Kelsier continued toward the center of the island. Whatever had "congealed" here, it was strikingly stonelike. And things grew on it. Kelsier passed scrubby plants sprouting from the otherwise hard ground—not misty, inchoate plants, but real ones full of color. They had broad brown leaves with—curiously—what seemed like *mist* rising from them. None of the plants reached higher than his knees, but there were still far more than he'd expected to find here.

As he passed through a field of the plants, he thought he caught something scurrying between them, rustling leaves in its passing.

*The world of the dead has plants and animals?* he thought. But that wasn't what Preservation had called it. The Cognitive Realm. How did these plants grow here? What watered them?

The farther he penetrated onto this island, the darker it became. Ruin was covering up that tiny sun, and Kelsier began to miss even the faint glow that had permeated the phantom mists in the city. Soon he was traveling in what seemed like twilight.

Eventually Preservation's ribbon grew thin, then vanished. Kelsier stopped near its tip, whispering, "Fuzz? You there?"

No response, the silence refuting Preservation's claim earlier that he was everywhere. Kelsier shook his head. Perhaps Preservation was listening, but wasn't *there* enough to give a reply. Kelsier continued forward, passing through a place where the plants had grown to waist height, mist rising from their broad leaves like steam from a hot plate.

Finally, ahead he spotted *light.* Kelsier pulled up. He'd fallen into a prowl naturally, led by instincts gained from a life spent on the con, literally since the day of his birth. He had no weapons. He knelt, feeling at the ground for a stone or stick, but these plants weren't big enough to provide anything substantial, and the ground was smooth, unbroken.

Preservation had promised him help, but he wasn't sure how much he trusted what Preservation said. Odd, that living through his own death should make him *more* hesitant to trust in God's word. He took off his belt for a weapon, but it evaporated in his hands and appeared back on his waist. Shaking his head, he prowled closer, approaching near enough to the fire to pick out two people. Alive, and in this Realm, not glowing souls or misty spirits.

The man wore skaa clothing—suspenders, shirt with sleeves rolled up—and tended a small dinner fire. He had short hair and a narrow, almost pinched face. That knife at his belt, nearly long enough to be a sword, would come in very handy.

The other person, who sat on a small folding chair, might have been Terris. There were some among their population who had a skin tone almost as dark as hers, though he'd also met some people from the various southern dominances who were dark. She certainly wasn't wearing Terris clothing—she had on a sturdy brown dress, with a large leather girdle around the waist, and wore her hair woven into tiny braids.

Two. He could handle two, couldn't he? Even without Allomancy or weapons. Regardless, best to be careful. He hadn't forgotten his humiliation at the hands of the Drifter. Kelsier made a careful decision, then stood up, straightened his coat, and strode into their camp.

"Well," he proclaimed, "this has been an unusual few days, I can tell you *that*."

The man at the fire scrambled backward, hand on his knife, gaping. The woman remained seated, though she reached for something at her side. A little tube with a handle on the bottom. She pointed it toward him, treating it like some kind of weapon.

"So," Kelsier said, glancing at the sky with its shifting, writhing mass of too-solid tendrils, "anyone else bothered by the voracious force of destruction in the air above us?"

"Shadows!" the man shouted. "It's *you*. You're dead!"

"Depends on your definition of dead," Kelsier said, strolling over to the fire. The woman trailed him with that odd weapon of hers. "What in the blazes are you *burning* for that fire?" He looked up at the two of them. "What?"

"How?" the man sputtered. "What? When . . ."

". . . Why?" Kelsier added helpfully.

"Yes, why!"

"I have a very delicate constitution, you see," Kelsier said. "And death seemed like it would be *rather* bad for the digestion. So I decided not to participate."

"One doesn't merely *decide* to become a shadow!" the man exclaimed. He had a faintly strange accent, one Kelsier couldn't place. "It's an important rite! With requirements and traditions. This . . . this is . . ." He threw his hands into the air. "This is a *bother*."

Kelsier smiled, meeting the gaze of the woman, who reached for a cup of something warm on the ground beside her. With her other hand she tucked her weapon away, as if it had never been there. She was perhaps in her mid-thirties.

"The Survivor of Hathsin," she said, musing.

"You seem to have me at a disadvantage," Kelsier said. "One problem with notoriety, unfortunately."

"I should assume there are many disadvantages to fame, for a thief. One doesn't particularly wish to be recognized while trying to lift pocketbooks."

"Considering how he's regarded by the people of this domain," the man said, still watching Kelsier with a wary eye, "I'd expect them to be delighted to discover him robbing them."

"Yes," Kelsier said dryly, "they practically lined up for the privilege. Must I repeat myself?"

She considered. "My name is Khriss, of Taldain." She nodded toward the other man, and he reluctantly replaced his knife. "That is Nazh, a man in my employ."

"Excellent," Kelsier said. "Any idea why Preservation would tell me to come talk to you?"

"*Preservation?*" Nazh said, stepping up and seizing Kelsier's arm. So, as with the Drifter, they could indeed touch Kelsier. "You've spoken directly with one of the *Shards*?"

"Sure," Kelsier said. "Fuzz and I go way back." He pulled his arm free of Nazh's grip and grabbed the other folding stool from beside the fire—two simple pieces of wood that folded together, a piece of cloth between them to sit on.

He settled it across from Khriss and sat down.

"I don't like this, Khriss," Nazh said. "He's dangerous."

"Fortunately," she replied, "so are we. The Shard Preservation, Survivor. How does he look?"

"Is that a test to see if I've actually spoken with him," Kelsier said, "or a sincere question as to the creature's status?"

"Both."

"He's dying," Kelsier said, spinning Nazh's knife in his fingers. He'd palmed it during their altercation a moment ago, and was curious to find that though it was made of metal, it didn't glow. "He's a short man with black hair—or he used to be. He's been . . . well, *unraveling.*"

"Hey," Nazh said, eyes narrowing at the knife. He looked at his belt, and the empty sheath. "*Hey!*"

"Unraveling," Khriss said. "So a slow death. Ati doesn't know how to Splinter another Shard? Or he hasn't the strength? Hmm . . ."

"Ati?" Kelsier asked. "Preservation mentioned that name too."

Khriss pointed at the sky with one finger while she sipped at her drink. "That's him. What he's become, at least."

"And . . . what is a Shard?" Kelsier asked.

"Are you a scholar, Mr. Survivor?"

"No," he said. "But I've killed a few."

"Cute. Well, you've stumbled into something far, far bigger than you, your politics, or your little planet."

"Bigger than you can handle, Survivor," Nazh said, swiping back his knife as Kelsier balanced it on his finger. "You should just bow out now."

"Nazh does have a point," Khriss said. "Your questions are dangerous. Once you step behind the curtain and see the actors as the people they are, it becomes harder to pretend the play is real."

"I . . ." Kelsier leaned forward, clasping his hands before him. Hell . . . that fire was warm, but it didn't seem to be *burning* anything. He stared at the flames and swallowed. "I woke up from death after having, deep down, expected there to be no afterlife. I found that God was real, but that he was dying. I need answers. *Please.*"

"Curious," she said.

He looked up, frowning.

"I have heard many stories of you, Survivor," she said. "They often laud your many admirable qualities. Sincerity is never one of those."

"I can steal something else from your manservant," Kelsier said, "if it will make you feel more comfortable that I am what you expected."

"You can try," Nazh said, walking around the fire, folding his arms and obviously trying to look intimidating.

"The Shards," Khriss said, drawing Kelsier's attention, "are not God, but they are *pieces* of God. Ruin, Preservation, Autonomy, Cultivation, Devotion . . . There are sixteen of them."

"Sixteen," Kelsier breathed. "There are fourteen *more* of these things running around?"

"The rest are on other planets."

"Other . . ." Kelsier blinked. "Other *planets.*"

"Ah, see," Nazh said. "You've broken him already, Khriss."

"Other planets," she repeated gently. "Yes, there are dozens of them. Many are inhabited by people much like you or me. There is an original, shrouded and hidden somewhere in the cosmere. I've yet to find it, but I *have* found stories.

"Anyway, there was a God. Adonalsium. I don't know if it was a force or a being, though I suspect the latter. Sixteen people, together, *killed* Adonalsium, ripping it apart and dividing its essence between them, becoming the first who Ascended."

"Who were they?" Kelsier said, trying to make sense of this.

"A diverse group," she said. "With equally diverse motives. Some wished for the power; others saw killing Adonalsium as the only good option left to them. Together they murdered a deity, and became divine themselves." She smiled in a kindly way, as if to prepare him for what came next. "Two of those created this planet, Survivor, including the people on it."

"So . . . my world, and everyone I know," Kelsier said, "is the creation of a pair of . . . half gods?"

"More like fractional gods," Nazh said. "And ones with no particular qualifications for deityhood, other than being conniving enough to murder the guy who had the job before."

"Oh, hell . . ." Kelsier breathed. "No wonder we're all so bloody messed up."

"Actually," Khriss noted, "people are generally like that, no matter who made them. If it's any consolation, Adonalsium originally created the first humans, therefore your gods had a pattern to use."

"So we're copies of a flawed original," Kelsier said. "Not terribly comforting." He looked upward. "And that thing? It used to be human?"

"The power . . . distorts," Khriss said. "There's a person in that somewhere, directing it. Or perhaps just riding it at this point."

Kelsier remembered the puppet Ruin had presented, the shape of a man. Now basically a shell filled with a terrible power. "So what happens if one of these things . . . dies?"

"I'm very curious to see," Khriss said. "I've never viewed it in person, and the past deaths were different. They were each a single, stunning event, the god's power shattered and dispersed. This is more like a strangulation, while those were like a beheading. This should be very instructive."

"Unless I stop it," Kelsier said.

She smiled at him.

"Don't be patronizing," Kelsier snapped, standing up, the stool falling down behind him. "I am going to stop it."

"This world is winding down, Survivor," Khriss said. "It is a true shame, but I know of no way to save it. I came with the hopes that I might be able to help, but I can't even reach the Physical Realm here any longer."

"Someone destroyed the gateway in," Nazh noted. "Someone *incredibly* foolhardy. Brash. Stupid. Didn't—"

"You're overselling it," Kelsier said. "The Drifter told me what I did."

"The . . . who?" Khriss asked.

"Fellow with white hair," Kelsier said. "Lanky, with a sharp nose and—"

"Damn," Khriss said. "Did he get to the Well of Ascension?"

"Stole something there," Kelsier said. "A bit of metal."

"*Damn,*" Khriss said, looking at her servant. "We need to go. I'm sorry, Survivor."

"But—"

"This isn't because of what you just told us," she said, rising and waving for Nazh to help gather their things. "We were leaving anyway. This planet is dying; as much as I wish to witness the death of a Shard, I don't dare risk doing it from up close. We'll observe from afar."

"Preservation thought you'd be able to help," Kelsier said. "Surely there is *something* you can do. Something you can tell me. It can't be over."

"I *am* sorry, Survivor," Khriss said softly. "Perhaps if I knew more, perhaps if I could convince the Eyree to answer my questions . . ." She shook her head. "It will happen slowly, Survivor, over months. But it is coming. Ruin will consume this world, and the man once known as Ati won't be able to stop it. If he even cared to."

"Everything," Kelsier whispered. "Everything I've known. Every person on my . . . my planet?"

Nearby, Nazh bent down and picked up the fire, making it *vanish.* The oversized flame just folded up upon itself in his palm, and Kelsier thought he saw a puff of mist when it did so. Kelsier picked up his stool with one finger, unscrewed the bolt on the bottom, and palmed it into his hand before handing the stool to Nazh.

Nazh then tugged on a hiking pack, tied with scroll cases across the top. He looked to Khriss.

"Stay," Kelsier said, turning back to Khriss. "Help me."

"Help you? I can't even help *myself,* Survivor. I'm in exile, and even if I weren't I wouldn't have the resources to stop a Shard. I probably should never have come." She hesitated. "And I'm sorry, but I cannot invite you to come with us. The eyes of your god will be upon you, Kelsier. He'll know where you are, as you have pieces of him within. It has been dangerous enough to speak here with you."

Nazh handed her a pack, and she slung it over her shoulder.

"I *am* going to stop this," Kelsier told them.

Khriss lifted a hand and curled her fingers in an unfamiliar gesture, bidding him farewell it seemed. She turned away from the clearing and strode away, into the brush. Nazh followed.

Kelsier sank down. They'd taken the stools, so he settled onto the ground, bowing his head. *This is what you deserve, Kelsier,* a piece of him thought. *You wished to dance with the divine and steal from gods. Should you now be surprised that you've found yourself in over your head?*

The sound of rustling leaves made him scramble back to his feet. Nazh emerged from the shadows. The shorter man stopped at the perimeter of the abandoned camp, then cursed softly before stepping forward and removing his side knife, sheath and all, and handing it toward Kelsier.

Hesitant, Kelsier accepted the leatherbound weapon.

"It's a bad state you and yours are in," Nazh said softly, "but I rather like this place. Damnable mists and all." He pointed westward. "They've set up out there."

"They?"

"The Eyree," he said. "They've been at this far longer than we have, Survivor. If someone will know how to help you, it will be the Eyree. Look for them where the land becomes solid again."

"Solid again . . ." Kelsier said. "Lake Tyrian?"

"Beyond. Far beyond, Survivor."

"The *ocean*? That's miles and miles away. Past Farmost!"

Nazh patted him on the shoulder, then turned back to hike after Khriss.

"Is there hope?" Kelsier called.

"What if I told you no?" Nazh said over his shoulder. "What if I said I figured you were damn well ruined, so to speak. Would it change what you were going to do?"

"No."

Nazh raised his fingers to his forehead in a kind of salute. "Farewell, Survivor. Take care of my knife. I'm fond of it."

He vanished into the darkness. Kelsier watched after him, then did the only rational thing.

He ate the bolt he'd taken from the bottom of the stool.

# 3

The bolt didn't do anything. He'd hoped he'd be able to make Allomancy work, but the bolt just settled into his stomach—a strange and uncomfortable weight. He couldn't burn it, despite trying. As he walked, he eventually coughed it back up and tossed it away.

He stepped to the transition from the island to the misty ground around Luthadel, and felt a new weight upon him. A doomed world, dying gods, and an entire universe he'd never known existed. His only hope now was . . . to journey to the ocean?

That was farther than he had ever gone, even during his travels with Gemmel. It would take months to walk that far. Did they have months?

He stepped off the island, crossing onto the soft ground of the misted banks. Luthadel loomed in the near distance, a shadowy wall of curling mist.

"Fuzz?" he called. "You out there?"

"I'm everywhere," Preservation said, appearing beside him.

"So you were listening?" Kelsier asked.

He nodded absently, form frayed, face indistinct. "I think . . . Surely I was . . ."

"They mentioned someone called the Eyes Ree?"

"Yes, the I-ree," Preservation said, pronouncing it in a slightly different way. "Three letters. I R E. It means something in their language, these people from another land. The ones who died, but did not. I have felt them crowding at the edges of my vision, like spirits in the night."

"Dead, but alive," Kelsier said. "Like me?"

"No."

"Then what?"

"Died, but did not."

*Great,* Kelsier thought. He turned toward the west. "They are supposedly at the ocean."

"The Ire built a city," Preservation said, softly. "In a place between worlds . . ."

"Well," Kelsier said, then took a deep breath. "That's where I'm going."

"Going?" Preservation said. "You're leaving me?"

The urgency of those words startled Kelsier. "If these people can help us, then I need to talk to them."

"They can't help us," Preservation said. "They're . . . they're callous. They plot over my corpse like scavenging insects waiting for the last beat of the heart. Don't go. Don't *leave me.*"

"You're everywhere. I can't leave you."

"No. They're beyond me. I . . . I cannot depart this land. I'm too Invested in it, in every rock and leaf." He pulsed, his already indistinct form spreading thinner. "We . . . grow attached easily, and it takes one who is particularly dedicated to leave."

"And Ruin?" Kelsier said, turning toward the west. "If he destroys everything, would he be able to escape?"

"Yes," Preservation said, very softly. "He could go then. But Kelsier, you can't abandon me. We . . . we're a team, right?"

Kelsier rested his hand on the creature's shoulder. Once so confident, now little more than a *smudge* in the air. "I'll be back as soon as I can. If I'm going to stop that thing, I'll need some kind of help."

"You pity me."

"I pity anyone who's not me, Fuzz. A hazard of being the man I am. But you *can* do this. Keep an eye on Ruin, and try to get word to Vin and that nobleman of hers."

"Pity," Preservation repeated. "Is that . . . is that what I've become? Yes . . . Yes, it is."

He reached up with a vaguely outlined hand and seized Kelsier's arm from underneath. Kelsier gasped, then cut off as Preservation grabbed him by the back of the neck with his other hand, locking his gaze with Kelsier's. Those eyes snapped into focus, fuzziness becoming suddenly distinct. A glow burst from them, silvery white, bathing Kelsier and blinding him.

Everything else was vaporized; nothing could withstand that terrible, wonderful light. Kelsier lost form, thought, very being. He transcended *self* and entered a place of flowing light. Ribbons of it exploded from him, and though he tried to scream, he had no voice.

Time didn't pass; time had no relevance here. It was not a place. Location had no relevance. Only Connection, person to person, man to world, Kelsier to god.

And that god was *everything*. The thing he had pitied was the very ground Kelsier walked upon, the air, the metals—his own soul. Preservation *was* everywhere. Beside it, Kelsier was insignificant. An afterthought.

The vision faded. Kelsier stumbled away from Preservation, who stood, placid, a blur in the air—but a representation of so much more. Kelsier put his hand to his chest and was pleased, for a reason he couldn't explain, to find that his heart was beating. His soul was learning to imitate a body, and somehow having a racing heart was comforting.

"I suppose I deserved that," Kelsier said. "Be careful how you use those visions, Fuzz. Reality isn't particularly healthy for a man's ego."

"I would call it very healthy," Preservation replied.

"I saw everything," Kelsier mumbled. "Everyone, everything. My Connection to them, and . . . and . . ."

*Spreading into the future,* he thought, grasping at an explanation. *Possibilities, so many possibilities . . . like atium.*

"Yes," Preservation said, sounding exhausted. "It can be trying to recognize one's true place in things. Few can handle the—"

"Send me back," Kelsier said, scrambling up to Preservation, taking him by the arms.

"What?"

"*Send me back.* I need to see that again."

"Your mind is too fragile. It will break."

"I broke that damn thing years ago, Fuzz. Do it. Please."

Preservation hesitantly gripped him, and this time his eyes took longer to start glowing. They flashed, his form trembling, and for a moment Kelsier thought the god would dissipate entirely.

Then the glow spurted to life, and in an instant Kelsier was consumed. This time he forced himself to look away from Preservation—though it was less a matter of *looking*, and more a matter of trying to sort through the horrible overload of information and sensation that assaulted him.

Unfortunately, in turning his attention away from Preservation he risked giving it to something else—something equally demanding. There was a second god here, black and terrible, the thing with the spines and spidery legs, sprouting from dark mists and reaching into everything throughout the land.

Including Kelsier.

In fact, his ties to Preservation were trivial by comparison to these hundreds of black fingers which attached him to that thing Beyond. He sensed a powerful satisfaction from it, along with an idea. Not words, just an undeniable fact.

*You are mine, Survivor.*

Kelsier rebelled at the thought, but in this place of perfect light, truth *had* to be acknowledged.

Straining, soul crumbling before that terrible reality, Kelsier turned toward the tendrils of light spreading into the distance. Possibilities upon possibilities, compounded upon one another. Infinite, overwhelming. The future.

He dropped out of the vision again, and this time fell to his knees panting. The glow faded, and he was again on the banks of Lake Luthadel. Preservation settled down beside him and rested his hand on Kelsier's back.

"I can't stop him," Kelsier whispered.

"I know," Preservation said.

"I could see thousands upon thousands of possibilities. In none of them did I defeat that thing."

"The ribbons of the future are never as useful as . . . as they should be," Preservation said. "I rode them much, in the past. It's too hard to see what is actually likely, and what is just a fragile . . . fragile, distant maybe. . . ."

"I can't stop it," Kelsier whispered. "I'm too like it. Everything I do serves *it*." Kelsier looked up, smiling.

"It broke you," Preservation said.

"No, Fuzz." Kelsier laughed, standing. "No. I can't stop it. No matter what I do, I can't stop it." He looked down at Preservation. "But *she* can."

"He knows this. You were right. He *has* been preparing her, infusing her."

"She can beat it."

"A frail possibility," Preservation said. "A false promise."

"No," Kelsier said softly. "A *hope*."

He held his hand out. Preservation took it and let Kelsier pull him to his feet. God nodded. "A hope. What is our plan?"

"I continue to the west," Kelsier said. "I saw, in the possibilities . . ."

"Do not trust what you saw," Preservation said, sounding far more firm than he had earlier. "It takes an infinite mind to even *begin* to glean information from those tendrils of the future. Even then you are likely to be wrong."

"The path I saw started by me going to the west," Kelsier said. "It's all I can think to do. Unless you have a better suggestion."

Preservation shook his head.

"You need to stay here, fight him off, resist—and try to get through to Vin. If not her, then Sazed."

"He . . . is not well."

Kelsier cocked his head. "Hurt in the fighting?"

"Worse. Ruin tries to break him."

*Damn.* But what could he do, except continue with his plan? "Do what you can," Kelsier said. "I'll seek these people to the west."

"They *won't* help."

"I'm not going to ask for their help," Kelsier said, then smiled. "I'm going to rob them."

# PART FOUR
# JOURNEY

# 1

KELSIER ran. He needed the urgency, the strength, of being in motion. A man running somewhere had a purpose.

He left the region around Luthadel, jogging alongside a canal for direction. Like the lake, the canal was reversed here—a long, narrow mound rather than a trough.

As he moved, Kelsier tried yet again to sort through the conflicting set of images, impressions, and ideas he'd experienced in that place where he could perceive everything. Vin *could* beat this thing. Of that Kelsier was certain, as certain as he was that he couldn't defeat Ruin himself.

From there however, his thoughts grew more vague. These people, the Ire, were working on something dangerous. Something he could use against Ruin . . . maybe.

That was all he had. Preservation was right; the threads in that place between moments were too knotted, too ephemeral, to give him much beyond a vague impression. But at least it was something he could do.

So he ran. He didn't have time to walk. He wished again for Allomancy, pewter to lend him strength and endurance. He'd had that power for such a short time, compared to the rest of his life, but it had become second nature to him very quickly.

He no longer had those abilities to lean on. Fortunately, without a body he did not seem to tire unless he stopped to think about the fact that he *should* be tiring. That was no problem. If there was one thing Kelsier was good at, it was lying to himself.

Hopefully Vin would be able to hold out long enough to save them all. It was a terrible weight to put on the shoulders of one person. He would lift what portion he could.

# 2

I KNOW *this place,* Kelsier thought, slowing his jog as he passed through a small canalside town. A waystop where canalmasters could rest their skaa, have a drink, and enjoy a warm bath for the night. It was one of many that dotted the dominances, all nearly identical. This one could be distinguished by the two crumbling towers on the opposite bank of the canal.

*Yes,* Kelsier thought, stopping on the street. Those towers were distinctive even in the dreamy, misted landscape of this Realm. Longsfollow. How could he have reached this place already? It was well outside the Central Dominance. How long had he been running?

Time had become a strange thing to him since his death. He had no need for food, and didn't feel tiredness beyond what his mind projected. With Ruin obstructing the sun, and the only light that of the misty ground, it was very difficult to judge the passing of days.

He'd been running . . . for a while. A long while?

He suddenly felt exhausted, his mind numbing, as if suffering the effects of a pewter drag. He groaned and sat down by the side of the canal mound, which was covered in tiny plants. Those plants seemed to grow anywhere water was present in the real world. He'd found them sprouting from misty cups.

Occasionally he'd found other, stranger plants in the landscape between towns—places where the springy ground grew more firm. Places without people: the extended, ashen emptiness between dots of civilization.

He heaved himself to his feet, fighting off the exhaustion. It was all in his head, quite literally. Reluctant to push himself back into a run for the moment, he strolled through Longsfollow. A town had grown up here around the canal stop. Well, a village. Noblemen who ran plantations farther out from the canal would come here to trade and to ship goods in toward Luthadel. It had become a hub of commerce, a bustling civic center.

Kelsier had killed seven men here.

Or had it been eight? He strolled, counting them off. The lord, both of his sons, his wife . . . Yes, seven, counting two guards and that cousin. That was right. He'd spared the cousin's wife, who had been with child.

He and Mare had been renting a room above the general store, over there, pretending to be merchants from a minor noble house. He walked up the steps outside the building, stopping at the door. He rested his fingers on it and sensed it in the Physical Realm, familiar even after all this time.

*We had plans!* Mare had said as they furiously packed. *How could you do this?*

"They murdered a child, Mare," Kelsier whispered. "Sank her in the canal with stones tied to her feet. Because she spilled their tea. Because she spilled the *damn tea*."

*Oh, Kell,* she'd said. *They kill people every day. It's terrible, but it's life. Are you going to bring retribution to* every *nobleman out there?*

"Yes," Kelsier whispered. He made a fist against the door. "I did it. I made the Lord Ruler himself pay, Mare."

And that boiling mass of writhing serpents in the sky . . . that had been the result. He'd seen the truth, in his moment between time with Preservation. The Lord Ruler would have prevented this doom for another thousand years.

Kill one man. Get vengeance, but cause how many more deaths? He and Mare had fled this village. He'd later learned that Inquisitors had come, torturing many of the people they'd known here, killing not a few in their search for answers.

Kill, and they killed in turn. Get revenge, and their vengeance returned tenfold.

*You are mine, Survivor.*

He gripped at the door handle, but couldn't do more than gain an impression of how it looked. He couldn't move it. Fortunately, he was able to push against the door and force himself through. He stumbled to a stop, and was shocked to see that the room was occupied. A solitary soul—glowing, so it was a person in the real world, not this one—lay on the cot in the corner.

He and Mare had left this place in a hurry, and had been forced to stash some of their possessions in a hole behind a stone in the hearth. Those were gone now; he'd pilfered them after Mare's death, following his escape from the Pits and his training with the strange old Allomancer named Gemmel.

He avoided the person and walked to the small hearth. When he'd returned for that hidden coin, he'd been on his way to Luthadel, his mind overflowing with grand plans and dangerous ideas. He'd retrieved the coin, but had found more than he intended. The pouch of coin, and beside it a journal of Mare's.

"If I'd died," Kelsier said, loudly, "if I'd let myself be pulled into that other place . . . I'd be with Mare now, wouldn't I?"

No reply.

"Preservation!" Kelsier shouted. "Do you know where she is? Did you see her pass into that darkness you spoke of, in that place where people go after this? I'd be with her, wouldn't I, if I'd let myself die?"

Again Preservation didn't reply. His mind certainly wasn't in all places, even if his essence was. Considering how erratic he'd been lately, his mind might not be completely in even *one* place. Kelsier sighed, looking around the small room.

Then he stepped back, realizing that the person on the cot had stood up and was looking about.

"What do you want?" Kelsier snapped.

The figure jumped. Had he *heard* that?

Kelsier walked up to the figure and touched him, gaining a vision of an old beggar, scraggly of beard and wild of eye. The man was muttering to himself, and Kelsier—while touching him—could make some of it out.

"In me head," the man muttered. "Geddouta me head."

"You can hear me," Kelsier said.

The figure jumped again. "Damn whispers," he said. "Geddouta me head!"

Kelsier lowered his hand. He'd seen this, in the pulses. Sometimes the mad whispered the things they had heard from Ruin. But it seemed they could hear Kelsier as well.

Could he use this man? *Gemmel muttered like that sometimes,* Kelsier realized, feeling a chill. *I always thought he was mad.*

Kelsier tried to speak further with the man, but the effort was fruitless. The man kept jumping and muttering, but wouldn't actually respond.

Eventually Kelsier made his way back out of the room. He'd been glad for the madman to distract him from his memories of this place. He fished in his pocket, but then remembered he didn't have the picture of Mare's flower any longer. He'd left it for Vin.

He knew the answer to the questions he'd asked of Preservation just before. In refusing to accept death, Kelsier had also given up returning to Mare. Unless there was nothing beyond the warping. Unless *that* death was real and final.

Surely she couldn't have expected him to just give in, to let the stretching darkness take him? *Everyone else I've seen passed willingly,* Kelsier thought. *Even the Lord Ruler. Why must I insist on remaining?*

Foolish questions. Useless. He couldn't go when the world was in such danger. And he wouldn't just let himself die, not even to be with her.

He left the town, turned his path to the west again, and continued running.

# 3

KELSIER knelt down beside an old cookfire, no longer burning, represented by a group of shadowy, cold logs in this Realm. He found it was important to stop every few weeks or so to catch a breather. He had been running . . . well, a long time now.

Today he intended to finally crack a puzzle. He seized the misted remains of the old cookfire. Immediately he gained a vision of them in the real world—but he pushed through that, feeling something beyond.

Not just images, but sensations. Almost emotions. Cold wood that somehow remembered warmth. This fire was dead in the real world, but it *wished* it could burn again.

It was a strange sensation, realizing that logs could have wishes. This flame had burned for years, feeding the families of many skaa. Countless generations had sat before this pit in the floor. They'd kept the fire burning almost perpetually. Laughing, savoring their brief moments of joy.

The fire had given them that. It longed to do so again. Unfortunately, the people had left. Kelsier was finding more and more villages abandoned these days. Ashfalls went on longer than usual, and Kelsier had felt occasional trembling in the ground, even in this Realm. Earthquakes.

He could give this fire something. *Burn again,* he told it. *Be warm again.*

It couldn't happen in the Physical Realm, but all things there could manifest here. The fire wasn't actually alive, but to the people who had once lived here, it had been almost so. A familiar, warm friend.

*Burn . . .*

Light burst from his fingers, pouring out of his hands, a flame appearing there. Kelsier dropped it quickly, stepping back, grinning at the crackling blaze. It looked very much like the fire that Nazh and Khriss had carried with them; the logs themselves had appeared on this side, with dancing flames.

Fire. He'd made *fire* in the world of the dead. *Not bad, Kell,* he thought, kneeling. After taking a deep breath, he pushed his hand into the fire and grabbed the center of the logs, then closed his fist, capturing the bit of mist that made up the essence of that cookfire. It all folded upon itself, vanishing.

He cupped the small handful of mist. He could feel it, like he could feel the ground beneath him. Springy, but real enough as long as he didn't push too hard. He tucked the soul of the cookfire away in his pocket, fairly certain it wouldn't burst alight unless he commanded it to do so.

He left the skaa hovel, stepping out into a plantation. He'd never been here before—this was farther west than he'd traveled with Gemmel. The plantations out here were made of odd rectangular buildings that were low and squat, but each had a large courtyard. He strolled out of this one, entering a street that ran among a dozen similar hovels.

All in all, skaa were better off out here than they were in the inner dominances. It was like saying that a man drowning in beer was better off than one drowning in acid.

Ash fell through the sky. Though he'd not been able to see it during his first days in this Realm, he'd learned to pick it out. It reflected like tiny curling bits of mist, almost invisible. Kelsier broke into a jog, and the ash streamed around him. Some passed through him, leaving him with the impression that *he* was ash. A burned-out husk, a corpse reduced to embers that drifted on the wind.

He passed far too much ash heaped up on the ground. It shouldn't be falling so heavily here. The ashmounts were distant; from what he'd learned in his travels, ash only fell once or twice a month out here. Or at least that was how it had been before Ruin's awakening. Some trees still lived here, shadowy, their souls manifesting as misty forms that glowed like the souls of men.

He approached people on the road who were making westward, toward the coastal towns. Likely their noblemen had already fled that direction, terrified by the sudden increase of ash and the other signs of destruction. As Kelsier passed the people, he stretched out his hand, letting it brush against them and give him impressions of each one.

A young mother lamed by a broken foot, carrying her new baby close to her breast.

An old woman, strong, as old skaa needed to be. The weak were often left to die.

A young, freckled man in a fine shirt. He'd stolen that from the lord's manor, most likely.

Kelsier watched for signs of madness or raving. He'd confirmed that those types could often hear him, though it didn't always require obvious madness. Many seemed unable to make out his specific words, but instead heard him as phantom whispers. Impressions.

He picked up speed, leaving the townspeople behind. He could tell that this was a well-traveled area from the light of the mists beneath him. During his months running, he'd come to understand—and to an extent even accept—the Cognitive Realm. There was a certain freedom to being able to move unhindered through walls. To being able to peek in at the people and their lives.

But he was so lonely.

He tried not to think about it. He focused on his run and the challenge ahead. Because of the way time blended here, it didn't feel to him as if months had passed. Indeed, this experience was far preferable to his sanity-grating year trapped at the Well.

But he missed the people. Kelsier needed people, conversation, friends. Without them he felt dried out. What he wouldn't have given for Preservation, unhinged as he was, to appear and speak to him. Even that white-haired *Drifter* would have been a welcome break from the wasteland of mists.

He tried to find madmen so he could at least have *some* interaction with other living beings, no matter how meaningless.

*At least I've gained something,* Kelsier thought. A campfire in his pocket. When he got out of this, and he *would* get out of it, he'd certainly have stories to tell.

# 4

KELSIER, the Survivor of Death, finally crested one last hill and beheld an incredible sight spread before him. Land.

It rose from the edge of the mists, an ominous, dark expanse. It felt less alive than the shifting white-grey mists beneath him, but oh was it a welcome sight.

He let out a long, relieved sigh. These last few weeks had been increasingly difficult. The thought of more running had started to nauseate him, and the loneliness had him seeing phantoms in the shifting mists, hearing voices in the lifeless nothing all around.

He was a much different figure from the one who had left Luthadel. He planted his staff on the ground beside him—he'd recovered that from the body of a dead refugee in the real world and coaxed it to life, giving it a new home and a new master to serve. Same for the enveloping cloak he wore, frayed at the edges almost like a mistcloak.

The pack he carried was different; he'd taken that from an abandoned store. No master had ever carried it. It considered its purpose to sit on a shelf and be admired. So far it had still made for a suitable companion.

Kelsier settled down, putting aside his staff and digging into his pack. He counted off his balls of mist, which he kept wrapped up tight in the pack. None had vanished this time; that was good. When an object was recovered—or worse, destroyed—in the Physical Realm, its Identity changed and the spirit would return to the location of its body.

Abandoned objects were best. Ones that had been owned for a long while, so they had a strong Identity, but that currently had nobody in the Physical Realm to care for them. He pulled out the ball of mist that was his campfire and unfolded it, bathing in its warmth. It was starting to fray, the logs pocked with misty holes. He could only guess that he'd carried it too far from its origin, and the distance was distressing it.

He pulled out another ball of mist, which unfolded in his hand, becoming a leather waterskin. He took a long drink. It didn't do him any real good; the water vanished soon after being poured out, and he didn't seem to need to drink.

He drank anyway. It felt good on his lips and throat, refreshing. It let him pretend to be alive.

He huddled on that hillside, overlooking the new frontier, sipping at phantom water beside the soul of a fire. His experience in the realm of gods, that moment between time, was a distant memory now . . . but, honestly, it had felt distant from the second he'd fallen out of it. The brilliant Connections and eternity-spanning revelations had immediately faded like mist before the morning sun.

He'd needed to reach this place. Beyond that . . . he had no idea. There were people out there, but how did he find them? And what did he do when he located them?

*I need what they have,* he thought, taking another pull on the waterskin. *But they won't give it to me.* He knew that for certain. But what was it they had? Knowledge? How could he con someone when he didn't even know if they'd speak his language?

"Fuzz?" Kelsier said, just as a test. "Preservation, you there?"

No reply. He sighed, packing away his waterskin. He glanced over his shoulder toward the direction he'd come from.

Then he scrambled to his feet, ripping his knife from the sheath at his side and spinning about, putting the fire between him and what stood there. The figure wore robes and had bright, flame-red hair. He bore a welcoming smile, but Kelsier could see spines beneath the surface of his skin. Pricking spider legs, thousands of them, pushing against the skin and causing it to pucker outward in erratic motions.

Ruin's puppet. The thing he'd seen the force construct and dangle toward Vin.

"Hello, Kelsier," Ruin said through the figure's lips. "My colleague is unavailable. But I will convey your requests, if you wish it of me."

"Stay back," Kelsier said, flourishing the knife, reaching by instinct for metals he could no longer burn. Damn, he missed that.

"Oh, Kelsier," Ruin said. "Stay back? I'm all around you—the air you pretend to breathe, the ground beneath your feet. I'm in that knife and in your very soul. How exactly am I to 'stay back'?"

"You can say what you wish," Kelsier said. "But you don't own me. I am *not* yours."

"Why do you resist so?" Ruin asked, strolling around the fire. Kelsier walked the other direction, keeping distance between himself and this creature.

"Oh, I don't know," Kelsier said. "Perhaps because you're an *evil force of destruction and pain.*"

Ruin pulled up, as if offended. "That was uncalled for!" He spread his hands. "Death is not evil, Kelsier. Death is necessary. Every clock must wind down, every day must end. Without *me* there is no life, and never could have been. Life is change, and I represent that change."

"And now you'll end it."

"It was a gift I gave," Ruin said, stretching out his hand toward Kelsier. "Life. Wondrous, *beautiful* life. The joy of the new child, the pride of a parent, the satisfaction of a job well done. These are from *me.*

"But it is done now, Kelsier. This planet is an elderly man, having lived his life in full, now wheezing his last breaths. It is not evil to give him the rest he demands. It's a *mercy.*"

Kelsier looked at that hand, which undulated with the pinprick pressing of the spiders inside.

"But who am I talking to?" Ruin said with a sigh, pulling back his hand. "The man who would not accept his own end, even though his soul longed for it, even though his wife longed for him to join her in the Beyond. No, Kelsier. I do not anticipate you will see the necessity of an ending. So continue to think me evil, if you must."

"Would it hurt so much," Kelsier said, "to give us a little more time?"

Ruin laughed. "Ever the thief, looking for what you can get away with. No, a reprieve has been granted time and time again. I assume you have no message for me to deliver, then?"

"Sure," Kelsier said. "Tell Fuzz he's to take something long, hard, and sharp, then ram it up your backside for me."

"As if he could harm even me. You realize that if he were in control, nobody would age? Nobody would think or live? If he had his way you'd all be frozen in time, unable to act lest you harm one another."

"So you're killing him."

"As I said," Ruin replied with a grin. "A mercy. For an old man well past his prime. But if all you plan to do is insult me, I must be going. It's a shame you'll be off on that island when the end comes. I assume you'd like to greet the others when they die."

"It can't be *that* close."

"It is, fortunately. But even if you could have done something to help, you're useless out here. A shame."

*Sure,* Kelsier thought. *And you came here to tell me that, rather than remaining quietly pleased that I was off being distracted by my quest.*

Kelsier recognized a hook when he saw one. Ruin wanted him to *believe* that the end was very near, that coming out here had been pointless.

Which meant it wasn't.

*Preservation said he couldn't leave to go where I'm going,* Kelsier thought. *And Ruin is similarly bound, at least until the world is destroyed.*

Maybe, for the first time in months, he'd be able to escape that squirming sky and the eyes of the destroyer. He saluted Ruin, tucked away his fire, then strode down the hill.

"Running, Kelsier?" Ruin said, appearing on the hillside with hands clasped as Kelsier passed him. "You cannot flee your fate. You are tied to this world, and to me."

Kelsier kept on walking, and Ruin appeared at the bottom of the hill, in the same pose.

"Those fools in the fortress won't be able to help you," Ruin noted. "I think that once this world reaches its end, I will pay them a visit. They've existed far too long past what is right."

Kelsier stopped at the edge of the new land of dark stone, like the lake that had become an island. This one was even larger. The ocean had become a continent.

"I will kill Vin while you're gone," Ruin whispered. "I will kill them all. Think about that, Kelsier, on your journey. When you come back, if there's anything left, I might have need of you. Thank you for all you've done on my behalf."

Kelsier stepped out onto the ocean continent, leaving Ruin behind on the shore. Kelsier could almost see the spindly threads of power that animated this puppet, providing a voice to the terrible force.

Damn. Its words were lies. He *knew* that.

They hurt anyway.

# PART FIVE
# IRE

# 1

HE'D hoped to have the sun back once Ruin vanished from the sky, but after walking far enough out, he seemed to leave his world behind—and the sun with it. The sky here was nothing but empty blackness. Kelsier eventually managed to use some vines to strap his flagging cookfire to the end of his staff, which became an improvised torch.

It was a strange experience, hiking through the darkened landscape, holding a staff with an entire *campfire* on the top. But the logs didn't fall apart, and the thing wasn't nearly as heavy as it should have been. Not as hot either, particularly if—when bringing it out—he didn't make it manifest fully.

Plant life grew all around him, real to his touch and eyes, though of strange varieties, some with brownish-red fronds and others with wide palms. Many trees—a jungle of exotic plants.

There were some bits of mist in here. If he knelt by the ground and looked for them, he could find little glowing spirits. Fish, sea plants. They manifested here above the ground, though in the ocean on the other side they were probably down within the depths. Kelsier stood up, holding the soul of some kind of massive deep-sea creature—like a fish, only as large as a building—in his hand, feeling its ponderous strength.

That was surreal, but so was his life these days. He dropped the fish's soul and continued onward, hiking through waist-high plants with a blazing staff lighting the way.

As he got farther from the shore, he felt a tugging at his soul. A manifestation of his ties to the world he'd left behind. He knew, without having to experiment, that this tug would ultimately grow strong enough that he wouldn't be able to continue outward.

He could use that. The tugging was a tool that let him judge if he was getting farther from his world, or if he'd gotten turned around in the darkness. Navigation was otherwise next to impossible, now that he didn't have the canals and roadways to guide him.

By judging the pull on his soul, he kept himself pointed directly outward, away from his homeland. He wasn't completely certain that was where he'd find his goal, but it seemed like his best bet.

He hiked through the jungle for days, but then it started to dwindle. Eventually he reached a place where plants grew only in occasional patches. They were replaced with strange formations of rock, like glassy sculptures. The jagged things were often some ten feet or more tall. He didn't know what to make of those. He had stopped passing the souls of fish, and nothing seemed to be alive out here in either Realm.

The pull tugging him backward was growing laborious to fight. He was beginning to worry he'd have to turn around when, at long last, he spotted something new.

A light on the horizon.

# 2

SNEAKING was a great deal easier when you didn't technically have a body.

Kelsier moved in silence, having dismissed his cloak and staff. He'd left his pack behind, and though there were a few plants out here, he could pass *through* them, not even rustling their leaves.

The lights ahead pulsed from a fortress crafted of white stone. It wasn't a city, but close enough for him. That light had an odd quality; it didn't burn or flicker like a flame. Some kind of limelight? He drew near and pulled up beside one of the odd rock formations that were common out here. It had hooked spikes drooping from it almost like branches.

The very walls of this fortress glowed faintly. Was that mist? It didn't seem to have the same hue to it; it was too blue. Keeping to the shadows of rock formations, Kelsier rounded the building toward a brighter light source at the back.

This turned out to be an enormous glowing cord as thick as a large tree trunk. It pulsed with a slow, rhythmic power, and the light it gave off was the same shade as the walls—only far more brilliant. It seemed to be some kind of energy conduit, and ran off into the far distance, visible in the darkness for miles.

The cord passed into the fortress through a large gate in the back. As Kelsier crept closer, he found that little lines of energy were running across the stone of the wall. They branched smaller and smaller, like a glowing web of veins.

The fortress was tall, imposing, like a keep—but without the ornamentation. It didn't have a separate fortification around it, but its walls were steep and sheer. Guards moved atop the roof, and as one passed, Kelsier pushed himself down into the ground. He was able to sink into it completely, becoming nearly invisible, though that required grabbing hold of the ground and pulling himself downward until only the top of his head was visible.

The guards didn't notice him. He climbed back out of the ground and inched up to the base of the fortress wall. He pressed his hand against the glowing stone and was given the impression of a rocky wall far from here, in another place. An unfamiliar land with striking *green* plants. He gasped, pulling his hand away.

These weren't stones, but the spirits of stones—like his spirit of a fire. They had been brought here and constructed into a building. Suddenly he didn't feel quite so clever at having found himself a staff and a sack.

He touched the stone again, looking at that green landscape. That was what Mare had talked about, a land with an open blue sky. *Another planet,* he decided. *One that didn't suffer our fate.*

For the moment he ignored the image of that place, pushing his fingers through the spirit of the stone. Strangely, the stone resisted. Kelsier gritted his teeth and pushed harder. He managed to get his fingers to sink in about two inches, but couldn't make them go any farther.

*It's that light,* he thought. It pushed back on him. *Looks a little like the light of souls.*

Well, he couldn't slip through the wall. What now? He retreated into the shadows to consider. Should he try to sneak in one of the gates? He rounded the building, contemplating this for a short time, before suddenly feeling foolish. He hurried forward to the wall again and pressed his hand against the stones, sinking his fingers in a few inches. Then he reached up and did the same with the other hand.

Then he proceeded to scale the wall.

Though he missed Steelpushing, this method proved quite effective. He could grip the wall basically anywhere he wanted, and his form didn't have much weight. Climbing was easy, as long as he maintained his concentration. Those images of a land with green plants were very distracting. Not a speck of ash in sight.

A piece of him had always considered Mare's flower a fanciful story. And while the place looked strange, it also attracted him with its alien beauty. There was something about it that was incredibly inviting. Unfortunately, the wall kept trying to spit his fingers back out, and maintaining his grip took a great deal of attention. He continued moving; he could revel in that luxurious scene of green grass and pleasant hills another time.

One of the upper levels had a window big enough to get through, which was good. The guards on the keep's top would have been difficult to dodge. Kelsier slipped in the window, entering a long stone corridor lit by the spiderwebs of power coursing across the walls, floor, and ceiling.

*The energy must keep the stones from evaporating*, Kelsier thought. All the souls he'd brought with him had begun to deteriorate, but these stones were solid and unbroken. Those tiny lines of power were somehow sustaining the spirits of the stone, and perhaps as a side effect keeping people like Kelsier from passing through the walls.

He crept down the corridor. He wasn't sure what he was searching for, but he wouldn't have learned anything more by sitting outside and waiting.

The power coursing through this place kept giving him visions of another world—and, he realized with discomfort, the energy seemed to be permeating him. Mixing with his soul's own energy, which had already been touched by the power at the Well. In a few brief moments, he had started to think that place with the green plants looked *normal.*

He heard voices echoing in the hallway, speaking a strange language with a nasal tone. Prepared for this, Kelsier scrambled out a window and clung there, just outside.

A pair of guards hurried through the hallway beside him, and after they passed he peeked in to see that they were wearing long white-blue tabards, pikes at their shoulders. They had fair skin and looked like they could have been from one of the dominances—except for their strange language. They spoke energetically, and as the words washed across him Kelsier thought . . . He thought he could make some of it out.

*Yes. They speak the language of open fields, of green plants. Of where these stones came from, and the source of this power . . .*

". . . is pretty sure he saw something, sir," one guard was saying.

The words struck Kelsier strangely. On one hand he felt they *should* be indecipherable. On the other hand he instantly knew what they meant.

"How would a Threnodite have made it all the way here?" the other guard snapped. "It defies reason, I tell you."

They passed through the doors at the other end of the hall. Kelsier climbed back into the corridor, curious. Had a guard seen him outside then? This didn't seem like a general alarm, so if he had been spotted, the glimpse had been brief.

He debated fleeing, but decided to follow the guards instead. Though most new thieves tried to avoid guards during an infiltration, Kelsier's experience showed that you generally wanted to tail them—for they'd always stick close to the things that were most important.

He wasn't certain if they could harm him in any way, though he figured it would be best not to find out, so he stayed a good distance back from the guards. After curving through a few stone corridors, they reached a door and went in. Kelsier crept up, cracked it, and was rewarded by the sight of a larger chamber where a small group of guards were setting up a strange device. A large yellow gemstone the size of Kelsier's fist shone in the center, glowing even more brightly than the walls. That gem was surrounded by a lattice of golden metal holding it in place. All told, it was the size of a desk clock.

Kelsier leaned forward, hidden just outside the door. That gemstone . . . that had to be worth a *fortune.*

A different door into the room—one opposite him—slammed open, causing several guards to jump, then salute. The creature that entered seemed . . . well, mostly human. Wizened, dried up, the woman had puckered lips, a bald scalp, and strange silvery-dark skin. She glowed faintly with the same quiet blue-white light as the walls.

"What is this?" the creature snapped in the language of the green plants.

The guard captain saluted. "Probably just a false alarm, ancient one. Maod says he saw something outside."

"Looked like a figure, ancient one," another guard piped up. "Saw it myself. It tested at the wall, sinking its fingers into the stone, but was rebuffed. Then it retreated, and I lost sight of it in the darkness."

So he *had* been seen. Damn. At least they didn't seem to know he'd crept into the building.

"Well, well," the ancient creature said. "My foresight does not seem so foolish now, does it, Captain? The powers of Threnody wish to join the main stage. Engage the device."

Kelsier had an immediate sinking feeling. Whatever that device did, he suspected it would not go well for him. He turned to bolt down the corridor, making for one of the windows. Behind him, the powerful golden light of the gemstone faded.

Kelsier felt nothing.

"Well," the captain said from behind, voice echoing. "Nobody from Threnody within a day's march of here. Looks like a false alarm after all."

Kelsier hesitated in the empty corridor. Then, cautious, he crept back to peek into the room. The guards and the wizened creature all stood around the device, seeming displeased.

"I do not doubt your foresight, ancient one," the guard captain continued. "But I *do* trust my forces on the Threnodite border. There are no shadows here."

"Perhaps," the creature said, resting her fingers on the gemstone. "Perhaps there was someone, but the guard was wrong about it being a Cognitive Shadow. Have the guards be on alert, and leave the device on just in case. This timing strikes me as too opportune to be coincidental. I must speak with the rest of the Ire."

As she said the word, this time Kelsier got a sense of its meaning in the language of the green plants. It meant "age," and he had a sudden impression of a strange symbol made from four dots and some lines that curved, like ripples in a river.

Kelsier shook his head, dispelling the vision. The creature was walking in Kelsier's direction. He scrambled away, barely reaching a window and climbing out as the creature pushed open the door and strode through the hallway.

*New plan,* Kelsier decided, hanging outside on the wall, feeling completely exposed. *Follow the weird lady giving orders.*

He let her get a distance ahead of him, then entered the corridor and followed silently. She rounded the outer corridor of the fortress before eventually reaching the end of it, where it stopped at a guarded door. She passed inside, and Kelsier thought for a moment, then climbed out another window.

He had to be careful; if the guards above weren't already keeping close watch on the walls, they soon would be. Unfortunately, he doubted he could get through that doorway without bringing every guard in the place down on him. Instead he climbed along the outside of the fortress until he reached the next window past the guarded door. This one was smaller than the others he'd gone through, more like an arrow slit than a true window. Fortunately, it looked into the room the strange woman had entered.

Inside, an entire group of the creatures sat in discussion. Kelsier pressed up against the slit of a window, peeking in, clinging precariously to the wall some fifty feet in the air. The beings all had that same silvery skin, though two were a shade darker than the rest. It was difficult to distinguish individuals among them; they were all so old, the men completely bald, the women nearly so. Each wore the same distinctive robe—white, with a hood that could be pulled up and silver embroidery around the cuffs.

Curiously, the light from the walls was dimmer in the room. The effect was particularly noticeable near where one of the creatures was sitting or standing. It was like . . . they themselves were drawing in the light.

He was at least able to pick out the woman from before, with her wizened lips and long fingers. Her robe had a thicker band of silver. "We must move up our timetable," she was saying to the others. "I do not believe this sighting was a coincidence."

"Bah," said a seated man who held a cup of glowing liquid. "You always jump at stories, Alonoe. Not every coincidence is a sign of someone drawing upon Fortune."

"And do you disagree that it is best to be careful?" Alonoe demanded. "We have come too far, worked too hard, to let the prize slip away now."

"Preservation's Vessel *has* nearly expired," another woman said. "Our window to strike is approaching."

"An entire Shard," Alonoe said. "Ours."

"And if that was an agent of Ruin the guards spotted?" asked the seated man. "If our plans have been discovered? The Vessel of Ruin could have his eyes upon us at this very moment."

Alonoe seemed disturbed by this, and she glanced upward as if to search the sky for the watching eyes of the Shard. She recovered, speaking firmly. "I will take the chance."

"We will draw his anger either way," another of the beings noted. "If one of us Ascends to Preservation, we will be safe. Only then."

Kelsier chewed on this as the creatures fell silent. *So someone else can take up the Shard. Fuzz is almost dead, but if someone were to seize his power as he died . . .*

But hadn't Preservation told Kelsier that such a thing was impossible? *You wouldn't be able to hold my power anyway,* Preservation had said. *You're not Connected enough to me.*

He'd seen that now firsthand, in the space between moments. Were these creatures somehow Connected enough to Preservation to take the power? Kelsier doubted it. So what was their plan?

"We move forward," the seated man said, looking to the others. One at a time, they nodded. "Devotion protect us. We move forward."

"You won't need Devotion, Elrao," Alonoe said. "You will have *me*."

*Over my dead body,* Kelsier thought. Or . . . well, something like that.

"The timetable is accelerated then," said Elrao, the man with the cup. He drank the glowing liquid, then stood. "To the vault?"

The others nodded. Together they left the room.

Kelsier waited until they were gone, then tried pushing himself through the window. It was too small for a person, but he wasn't completely a person any longer. He could meld a few inches with the stone, and with effort he was able to contort his shape and *squeeze* through the wide slit.

He finally tumbled into the room, shoulders popping into their previous shape. The experience left him with a splitting headache. He sat up, back to the wall, and waited for the pain to fade before standing to give this room a thorough ransacking.

He didn't come up with much. A few bottles of wine, a handful of gemstones left casually in one of the drawers. Both were real, not souls pulled through to this Realm.

The room had a door leading into the inner parts of the fortress, and so—after peeking through—he slipped in. This next room looked more promising. It was a bedroom. He rifled through the drawers, discovering several robes like the ones the wizened people had been wearing. And then, in the small table by the hearth, the jackpot. A book of sketches filled with strange symbols like the one he had visualized. Symbols that he felt, vaguely, he could understand.

Yes . . . These were writing, though most of the pages were filled with terms he couldn't begin to comprehend, even once he began to be able to read the symbols themselves. Terms like "Adonalsium," "Connection," "Realmatic Theory."

The end pages, however, described the culmination of the notes and sketches. A kind of arcane device in the shape of a sphere. You could break it and absorb the power within, which would briefly Connect you to Preservation—like the lines he'd seen in the space between moments.

That was their plan. Travel to the location of Preservation's death, prime themselves with this device, and absorb his power—Ascending to take his place.

Bold. Exactly the kind of plan Kelsier admired. And now, he finally knew what he was going to steal from them.

# 3

THIEVERY was the most authentic form of flattery.

What could be more satisfying than knowing the things you possessed were intriguing, captivating, or valuable enough to provoke another man to risk everything to obtain them? This was Kelsier's purpose in life, to remind people of the value of the things they loved. By taking them away.

These days, he didn't care for the *little* thieveries. Yes, he'd pocketed the gemstones he'd found up above, but that was more out of pragmatism than anything else. Ever since the Pits of Hathsin, he hadn't been interested in stealing common possessions.

No, these days he stole something far greater. Kelsier stole dreams.

He crouched outside the fortress, hidden between two spires of twisting black rock. He now understood the purpose of creating such a powerful building, here at the reaches of Preservation and Ruin's dominion. That fortress protected a vault, and inside that vault lay an incredible opportunity. The seed that would make a person, under the right circumstances, into a god.

Getting to it would be nearly impossible. They'd have guards, locks, traps, and arcane devices he couldn't plan for or expect. Sneaking in and robbing that vault would test his skills to their utmost, and even then he was likely to fail.

He decided not to try.

That was the thing about big, defended vaults. You couldn't realistically leave most possessions in them forever. Eventually you had to use what you guarded—and that provided men such as Kelsier with an opportunity. And so he waited, prepared, and planned.

It took a week or so—counting days by judging the schedules of the guards—but at long last an expedition sallied forth from the keep. The grand procession of twenty people rode on horseback, holding aloft lanterns.

*Horses,* Kelsier thought, slipping through the darkness to keep pace with the procession. *Hadn't expected that.*

Well, they weren't moving terribly quickly even with the mounts. He was able to keep up with them easily, particularly since he didn't tire as he had when alive.

He counted five of the wizened ancients and a force of fifteen soldiers. Curiously, each of the ancients was dressed almost exactly the same, in their similar robes with hoods up and leather satchels over their shoulders, the same style of saddlebags on each horse.

*Decoys,* Kelsier decided. *If someone attacks, they can split up. Their enemy might not know which of them to follow.*

Kelsier could use that, particularly since he was relatively certain who carried the Connection device. Alonoe, the imperious woman who seemed to be in charge, wasn't the type to let power slip through her spindly fingertips. She intended to become Preservation; letting one of her colleagues carry the device would be too risky. What if they got ideas? What if they used it themselves?

No, she'd have the weapon on her somewhere. The only question was how to get it from her.

Kelsier gave it some time. Days of travel through the darkened landscape, keeping pace with the caravan while he planned.

There were three basic types of thievery. The first involved a knife to the throat and a whispered threat. The second involved pilfering in the night. And the third . . . well, that was Kelsier's favorite. It involved a tongue coated with zinc. Instead of a knife it used confusion, and instead of prowling it worked in the open.

The best kind of thievery left your target uncertain whether anything had happened at all. Getting away with the prize was all well and good, but it didn't mean much if the city guard came pounding on your door the next day. He'd rather escape with half as many boxings, but the confidence that his trickery wouldn't be discovered for weeks to come.

And the *real* trophy was to pull off a heist so clever, the target didn't ever discover you'd taken something from them.

Each "night" the caravan made camp in an anxious little cluster of bedrolls around a campfire much like the one in Kelsier's pack. The ancients got out jars of light, drinking and restoring the luminance to their skin. They didn't chat much; these people seemed less like friends and more like a group of noblemen who considered one another allies by necessity.

Soon after their meal each night, the ancients retired to their bedrolls. They set guards, but didn't sleep in tents. Why would you need a tent out here? There was no rain to keep off, and practically no wind to block. Just darkness, rustling plants, and a dead man.

Unfortunately, Kelsier couldn't figure out a way to get to the weapon. Alonoe slept with her satchel in her hands, watched over by two guards. Each morning she checked to make sure the weapon was still there. Kelsier managed to get a glimpse of it one morning, and saw the glowing light inside, making him reasonably certain her satchel wasn't a decoy.

Well, that would come. His first step was to sow a little misdirection. He waited for an appropriate night, then pushed himself down into the ground, sinking his essence beneath the surface. Then he pulled himself through the rock. It was like swimming through very thick liquid dirt.

He came up near where Alonoe had just settled down to sleep, and stuck only his lips out of the ground. *Dox would have had a fit of laughter seeing this,* Kelsier thought. Well, Kelsier was far too arrogant to worry about his pride.

"So," he whispered to Alonoe in her own language, "you presume to hold Preservation's power. You think you'll fare better than he did at resisting me?"

He then pulled himself down under the ground. It was black as night under there, but he could hear the thumping of feet and the cries of shock from what he'd said. He swam out a distance, then lifted an ear from the ground.

"It was Ruin!" Alonoe was saying. "I swear, it must have been his Vessel. Speaking to me."

"So he does know," said another of the ancient ones. Kelsier thought it was Elrao, the man who had challenged her back in the fortress.

"Your wards were supposed to prevent this!" Alonoe said. "You told me they'd stop him from sensing the device!"

"There are ways for him to know of us without having sensed the orb, Alonoe," another female said. "My art is exacting."

"How he found us is not the problem," Elrao said. "The question is why he hasn't destroyed us."

"Preservation's Vessel still lives," the other woman said, musing. "That might be preventing Ruin's direct interference."

"I don't like it," Elrao said. "I think we should turn back."

"We have committed," Alonoe replied. "We press forward. No quarreling."

The stir in the camp eventually quieted down and the ancient ones turned back to their bedrolls, though more of the guards stayed awake than usual. Kelsier smiled, then pushed himself over beside Alonoe's head again.

"How would you like to die, Alonoe?" he whispered to her, then ducked beneath the earth.

This time they didn't go back to sleep. The next day it was a bleary-eyed party that set off across the dark landscape. That night, Kelsier prodded them again. And again. He made the next week a hell for the group, whispering to different members, promising them terrible things. He was quite proud of the various ways he came up with to distract, frighten, and unnerve them. He didn't get a chance to grab Alonoe's satchel—if anything, they were more careful with it than they had been. He did manage to snatch one of the other ones while they were breaking down camp one morning. It was empty save for a fake glass orb.

Kelsier continued his campaign of discord, and by the time the group reached the jungle of strange trees their patience had unraveled. They snapped at one another and spent less time each morning or night resting. Half the party was convinced they should turn back, though Alonoe insisted that the fact that "Ruin" only *spoke* to them was proof he couldn't stop them. She pressed the increasingly divided group forward, into the trees.

Which was exactly where Kelsier wanted them. Staying ahead of the horses would be easy in this snarl of a jungle, where he could pass through foliage as if it weren't there. He slipped on ahead and set up a little surprise for the group, then came back to find them bickering again. Perfect.

He pushed himself into the center of one of the trees, keeping only his hand outside, tucked at the back, holding the knife that Nazh had given him. As the line of horses passed, he reached out and swiped one of the animals on the flank.

The creature let out a scream of pain, and chaos broke out in the line. The people near the front—their nerves taut from a week spent being tormented by Kelsier's whispers—gave their horses their heads. Soldiers shouted, warning they were under attack. Ancient ones urged their beasts in different directions, some collapsing as the animals tripped in the underbrush.

Kelsier darted through the jungle, catching up to those in the front. Alonoe had kept her horse mostly under control, but it was even darker in these trees than outside, and the lanterns jostled wildly as the animals moved. Kelsier dashed past Alonoe to a point ahead where he'd strung his cloak between two trees and lashed it in place with vines.

He climbed a tree and reached into the cloak as the front of the line—haggard and reduced in numbers—arrived. He'd lashed his fire inside the cloak, and he brought it alive as they neared. The result was a burning, cloaked figure, appearing suddenly in the air above the already frazzled group.

They screamed, calling that Ruin had found them, and split apart, running their horses in a chaotic jumble—some in one direction, some in another.

Kelsier dropped to the ground and slipped through the darkness, staying parallel to Alonoe and the guard who managed to remain with her. The woman soon caught her horse in a snarl of undergrowth. Perfect. Kelsier ducked away and recovered his stash of supplies, then threw on one of the robes he'd found in the fortress. He scrambled through the brush, the robe catching on things, until he was just close enough for Alonoe to see.

Then he stepped out where she could see him and called to her, waving his hand. Thinking she'd found a larger group of her people, she and her lone guard trotted their horses toward him. That, however, only served to draw them away from the rest of the group. Kelsier led her farther from the others, then ducked away into the darkness, losing her and leaving her and her guard isolated.

From there he scrambled through the dark underbrush toward the rest of the group, his phantom heart pounding.

*This.* He'd *missed* this.

The con. The excitement of playing people like flutes, twisting them about themselves, tying their minds in knots. He hurried through the forest, listening to the shouts of fright, the calls of soldiers to one another, the snorts and cries of the horses. The patch of dense vegetation had become demonic disharmony.

Nearby, one of the wizened men was gathering soldiers and his colleagues, calling for them to keep their heads, and started leading them back in the direction they'd come, perhaps to regroup with those who had been lost when the line first scattered.

Kelsier—still wearing the robe and holding his stolen satchel over his shoulder—lay down on the ground in their path, and waited until someone spotted him.

"There!" a guard said. "It's—"

Kelsier sank himself down into the ground, leaving the robe and satchel behind. The guard screamed at the sight of one of the ancients apparently *melting* to nothing.

Kelsier crept up out of the ground a short distance away as the group gathered around his robe and satchel. "She *disintegrated,* ancient one!" the guard said. "I watched it with my own eyes."

"That's one of Alonoe's robes," a woman whispered, hand pulled to her breast in shock.

Another of the ancients looked in the satchel. "Empty," he said. "Merciful Domi . . . What were we thinking?"

"Back," Elrao said. "Back! Everyone get your horses! We're leaving. Curse Alonoe and this idea of hers!"

They were gone in moments. Kelsier strolled through the forest, stepping up beside the discarded robe—which they'd left—listening to the main bulk of the expedition crash through the jungle in their haste to escape him.

He shook his head, then took a short walk through the underbrush to where Alonoe and her lone guard were now trying to follow the sounds of the main body. They were doing a pretty good job of it, all things considered.

When the ancient one wasn't looking, Kelsier grabbed the guard around the neck and hauled him into the darkness. The man thrashed, but Kelsier got him in a quick lock and hold, knocking the man out without too much trouble. He pulled the body back quietly, then returned to find the solitary ancient one standing with lantern in hand beside her horse, turning frantically.

The jungle had become eerily still. "Hello?" she called. "Elrao? Riina?"

Kelsier waited in shadow as the calls became more and more frantic. Eventually the woman's voice gave out. She slumped down in the forest, exhausted.

"Leave it," Kelsier whispered.

She looked up, red-eyed, frightened. Ancient or not, she could obviously still feel fear. Her eyes darted to one side, then the other, but he was too well hidden for her to spot him.

"*Leave it,*" Kelsier repeated.

He didn't need to ask again. She nodded, trembling, then took off her satchel and opened it, dumping out a large glass orb. The light from it was brilliant, and Kelsier had to step back lest it reveal him. Yes, there was power in that orb, great power. It was filled with glowing liquid that was far purer, and far brighter, than what the ancients had been drinking.

Exhaustion evident in her every move, the woman went to climb back onto her horse.

"Walk," Kelsier commanded.

She looked toward the darkness, searching, but didn't see him. "I . . ." she said, then licked her wizened lips. "I could serve you, Vessel. I—"

"*Go,*" Kelsier ordered.

Wincing, she unhooked the saddlebags and—lethargically—threw them over her shoulder. He didn't stop her. She probably needed those jars of glowing liquid to survive, and he didn't want her dead. He just wanted her to be slower than her companions. Once she found them, they might compare stories and realize they'd been had.

Or perhaps not. Alonoe struck out into the jungle. Hopefully they'd all conclude that Ruin had indeed bested them. Kelsier waited until she was gone, then strolled over and picked up the large glass orb. It showed no discernible way of being opened, other than shattering it.

He held the glowing orb before him and shook it, gazing at the incredible, mesmerizing liquid light within.

That was the most fun he'd had in ages.

# PART SIX
# HERO

# 1

KELSIER ran across a broken world. The trouble had been apparent the moment he left the ocean, stepping back onto the misty ground that made up the Final Empire. Here he'd found the wreckage of a coastal city. Smashed buildings, shattered streets. The entire city seemed to have *slid* into the ocean, a fact he wasn't able to fully piece together until he stood above the town and noticed the shadowy remains of buildings sticking from the ocean island farther up the coast.

From there it only grew worse. Empty towns. Vast piles of ash, which manifested on this side as rolling hills that he ran across for a time before realizing what they were.

Several days into his run home, he passed a small village where a few glowing souls huddled together in a building. As he watched, horrified, the roof collapsed, dumping ash on them. Three glows winked out immediately, and the souls of three ashen skaa appeared in the Cognitive Realm, their strings to the physical world cut.

Preservation didn't appear to greet them.

Kelsier grabbed one of them, an aged woman who—as he took her hand—started and looked at him with wide eyes. "Lord Ruler!"

"No," Kelsier said. "But close. What is happening?"

She started to stretch away. Her companions had already vanished.

"It's ending . . ." she whispered. "All ending . . ."

And she was gone. Kelsier was left holding empty air, disturbed.

He started running again. He'd felt guilty leaving the horse behind in the forest, but surely the animal was better off there than it would have been here.

Was he too late? Was Preservation already dead?

He ran himself hard, the heft of the glass orb weighing down his pack. Perhaps it was the urgency, but his course became even more single-minded than it had been during his trip out. He didn't want to see the failing world, the death all around him. Compared to that the exhaustion of the run was preferable, and so he sought it, running himself ragged.

He traveled for days upon days. Weeks upon weeks. Never stopping, never looking. Until . . .

*Kelsier.*

He jolted to a halt on a field of windswept ash. He had the distinct impression of mist in the physical world. Glowing mist. *Power.* He could not see that here, but he could sense it all around him.

"Fuzz?" he said, raising a hand to his forehead. Had he imagined that voice?

*Not that way, Kelsier,* the voice said, sounding distant. But yes, it *was* Preservation. *We aren't . . . aren't . . . there. . . .*

The crushing weight of fatigue hit Kelsier. Where was he? He spun about, looking for some kind of landmark, but those were difficult to find out here. The ash had buried the canals; a few weeks back he remembered swimming down through the ground to find them. Lately . . . he'd just been running. . . .

"Where?" Kelsier demanded. "Fuzz?"

*So . . . tired . . .*

"I know," Kelsier whispered. "I know, Fuzz."

*Fadrex. Come to Fadrex. You are close. . . .*

Fadrex City? Kelsier had been there before, in his youth. It was just south of . . .

There. Just barely visible in the Cognitive Realm, he made out the shadowy tip of Mount Morag in the distance. That direction was north.

He turned his back toward the ashmount and ran for everything he was worth. It seemed a brief eyeblink before he reached the city and was given a welcome, warming sight. Souls.

The city was alive. Guards in the towers and on the tall rock formations surrounding the city. People in the streets, sleeping in their beds, clogging the buildings with beautiful, shining light. Kelsier walked right through the city gates, entering a wonderful, radiant city where people still fought on.

In the warmth of that glow, he knew he was not too late.

Unfortunately, his was not the only attention focused here. He had resisted looking upward during his run, but he could not help but do so now, confronting the churning, boiling mass. Shapes like black snakes slithered across one another, stretching to the horizon in all directions. It was watching. It was here.

So where was Preservation? Kelsier walked through the city, basking in the presence of other souls, recovering from his extended run. He stopped at one street corner, then spotted something. A tiny line of light, like a very long piece of hair, near his feet. He knelt, picking at it, and found that it stretched all the way along the street—impossibly thin, glowing faintly, yet too strong for him to break.

"Fuzz?" Kelsier said, following the strand, finding where it connected to another—it seemed a lattice that spread through the whole city.

*Yes. I . . . I'm trying. . . .*

"Nice work."

*I can't talk to them . . .* Fuzz said. *I'm dying, Kelsier. . . .*

"Hang on," Kelsier said. "I've found something; it's here in my pack. I took it from those creatures you mentioned. The Eyree."

*I do not sense anything,* Fuzz said.

Kelsier hesitated. He didn't want to reveal the object to Ruin. Instead he picked up the thread, which had enough slack for him to slip it into the pack and press it against the orb.

"How about that?"

*Ahh . . . Yes . . .*

"Can this help you somehow?"

*No, unfortunately.*

Kelsier felt his heart sink further.

*The power . . . the power is hers. . . . But Ruin has her, Kelsier. I can't . . . I can't give it. . . .*

"Hers?" Kelsier asked. "Vin? Is she here?"

The thread vibrated in Kelsier's fingers like the string of an instrument. Waves came along it from one direction.

Kelsier followed them, noticing again how Preservation had covered this city with his essence. Perhaps he figured that if he was going to be strung out anyway, he should lie down like a protective blanket.

Preservation led him to a small city square clogged with glowing souls and bits of metal on the walls. They glowed so brightly, particularly in contrast to the darkness of his months out alone. Was one of these souls Vin?

No, they were beggars. He moved among them, feeling at their souls with his fingertips, catching glimpses of them in the other Realm. Huddled in the ash, coughing and shivering. The fallen men and women of the Final Empire, the people even the common skaa tended to dismiss. For all his grand plans, he hadn't made the lives of these people better, had he?

He stopped in place.

That last beggar, sitting against an old brick wall . . . there was something about him. Kelsier backed up, touching the beggar's soul again, seeing a vision of a man with hands and face wrapped in bandages, white hair sticking out from beneath. Stark white hair, a fact not quite hidden by the ash that had been rubbed into it.

Kelsier felt a sudden shock, a painful *spike* that ran up his fingers into his soul. He jumped back as the beggar glanced his direction.

"You!" Kelsier said. "Drifter!"

The beggar shifted in place, but then glanced another direction, searching the square.

"What are you doing here?" Kelsier demanded.

The glowing figure gave no response.

Kelsier whipped his hand back and forth, trying to shake out the pain. His fingers had actually gone *numb.* What had that been? And how had the white-haired Drifter managed to affect him in *this* Realm?

A small glowing figure landed on a rooftop nearby.

"Oh, *hell,*" Kelsier said, looking from Vin to the Drifter. He responded immediately, throwing himself toward the wall of the building and climbing desperately up it to Vin's side. "Vin. Vin, stay *away* from that man."

Of course yelling was pointless. She couldn't hear him.

Still, Kelsier seized her by the shoulders, seeing her in the Physical Realm. When had she grown so confident, so knowing? Those shoulders of hers had once cringed, but now they gave her the posture of a woman fully in control. Those eyes that had once widened in wonder were now narrowed with keen perception. Her hair was longer, but her slight build somehow seemed far more *powerful* than it had when he'd first met her.

"Vin," Kelsier said. "Vin! Listen, please. That man is trouble. Don't approach him. Don't—"

Vin cocked her head, then leaped off the roof, *away* from the Drifter.

"Hell," Kelsier said. "Did she actually hear me?"

Or was it a coincidence? Kelsier leaped after Vin, tossing himself carelessly from the building. He didn't have Allomancy, but he was light, and could fall without getting hurt. He landed softly and sprinted across the springy ground, tailing Vin as best he could, running *through* buildings, ignoring walls, trying to stay close. She still got ahead of him.

*Kelsier* . . . Preservation's voice whispered at him.

Something thrummed through him, a familiar jolt of power, a warmth within. It reminded him of burning metals. Preservation's own essence, empowering him.

He ran faster, jumped farther. It wasn't true Allomancy, but instead was something more raw and primal. It surged through Kelsier, warming his soul, letting him reach Vin—who had stopped in the street before a large building. Soon after he reached her, she took off again down the street, but this time Kelsier managed to keep pace, barely.

And she knew he was there. He could sense it in the way she leaped, trying to shake a tail, or at least catch sight of one. She was good, but this was a game he'd been playing for decades before she was born.

She *could* sense him. Why? How?

She sped up and he followed, with difficulty. His motions were clumsy;

he had Preservation pushing him along, but he didn't have the finesse of true Allomancy. He couldn't Push or Pull; he merely jumped, grabbing hold of the shadowed walls of buildings, then throwing himself off in prowling leaps.

Still, he grinned widely. He hadn't realized how much he had missed training with Vin in the mists, matching himself against another Mistborn, watching his protégé inch toward excellence. She was good now. Fantastic even. Remarkable at judging the force of each Push, at balancing her own weight against her anchors.

This was energy; this was excitement. Almost he forgot the troubles he faced. Almost this was enough. If he could dance the mists with Vin at night, then finding a way to recapture his life in the Physical Realm might not matter so much.

They hit an intersection and turned toward the city's perimeter. Vin bounded ahead on lines of steel; Kelsier hit the ground, thrumming with Preservation's power, and prepared to jump.

Something descended around him. A blackness of shredding spikes, of spider-leg scratches in the air, of jet-black mist.

"Well," Ruin said from all sides. "Well, well. Kelsier? How did I not see you earlier?"

The power suffocated him, pushing him toward the ground. Ahead, a small figure bounded after Vin, created of black mist and pulsing with a similar rhythm to what Kelsier had displayed. A decoy of some sort.

*Like he did before,* Kelsier thought. *Imitating Fuzz to trick Vin.* He struggled, frustrated, against his bonds.

Preservation, in turn, whimpered like a child in Kelsier's mind, then withdrew from him. The warming power faded from within Kelsier. Remarkably, as the power dampened, so did Ruin's ability to hold Kelsier down. Ruin's strength became less oppressive, and Kelsier was able to struggle to his feet and push through the veil of sharp mists, stumbling onto the street.

"Where *have* you been?" Ruin asked. The power behind Kelsier condensed, forming into the shape of the man he'd seen before, with the red hair. The motions beneath the man's skin were more subdued this time.

"Here and there," Kelsier said, glancing after Vin. He'd never catch up to her now. "I thought I'd see the sights. Find out what death has to offer."

"Ah, very coy. Did you visit the Ire? And got turned away from them, I assume. Yes, I can guess at that. What I want to know is why you returned. I thought for certain you would flee. Your part in this is done; you did what I needed you to."

Kelsier set down his pack, hopefully keeping hidden the orb of light inside. He walked forward, strolling around Ruin's manifestation. "My part?"

"The Eleventh Metal," Ruin said, amused. "You think that was a coincidence? A story nobody else had heard of, a secret way to kill an immortal emperor? It fell right in your lap."

Kelsier took it in stride. He'd already figured that Gemmel had been touched by Ruin, that Kelsier himself had been a pawn of the creature. *But why could Vin hear me?* What was he missing? He looked after Vin again.

"Ah," Ruin said. "The child. You still think she's going to defeat me, do you? Even after she set me free?"

Kelsier spun toward Ruin. Damn. How much did the creature know? Ruin smiled and stepped up to Kelsier.

"Leave Vin alone," Kelsier hissed.

"Leave her alone? She's mine, Kelsier. Just as you are. I've known that child since the day of her birth, and have been preparing her for even longer."

Kelsier gritted his teeth.

"So cute," Ruin said. "You actually thought this was all your idea, didn't you? The fall of the Final Empire, the end of the Lord Ruler . . . recruiting Vin in the first place?"

"Ideas are never original," Kelsier said. "Only one thing is."

"And what is that?"

"Style," Kelsier said.

Then he punched Ruin across the face.

Or he tried to. Ruin evaporated as his fist drew close, and a copy of him formed beside Kelsier a moment later. "Ah, Kelsier," he said. "Was that wise?"

"No," Kelsier said. "It was merely thematic. Leave her alone, Ruin."

Ruin smiled at him in a pitying way, then a thousand spindly, needle-like black spikes shot from the creature's body, ripping through the robes that made up its clothing. They pierced Kelsier like spears, fraying his soul, bringing a blinding wave of pain.

He screamed, falling to his knees. It was like the stretching when he'd first entered this place, only *forced, intrusive.*

He dropped to the ground, spasming, his soul leaking curls of mist. The spikes were gone, as was Ruin. But of course the creature was never *truly* gone. It watched from that undulating sky, covering everything.

*Nothing can be destroyed, Kelsier,* Ruin's voice whispered, intruding directly into his mind. *That's something humans can't understand. All things merely change, break down, become something new . . . something perfect. Preservation and I, we're two sides to the same coin, really. For when I am done, he shall finally have his desired stillness, unchangingness. And there won't be anything, body or soul, to disturb it.*

Kelsier breathed in and out, using familiar motions from when he'd been alive to calm himself. Finally he groaned and rolled to his knees.

"You deserved that," Preservation noted, his voice distant.

"Sure did," Kelsier said, stumbling to his feet. "It was worth trying anyway."

# 2

OVER the next few days, Kelsier tried to replicate his success in getting Vin to listen to him. Unfortunately, Ruin was watching for him now. Each time Kelsier got close, Ruin interfered, surrounding him, holding him back. Choking him with black smoke and driving him away.

Ruin seemed amused to keep Kelsier around the periphery of Vin's camp outside Fadrex, and didn't drive him away. But anytime Kelsier tried to speak directly with her, Ruin punished him. Like a parent slapping a child's hand for getting too close to the flame.

It was infuriating, more so because of the way Ruin's words dug at him. Everything Kelsier had accomplished had merely been part of this *thing's* master plan to be freed. And the creature *did* have some kind of hold on Vin. It could appear to her, as reinforced by how it led her away from the camp one day, in a sudden motion that confused Kelsier.

He tried to follow, running after the phantom that Ruin had made. It bounded like a Mistborn and Vin followed, obviously convinced that she'd discovered a spy. They left the camp behind entirely.

Kelsier slowed, feeling useless, standing on the misty ground outside the city and watching them vanish into the distance. She could sense that thing, and as long as it was here it overshadowed Kelsier. He'd never be able to speak with her.

Ruin's reason for leading Vin away soon manifested. Something launched an assault on Vin and Elend's army of koloss. Kelsier figured it out from the bustling of the camp, and was able to reach the scene faster than the people in the Physical Realm. It looked like siege equipment had been rolled out onto a ridge above where the koloss camped.

It rained down death upon the beasts. Kelsier couldn't do anything but watch as the sudden attack killed thousands of them. He couldn't feel any real regret when the koloss were destroyed, but it did seem a waste.

The koloss raged in frustration, unable to reach their enemy. Curiously, their souls started to appear in the Cognitive Realm.

And they were human.

Not koloss at all, but *people,* dressed in a variety of outfits. Many were skaa, but there were soldiers, merchants, and even nobility among them. Both male and female.

Kelsier gaped. He had never quite known what koloss were, but he had not expected this. Common people, made beasts somehow? He rushed among the dying souls as they faded.

"What happened to you," he demanded of one woman. "How did this happen to you?"

She regarded him with a bemused expression. "Where," she said, "where am I?"

In a moment she was gone. It seemed the transition was too much of a shock. The others showed similar confusion, holding out their hands as if surprised to find themselves human again—though not a few seemed relieved. Kelsier watched as thousands of these figures appeared, then faded away. It was a slaughter on the other side, stones crashing down all around. One passed right through Kelsier before rolling away, breaking bodies.

He could use this, but he would need something specific. Not a skaa peasant, or even a crafty lord. He needed someone who . . .

There.

He dashed through fading spirits and dodged between the glowing souls of creatures not yet dead, making for a particular spirit who had just appeared. Bald, with tattoos circling his eyes. An obligator. This man seemed less surprised by events, and more resigned. By the time Kelsier arrived, the lanky obligator was already starting to stretch away.

"How?" Kelsier demanded, counting on the obligator to understand more about the koloss. "How did this happen to you?"

"I don't know," the man said.

Kelsier felt his heart sink.

"The beasts," the man continued, "should have known better than to take an obligator! I was their keeper, and they did this to me? This world is ruined."

Should have known better? Kelsier clutched the obligator's shoulder as the man stretched toward nothingness. "How? Please, *how* is it done? Men become koloss?"

The obligator looked to him and, vanishing, said one word.

"Spikes."

Kelsier gaped again. Around him on the misty plain, souls blazed bright, flashed, and were dumped into this Realm—before finally fading to nothing. Like human bonfires being extinguished.

Spikes. Like Inquisitor spikes?

He walked to the slumped-over corpses of the dead and knelt, inspecting them. Yes, he could see it. Metal glowed on this side, and among those corpses were little spikes—like embers, small but glowing fiercely.

They were much harder to make out on the living koloss, because of the way the soul blazed, but it seemed to him that the spikes pierced into the soul. Was that the secret? He shouted at a pair of koloss, and they looked toward him, then glanced about, confused.

*The spikes transform them*, Kelsier thought, *like Inquisitors. Is that how they're controlled? Through piercings in the soul?*

What of madmen? Were their souls cracked open, allowing something similar? Troubled, he left the field and its dying, although the battle—or rather the slaughter—seemed to be ending.

Kelsier crossed the misty field outside Fadrex, then lingered out here alone, away from the souls of men until Vin returned, trailed by a shadow she didn't seem to know was there this time. She passed by, then disappeared into the camp.

Kelsier settled down near one of the little tendrils of Preservation, and touched it. "He has his fingers in everything, doesn't he, Fuzz?"

"Yes," Preservation said, his voice frail, tiny. "See."

Something appeared in Kelsier's mind, a sequence of images: Inquisitors listening with heads raised toward Ruin's voice. Vin in the creature's shadow. A man he didn't know sitting on a burning throne and watching Luthadel, a twisted smile on his lips.

Then, little Lestibournes. Spook wore a burned cloak that seemed too big for him, and Ruin crouched nearby, whispering with Kelsier's *own voice* into the poor lad's ear.

After him, Kelsier saw Marsh standing among falling ash, spiked eyes staring sightlessly across the landscape. He didn't seem to be moving; the ash was piling up on his shoulders and head.

Marsh . . . Seeing his brother like that made Kelsier sick. Kelsier's plan had required Marsh to join the obligators. He had deduced what must have happened next. Marsh's Allomancy had been noticed, as had the fervent way he lived his life.

Passion and care. Marsh had never been as capable as Kelsier. But he had always, *always* been a better man.

Preservation showed him dozens of others, mostly people in power leading their followers to doom, laughing and dancing as ash piled high and crops withered in the mists. Each one was a person either pierced by metal or influenced by people around them who were pierced by metal. He should have made the connection back at the Well of Ascension, when he'd seen in the pulses that Ruin could speak to Marsh and the other Inquisitors.

Metal. It was the key to everything.

"So much destruction," Kelsier whispered at the visions. "We can't survive this, can we? Even if we stop Ruin, we are doomed."

"No," Preservation said. "Not doomed. Remember . . . hope, Kelsier. You said, I . . . I . . . am . . ."

"I am hope," Kelsier whispered.

"I cannot save you. But we must trust."

"In what?"

"In the man I was. In the . . . the plan . . . The sign . . . and the Hero . . ."

"Vin. He has her, Fuzz."

"He doesn't know as much as he thinks," Preservation whispered. "That is his weakness. The . . . weakness . . . of all clever men . . ."

"Except me, of course."

Preservation had enough spark left to chuckle at that, which did Kelsier some good. He stood up, dusting off his clothing. Which was somewhat pointless, seeing as how there was no dust here—not to mention no actual clothing. "Come now, Fuzz, when have you known me to be wrong?"

"Well, there was—"

"Those don't count. I wasn't fully myself back then."

"And . . . when did you become . . . fully yourself?"

"Only just now," Kelsier said.

"You could . . . you could use that excuse . . . anytime. . . ."

"Now you're catching on, Fuzz." Kelsier put his hands on his hips. "We use the plan you set in motion when you were sane, eh? All right then. How can I help?"

"Help? I . . . I don't . . ."

"No, be decisive. Bold! A good crewleader is always sure of himself, even when he isn't. *Especially* when he isn't."

"That doesn't make . . . sense. . . ."

"I'm dead. I don't need to make sense anymore. Ideas? You're crewleader now."

". . . Me?"

"Sure. Your plan. You're in charge. I mean, you *are* a god. That should count for something, I suppose."

"Thank you for . . . finally . . . acknowledging that. . . ."

Kelsier deliberated, then set his pack on the ground. "You're sure this can't help? It builds links between people and gods. I'd think it could heal you or something."

"Oh, Kelsier," Preservation said. "I've told you that I am dead already. You cannot . . . save me. Save my . . . successor instead."

"Then I will give it to Vin. Would that help?"

"No. You must tell . . . her. You can reach . . . through the gaps in souls . . . when I cannot. Tell her that she must not trust . . . pierced by metal. You must free her to take . . . my power. All of it."

"Right," Kelsier said, tucking away the glass globe. "Free Vin. Easy."

He just had to find a way past Ruin.

# 3

So, Midge," Kelsier whispered to the dozing man. "You got that?"

"Mission . . ." the scruffy soldier mumbled. "Survivor . . ."

"You can't trust anyone pierced by metal," Kelsier said. "Tell her that. Those exact words. It's a mission for you from the Survivor."

The man snorted awake; he was supposed to have been on watch, and he stumbled to his feet as his replacement approached. Kelsier regarded the glowing beings, anxious. It had taken precious days—during which Ruin had kept him far from Vin—to search out someone in the army who was touched in the head, someone with that distinctive soul of madness.

It wasn't that they were broken, as he had once guessed. They were merely . . . open. This man, Midge, seemed perfect. He responded to Kelsier's words, but he wasn't so unhinged that the others ignored him.

Kelsier followed Midge eagerly through camp to one of the cookfires, where Midge started chatting, animatedly, with the others there.

*Tell them,* Kelsier thought. *Spread the news through camp. Let Vin hear it.*

Midge continued speaking. Others stood up around the fire. They were listening! Kelsier touched Midge, trying to hear what he was saying. He couldn't make it out though, until a thread of Preservation touched him—then the words started to vibrate through his soul, faintly audible to his ears.

"That's right," Midge said. "He talked to me. Said I'm special. Said we shouldn't trust none of you. I'm holy, and you just ain't."

"What?" Kelsier snapped. "Midge, you *idiot.*"

It went downhill from there. Kelsier stepped back as men around the cookfire squabbled and started shoving one another, then began a full-on brawl. With a sigh, Kelsier settled down on the misty shadow of a boulder and watched several days' worth of work evaporate.

Someone laid a hand on his shoulder, and he glanced toward Ruin, who had appeared there.

"Careful," Kelsier said, "you'll get *you* on my shirt."

Ruin chuckled. "I was worried, leaving you alone, Kelsier. But it seems you've been serving me well in my absence." One of the brawlers punched Demoux right across the face, and Ruin winced. "Nice."

"Needs to follow through more," Kelsier mumbled. "You need to really commit to a punch."

Ruin smiled a deep, knowing, insufferable smile. *Hell,* Kelsier thought. *I hope that's not what I look like.*

"You must realize by now, Kelsier," Ruin said, "that anything you do, I will counter. Struggle serves only Ruin."

Elend Venture arrived on the scene, gliding on a Steelpush that Kelsier envied, looking properly regal. That boy had grown into more of a man than Kelsier had ever expected he would. Despite that stupid beard.

Kelsier frowned. "Where is Vin?"

"Hm?" Ruin said. "Oh, I have her."

"Where?" Kelsier demanded.

"Away. Where I can keep her in hand." He leaned toward Kelsier. "Good job wasting time on the madman." He vanished.

*I absolutely hate that man,* Kelsier thought. Ruin . . . he was no more impressive, deep down, than Preservation was. *Hell,* Kelsier thought, *I'm better at this god stuff than they are.* At least he had inspired people.

Including Midge and the rest of the brawlers, unfortunately. Kelsier stood up from the rock and finally acknowledged a fact he'd been wanting to avoid. He couldn't do anything here, not with Ruin so focused on Vin and Elend right now. Kelsier had to get to someone else. Sazed maybe? Or perhaps Marsh. If he could get through to his brother while Ruin was distracted . . .

He had to hope that the wards on that orb would shade him from the dark god's eyes, as they had when Kelsier had first arrived at Fadrex. He needed to leave this place, strike out, lose Ruin's interest and then try to contact Marsh or Spook, get them to relay a message to Vin.

It hurt him to leave her behind in Ruin's clutches, but there was nothing more he could do.

Kelsier left that very hour.

# 4

KELSIER was nowhere in particular when God finally died.

He couldn't place the location. No town nearby, at least not one that hadn't been buried in ash. He had intended to head toward Luthadel, but with all the landmarks covered over—and with no sun to guide him—he wasn't certain he'd been going the right direction.

The land trembled, the misty ground quivering. Kelsier pulled up short, looking at the sky, at first expecting that Ruin was causing this tremor.

Then he felt it. Perhaps it was the small Connection he had to Preservation from his time at the Well of Ascension. Or maybe it was the piece inside him that the god had placed, the piece inside them all. The light of the soul.

Whatever the reason, Kelsier felt the end like a long, drawn-out sigh. It sent a chill up his spine, and he scrambled to find a thread of Preservation. They had been all over the ground earlier in his trip, but now he found nothing.

"Fuzz!" he screamed. "Preservation!"

*Kelsier . . .* The voice vibrated through him. *Goodbye.*

"Hell, Fuzz," Kelsier said, searching the sky. "I'm sorry. I . . ." He swallowed.

*Odd*, the voice said. *After all these years appearing for others as they died, I never expected . . . that my own passing would be so cold and lonely. . . .*

"I'm here for you," Kelsier said.

*No. You weren't. Kelsier, he's splitting my power. He's breaking it apart. It will be gone . . . Splintered. . . . He'll destroy it.*

"Like hell he will," Kelsier said, dropping his pack. He reached inside, gripping the glowing orb filled with liquid.

*It's not for you, Kelsier,* Preservation said. *It's not yours. It belongs to another.*

"I'll get it to her," Kelsier said, taking up the sphere. He drew in a deep breath, then used Nazh's knife to smash the orb, spraying his arm and body with the glowing liquid.

Lines like threads burst out from him. Glowing, effulgent. Like the lines from burning steel or iron, except they pointed at everything.

*Kelsier!* Preservation said, his voice strengthening. *Do better than you have before! They called you their god, and you were casual with their faith! The hearts of men are NOT YOUR TOYS.*

"I . . ." Kelsier licked his lips. "I understand. My Lord."

*Do better, Kelsier,* Preservation commanded, his voice fading. *If the end comes, get them below ground. It might help. And remember . . . remember what I told you, so long ago. . . . Do what I cannot, Kelsier. . . .*

*SURVIVE.*

The word vibrated through him, and Kelsier gasped. He knew that feeling, remembered that exact command. He'd heard that voice in the Pits. Waking him, driving him forward.

Saving him.

Kelsier bowed his head as he felt Preservation fade, finally, and stretch into the darkness.

Then, full of borrowed light, Kelsier seized the threads spinning around him and *Pulled*. The power resisted. He didn't know why—he had only a rudimentary understanding of what he was doing. Why did the power attune to some people and not others?

Well, he'd Pulled on stubborn anchors before. He yanked with all his might, drawing the power toward him. It struggled, defying him almost like it was alive . . . until . . .

It broke, flooding into him.

And Kelsier, the Survivor of Death, Ascended.

With a cry of exultation, he felt the power flow through him, like Allomancy a hundred times over. A feverish, molten, burning energy that washed through his soul. He laughed, rising into the air, expanding, becoming everywhere and everything.

*What is this?* Ruin's voice demanded.

Kelsier found himself confronted by the opposing god, their forms extending into eternity—one the icy coolness of life frozen, unmoving; the other the scrabbling, crumbling, violent blackness of decay. Kelsier grinned as he felt utter and complete *shock* from Ruin.

"What was it," Kelsier asked, "that you said before? Anything I can do, you will counter? How about this?"

Ruin raged, power flaring in a cyclone of anger. The persona cracked apart, revealing the *thing,* the raw energy that had plotted and planned for so long, only to be stopped now. Kelsier's grin widened, and he imagined—with delight—the sensation of ripping apart this monster that had killed Preservation. This useless, outdated waste of energy. Crushing it would be so *satisfying.* He willed his boundless power to attack.

And nothing happened.

Preservation's power resisted him still. It shied away from his murderous intent, and push though he would, he couldn't make it hurt Ruin.

His enemy vibrated, quivering, and the shaking became a sound like laughter. The churning dark mists recovered, transforming back into the image of a deific man stretching through the sky. "Oh, Kelsier!" Ruin cried. "You think I mind what you have done? Why, I'd have chosen for *you* to take the power! It's perfect! You're merely an aspect of me, after all."

Kelsier gritted his teeth, then stretched forth fingers made of rushing wind, as if to grab Ruin and *throttle* him.

The creature merely laughed louder. "You can barely control it," Ruin said. "Even assuming it could harm me, you couldn't accomplish such a task. Look at you, Kelsier! You haven't form or shape. You're not alive, you're an *idea.* A *memory* of a man holding the power will never be as potent as a real one with ties to all three Realms."

Ruin shoved him aside with ease, though Kelsier felt a *crackling* at the thing's touch. These powers reacted to one another like flame and water. That made Kelsier certain there *was* a way to use the power he held to destroy Ruin. If he could figure it out.

Ruin turned his attention from Kelsier, and so Kelsier took to trying to acquaint himself with the power. Unfortunately, each thing he tried was met with resistance—both from Ruin's energy and from the power of Preservation itself. He could see himself now, in the Spiritual Realm—and those black lines were still there, tying him to Ruin.

The power he held didn't like that at all. It tumbled inside him, churning, trying to break free. He could hold on, but he knew that if he let go, it would escape him and he would never be able to recapture it.

Still, it was grand to be more than just a spirit. He could see into the Physical Realm again, though metal continued to glow brightly to his eyes. It was a relief to be able to see something other than misty shadows and glowing souls.

He wished that view were more encouraging. Endless seas of ash. Very few cities, dug out like craters. Burning mountains that spewed not only ash, but lava and brimstone. The land had cracked, creating rifts.

He tried not to think of that, but of the people. He could feel them, like he felt the very crust and core of the planet. He easily found which ones had souls that were open to him, and eagerly he swung down in. Surely among these he could find one who could deliver a message to Vin.

Yet they didn't seem to be able to hear him, no matter how he whispered to them. It was frustrating and baffling. He held the powers of eternity. How could he have lost the ability he'd had before, the ability to communicate with his people?

Around him, Ruin laughed.

"You think your predecessor didn't try that?" Ruin asked. "Your power cannot leak through those cracks, Preservation. It tries too hard to shore them up, to protect them. Only *I* can widen cracks."

Whether his reasoning was correct or not, Kelsier couldn't tell. But he did confirm time and time again that madmen could no longer hear him.

However, now *he* could hear people.

Everyone, not just the mad. He could hear their thoughts like voices—their hopes, their worries, their terrors. If he focused too long on them, directed his attention to a city, the multitude of thoughts threatened to overwhelm him. It was a buzz, a rush, and he found it difficult to separate individuals from the mess.

Above it all—land, cities, ash—hung the mists. They coated everything, even in the daytime. While trapped entirely in the Cognitive Realm, he hadn't seen how pervasive they were.

*That's power,* he thought, gazing upon it. *My power. I should be able to hold that, manipulate it.*

He couldn't. That left Ruin far stronger than he was. Why had Preservation left the mists untouched like that? It was still part of him, of course, but it was like . . . like a diffused army, spread as scouts throughout the kingdom, rather than gathered for war.

Ruin wasn't so inhibited. Kelsier could see his power at work now, revealed in ways that had been too grand for him to recognize before Ascending. Ruin ripped open the tops of ashmounts, holding them pried apart, letting death spew forth. He touched koloss all across the empire, driving them to murderous frenzies. When they ran out of people to kill, he gleefully turned them against one another.

He had hold of multiple people in every remaining city. His machinations were incredible—complex, subtle. Kelsier couldn't even follow all the threads, but the result was obvious: chaos.

Kelsier could do nothing about it. He held unimaginable power, yet he was *still* impotent. But importantly, Ruin had to *act* to counter him.

That was an important revelation. He and Ruin were both everywhere; their souls were the very bones of the planet. But their attention . . . that could only be divided so far.

If Kelsier tried to change things where Ruin was focused, he always lost. When Kelsier tried to stop the ashmounts, Ruin's arms ripping them open were stronger than his trying to seal them. When he tried to bolster Vin's armies with a sense of encouragement, Ruin acted like a blockade, keeping him away.

In a desperate attempt, he made a push to approach Vin herself. He wasn't certain what he could do, but he wanted to try battering Ruin away—push himself, and see what he was capable of doing.

He threw everything he had into it, straining against Ruin—feeling the friction of their essences meeting as he drew nearer to Vin, who was locked in a room within the palace of Fadrex. His essence meeting Ruin's caused shocks through the land, trembles. An earthquake.

He was able to draw close. He could feel Vin's mind, hear her thoughts. She knew so little—like he had known so little when he'd begun this. She didn't know about Preservation.

The clashing pushed Kelsier's essence away, ripping Preservation back from him, exposing his core—like a grinning skull as the flesh was torn free. A soul lined with darkness, but which was *Connected* to Vin somehow. Tied to her by the inscrutable lines that made up the Spiritual Realm.

"Vin!" he shouted, in agony, straining. The fight between him and Ruin caused the earthquake to intensify, and Ruin exulted in that destruction. It weakened his attention for a brief moment.

"Vin!" Kelsier said, getting closer. "Another god, Vin! There's another force!"

Confusion. She didn't see. Something leaked from Kelsier, drawing toward her. And with a shock, Kelsier saw a terrible sight, something he'd never suspected. A glowing spot of metal in Vin's ear, so similar to the color of her brilliant soul that he had missed it until he'd gotten very close.

Vin was spiked.

"What's the first rule of Allomancy, Vin!" Kelsier screamed. "The first thing I taught you!"

Vin looked up. Had she *heard*?

"Spikes, Vin!" Kelsier began. "You can't trust—"

Ruin returned and shoved Kelsier with a fierce burst of power, interrupting him. To hold on longer would have meant letting Ruin rip the power of Preservation away from him completely, and so he let himself go.

Ruin shoved him out of the building, out of the city entirely. Their clash brought incredible pain to Kelsier, and he couldn't help bearing the impression that—divine though he was—he was *limping* as he left the city.

Ruin was too focused on this place. Too strong here. He had almost all of his attention pointed at Vin and this city of Fadrex. He was even bringing in Marsh.

Maybe . . .

Kelsier tried to get close to Marsh, focusing his attention on his brother. Those same lines were there as had been with Vin, lines of Connection linking Kelsier's soul to his brother. Perhaps he could get through to Marsh too.

Unfortunately, Ruin spotted this too easily, and Kelsier was too weakened—too sore—from the previous clash. Ruin rebuffed him with ease, but not before Kelsier heard something emanating from Marsh.

*Remember yourself,* Marsh's thoughts whispered. *Fight, Marsh, FIGHT. Remember who you are.*

Kelsier felt a swelling of pride as he fled from Ruin. Something within Marsh, something of his brother, had survived. However, there was nothing Kelsier could do to help now. Whatever Ruin wanted in Fadrex, Kelsier would have to let him have it. To confront Ruin here was impossible, for Ruin could best Kelsier in a direct confrontation.

Fortunately, Kelsier had made a career of knowing when to avoid a fair fight. The con was on, and when the house guard was alert, your best bet was to lie low for a while.

Ruin watched Fadrex so intently, it would leave chinks elsewhere.

# 5

*Do better, Kelsier.*

He watched and waited. He could be careful.

*The hearts of men are not your toys.*

He floated, becoming the mists, observing how Ruin moved his pieces. The Inquisitors were his primary hands. Ruin positioned them deliberately.

*The weakness of all clever men.*

An opening. Kelsier needed an opening.

*Survive.*

Ruin thought he was in control all across the Final Empire. So sure of himself. But there were holes. He was devoting less and less attention to the broken city of Urteau, with its empty canals and starving people. One of his threads revolved around a young man who wore cloth wrapping his eyes and a burned cloak on his back.

Yes, Ruin thought he had this city in hand.

But Kelsier . . . Kelsier *knew* that boy.

Kelsier focused his attention on Spook as the young man—overwhelmed and driven to the brink of madness—stumbled onto a stage before a crowd. Ruin had driven him to this point by wearing Kelsier's form. He was trying to make an Inquisitor of the boy, while at the same time setting up the city to burn in riots and bedlam.

But his actions in this city were like so many others. His attention was too divided, with his only real focus on Fadrex. He worked in Urteau, but didn't *prioritize* it. He'd already set his plans in motion: Ruin the hopes of this people, burn the city to the ground. All it required was for a confused boy to commit a murder.

Spook stood onstage, prepared to kill in front of the crowd. Kelsier drew his attention in like a puff of mist, careful, quiet. He was the pulsing of the boards beneath Spook's feet, he was the air being breathed, he was the flame and fire.

Ruin was here, raging, demanding that Spook murder. It wasn't the careful, smiling persona. This was a purer, rawer form of the power. This piece of him had little of Ruin's attention, and he hadn't brought his full power to bear.

It didn't notice Kelsier as he drew back from the power, exposing his own soul and drawing it close to Spook. Those lines were there, the lines of familiarity, family, and Connection. Strangely, they were even *stronger* for Spook than they'd been for Marsh and Vin. Why would that be?

*Now, you must kill her,* Ruin said to Spook.

Under that anger, Kelsier whispered to Spook's broken soul. *Hope.*

*You want power, Spook?* Ruin thundered. *You want to be a better Allomancer? Well, power must come from somewhere. It is never free. This woman is a Coinshot. Kill her, and you can have her ability. I will give it to you.*

*Hope,* Kelsier said.

Back and forth. *Kill.* Ruin sent impressions, words. *Murder, destroy. Ruin.*

*Hope.*

Spook reached for the metal at his chest.

*No!* Ruin shouted, sounding shocked. *Spook, do you want to go back to being normal? Do you want to be useless again? You'll lose your pewter, and go back to being weak, like you were when you let your uncle die!*

Spook looked at Ruin, grimaced, then cut into his body and pulled the spike free.

*Hope.*

Ruin screamed in denial, his figure fuzzing, spider-leg knives spearing out of the broken shape he wore. Destruction sprouted from the figure and became black mist.

Spook sank down onto the platform, slumping to his knees, then fell forward. Kelsier knelt and held him, drawing Preservation's power back to himself. "Oh, Spook," he whispered. "You poor, poor child."

He could feel the youth's spirit sputtering. *Broken.* Cracked through to the core. The boy's thoughts drifted to Kelsier. Thoughts of a woman he loved. Thoughts of his own failures. Confused thoughts.

Deep down, this boy had been following Ruin because he'd wished so desperately for Kelsier to guide him. He'd tried so hard to be like Kelsier himself.

It twisted Kelsier about, seeing the faith of this youth. Faith in him. Kelsier, the Survivor.

A pretend god.

"Spook," Kelsier whispered, touching Spook's soul with his own again. He choked on the words, but forced them out. "Spook, her city is burning."

Spook trembled.

"Thousands will die in the flames," Kelsier whispered. He touched the boy's cheek. "Spook, child. You want to be like me? Really like me? Then fight when you are beaten!"

Kelsier looked up at the spiraling, churning form of Ruin, angered. More of Ruin's attention was focusing in this direction. It would soon rebuff Kelsier.

Beating it here was only a small victory, but it was proof. This thing could be resisted. Spook had done it.

And would do it again.

Kelsier looked down at the child in his arms. No, not a child any longer. He opened himself to Spook, and spoke a single, all-powerful command.

"Survive!"

Spook screamed, burning his metal, startling himself to lucidity. Kelsier stood up, triumphant. Spook lurched to his knees, his spirit strengthening.

"Whatever you do," Ruin said to Kelsier, as if seeing him there for the first time, "I counter."

The force of destruction exploded outward, sending tendrils of darkness into the city. He didn't push Kelsier away. Kelsier wasn't certain if that was because his attention was still too focused elsewhere, or if he just didn't care whether Kelsier stayed to witness the end of this city.

Fires. Death. Kelsier saw the thing's plan in a flashing moment: Burn this city to the ground, extinguish all signs of Ruin's failure. End the people here.

Spook was already moving, confronting the people around him, giving orders as if he were the Lord Ruler himself. And was that . . .

Sazed!

Kelsier felt a comforting warmth upon seeing the quiet Terrisman stepping up to Spook. Sazed always had answers. But here he looked haggard, confused, *exhausted.*

"Oh, my friend," Kelsier whispered. "What has he done to you?"

The group obeyed Spook's orders, rushing off. Spook lagged behind them, walking down the street. Kelsier could see the threads of the future, in the Spiritual Realm. Coated in darkness, a city destroyed. Possibilities ending.

But a few lines of light remained. Yes, it was still possible. First this boy had to save his city.

"Spook," Kelsier said, forming himself a body of power. Nobody could see him, but that didn't matter. He fell into step beside Spook, who practically stumbled along. One foot after the other, barely moving.

"Keep moving," Kelsier encouraged. He could feel this man's pain, his anguish and confusion. His faith battered. And somehow, through Connection, Kelsier could talk to him as he'd not been able to do to others.

Kelsier shared in Spook's exhaustion with each trembling, agonized step. He whispered the words over and over. *Keep moving.* It became a mantra. Spook's young woman arrived, helping him. Kelsier walked on his other side. *Keep moving.*

Blessedly, he did. Somehow the exhausted young man stumbled all the way to a burning building. He stopped outside, where Sazed had been forced to shy away. Kelsier read their attitudes in the slump of their shoulders, the fear in their eyes, reflecting flames. He heard their thoughts, pulsing from them, quiet and afraid.

This city was doomed, and they knew it.

Spook let the others pull him back from the fires. Emotions, memories, ideas rose from the boy.

*Kelsier didn't care about me,* Spook thought. *He didn't think of me. He remembered the others, but not me. Gave them jobs to do. I didn't matter to him. . . .*

"I named you, Spook," Kelsier whispered. "You were my friend. Isn't that enough?"

Spook stopped in place, pulling against the grip of the others.

"I'm sorry," Kelsier said, weeping, "for what you must do. Survivor."

Spook pulled from the grip of the others. And as Ruin raged above, sputtering and screaming—finally bringing in his attention to begin forcing Kelsier back—this young man entered the flames.

And saved the city.

# 6

KELSIER sat on a strange, verdant field. Green grass everywhere. So odd. So beautiful.

Spook walked over and settled down next to him. The boy removed the cloth from his eyes and shook his head, then ran his fingers through his hair. "What is this?"

"Half dream," Kelsier said, plucking a piece of grass and chewing on it.

"Half dream?" Spook asked.

"You're almost dead, kid," Kelsier said. "Smashed your spirit up pretty good. Lots of cracks." He smiled. "That let me in."

There was more to it. This young man was special. At the very least, their relationship was special. Spook believed in him as no other had.

Kelsier thought on this as he plucked another piece of grass and chewed on it.

"What are you doing?" Spook asked.

"It looks so strange," Kelsier said. "Like Mare always said it would."

"So you're *eating* it?"

"Chewing it, mostly," Kelsier said, then spat it to the side. "Just curious."

Spook puffed in and out. "Doesn't matter. None of this matters. You're not real."

"Well, that's partially right," Kelsier said. "I'm not completely real. Haven't been since I died. But then I'm also a god now . . . I think. It's complicated."

Spook looked at him, frowning.

"I needed someone I could chat with," Kelsier said. "I needed you. Someone who was broken, but who had resisted *him*."

"The other you."

Kelsier nodded.

"You always were so harsh, Kelsier," Spook said, staring out over the rolling green fields. "I could see that deep down, you *really* hated the nobility. I thought that hatred was why you were so strong."

"Strong like scar tissue," Kelsier whispered. "Functional, but stiff. It's a strength I'd rather you never need."

Spook nodded, and seemed to understand.

"I'm proud of you, kid," Kelsier said, giving him a fond punch to the arm.

"I almost ruined everything," he said, eyes downcast.

"Spook, if you knew how many times *I've* almost destroyed a city, you'd be embarrassed to talk like that. Hell, you barely even broke that place. They've put out the fires, rescued most of the population. You're a hero."

Spook looked up, smiling.

"Here's the thing, kid," Kelsier said. "Vin doesn't know."

"Know what?"

"The spikes, Spook. I can't get the message to her. She needs to know. And Spook, she . . . she has a spike in her too."

"Lord Ruler . . ." Spook whispered. "Vin?"

Kelsier nodded. "Listen to me. You're going to wake soon. I need you to remember this part, even if you forget everything else about the dream. When the end comes, get people underground. Send a message to Vin. Scratch the message in metal, for anything not set in metal cannot be trusted.

"Vin needs to know about Ruin and his false faces. She needs to know about the spikes, that metal buried within a person lets Ruin whisper to them. Remember it, Spook. Don't trust anyone pierced by metal! Even the smallest bit can taint a man."

Spook began to fuzz, waking.

"Remember," Kelsier said. "Vin is hearing Ruin. She doesn't know who to trust, and that's why you absolutely must get that message sent, Spook. The pieces of this thing are all spinning about, cast to the wind. You have a clue that nobody else does. Send it flying for me."

Spook nodded as he woke up.

"Good lad," Kelsier whispered, smiling. "You did well, Spook. I'm proud."

# 7

A MAN left Urteau, forging outward through the mists and the ash, starting the long trip toward Luthadel.

Kelsier didn't know this man, Goradel, personally. However, the power knew him. Knew how he'd joined the Lord Ruler's guards as a youth, hoping for a better life for himself and his family. This was a man whom Kelsier, if he'd been given the chance, would have killed without mercy.

Now Goradel might just save the world. Kelsier soared behind him, feeling the anticipation of the mists build. Goradel carried a metal plate bearing the secret.

Ruin rolled across the land like a shadow, dominating Kelsier. He laughed as he saw Goradel fighting through the ash, piled as high as snow in the mountains.

"Oh, Kelsier," Ruin said. "This is the best you can do? All that work with the child in Urteau, for this?"

Kelsier grunted as tendrils of Ruin's power sought out a pair of hands and brought them calling. In the real world hours passed, but to the eyes of gods time was a mutable thing. It flowed as you wished it to.

"Did you ever play card tricks, Ruin?" Kelsier asked. "Back when you were a common man?"

"I was never a common man," Ruin said. "I was but a Vessel awaiting my power."

"So what did that Vessel do with its time?" Kelsier asked. "Play card tricks?"

"Hardly," Ruin said. "I was a far better man than that."

Kelsier groaned as Ruin's hands eventually arrived, soaring high through the falling ash. A figure with spikes through his eyes, lips drawn back in a sneer.

"I was pretty good at card tricks," Kelsier said softly, "when I was a child. My first cons were with cards. Not three-card spin; that was too simple. I preferred the tricks where it was you, a deck of cards, and a mark who was watching your every move."

Below, Marsh struggled with—then finally slaughtered—the hapless Goradel. Kelsier winced as his brother didn't just murder, but reveled in the death, driven to madness by Ruin's taint. Strangely, Ruin worked to hold him *back.* As if in the moment, he'd lost control of Marsh.

Ruin was careful not to let Kelsier get too close. He couldn't even draw near enough to hear his brother's thoughts. Ruin laughed as, awash in the gore of the murder, Marsh finally retrieved the letter Spook had sent.

"You think," Ruin said, "you're so clever, Kelsier. Words in metal. I can't read them, but my minion can."

Kelsier sank down as Marsh felt at the plate Spook had ordered carved, reading the words out loud for Ruin to hear. Kelsier formed a body for himself and knelt in the ash, slumping forward, beaten.

Ruin formed beside him. "It's all right, Kelsier. This is the way things were *meant* to be. The reason they were created! Do not mourn the deaths that come to us; celebrate the lives that have passed."

He patted Kelsier, then evaporated. Marsh stumbled to his feet, ash sticking to the still-wet blood on his clothing and face. He then leaped after Ruin, following his master's call. The end was approaching quickly now.

Kelsier knelt by the corpse of the fallen man, who was slowly being covered in ash. Vin had spared him, and Kelsier had gotten him killed after all. He reached into the Cognitive Realm, where the man's spirit had stumbled in the place of mist and shadows, and was now looking skyward.

Kelsier approached and clasped the man's hand. "Thank you," he said. "And I'm sorry."

"I've failed," Goradel said as he stretched away.

It twisted Kelsier inside, but he didn't dare contradict the man. *Forgive me.*

Now, to be quiet. Kelsier let himself drift again, spread out. No longer did he try to stop Ruin's influence. In withdrawing, he saw that he *had* been helping a tiny bit. He'd held back some earthquakes, slowed the flow of lava. An insignificant amount, but at least he'd done something.

Now he let it go and gave Ruin free rein. The end accelerated, twisting about the motions of one young woman, who arrived back in Luthadel at the advent of a storm.

Kelsier closed his eyes, feeling the world hush, as if the land itself were holding its breath. Vin fought, danced, and pushed herself to the limits of her abilities—and then beyond. She stood against Ruin's assembled might of Inquisitors, and fought with such majesty that Kelsier was astonished. She was better than the Inquisitor he'd fought, better than any man he'd seen. Better than Kelsier himself.

Unfortunately, against an entire murder of Inquisitors, it was not nearly enough.

Kelsier forced himself to hold back. And *hell,* was it difficult. He let Ruin reign, let his Inquisitors beat Vin to submission. The fight was over too soon, and ended with Vin broken and defeated, at Marsh's mercy.

Ruin stepped close, whispering to her. *Where is the atium, Vin?* he said. *What do you know of it?*

Atium? Kelsier drew himself near as Marsh knelt by Vin and prepared to hurt her. Atium. Why . . .

It all came together for him. Ruin wasn't complete either. There in the broken city of Luthadel—rain washing down, ash clogging the streets, Inquisitors roosting and watching with expressionless spiked eyes—Kelsier understood.

Preservation's plan. It could work!

Marsh snapped Vin's arm, and grinned.

*Now.*

Kelsier hit Ruin with the full strength of his power. It wasn't much, and he was a poor master of it. But it *was* unexpected, and it drew away Ruin's attention. The powers met, and the friction—the opposition—caused them to grind.

Pain coursed through Kelsier. The ground throughout the city trembled.

"Kelsier, Kelsier," Ruin said.

Below, Marsh laughed.

"Do you know," Kelsier said, "why I always won at card tricks, Ruin?"

"Please," Ruin said. "Does this matter?"

"It's because," Kelsier said, grunting in pain, his power taut, "I could always. Force. People to choose. The card *I wanted them to.*"

Ruin paused, then looked down. The letter—delivered by Goradel not to Vin, but to Marsh—did its job.

Marsh ripped free Vin's earring.

The world froze. Ruin, vast and immortal, looked on with complete and utter horror.

"You made the wrong one of us into your Inquisitor, Ruin," Kelsier hissed. "You shouldn't have picked the *good* brother. He always *did* have a nasty habit of doing what was right instead of what was smart."

Ruin looked to Kelsier, turning his full, incredible attention on him.

Kelsier smiled. Gods, it appeared, could still fall for a classic misdirection con.

Vin reached to the mists, and Kelsier felt the power within him tremble, eager. This was what they'd been meant for; this was their purpose. He felt Vin's yearning, and felt her question. Where had she felt this power before?

Kelsier rammed himself against Ruin, the powers clashing, exposing his soul. His darkened, battered soul.

"The power came from the Well of Ascension, of course," Kelsier said to Vin. "It's the same power, after all. Solid in the metal you fed to Elend. Liquid in the pool you burned. And vapor in the air, confined to night. Hiding you. Protecting you . . ."

Kelsier took a deep breath. He felt Preservation's energy being ripped from him. He felt Ruin's fury pummeling him, flaying him, ravenous to destroy him. For one last moment he felt the world. The farthest ashfall, the people in the distant south, the curling winds, and the life straining—struggling—to continue on this planet.

Then Kelsier did the most difficult thing he'd ever done.

"Giving you power!" he roared to Vin, letting go of Preservation's essence so she could take it up.

Vin drew in the mists.

And Ruin's full fury came against Kelsier, slamming him down, ripping into his soul. Tearing him apart.

# 8

KELSIER was cloven asunder with a rending, pervasive pain—like that of a bone being pulled from a socket. He tumbled, unable to see or think—unable to do more than scream at the attack.

He ended up someplace surrounded by mist, blind to anything beyond its shifting. Death, for real this time? No . . . but he was very close. He could feel the stretching coming upon him again, coaxing him, trying to pull him toward that distant point where everyone else had gone.

He wanted to go. He hurt *so much.* He wanted it all to end, to go away. Everything. He just wanted it to stop.

He had felt this despair before, in the Pits of Hathsin. He didn't have Preservation's voice to guide him now, as he had then, but—weeping, trembling—he sank his hands into the misty expanse around him and *held on.* Clinging to it, refusing to go. Denying that force that called to him, promising peace and an ending.

Eventually it stilled, and the stretching sensation faded away. He had held the power of deity. The final death could not take him unless he wanted it to.

Or unless he was completely destroyed. He shuddered in the mists, thankful for their embrace, but still uncertain where he was—and uncertain why Ruin hadn't finished the job. He'd planned to; Kelsier had felt that. Fortunately, Kelsier's destruction had become an afterthought in the face of a new threat.

Vin. She'd done it! She'd Ascended!

Groaning, Kelsier pulled himself upward, finding he'd been hit so hard by Ruin's attack that he'd been driven far down into the springy, misty ground of the Cognitive Realm. He was able to pull himself out, with difficulty, and collapsed onto the surface. His soul was distorted, mangled, like a body struck by a boulder. It leaked dark smoke from a thousand holes.

As he lay there it slowly re-formed, and the pain—at long last—faded. Time had passed. He didn't know how much, but it had been hours upon hours. He wasn't in Luthadel. De-Ascending—then being crushed by Ruin's power—had flung his soul far from the city.

He blinked phantom eyes. Above him the sky was a tempest of white and black tendrils, like clouds attacking one another. In the distance he could hear something that made the Realm tremble. He forced himself to his feet and walked, eventually cresting a hill where he saw—below—that figures made of light were locked in battle. A war, men against koloss.

Preservation's plan. He'd seen it, understood it in those last moments. Ruin's body was atium. The plan was to create something special and new—people who could *burn away* Ruin's body in an attempt to get rid of it.

Below, men fought for their lives, and he saw them transcending the Physical Realm because of the body of the god that they burned. Above, Ruin and Preservation clashed. Vin did a much better job of it than Kelsier had; she had the full power of the mists, and beyond that there was something *natural* about the way she held that power.

Kelsier dusted himself off and adjusted his clothing. Still the same shirt and trousers he'd been wearing during his fight with the Inquisitor long ago. What had happened to his pack and the knife Nazh had given him? Those were lost somewhere on the endless fields of ash between here and Fadrex.

He crossed through the battle, stepping out of the way of raging koloss and transcendent men who could see into the Spiritual Realm, if only in a very limited way.

Kelsier reached the top of a hill and stopped. On another hill beyond, distant but close enough to make out, Elend Venture stood among a pile of corpses, clashing with Marsh. Vin hovered above, expansive and incredible, a figure of glowing light and awesome power—like an inspiration for the sun and clouds.

Elend Venture raised his hand, and then *exploded* with light. Lines of white scattered from him in all directions, lines that drilled through all things. Lines that Connected him to Kelsier, to the future, and to the past.

*He's seeing it fully,* Kelsier thought. *That place between moments.*

Elend ended with a sword in Marsh's neck, and looked directly at Kelsier, transcending the three Realms.

Marsh slammed an axe into Elend's chest.

"No!" Kelsier screamed. "*No!*" He stumbled down the hillside, running for Venture. He climbed over corpses, shadowy on this side, and scrambled toward where Elend had died.

He hadn't reached the position yet when Marsh took off Elend's head.

*Oh, Vin. I'm sorry.*

Vin's full attention coursed around the fallen man. Kelsier pulled to a stop, numb. She would rage. She would lose control. She would . . .

Rise in glory?

He watched, awed, as Vin's strength coalesced. There was no hatred in the thrumming that washed from her, calming all things. Above her Ruin laughed, again assuming he knew so much. That laughter cut off as Vin rose against him, a glorious, radiant spear of power—controlled, loving, compassionate, but *unyielding.*

Kelsier knew then why she, and not he, had needed to do this.

Vin crashed her power against Ruin's, suffocating him. Kelsier stepped up to the top of the hill, watching, feeling a familiarity with that power. A kinship that warmed him deep within as Vin performed the ultimate act of heroism.

She brought destruction to the destroyer.

It ended in an eruption of light. Wisps of mist, both dark and white, streamed down from the sky. Kelsier smiled, knowing that at long last it was finished. In a rush, the mists swirled in twin columns, impossibly high. The powers had been released. They quivered, uncertain, like a storm brewing.

*Nobody is holding them. . . .*

Kelsier reached out, timid, trembling. He could . . .

Elend Venture's spirit stumbled into the Cognitive Realm beside him, tripping and collapsing to the ground. He groaned, and Kelsier grinned at him.

Elend blinked as Kelsier held out a hand. "I always imagined death," Elend said, letting Kelsier help him to his feet, "as being greeted by everyone I've ever loved in life. I hadn't imagined that would include *you*."

"You need to pay better attention, kid," Kelsier said, looking him over. "Nice uniform. Did you *ask* them to make you look like a cheap knockoff of the Lord Ruler, or was it more an accident?"

Elend blinked. "Wow. I hate you already."

"Give it time," Kelsier said, slapping him on the back. "For most that eventually fades to a sense of mild exasperation." He looked at the power still coursing around them, then frowned as a figure made of glowing light scrambled across the field. Its shape was familiar to him. It stepped up to Vin's corpse, which had fallen to the ground.

"Sazed," Kelsier whispered, then touched him. He was not prepared for the rush of emotion brought on by seeing his friend in this state. Sazed was frightened. Disbelieving. Crushed. Ruin was dead, but the world was still ending. Sazed had thought that Vin would save them. Honestly, so had Kelsier.

But it seemed there was yet another secret.

"It's him," Kelsier whispered. "He's the Hero."

Elend Venture placed a hand on Kelsier's shoulder. "You need to pay better attention," he noted. "Kid." He pulled Kelsier away as Sazed reached for the powers, one with each hand.

Kelsier stood in awe of the way they combined. He'd always seen these powers as opposites, yet as they swirled around Sazed it seemed that they actually *belonged* to one another. "How?" he whispered. "How is he Connected to them both, so evenly? Why not just Preservation?"

"He has changed, this last year," Elend said. "Ruin is more than death and destruction. It is peace with these things."

The transformation continued, but awesome though it was, Kelsier's attention was drawn by something else. A coalescing of power near him on the hilltop. It formed into the shape of a young woman who slipped easily into the Cognitive Realm. She didn't so much as stumble, which was both appropriate and horribly unfair.

Vin glanced at Kelsier and smiled. A welcoming, warm smile. A smile of joy and acceptance, which filled him with pride. How he wished he'd been able to find her earlier, when Mare was still alive. When she'd needed parents.

She went to Elend first, and seized him in a long embrace. Kelsier glanced at Sazed, who was expanding to become everything. Well, good for him. It was a tough job; Sazed could have it.

Elend nodded to Kelsier, and Vin walked over. "Kelsier," she said to him, "oh, Kelsier. You always did make your own rules."

Hesitant, he didn't embrace her. He reached out his hand, feeling oddly reverent. Vin took it, the tips of her fingers curling into his palm.

Nearby another figure had coalesced from the power, but Kelsier ignored him. He stepped closer to Vin. "I . . ." What did he say? Hell, he didn't know.

For once, he didn't know.

She embraced him, and he found himself weeping. The daughter he'd never had, the little child of the streets. Though she was still small, she'd outgrown him. And she loved him anyway. He held his daughter close against his own broken soul.

"You did it," he finally whispered. "What nobody else could have done. You gave yourself up."

"Well," she said, "I had such a good example, you see."

He pulled her tight and held her for a moment longer. Unfortunately, he eventually had to let go.

Ruin stood up nearby, blinking. Or . . . no, it wasn't Ruin any longer. It was just the Vessel, Ati. The man who had held the power. Ati ran his hand through his red hair, then looked about. "Vax?" he said, sounding confused.

"Excuse me," Kelsier said to Vin, then released her and trotted over to the red-haired man.

Whereupon he decked the man across the face, laying him out completely.

"Excellent," Kelsier said, shaking his hand. At his feet, the man looked at him, then closed his eyes and sighed, stretching away into eternity.

Kelsier walked back to the others, passing a figure in Terris robes standing with hands clasped before him, draping sleeves covering them. "Hey," Kelsier said, then looked at the sky and the glowing figure there. "Aren't you . . ."

"Part of me is," Sazed replied. He looked to Vin and Elend and held out his hands, one toward each of them. "Thank you both for this new beginning. I have healed your bodies. You can return to them, if you wish."

Vin looked to Elend. To Kelsier's horror, he had begun to stretch out. He turned toward something Kelsier couldn't see, something Beyond, and smiled, then stepped in that direction.

"I don't think it works that way, Saze," Vin said, then kissed him on the cheek. "Thank you." She turned, took Elend's hand, and began to stretch toward that unseen, distant point.

"Vin!" Kelsier cried, grabbing her other hand, clutching it. "No, Vin. You held the power. You don't have to go."

"I know," she said, looking back over her shoulder at him.

"Please," Kelsier said. "Don't go. Stay. With me."

"Ah, Kelsier," she said. "You have a lot to learn about love, don't you?"

"I know love, Vin. Everything I've done—the fall of the empire, the power I've given up—that was all *about* love."

She smiled. "Kelsier. You are a great man, and should be proud of what you've done. And you do love. I know you do. But at the same time, I don't think you understand it."

She turned her gaze toward Elend, who was vanishing, only his hand—in hers—still visible. "Thank you, Kelsier," she whispered, looking back at him, "for all you have done. Your sacrifice was amazing. But to do the things you had to do, to defend the world, you had to become something. Something that worries me.

"Once, you taught me an important lesson about friendship. I need to return that lesson. A last gift. You need to know, you need to ask. How much of what you've done was about love, and how much was about proving something? That you hadn't been betrayed, bested, beaten? Can you answer honestly, Kelsier?"

He met her eyes, and saw the implicit question.

*How much was about us?* it asked. *And how much was about you?*

"I don't know," he said to her.

She squeezed his hand and smiled—that smile she'd never have been able to give when he first found her.

That, more than anything, made him proud of her.

"Thank you," she whispered again.

Then she let go of his hand and followed Elend into the Beyond.

# 9

THE land shook and groaned as it died, and was reborn.

Kelsier walked it, hands shoved in his pockets. He strolled through the end of the world, power spraying in all directions, giving him visions of all three Realms.

Fires burned from the heavens. Stones crashed together, then ripped back apart. Oceans boiled, and their steam became a new mist in the air.

Still Kelsier walked. He walked as if his feet could carry him from one world to the next, from one life to the next. He didn't feel abandoned, but he did feel alone. Like he was the only man left in all the world, and the last witness of eras.

Ash was consumed by a land of stones made liquid. Mountains crashed from the ground behind Kelsier, in rhythm to his footsteps. Rivers washed down from the heights and oceans filled. Life sprang up, trees sprouting and shooting toward the sky, making a forest around him. Then that passed, and he was in a desert, quickly drying, sand boiling from the depths of the land as Sazed created it.

A dozen different settings passed him in an eyeblink, the land growing in his wake, his shadow. Kelsier finally stopped on a lofty highland plateau overlooking a new world, winds from three Realms ruffling his clothing. Grass grew beneath his feet, then blossoms sprouted. Mare's flowers.

He knelt and bowed his head, resting his fingers on one of them.

Sazed appeared beside him. Slowly, Kelsier's vision of the real world faded, and he was trapped again in the Cognitive Realm. All became mist around him.

Sazed sat down next to him. "I will be honest, Kelsier. This is not the end I had in mind when I joined your crew."

"The rebellious Terrisman," Kelsier said. Though he was in the world of mist, he could see clouds—vaguely—in the real world. They passed beneath his feet, surging around the base of the mountain. "You were a living contradiction even then, Saze. I should have seen it."

"I can't bring them back," Sazed said softly. "Not yet . . . perhaps not ever. The Beyond is a place I can't reach."

"It's all right," Kelsier said. "Do me a favor. Will you see what you can do for Spook? His body is in rough shape. He's pushed it too hard. Fix him up a little? Maybe make him Mistborn while you're at it. They're going to need some Allomancers in the world that comes."

"I'll consider it," Sazed said.

They sat there together. Two friends at the edge of the world, at the end and start of time. Eventually, Sazed stood and bowed to Kelsier. A reverent motion for one who was himself divine.

"What do you think, Saze?" Kelsier asked, staring out over the world. "Is there a way for me to get out of this, and live again in the Physical Realm?"

Sazed hesitated. "No. I do not think so." He patted Kelsier on the shoulder, then vanished.

*Huh,* Kelsier thought. *He holds the powers of creation in twain, a god among gods.*

*And he's still a terrible liar.*

# EPILOGUE

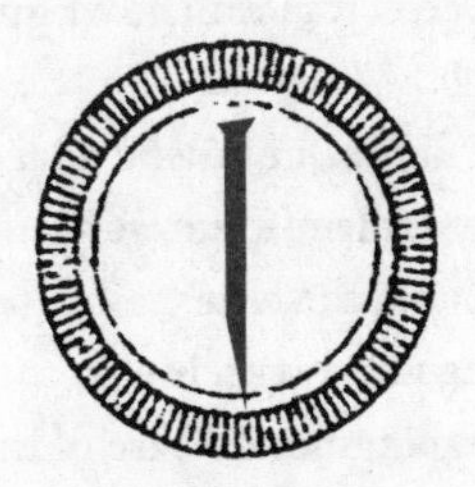

SPOOK felt uncomfortable living in a mansion when everyone else had so little. But they had insisted—and besides, it wasn't much of a mansion. Yes, it was a log house of two stories, when most lived in shanties. And yes, he had his own room. But that room was small, and it felt muggy at night. They didn't have glass for windows, and if he left the shutters open, insects got in.

This perfect new world had a disappointing amount of normalcy to it.

He yawned, closing his door. The room held a cot and a desk. No candles or lamps; they didn't yet have the resources to spare those. His head was full of Breeze's instructions on how to be a king, and his arms hurt from training with Ham. Beldre would expect him for dinner shortly.

Downstairs a door thumped, and Spook jumped. He kept expecting loud noises to hurt his ears more than they did, and even after all these weeks he still wasn't used to walking around with his eyes uncovered. On his desk one of his aides had left a little writing board—they didn't have paper—scratched on with charcoal, listing a few of his appointments for the next day. And at the bottom was a quick note.

*I finally got the smith to make this as you requested, though he was timid about handling Inquisitor spikes. Not sure why you want it so much, Your Majesty. But here you go.*

At the base of the board was a tiny spike shaped like an earring. Hesitant, Spook picked it up and held it before him. Why *did* he want this, again? He remembered something, whispers in his dreams. *Get a spike forged, an earring. An old Inquisitor spike will work. You can find one in the caverns that used to be beneath Kredik Shaw. . . .*

A dream? He considered, then—perhaps against his better judgment—jabbed the thing through his ear.

Kelsier appeared in the room with him.

"Gah!" Spook said, leaping back. "You! You're dead. Vin killed you. Saze's book says—"

"It's okay, kid," Kelsier said. "I'm the real one."

"I . . ." Spook stammered. "It . . . Gah!"

Kelsier walked over and put his arm around Spook's shoulders. "See, I knew this would work. You've got them both now. Broken mind, Hemalurgic spike. You can see just enough into the Cognitive Realm. That means we can work together, you and I."

"Oh hell," Spook said.

"Now, don't be like that," Kelsier said. "Our work is important. *Vital.* We're going to unravel the mysteries of the universe. The cosmere, as it is called."

"What . . . what do you mean?"

Kelsier smiled.

"I think I'm going to be sick," Spook said.

"It's a big, big place out there, kid," Kelsier said. "Bigger than I ever knew. Ignorance almost lost us everything. I'm not going to let that happen again." He tapped at Spook's ear. "While dead, I had an opportunity. My mind expanded, and I learned some things. My focus wasn't on these spikes; I think I could have worked it all out, if it had been. I still learned enough to be dangerous, and the two of us are going to figure the rest out."

Spook pulled back. He was his own man now! He didn't need to just do whatever Kelsier said. Hell, he didn't even know if this really *was* Kelsier. He'd been fooled once before.

"Why?" Spook demanded. "Why would I care?"

Kelsier shrugged. "The Lord Ruler was immortal, you know. By a combination of the powers, he managed to make himself unable to age—unable to die, under most circumstances. You're Mistborn, Spook. Half-way there. Aren't you curious about what else is possible? I mean, we have a little pile of Inquisitor spikes, and nothing to do with them. . . ."

*Immortal.*

"And you?" Spook asked. "What do you get from this?"

"Nothing big," Kelsier said. "Just a little thing. Someone once explained my problem. My string has been cut, the thing holding me to the physical world." His smile broadened. "Well, we're just going to have to find me a new string."

# POSTSCRIPT

I started planning this story while writing the original trilogy. By then, I'd pitched the idea of a "trilogy of trilogies" to my editor. (This is the idea that Mistborn, as a series, would change epochs and tech levels as the Cosmere matured.) I also knew that Kelsier would be playing a major role in future books in the series.

I'm not opposed to letting characters die; I believe that every series I've done has had some major, permanent casualties among viewpoint characters. At the same time, I was well aware that Kelsier's story was not finished. The person he was at the end of the first volume had learned some things, but hadn't completed his journey.

So, early on I began planning how to bring him back. I saturated *The Hero of Ages* with hints as to what he was doing behind the scenes, and even managed to slip in a few earlier hints here and there. I made very clear to fans who asked me that Kelsier was never good at doing what he was supposed to.

I am very aware of character resurrection as a dangerous trope, the balance of which I'm still figuring out. I didn't think this one was particularly controversial, in part because of the foreshadowing I'd done. But I do want death to be a very real danger, or consequence, in my stories.

That said, Kelsier from the start was coming back—though at times I wavered on whether I was going to write this story or not. I was worried that if I wrote it out, it would feel disjointed, as so much time passes and so many different phases of storytelling had to occur. I started writing for it a few years before I finally published it, tweaking scenes off and on, here and there.

Once I wrote *The Bands of Mourning*, it became clear to me that I'd need to get an explanation to readers out sooner rather than later. This set me to working on the story more diligently. In the end, I'm very pleased with how it turned out. It is a little disjointed, as I worried. However, the chance to finally talk about some of the behind-the-scenes stories going on in the Cosmere was very rewarding, both for myself and for fans.

To forestall questions, I do know what Kelsier and Spook were up to directly following this story. And I also know what Kelsier was doing during the era of the Wax and Wayne books. (There are some hints in those, as the original books have hints at this story.)

I can't promise that I'll write *Secret History 2* or *3*. There's already a lot on my plate. However, the possibility is in the back of my mind.

# THE TALDAIN SYSTEM

The Taldain System
The Particulate Ring
Taldain
Darkside
Dayside
NizhDa

# THE TALDAIN SYSTEM

Taldain is one of the most bizarre planets in the cosmere, a fact that, in turn, feels bizarre to me. Having grown up on Taldain's Darkside, there is a part of me—even all these years later—that instinctively feels that the way of this planet is the normal, natural one.

Taldain is a tidally locked planet trapped between the gravitational forces of two stars in a binary system. The smaller star is a weak white dwarf that, enveloped in a particulate ring, is barely visible from the dark side of the planet. Those of us originating from this side of the planet consider a uniform darkness (what most might consider a twilight similar to the sky just after a sun has set) to be the natural state.

Our planet is not grim, and assumptions otherwise are simple ignorance. The ultraviolet light that shines through the ring causes a certain reflective luminescence in much of the plant and animal life. Indeed, the few visitors to the planet that I've met often found it somewhere between striking and garish.

On the other side of the planet is Dayside, which faces the larger of the two stars, a blue-white supergiant around which the dwarf orbits. The sun is a dominating fixture of Dayside, which is primarily a vast sandy desert, with most of the flora and fauna living beneath the surface.

For years we assumed that our Shard, Autonomy, had Invested only Dayside, through the sunlight itself. We know now it is not as simple as this, though the mechanism is best explained under those assumptions. The Investiture beats down from the sky, and is absorbed by a microflora that grows like a lichen on the surface of the sand, giving it its brilliant white color (when fully Invested) or deep blackness (when that Investiture is depleted).

Giving water to the tiny plant causes a chain reaction of sudden growth, energy, and Realmic transition. Certain people can control this reaction, using the water from their own bodies to forge a brief Cognitive bond. They can draw Investiture (in very small amounts) directly from the Spiritual Realm, and use that to control the sand.

Though the effect is dramatic, the actual power used is quite small. This is a magic more about finesse than raw strength.

Dayside is home to two prominent cultures, while Darkside is more hospitable and varied. The flora and fauna of both sides are remarkable, though currently prospective visitors are—unfortunately—unable to experience them directly. Autonomy's policy of isolationism in recent times (in direct contrast to her interference with other planets, I might add) has prevented travel to and from Taldain for many, many years.

A fact of which I am all too aware.

# WHITE SAND

This excerpt of the 2016 graphic novel is followed by the beginning of the 1999 draft that formed the basis of the graphic adaptation.

SO...
...THE MASTREL PATH. REMIND
AGAIN WHY I THO
THIS WOULD BE
SMART IDEA
WHITE SAN
STORY: BRANDON SANDERS
SCRIPT: RIK HOS
ART: JULIUS GO
COLORS: ROSS CAMPB
LETTERS: MARSHALL DILL
EDITS: RICH YOU
I GUESS I'VE ALWAYS BEEN TRYING TO PROVE SOMETHING TO MY FATHER, THE LORD MASTRELL.
"AND THIS ONE, SENIOR MASTRELL TENDEL? DOES HE SHOW PROMISE?"
"YES, LORD MASTRELL. HE'S ONE IN A VERY STRONG GROUP THIS YEAR."
WELL, CHILD? TELL THE LORD MASTRELL YOUR NAME.
TRAIBEN, SIR.
NOW SHOW US YOUR MASTERY SO FAR.

...
YOU
E AWARE
AT YOU
Y BEGIN,
AIBEN?
NNGHFF!
A GOOD START.
THE LORD MASTRELL WILL FIND A PLACE FOR YOU IN THE *DIEM* WHERE YOU WILL LEARN PROPER MASTERY OF SAND.
ND SO IT WENT,
ACH WOULD-BE
OLENT PROVING
F RAW ABILITIES
EFORE BEING
INDUCTED.
SOME *WEAK*.
SOME *STRONG*.
VOOM
A REMARKABLE DISPLAY. I HAVEN'T SEEN ONE SO POWERFUL IN YEARS. WHO IS THAT?
DRILE, SON OF REENST RILE.
*HMMM.* A PROFITABLE CATCH THEN, IN MORE THAN ONE WAY.

AND THEN IT WAS MY TURN.
AND THE LAST WOULD-BE ACOLENT IS YOUR SON-- KENTON.
MY FATHER SAID NOTHING, OF COURSE. AS HIS YOUNGEST SON, I WAS THE LAST IN A LONG LINE OF DISAPPOINTMENTS, NOT A SINGLE ONE OF US EXHIBITING ANY TALENT FOR SAND MASTERY.
MY FATHER, THE L MASTRELL, UNAB TO PRODUCE SINGLE SAN MASTER CHILD- WAS UNHEARD SCANDALOU
RUMORS HAD IT THAT IT WAS BECA OUR MOTHER WAS FROM DARKSID AND THAT SHE HAD POLLUTED T FAMILY LINE FOREVER, POISONING T FAMILY TREE AT ITS ROOTS.
I WAS THERE TO PROVE THEM WRONG. TO PROVE ALL OF THEM WRONG.
FZZZT
THE TROUBLE WITH ALL THAT PENT-UP DETERMINATION AND RIGHTEOUSNESS--
--IS IT'S SUBSTITU FOR ACTU ABILITY.
HUFF HUFF HUFF HUFF
I'M... SORRY, LORD MASTRELL.
IT IS NOTHING. NOT EVERY BOY IS MEANT TO BE A SAND MASTER.
BUT... THIS WAS--
YES.

AKE THEM AWAY.
GE WHO HAVE ANY
L MAY ENTER THE
M; THE REST WILL
OOSE ANOTHER
PROFESSION.
I WILL BE A SAND MASTER! AS IS MY RIGHT!
YOU HAVE NO TALENT FOR SAND MASTERY, BOY! GO HOME.
YOU SAW.
THE LAW SAYS I HAVE ENOUGH!
YOU'VE STUDIED THE LAW, HAVE YOU, BOY? THEN YOU KNOW THAT, AS LORD MASTRELL, I AM THE ONLY ONE WHO CAN GRANT ADVANCEMENT IN THE DIEM--
--AND THAT IT IS I WHO MUST GIVE HIS APPROVAL BEFORE ANY SAND MASTER CAN BE ASSIGNED A RANK.
FOR EVERY RANK BUT THE FIRST!
YOU WOULD NOT FIND IT EASY IN THE DIEM, BOY.
BUT YOU MAY JOIN IF THAT IS YOUR DESIRE.
JOIN AND FAIL-- THAT'S WHAT HE MEANT.

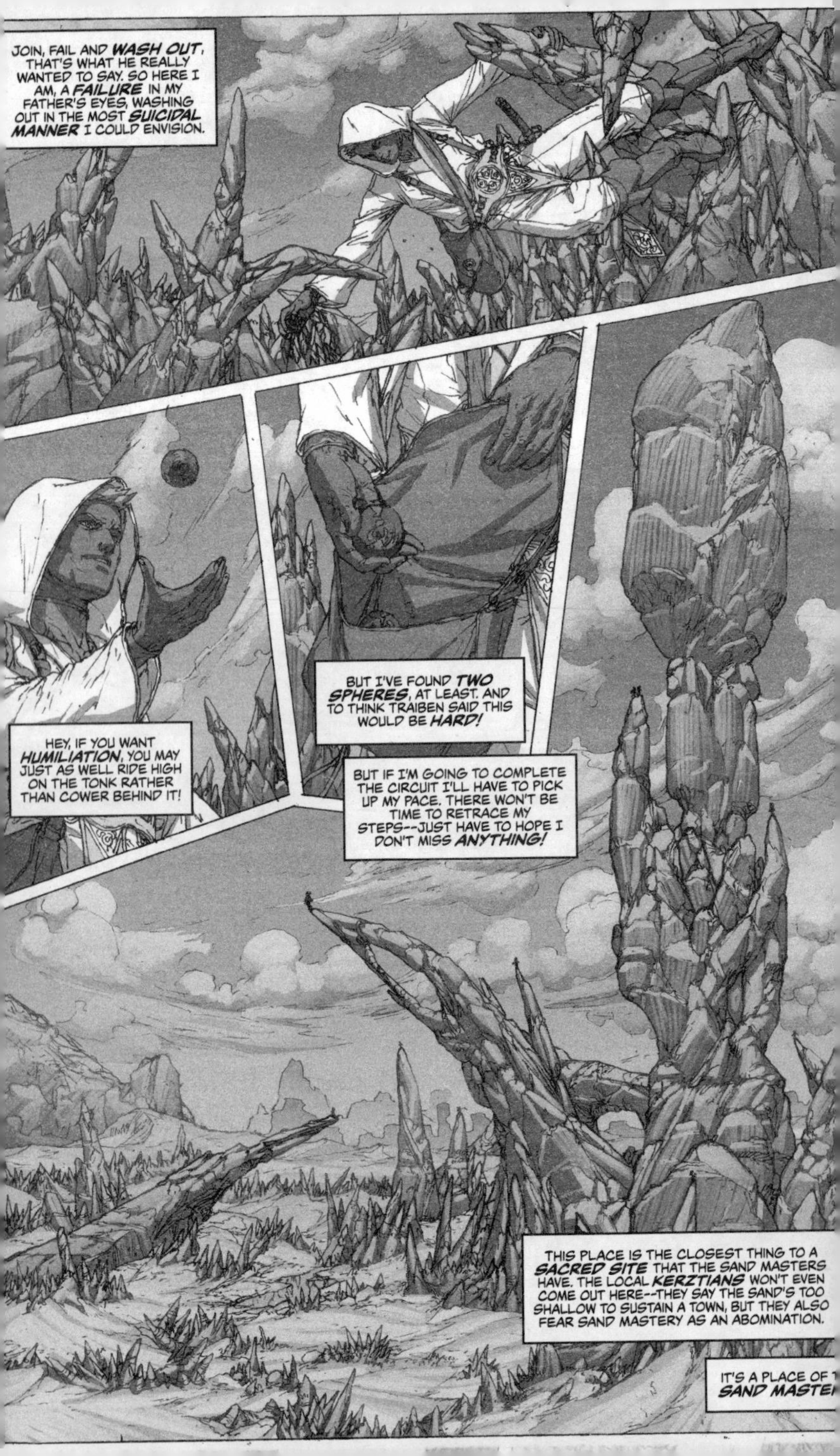
JOIN, FAIL AND WASH OUT, THAT'S WHAT HE REALLY WANTED TO SAY. SO HERE I AM, A FAILURE IN MY FATHER'S EYES, WASHING OUT IN THE MOST SUICIDAL MANNER I COULD ENVISION.
HEY, IF YOU WANT HUMILIATION, YOU MAY JUST AS WELL RIDE HIGH ON THE TONK RATHER THAN COWER BEHIND IT!
BUT I'VE FOUND TWO SPHERES, AT LEAST. AND TO THINK TRAIBEN SAID THIS WOULD BE HARD!
BUT IF I'M GOING TO COMPLETE THE CIRCUIT I'LL HAVE TO PICK UP MY PACE. THERE WON'T BE TIME TO RETRACE MY STEPS--JUST HAVE TO HOPE I DON'T MISS ANYTHING!
THIS PLACE IS THE CLOSEST THING TO A SACRED SITE THAT THE SAND MASTERS HAVE. THE LOCAL KERZTIANS WON'T EVEN COME OUT HERE--THEY SAY THE SAND'S TOO SHALLOW TO SUSTAIN A TOWN, BUT THEY ALSO FEAR SAND MASTERY AS AN ABOMINATION.
IT'S A PLACE OF

AY, BIG DROP. GER THAN I WAS ECTING, BUT THIS THE PATH ALL T--MARKER FLAG NFIRMS IT. SO W THE REAL ST BEGINS.
SAND MASTERS, POWER IS EVERYTHING. I EARNED THAT YOUNG, AS OON AS I WAS INDUCTED INTO THE DIEM.
NEW STUDENTS ARE ASSIGNED THEIR POSITION BASED ON THEIR ABILITY.
MY PALTRY ABILITY PLUNGED ME TO A SOCIAL POSITION AT THE BOTTOM OF A CHASM TWICE AS DEEP AS THIS ONE.

BUT THE WAY I SEE THINGS...
...THERE'S ABILITY...
...AND THEN THERE'S CONTROL.
SURE, THE WAY I DO IT MAY NOT BE FLASHY--
--BUT IT GETS THE JOB DONE.
ONCE USED, SA
NO LONGER
WHITE--IT'S BL
THAT MEANS
ENERGY IS SP
IT'S A GOOD
REMINDER THAT
NOT JUST THE
SAND'S ENERG
HAVE TO WATCH
HERE--IT'S MIN
MY MOUTH IS
THE FIRST SIGN
DEHYDRATION.
MASTERY DOES
JUST TAKE
STRENGTH--
REQUIRES WAT
SUCKING THE
PRECIOUS LIQU
FROM THE BODY
A MASTER.

HE FIRST G A SAND ASTER RNS IS TO EP TRACK OF HIS WATER.
HE HAS TO BE CAREFUL NOT TO MASTER TO THE POINT THAT HIS BODY TAKES PERMANENT DAMAGE FROM DEHYDRATION.
THIS HAD BETTER WORK!
WHAT IS HE DOING?!!
SAND MASTERS SHOULD FLOW AND DANCE, SOARING THROUGH THE AIR IN CLOUDS OF RADIANT SAND--NOT CREEP UP A WALL LIKE A DROWSY SANDLING!
I CAN'T LIFT MYSELF VERY FAR--THAT TAKES A GREATER AMOUNT OF SAND THAN I CAN COMMAND.
IT HAS ITS ADVANTAGES THOUGH--TAKING THE LONG WAY MEANS YOU GET TO SEE THE SIGHTS!

AND SO IT GOES. THE THIRD SPHERE PROVES EASY TO FIND AND THE SPENT SAND SHOWS WHERE THE FOURTH HAS BEEN HIDDEN AS CLEARLY AS ANY MAN-MADE MARKER.
IT TAKES THE SUNLIGHT FOUR HOURS TO REPLENISH THE SAND AND TURN IT WHITE AGAIN AFTER IT'S BEEN MANIPULATED. FOUR HOURS IT HASN'T HAD SINCE SOME SAND MASTER HID THIS SPHERE HERE.
BUT REACHING THE SPHERES TAKES TIME, TIME I CAN'T AFFORD TO WASTE. NO MATTER HOW HARD I TRY, I HAVE ALMOST NO TIME LEFT AND MY BODY'S OUT OF WATER.
IF ONLY I COULD SLATRIFY.
SO STUPID. MY FATHER IS AS HARSH AS THE SANDS THEMSELVES. HE WOULD NEVER HAVE LET ME BECOME A MASTRELL, EVEN IF I'D FOUND ALL...
...FIVE...?
INCREDIBLE. THIS IS THE LAST SPHERE. I'VE DONE IT!

WOULD YOU LOOK AT THIS PLACE? HOW MANY YEARS DID IT TAKE THE KERLA WINDS TO CARVE THIS?
PHEW.
I HAD EXPECTED THE LAST SPHERE WOULD HAVE BEEN THE BEST HIDDEN, THE MOST DIFFICULT TO FIND. BUT IT'S RIGHT IN THE...
...DEEP SAND!
FEW PEOPLE--EVEN KERZTIANS--ARE FOOLISH ENOUGH TO WANDER ONTO DEEP SAND.
AISHA!
SOMETHING'S WRONG.
SOMETHING'S VERY, VERY WRONG.
SHHHHHH

NOW I REMEMBER WHY KERZTIANS DON'T VENTURE ONTO DEEP SAND!
BECAUSE OF THESE THINGS-- SANDLINGS. PREDATORS WHO GLIDE EFFORTLESSLY THROUGH SAND. THEY'RE FAST AND NEAR INDESTRUCTIBLE, LIVING IN THE DEEP SAND AND ONLY EMERGING TO HUNT.

THEY DON'T REALLY SEE-- THEY FEEL. THE KERZTIANS BELIEVE THAT THEY EVEN SPEAK TO THE SAND.

I'M SUDDENLY THANKFUL FOR ALL THE HOURS I SPENT SPARRING WITH SOLDIERS FROM THE TOWER. DAYS HONING REFLEXES ARE ALL THAT'S KEPT ME ALIVE FOR THE PAST FIVE SECONDS.
LET'S SEE IF
LAST FIVE
AMBITIOUS GOAL, IT SEEMS.
CLANG
KENTON! WE CANNOT INTERCEDE UNLESS YOU ASK!
I MAY NOT BE ABLE TO CONTROL DOZENS OF LINES AT ONCE, BUT WHEN IT COMES TO A SINGLE RIBBON--
--I'M
IN SPEED

F COURSE, THIS DLING IS TERKEN-- IMPERVIOUS TO ND MASTERY. ITS UCH KILLS THE SAND'S ENERGY.
DIDN'T YOU HEAR ME, LAD? ASK US TO BRING YOU OUT!
NO.
IT'S CLEAR WHAT I'M SUPPOSED TO DO. ALL SANDLINGS HAVE ONE POWERFUL WEAKNESS: WATER. THE LIQUID DISSOLVES THEIR SHELL AND SKIN.
THE FINAL CHALLENGE IN THE MASTRELL'S PATH TESTS THE MOST POWERFUL SAND MASTERY SKILL--SLATRIFICATION.
LORD ASTRELL, MUST CALL TOP TO THIS W. YOUR SON ILL DIE IF OU DON'T--
THE RULES ARE CLEAR, ELORIN. KENTON MUST REQUEST THE INTERVENTION.

SLATRIFICATION IS THE ONE THING I CAN'T DO.
BUT I HAVE OTHER TRICKS.
EVEN CONTROLLI JUST ONE RIBBO A TIME CAN SEEM A MULTITUDE, IF DO IT QUICKLY ENO
BUT I'M USING UP VALUABLE RESOURCES TO REACH THAT SPHERE. I'M STARTING TO DRY OUT. FIRST LESSON, FIRST DAY: FOR THE GOOD OF THE DIEM, ONE MUSTN'T EVEN COME CLOSE TO OVERMASTERY.
THERE!
BUT... WAIT!
ANOTHER SPHERE?! BUT THAT'S IMPOSSIBLE!

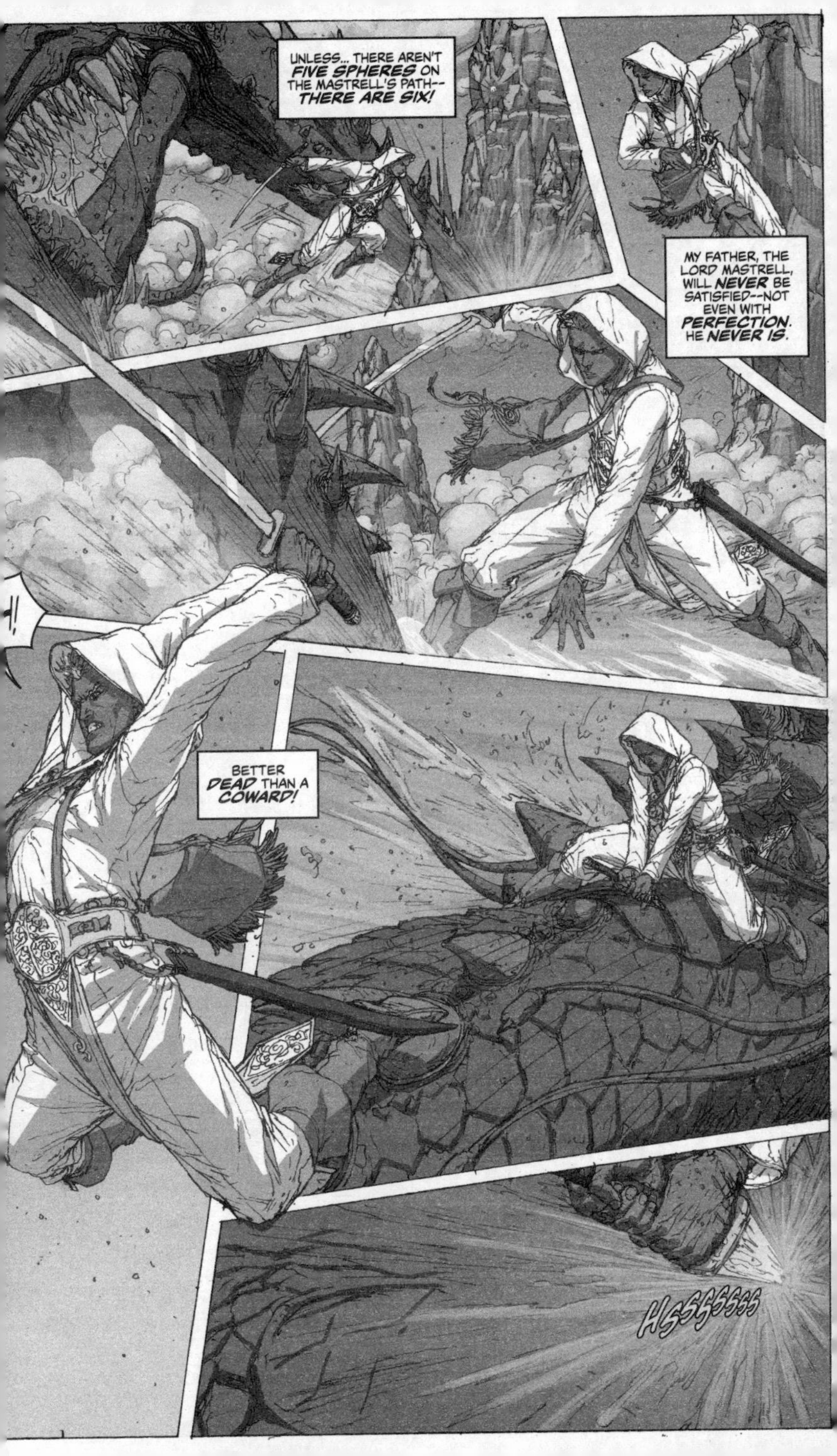
UNLESS... THERE AREN'T FIVE SPHERES ON THE MASTRELL'S PATH-- THERE ARE SIX!
MY FATHER, THE LORD MASTRELL, WILL NEVER BE SATISFIED--NOT EVEN WITH PERFECTION. HE NEVER IS.
BETTER DEAD THAN A COWARD!
HSSSSSSS

UNGH!
HSSSSSSSS
I COMMAND MY RIBBON TO EXPLORE THE CUT IN THE SANDLING'S SHELL--
--TO HURT THIS BEAUTIFUL, TERRIBLE CREATURE THAT RULES FAR BELOW THE KERLA.
IT WRITHES A MOMENT TH SEEMS TO LA FOREVER, A LIF COUNTLES YEARS FINA ENDING.

MY TIME IS ALMOST UP TOO, BUT I HAVE TO FINISH THIS.
SIX SPHERES! IT'S IMPOSSIBLE!
I LAID FIVE. WHERE DID THE SIXTH COME FROM?
WATER! BRING THE LAD WATER!
FWUMP
HE'S PUSHED HIMSELF TO THE EXTREME--THANK THE SAND LORD HE SURVIVED. YOU MUST BE PROUD OF YOUR SON, LORD MASTRELL.
MUST I?
TO BE CONTINUED.

# PROLOGUE

THE wind caressed the stark dunes with a whispering touch, catching fine grains of sand between its fingers and bearing them forth like thousands of tiny charioteers. The sand, like the dunes it sculpted, was bone white. It had been bleached by the sun's harsh stare—a stare that never slackened, for here, in the empire of the white sand, the sun never set. It hung motionless, neither rising nor falling, ever watching the dunes like a jealous monarch.

Praxton could feel the wind-borne grains of sand biting into his cheek. He pulled up the hood of his robe, but it seemed to make little difference. He could still feel the particles attacking the side of his face like furious insects. The sand masters would have to hurry—the winds could whip the Kerla sands from stagnation to a whirling typhoon in a matter of minutes.

A dozen forms stood a short distance away, clothed in brown robes. They had their hoods pulled up against the wind, but it was easy to tell from their small frames that they were children, barely into their second decade of life. The boys stood uncomfortably, shuffling with nervous feet as the winds whipped at their robes. They knew how important this day was. They couldn't understand as Praxton did; they couldn't know how many times they would look back on the event, how often the results of the testing would determine the course of their lives. Still, they could sense the significance of what was about to happen.

At the bidding of a white-robed mastrell, the boys reached into their robes and pulled out small cloth bags. Praxton watched the event with a stern face—the face he usually wore—presiding over the ceremony as Lord Mastrell, leader of the sand masters. He watched with emotionless eyes as each boy pulled a handful of white sand from within his bag. They had to hold tightly to keep the increasingly powerful wind from tearing the sand away and scattering it across the Kerla.

Praxton frowned, as if his simple displeasure could force the wind to abate. The testing took place close to the mountain KraeDa—one of the few places in the Kerla where stone jutted free from the sand. Here the wind was usually blocked by both mountain and surrounding cliffs.

He shook his head, taking his mind off the wind as the first boy began the testing. Two mastrells stood before him, instructing him in quiet voices that were lost upon the wind. Praxton saw the results, even if he couldn't hear the voices—the boy stared at the sand in his hand for a moment, a brief flutter of wind revealing the look of concentration on his face. The sand, cupped protectively in his open palm, began to glow faintly for a moment, then turned a dull black, like the charred remnants of a fire.

"A good start," one of the senior mastrells, Tendel, muttered from behind him. Praxton nodded silently—Tendel was correct; it was a good sign. The boy—Praxton thought he recognized him as Traiben, son of a lower sand master—had been able to make the sand glow bright enough to be seen even from a short distance, which meant he had at least moderate power.

The testing continued, some of the boys producing glows similar to Traiben's, some barely managing to turn the sand black. Overall, however, it was an unusually strong batch. They would bring much strength to the Diem.

There was a sudden flash, one so bright that it produced an explosive crack loud enough to be heard even over the wind. Praxton blinked in surprise, trying to clear the bright afterimage from his eyes. The two mastrells performing the test stood stunned before a small child with a shaking hand.

Tendel whistled beside Praxton. "I haven't seen one so powerful in years," the old mastrell said. "Who is that?"

"Drile," Praxton said despite himself. "Son of Reenst Rile."

"A profitable catch in more than one way, then," Tendel noted.

The testing mastrells recovered from their surprise and moved on to the next, and final, boy. Despite his age, his determined calmness, and his stern nature, Praxton felt his heart beat a little more quickly as the final child listened to their instructions.

*Oh please,* he felt himself mutter in a half-conscious prayer. He was not a religious man, but this was his final opportunity. He had failed so many times before. . . .

The boy looked at his sand. His hood had fallen to the wind, and his face, round and topped with a pile of short blond hair, adopted a look of total concentration. Praxton held his breath, waiting, excited in spite of himself.

The boy stared at the sand, his teeth clenched. Praxton felt his excitement dribble away as nothing happened. Finally, the sand gave a very weak glimmer—one so dark Praxton couldn't be certain he hadn't just imagined it—then faded to a dun black.

Though he knew he betrayed no look of disappointment, Praxton felt the senior mastrells around him grow stiff with anticipation.

"I'm . . . sorry, Lord Mastrell," Tendel said beside him.

"It is nothing," Praxton replied with a dismissive wave of his hand. "Not every boy is meant to be a sand master."

"But . . . this was your last son," Tendel pointed out—a rather unnecessary acknowledgment, in Praxton's estimation.

"Take them away," Praxton ordered in a loud voice. *So, this will be my legacy,* he thought to himself. *A Lord Mastrell who couldn't produce a single sand master child. I will be remembered as the man who married a woman from Darkside, thereby sullying his line.*

He sighed, continuing. "Those who have skill may enter the Diem; the rest will choose another Profession."

The sand masters moved quickly, their feet sinking easily into the swirling, fine-grained dunes beneath. They were eager to seek refuge from the furious elements. One form, however, did not follow the white-robed mastrells. Small and slight of frame, the boy stood in the increasingly violent wind. His robe whipped around him, writhing like a beast in the throes of a gruesome death.

"Kenton," Praxton said under his breath.

"I will be a sand master!" the young boy said, his voice barely audible over the wind. A short distance away the line of retreating mastrells and boys paused, several heads turning in surprise.

"You have no talent for sand mastery, boy!" Praxton spat, waving for the group to continue moving. They made only a perfunctory show of obeying the order. Few people ever challenged the Lord Mastrell, especially not young boys. Such a sight was worth standing in a sandstorm to watch.

"The Law says I have enough!" Kenton rebutted, his small voice nearly a scream.

Praxton frowned. "You've studied the Law, have you, boy?"

"I have."

"Then you know that I am the only one who can grant advancement in the Diem," Praxton said, growing more and more furious at the challenge to his authority. It looked bad to be confronted by a child, especially his own son. "The Lord Mastrell must give his approval before any sand master can increase in rank."

"Every rank but the first!" Kenton shouted back.

Praxton paused, feeling his rage build. Everything beat against him—the insufferable wind, the boy's insolence, the other sand masters' eyes. . . . The worst of it was his own knowledge. Knowledge that the boy was right. Anyone who could make the sand glow was technically allowed to join the Diem. Boys with less power than Kenton had become sand masters. Of course, none of them had been children of the Lord Mastrell. If Kenton joined the Diem, his inability would weaken Praxton's authority by association.

The boy continued to stand, his posture determined. The windblown sand was piling around his legs, burying him up to the knees in a shifting barrow.

"You will not find it easy in the Diem, boy," Praxton hissed. "By the sands, see reason!"

Kenton did not move.

Praxton sighed. "Fine!" he declared. "You may join."

Kenton smiled in victory, pulling his legs free from the dune and scrambling over to join the line of students. Praxton watched motionlessly as the boy moved.

The buffeting wind tore at his robes, sand scraping its way into his eyes and between his lips. Such discomfort would be little compared to the pain Kenton would soon know—the Diem was a place of unforgiving politics, and sheer power was often the means by which a sand master was judged. No, life would not be easy for one so weak, especially since his father was so powerful. No matter what Praxton did, the other students would resent Kenton for supposed coddlings or favoritism.

Oblivious to the trials ahead of him, the young boy made his way to the caves a short distance away. It appeared as if Praxton's final child would also prove to be his largest embarrassment.

# CHAPTER ONE

It almost seemed to Kenton as if the sands were breathing. Heat from the immobile sun reflected off the grains, distorting the air—making the dunes seem like they were composed of tiny coals, white-hot with energy. In the distance, Kenton could hear wind moaning through crevices in the rock. There was only one place in the enormous dune-covered expanse of the Kerla that such rock protrusions could be found: here, beside Mount KraeDa, in the place sacred to the sand masters. Everywhere else the sands were far too deep.

Kenton, now a man, once again stood before a group of mastrells. In many ways he was very similar to the boy who had stood in this exact place eight years before. He had the same close-cropped blondish hair, the same roundish face and determined expression, and—most importantly—the same look of rebellious conviction in his eyes. He now wore the white robes of a sand master, but, unlike most others of his kind, he wore no colored sash. His sash was plain white—the sign of a student who hadn't yet been assigned a rank in the Diem. Tied at his waist was another oddity—a sword. He was the only person in the group of sand masters who was armed.

"Don't tell me you intend to go through with this foolishness?" the man in front of Kenton demanded. Praxton, looking older than the sand itself, stood at the head of the Diem's twenty gold-sashed mastrells. Though he had seen barely sixty years, Praxton's skin was dry, wrinkled like a fruit that had been left out in the sun. Like most sand masters, he wore no beard.

Kenton looked back defiantly, something he had grown very good at doing over the last eight years. Praxton regarded his son with a mixture of disgust and embarrassment. Then, with a sigh, the old man did something unexpected. He moved away from the rest of the mastrells, who stood silently on the rock plateau. Kenton watched with confusion as Praxton waved him over, standing far enough away from the others that the two could have a private conversation. For once, Kenton did as commanded, moving over to hear what the Lord Mastrell had to say.

Praxton looked back at the mastrells, then turned back to Kenton. His eyes only briefly shot down at the sword tied at Kenton's waist before coming up to stare him in the eyes.

"Look, boy," Praxton said, his voice cracking slightly as he spoke. "I have suffered your insolence and games for eight years. The Sand Lord only knows how much trouble you've caused. Why must you constantly defy me?"

Kenton shrugged. "Because I'm good at it?"

Praxton scowled.

"Lord Mastrell," Kenton continued, more serious but no less defiant. "Once a sand master has accepted a rank, he's forever frozen in that place."

"So?" Praxton demanded.

Kenton didn't answer. He had refused advancement four times now, a move that had made him into a fool and a novelty before the rest of the Diem. Inept students were sometimes forced to spend five years as an acolent, but never in the history of sand mastery had anyone remained a student for eight.

Praxton sighed again, reaching down to take a sip of water from his qido. "All right, boy," Praxton finally said. "Despite the pain—despite the shame—I will admit that you've worked hard. The Sand Lord knows you haven't any talent to speak of, but at least you did something with the small amount you have. Give up this stupid decision to run the Path, and tomorrow I'll offer you the rank of fen."

Fen. It was the next to lowest of the nine sand master ranks; only underfen—the rank Kenton had been offered the four previous years—was beneath it.

"No," Kenton said. "I think I want to be a mastrell."

"*Aisha!*" Praxton cursed.

"Don't swear now, Father," Kenton suggested. "Wait until I run the Path successfully. Then what will you do?"

Kenton's defiant words were more optimistic than his heart, however. Even as his father raged, Kenton felt the questions resurfacing.

*What on the sands am I doing? Eight years ago no one thought I could even be a sand master, and now I've been offered a respectable rank in the Diem. It isn't what I wanted, but . . .*

"Boy, you're inept enough to make the Hundred Idiots look brilliant. Running the Mastrell's Path won't prove anything. It's meant for mastrells—not for simple acolents."

"The Law doesn't say a student cannot run it," Kenton said, thoughts of his inadequacy still strong in his mind.

"I won't make you a mastrell," Praxton warned. "Even if you find all five spheres, I won't do it. The Path is not a test or a proof. Mastrells run it if they want to, but only after they've been advanced. Your success will mean nothing. You'll never be a mastrell—you aren't even worthy to be a sand master!"

Praxton's words burned away Kenton's doubts like water in the sun. If there was one person who could fuel Kenton's sense of defiance, it was Praxton.

"Then I'll be an acolent until the day I die, Lord Mastrell," Kenton replied, folding his arms.

"You can't be a mastrell," Praxton reiterated. "You don't have the power."

"I don't believe in power, Father. I believe in ability. I can do anything a mastrell can; I just have different methods." It was an old argument, one he had been making for the last eight years.

"Can you slatrify?"

Kenton paused. No, that was one thing he couldn't do. Slatrification, the ability to change sand into water, was the ultimate art of sand mastery. It was wildly different from sand mastery's other abilities, and none of Kenton's creativity or ingenuity could replicate it.

"There have been mastrells who couldn't slatrify," Kenton replied weakly.

"Only two," Praxton replied. "And both were able to control over two dozen ribbons of sand at once. How many can you control, boy?"

Kenton ground his teeth. It was a direct question, however, and he couldn't refuse to respond. "One," he finally admitted.

"One," Praxton repeated. "One ribbon. I've never known a mastrell who couldn't control at least fifteen. You're telling me you can do as much with one as they can with fifteen? Why can't you see how preposterous that is?"

Kenton smiled slightly. *Thank you for the encouragement, Father.* "Well, I'll just have to prove it to you then, Lord Mastrell," he said with a mocking bow, turning away from his father.

"The Path was meant for mastrells, boy," Praxton's cracking voice repeated behind him. "Most of them don't even use it—it's too dangerous."

Kenton ignored the old man, instead approaching another sand master who was standing a short distance away. His short frame cast no shadow, for the sun was directly overhead here, in the jagged rocklands south of Mount KraeDa. The sand master was bald and had a slightly fat, oval face. Around his waist was tied the yellow sash of an undermastrell, the rank directly below mastrell. The man smiled as Kenton approached.

"Are you sure you want to do this, Kenton?"

Kenton nodded. "Yes, Elorin, I do."

"Your father's objections are well founded," Elorin cautioned. "The Mastrell's Path was created by a group of men with inflated egos who wanted very desperately to prove themselves better than their peers. It was designed for those with massive power. Mastrells have died running it before."

"I understand," Kenton said, but inwardly he was curious. No one who had run the Path was allowed to reveal its secrets, and for all his studying, Kenton hadn't been able to determine what could be so dangerous about a simple race through the Kerla. Was it the lack of water? Steep cliffs? Neither should have provided much of a challenge to well-trained sand masters.

Elorin continued. "All right then. The Lord Mastrell has asked me to mediate your run. A group of us will watch as you move through the Path, evaluating your progress and making certain you don't cheat. We cannot help you unless you ask, and if we do the intervention will end your run where it stands."

The shorter man reached into his white sand master's robes, pulling out a small red sphere. "There are five of these hidden on the Path," he explained. "Your goal is to find all five. You may start when I say so. You have until the moon passes behind the mountain and reappears on the other side. The test is over the moment you either run out of time or find the fifth sphere."

Kenton looked up. The moon circled the sky once per day, hovering just above the horizon the entire time. Soon it would pass behind Mount KraeDa. He would probably have about an hour, a hundred minutes, to run the Path.

"So I don't have to make it back to the starting point?" Kenton clarified.

Elorin shook his head. "The moment the moon reappears, your run is over. We will count the spheres you have found, and that is your score."

Kenton nodded.

"You may not take your qido with you," Elorin informed him, reaching out a hand to take Kenton's water bottle from his side.

"The sword too," Praxton called from behind, his lips curled downward in their characteristic look of disapproval.

"That is not in the rules, old man," Kenton objected, his hand falling to the hilt.

"A true sand master has no need of such a clumsy weapon," Praxton argued.

"It's not in the rules," Kenton repeated.

"He is right, Lord Mastrell," Elorin agreed. He was frowning too—as kind as the undermastrell was, even he didn't agree with Kenton's insistence on carrying a sword. In the eyes of most sand masters, weapons were crass things, meant for lowly Professions such as soldiers.

Praxton rolled his eyes in a look of frustration, but made no further objections. A few minutes later the last bit of the moon's sphere disappeared behind the mountain.

"May the Sand Lord protect you, young Kenton," Elorin offered.

The Path started simply enough, and Kenton quickly found the first two spheres. The red sandstone globes had been so easy to locate, in fact, that he began to worry that he had missed something. Unfortunately, Kenton knew that he didn't have time to go back and recheck his steps. Either he found them all on the first try, or he failed.

That determination drove Kenton forward as he ran across the top of a rock ledge. Around him the strange formations of stone jutted from the sand floor, some rising hundreds of feet into the air, others barely breaking the surface. The scenery was familiar to him—the sand masters came to this place every year to choose new members and award merits to old ones. It was almost a sacred place, though sand masters tended to be irreligious. None of the Kerla's Kerztian inhabitants came to this place—its sand was far too shallow to sustain a town. In fact, few even knew of its existence. It was a place of the sand masters.

And, for four years, it had been a place of embarrassment—to Kenton at least. Four years of standing before the entire population of the Diem, presenting himself for an advancement that would not be granted. He knew that most of the others considered him a fool—an arrogant fool. At times, he wondered if they might be right. Why did he keep pushing for a rank he did not deserve? Why not be satisfied with what Praxton was willing to give him?

Life in the Diem had not been easy for Kenton. Sand master society was ancient and stratified—new students were immediately given positions of leadership and favor based on their power. Those with lesser ability were made the virtual servants and attendants of those more talented—and such was a situation that continued up through the entire sand master hierarchy.

To them, power was everything. Kenton had watched the other acolents in his group, and seen how easily sand mastery came to them. They didn't have to stretch themselves, didn't have to learn how to control their sand. Their answer to any problem was to throw a dozen ribbons at it and hope it went away. Today, Kenton intended to prove that there was a better way.

Kenton paused, stopping abruptly. He had run out of ground—directly in front of him the sand-covered earth ended in a steep chasm. It rose again perhaps fifty feet away. He could barely make out a flag flapping on the other side of the gorge—a marker to indicate the direction he was to take.

*And so the real test begins,* Kenton thought, reaching down to grab a handful of sand from the ground. Another sand master, one more powerful, could have leapt the chasm, propelling himself through the air on a stream of sand. Kenton didn't have that option.

So, instead, he jumped off the cliff.

He plummeted toward the ground, his white robes flapping in the sudden wind. He didn't look down, instead concentrating on the sand clutched in his fist.

The sand burst to life.

With an explosion of light, the sand changed from bone white to shimmering mother-of-pearl. Kenton opened his hand as he fell, commanding the sand to move. It shot forward, forming into a ribbon of light that extended from his palm toward the quickly approaching dunes below.

When the sand had reached the ground, he commanded it to gather mass from the dunes below and move back up. A second later there was a shimmering line of mastered sand extending from Kenton to the ground. He was still falling, but as he commanded the sand to push, his descent slowed. The sand worked like a shimmering coil, slowing him more and more as he approached the ground. He came to a stop just a foot above the surface of the dunes, then stepped off the ribbon and dropped to the ground. As he did so, he released the ribbon from his control, and the shimmering sand immediately darkened and fell dead. No longer white, it was now a dull black, its energy spent.

Kenton jogged along the bottom of the ravine, forcing himself not to slow despite the fatigue of sand mastery. He was beginning to regret his insistence on bringing his sword—the weapon seemed to grow more and more heavy as he ran, dragging at his side.

Going along the bottom of the chasm instead of jumping was costing him precious time. He had already wasted about sixty minutes of his hour. He licked his lips, which were growing dry. Sand mastery didn't just take strength, it required water, sucking the precious liquid from the body of the sand master. A sand master had to be careful not to master to the point that his body took permanent damage from dehydration.

Kenton reached the second cliff and looked up, gathering his strength. In the distance he could see a group of white-robed forms. The mastrells, evaluating his progress. Even at a distance, Kenton could sense the finality in their postures. They assumed he was stuck—it was well known that Kenton could barely lift himself a few feet with his sand. Of course, that much in itself was amazing—no other sand master could do so much with only a single ribbon. Amazing or not, however, it wasn't enough to get him to the top of the cliff, which was at least a hundred feet tall.

The mastrells were turning their heads, discussing among themselves in voices far too distant to hear. Ignoring them, Kenton reached down and grabbed another handful of sand. He called it to life, feeling it begging to squirm and shimmer in his hand. The sand shone brightly—more brightly, even, than that of a mastrell. Kenton could only control one ribbon, but it was by far the most powerful ribbon any sand master had ever created.

*This had better work . . .* Kenton thought to himself.

He let the sand slip forward, dropping to the ground like a stream of water. There, he gathered more sand, calling to life as much as he could handle—enough to make a thin string perhaps twenty feet long. This time, however, he didn't form the sand into the ribbon. Instead he created a step.

He couldn't lift himself very far, true. The higher a sand master lifted himself in the air, the more sand was required, and Kenton could only control a relatively small amount. He could, however, hold himself in place.

Taking a breath, he stepped onto his small platform of sand, pressing his body against the rough stone cliff face. Then, holding on as best he could and not looking down, he began to inch sideways, dropping sand off one edge of the platform and replacing it on the other. He concentrated on making his sand cling to the cliff wall, slipping in cracks and holding to its imperfections, rather than pushing it against the ground. Slowly, Kenton moved to the side, sloping his platform of sand just enough that he moved in a diagonal direction up the wall.

He must have looked incredibly silly. Sand masters were supposed to flow and dance, soaring through the air in clouds of radiant sand, not creep up the side of a wall like a sleepy sandling. Still, the process worked, and barely a few minutes later he was nearing the top of the chasm. It was then that he noticed something—a small ledge about ten feet down the side of the cliff. Perched on the ledge was a small red sphere.

Kenton smiled in triumph, maladroitly climbing onto the top of the ledge. He then shook his rectangle of sand into a ribbon and sent it to collect the sphere. Guided by his commands, the rope of sand wrapped around the sphere and brought it back to its master. There were only two spheres left to find. Unfortunately, he had just over thirty minutes to do so.

The group of mastrells watched him with dumbfounded frowns as he jogged past the marking flag and located the next one in the distance. The rocks were growing more and more frequent now, forming caverns and walls of stone. Kenton moved along on the sandy ground, his eyes searching for any hints of red. The next sphere couldn't be far away—if he guessed right, the Path wound in a circle, and he was nearing the place where he had started. For a moment, his horror returned—had he missed two entire spheres?

A short distance away several lines of glimmering sand marked his silent followers. True to mastrell form, each of them was making a huge display of power, gathering as many ribbons of sand around them as they could manage. While it wasn't actually possible to fly with sand mastery, powerful mastrells could launch themselves in extended leaps that could span hundreds of feet. Each jumping mastrell left a trail of sand behind him—sand pushing against the ground to form a means of propulsion.

The mastrells stopped atop a pillar of rock a short distance away. Kenton slowed his jog to a walk, watching them with careful eyes. The place they landed looked too predetermined to be random—the sphere had to be somewhere close. Kenton searched around him, his eyes seeking out shadows and places that could hide one of the diminutive spheres. Unfortunately, there was no shortage of options.

A short distance away a large wall-like section of rock extended from the sand. It was filled with fist-sized holes, each one extending back into darkness. With a sinking feeling, Kenton realized that this was his next test.

*Any one of them could hold a sphere!* he thought with an internal moan. If he had been able to control two dozen ribbons, searching through the holes would have taken no time at all. However, using his single ribbon to do the same would probably take longer than he had left.

Yet, it appeared as if that were his only choice. Sighing, Kenton brought a handful of sand to life. Perhaps he would get lucky and choose the right hole. He paused, however, as he prepared to send the ribbon forth. There had to be a better way.

His eyes skimmed the rock wall. Ironically, one thing he had learned from his lack of ability was that sometimes sand mastery wasn't the answer. His eyes almost passed over the solution before his brain registered it. A small pile of black sand. There were only two things that could change sand from white to black—water or sand mastery.

Kenton smiled, approaching the discolored sand. It wasn't pure black, more of a dull grey. It had probably been recharging in the sunlight for a couple of hours now—a few more and it would be completely indistinguishable from the white sand around it. Kenton raised his eyes from the sand, looking at the wall directly above it. Just over his head he noticed a trail of black grains sitting on the lip of one of the holes.

Kenton reached into the hole, retrieving the red sandstone sphere that was hidden in its depths. Though there was a smile on his lips when he turned to look back at the mastrells, inwardly Kenton was worried. If the sand master who had hidden the spheres hadn't been careless—if he had used his hands instead of sand mastery—Kenton would never have found the sphere.

Still, he couldn't help feeling a sense of satisfaction as the mastrells jumped away, twisting ribbons of sand carrying them into the air. Now there was only one sphere left. If Kenton found it, he would have succeeded in a task that baffled many mastrells.

As he moved to begin running again, Kenton noticed that one of the mastrells had stayed behind. Even though the column of rock was far away, somehow Kenton knew that the stooped-over form belonged to his father. The wind wailed through rock hollows around Kenton as he stared up at Praxton's face.

The Lord Mastrell was not pleased. Kenton stared at him for a long moment, trying to project his defiance. Eventually, Praxton raised his hands, summoning a dozen strings of sand from the floor below. They twisted around him like living creatures, their bright translucent glow shifting from color to color in the way of mastered sand. When Praxton jumped, the ribbons threw him into the air, and Kenton was left alone beside the rock wall.

*One more.* Kenton took a deep breath and started to move again. He was running out of time—not only would the moon soon reappear, but he was beginning to feel the effects of his sand mastery. His mouth was parched, refusing to salivate, and his eyes were beginning to burn. His brow, which had been slick with sweat during the beginning of the run, was now crusted with salty residue. The price a sand master had to pay, the fuel that his art burned, was the water from his own body.

The dry mouth and eyes were the first signs that he was getting close to doing permanent damage to himself. The first thing a sand master learned was to keep track of his water, to pace himself so he didn't overmaster. Students who even approached the point of overmastery were severely punished.

*If only I could slatrify,* he thought, not for the first time. There was a reason the ability to change sand into water was the most valuable of sand mastery's skills.

Casting such thoughts aside, Kenton continued to jog. The rock walls were rising high around him again. Even as he began to think the area looked familiar, he rounded a corner and stopped. Up ahead he could just barely make out the rock plateau where he had begun the Path. The mastrells stood atop it, waiting for him to approach.

Kenton paused with a groan, leaning against the smooth rock wall.

His breath was beginning to come with more and more difficulty; both running and sand mastery sapped strength, and his dry throat made each breath painful. The mastrells held his qido and its water—he anticipated that first drink with such ferocity that he almost didn't care that he had failed.

And he had failed. Somewhere, back on the Path, he had missed one of the spheres. He had done well—four out of five was a respectable number. Some of the mastrells he knew had only found three. Unfortunately, Kenton couldn't afford anything less than perfection. Praxton wouldn't see the four spheres his son had found, but the one he had missed.

Kenton rested the back of his head against the rock for a moment. He briefly considered turning back to try to find the sphere, but he probably only had ten minutes left. That was barely enough time to make it back to the rock wall where he had found the last sphere. He opened his eyes and stood upright. He knew he had done better than anyone could have assumed.

Kenton kicked away the windblown sand that had gathered at his feet, striding out into the middle of the basin. Realistically, he knew that even a successful run of the Path wouldn't have changed Praxton's mind. The Lord Mastrell was as harsh as the sands themselves; few things impressed him.

Kenton picked up a handful of sand—he would have to use his step method to climb up the back of the rock basin and join the mastrells. He only paused for a moment to regard the strange rock formation around him. The sides were smooth and steep, almost forming a pit with a sand-filled bottom, perhaps fifty feet across. How many years had it taken the Kerla's dry winds to carve such an odd bowl-like formation?

Kenton froze, his abrupt stop kicking up a small spray of sand. As his eyes had scanned the basin, they fell on something so dumbfounding it almost caused him to trip in surprise. There, sitting in the middle of the circular flooring of sand, was a speck of red. It sat like a drop of blood, stark against the white background. Ripples in the sand had caused him to miss it earlier, but now there was no mistaking the red sphere.

Kenton looked up at the mastrells with confusion. They stood along the rim of the basin, their white robes fluttering, as if in unison, before the wind.

*Something's wrong.* There had to be more—some test. This was the last sphere. It should have been the most difficult to find.

Only a moment later he felt the sand begin to shift beneath his feet.

"*Aisha!*" Kenton yelped in surprise, jumping backward. It couldn't be . . .

The sand near the sphere began to churn like boiling water. There was something beneath it—something that was rising.

*Deep sand!* Kenton thought with shock. The sand-filled pit must go down farther than he had assumed.

A black form burst from the ground, burying the sphere in a wave of sand. Kenton gasped in amazement as he regarded the creature that slid from the ground. Sand streamed like water off the twenty-foot-tall monstrosity's carapace as it rose into the air. Its body was formed of bulbous, chitinous segments stacked on top of one another. A pair of arms sprouted from each "waist" where segments met, arms that were tipped with thick, jagged claws. Its head—if that was the right term—was little more than a box with deep black spots instead of eyes, with no visible mouth. The worst thing was, Kenton knew that the bulk of the creature's body was probably still hidden beneath the sands.

He was so busy staring that he was almost crushed as the creature swiped a claw in his direction. Kenton yelped, dodging to the side, dashing toward the wall of the basin. The sandling's body was huge—perhaps ten feet wide. Kenton was going to have a difficult time staying out of its way.

His body, invigorated by adrenaline and excitement, no longer responded sluggishly. His heart began to race, but his mind worked even faster. Kenton had read of deep sandlings, and even seen drawings of them, but he had never visited deep sand in person. Few people—even Kerztians—were foolish enough to wander onto deep sand. Mentally, he ran through the catalogue of deep sandlings he had studied, but this one didn't seem to fit any of the descriptions. Kenton dodged again as the sandling reached for him. The creature seemed to glide through the sand as if it were water—Kenton could barely see the thousands of tiny hairlike tentacles that lined the beast's carapace, the means by which it moved.

All observation was abandoned as the creature's claw slammed down in front of him. Kenton dropped to the sand, barely rolling out of the way as a second claw swiped through the air above him. The creature was incredibly fast—there was a reason deep sand was regarded with terror. The creatures that lurked within its depths were said to be nearly indestructible.

Kenton rolled to his feet, thankful for the hours he had spent sparring with soldiers from the Tower. His movements were quick and dexterous as he whipped his sword free with his left hand and grabbed a handful of sand in the other.

"We cannot intercede unless you ask!" a voice came from above. Kenton didn't spare a look upward, instead focusing on his foe. The creature had eyespots on each side of its head—it would not be easy to surprise. Of course, sandlings were said to have poorly developed sight. Their true sense was the sand itself. It was more than an ability to feel movement; for some reason sandlings could sense the location of even a completely still body. The Kerztians said deep sandlings could actually speak with the sand, though few from Lossand gave credence to their mysticisms.

"Didn't you hear me?" the voice repeated as Kenton dodged again. "Ask us to bring you out!" It belonged to Elorin. Kenton ignored him, calling his sand to life as he spun away from a claw. He raised his sword, deflecting a second attack. The creature's strength was such that his parry barely seemed to do much good, but it did allow him to dodge the attack just long enough to strike.

Even as he turned, Kenton raised his fist, commanding his sand forward. The sand tore out of his palm, streaking toward the sandling's head. It extended like a spear from Kenton's hand, leaving a glowing trail behind. The sand moved so quickly it seemed to scream in the air—Kenton might not be able to control dozens of lines at once, but when it came to a single ribbon, he was unmatched. No sand master could move sand with half as much speed or precision.

The sand snapped against the creature's shell of a head and immediately lost its luster, spraying to the sides like a stream of water hitting a stone wall. Kenton stood in confusion, so stunned that the creature's next attack took him in the side, throwing him back against the stone wall and ripping a deep gash in his shoulder. Kenton's sword dropped to the sand, slipping from stunned fingers.

The sandling was terken. It was impervious to sand mastery.

Kenton cursed again, feeling blood begin to flow from his shoulder. He had, of course, read of terken creatures, but they were supposed to be extremely rare. Only the most ancient and feared of deep sandlings—creatures said to be protected by the Sand Lord himself—had terken shells. How had one come to live here, in the middle of shallow sands and rock formations?

Regardless, it was obvious what he was supposed to do. All sandlings, whether from the deep sands or not, had one powerful weakness: water. The liquid could dissolve their carapaces, melting away their shell and skin, leaving behind nothing but sludge.

It made sense. The final challenge in the Mastrell's Path would test the most powerful of sand mastery's skills—the ability to change sand into water. With slatrification, a sand master could melt away the sandling's shell with barely a thought. Unfortunately, Kenton couldn't slatrify. Suddenly Elorin's suggestion that he escape made a great deal of sense.

Kenton cast his speculations aside, concentrating on staying alive. He was moving more and more slowly; he could feel himself weakening. Trying to ignore the pain of his shoulder, he stooped as he ran, grabbing another handful of sand. As the next attack came he used the mastered sand to give himself a boost, jumping high into the air and tumbling over the claws.

Kenton dropped heavily to the sand, then scrambled in the direction of the sandling's original position. Somewhere in that sand was the sphere. He didn't really need to kill the sandling; he just needed to find the sphere and get away.

He released his sand, dropping it to the ground black and stale. Instead, he placed his hand on the ground near where he had last seen the sphere. He called ribbon after ribbon to life, commanding them to jump away and then releasing them. Sand flew from the ground where he knelt; he commanded and released ribbons in such quick succession that it almost seemed like he could control more than one at a time.

Unfortunately, the sandling did not leave him to his digging. Kenton's jump had confused it, but it quickly reoriented itself. It came at him, the only sound of its movement that of sand rubbing against sand. Kenton continued to dig until the last moment, then dashed away, running desperately. He could feel the dryness on his skin, and each time he blinked his lids seemed to stick to his eyes. His lungs were beginning to burn, and his breaths came painfully. He was approaching the last of his water reserves—he would probably even be chastised for going this far. *For the good of the Diem, one mustn't even come close to overmastery,* the familiar teaching claimed. It was time to give up.

Just as he made the determination to escape, however, he saw it. Resting beside the far wall of the basin was a speck of red, brighter than the dark drops of his own blood that ran behind him. Crying out, Kenton switched directions, ducking beneath the sandling's arms and dashing so close to its body that he could smell the sulfurous pungency of its carapace.

And, as he ran by the creature, feeling the sand slither beneath his feet from the sandling's motion, he noticed an incredulous sight. There, trapped between two bowl-like chinks in the sandling's carapace, was another red sphere.

Kenton continued his dash, his mind confused. He stopped beside the wall, digging in the sand until his fingers found something round and hard. He pulled the sphere free, looking at it with a frown, then turned his eyes back on the sandling. From this angle he could see it distinctly—a red sphere, just like the five he had already found. There weren't five spheres on the Path, but six.

Kenton dropped the sphere into the pouch at his side, then turned eyes up to the edge of the cliff. Directly above he could see the faces of twenty mastrells looking down at him. He could escape now; his time was probably all but up anyway. He had won—he had found all five spheres. What was he waiting for?

For some reason he looked back at the sandling. Its shell and skin were terken, but its insides . . .

Kenton knew his father wouldn't be satisfied with perfection—he never was. Praxton would demand more. Well, Kenton would give him more.

The mastrells cried out in surprise as Kenton dashed away from the wall, his face resolute.

"Idiot boy!" Praxton's voice sounded behind him.

Kenton brought sand to life, whipping it past the creature and using it to snatch his discarded sword from the sand floor. The blade flashed through the air, carried on fingers of sand. Kenton caught it as he ducked beneath the sandling's first attack, grabbing a second handful of sand as he came up barely inches from the creature's chest.

With a cry of determination, Kenton slammed his sword into the creature's side. The blade slipped off a segment of carapace and crunched through a less-protected line of skin, digging deeply into the soft area between plates. Kenton jammed the weapon in with all the strength he had left.

Suddenly, his sword jerked, then ripped free from his hands, blasted backward by a powerful force. A loud hissing sound exploded from the cut. He had pierced the skin. Kenton caught a faceful of acrid gas—what sandlings had instead of blood—just before one of the monster's legs caught him full in the chest, flinging him into the air.

Even as he soared away from the creature, Kenton called the sand in his fist to life. He commanded it forward, driving it with all of his skill. Kenton slammed against the rock wall at the same time that his sand hit the creature's chest, yet he did not release control of his ribbon. He felt his body slump to the ground, but ignored the pain, commanding his sand to find the cut, to wiggle past the terken carapace into the creature's cavernous insides. He had to fight against air pressure and his own approaching unconsciousness, but he refused to release the sand.

He felt it break through, the resistance of the air pressure suddenly vanishing. With a final surge of effort, Kenton ordered the ribbon around wildly, slicing it through organs inside the monster's chest. The sandling began to shake and spasm as Kenton commanded the sand to move vaguely upward. A second later Kenton found the head, and the sandling grew rigid in a sudden motion, throwing sand in all directions. Then, as silent in death as it had been in life, the creature slumped to the side, its corpse sinking slightly in the sand before coming to a rest.

Kenton didn't know where he found the strength to stumble to his feet and cross the sand. He only vaguely remembered retrieving his sword and using it to pry the sixth sphere free from the creature's carapace.

One image remained stark in his mind, however—that of looking up at the ridge and seeing his father's hard, angry face. Just behind the Lord Mastrell, the enormous Mount KraeDa towered in the distance. As Kenton watched, the silvery edge of the moon began to peek out from behind the mountain.

# POSTSCRIPT

I was thinking that *Mistborn: Secret History* was the story in this collection that had the longest time between original idea and final publication, but then I remembered that this is in here.

What to say about *White Sand*? I'm thrilled to, at long last, be publishing this graphic novel. (And I'm very thankful to Dynamite, the publisher, for letting us include this excerpt in the collection.) *White Sand* started very long ago as a simple image: finding a body buried in the sand. The novel was the first I ever wrote—and also the eighth, as I started it over from scratch to try again once I'd learned more about writing. The excerpt you have here is from the 1999 version, not the 1995 version.

It's been a long, long road to publication for this story. I'm still very enamored of the world, and consider it a major part of the Cosmere. (The fact that Khriss is an important figure in the unfolding of these things should indicate that.) However, it was getting hard to plan when I'd be able to squeeze the novel in. I still have to finish so many books, I had no idea where to slot this trilogy in. Then Dynamite came to us and suggested the graphic novel. I was up for this from the get-go, as it was a way to get a canonical version of the story on shelves for readers faster than my schedule would otherwise allow.

As for the scene in question—well, you can see from it that my writing style starting with my very first book was focused on magic systems. At that point, I was reading a lot of The Wheel of Time and other similar books. I loved how powerful the characters were, but I wanted to create something that showed off someone who *wasn't* particularly powerful in the magic. Kenton was born out of me trying to figure out a magic where finesse would be as valuable as raw strength, and sand mastery grew completely out of that.

The idea of a test he had to complete (one many believed he wouldn't be able to pass) using the magic seemed the perfect way to show this off. Indeed, it worked out great—and boy does it pop off the page in graphic novel form. Of all my magic systems, this one seems the best for this medium, because it's so visual.

# THE THRENODITE SYSTEM

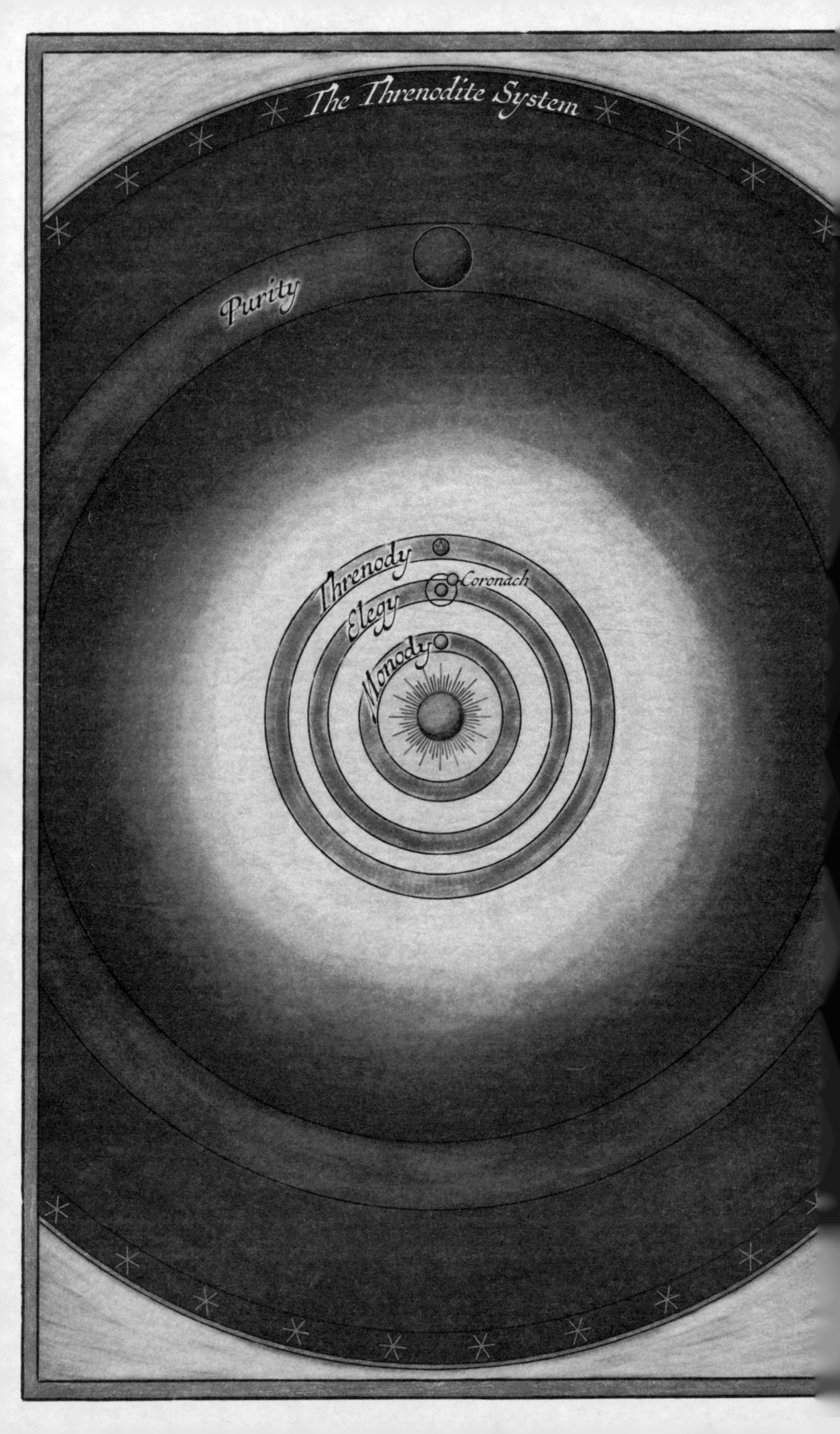

The Threnodite System
Purity
Threnody
Coronach
Elegy
Monody

# THE THRENODITE SYSTEM

The Threnodite system is a site warped by an ancient conflict. Long ago, soon after the Shattering, Odium clashed with (and mortally wounded) the Shard Ambition here. Ambition would later be Splintered, though that final act took place in a different location.

The direct clash between two Shards of Adonalsium had a profound effect on the planets of this system. Though the actual battle took place in the vast space between planets—and though the true contest happened mostly in other Realms—the ripples of destruction and change washed through the system. Investigations into how this changed the other planets of the system have been fruitless, as none of them have perpendicularities to allow physical visitation.

Fortunately I have personal access to someone from Threnody, the third planet in the system. Judging by the records that Nazh has provided, I have concluded that some measure of Investiture must have existed on this planet before the battle between Shards. However, the waves of destruction—carrying ripped-off chunks of Ambition's power—twisted both the people and the planet of Threnody.

The planet is home to two separate continents. The larger of the two has been abandoned to something known as "the Evil," a force that even Nazh can speak of only in vague terms. A creeping darkness, a terrible force that consumed the entirety of the continent, feasting upon the souls of men. I do not know how much of this is metaphoric, and how much literal. Expeditions sent from the smaller continent to explore have vanished, and the place is dangerous to visit even in the Cognitive Realm.

The smaller continent is a frontier, mostly unexplored and unnamed, with several bastions of civilization. I have visited one of the largest of these, and even it feels unfinished—set up haphazardly by refugees fleeing across the ocean, lacking some basic necessities. They focused on making it a fortress first, and a home second. This makes sense, as the people there live in constant fear that the Evil will find a way across the ocean.

Or perhaps they fear the spirits of the dead. People on Threnody are afflicted with a particular ailment that—upon death—sometimes turns them into what we call a Cognitive Shadow. I will leave aside the nature of whether or not a Cognitive Shadow is actually the soul of the person—this is a question for a theologian or a philosopher.

I can, however, explain what is happening magically. A spirit infused with extra Investiture will often imprint upon that very power. Much as the spren of Roshar become self-aware over time because of people's focus on the Surges as being alive, this excess Investiture can attain the ability to remain sapient after being separated from its Physical form.

Locally they think of these things as ghosts, though really they are instantiations of self-aware (well, in this case, barely self-aware) Investiture. This is an area deserving of more research. Unfortunately, visiting the planet is difficult, as there is no stable perpendicularity—only very unstable ones that cannot be predicted easily, and have a somewhat morbid origin.

# SHADOWS FOR SILENCE IN THE FORESTS OF HELL

"THE one you have to watch for is the White Fox," Daggon said, sipping his beer. "They say he shook hands with the Evil itself, that he visited the Fallen World and came back with strange powers. He can kindle fire on even the deepest of nights, and no shade will dare come for his soul. Yes, the White Fox. Meanest bastard in these parts for sure. Pray he doesn't set his eyes on you, friend. If he does, you're dead."

Daggon's drinking companion had a neck like a slender wine bottle and a head like a potato stuck sideways on the top. He squeaked as he spoke, a Lastport accent, voice echoing in the eaves of the waystop's common room. "Why . . . why would he set his eyes on me?"

"That depends, friend," Daggon said, looking about as a few overdressed merchants sauntered in. They wore black coats, ruffled lace poking out the front, and the tall-topped, wide-brimmed hats of fortfolk. They wouldn't last two weeks out here in the Forests.

"It depends?" Daggon's dining companion prompted. "It depends on what?"

"On a lot of things, friend. The White Fox is a bounty hunter, you know. What crimes have you committed? What have you done?"

"Nothing." That squeak was like a rusty wheel.

"Nothing? Men don't come out into the Forests to do 'nothing,' friend."

His companion glanced from side to side. He'd given his name as Earnest. But then, Daggon had given his name as Amity. Names didn't mean a whole lot in the Forests. Or maybe they meant everything. The right ones, that was.

Earnest leaned back, scrunching down that fishing-pole neck of his as if trying to disappear into his beer. He'd bite. People liked hearing about the White Fox, and Daggon considered himself an expert. At least, he was an expert at telling stories to get ratty men like Earnest to pay for his drinks.

*I'll give him some time to stew,* Daggon thought, smiling to himself. *Let him worry.* Earnest would ply him for more information in a bit.

While he waited, Daggon leaned back, surveying the room. The merchants were making a nuisance of themselves, calling for food, saying they meant to be on their way in an hour. That *proved* them to be fools. Traveling at night in the Forests? Good homesteader stock would do it. Men like these, though . . . they'd probably take less than an hour to violate one of the Simple Rules and bring the shades upon them. Daggon put the idiots out of his mind.

That fellow in the corner, though . . . dressed all in brown, still wearing his hat despite being indoors. That fellow looked truly dangerous. *I wonder if it's him,* Daggon thought. So far as he knew, nobody had ever seen the White Fox and lived. Ten years, over a hundred bounties turned in. Surely someone knew his name. The authorities in the forts paid him the bounties, after all.

The waystop's owner, Madam Silence, passed by the table and deposited Daggon's meal with an unceremonious thump. Scowling, she topped off his beer, spilling a sudsy dribble onto his hand, before limping off. She was a stout woman. Tough. Everyone in the Forests was tough. The ones that survived, at least.

He'd learned that a scowl from Silence was just her way of saying hello. She'd given him an extra helping of venison; she often did that. He liked to think that she had a fondness for him. Maybe someday . . .

*Don't be a fool,* he thought to himself as he dug into the heavily gravied food and took a few gulps of his beer. Better to marry a stone than Silence Montane. A stone showed more affection. Likely she gave him the extra slice because she recognized the value of a repeat customer. Fewer and fewer people came this way lately. Too many shades. And then there was Chesterton. Nasty business, that.

"So . . . he's a bounty hunter, this Fox?" The man who called himself Earnest seemed to be sweating.

Daggon smiled. Hooked right good, this one was. "He's not just a bounty hunter. He's *the* bounty hunter. Though the White Fox doesn't go for the small-timers—and no offense, friend, but you seem pretty small-time."

His friend grew more nervous. What *had* he done? "But," the man stammered, "he wouldn't come for me—er, pretending I'd done something, of course—anyway, he wouldn't come in here, would he? I mean, Madam Silence's waystop, it's protected. Everyone knows that. Shade of her dead husband lurks here. I had a cousin who saw it, I did."

"The White Fox doesn't fear shades," Daggon said, leaning in. "Now, mind you, I don't *think* he'd risk coming in here—but not because of some shade. Everyone knows this is neutral ground. You've got to have some safe places, even in the Forests. But . . ."

Daggon smiled at Silence as she passed him by, on the way to the kitchens again. This time she didn't scowl at him. He was getting through to her for certain.

"But?" Earnest squeaked.

"Well . . ." Daggon said. "I could tell you a few things about how the White Fox takes men, but you see, my beer is nearly empty. A shame. I think you'd be very interested in how the White Fox caught Makepeace Hapshire. Great story, that."

Earnest squeaked for Silence to bring another beer, though she bustled into the kitchen and didn't hear. Daggon frowned, but Earnest put a coin on the side of the table, indicating he'd like a refill when Silence or her daughter returned. That would do. Daggon smiled to himself and launched into the story.

---

Silence Montane closed the door to the common room, then turned and pressed her back against it. She tried to still her racing heart by breathing in and out. Had she made any obvious signs? Did they know she'd recognized them?

William Ann passed by, wiping her hands on a cloth. "Mother?" the young woman asked, pausing. "Mother, are you—"

"Fetch the book. Quickly, child!"

William Ann's face went pale, then she hurried into the back pantry. Silence clutched her apron to still her nerves, then joined William Ann as the girl came out of the pantry with a thick, leather satchel. White flour dusted its cover and spine from the hiding place.

Silence took the satchel and opened it on the high kitchen counter, revealing a collection of loose-leaf papers. Most had faces drawn on them. As Silence rifled through the pages, William Ann moved to the peephole for spying into the common room.

For a few moments, the only sound to accompany Silence's thumping heart was that of hastily turned pages.

"It's the man with the long neck, isn't it?" William Ann asked. "I remember his face from one of the bounties."

"That's just Lamentation Winebare, a petty horse thief. He's barely worth two measures of silver."

"Who, then? The man in the back, with the hat?"

Silence shook her head, finding a sequence of pages at the bottom of her pile. She inspected the drawings. *God Beyond,* she thought. *I can't decide if I want it to be them or not.* At least her hands had stopped shaking.

William Ann scurried back and craned her neck over Silence's shoulder. At fourteen, the girl was already taller than her mother. A fine thing to suffer, a child taller than you. Though William Ann grumbled about being awkward and lanky, her slender build foreshadowed a beauty to come. She took after her father.

"Oh, God *Beyond*," William Ann said, raising a hand to her mouth. "You mean—"

"Chesterton Divide," Silence said. The shape of the chin, the look in the eyes . . . they were the same. "He walked right into our hands, with four of his men." The bounty on those five would be enough to pay her supply needs for a year. Maybe two.

Her eyes flickered to the words below the pictures, printed in harsh, bold letters. **Extremely dangerous. Wanted for murder, rape, extortion.** And, of course, there was the big one at the end: **And assassination.**

Silence had always wondered if Chesterton and his men had intended to kill the governor of the most powerful fort city on this continent, or if it had been an accident. A simple robbery gone wrong. Either way, Chesterton understood what he'd done. Before the incident, he had been a common—if accomplished—highway bandit.

Now he was something greater, something far more dangerous. Chesterton knew that if he were captured, there would be no mercy, no quarter. Lastport had painted Chesterton as an anarchist, a menace, and a psychopath.

Chesterton had no reason to hold back. So he didn't.

*Oh, God Beyond,* Silence thought, looking at the continuing list of his crimes on the next page.

Beside her, William Ann whispered the words to herself. "He's out there?" she asked. "But where?"

"The merchants," Silence said.

"*What?*" William Ann rushed back to the peephole. The wood there—indeed, all around the kitchen—had been scrubbed so hard that it had been bleached white. Sebruki had been cleaning again.

"I can't see it," William Ann said.

"Look closer." Silence hadn't seen it at first either, even though she spent each night with the book, memorizing its faces.

A few moments later William Ann gasped, raising her hand to her mouth. "That seems so *foolish* of him. Why is he going about perfectly visible like this? Even in disguise."

"Everyone will remember just another band of fool merchants from the fort who thought they could brave the Forests. It's a clever ruse. When they vanish from the paths in a few days, it will be assumed—if anyone cares to wonder—that the shades got them. Besides, this way Chesterton can travel quickly and in the open, visiting waystops and listening for information."

Was this how Chesterton discovered good targets to hit? Had they come through her waystop before? The thought made her stomach turn. She had fed criminals many times; some were regulars. Every man was probably a criminal out in the Forests, if only for ignoring taxes imposed by the fortfolk.

Chesterton and his men were different. She didn't need the list of crimes to know what they were capable of doing.

"Where's Sebruki?" Silence said.

William Ann shook herself, as if coming out of a stupor. "She's feeding the pigs. Shadows! You don't think they'd recognize her, do you?"

"No," Silence said. "I'm worried she'll recognize them." Sebruki might only be eight, but she could be shockingly—disturbingly—observant.

Silence closed the book of bounties. She rested her fingers on the satchel's leather.

"We're going to kill them, aren't we?" William Ann asked.

"Yes."

"How much are they worth?"

"Sometimes, child, it's not about what a man is worth." Silence heard the faint lie in her voice. Times were increasingly tight, with the price of silver from both Bastion Hill and Lastport on the rise.

Sometimes it wasn't about what a man was worth. But this wasn't one of those times.

"I'll get the poison." William Ann left the peephole and crossed the room.

"Something light, child," Silence cautioned. "These are dangerous men. They'll notice if things are out of the ordinary."

"I'm not a fool, Mother," William Ann said dryly. "I'll use fenweed. They won't taste it in the beer."

"Half dose. I don't want them collapsing at the table."

William Ann nodded, entering the old storage room, where she closed the door and began prying up floorboards to get to the poisons. Fenweed would leave the men cloudy-headed and dizzy, but wouldn't kill them.

Silence didn't dare risk something more deadly. If suspicion ever came back to her waystop, her career—and likely her life—would end. She needed to remain, in the minds of travelers, the crotchety but fair innkeeper who didn't ask too many questions. Her waystop was a place of perceived safety, even for the roughest of criminals. She bedded down each night with a heart full of fear that someone would realize a suspicious number of the White Fox's bounties stayed at Silence's waystop in the days preceding their demise.

She went into the pantry to put away the bounty book. Here, too, the walls had been scrubbed clean, the shelves freshly sanded and dusted. That child. Who had heard of a child who would rather clean than play? Of course, given what Sebruki had been through . . .

Silence could not help reaching onto the top shelf and feeling the crossbow she kept there. Silver boltheads. She kept it for shades, and hadn't yet turned it against a man. Drawing blood was too dangerous in the Forests. It still comforted her to know that in case of a true emergency, she had the weapon at hand.

Bounty book stowed, she went to check on Sebruki. The child was indeed caring for the pigs. Silence liked to keep a healthy stock, though of course not for eating. Pigs were said to ward away shades. She used any tool she could to make the waystop seem more safe.

Sebruki knelt inside the pig shack. The short girl had dark skin and long, black hair. Nobody would have taken her for Silence's daughter, even if they hadn't heard of Sebruki's unfortunate history. The child hummed to herself, scrubbing at the wall of the enclosure.

"Child?" Silence asked.

Sebruki turned to her and smiled. What a difference one year could make. Once, Silence would have sworn that this child would never smile again. Sebruki had spent her first three months at the waystop staring at walls. No matter where Silence had put her, the child had moved to the nearest wall, sat down, and stared at it all day. Never speaking a word. Eyes dead as those of a shade . . .

"Aunt Silence?" Sebruki asked. "Are you well?"

"I'm fine, child. Just plagued by memories. You're . . . cleaning the *pig shack* now?"

"The walls need a good scrubbing," Sebruki said. "The pigs do so like it to be clean. Well, Jarom and Ezekiel prefer it that way. The others don't seem to care."

"You don't need to clean so hard, child."

"I like doing it," Sebruki said. "It feels good. It's something I can do. To help."

Well, it was better to clean the walls than stare blankly at them all day. Today, Silence was happy for anything that kept the child busy. Anything, so long as she didn't enter the common room.

"I think the pigs will like it," Silence said. "Why don't you keep at it in here for a while?"

Sebruki eyed her. "What's wrong?"

Shadows. She was so observant. "There are some men with rough tongues in the common room," Silence said. "I won't have you picking up their cussing."

"I'm not a child, Aunt Silence."

"Yes you are," Silence said firmly. "And you'll obey. Don't think I won't take a switch to your backside."

Sebruki rolled her eyes, but went back to work and began humming to herself. Silence let a little of her grandmother's ways out when she spoke with Sebruki. The child responded well to sternness. She seemed to crave it, perhaps as a symbol that someone was in control.

Silence wished she actually were in control. But she was a Forescout—the surname taken by her grandparents and the others who had left Homeland first and explored this continent. Yes, she was a Forescout, and she'd be damned before she'd let anyone know how absolutely powerless she felt much of the time.

Silence crossed the backyard of the large inn, noting William Ann inside the kitchen mixing a paste to dissolve in the beer. Silence passed her by and looked in on the stable. Unsurprisingly, Chesterton had said they'd be leaving after their meal. While a lot of folk sought the relative safety of a waystop at night, Chesterton and his men would be accustomed to sleeping in the Forests. Even with the shades about, they would feel more comfortable in a camp of their own devising than they would in a waystop bed.

Inside the stable, Dob—the old stable hand—had just finished brushing down the horses. He wouldn't have watered them. Silence had a standing order to not do that until last.

"This is well done, Dob," Silence said. "Why don't you take your break now?"

He nodded to her with a mumbled, "Thank'ya, mam." He'd find the front porch and his pipe, as always. Dob hadn't two wits to rub together, and he hadn't a clue about what she really did at the waystop, but he'd been with her since before William's death. He was as loyal a man as she'd ever found.

Silence shut the door after him, then fetched some pouches from the locked cabinet at the rear of the stable. She checked each one in the dim light, then set them on the grooming table and heaved the first saddle onto its owner's back.

She was near finished with the saddling when the door eased open. She froze, immediately thinking of the pouches on the table. Why hadn't she stuffed them in her apron? Sloppy!

"Silence Forescout," a smooth voice said from the doorway.

Silence stifled a groan and turned to confront her visitor. "Theopolis," she said. "It's not polite to sneak about on a woman's property. I should have you thrown out for trespassing."

"Now, now. That would be rather like . . . the horse kicking at the man who feeds him, hmmm?" Theopolis leaned his gangly frame against the doorway, folding his arms. He wore simple clothing, no markings of his station. A fort tax collector often didn't want random passers to know of his profession. Clean-shaven, his face always had that same patronizing smile on it. His clothing was too clean, too new to be that of one who lived out in the Forests. Not that he was a dandy, nor was he a fool. Theopolis was dangerous, just a different kind of dangerous from most.

"Why are you here, Theopolis?" she said, hefting the last saddle onto the back of a snorting roan gelding.

"Why do I always come to you, Silence? It's not because of your cheerful countenance, hmmm?"

"I'm paid up on taxes."

"That's because you're mostly exempt from taxes," Theopolis said. "But you haven't paid me for last month's shipment of silver."

"Things have been a little dry lately. It's coming."

"And the bolts for your crossbow?" Theopolis asked. "One wonders if you're trying to forget about the price of those silver boltheads, hmmm? And the shipment of replacement sections for your protection rings?"

His whining accent made her wince as she buckled the saddle on. Theopolis. Shadows, what a day!

"Oh my," Theopolis said, walking over to the grooming table. He picked up one of the pouches. "What are these, now? That looks like wetleek sap. I've heard that it glows at night if you shine the right kind of light upon it. Is this one of the White Fox's mysterious secrets?"

She snatched the pouch away. "Don't say that name," she hissed.

He grinned. "You have a bounty! Delightful. I have always wondered how you tracked them. Poke a pinhole in that, attach it to the underside of the saddle, then follow the dripping trail it leaves? Hmmm? You could probably track them a long way, kill them far from here. Keep suspicion off the little waystop?"

Yes, Theopolis was dangerous, but she needed *someone* to turn in her bounties for her. Theopolis was a rat, and like all rats he knew the best holes, troughs, and crannies. He had connections in Lastport, and had managed to get her the money in the name of the White Fox without revealing her.

"I've been tempted to turn you in lately, you know," Theopolis said. "Many a group keeps a betting pool on the identity of the infamous Fox. I could be a rich man with this knowledge, hmmm?"

"You're already a rich man," she snapped. "And though you're many things, you are not an idiot. This has worked just fine for a decade. Don't tell me you'd trade wealth for a little notoriety?"

He smiled, but did not contradict her. He kept half of what she earned from each bounty. It was a fine arrangement for Theopolis. No danger to him, which was how she knew he liked it. He was a civil servant, not a bounty hunter. The only time she'd seen him kill, the man he'd murdered couldn't fight back.

"You know me too well, Silence," Theopolis said with a laugh. "Too well indeed. My, my. A bounty! I wonder who it is. I'll have to go look in the common room."

"You'll do nothing of the sort. Shadows! You think the face of a tax collector won't spook them? Don't you go walking in and spoiling things."

"Peace, Silence," he said, still grinning. "I obey your rules. I am careful not to show myself around here often, and I don't bring suspicion to you. I couldn't stay today anyway; I merely came to give you an offer. Only now you probably won't need it! Ah, such a pity. After all the trouble I went to in your name, hmmm?"

She felt cold. "What help could you possibly give me?"

He took a sheet of paper from his satchel, then carefully unfolded it with too-long fingers. He moved to hold it up, but she snatched it from him.

"What is this?"

"A way to relieve you of your debt, Silence! A way to prevent you from ever having to worry again."

The paper was a writ of seizure, an authorization for Silence's creditors—Theopolis—to claim her property as payment. The forts claimed jurisdiction over the roadways and the land to either side of them. They did send soldiers out to patrol them. Occasionally.

"I take it back, Theopolis," she spat. "You most certainly *are* a fool. You'd give up everything we have for a greedy land snatch?"

"Of course not, Silence. This wouldn't be giving up anything at all! Why, I *do* so feel bad seeing you constantly in my debt. Wouldn't it be more efficient if I took over the finances of the waystop? You would remain working here, and hunting bounties, as you always have. Only, you would no longer have to worry about your debts, hmmm?"

She crumpled the paper in her hand. "You'd turn me and mine into slaves, Theopolis."

"Oh, don't be so dramatic. Those in Lastport have begun to worry that such an important waypoint as this is owned by an unknown element. You are drawing attention, Silence. I should think that is the last thing you want."

Silence crumpled the paper further in her hand, fist tight. Horses shuffled in their stalls. Theopolis grinned.

"Well," he said. "Perhaps it won't be needed. Perhaps this bounty of yours is a big one, hmmm? Any clues to give me, so I don't sit wondering all day?"

"Get out," she whispered.

"Dear Silence," he said. "Forescout blood, stubborn to the last breath. They say your grandparents were the first of the first. The first people to come scout this continent, the first to homestead the Forests . . . the first to stake a claim on hell itself."

"Don't call the Forests that. This is my home."

"But it is how men saw this land, before the Evil. Doesn't that make you curious? Hell, land of the damned, where the shadows of the dead made their home. I keep wondering: Is there really a shade of your departed husband guarding this place, or is it just another story you tell people? To make them feel safe, hmmm? You spend a fortune in silver. That offers the real protection, and I never *have* been able to find a record of your marriage. Of course, if there wasn't one, that would make dear William Ann a—"

"*Go.*"

He grinned, but tipped his hat to her and stepped out. She heard him climb into the saddle, then ride off. Night would soon fall; it was probably too much to hope that the shades would take Theopolis. She'd long suspected that he had a hiding hole somewhere near, probably a cavern he kept lined with silver.

She breathed in and out, trying to calm herself. Theopolis was frustrating, but he didn't know everything. She forced her attention back to the horses and got out a bucket of water. She dumped the contents of the pouches into it, then gave a hearty dose to the horses, who each drank thirstily.

Pouches that dripped sap in the way Theopolis indicated would be too easy to spot. What would happen when her bounties removed their saddles at night and found the pouches? They'd know someone was coming for them. No, she needed something less obvious.

"How am I going to manage this?" she whispered as a horse drank from her bucket. "Shadows. They're reaching for me on all sides."

*Kill Theopolis.* That was probably what Grandmother would have done. She considered it.

*No,* she thought. *I won't become that. I won't become her.* Theopolis was a thug and a scoundrel, but he had not broken any laws, nor had he done anyone direct harm that she knew. There had to be rules, even out here.

There had to be lines. Perhaps in that respect, she wasn't so different from the fortfolk.

She'd find another way. Theopolis only had a writ of debt; he had been required to show it to her. That meant she had a day or two to come up with his money. All neat and orderly. In the fort cities, they claimed to have civilization. Those rules gave her a chance.

She left the stable. A glance through the window into the common room showed her William Ann delivering drinks to the "merchants" of Chesterton's gang. Silence stopped to watch.

Behind her, the Forests shivered in the wind.

Silence listened, then turned to face them. You could tell fortfolk by the way they refused to face the Forests. They averted their eyes, never looking into the depths. Those solemn trees covered almost every inch of this continent, those leaves shading the ground. Still. Silent. Animals lived out there, but fort surveyors declared that there were no predators. The shades had gotten those long ago, drawn by the shedding of blood.

Staring into the Forests seemed to make them . . . retreat. The darkness of their depths withdrew, the stillness gave way to the sound of rodents picking through fallen leaves. A Forescout knew to look the Forests straight on. A Forescout knew that the surveyors were wrong. There *was* a predator out there. The Forest itself was one.

Silence turned and walked to the door into the kitchen. Keeping the waystop had to be her first goal, so she was committed to collecting Chesterton's bounty now. If she couldn't pay Theopolis, she had little faith that everything would stay the same. He'd have a hand around her throat, as she couldn't leave the waystop. She had no fort citizenship, and times were too tight for the local homesteaders to take her in. No, she'd *have* to stay and work the waystop for Theopolis, and he would squeeze her dry, taking larger and larger percentages of the bounties.

She pushed open the door to the kitchen. It—

Sebruki sat at the kitchen table holding the crossbow in her lap.

"God Beyond!" Silence gasped, pulling the door closed as she stepped inside. "Child, what are you—"

Sebruki looked up at her. Those haunted eyes were back, eyes void of life and emotion. Eyes like a shade's.

"We have visitors, Aunt Silence," Sebruki said in a cold, monotone voice. The crossbow's winding crank sat next to her. She had managed to load the thing and cock it, all on her own. "I coated the bolt's tip with blackblood. I did that right, didn't I? That way, the poison will kill him for sure."

"Child . . ." Silence stepped forward.

Sebruki turned the crossbow in her lap, holding it at an angle to support it, one small hand on the trigger. The point turned toward Silence.

Sebruki stared ahead, eyes blank.

"This won't work, Sebruki," Silence said, stern. "Even if you were able to lift that thing into the common room, you wouldn't hit him—and even if you did, his men would kill us all in retribution!"

"I wouldn't mind," Sebruki said softly. "So long as I got to kill him. So long as I pulled the trigger."

"You care nothing for us?" Silence snapped. "I take you in, give you a home, and this is your payment? You steal a weapon? You *threaten* me?"

Sebruki blinked.

"What is wrong with you?" Silence said. "You'd shed blood in this place of sanctuary? Bring the shades down upon us, beating at our protections? If they got through, they'd kill everyone under my roof! People I've promised safety. How *dare* you!"

Sebruki shook, as if coming awake. Her mask broke and she dropped the crossbow. Silence heard a snap, and the catch released. She felt the bolt pass within an inch of her cheek, then break the window behind.

Shadows! Had the bolt grazed Silence? Had Sebruki *drawn blood*? Silence reached up with a shaking hand, but blessedly felt no blood. The bolt hadn't hit her.

A moment later Sebruki was in her arms, sobbing. Silence knelt down, holding the child close. "Hush, dear one. It's all right. It's all right."

"I heard it all," Sebruki whispered. "Mother never cried out. She knew I was there. She was strong, Aunt Silence. That was why I could be strong, even when the blood came down. Soaking my hair. I heard it. *I heard it all.*"

Silence closed her eyes, holding Sebruki tight. She herself had been the only one willing to investigate the smoking homestead. Sebruki's father had stayed at the waystop on occasion. A good man. As good a man as was left after the Evil took Homeland, that was.

In the smoldering remains of the homestead, Silence had found the corpses of a dozen people. Each family member had been slaughtered by Chesterton and his men, right down to the children. The only one left had been Sebruki, the youngest, who had been shoved into the crawl space under the floorboards in the bedroom.

She'd lain there, soaked in her mother's blood, soundless even as Silence found her. She'd only discovered the girl because Chesterton had been careful, lining the room with silver dust to protect against shades as he prepared to kill. Silence had tried to recover some of the dust that had trickled between the floorboards, and had run across eyes staring up at her through the slits.

Chesterton had burned thirteen different homesteads over the last year. Over fifty people murdered. Sebruki was the only one who had escaped him.

The girl trembled as she heaved with sobs. "Why . . . Why?"

"There is no reason. I'm sorry." What else could she do? Offer some foolish platitude or comfort about the God Beyond? These were the Forests. You didn't survive on platitudes.

Silence did hold the girl until her crying began to subside. William Ann entered, then stilled beside the kitchen table, holding a tray of empty mugs. Her eyes flickered toward the fallen crossbow, then at the broken window.

"You'll kill him?" Sebruki whispered. "You'll bring him to justice?"

"Justice died in Homeland," Silence said. "But yes, I'll kill him. I promise it to you, child."

Stepping timidly, William Ann picked up the crossbow, then turned it, displaying its now broken bow. Silence breathed out. She should never have left the thing where Sebruki could get to it.

"Care for the patrons, William Ann," Silence said. "I'll take Sebruki upstairs."

William Ann nodded, glancing at the broken window again.

"No blood was shed," Silence said. "We will be fine. Though if you get a moment, see if you can find the bolt. The head is silver." This was hardly a time when they could afford to waste money.

William Ann stowed the crossbow in the pantry as Silence carefully set Sebruki on a kitchen stool. The girl clung to her, refusing to let go, so Silence relented and held her for a time longer.

William Ann took a few deep breaths, as if to calm herself, then pushed back out into the common room to distribute drinks.

Eventually, Sebruki let go long enough for Silence to mix a draught. She carried the girl up the stairs to the loft above the common room, where the three of them made their beds. Dob slept in the stable and the guests in the nicer rooms on the second floor.

"You're going to make me sleep," Sebruki said, regarding the cup with reddened eyes.

"The world will seem a brighter place in the morning," Silence said. *And I can't risk you sneaking out after me tonight.*

The girl reluctantly took the draught, then drank it down. "I'm sorry. About the crossbow."

"We will find a way for you to work off the cost of fixing it."

That seemed to comfort Sebruki. She was a homesteader, Forests born. "You used to sing to me at night," Sebruki said softly, closing her eyes, lying back. "When you first brought me here. After . . . After . . ." She swallowed.

"I wasn't certain you noticed." Silence hadn't been certain Sebruki noticed anything, during those times.

"I did."

Silence sat down on the stool beside Sebruki's cot. She didn't feel like singing, so she began humming. It was the lullaby she'd sung to William Ann during the hard times right after her birth.

Before long, the words came out, unbidden:

"Hush now, my dear one . . . be not afraid. Night comes upon us, but sunlight will break. Sleep now, my dear one . . . let your tears fade. Darkness surrounds us, but someday we'll wake. . . ."

She held Sebruki's hand until the child fell asleep. The window by the bed overlooked the courtyard, so Silence could see as Dob brought out Chesterton's horses. The five men in their fancy merchant clothing stomped down off the porch and climbed into their saddles.

They rode in a file out onto the roadway; then the Forests enveloped them.

One hour after nightfall, Silence packed her rucksack by the light of the hearth.

Her grandmother had kindled that hearth's flame, and it had been burning ever since. She'd nearly lost her life lighting the fire, but she hadn't been willing to pay any of the fire merchants for a start. Silence shook her head. Grandmother always had bucked convention. But then, was Silence any better?

*Don't kindle flame, don't shed the blood of another, don't run at night. These things draw shades.* The Simple Rules, by which every homesteader lived. She'd broken all three on more than one occasion. It was a wonder she hadn't been withered away into a shade by now.

The fire's warmth seemed a distant thing as she prepared to kill. Silence glanced at the old shrine, really just a closet, that she kept locked. The flames reminded her of her grandmother. At times, she thought of the fire *as* her grandmother. Defiant of both the shades and the forts, right until the end. She'd purged the waystop of other reminders of Grandmother, all save the shrine to the God Beyond. That was set behind a locked door beside the pantry, and next to the door had once hung her grandmother's silver dagger, symbol of the old religion.

That dagger was etched with the symbols of divinity as a warding. Silence now carried it in a sheath at her side, not for its wardings, but because it was silver. One could never have too much silver in the Forests.

She packed the sack carefully, first putting in her medicine kit and then a good-sized pouch of silver dust to heal withering. She followed that with ten empty sacks of thick burlap, tarred on the inside to prevent their contents from leaking. Finally, she added an oil lamp. She wouldn't want to use it, as she didn't trust fire. Fire could draw shades. However, she'd found it useful to have on prior outings, so she brought it. She'd only light it if she ran across someone who already had a fire started.

Once done, she hesitated, then went to the old storage room. She removed the floorboards and took out the small, dry-packed keg that lay beside the poisons.

Gunpowder.

"Mother?" William Ann asked, causing her to jump. She hadn't heard the girl enter the kitchen.

Silence nearly dropped the keg in her startlement, and that nearly stopped her heart. She cursed herself for a fool, tucking the keg under her arm. It couldn't explode without fire. She knew that much.

"Mother!" William Ann said, looking at the keg.

"I probably won't need it."

"But—"

"I know. Hush." She walked over and placed the keg into her sack. Attached to the side of the keg, with cloth stuffed between the metal arms, was her grandmother's firestarter. Igniting gunpowder counted as kindling flames, at least in the eyes of the shades. It drew them almost as quickly as blood did, day or night. The early refugees from Homeland had discovered that in short order.

In some ways, blood was easier to avoid. A simple nosebleed or issue of blood wouldn't draw the shades; they wouldn't even notice. It had to be the blood of another, shed by your hands—and they would go for the one who shed the blood first. Of course, after that person was dead, they often didn't care who they killed next. Once enraged, shades were dangerous to all nearby.

Only after Silence had the gunpowder packed did she notice that William Ann was dressed for traveling in trousers and boots. She carried a sack like Silence's.

"What do you think you're about, William Ann?" Silence asked.

"You intend to kill five men who had only half a dose of fenweed by yourself, Mother?"

"I've done similar before. I've learned to work on my own."

"Only because you didn't have anyone else to help." William Ann slung her sack onto her shoulder. "That's no longer the case."

"You're too young. Go back to bed; watch the waystop until I return."

William Ann showed no signs of budging.

"Child, I told you—"

"Mother," William Ann said, taking her arm firmly, "you aren't a *youth* anymore! You think I don't see your limp getting worse? You can't do everything by yourself! You're going to have to start letting me help you sometime, dammit!"

Silence regarded her daughter. Where had that fierceness come from? It was hard to remember that William Ann, too, was Forescout stock. Grandmother would have been disgusted by her, and that made Silence proud. William Ann had actually had a childhood. She wasn't weak, she was just . . . normal. A woman could be strong without having the emotions of a brick.

"Don't you cuss at your mother," Silence finally told the girl.

William Ann raised an eyebrow.

"You may come," Silence said, prying her arm out of her daughter's grip. "But you *will* do as you are told."

William Ann let out a deep breath, then nodded eagerly. "I'll warn Dob we're going." She walked out, adopting the natural slow step of a homesteader as she entered the darkness. Even though she was within the protection of the waystop's silver rings, she knew to follow the Simple Rules. Ignoring them when you were safe led to lapses when you weren't.

Silence got out two bowls, then mixed two different types of glowpaste. When finished, she poured them into separate jars, which she packed into her sack.

She stepped outside into the night. The air was crisp, chill. The Forests had gone silent.

The shades were out, of course.

A few of them moved across the grassy ground, visible by their own soft glow. Ethereal, translucent, the ones nearby right now were old shades; they barely had human forms any longer. The heads rippled, faces shifting like smoke rings. They trailed waves of whiteness about an arm's length behind them. Silence had always imagined that as the tattered remains of their clothing.

No woman, not even a Forescout, looked upon shades without feeling a coldness inside of her. The shades were about during the day, of course; you just couldn't see them. Kindle fire, draw blood, and they'd come for you even then. At night, though, they were different. Quicker to respond to infractions. At night they also responded to rapid motions, which they never did during the day.

Silence took out one of the glowpaste jars, bathing the area around her in a pale green light. The light was dim, but was even and steady, unlike torchlight. Torches were unreliable, since you couldn't relight them if they went out.

William Ann waited at the front with the lantern poles. "We will need to move quietly," Silence told her while affixing the jars to the poles. "You may speak, but do so in a whisper. I said you will obey me. You will, in all things, immediately. These men we're after . . . they will kill you, or worse, without giving the deed a passing thought."

William Ann nodded.

"You're not scared enough," Silence said, slipping a black covering around the jar with the brighter glowpaste. That plunged them into darkness, but the Starbelt was high in the sky today. Some of that light would filter down through the leaves, particularly if they stayed near the road.

"I—" William Ann began.

"You remember when Harold's hound went mad last spring?" Silence asked. "Do you remember that look in the hound's eyes? No recognition? Eyes that lusted for the kill? Well, that's what these men are, William Ann. Rabid. They need to be put down, same as that hound. They won't see you as a person. They'll see you as meat. Do you understand?"

William Ann nodded. Silence could see that she was still more excited than afraid, but there was no helping that. Silence handed William Ann the pole with the darker glowpaste. It had a faint blue light to it but didn't illuminate much. Silence put the other pole to her right shoulder, sack over her left, then nodded toward the roadway.

Nearby, a shade drifted toward the boundary of the waystop. When it touched the thin barrier of silver on the ground, the silver crackled like sparks and drove the thing backward with a sudden jerk. The shade floated the other way.

Each touch like that cost Silence money. The touch of a shade ruined silver. That was what her patrons paid for: a waystop whose boundary had not been broken in over a hundred years, with a long-standing tradition that no unwanted shades were trapped within. Peace, of a sort. The best the Forests offered.

William Ann stepped across the boundary, which was marked by the curve of the large silver hoops jutting from the ground. They were anchored below by concrete so you couldn't just pull one up. Replacing an overlapping section from one of the rings—she had three concentric ones surrounding her waystop—required digging down and unchaining the section. It was a lot of work, which Silence knew intimately. A week didn't pass that they didn't rotate or replace one section or another.

The shade nearby drifted away. It didn't acknowledge them. Silence didn't know if regular people were invisible to them unless the rules were broken, or if the people just weren't worthy of attention until then.

She and William Ann moved out onto the dark roadway, which was somewhat overgrown. No road in the Forests was well maintained. Perhaps if the forts ever made good on their promises, that would change. Still, there was travel. Homesteaders traveling to one fort or another to trade food. The grains grown out in Forest clearings were richer, tastier than what could be produced up in the mountains. Rabbits and turkeys caught in snares or raised in hutches could be sold for good silver.

Not hogs. Only someone in one of the forts would be so crass as to eat a pig.

Anyway, there *was* trade, and that kept the roadway worn, even if the trees around did have a tendency to reach down their boughs—like grasping arms—to try to cover up the pathway. Reclaim it. The Forests did not like that people had infested them.

The two women walked carefully and deliberately. No quick motions. Walking so, it seemed an eternity before something appeared on the road in front of them.

"There!" William Ann whispered.

Silence released her tension in a breath. Something glowing blue marked the roadway in the light of the glowpaste. Theopolis's guess at how she tracked her quarries had been a good one, but incomplete. Yes, the light of the paste also known as Abraham's Fire did make drops of wetleek sap glow. By coincidence, wetleek sap *also* caused a horse's bladder to loosen.

Silence inspected the line of glowing sap and urine on the ground. She'd been worried that Chesterton and his men would set off into the Forests soon after leaving the waystop. That hadn't been likely, but still she'd worried.

Now she was sure she had the trail. If Chesterton cut into the Forests, he'd do it a few hours after leaving the waystop, to be more certain their cover was safe. She closed her eyes and breathed a sigh of relief, then found herself offering a prayer of thanks by rote. She hesitated. Where had that come from? It had been a long time.

She shook her head, rising and continuing down the road. By drugging all five horses, she got a steady sequence of markings to follow.

The Forests felt . . . dark this night. The light of the Starbelt above didn't seem to filter through the branches as well as it should. And there seemed to be more shades than normal, prowling between the trunks of trees, glowing just faintly.

William Ann clung to her lantern pole. The child had been out in the night before, of course. No homesteader looked forward to doing so, but none shied away from it either. You couldn't spend your life trapped inside, frozen by fear of the darkness. Live like that, and . . . well, you were no better off than the people in the forts. Life in the Forests was hard, often deadly. But it was also free.

"Mother," William Ann whispered as they walked. "Why don't you believe in God anymore?"

"Is this really the time, girl?"

William Ann looked down as they passed another line of urine, glowing blue on the roadway. "You always say something like that."

"And I'm usually trying to avoid the question when you ask it," Silence said. "But I'm also not usually walking the Forests at night."

"It just seems important to me now. You're wrong about me not being afraid enough. I can hardly breathe, but I do know how much trouble the waystop is in. You're always so angry after Master Theopolis visits. You don't change our border silver as often as you used to. One out of two days, you don't eat anything but bread."

"And you think this has to do with God . . . why?"

William Ann kept looking down.

*Oh, shadows,* Silence thought. *She thinks we're being punished.* Fool girl. Foolish as her father.

They passed the Old Bridge, walking its rickety wooden planks. When the light was better, you could still pick out timbers from the New Bridge down in the chasm below, representing the promises of the forts and their gifts, which always looked pretty but frayed before long. Sebruki's father had been one of those who had come put the Old Bridge back up.

"I believe in the God Beyond," Silence said, after they reached the other side.

"But—"

"I don't worship," Silence said, "but that doesn't mean I don't believe. The old books, they called this land the home of the damned. I doubt that worshipping does any good if you're already damned. That's all."

William Ann didn't reply.

They walked another good two hours. Silence considered taking a shortcut through the woods, but the risk of losing the trail and having to double back felt too dangerous. Besides. Those markings, glowing a soft blue-white in the unseen light of the glowpaste . . . those were something *real.* A lifeline of light in the shadows all around. Those lines represented safety for her and her children.

With both of them counting the moments between urine markings, they didn't miss the turnoff by much. A few minutes walking without seeing a mark, and they turned back without a word, searching the sides of the path. Silence had worried this would be the most difficult part of the hunt, but they easily found where the men had turned into the Forests. A glowing hoofprint formed the sign; one of the horses had stepped in another's urine on the roadway, then tracked it into the Forests.

Silence set down her pack and opened it to retrieve her garrote, then held a finger to her lips and motioned for William Ann to wait by the road. The girl nodded. Silence couldn't make out much of her features in the darkness, but she did hear the girl's breathing grow more rapid.

Being a homesteader and accustomed to going out at night was one thing. Being alone in the Forests . . .

Silence took the blue glowpaste jar and covered it with her handkerchief. Then she took off her shoes and stockings and crept out into the night. Each time she did this, she felt like a child again, going into the Forests with her grandfather. Toes in the dirt, testing for crackling leaves or twigs that would snap and give her away.

She could almost hear his voice giving instructions, telling her how to judge the wind and use the sound of rustling leaves to mask her as she crossed noisy patches. He'd loved the Forests until the day they'd claimed him. *Never call this land hell,* he had said. *Respect the land as you would a dangerous beast, but do not hate it.*

Shades slid through the trees nearby, almost invisible with nothing to illuminate them. She kept her distance, but even so, she occasionally turned to see one of the things drifting past her. Stumbling into a shade could kill you, but that kind of accident was uncommon. Unless enraged, shades moved away from people who got too close, as if blown by a soft breeze. So long as you were moving slowly—and you *should* be—you would be all right.

She kept the handkerchief around the jar except when she wanted to check specifically for any markings. Glowpaste illuminated shades, and shades that glowed too brightly might give warning of her approach.

A groan sounded nearby. Silence froze, heart practically bursting from her chest. Shades made no sound; that had been a man. Tense, silent, she searched until she caught sight of him, well hidden in the hollow of a tree. He moved, massaging his temples. The headaches from William Ann's poison were upon him.

Silence considered, then crept around the back of the tree. She crouched down, then waited a painful five minutes for him to move. He reached up again, rustling the leaves.

Silence snapped forward and looped her garrote around his neck, then pulled tight. Strangling wasn't the best way to kill a man in the Forests. It was so slow.

The guard started to thrash, clawing at his throat. Shades nearby halted.

Silence pulled tighter. The guard, weakened by the poison, tried to kick at her with his legs. She shuffled backward, still holding tightly, watching those shades. They looked around like animals sniffing the air. A few of them started to dim, their own faint natural luminescence fading, their forms bleeding from white to black.

Not a good sign. Silence felt her heartbeat like thunder inside. *Die, damn you!*

The man finally stopped jerking, motions growing more lethargic. After he trembled one final time and fell still, Silence waited there for a painful eternity, holding her breath. Finally the shades nearby faded back to white, then drifted off in their meandering directions.

She unwound the garrote, breathing out in relief. After a moment to get her bearings, she left the corpse and crept back to William Ann.

The girl did her proud; she'd hidden herself so well that Silence didn't see her until she whispered, "Mother?"

"Yes," Silence said.

"Thank the God Beyond," William Ann said, crawling out of the hollow where she'd covered herself in leaves. She took Silence by the arm, trembling. "You found them?"

"Killed the man on watch," Silence said with a nod. "The other four should be sleeping. This is where I'll need you."

"I'm ready."

"Follow."

They moved back along the path Silence had taken. They passed the heap of the lookout's corpse, and William Ann inspected it, showing no pity. "It's one of them," she whispered. "I recognize him."

"Of course it's one of them."

"I just wanted to be sure. Since we're . . . you know."

Not far beyond the guard post, they found the camp. Four men in bedrolls slept amid the shades as only true Forestborn would ever try. They had set a small jar of glowpaste at the center of the camp, inside a pit so it wouldn't glow too brightly and give them away, but it was enough light to show the horses tethered a few feet away on the other side of the camp. The green light also showed William Ann's face, and Silence was shocked to see not fear but intense anger in the girl's expression. She had taken quickly to being a protective older sister to Sebruki. She was ready to kill after all.

Silence gestured toward the rightmost man, and William Ann nodded. This was the dangerous part. On only a half dose, any of these men could still wake to the noise of their partners dying.

Silence took one of the burlap sacks from her pack and handed it to William Ann, then removed her hammer. It wasn't some war weapon, like her grandfather had spoken of. Just a simple tool for pounding nails. Or other things.

Silence stooped over the first man. Seeing his sleeping face sent a shiver through her. A primal piece of her waited, tense, for those eyes to snap open.

She held up three fingers to William Ann, then lowered them one at a time. When the third finger went down, William Ann shoved the sack over the man's head. As he jerked, Silence pounded him hard on the side of the temple with the hammer. The skull cracked and the head sank in a little. The man thrashed once, then grew limp.

Silence looked up, tense, watching the other men as William Ann pulled the sack tight. The shades nearby paused, but this didn't draw their attention as much as the strangling had. So long as the sack's lining of tar kept the blood from leaking out, they should be safe. Silence hit the man's head twice more, then checked for a pulse. There was none.

They carefully did the next man in the row. It was brutal work, like slaughtering animals. It helped to think of these men as rabid, as she'd told William Ann earlier. It did not help to think of what the men had done to Sebruki. That would make her angry, and she couldn't afford to be angry. She needed to be cold, quiet, and efficient.

The second man took a few more knocks to the head to kill, but he woke more slowly than his friend. Fenweed made men groggy. It was an excellent drug for her purposes. She just needed them sleepy, a little disoriented. And—

The next man sat up in his bedroll. "What . . . ?" he asked in a slurred voice.

Silence leaped for him, grabbing him by the shoulders and slamming him to the ground. Nearby shades spun about as if at a loud noise.

Silence pulled her garrote out as the man heaved at her, trying to push her aside, and William Ann gasped in shock.

Silence rolled around, wrapping the man's neck. She pulled tight, straining while the man thrashed, agitating the shades. She almost had him dead when the last man leaped from his bedroll. In his dazed alarm, he chose to dash away.

Shadows! That last one was Chesterton himself. If he drew the shades . . .

Silence left the third man gasping and threw caution aside, racing after Chesterton. If the shades withered him to dust, she'd have *nothing.* No corpse to turn in meant no bounty.

The shades around the campsite faded from view as Silence reached Chesterton, catching him at the perimeter of the camp by the horses. She desperately tackled him by the legs, throwing the groggy man to the ground.

"You bitch," he said in a slurred voice, kicking at her. "You're the innkeeper. You poisoned me, you *bitch*!"

In the forest, the shades had gone completely black. Green eyes burst alight as they opened their earthsight. The eyes trailed a misty light.

Silence battered aside Chesterton's hands as he struggled.

"I'll pay you," he said, clawing at her. "I'll pay you—"

Silence slammed her hammer into his arm, causing him to scream. Then she brought it down on his face with a crunch. She ripped off her sweater as he groaned and thrashed, somehow wrapping it around his head and the hammer.

"William Ann!" she screamed. "I need a bag. A bag, girl! Give me—"

William Ann knelt beside her, pulling a sack over Chesterton's head as the blood soaked through the sweater. Silence reached to the side with a frantic hand and grabbed a stone, then smashed it into the sack-covered head. The sweater muffled Chesterton's screams, but also muffled the rock. She had to beat again and again.

He finally fell still. William Ann held the sack against his neck to keep the blood from flowing out, her breath coming in quick gasps. "Oh, God Beyond. Oh, *God* . . ."

Silence dared look up. Dozens of green eyes hung in the forest, glowing like little fires in the blackness. William Ann squeezed her eyes shut and whispered a prayer, tears leaking down her cheeks.

Silence reached slowly to her side and took out her silver dagger. She remembered another night, another sea of glowing green eyes. Her grandmother's last night. *Run, girl! RUN!*

That night, running had been an option. They'd been close to safety. Even then, Grandmother hadn't made it. She might have, but she hadn't.

That night horrified Silence. What Grandmother had done. What Silence had done . . . Well, tonight she had only one hope. Running would not save them. Safety was too far away.

Slowly, blessedly, the eyes started to fade away. Silence sat back and let the silver knife slip out of her fingers to the ground.

William Ann opened her eyes. "Oh, God Beyond!" she said as the shades faded back into view. "A miracle!"

"Not a miracle," Silence said. "Just luck. We killed him in time. Another second, and they'd have enraged."

William Ann wrapped her arms around herself. "Oh, shadows. Oh, shadows. I thought we were dead. Oh, shadows."

Suddenly, Silence remembered something. The third man. She hadn't finished strangling him before Chesterton ran. She stumbled to her feet, turning.

He lay there, immobile.

"I finished him off," William Ann said. "Had to strangle him with my hands. My hands . . ."

Silence glanced back at her. "You did well, girl. You probably saved our lives. If you hadn't been here, I'd never have killed Chesterton without enraging the shades."

The girl still stared out into the woods, watching the placid shades. "What would it take?" she asked. "For you to see a miracle instead of a coincidence?"

"It would take a miracle, obviously," Silence said, picking up her knife. "Instead of just a coincidence. Come on. Let's put a second sack on these fellows."

William Ann joined her, lethargic as she helped put sacks on the heads of the bandits. Two sacks each, just in case. Blood was the most dangerous. Running drew shades, but slowly. Fire enraged them immediately, but it also blinded and confused them.

Blood, though . . . blood shed in anger, exposed to the open air . . . a single drop could make the shades slaughter you, and then everything else within their sight.

Silence checked each man for a heartbeat, just in case, and found none. They saddled the horses and heaved the corpses, including the lookout, into the saddles and tied them in place. They took the bedrolls and other equipment too. Hopefully the men would have some silver on them. Bounty laws let Silence keep what she found unless there was specific mention of something stolen. In this case, the forts just wanted Chesterton dead. Pretty much everyone did.

Silence pulled a rope tight, then paused.

"Mother!" William Ann said, noticing the same thing. Leaves rustling out in the Forests. They'd uncovered their jar of green glowpaste to join that of the bandits, so the small campsite was well illuminated as a gang of eight men and women on horseback rode in through the Forests.

They were from the forts. The nice clothing, the way they kept looking into the Forests at the shades . . . Fortfolk for certain. Silence stepped forward, wishing she had her hammer to look at least a little threatening. That was still tied in the sack around Chesterton's head. It would have blood on it, so she couldn't get it out until that dried or she was in someplace very, *very* safe.

"Now, look at this," said the man at the front of the newcomers. "I couldn't believe what Tobias told me when he came back from scouting, but it appears to be true. All five men in Chesterton's gang, killed by a couple of Forest homesteaders?"

"Who are you?" Silence asked.

"Red Young," the man said with a tip of the hat. "I've been tracking this lot for the last four months. I can't thank you enough for taking care of them for me." He waved to a few of his people, who dismounted.

"Mother!" William Ann hissed.

Silence studied Red's eyes. He was armed with a cudgel, and one of the women behind him had one of those new crossbows with the blunt tips. They cranked fast and hit hard, but didn't draw blood.

"Step away from the horses, child," Silence said.

"But—"

"Step away." Silence dropped the rope of the horse she was leading. Three fort city people gathered up the ropes, one of the men leering at William Ann.

"You're a smart one," Red said, leaning down and studying Silence. One of his women walked past, towing Chesterton's horse with the man's corpse slumped over the saddle.

Silence stepped up, resting a hand on Chesterton's saddle. The woman towing it paused, then looked at her boss. Silence slipped her knife from its sheath.

"You'll give us something," Silence said to Red, knife hand hidden. "After what we did. One quarter, and I don't say a word."

"Sure," he said, tipping his hat to her. He had a fake kind of grin, like one in a painting. "One quarter it is."

Silence nodded. She slipped the knife against one of the thin ropes that held Chesterton in the saddle. That gave her a good cut on it as the woman pulled the horse away. Silence stepped back, resting her hand on William Ann's shoulder while covertly moving the knife back into its sheath.

Red tipped his hat to her again. In moments, the bounty hunters had retreated back through the trees toward the roadway.

"One quarter?" William Ann hissed. "You think he'll pay it?"

"Hardly," Silence said, picking up her pack. "We're lucky he didn't just kill us. Come on." She moved out into the Forests. William Ann walked with her, both moving with the careful steps the Forests demanded. "It might be time for you to return to the waystop, William Ann."

"And what are you going to do?"

"Get our bounty back." She was a Forescout, dammit. No prim fort man was going to steal from her.

"You mean to cut them off at the white span, I assume. But what will you do? We can't fight so many, Mother."

"I'll find a way." That corpse meant freedom—*life*—for her daughters. She would not let it slip away like smoke between the fingers. They entered the darkness, passing shades that had, just a short time before, been almost ready to wither them. Now the shades drifted away, completely indifferent toward their flesh.

*Think, Silence. Something is very wrong here.* How had those men found the camp? The light? Had they overheard her and William Ann talking? They'd claimed to have been chasing Chesterton for months. Shouldn't she have caught wind of them before now? These men and women looked too crisp to have been out in the Forests for months trailing killers.

It led to a conclusion she did not want to admit. One man had known she was hunting a bounty today and had seen how she was planning to track that bounty. One man had cause to see that bounty stolen from her.

*Theopolis, I hope I'm wrong,* she thought. *Because if you're behind this . . .*

Silence and William Ann trudged through the guts of the Forest, a place where the gluttonous canopy above drank in all of the light, leaving the ground below barren. Shades patrolled these wooden halls like blind sentries. Red and his bounty hunters were of the forts. They would keep to the roadways, and that was her advantage. The Forests were no friend to a homesteader, no more than a familiar chasm was any less dangerous a drop.

But Silence was a sailor on this abyss. She could ride its winds better than any fortdweller. Perhaps it was time to make a storm.

What homesteaders called the "white span" was a section of roadway lined by mushroom fields. It took about an hour through the Forests to reach the span, and Silence was feeling the price of a night without sleep by the time she arrived. She ignored the fatigue, tromping through the field of mushrooms, holding her jar of green light and giving an ill cast to trees and furrows in the land.

The roadway bent around through the Forests, then came back this way. If the men were heading toward Lastport or any of the other nearby forts, they would come this direction. "You continue on," Silence said to William Ann. "It's only another hour's hike back to the waystop. Check on things there."

"I'm not leaving you, Mother."

"You promised to obey. Would you break your word?"

"And you promised to let me help you. Would you break yours?"

"I don't need you for this," Silence said. "And it will be dangerous."

"What are you going to do?"

Silence stopped beside the roadway, then knelt, fishing in her pack. She came out with the small keg of gunpowder. William Ann went as white as the mushrooms.

"Mother!"

Silence untied her grandmother's firestarter. She didn't know for certain if it still worked. She'd never dared compress the two metal arms, which looked like tongs. Squeezing them together would grind the ends against one another, making sparks, and a spring at the joint would make them come back apart.

Silence looked up at her daughter, then held the firestarter up beside her head. William Ann stepped back, then glanced to the sides, toward nearby shades.

"Are things really that bad?" the girl whispered. "For us, I mean?"

Silence nodded.

"All right then."

Fool girl. Well, Silence wouldn't send her away. The truth was, she probably *would* need help. She intended to get that corpse. Bodies were heavy, and there wasn't any way she'd be able to cut off just the head. Not out in the Forests, with shades about.

She dug into her pack, pulling out her medical supplies. They were tied between two small boards, intended to be used as splints. It was not difficult to tie the two boards to either side of the firestarter. With her hand trowel, she dug a small hole in the roadway's soft earth, about the size of the powder keg.

She then opened the plug to the keg and set it into the hole. She soaked her handkerchief in the lamp oil, stuck one end in the keg, then positioned the firestarter boards on the road with the end of the kerchief next to the spark-making heads. After covering the contraption with some leaves, she had a rudimentary trap. If someone stepped on the top board, that would press it down and grind out sparks to light the kerchief. Hopefully.

She couldn't afford to light the fire herself. The shades would come first for the one who made the fire.

"What happens if they don't step on it?" William Ann asked.

"Then we move it to another place on the road and try again," Silence said.

"That could shed blood, you realize."

Silence didn't reply. If the trap was triggered by a footfall, the shades wouldn't see Silence as the one causing it. They'd come first for the one who triggered the trap. But if blood was drawn, they would enrage. Soon after, it wouldn't matter who had caused it. All would be in danger.

"We have hours of darkness left," Silence said. "Cover your glowpaste."

William Ann nodded, hastily putting the cover on her jar. Silence inspected her trap again, then took William Ann by the shoulder and pulled her to the side of the roadway. The underbrush was thicker there, as the road tended to wind through breaks in the canopy. People sought out places in the Forests where they could see the sky.

The bounty hunters came along eventually. Silent, illuminated by a jar of glowpaste each. Fortfolk didn't talk at night. They passed the trap, which Silence had placed on the narrowest section of roadway. She held her breath, watching the horses pass, step after step missing the lump that marked the board. William Ann covered her ears, hunkering down.

A hoof hit the trap. Nothing happened. Silence released an annoyed breath. What would she do if the firestarter was broken? Could she find another way to—

The explosion struck her, the wave of force shaking her body. Shades vanished in a blink, green eyes snapping open. Horses reared and whinnied, men and women yelling.

Silence shook off her stupefaction, grabbing William Ann by the shoulder and pulling her out of hiding. Her trap had worked better than she'd assumed; the burning rag had allowed the horse who had triggered the trap to take a few steps before the blast hit. No blood, just a lot of surprised horses and confused people. The little keg of gunpowder hadn't done as much damage as she'd anticipated—the stories of what gunpowder could do were often as fanciful as stories of the Homeland—but the sound had been incredible.

Silence's ears rang as she fought through the confused fortfolk, finding what she'd hoped to see. Chesterton's corpse lay on the ground, dumped from saddleback by a bucking horse and a frayed rope. She grabbed the corpse under the arms and William Ann took the legs. They moved sideways into the Forests.

"Idiots!" Red bellowed from amid the confusion. "Stop her! It—"

He cut off as shades swarmed the roadway, descending upon the men. Red had managed to keep his horse under control, but now he had to dance it back from the shades. Enraged, they had turned pure black, though the blast of light and fire had obviously left them dazed. They fluttered about, like moths at a flame. Green eyes. A small blessing. If those turned red . . .

One bounty hunter, standing on the road and spinning about, was struck. His back arched, black-veined tendrils crisscrossing his skin. He dropped to his knees, screaming as the flesh of his face shrank around his skull.

Silence turned away. William Ann watched the fallen man with a horrified expression.

"Slowly, child," Silence said in what she hoped was a comforting voice. She hardly felt comforting. "Carefully. We can move away from them. William Ann. Look at me."

The girl turned to look at her.

"Hold my eyes. Move. That's right. Remember, the shades will go to the source of the fire first. They are confused, stunned. They can't smell fire like they do blood, and they'll look from it to the nearest rapid motion. Slowly, easily. Let the scrambling fortfolk distract them."

The two of them eased into the Forests with excruciating deliberateness. In the face of so much chaos, so much danger, their pace felt like a crawl. Red organized a resistance. Fire-crazed shades could be fought, destroyed, with silver. More and more would come, but if the bounty hunters were clever and lucky, they'd be able to destroy those nearby and then move slowly away from the source of the fire. They could hide, survive. Maybe.

Unless one of them accidentally drew blood.

Silence and William Ann stepped through a field of mushrooms that glowed like the skulls of rats and broke silently beneath their feet. Luck was not completely with them, for as the shades shook off their disorientation from the explosion, a pair of them on the outskirts turned and struck out toward the fleeing women.

William Ann gasped. Silence deliberately set down Chesterton's shoulders, then took out her knife. "Keep going," she whispered. "Pull him away. Slowly, girl. *Slowly.*"

"I won't leave you!"

"I will catch up," Silence said. "You aren't ready for this."

She didn't look to see if William Ann obeyed, for the shades—figures of jet black streaking across the white-knobbed ground—were upon her. Strength was meaningless against shades. They had no real substance. Only two things mattered: your speed and not letting yourself be frightened.

Shades *were* dangerous, but so long as you had silver, you could fight. Many a man died because he ran, drawing even more shades, rather than standing his ground.

Silence swung at the shades as they reached her. *You want my daughter, hellbound?* she thought with a snarl. *You should have tried for the fortfolk instead.*

She swept her knife through the first shade, as Grandmother had taught. *Never creep back and cower before shades. You're Forescout blood. You claim the Forests. You are their creature as much as any other. As am I. . . .*

Her knife passed through the shade with a slight tugging feeling, creating a shower of bright white sparks that sprayed out of the shade. The shade pulled back, its black tendrils writhing about one another.

Silence spun on the other. The pitch sky let her see only the thing's eyes, a horrid green, as it reached for her. She lunged.

Its spectral hands were upon her, the icy cold of its fingers gripping her arm below the elbow. She could feel it. Shade fingers had substance; they could grab you, hold you back. Only silver warded them away. Only with silver could you fight.

She rammed her arm in farther. Sparks shot out its back, spraying like a bucket of washwater. Silence gasped at the horrid, icy pain. Her knife slipped from fingers she could no longer feel. She lurched forward, falling to her knees as the second shade fell backward, then began spinning about in a mad spiral. The first one flopped on the ground like a dying fish, trying to rise, its top half falling over.

The cold of her arm was so *bitter.* She stared at the wounded arm, watching the flesh of her hand wither upon itself, pulling in toward the bone.

She heard weeping.

*You stand there, Silence.* Grandmother's voice. Memories of the first time she'd killed a shade. *You do as I say. No tears! Forescouts don't cry. Forescouts DON'T CRY.*

She had learned to hate her that day. Ten years old, with her little knife, shivering and weeping in the night as her grandmother had enclosed her and a drifting shade in a ring of silver dust.

Grandmother had run around the perimeter, enraging it with motion. While Silence was trapped in there. With death.

*The only way to learn is to do, Silence. And you'll learn, one way or another!*

"Mother!" William Ann said.

Silence blinked, coming out of the memory as her daughter dumped silver dust on the exposed arm. The withering stopped as William Ann, choking against her thick tears, dumped the entire pouch of emergency silver over the hand. The metal reversed the withering, and the skin turned pink again, the blackness melting away in sparks of white.

*Too much,* Silence thought. William Ann had used all of the silver dust in her haste, far more than one wound needed. It was difficult to summon any anger, for feeling flooded back into her hand and the icy cold retreated.

"Mother?" William Ann asked. "I left you, as you said. But he was so heavy, I didn't get far. I came back for you. I'm sorry. I came back for you!"

"Thank you," Silence said, breathing in. "You did well." She reached up and took her daughter by the shoulder, then used the once-withered hand to search in the grass for Grandmother's knife. When she brought it up, the blade was blackened in several places, but still good.

Back on the road, the fortfolk had made a circle and were holding off the shades with silver-tipped spears. The horses had all fled or been consumed. Silence fished on the ground, coming up with a small handful of silver dust. The rest had been expended in the healing. Too much.

*No use worrying about that now,* she thought, stuffing the handful of dust in her pocket. "Come," she said, hauling herself to her feet. "I'm sorry I never taught you to fight them."

"Yes you did," William Ann said, wiping her tears. "You've told me all about it."

Told. Never shown. *Shadows, Grandmother. I know I disappoint you, but I won't do it to her. I can't. But I am a good mother. I* will *protect them.*

The two left the mushrooms, taking up their grisly prize again and tromping through the Forests. They passed more darkened shades floating toward the fight. All of those sparks would draw them. The fortfolk were dead. Too much attention, too much struggle. They'd have a thousand shades upon them before the hour was out.

Silence and William Ann moved slowly. Though the cold had mostly retreated from Silence's hand, there was a lingering . . . something. A deep shiver. A limb touched by the shades wouldn't feel right for months.

That was far better than what could have happened. Without William Ann's quick thinking, Silence could have become a cripple. Once the withering settled in—that took a little time, though it varied—it was irreversible.

Something rustled in the woods. Silence froze, causing William Ann to stop and glance about.

"Mother?" William Ann whispered.

Silence frowned. The night was so black, and they'd been forced to leave their lights. *Something's out there,* she thought, trying to pierce the darkness. *What are you?* God Beyond protect them if the fighting had drawn one of the Deepest Ones.

The sound did not repeat. Reluctantly, Silence continued on. They walked for a good hour, and in the darkness Silence hadn't realized they'd neared the roadway again until they stepped onto it.

Silence heaved out a breath, setting down their burden and rolling her tired arms in their joints. Some light from the Starbelt filtered down upon them, illuminating something like a large jawbone to their left.

The Old Bridge. They were almost home. The shades here weren't even agitated; they moved with their lazy, almost butterfly, gaits.

Her arms felt so sore. That body felt as if it were getting heavier every moment. People often didn't realize how heavy a corpse was. Silence sat down. They'd rest for a time before continuing on. "William Ann, do you have any water left in your canteen?"

William Ann whimpered.

Silence started, then scrambled to her feet. Her daughter stood beside the bridge, and something dark stood behind her. A green glow suddenly illuminated the night as the figure took out a small vial of glowpaste. By that sickly light, Silence could see that the figure was Red.

He held a dagger to William Ann's neck. The fort man had not fared well in the fighting. One eye was now a milky white, half his face blackened, his lips pulled back from his teeth. A shade had gotten him across the face. He was lucky to be alive.

"I figured you'd come back this way," he said, the words slurred by his shriveled lips. Spittle dripped from his chin. "Silver. Give me your silver."

His knife . . . it was common steel.

"*Now!*" he roared, pulling the knife closer to William Ann's neck. If he so much as nicked her, the shades would be upon them in heartbeats.

"I only have the knife," Silence lied, taking it out and tossing it to the ground before him. "It's too late for your face, Red. That withering has set in."

"I don't care," he hissed. "Now the body. Step away from it, woman. Away!"

Silence stepped to the side. Could she get to him before he killed William Ann? He'd have to grab that knife. If she sprang just right . . .

"You killed my crew," Red growled. "They're dead, all of them. God, if I hadn't rolled into the hollow . . . I had to *listen* to it. Listen to them being slaughtered!"

"You were the only smart one," she said. "You couldn't have saved them, Red."

"Bitch! You killed them."

"They killed themselves," she whispered. "You come to my Forests, take what is mine? It was your crew or my children, Red."

"Well, if you want your child to live through this, you'll stay very still. Girl, pick up that knife."

Whimpering, William Ann knelt. Red mimicked her, staying just behind her, watching Silence, holding the knife steady. William Ann picked up the knife in trembling hands.

Red pulled the silver knife from William Ann, then held it in one hand, the common knife at her neck in the other. "Now, the girl is going to carry the corpse, and you're going to wait right there. I don't want you coming near."

"Of course," Silence said, already planning. She couldn't afford to strike right now. He was too careful. She would follow through the Forests, along the road, and wait for a moment of weakness. Then she'd strike.

Red spat to the side.

Then a padded crossbow bolt shot from the night and took him in the shoulder, jolting him. His blade slid across William Ann's neck, and a dribble of blood ran down it. The girl's eyes widened in horror, though it was little more than a nick. The danger to her throat wasn't important.

The blood was.

Red tumbled back, gasping, hand to his shoulder. A few drops of blood glistened on his knife. The shades in the Forests around them went black. Glowing green eyes burst alight, then deepened to crimson.

Red eyes in the night. Blood in the air.

"Oh, hell!" Red screamed. "Oh, *hell.*" Red eyes swarmed around him. There was no hesitation here, no confusion. They went straight for the one who had drawn blood.

Silence reached for William Ann as the shades descended. Red grabbed the girl and shoved her through a shade, trying to stop it. He spun and dashed the other direction.

William Ann passed through the shade, her face withering, skin pulling in at the chin and around the eyes. She stumbled through the shade and into Silence's arms.

Silence felt an immediate, overwhelming panic.

"No! Child, no. No. *No* . . ."

William Ann worked her mouth, making a choking sound, her lips pulling back toward her teeth, her eyes open wide as her skin tightened and her eyelids shriveled.

*Silver. I need silver. I can save her.* Silence snapped her head up, clutching William Ann. Red ran down the roadway, slashing the silver dagger all about, spraying light and sparks. Shades surrounded him. Hundreds, like ravens flocking to a roost.

Not that way. The shades would finish with him soon and would look for flesh—any flesh. William Ann still had blood on her neck. They'd come for her next. Even without that, the girl was withering fast.

The dagger wouldn't be enough to save William Ann. Silence needed dust, silver dust, to force down her daughter's throat. Silence fumbled in her pocket, coming out with the small bit of silver dust there.

Too little. She *knew* that would be too little. Her grandmother's training calmed her mind, and everything became immediately clear.

The waystop was close. She had more silver there.

"M . . . Mother . . ."

Silence heaved William Ann into her arms. Too light, the flesh drying. Then she turned and ran with everything she had across the bridge.

Her arms stung, weakened from having hauled the corpse so far. The corpse . . . she couldn't lose it!

No. She couldn't think on that. The shades would have it, as warm enough flesh, soon after Red was gone. There would be no bounty. She had to focus on William Ann.

Silence's tears felt cold on her face as she ran, wind blowing her. Her daughter trembled and shook in her arms, spasming as she died. She'd become a shade if she died like this.

"I won't lose you!" Silence said into the night. "Please. I won't lose you. . . ."

Behind her, Red screamed a long, wailing screech of agony that cut off at the end as the shades feasted. Near her, other shades stopped, eyes deepening to red.

Blood in the air. Eyes of crimson.

"I hate you," Silence whispered into the air as she ran. Each step was agony. She *was* growing old. "I hate you! What you did to me. What you did to us."

She didn't know if she was speaking to Grandmother or the God Beyond. So often, they were the same in her mind. Had she ever realized that before?

Branches lashed at her as she pushed forward. Was that light ahead? The waystop?

Hundreds upon hundreds of red eyes opened in front of her. She stumbled to the ground, spent, William Ann like a heavy bundle of branches in her arms. The girl trembled, her eyes rolled back in her head.

Silence held out the small bit of silver dust she'd recovered earlier. She longed to pour it on William Ann, save her a little pain, but she knew with clarity that was a waste. She looked down, crying, then took the dust and made a small circle around the two of them. What else could she do?

William Ann shook with a seizure as she rasped, drawing in breaths and clawing at Silence's arms. The shades came by the dozens, huddling around the two of them, smelling the blood. The flesh.

Silence pulled her daughter close. She should have gone for the knife after all; it wouldn't heal William Ann, but she could have at least fought with it.

Without that, without anything, she failed. Grandmother had been right all along.

"Hush now, my dear one . . ." Silence whispered, squeezing her eyes shut. "Be not afraid."

Shades came at her frail barrier, throwing up sparks, making Silence open her eyes. They backed away, then others came, beating against the silver, their red eyes illuminating writhing black forms.

"Night comes upon us . . ." Silence whispered, choking at the words, ". . . but sunlight will break."

William Ann arched her back, then fell still.

"Sleep now . . . my . . . my dear one . . . let your tears fade. Darkness surrounds us, but someday . . . we'll wake. . . ."

So tired. *I shouldn't have let her come.*

If she hadn't, Chesterton would have gotten away from her, and she'd have probably fallen to the shades then. William Ann and Sebruki would have become slaves to Theopolis, or worse.

No choices. No way out.

"Why did you send us here?" she screamed, looking up past hundreds of glowing red eyes. "What is the point?"

There was no answer. There was never an answer.

Yes, that *was* light ahead; she could see it through the low tree branches in front of her. She was only a few yards from the waystop. She would die, like Grandmother had, mere paces from her home.

She blinked, cradling William Ann as the tiny silver barrier failed.

That . . . that branch just in front of her. It had such a very odd shape. Long, thin, no leaves. Not like a branch at all. Instead, like . . .

Like a crossbow bolt.

It had lodged into the tree after being fired from the waystop earlier in the day. She remembered facing down that bolt earlier, staring at its reflective end.

Silver.

Silence Montane crashed through the back door of the waystop, hauling a desiccated body behind her. She stumbled into the kitchen, barely able to walk, and dropped the silver-tipped bolt from a withered hand.

Her skin continued to pull tight, her body shriveling. She had not been able to avoid withering, not when fighting so many shades. The crossbow bolt had merely cleared a path, allowing her to push forward in a last, frantic charge.

She could barely see. Tears streamed from her clouded eyes. Even with the tears, her eyes felt as dry as if she had been standing in the wind for an hour while holding them wide open. Her lids refused to blink, and she couldn't move her lips.

She had . . . powder. Didn't she?

Thought. Mind. What?

She moved without thought. Jar on the windowsill. In case of broken circle. She unscrewed the lid with fingers like sticks. Seeing them horrified a distant part of her mind.

*Dying. I'm dying.*

She dunked the jar of silver powder in the water cistern and pulled it out, then stumbled to William Ann. She fell to her knees beside the girl, spilling much of the water. The rest she dumped on her daughter's face with a shaking arm.

*Please. Please.*

Darkness.

•

"We were sent here to be strong," Grandmother said, standing on the cliff edge overlooking the waters. Her whited hair curled in the wind, writhing like the wisps of a shade.

She turned back to Silence, and her weathered face was covered in droplets of water from the crashing surf below. "The God Beyond sent us. It's part of the plan."

"It's so easy for you to say that, isn't it?" Silence spat. "You can fit anything into that nebulous *plan*. Even the destruction of the world itself."

"I won't hear blasphemy from you, child." A voice like boots stepping in gravel. She walked toward Silence. "You can rail against the God Beyond, but it will change nothing. William was a fool and an idiot. You are better off. We are *Forescouts*. We *survive*. We will be the ones to defeat the Evil, someday." She passed Silence by.

Silence had never seen a smile from Grandmother, not since her husband's death. Smiling was wasted energy. And love . . . love was for the people back in Homeland. The people who'd perished from the Evil.

"I'm with child," Silence said.

Grandmother stopped. "William?"

"Who else?"

Grandmother continued on.

"No condemnations?" Silence asked, turning, folding her arms.

"It's done," Grandmother said. "We are Forescouts. If this is how we must continue, so be it. I'm more worried about the waystop, and meeting our payments to those damn forts."

*I have an idea for that,* Silence thought, considering the lists of bounties she'd begun collecting. *Something even you wouldn't dare. Something dangerous. Something unthinkable.*

Grandmother reached the woods and looked at Silence, scowled, then pulled on her hat and stepped into the trees.

"I will not have you interfering with my child," Silence called after her. "I will raise my own as I will!"

Grandmother vanished into the shadows.

*Please. Please.*

"I *will*!"

*I won't lose you. I won't . . .*

---

Silence gasped, coming awake and clawing at the floorboards, staring upward.

Alive. She was alive!

Dob the stableman knelt beside her, holding the jar of powdered silver. She coughed, lifting fingers—plump, the flesh restored—to her neck. It was hale, though ragged from the flakes of silver that had been forced down her throat. Her skin was dusted with black bits of ruined silver.

"William Ann!" she said, turning.

The child lay on the floor beside the door. William Ann's left side, where she'd first touched the shade, was blackened. Her face wasn't too bad, but her hand was a withered skeleton. They'd have to cut that off. Her leg looked bad too. Silence couldn't tell how bad without tending the wounds.

"Oh, child . . ." Silence knelt beside her.

But the girl breathed in and out. That was enough, all things considered.

"I tried," Dob said. "But you'd already done what could be done."

"Thank you," Silence said. She turned to the aged man, with his high forehead and dull eyes.

"Did you get him?" Dob asked.

"Who?"

"The bounty."

"I . . . yes, I did. But I had to leave him."

"You'll find another," Dob said in his monotone, climbing to his feet. "The Fox always does."

"How long have you known?"

"I'm an idiot, mam," he said. "Not a fool." He bowed his head to her, then walked away, slump-backed as always.

Silence climbed to her feet, then groaned, picking up William Ann. She lifted her daughter to the rooms above and saw to her.

The leg wasn't as bad as Silence had feared. A few of the toes would be lost, but the foot itself was hale enough. The entire left side of William Ann's body was blackened, as if burned. That would fade, with time, to grey.

Everyone who saw her would know exactly what had happened. Many men would never touch her, fearing her taint. This might just doom her to a life alone.

*I know a little about such a life,* Silence thought, dipping a cloth into the water bin and washing William Ann's face. The youth would sleep through the day. She had come very close to death, to becoming a shade herself. The body did not recover quickly from that.

Of course, Silence had been close to that too. She, however, had been there before. Another of Grandmother's preparations. Oh, how she hated that woman. Silence owed who she was to how that training had toughened her. Could she be thankful for Grandmother and hateful, both at once?

Silence finished washing William Ann, then dressed her in a soft nightgown and left her in her bunk. Sebruki still slept off the draught Silence had given her.

So she went downstairs to the kitchen to think difficult thoughts. She'd lost the bounty. The shades would have had at that body; the skin would be dust, the skull blackened and ruined. She had no way to prove that she'd taken Chesterton.

She settled against the kitchen table and laced her hands before her. She wanted to have at the whiskey instead, to dull the horror of the night.

She thought for hours. Could she pay Theopolis off some way? Borrow from someone else? Who? Maybe find another bounty. But so few people came through the waystop these days. Theopolis had already given her warning, with his writ. He wouldn't wait more than a day or two for payment before claiming the waystop as his own.

Had she really gone through so much, still to lose?

Sunlight fell on her face and a breeze from the broken window tickled her cheek, waking her from her slumber at the table. Silence blinked, stretching, limbs complaining. Then she sighed, moving to the kitchen counter. She'd left out all of the materials from the preparations last night, her clay bowls thick with glowpaste that still shone faintly. The silver-tipped crossbow bolt lay by the back door where she'd dropped it. She'd need to clean up and get breakfast ready for her few guests. Then, think of *some* way to . . .

The back door opened and someone stepped in.

. . . to deal with Theopolis. She exhaled softly, looking at him in his clean clothing and condescending smile. He tracked mud onto her floor as he entered. "Silence Montane. Nice morning, hmmm?"

*Shadows,* she thought. *I don't have the mental strength to deal with him right now.*

He moved to close the window shutters.

"What are you doing?" she demanded.

"Hmmm? Haven't you warned me before that you loathe that people might see us together? That they might get a hint that you are turning in bounties to me? I'm just trying to protect you. Has something happened? You look awful, hmmm?"

"I know what you did."

"You do? But, see, I do many things. About what do you speak?"

Oh, how she'd like to cut that grin from his lips and cut out his throat, stomp out that annoying Lastport accent. She couldn't. He was just so blasted *good* at acting. She had guesses, probably good ones. But no proof.

Grandmother would have killed him right then. Was she so desperate to prove him wrong that she'd lose everything?

"You were in the Forests," Silence said. "When Red surprised me at the bridge, I assumed that the thing I'd heard—rustling in the darkness—had been him. It wasn't. He implied he'd been waiting for us at the bridge. That thing in the darkness, it was you. *You* shot him with the crossbow to jostle him, make him draw blood. Why, Theopolis?"

"Blood?" Theopolis said. "In the night? And you *survived*? You're quite fortunate, I should say. Remarkable. What else happened?"

She said nothing.

"I have come for payment of debt," Theopolis said. "You have no bounty to turn in then, hmmm? Perhaps we will need my document after all. So kind of me to bring another copy. This really will be wonderful for us both. Do you not agree?"

"Your feet are glowing."

Theopolis hesitated, then looked down. There, the mud he'd tracked in shone very faintly blue in the light of the glowpaste remnants.

"You followed me," she said. "You *were* there last night."

He looked up at her with a slow, unconcerned expression. "And?" He took a step forward.

Silence backed away, her heel hitting the wall behind her. She reached around, taking out the key and unlocking the door behind her. Theopolis grabbed her arm, yanking her away as she pulled open the door.

"Going for one of your hidden weapons?" he asked with a sneer. "The crossbow you keep on the pantry shelf? Yes, I know of that. I'm disappointed, Silence. Can't we be civil?"

"I will never sign your document, Theopolis," she said, then spat at his feet. "I would sooner die, I would sooner be put out of house and home. You can take the waystop by force, but I will *not* serve you. You can be damned, for all I care, you bastard. You—"

He slapped her across the face. A quick but unemotional gesture. "Oh, do shut up."

She stumbled back.

"Such dramatics, Silence. I can't be the only one to wish you lived up to your name, hmmm?"

She licked her lip, feeling the pain of his slap. She lifted her hand to her face. A single drop of blood colored her fingertip when she pulled it away.

"You expect me to be frightened?" Theopolis asked. "I know we're safe in here."

"Fort city fool," she whispered, then flipped the drop of blood at him. It hit him on the cheek. "Always follow the Simple Rules. Even when you think you don't have to. And I wasn't opening the pantry, as you thought."

Theopolis frowned, then glanced over at the door she had opened. The door into the small old shrine. Her grandmother's shrine to the God Beyond.

The bottom of the door was rimmed in silver.

Red eyes opened in the air behind Theopolis, a jet-black form coalescing in the shadowed room. Theopolis hesitated, then turned.

He didn't get to scream as the shade took his head in its hands and drew his life away. It was a newer shade, its form still strong despite the writhing blackness of its clothing. A tall woman, hard of features, with curling hair. Theopolis opened his mouth, then his face withered away, eyes sinking into his head.

"You should have run, Theopolis," Silence said.

His head began to crumble. His body collapsed to the floor.

"Hide from the green eyes, run from the red," Silence said, retrieving the silver-tipped crossbow bolt from where it lay by the back door. "Your rules, Grandmother."

The shade turned to her. Silence shivered, looking into those dead, glassy eyes of a matriarch she loathed and loved.

"I hate you," Silence said. "Thank you for making me hate you." She held the crossbow bolt before her, but the shade did not strike. Silence edged around, forcing the shade back. It floated away from her, back into the shrine lined with silver at the bottom of its three walls, where Silence had trapped it years ago.

Her heart pounding, Silence closed the door, completing the barrier, and locked it again. No matter what happened, that shade left Silence alone. Almost, she thought it remembered. And almost, Silence felt guilty for trapping that soul inside the small closet for all these years.

Silence found Theopolis's hidden cave after six hours of hunting.

It was about where she'd expected it to be, in the hills not far from the Old Bridge. It included a silver barrier. She could harvest that. Good money there.

Inside the small cavern, she found Chesterton's corpse, which Theopolis had dragged to the cave while the shades killed Red and then hunted Silence. *I'm so glad, for once, you were a greedy man, Theopolis.*

She would have to find someone else to start turning in bounties for her. That would be difficult, particularly on short notice. She dragged the corpse out and threw it over the back of Theopolis's horse. A short hike took her back to the road, where she paused, then walked up and located Red's fallen corpse, withered down to just bones and clothing.

She fished out her grandmother's dagger, scored and blackened from the fight. It fit back into the sheath at her side. She trudged, exhausted, back to the waystop and hid Chesterton's corpse in the cold cellar out behind the stable, beside where she'd put Theopolis's remains. She hiked back into the kitchen. Beside the shrine's door where her grandmother's dagger had once hung, she had placed the silver crossbow bolt that Sebruki had unknowingly sent her.

What would the fort authorities say when she explained Theopolis's death to them? Perhaps she could claim to have found him like that. . . .

She paused, then smiled.

"Looks like you're lucky, friend," Daggon said, sipping at his beer. "The White Fox won't be looking for you anytime soon."

The spindly man, who still insisted his name was Earnest, hunkered down a little farther in his seat.

"How is it you're still here?" Daggon asked. "I traveled all the way to Lastport. I hardly expected to find you here on my path back."

"I hired on at a homestead nearby," said the slender-necked man. "Good work, mind you. Solid work."

"And you pay each night to stay here?"

"I like it. It feels peaceful. The homesteads don't have good silver protection. They just . . . let the shades move about. Even inside." The man shuddered.

Daggon shrugged, lifting his drink as Silence Montane limped by. Yes, she was a healthy-looking woman. He really *should* court her, one of these days. She scowled at his smile and dumped his plate in front of him.

"I think I'm wearing her down," Daggon said, mostly to himself, as she left.

"You will have to work hard," Earnest said. "Seven men have proposed to her during the last month."

"What!"

"The reward!" the spindly man said. "The one for bringing in Chesterton. Lucky woman, Silence Montane, finding the White Fox's lair like that."

Daggon dug into his meal. He didn't much like how things had turned out. That dandy Theopolis had been the White Fox all along? Poor Silence. How had it been, stumbling upon his cave and finding him inside, all withered away?

"They say that this Theopolis spent his last strength killing Chesterton," Earnest said, "then dragging him into the hole. Theopolis withered before he could get to his silver powder. Very like the White Fox, always determined to get the bounty, no matter what. We won't soon see a hunter like him again."

"I suppose not," Daggon said, though he'd much rather that the man had kept his skin. Now who would Daggon tell his tales about? He didn't fancy paying for his own beer.

Nearby, a greasy-looking fellow rose from his meal and shuffled out of the front door, looking half drunk already, though it was only noon.

Some people. Daggon shook his head. "To the White Fox," he said, raising his drink.

Earnest clinked his mug to Daggon's. "The White Fox, meanest bastard the Forests have ever known."

"May his soul know peace," Daggon said, "and may the God Beyond be thanked that he never decided we were worth his time."

"Amen," Earnest said.

"Of course," Daggon said, "there *is* still Bloody Kent. Now *he's* a right nasty fellow. You'd better hope he doesn't get your number, friend. And don't you give me that innocent look. These are the Forests. Everybody here has done something, now and then, that you don't want others to know about. . . ."

# POSTSCRIPT

This story started when George R. R. Martin leaned over at a book signing the two of us were doing and said, "Hey, do you do short fiction?"

I told him I did *long* short fiction. He then invited me into one of his anthologies—which was a true honor. The anthologies he and Gardner Dozois do are kind of a "who's who" of speculative fiction writers, and though George is famous for his novels these days, he's always been known in the industry for his editorial skills. (Gardner, by the way, is equally famous—so it's a real privilege to get an invitation from them.)

I thought a long time about the nature of an anthology called *Dangerous Women.* I worried that stories submitted to it might fall into the trope of making women dangerous all in the same way. (This turned out to not be the case, fortunately.) I didn't want to write just another clichéd story about a femme fatale, or a woman soldier who was basically a man with breasts.

What other ways could someone be dangerous? I knew early on that I wanted my protagonist to be a middle-aged mother. Threnody was a fully built world already, as I knew it was important to the Cosmere. I toyed with setting the story there, and the final piece came when I was doing genealogy for religious purposes and ran across a woman named Silence.

Who would name their daughter Silence? It seemed one of those beautifully Puritan names that wouldn't fly in most settings—but it was perfect for Threnody. (Someday, someone will pull out of us what Nazh's real name is.) The story grew from there.

A few cool notes about this story. First, the rules for how to deal with the ghosts are (vaguely) based on Jewish laws of what you can and can't do on the Sabbath. Isaac, our tireless cartographer, named the planet

Threnody (he named Nazh as well). The frame story with the men in Silence's inn was nearly cut two or three times—even Gardner was skeptical about it when he started reading. In the end, it proved worth its space because of the punch it gives transitioning into Silence's viewpoint, and because of the nice way it wraps up the story at the end. I think it's necessary, but it also means the story starts with what I consider a weaker section.

You'll see more of this world in the future, most likely.

# THE DROMINAD SYSTEM

The Drominad System
Seventh of the Sun
Sixth of the Sun
Fifth of the Sun
asteroid belt
Fourth of the Sun
Third of the Sun
Second of the Sun
First of the Sun
First of the First

# THE DROMINAD SYSTEM

THERE are many planets in the cosmere that are inhabited, but upon which no Shards currently reside. Though the lives, passions, and beliefs of the people are, of course, important regardless of which planet they reside on, only a few of these planets have relevance to the greater cosmere at large.

This is mostly due to the fact that travel on and off the planets (at least in the Physical Realm) is dependent upon perpendicularities—places where a person can transition from Shadesmar onto the planet itself. If a world doesn't have a perpendicularity, then it can be studied from the Cognitive Realm, but cannot truly be visited.

In general, perpendicularities are created by the presence of a Shard on the planet. The concentration of so much Investiture on the Cognitive and Physical Realms creates points of . . . friction, where a kind of tunneling exists. At these points, Physical matter, Cognitive thought, and Spiritual essence become one—and a being can slide between Realms.

The existence of a perpendicularity (which often take the form of pools of concentrated power on the Physical Realm) on a planet is a hallmark of a Shard's presence. This is what makes First of the Sun so interesting.

The system, nicknamed Drominad, has a remarkable three planets inhabited by fully developed human societies. (There is also a fourth planet in the habitable zone.) This is unique in the cosmere; only the Rosharan system can rival it, and there one of the planets is inhabited solely by Splinters.

All four of these planets have water as a dominant feature. And one of them, the first planet, has a perpendicularity.

I have not been able to discover why, or how, this perpendicularity exists. There is certainly no Shard residing in the system. I cannot say what is happening, only that this feature must hint at things that occurred in the past of the planet. There is likely Investiture here somewhere as well, though I have not yet had a chance to investigate First of the Sun myself. The area around the perpendicularity is extremely dangerous, and the few expeditions sent there from Silverlight have not returned.

# SIXTH OF THE DUSK

DEATH hunted beneath the waves. Dusk saw it approach, an enormous blackness within the deep blue, a shadowed form as wide as six narrowboats tied together. Dusk's hands tensed on his paddle, his heartbeat racing as he immediately sought out Kokerlii.

Fortunately, the colorful bird sat in his customary place on the prow of the boat, idly biting at one clawed foot raised to his beak. Kokerlii lowered his foot and puffed out his feathers, as if completely unmindful of the danger beneath.

Dusk held his breath. He always did, when unfortunate enough to run across one of these things in the open ocean. He did not know what they looked like beneath those waves. He hoped to never find out.

The shadow drew closer, almost to the boat now. A school of slimfish passing nearby jumped into the air in a silvery wave, spooked by the shadow's approach. The terrified fish showered back to the water with a sound like rain. The shadow did not deviate. The slimfish were too small a meal to interest it.

A boat's occupants, however . . .

It passed directly underneath. Sak chirped quietly from Dusk's shoulder;

the second bird seemed to have some sense of the danger. Creatures like the shadow did not hunt by smell or sight, but by sensing the minds of prey. Dusk glanced at Kokerlii again, his only protection against a danger that could swallow his ship whole. He had never clipped Kokerlii's wings, but at times like this he understood why many sailors preferred Aviar that could not fly away.

The boat rocked softly; the jumping slimfish stilled. Waves lapped against the sides of the vessel. Had the shadow stopped? Hesitated? Did it sense them? Kokerlii's protective aura had always been enough before, but . . .

The shadow slowly vanished. It had turned to swim downward, Dusk realized. In moments, he could make out nothing through the waters. He hesitated, then forced himself to get out his new mask. It was a modern device he had acquired only two supply trips back: a glass faceplate with leather at the sides. He placed it on the water's surface and leaned down, looking into the depths. They became as clear to him as an undisturbed lagoon.

Nothing. Just that endless deep. *Fool man,* he thought, tucking away the mask and getting out his paddle. *Didn't you just think to yourself that you never wanted to see one of those?*

Still, as he started paddling again, he knew that he'd spend the rest of this trip feeling as if the shadow were down there, following him. That was the nature of the waters. You never knew what lurked below.

He continued on his journey, paddling his outrigger canoe and reading the lapping of the waves to judge his position. Those waves were as good as a compass for him—once, they would have been good enough for any of the Eelakin, his people. These days, just the trappers learned the old arts. Admittedly, though, even *he* carried one of the newest compasses, wrapped up in his pack with a set of the new sea charts—maps given as gifts by the Ones Above during their visit earlier in the year. They were said to be more accurate than even the latest surveys, so he'd purchased a set just in case. You could not stop times from changing, his mother said, no more than you could stop the surf from rolling.

It was not long, after the accounting of tides, before he caught sight of the first island. Sori was a small island in the Pantheon, and the most commonly visited. Her name meant "child"; Dusk vividly remembered training on her shores with his uncle.

It had been long since he'd burned an offering to Sori, despite how well she had treated him during his youth. Perhaps a small offering would not be out of line. Patji would not grow jealous. One could not be jealous of Sori, the least of the islands. Just as every trapper was welcome on Sori, every other island in the Pantheon was said to be affectionate of her.

Be that as it may, Sori did not contain much valuable game. Dusk continued rowing, moving down one leg of the archipelago his people knew as the Pantheon. From a distance, this archipelago was not so different from the homeisles of the Eelakin, now a three-week trip behind him.

From a distance. Up close, they were very, very different. Over the next five hours, Dusk rowed past Sori, then her three cousins. He had never set foot on any of those three. In fact, he had not landed on many of the forty-some islands in the Pantheon. At the end of his apprenticeship, a trapper chose one island and worked there all his life. He had chosen Patji—an event some ten years past now. Seemed like far less.

Dusk saw no other shadows beneath the waves, but he kept watch. Not that he could do much to protect himself. Kokerlii did all of that work as he roosted happily at the prow of the ship, eyes half closed. Dusk had fed him seed; Kokerlii did like it so much more than dried fruit.

Nobody knew why beasts like the shadows only lived here, in the waters near the Pantheon. Why not travel across the seas to the Eelakin Islands or the mainland, where food would be plentiful and Aviar like Kokerlii were far more rare? Once, these questions had not been asked. The seas were what they were. Now, however, men poked and prodded into everything. They asked, "Why?" They said, "We should explain it."

Dusk shook his head, dipping his paddle into the water. That sound—wood on water—had been his companion for most of his days. He understood it far better than he did the speech of men.

Even if sometimes their questions got inside of him and refused to go free.

After the cousins, most trappers would have turned north or south, moving along branches of the archipelago until reaching their chosen island. Dusk continued forward, into the heart of the islands, until a shape loomed before him. Patji, largest island of the Pantheon. It towered like a wedge rising from the sea. A place of inhospitable peaks, sharp cliffs, and deep jungle.

*Hello, old destroyer,* he thought. *Hello, Father.*

Dusk raised his paddle and placed it in the boat. He sat for a time, chewing on fish from last night's catch, feeding scraps to Sak. The black-plumed bird ate them with an air of solemnity. Kokerlii continued to sit on the prow, chirping occasionally. He would be eager to land. Sak seemed never to grow eager about anything.

Approaching Patji was not a simple task, even for one who trapped his shores. The boat continued its dance with the waves as Dusk considered which landing to make. Eventually, he put the fish away, then dipped his paddle back into the waters. Those waters remained deep and blue, despite the proximity to the island. Some members of the Pantheon had sheltered bays and gradual beaches. Patji had no patience for such foolishness. His beaches were rocky and had steep drop-offs.

You were never safe on his shores. In fact, the beaches were the most dangerous part—upon them, not only could the horrors of the land get to you, but you were still within reach of the deep's monsters. Dusk's uncle had cautioned him about this time and time again. Only a fool slept on Patji's shores.

The tide was with him, and he avoided being caught in any of the swells that would crush him against those stern rock faces. Dusk approached a partially sheltered expanse of stone crags and outcroppings, Patji's version of a beach. Kokerlii fluttered off, chirping and calling as he flew toward the trees.

Dusk immediately glanced at the waters. No shadows. Still, he felt naked as he hopped out of the canoe and pulled it up onto the rocks, warm water washing against his legs. Sak remained in her place on Dusk's shoulder.

Nearby in the surf, Dusk saw a corpse bobbing in the water.

*Beginning your visions early, my friend?* he thought, glancing at Sak.

The Aviar usually waited until they'd fully landed before bestowing her blessing.

The black-feathered bird just watched the waves.

Dusk continued his work. The body he saw in the surf was his own. It told him to avoid that section of water. Perhaps there was a spiny anemone that would have pricked him, or perhaps a deceptive undercurrent lay in wait. Sak's visions did not show such detail; they gave only warning.

Dusk got the boat out of the water, then detached the floats, tying them more securely onto the main part of the canoe. Following that, he worked the vessel carefully up the shore, mindful not to scrape the hull on sharp rocks. He would need to hide the canoe in the jungle. If another trapper discovered it, Dusk would be stranded on the island for several extra weeks preparing his spare. That would—

He stopped as his heel struck something soft as he backed up the shore. He glanced down, expecting a pile of seaweed. Instead he found a damp piece of cloth. A shirt? Dusk held it up, then noticed other, more subtle signs across the shore. Broken lengths of sanded wood. Bits of paper floating in an eddy.

*Those fools,* he thought.

He returned to moving his canoe. Rushing was never a good idea on a Pantheon island. He did step more quickly, however.

As he reached the tree line, he caught sight of his corpse hanging from a tree nearby. Those were cutaway vines lurking in the fernlike treetop. Sak squawked softly on his shoulder as Dusk hefted a large stone from the beach, then tossed it at the tree. It thumped against the wood, and sure enough, the vines dropped like a net, full of stinging barbs.

They would take a few hours to retract. Dusk pulled his canoe over and hid it in the underbrush near the tree. Hopefully, other trappers would be smart enough to stay away from the cutaway vines—and therefore wouldn't stumble over his boat.

Before placing the final camouflaging fronds, Dusk pulled out his pack. Though the centuries had changed a trapper's duties very little, the modern world did offer its benefits. Instead of a simple wrap that left his legs and chest exposed, he put on thick trousers with pockets on the legs and a buttoning shirt to protect his skin against sharp branches and leaves. Instead of sandals, Dusk tied on sturdy boots. And instead of a tooth-lined club, he bore a machete of the finest steel. His pack contained luxuries like a steel-hooked rope, a lantern, and a firestarter that created sparks simply by pressing the two handles together.

He looked very little like the trappers in the paintings back home. He didn't mind. He'd rather stay alive.

Dusk left the canoe, shouldering his pack, machete sheathed at his side. Sak moved to his other shoulder. Before leaving the beach, Dusk paused, looking at the image of his translucent corpse, still hanging from unseen vines by the tree.

Could he really have ever been foolish enough to be caught by cutaway vines? Near as he could tell, Sak only showed him plausible deaths. He liked to think that most were fairly unlikely—a vision of what could have happened if he'd been careless, or if his uncle's training hadn't been so extensive.

Once, Dusk had stayed away from any place where he saw his corpse. It wasn't bravery that drove him to do the opposite now. He just . . . needed to confront the possibilities. He needed to be able to walk away from this beach knowing that he could still deal with cutaway vines. If he avoided danger, he would soon lose his skills. He could not rely on Sak too much.

For Patji would try on every possible occasion to kill him.

Dusk turned and trudged across the rocks along the coast. Doing so went against his instincts—he normally wanted to get inland as soon as possible. Unfortunately, he could not leave without investigating the origin of the debris he had seen earlier. He had a strong suspicion of where he would find their source.

He gave a whistle, and Kokerlii trilled above, flapping out of a tree nearby and winging over the beach. The protection he offered would not be as strong as it would be if he were close, but the beasts that hunted minds on the island were not as large or as strong of psyche as the shadows of the ocean. Dusk and Sak would be invisible to them.

About a half hour up the coast, Dusk found the remnants of a large camp. Broken boxes, fraying ropes lying half submerged in tidal pools, ripped canvas, shattered pieces of wood that might once have been walls. Kokerlii landed on a broken pole.

There were no signs of his corpse nearby. That could mean that the area wasn't immediately dangerous. It could also mean that whatever might kill him here would swallow the corpse whole.

Dusk trod lightly on wet stones at the edge of the broken campsite. No. Larger than a campsite. Dusk ran his fingers over a broken chunk of wood, stenciled with the words *Northern Interests Trading Company*. A powerful mercantile force from his homeland.

He had told them. He had *told* them. Do not come to Patji. Fools. And they had camped here on the beach itself! Was nobody in that company capable of listening? He stopped beside a group of gouges in the rocks, as wide as his upper arm, running some ten paces long. They led toward the ocean.

*Shadow,* he thought. *One of the deep beasts.* His uncle had spoken of seeing one once. An enormous . . . *something* that had exploded up from the depths. It had killed a dozen krell that had been chewing on ocean-side weeds before retreating into the waters with its feast.

Dusk shivered, imagining this camp on the rocks, bustling with men unpacking boxes, preparing to build the fort they had described to him. But where was their ship? The great steam-powered vessel with an iron hull they claimed could rebuff the attacks of even the deepest of shadows? Did it now defend the ocean bottom, a home for slimfish and octopus?

There were no survivors—nor even any corpses—that Dusk could see. The shadow must have consumed them. He pulled back to the slightly safer locale of the jungle's edge, then scanned the foliage, looking for signs that people had passed this way. The attack was recent, within the last day or so.

He absently gave Sak a seed from his pocket as he located a series of broken fronds leading into the jungle. So there were survivors. Maybe as many as a half dozen. They had each chosen to go in a different direction, in a hurry. Running from the attack.

Running through the jungle was a good way to get dead. These company types thought themselves rugged and prepared. They were wrong.

He'd spoken to a number of them, trying to persuade as many of their "trappers" as possible to abandon the voyage.

It had done no good. He wanted to blame the visits of the Ones Above for causing this foolish striving for progress, but the truth was the companies had been talking of outposts on the Pantheon for years. Dusk sighed. Well, these survivors were likely dead now. He should leave them to their fates.

Except . . . The thought of it, outsiders on Patji, it made him shiver with something that mixed disgust and anxiety. They were *here.* It was wrong. These islands were sacred, the trappers their priests.

The plants rustled nearby. Dusk whipped his machete about, leveling it, reaching into his pocket for his sling. It was not a refugee who left the bushes, or even a predator. A group of small, mouselike creatures crawled out, sniffing the air. Sak squawked. She had never liked meekers.

*Food?* the three meekers sent to Dusk. *Food?*

It was the most rudimentary of thoughts, projected directly into his mind. Though he did not want the distraction, he did not pass up the opportunity to fish out some dried meat for the meekers. As they huddled around it, sending him gratitude, he saw their sharp teeth and the single pointed fang at the tips of their mouths. His uncle had told him that once, meekers had been dangerous to men. One bite was enough to kill. Over the centuries, the little creatures had grown accustomed to trappers. They had minds beyond those of dull animals. Almost he found them as intelligent as the Aviar.

*You remember?* he sent them through thoughts. *You remember your task?*

*Others,* they sent back gleefully. *Bite others!*

Trappers ignored these little beasts; Dusk figured that maybe with some training, the meekers could provide an unexpected surprise for one of his rivals. He fished in his pocket, fingers brushing an old stiff piece of feather. Then, not wanting to pass up the opportunity, he got a few long, bright green and red feathers from his pack. They were mating plumes, which he'd taken from Kokerlii during the Aviar's most recent molting.

He moved into the jungle, meekers following with excitement. Once he neared their den, he stuck the mating plumes into some branches, as if they had fallen there naturally. A passing trapper might see the plumes and assume that Aviar had a nest nearby, fresh with eggs for the plunder. That would draw them.

*Bite others,* Dusk instructed again.

*Bite others!* they replied.

He hesitated, thoughtful. Had they perhaps seen something from the company wreck? Point him in the right direction. *Have you seen any others?* Dusk sent them. *Recently? In the jungle?*

*Bite others!* came the reply.

They were intelligent . . . but not *that* intelligent. Dusk bade the animals farewell and turned toward the forest. After a moment's deliberation, he found himself striking inland, crossing—then following—one of the refugee trails. He chose the one that looked as if it would pass uncomfortably close to one of his own safecamps, deep within the jungle.

It was hotter here beneath the jungle's canopy, despite the shade. Comfortably sweltering. Kokerlii joined him, winging up ahead to a branch where a few lesser Aviar sat chirping. Kokerlii towered over them, but sang at them with enthusiasm. An Aviar raised around humans never quite fit back in among their own kind. The same could be said of a man raised around Aviar.

Dusk followed the trail left by the refugee, expecting to stumble over the man's corpse at any moment. He did not, though his own dead body did occasionally appear along the path. He saw it lying half eaten in the mud or tucked away in a fallen log with only the foot showing. He could never grow too complacent, with Sak on his shoulder. It did not matter if Sak's visions were truth or fiction; he needed the constant reminder of how Patji treated the unwary.

He fell into the familiar, but not comfortable, lope of a Pantheon trapper. Alert, wary, careful not to brush leaves that could carry biting insects. Cutting with the machete only when necessary, lest he leave a trail another could follow. Listening, aware of his Aviar at all times, never outstripping Kokerlii or letting him drift too far ahead.

The refugee did not fall to the common dangers of the island—he cut across game trails, rather than following them. The surest way to encounter predators was to fall in with their food. The refugee did not know how to mask his trail, but neither did he blunder into the nest of firesnap lizards, or brush the deathweed bark, or step into the patch of hungry mud.

Was this another trapper, perhaps? A youthful one, not fully trained? That seemed something the company would try. Experienced trappers were beyond recruitment; none would be foolish enough to guide a group of clerks and merchants around the islands. But a youth, who had not yet chosen his island? A youth who, perhaps, resented being required to practice only on Sori until his mentor determined his apprenticeship complete? Dusk had felt that way ten years ago.

So the company had hired itself a trapper at last. That would explain why they had grown so bold as to finally organize their expedition. *But Patji himself?* he thought, kneeling beside the bank of a small stream. It had no name, but it was familiar to him. *Why would they come here?*

The answer was simple. They were merchants. The biggest, to them, would be the best. Why waste time on lesser islands? Why not come for the Father himself?

Above, Kokerlii landed on a branch and began pecking at a fruit. The refugee had stopped by this river. Dusk had gained time on the youth. Judging by the depth the boy's footprints had sunk in the mud, Dusk could imagine his weight and height. Sixteen? Maybe younger? Trappers apprenticed at ten, but Dusk could not imagine even the company trying to recruit one so ill trained.

*Two hours gone,* Dusk thought, turning a broken stem and smelling the sap. The boy's path continued on toward Dusk's safecamp. How? Dusk had never spoken of it to anyone. Perhaps this youth was apprenticing under one of the other trappers who visited Patji. One of them could have found his safecamp and mentioned it.

Dusk frowned, considering. In ten years on Patji, he had seen another trapper in person only a handful of times. On each occasion, they had both turned and gone a different direction without saying a word. It was the way of such things. They would try to kill one another, but they didn't do it in person. Better to let Patji claim rivals than to directly stain one's hands. At least, so his uncle had taught him.

Sometimes, Dusk found himself frustrated by that. Patji would get them all eventually. Why help the Father out? Still, it was the way of things, so he went through the motions. Regardless, this refugee was making directly for Dusk's safecamp. The youth might not know the proper way of things. Perhaps he had come seeking help, afraid to go to one of his master's safecamps for fear of punishment. Or . . .

No, best to avoid pondering it. Dusk already had a mind full of spurious conjectures. He would find what he would find. He had to focus on the jungle and its dangers. He started away from the stream, and as he did so, he saw his corpse appear suddenly before him.

He hopped forward, then spun backward, hearing a faint hiss. The distinctive sound was made by air escaping from a small break in the ground, followed by a flood of tiny yellow insects, each as small as a pinhead. A new deathant pod? If he'd stood there a little longer, disturbing their hidden nest, they would have flooded up around his boot. One bite, and he'd be dead.

He stared at that pool of scrambling insects longer than he should have. They pulled back into their nest, finding no prey. Sometimes a small bulge announced their location, but today he had seen nothing. Only Sak's vision had saved him.

Such was life on Patji. Even the most careful trapper could make a mistake—and even if they didn't, death could still find them. Patji was a domineering, vengeful parent who sought the blood of all who landed on his shores.

Sak chirped on his shoulder. Dusk rubbed her neck in thanks, though her chirp sounded apologetic. The warning had come almost too late. Without her, Patji would have claimed him this day. Dusk shoved down those itching questions he should not be thinking, and continued on his way.

He finally approached his safecamp as evening settled upon the island. Two of his tripwires had been cut, disarming them. That was not surprising; those were meant to be obvious. Dusk crept past another deathant nest in the ground—this larger one had a permanent crack as an opening they could flood out of, but the rift had been stoppered with a smoldering twig. Beyond it, the nightwind fungi that Dusk had spent years cultivating here had been smothered in water to keep the spores from escaping. The next two tripwires—the ones not intended to be obvious—had *also* been cut.

*Nice work, kid,* Dusk thought. He hadn't just avoided the traps, but disarmed them, in case he needed to flee quickly back this direction. However, someone really needed to teach the boy how to move without being trackable. Of course, those tracks could be a trap unto themselves—an attempt to make Dusk himself careless. And so, he was extra careful as he edged forward. Yes, here the youth had left more footprints, broken stems, and other signs. . . .

Something moved up above in the canopy. Dusk hesitated, squinting. A *woman* hung from the tree branches above, trapped in a net made of jellywire vines—they left someone numb, unable to move. So, one of his traps had finally worked.

"Um, hello?" she said.

*A woman,* Dusk thought, suddenly feeling stupid. *The smaller footprint, lighter step . . .*

"I want to make it perfectly clear," the woman said. "I have no intention of stealing your birds or infringing upon your territory."

Dusk stepped closer in the dimming light. He recognized this woman. She was one of the clerks who had been at his meetings with the company. "You cut my tripwires," Dusk said. Words felt odd in his mouth, and they came out ragged, as if he'd swallowed handfuls of dust. The result of weeks without speaking.

"Er, yes, I did. I assumed you could replace them." She hesitated. "Sorry?"

Dusk settled back. The woman rotated slowly in her net, and he noticed an Aviar clinging to the outside—like his own birds, it was about as tall as three fists atop one another, though this one had subdued white and green plumage. A streamer, which was a breed that did not live on Patji. He did not know much about them, other than that like Kokerlii, they protected the mind from predators.

The setting sun cast shadows, the sky darkening. Soon, he would need to hunker down for the night, for darkness brought out the island's most dangerous of predators.

"I promise," the woman said from within her bindings. What was her name? He believed it had been told to him, but he did not recall. Something untraditional. "I really don't want to steal from you. You remember me, don't you? We met back in the company halls?"

He gave no reply.

"Please," she said. "I'd really rather not be hung by my ankles from a tree, slathered with blood to attract predators. If it's all the same to you."

"You are not a trapper."

"Well, no," she said. "You may have noticed my gender."

"There have been female trappers."

"One. One female trapper, Yaalani the Brave. I've heard her story a hundred times. You may find it curious to know that almost every society has its myth of the female role reversal. She goes to war dressed as a man, or leads her father's armies into battle, or traps on an island. I'm convinced that such stories exist so that parents can tell their daughters, 'You are not Yaalani.'"

This woman spoke. A lot. People did that back on the Eelakin Islands. Her skin was dark, like his, and she had the sound of his people. The slight accent to her voice . . . he had heard it more and more when visiting the homeisles. It was the accent of one who was educated.

"Can I get down?" she asked, voice bearing a faint tremor. "I cannot feel my hands. It is . . . unsettling."

"What is your name?" Dusk asked. "I have forgotten it." This was too much speaking. It hurt his ears. This place was supposed to be soft.

"Vathi."

*That's right.* It was an improper name. Not a reference to her birth order and day of birth, but a name like the mainlanders used. That was not uncommon among his people now.

He walked over and took the rope from the nearby tree, then lowered the net. The woman's Aviar flapped down, screeching in annoyance, favoring one wing, obviously wounded. Vathi hit the ground, a bundle of dark curls and green linen skirts. She stumbled to her feet, but fell back down again. Her skin would be numb for some fifteen minutes from the touch of the vines.

She sat there and wagged her hands, as if to shake out the numbness. "So . . . uh, no ankles and blood?" she asked, hopeful.

"That is a story parents tell to children," Dusk said. "It is not something we actually do."

"Oh."

"If you had been another trapper, I would have killed you directly, rather than leaving you to avenge yourself upon me." He walked over to her Aviar, which opened its beak in a hissing posture, raising both wings as if to be bigger than it was. Sak chirped from his shoulder, but the bird didn't seem to care.

Yes, one wing was bloody. Vathi knew enough to care for the bird, however, which was pleasing. Some homeislers were completely ignorant of their Aviar's needs, treating them like accessories rather than intelligent creatures.

Vathi had pulled out the feathers near the wound, including a blood feather. She'd wrapped the wound with gauze. That wing didn't look good, however. Might be a fracture involved. He'd want to wrap both wings, prevent the creature from flying.

"Oh, Mirris," Vathi said, finally finding her feet. "I tried to help her. We fell, you see, when the monster—"

"Pick her up," Dusk said, checking the sky. "Follow. Step where I step."

Vathi nodded, not complaining, though her numbness would not have passed yet. She collected a small pack from the vines and straightened her skirts. She wore a tight vest above them, and the pack had some kind of metal tube sticking out of it. A map case? She fetched her Aviar, who huddled happily on her shoulder.

As Dusk led the way, she followed, and she did not attempt to attack him when his back was turned. Good. Darkness was coming upon them, but his safecamp was just ahead, and he knew by heart the steps to approach along this path. As they walked, Kokerlii fluttered down and landed on the woman's other shoulder, then began chirping in an amiable way.

Dusk stopped, turning. The woman's own Aviar moved down her dress away from Kokerlii to cling near her bodice. The bird hissed softly, but Kokerlii—oblivious, as usual—continued to chirp happily. It was fortunate his breed was so mind-invisible, even deathants would consider him no more edible than a piece of bark.

"Is this . . ." Vathi said, looking to Dusk. "Yours? But of course. The one on your shoulder is not Aviar."

Sak settled back, puffing up her feathers. No, her species was not Aviar. Dusk continued to lead the way.

"I have never seen a trapper carry a bird who was not from the islands," Vathi said from behind.

It was not a question. Dusk, therefore, felt no need to reply.

This safecamp—he had three total on the island—lay atop a short hill following a twisting trail. Here, a stout gurratree held aloft a single-room structure. Trees were one of the safer places to sleep on Patji. The treetops were the domain of the Aviar, and most of the large predators walked.

Dusk lit his lantern, then held it aloft, letting the orange light bathe his home. "Up," he said to the woman.

She glanced over her shoulder into the darkening jungle. By the lantern-light, he saw that the whites of her eyes were red from lack of sleep, despite the unconcerned smile she gave him before climbing up the stakes he'd planted in the tree. Her numbness should have worn off by now.

"How did you know?" he asked.

Vathi hesitated, near to the trapdoor leading into his home. "Know what?"

"Where my safecamp was. Who told you?"

"I followed the sound of water," she said, nodding toward the small spring that bubbled out of the mountainside here. "When I found traps, I knew I was coming the right way."

Dusk frowned. One could not hear this water, as the stream vanished only a few hundred yards away, resurfacing in an unexpected location. Following it here . . . that would be virtually impossible.

So was she lying, or was she just lucky?

"You wanted to find me," he said.

"I wanted to find *someone*," she said, pushing open the trapdoor, voice growing muffled as she climbed up into the building. "I figured that a trapper would be my only chance for survival." Above, she stepped up to one of the netted windows, Kokerlii still on her shoulder. "This is nice. Very roomy for a shack on a mountainside in the middle of a deadly jungle on an isolated island surrounded by monsters."

Dusk climbed up, holding the lantern in his teeth. The room at the top was perhaps four paces square, tall enough to stand in, but only barely. "Shake out those blankets," he said, nodding toward the stack and setting down the lantern. "Then lift every cup and bowl on the shelf and check inside of them."

Her eyes widened. "What am I looking for?"

"Deathants, scorpions, spiders, bloodscratches . . ." He shrugged, putting Sak on her perch by the window. "The room is built to be tight, but this is Patji. The Father likes surprises."

As she hesitantly set aside her pack and got to work, Dusk continued up another ladder to check the roof. There, a group of bird-size boxes, with nests inside and holes to allow the birds to come and go freely, lay arranged in a double row. The animals would not stray far, except on special occasions, now that they had been raised with him handling them.

Kokerlii landed on top of one of the homes, trilling—but softly, now that night had fallen. More coos and chirps came from the other boxes. Dusk climbed out to check each bird for hurt wings or feet. These Aviar pairs were his life's work; the chicks each one hatched became his primary stock-in-trade. Yes, he would trap on the island, trying to find nests and wild chicks—but that was never as efficient as raising nests.

"Your name was Sixth, wasn't it?" Vathi said from below, voice accompanied by the sound of a blanket being shaken.

"It is."

"Large family," Vathi noted.

An ordinary family. Or, so it had once been. His father had been a twelfth and his mother an eleventh.

"Sixth of what?" Vathi prompted below.

"Of the Dusk."

"So you were born in the evening," Vathi said. "I've always found the traditional names so . . . uh . . . *descriptive.*"

*What a meaningless comment,* Dusk thought. *Why do homeislers feel the need to speak when there is nothing to say?*

He moved on to the next nest, checking the two drowsy birds inside, then inspecting their droppings. They responded to his presence with happiness. An Aviar raised around humans—particularly one that had lent its talent to a person at an early age—would always see people as part of their flock. These birds were not his companions, like Sak and Kokerlii, but they were still special to him.

"No insects in the blankets," Vathi said, sticking her head up out of the trapdoor behind him, her own Aviar on her shoulder.

"The cups?"

"I'll get to those in a moment. So these are your breeding pairs, are they?"

Obviously they were, so he didn't need to reply.

She watched him check them. He felt her eyes on him. Finally, he spoke. "Why did your company ignore the advice we gave you? Coming here was a disaster."

"Yes."

He turned to her.

"Yes," she continued, "this whole expedition will likely be a disaster—a disaster that takes us a step closer to our goal."

He checked Sisisru next, working by the light of the now-rising moon. "Foolish."

Vathi folded her arms before her on the roof of the building, torso still disappearing into the lit square of the trapdoor below. "Do you think that our ancestors learned to wayfind on the oceans without experiencing a few disasters along the way? Or what of the first trappers? You have knowledge passed down for generations, knowledge learned through trial and error. If the first trappers had considered it too 'foolish' to explore, where would you be?"

"They were single men, well-trained, not a ship full of clerks and dockworkers."

"The world is changing, Sixth of the Dusk," she said softly. "The people of the mainland grow hungry for Aviar companions; things once restricted to the very wealthy are within the reach of ordinary people. We've learned so much, yet the Aviar are still an enigma. Why don't chicks raised on the homeisles bestow talents? Why—"

"Foolish arguments," Dusk said, putting Sisisru back into her nest. "I do not wish to hear them again."

"And the Ones Above?" she asked. "What of their technology, the wonders they produce?"

He hesitated, then he took out a pair of thick gloves and gestured toward her Aviar. Vathi looked at the white and green Aviar, then made a comforting clicking sound and took her in two hands. The bird suffered it with a few annoyed half bites at Vathi's fingers.

Dusk carefully took the bird in his gloved hands—for him, those bites would not be as timid—and undid Vathi's bandage. Then he cleaned the wound—much to the bird's protests—and carefully placed a new bandage. From there, he wrapped the bird's wings around its body with another bandage, not too tight, lest the creature be unable to breathe.

She didn't like it, obviously. But flying would hurt that wing more, with the fracture. She'd eventually be able to bite off the bandage, but for now, she'd get a chance to heal. Once done, he placed her with his other Aviar, who made quiet, friendly chirps, calming the flustered bird.

Vathi seemed content to let her bird remain there for the time, though she watched the entire process with interest.

"You may sleep in my safecamp tonight," Dusk said, turning back to her.

"And then what?" she asked. "You turn me out into the jungle to die?"

"You did well on your way here," he said, grudgingly. She was not a trapper. A scholar should not have been able to do what she did. "You will probably survive."

"I got lucky. I'd never make it across the entire island."

Dusk paused. "Across the island?"

"To the main company camp."

"There are *more* of you?"

"I . . . Of course. You didn't think . . ."

"What happened?" *Now who is the fool?* he thought to himself. *You should have asked this first.* Talking. He had never been good with it.

She shied away from him, eyes widening. Did he look dangerous? Perhaps he had barked that last question forcefully. No matter. She spoke, so he got what he needed.

"We set up camp on the far beach," she said. "We have two ironhulls armed with cannons watching the waters. Those can take on even a deepwalker, if they have to. Two hundred soldiers, half that number in scientists and merchants. We're determined to find out, once and for all, why the Aviar must be born on one of the Pantheon Islands to be able to bestow talents.

"One team came down this direction to scout sites to place another fortress. The company is determined to hold Patji against other interests. I thought the smaller expedition a bad idea, but had my own reasons for wanting to circle the island. So I went along. And then, the deepwalker . . ." She looked sick.

Dusk had almost stopped listening. Two *hundred* soldiers? Crawling across Patji like ants on a fallen piece of fruit. Unbearable! He thought of the quiet jungle broken by the sounds of their racketous voices. The sound of humans yelling at each other, clanging on metal, stomping about. Like a city.

A flurry of dark feathers announced Sak coming up from below and landing on the lip of the trapdoor beside Vathi. The black-plumed bird limped across the roof toward Dusk, stretching her wings, showing off the scars on her left. Flying even a dozen feet was a chore for her.

Dusk reached down to scratch her neck. It was happening. An invasion. He had to find a way to stop it. Somehow . . .

"I'm sorry, Dusk," Vathi said. "The trappers are fascinating to me; I've read of your ways, and I respect them. But this was *going* to happen someday; it's inevitable. The islands *will* be tamed. The Aviar are too valuable to leave in the hands of a couple hundred eccentric woodsmen."

"The chiefs . . ."

"All twenty chiefs in council agreed to this plan," Vathi said. "I was there. If the Eelakin do not secure these islands and the Aviar, someone else will."

Dusk stared out into the night. "Go and make certain there are no insects in the cups below."

"But—"

"*Go,*" he said, "and make *certain* there are no insects in the cups below!"

The woman sighed softly, but retreated into the room, leaving him with his Aviar. He continued to scratch Sak on the neck, seeking comfort in the familiar motion and in her presence. Dared he hope that the shadows would prove too deadly for the company and its iron-hulled ships? Vathi seemed confident.

*She did not tell me why she joined the scouting group.* She had seen a shadow, witnessed it destroying her team, but had still managed the presence of mind to find his camp. She was a strong woman. He would need to remember that.

She was also a company type, as removed from his experience as a person could get. Soldiers, craftsmen, even chiefs he could understand. But these soft-spoken scribes who had quietly conquered the world with a sword of commerce, they baffled him.

"Father," he whispered. "What do I do?"

Patji gave no reply beyond the normal sounds of night. Creatures moving, hunting, rustling. At night, the Aviar slept, and that gave opportunity to the most dangerous of the island's predators. In the distance a nightmaw called, its horrid screech echoing through the trees.

Sak spread her wings, leaning down, head darting back and forth. The sound always made her tremble. It did the same to Dusk.

He sighed and rose, placing Sak on his shoulder. He turned, and almost stumbled as he saw his corpse at his feet. He came alert immediately. What was it? Vines in the tree branches? A spider, dropping quietly from above? There wasn't supposed to be anything in his safecamp that could kill him.

Sak screeched as if in pain.

Nearby, his other Aviar cried out as well, a cacophony of squawks, screeches, chirps. No, it wasn't just them! All around . . . echoing in the distance, from both near and far, wild Aviar squawked. They rustled in their branches, a sound like a powerful wind blowing through the trees.

Dusk spun about, holding his hands to his ears, eyes wide as corpses appeared around him. They piled high, one atop another, some bloated, some bloody, some skeletal. Haunting him. Dozens upon *dozens.*

He dropped to his knees, yelling. That put him eye-to-eye with one of his corpses. Only this one . . . this one was not quite dead. Blood dripped from its lips as it tried to speak, mouthing words that Dusk did not understand.

It vanished.

They all did, every last one. He spun about, wild, but saw no bodies. The sounds of the Aviar quieted, and his flock settled back into their nests. Dusk breathed in and out deeply, heart racing. He felt tense, as if at any moment a shadow would explode from the blackness around his camp and consume him. He anticipated it, felt it coming. He wanted to run, run *somewhere*.

What had that been? In all of his years with Sak, he had never seen anything like it. What could have upset all of the Aviar at once? Was it the nightmaw he had heard?

*Don't be foolish,* he thought. *This was different, different from anything you've seen. Different from anything that has been seen on Patji.* But what? What had changed . . .

Sak had not settled down like the others. She stared northward, toward where Vathi had said the main camp of invaders was setting up.

Dusk stood, then clambered down into the room below, Sak on his shoulder. "What are your people doing?"

Vathi spun at his harsh tone. She had been looking out of the window, northward. "I don't—"

He took her by the front of her vest, pulling her toward him in a two-fisted grip, meeting her eyes from only a few inches away. "*What are your people doing?*"

Her eyes widened, and he could feel her tremble in his grip, though she set her jaw and held his gaze. Scribes were not supposed to have grit like this. He had seen them scribbling away in their windowless rooms. Dusk tightened his grip on her vest, pulling the fabric so it dug into her skin, and found himself growling softly.

"Release me," she said, "and we will speak."

"Bah," he said, letting go. She dropped a few inches, hitting the floor with a thump. He hadn't realized he'd lifted her off the ground.

She backed away, putting as much space between them as the room would allow. He stalked to the window, looking through the mesh screen at the night. His corpse dropped from the roof above, hitting the ground below. He jumped back, worried that it was happening again.

It didn't, not the same way as before. However, when he turned back into the room, his corpse lay in the corner, bloody lips parted, eyes staring sightlessly. The danger, whatever it was, had not passed.

Vathi had sat down on the floor, holding her head, trembling. Had he frightened her that soundly? She did look tired, exhausted. She wrapped her arms around herself, and when she looked at him, there was a cast to her eyes that hadn't been there before—as if she were regarding a wild animal let off its chain.

That seemed fitting.

"What do you know of the Ones Above?" she asked him.

"They live in the stars," Dusk said.

"We at the company have been meeting with them. We don't understand their ways. They look like us; at times they talk like us. But they have . . . rules, laws that they won't explain. They refuse to sell us their marvels, but in like manner, they seem forbidden from taking things from us, even in trade. They promise it, someday when we are more advanced. It's like they think we are children."

"Why should we care?" Dusk said. "If they leave us alone, we will be better for it."

"You haven't seen the things they can do," she said softly, getting a distant look in her eyes. "We have barely worked out how to create ships that can sail on their own, against the wind. But the Ones Above . . . they can sail the skies, sail the *stars themselves.* They know so much, and they won't *tell* us any of it."

She shook her head, reaching into the pocket of her skirt. "They are after something, Dusk. What interest do we hold for them? From what I've heard them say, there are many other worlds like ours, with cultures that cannot sail the stars. We are not unique, yet the Ones Above come back here time and time again. They *do* want something. You can see it in their eyes. . . ."

"What is that?" Dusk asked, nodding to the thing she took from her pocket. It rested in her palm like the shell of a clam, but had a mirror-like face on the top.

"It is a machine," she said. "Like a clock, only it never needs to be wound, and it . . . shows things."

"What things?"

"Well, it translates languages. Ours into that of the Ones Above. It also . . . shows the locations of Aviar."

"*What?*"

"It's like a map," she said. "It points the way to Aviar."

"That's how you found my camp," Dusk said, stepping toward her.

"Yes." She rubbed her thumb across the machine's surface. "We aren't supposed to have this. It was the possession of an emissary sent to work with us. He choked while eating a few months back. They *can* die, it appears, even of mundane causes. That . . . changed how I view them.

"His kind have asked after his machines, and we will have to return them soon. But this one tells us what they are after: the Aviar. The Ones Above are always fascinated with them. I think they want to find a way to trade for the birds, a way their laws will allow. They hint that we might not be safe, that not everyone Above follows their laws."

"But why did the Aviar react like they did, just now?" Dusk said, turning back to the window. "Why did . . ." *Why did I see what I saw? What I'm still seeing, to an extent?* His corpse was there, wherever he looked. Slumped by a tree outside, in the corner of the room, hanging out of the trapdoor in the roof. Sloppy. He should have closed that.

Sak had pulled into his hair like she did when a predator was near.

"There . . . is a second machine," Vathi said.

"Where?" he demanded.

"On our ship."

The direction the Aviar had looked.

"The second machine is much larger," Vathi said. "This one in my hand has limited range. The larger one can create an enormous map, one of an entire island, then *write* out a paper with a copy of that map. That map will include a dot marking every Aviar."

"And?"

"And we were going to engage the machine tonight," she said. "It takes hours to prepare—like an oven, growing hot—before it's ready. The schedule was to turn it on tonight just after sunset so we could use it in the morning."

"The others," Dusk demanded, "they'd use it without you?"

She grimaced. "Happily. Captain Eusto probably did a dance when I didn't return from scouting. He's been worried I would take control of this expedition. But the machine isn't harmful; it merely locates Aviar."

"Did it do *that* before?" he demanded, waving toward the night.

"When you last used it, did it draw the attention of all the Aviar? Discomfort them?"

"Well, no," she said. "But the moment of discomfort has passed, hasn't it? I'm sure it's nothing."

Nothing. Sak quivered on his shoulder. Dusk saw death all around him. The moment they had engaged that machine, the corpses had piled up. If they used it again, the results would be horrible. Dusk knew it. He could *feel* it.

"We're going to stop them," he said.

"What?" Vathi asked. "*Tonight?*"

"Yes," Dusk said, walking to a small hidden cabinet in the wall. He pulled it open and began to pick through the supplies inside. A second lantern. Extra oil.

"That's insane," Vathi said. "Nobody travels the islands at night."

"I've done it once before. With my uncle."

His uncle had died on that trip.

"You can't be serious, Dusk. The nightmaws are out. I've heard them."

"Nightmaws track minds," Dusk said, stuffing supplies into his pack. "They are almost completely deaf, and close to blind. If we move quickly and cut across the center of the island, we can be to your camp by morning. We can stop them from using the machine again."

"But why would we *want* to?"

He shouldered the pack. "Because if we don't, it will destroy the island."

She frowned at him, cocking her head. "You can't know that. Why do you think you know that?"

"Your Aviar will have to remain here, with that wound," he said, ignoring the question. "She would not be able to fly away if something happened to us." The same argument could be made for Sak, but he would not be without the bird. "I will return her to you after we have stopped the machine. Come." He walked to the floor hatch and pulled it open.

Vathi rose, but pressed back against the wall. "I'm staying here."

"The people of your company won't believe me," he said. "You will have to tell them to stop. You are coming."

Vathi licked her lips in what seemed to be a nervous habit. She glanced to the sides, looking for escape, then back at him. Right then,

Dusk noticed his corpse hanging from the pegs in the tree beneath him. He jumped.

"What was that?" she demanded.

"Nothing."

"You keep glancing to the sides," Vathi said. "What do you think you see, Dusk?"

"We're going. Now."

"You've been alone on the island for a long time," she said, obviously trying to make her voice soothing. "You're upset about our arrival. You aren't thinking clearly. I understand."

Dusk drew in a deep breath. "Sak, show her."

The bird launched from his shoulder, flapping across the room, landing on Vathi. She turned to the bird, frowning.

Then she gasped, falling to her knees. Vathi huddled back against the wall, eyes darting from side to side, mouth working but no words coming out. Dusk left her to it for a short time, then raised his arm. Sak returned to him on black wings, dropping a single dark feather to the floor. She settled in again on his shoulder. That much flying was difficult for her.

"What was *that*?" Vathi demanded.

"Come," Dusk said, taking his pack and climbing down out of the room.

Vathi scrambled to the open hatch. "No. Tell me. What *was* that?"

"You saw your corpse."

"All about me. Everywhere I looked."

"Sak grants that talent."

"There is no such talent."

Dusk looked up at her, halfway down the pegs. "You have seen your death. That is what will happen if your friends use their machine. Death. All of us. The Aviar, everyone living here. I do not know why, but I know that it *will* come."

"You've discovered a new Aviar," Vathi said. "How . . . When . . . ?"

"Hand me the lantern," Dusk said.

Looking numb, she obeyed, handing it down. He put it into his teeth and descended the pegs to the ground. Then he raised the lantern high, looking down the slope.

The inky jungle at night. Like the depths of the ocean.

He shivered, then whistled. Kokerlii fluttered down from above, landing on his other shoulder. He would hide their minds, and with that, they had a chance. It would still not be easy. The things of the jungle relied upon mind sense, but many could still hunt by scent or other senses.

Vathi scrambled down the pegs behind him, her pack over her shoulder, the strange tube peeking out. "You have two Aviar," she said. "You use them both at once?"

"My uncle had three."

"How is that even possible?"

"They like trappers." So many questions. Could she not think about what the answers might be before asking?

"We're actually going to do this," she said, whispering, as if to herself. "The jungle at night. I should stay. I should refuse . . ."

"You've seen your death if you do."

"I've seen what you claim is my death. A new Aviar . . . It has been centuries." Though her voice still sounded reluctant, she walked after him as he strode down the slope and passed his traps, entering the jungle again.

His corpse sat at the base of a tree. That made him immediately look for what could kill him here, but Sak's senses seemed to be off. The island's impending death was so overpowering, it seemed to be smothering smaller dangers. He might not be able to rely upon her visions until the machine was destroyed.

The thick jungle canopy swallowed them, hot, even at night; the ocean breezes didn't reach this far inland. That left the air feeling stagnant, and it dripped with the scents of the jungle. Fungus, rotting leaves, the perfumes of flowers. The accompaniment to those scents was the sounds of an island coming alive. A constant crinkling in the underbrush, like the sound of maggots writhing in a pile of dry leaves. The lantern's light did not seem to extend as far as it should.

Vathi pulled up close behind him. "Why did you do this before?" she whispered. "The other time you went out at night?"

More questions. But sounds, fortunately, were not too dangerous.

"I was wounded," Dusk whispered. "We had to get from one safe-camp to the other to recover my uncle's store of antivenom." Because Dusk, hands trembling, had dropped the other flask.

"You survived it? Well, obviously you did, I mean. I'm surprised, is all."

She seemed to be talking to fill the air.

"They could be watching us," she said, looking into the darkness. "Nightmaws."

"They are not."

"How can you know?" she asked, voice hushed. "Anything could be out there, in that darkness."

"If the nightmaws had seen us, we'd be dead. That is how I know." He shook his head, sliding out his machete and cutting away a few branches before them. Any could hold deathants skittering across their leaves. In the dark, it would be difficult to spot them, and so brushing against foliage seemed a poor decision.

*We won't be able to avoid it,* he thought, leading the way down through a gully thick with mud. He had to step on stones to keep from sinking in. Vathi followed with remarkable dexterity. *We have to go quickly. I can't cut down every branch in our way.*

He hopped off a stone and onto the bank of the gully, and there passed his corpse sinking into the mud. Nearby, he spotted a second corpse, so translucent it was nearly invisible. He raised his lantern, hoping it wasn't happening again.

Others did not appear. Just these two. And the very faint image . . . yes, that was a sinkhole there. Sak chirped softly, and he fished in his pocket for a seed to give her. She had figured out how to send him help. The fainter images were immediate dangers—he would have to watch for those.

"Thank you," he whispered to her.

"That bird of yours," Vathi said, speaking softly in the gloom of night, "are there others?"

They climbed out of the gully, continuing on, crossing a krell trail in the night. He stopped them just before they wandered into a patch of deathants. Vathi looked at the trail of tiny yellow insects, moving in a straight line.

"Dusk?" she asked as they rounded the ants. "Are there others? Why haven't you brought any chicks to market?"

"I do not have any chicks."

"So you found only the one?" she asked.

Questions, questions. Buzzing around him like flies.

*Don't be foolish,* he told himself, shoving down his annoyance. *You would ask the same, if you saw someone with a new Aviar.* He had tried to keep Sak a secret; for years, he hadn't even brought her with him when he left the island. But with her hurt wing, he hadn't wanted to abandon her.

Deep down, he'd known he couldn't keep his secret forever. "There are many like her," he said. "But only she has a talent to bestow."

Vathi stopped in place as he continued to cut them a path. He turned back, looking at her alone on the new trail. He had given her the lantern to hold.

"That's a mainlander bird," she said. She held up the light. "I knew it was when I first saw it, and I assumed it wasn't an Aviar, because mainlander birds can't bestow talents."

Dusk turned back and continued cutting.

"You brought a mainlander chick to the Pantheon," Vathi whispered behind. "And it *gained a talent.*"

With a hack he brought down a branch, then continued on. Again, she had not asked a question, so he needed not answer.

Vathi hurried to keep up, the glow of the lantern tossing his shadow before him as she stepped up behind. "Surely someone else has tried it before. Surely . . ."

He did not know.

"But why would they?" she continued, quietly, as if to herself. "The Aviar are special. Everyone knows the separate breeds and what they do. Why assume that a fish would learn to breathe air, if raised on land? Why assume a non-Aviar would become one if raised on Patji. . . ."

They continued through the night. Dusk led them around many dangers, though he found that he needed to rely greatly upon Sak's help. *Do not follow that stream, which has your corpse bobbing in its waters. Do not touch that tree; the bark is poisonous with rot. Turn from that path. Your corpse shows a deathant bite.*

Sak did not speak to him, but each message was clear. When he stopped to let Vathi drink from her canteen, he held Sak and found her trembling. She did not peck at him as was usual when he enclosed her in his hands.

They stood in a small clearing, pure dark all around them, the sky shrouded in clouds. He heard distant rainfall on the trees. Not uncommon, here.

Nightmaws screeched, one then another. They only did that when they had made a kill or when they were seeking to frighten prey. Often, krell herds slept near Aviar roosts. Frighten away the birds, and you could sense the krell.

Vathi had taken out her tube. Not a scroll case—and not something scholarly at all, considering the way she held it as she poured something into its end. Once done, she raised it like one would a weapon. Beneath her feet, Dusk's body lay mangled.

He did not ask after Vathi's weapon, not even as she took some kind of short, slender spear and fitted it into the top end. No weapon could penetrate the thick skin of a nightmaw. You either avoided them or you died.

Kokerlii fluttered down to his shoulder, chirping away. He seemed confused by the darkness. Why were they out like this, at night, when birds normally made no noise?

"We must keep moving," Dusk said, placing Sak on his other shoulder and taking out his machete.

"You realize that your bird changes everything," Vathi said quietly, joining him, shouldering her pack and carrying her tube in the other hand.

"There will be a new kind of Aviar," Dusk whispered, stepping over his corpse.

"That's the *least* of it. Dusk, we assumed that chicks raised away from these islands did not develop their abilities because they were not around others to train them. We assumed that their abilities were innate, like our ability to speak—it's inborn, but we require help from others to develop it."

"That can still be true," Dusk said. "Other species, such as Sak, can merely be trained to speak."

"And your bird? Was it trained by others?"

"Perhaps." He did not say what he really thought. It was a thing of trappers. He noted a corpse on the ground before them.

It was not his.

He held up a hand immediately, stilling Vathi as she continued on to ask another question. What was *this*? The meat had been picked off much of the skeleton, and the clothing lay strewn about, ripped open by animals that feasted. Small, funguslike plants had sprouted around the ground near it, tiny red tendrils reaching up to enclose parts of the skeleton.

He looked up at the great tree, at the foot of which rested the corpse. The flowers were not in bloom. Dusk released his breath.

"What is it?" Vathi whispered. "Deathants?"

"No. Patji's Finger."

She frowned. "Is that . . . some kind of curse?"

"It is a name," Dusk said, stepping forward carefully to inspect the corpse. Machete. Boots. Rugged gear. One of his colleagues had fallen. He *thought* he recognized the man from the clothing. An older trapper named First of the Sky.

"The name of a person?" Vathi asked, peeking over his shoulder.

"The name of a tree," Dusk said, poking at the corpse's clothing, careful of insects that might be lurking inside. "Raise the lamp."

"I've never heard of that tree," she said skeptically.

"They are only on Patji."

"I have read a lot about the flora on these islands. . . ."

"Here you are a child. Light."

She sighed, raising it for him. He used a stick to prod at pockets on the ripped clothing. This man had been killed by a pack of tuskrun, larger predators—almost as large as a man—that prowled mostly by day. Their movement patterns were predictable unless one happened across one of Patji's Fingers in bloom.

There. He found a small book in the man's pocket. Dusk raised it, then backed away. Vathi peered over his shoulder. Homeislers stood so *close* to each other. Did she need to stand right by his elbow?

He checked the first pages, finding a list of dates. Yes, judging by the last date written down, this man was only a few days dead. The pages after that detailed the locations of Sky's safecamps, along with explanations of the traps guarding each one. The last page contained the farewell.

*I am First of the Sky, taken by Patji at last. I have a brother on Suluko. Care for them, rival.*

Few words. Few words were good. Dusk carried a book like this himself, and he had said even less on his last page.

"He wants you to care for his family?" Vathi asked.

"Don't be stupid," Dusk said, tucking the book away. "His birds."

"That's sweet," Vathi said. "I had always heard that trappers were incredibly territorial."

"We are," he said, noting how she said it. Again, her tone made it seem as if she considered trappers to be like animals. "But our birds might die without care—they are accustomed to humans. Better to give them to a rival than to let them die."

"Even if that rival is the one who killed you?" Vathi asked. "The traps you set, the ways you try to interfere with one another . . ."

"It is our way."

"That is an awful excuse," she said, looking up at the tree.

She was right.

The tree was massive, with drooping fronds. At the end of each one was a large closed blossom, as long as two hands put together. "You don't seem worried," she noted, "though the plant seems to have killed that man."

"These are only dangerous when they bloom."

"Spores?" she asked.

"No." He picked up the fallen machete, but left the rest of Sky's things alone. Let Patji claim him. Father did so like to murder his children. Dusk continued onward, leading Vathi, ignoring his corpse draped across a log.

"Dusk?" Vathi asked, raising the lantern and hurrying to him. "If not spores, then how does the tree kill?"

"So many questions."

"My life is about questions," she replied. "And about answers. If my people are going to work on this island . . ."

He hacked at some plants with the machete.

"It *is* going to happen," she said, more softly. "I'm sorry, Dusk. You can't stop the world from changing. Perhaps my expedition will be defeated, but others will come."

"Because of the Ones Above," he snapped.

"They may spur it," Vathi said. "Truly, when we finally convince them we are developed enough to be traded with, we will sail the stars as they do. But change will happen even without them. The world is progressing. One man cannot slow it, no matter how determined he is."

He stopped in the path.

*You cannot stop the tides from changing, Dusk. No matter how determined you are.* His mother's words. Some of the last he remembered from her.

Dusk continued on his way. Vathi followed. He would need her, though a treacherous piece of him whispered that she would be easy to end. With her would go her questions, and more importantly her answers. The ones he suspected she was very close to discovering.

*You cannot change it. . . .*

He could not. He hated that it was so. He wanted so badly to protect this island, as his kind had done for centuries. He worked this jungle, he loved its birds, was fond of its scents and sounds—despite all else. How he wished he could prove to Patji that he and the others were worthy of these shores.

Perhaps. Perhaps then . . .

Bah. Well, killing this woman would not provide any real protection for the island. Besides, had he sunk so low that he would murder a helpless scribe in cold blood? He would not even do that to another trapper, unless they approached his camp and did not retreat.

"The blossoms can think," he found himself saying as he turned them away from a mound that showed the tuskrun pack had been rooting here. "The Fingers of Patji. The trees themselves are not dangerous, even when blooming—but they attract predators, imitating the thoughts of a wounded animal that is full of pain and worry."

Vathi gasped. "A *plant*," she said, "that broadcasts a mental signature? Are you certain?"

"Yes."

"I need one of those blossoms." The light shook as she turned to go back.

Dusk spun and caught her by the arm. "We must keep moving."

"But—"

"You will have another chance." He took a deep breath. "Your people will soon infest this island like maggots on carrion. You will see other trees. Tonight, we must *go.* Dawn approaches."

He let go of her and turned back to his work. He had judged her wise, for a homeisler. Perhaps she would listen.

She did. She followed behind.

Patji's Fingers. First of the Sky, the dead trapper, should not have died in that place. Truly, the trees were not that dangerous. They lived by opening many blossoms and attracting predators to come feast. The predators would then fight one another, and the tree would feed off the corpses. Sky must have stumbled across a tree as it was beginning to flower, and got caught in what came.

His Aviar had not been enough to shield so many open blossoms. Who would have expected a death like that? After years on the island, surviving much more terrible dangers, to be caught by those simple flowers. It almost seemed a mockery, on Patji's part, of the poor man.

Dusk and Vathi's path continued, and soon grew steeper. They'd need to go uphill for a while before crossing to the downward slope that would lead to the other side of the island. Their trail, fortunately, would avoid Patji's main peak—the point of the wedge that jutted up the easternmost side of the island. His camp had been near the south, and Vathi's would be to the northeast, letting them skirt around the base of the wedge before arriving on the other beach.

They fell into a rhythm, and she was quiet for a time. Eventually, atop a particularly steep incline, he nodded for a break and squatted down to drink from his canteen. On Patji one did not simply sit, without care, upon a stump or log to rest.

Consumed by worry, and not a little frustration, he didn't notice what Vathi was doing until it was too late. She'd found something tucked into a branch—a long colorful feather. A mating plume.

Dusk leaped to his feet.

Vathi reached up toward the lower branches of the tree.

A set of spikes on ropes dropped from a nearby tree as Vathi pulled the branch. They swung down as Dusk reached her, one arm thrown in the way. A spike hit, the long, thin nail ripping into his skin and jutting out the other side, bloodied, and stopping a hair from Vathi's cheek.

She screamed.

Many predators on Patji were hard of hearing, but still that wasn't wise. Dusk didn't care. He yanked the spike from his skin, unconcerned with the bleeding for now, and checked the other spikes on the drop-rope trap.

No poison. Blessedly, they had not been poisoned.

"Your arm!" Vathi said.

He grunted. It didn't hurt. Yet. She began fishing in her pack for a bandage, and he accepted her ministrations without complaint or groan, even as the pain came upon him.

"I'm so sorry!" Vathi sputtered. "I found a mating plume! That meant an Aviar nest, so I thought to look in the tree. Have we stumbled across another trapper's safecamp?"

She was babbling out words as she worked. Seemed appropriate. When he grew nervous, he grew even more quiet. She would do the opposite.

She was good with a bandage, again surprising him. The wound had not hit any major arteries. He would be fine, though using his left hand would not be easy. This would be an annoyance. When she was done, looking sheepish and guilty, he reached down and picked up the mating plume she had dropped.

"This," he said with a harsh whisper, holding it up before her, "is the symbol of your ignorance. On the Pantheon Islands, nothing is easy, nothing is simple. That plume was placed by another trapper to catch someone who does not deserve to be here, someone who thought to find an easy prize. You cannot be that person. Never move without asking yourself, is this too easy?"

She paled. Then she took the feather in her fingers.

"Come."

He turned and walked on their way. That was the speech for an apprentice, he realized. Upon their first major mistake. A ritual among trappers. What had possessed him to give it to her?

She followed behind, head bowed, appropriately shamed. She didn't realize the honor he had just paid her, if unconsciously. They walked onward, an hour or more passing.

By the time she spoke, for some reason, he almost welcomed the words breaking upon the sounds of the jungle. "I'm sorry."

"You need not be sorry," he said. "Only careful."

"I understand." She took a deep breath, following behind him on the path. "And I *am* sorry. Not just about your arm. About this island. About what is coming. I think it inevitable, but I do wish that it did not mean the end of such a grand tradition."

"I . . ."

Words. He hated trying to find words.

"It . . . was not dusk when I was born," he finally said, then hacked down a swampvine and held his breath against the noxious fumes that it released toward him. They were only dangerous for a few moments.

"Excuse me?" Vathi asked, keeping her distance from the swampvine. "You were born . . ."

"My mother did not name me for the time of day. I was named because my mother saw the dusk of our people. The sun will soon set on us, she often told me." He looked back to Vathi, letting her pass him and enter a small clearing.

Oddly, she smiled at him. Why had he found those words to speak? He followed into the clearing, concerned at himself. He had not given those words to his uncle; only his parents knew the source of his name.

He was not certain why he'd told this scribe from an evil company. But . . . it did feel good to have said them.

A nightmaw broke through between two trees behind Vathi.

The enormous beast would have been as tall as a tree if it had stood upright. Instead it leaned forward in a prowling posture, powerful legs behind bearing most of its weight, its two clawed forelegs ripping up the ground. It reached forward its long neck, beak open, razor-sharp and deadly. It looked like a bird—in the same way that a wolf looked like a lapdog.

He threw his machete. An instinctive reaction, for he did not have time for thought. He did not have time for fear. That snapping beak—as tall as a door—would have the two of them dead in moments.

His machete glanced off the beak and actually cut the creature on the side of the head. That drew its attention, making it hesitate for just a moment. Dusk leaped for Vathi. She stepped back from him, setting the butt of her tube against the ground. He needed to pull her away, to—

The explosion deafened him.

Smoke bloomed around Vathi, who stood—wide-eyed—having dropped the lantern, oil spilling. The sudden sound stunned Dusk, and he almost collided with her as the nightmaw lurched and fell, skidding, the ground *thumping* from the impact.

Dusk found himself on the ground. He scrambled to his feet, backing away from the twitching nightmaw mere inches from him. Lit by flickering lanternlight, it was all leathery skin that was bumpy like that of a bird who had lost her feathers.

It was dead. Vathi had killed it.

She said something.

Vathi had *killed* a nightmaw.

"Dusk!" Her voice seemed distant.

He raised a hand to his forehead, which had belatedly begun to prickle with sweat. His wounded arm throbbed, but he was otherwise tense. He felt as if he should be running. He had never wanted to be so close to one of these. *Never.*

She'd actually killed it.

He turned toward her, his eyes wide. Vathi was trembling, but she covered it well. "So, that worked," she said. "We weren't certain it would, even though we'd prepared these specifically for the nightmaws."

"It's like a cannon," Dusk said. "Like from one of the ships, only in your *hands*."

"Yes."

He turned back toward the beast. Actually, it *wasn't* dead, not completely. It twitched, and let out a plaintive screech that shocked him, even with his hearing muffled. The weapon had fired that spear right into the beast's chest.

The nightmaw quaked and thrashed a weak leg.

"We could kill them all," Dusk said. He turned, then rushed over to Vathi, taking her with his right hand, the arm that wasn't wounded.

"With those weapons, we could kill them *all.* Every nightmaw. Maybe the shadows too!"

"Well, yes, it has been discussed. However, they are important parts of the ecosystem on these islands. Removing the apex predators could have undesirable results."

"Undesirable results?" Dusk ran his left hand through his hair. "They'd be gone. All of them! I don't care what other problems you think it would cause. They would all be *dead.*"

Vathi snorted, picking up the lantern and stamping out the fires it had started. "I thought trappers were connected to nature."

"We are. That's how I know we would all be better off without any of these things."

"You are disabusing me of many romantic notions about your kind, Dusk," she said, circling the dying beast.

Dusk whistled, holding up his arm. Kokerlii fluttered down from high branches; in the chaos and explosion, Dusk had not seen the bird fly away. Sak still clung to his shoulder with a death grip, her claws digging into his skin through the cloth. He hadn't noticed. Kokerlii landed on his arm and gave an apologetic chirp.

"It wasn't your fault," Dusk said soothingly. "They prowl the night. Even when they cannot sense our minds, they can smell us." Their sense of smell was said to be incredible. This one had come up the trail behind them; it must have crossed their path and followed it.

Dangerous. His uncle always claimed the nightmaws were growing smarter, that they knew they could not hunt men only by their minds. *I should have taken us across more streams,* Dusk thought, reaching up and rubbing Sak's neck to soothe her. *There just isn't time. . . .*

His corpse lay wherever he looked. Draped across a rock, hanging from the vines of trees, slumped beneath the dying nightmaw's claw . . .

The beast trembled once more, then amazingly it lifted its gruesome head and let out a last screech. Not as loud as those that normally sounded in the night, but bone-chilling and horrid. Dusk stepped back despite himself, and Sak chirped nervously.

Other nightmaw screeches rose in the night, distant. That sound . . . he had been trained to recognize that sound as the sound of death.

"We're going," he said, stalking across the ground and pulling Vathi away from the dying beast, which had lowered its head and fallen silent.

"Dusk?" She did not resist as he pulled her away.

One of the other nightmaws sounded again in the night. Was it closer? *Oh, Patji, please,* Dusk thought. *No. Not this.*

He pulled her faster, reaching for his machete at his side, but it was not there. He had thrown it. He took out the one he had gathered from his fallen rival, then dragged her out of the clearing, back into the jungle, moving quickly. He could no longer worry about brushing against deathants.

A greater danger was coming.

The calls of death came again.

"Are those getting *closer*?" Vathi asked.

Dusk did not answer. It was a question, but he did not know the answer. At least his hearing was recovering. He released her hand, moving more quickly, almost at a trot—faster than he ever wanted to go through the jungle, day or night.

"Dusk!" Vathi hissed. "Will they come? To the call of the dying one? Is that something they do?"

"How should I know? I have never known one of them to be killed before." He saw the tube, again carried over her shoulder, lit by the light of the lantern she carried.

That gave him pause, though his instincts screamed at him to keep moving and he felt a fool. "Your weapon," he said. "You can use it again?"

"Yes," she said. "Once more."

"*Once* more?"

A half dozen screeches sounded in the night.

"Yes," she replied. "I only brought three spears and enough powder for three shots. I tried firing one at the shadow. It didn't do much."

He spoke no further, ignoring his wounded arm—the bandage was in need of changing—and towing her through the jungle. The calls came again and again. Agitated. How did one escape nightmaws? His Aviar clung to him, a bird on each shoulder. He had to leap over his corpse as they traversed a gulch and came up the other side.

*How do you escape them?* he thought, remembering his uncle's training. *You don't draw their attention in the first place!*

They were fast. Kokerlii would hide his mind, but if they picked up his trail at the dead one . . .

*Water.* He stopped in the night, turning right, then left. Where would he find a stream? Patji was an island. Fresh water came from rainfall, mostly. The largest lake . . . the only one . . . was up the wedge. Toward the peak. Along the eastern side, the island rose to some heights with cliffs on all sides. Rainfall collected there, in Patji's Eye. The river was his tears.

It was a dangerous place to go with Vathi in tow. Their path had skirted the slope up the heights, heading across the island toward the northern beach. They were close. . . .

Those screeches behind spurred him on. Patji would just have to forgive him for what came next. Dusk seized Vathi's hand and towed her in a more eastern direction. She did not complain, though she did keep looking over her shoulder.

The screeches grew closer.

He ran. He ran as he had never expected to do on Patji, wild and reckless. Leaping over troughs, around fallen logs coated in moss. Through the dark underbrush, scaring away meekers and startling Aviar slumbering in the branches above. It was foolish. It was crazy. But did it matter? Somehow, he knew those other things would not claim him. The kings of Patji hunted him; lesser dangers would not dare steal from their betters.

Vathi followed with difficulty. Those skirts were trouble, but she caught up to him each time Dusk had to occasionally stop and cut their way through underbrush. Urgent, frantic. He expected her to keep up, and she did. A piece of him—buried deep beneath the terror—was impressed. This woman would have made a fantastic trapper. Instead she would probably destroy all trappers.

He froze as screeches sounded behind, so close. Vathi gasped, and Dusk turned back to his work. Not far to go. He hacked through a dense patch of undergrowth and ran on, sweat streaming down the sides of his face. Jostling light came from Vathi's lantern behind; the scene before him was one of horrific shadows dancing on the jungle's boughs, leaves, ferns, and rocks.

*This is your fault, Patji,* he thought with an unexpected fury. The screeches seemed almost on top of him. Was that breaking brush he could hear behind? *We are your priests, and yet you hate us! You hate all.*

Dusk broke from the jungle and out onto the banks of the river. Small by mainland standards, but it would do. He led Vathi right into it, splashing into the cold waters.

He turned upstream. What else could he do? Downstream would lead closer to those sounds, the calls of death.

*Of the Dusk,* he thought. *Of the Dusk.*

The waters came only to their calves, bitter cold. The coldest water on the island, though he did not know why. They slipped and scrambled as they ran, best they could, upriver. They passed through some narrows, with lichen-covered rock walls on either side twice as tall as a man, then burst out into the basin.

A place men did not go. A place he had visited only once. A cool emerald lake rested here, sequestered.

Dusk towed Vathi to the side, out of the river, toward some brush. Perhaps she would not see. He huddled down with her, raising a finger to his lips, then turned down the light of the lantern she still held. Nightmaws could not see well, but perhaps the dim light would help. In more ways than one.

They waited there, on the shore of the small lake, hoping that the water had washed away their scent—hoping the nightmaws would grow confused or distracted. For one thing about this place was that the basin had steep walls, and there was no way out other than the river. If the nightmaws came up it, Dusk and Vathi would be trapped.

Screeches sounded. The creatures had reached the river. Dusk waited in near darkness, and so squeezed his eyes shut. He prayed to Patji, whom he loved, whom he hated.

Vathi gasped softly. "What . . . ?"

So she had seen. Of course she had. She was a seeker, a learner. A questioner.

Why must men ask so many questions?

"Dusk! There are Aviar here, in these branches! Hundreds of them." She spoke in a hushed, frightened tone. Even as they awaited death itself, she saw and could not help speaking. "Have you seen them? What is this place?" She hesitated. "So many juveniles. Barely able to fly . . ."

"They come here," he whispered. "Every bird from every island. In their youth, they must come here."

He opened his eyes, looking up. He had turned down the lantern, but it was still bright enough to see them roosting there. Some stirred at the light and the sound. They stirred more as the nightmaws screeched below.

Sak chirped on his shoulder, terrified. Kokerlii, for once, had nothing to say.

"Every bird from every island . . ." Vathi said, putting it together. "They all come here, to this place. Are you certain?"

"Yes." It was a thing that trappers knew. You could not capture a bird before it had visited Patji.

Otherwise it would be able to bestow no talent.

"They come here," she said. "We knew they migrated between islands. . . . Why do they come here?"

Was there any point in holding back now? She would figure it out. Still, he did not speak. Let her do so.

"They gain their talents here, don't they?" she asked. "How? Is it where they are trained? Is this how you made a bird who was not an Aviar into one? You brought a hatchling here, and then . . ." She frowned, raising her lantern. "I recognize those trees. They are the ones you called Patji's Fingers."

A dozen of them grew here, the largest concentration on the island. And beneath them, their fruit littered the ground. Much of it eaten, some of it only halfway so, bites taken out by birds of all stripes.

Vathi saw him looking, and frowned. "The fruit?" she asked.

"Worms," he whispered in reply.

A light seemed to go on in her eyes. "It's not the birds. It never has been . . . it's a parasite. They carry a parasite that bestows talents! That's why those raised away from the islands cannot gain the abilities, and why a mainland bird you brought here could."

"Yes."

"This changes everything, Dusk. Everything."

"Yes."

Of the Dusk. Born during that dusk, or bringer of it? What had he done?

Downriver, the nightmaw screeches drew closer. They had decided to search upriver. They were clever, more clever than men off the islands thought them to be. Vathi gasped, turning toward the small river canyon.

"Isn't this dangerous?" she whispered. "The trees are blooming. The nightmaws will come! But no. So many Aviar. They can hide those blossoms, like they do a man's mind?"

"No," he said. "All minds in this place are invisible, always, regardless of Aviar."

"But . . . how? Why? The worms?"

Dusk didn't know, and for now didn't care. *I am trying to protect you, Patji!* Dusk looked toward Patji's Fingers. *I need to stop the men and their device. I know it! Why? Why do you hunt me?*

Perhaps it was because he knew so much. Too much. More than any man had known. For he had asked questions.

Men. And their questions.

"They're coming up the river, aren't they?" she asked.

The answer seemed obvious. He did not reply.

"No," she said, standing. "I won't die with this knowledge, Dusk. I *won't*. There must be a way."

"There is," he said, standing beside her. He took a deep breath. *So I finally pay for it.* He took Sak carefully in his hand, and placed her on Vathi's shoulder. He pried Kokerlii free too.

"What are you doing?" Vathi asked.

"I will go as far as I can," Dusk said, handing Kokerlii toward her. The bird bit with annoyance at his hands, although never strong enough to draw blood. "You will need to hold him. He will try to follow me."

"No, wait. We can hide in the lake, they—"

"They will find us!" Dusk said. "It isn't deep enough by far to hide us."

"But you can't—"

"They are nearly here, woman!" he said, forcing Kokerlii into her hands. "The men of the company will not listen to me if I tell them to turn off the device. You are smart, you can make them stop. You can reach them. With Kokerlii you can reach them. Be ready to go."

She looked at him, stunned, but she seemed to realize that there was no other way. She stood, holding Kokerlii in two hands as he pulled out the journal of First of the Sky, then his own book that listed where his Aviar were, and tucked them into her pack. Finally, he stepped back into the river. He could hear a rushing sound downstream. He would have to go quickly to reach the end of the canyon before they arrived. If he could draw them out into the jungle even a short ways to the south, Vathi could slip away.

As he entered the stream, his visions of death finally vanished. No more corpses bobbing in the water, lying on the banks. Sak had realized what was happening.

She gave a final chirp.

He started to run.

One of Patji's Fingers, growing right next to the mouth of the canyon, was blooming.

"Wait!"

He should not have stopped as Vathi yelled at him. He should have continued on, for time was so slim. However, the sight of that flower—along with her yell—made him hesitate.

*The flower . . .*

It struck him as it must have struck Vathi. An idea. Vathi ran for her pack, letting go of Kokerlii, who immediately flew to his shoulder and started chirping at him in annoyed chastisement. Dusk didn't listen. He yanked the flower off—it was as large as a man's head, with a large bulging part at the center.

It was invisible in this basin, like they all were.

"A flower that can think," Vathi said, breathing quickly, fishing in her pack. "A flower that can draw the attention of predators."

Dusk pulled out his rope as she brought out her weapon and prepared it. He lashed the flower to the end of the spear sticking out slightly from the tube.

Nightmaw screeches echoed up the cavern. He could see their shadows, hear them splashing.

He stumbled back from Vathi as she crouched down, set the weapon's butt against the ground, and pulled a lever at the base.

The explosion, once again, nearly deafened him.

Aviar all around the rim of the basin screeched and called in fright, taking wing. A storm of feathers and flapping ensued, and through the middle of it, Vathi's spear shot into the air, flower on the end. It arced out over the canyon into the night.

Dusk grabbed her by the shoulder and pulled her back along the river, into the lake itself. They slipped into the shallow water, Kokerlii on his shoulder, Sak on hers. They left the lantern burning, giving a quiet light to the suddenly empty basin.

The lake was not deep. Two or three feet. Even crouching, it didn't cover them completely.

The nightmaws stopped in the canyon. His lanternlight showed a couple of them in the shadows, large as huts, turning and watching the sky. They were smart, but like the meekers, not as smart as men.

*Patji,* Dusk thought. *Patji, please . . .*

The nightmaws turned back down the canyon, following the mental signature broadcast by the flowering plant. And, as Dusk watched, his corpse bobbing in the water nearby grew increasingly translucent.

Then faded away entirely.

Dusk counted to a hundred, then slipped from the waters. Vathi, sodden in her skirts, did not speak as she grabbed the lantern. They left the weapon, its shots expended.

The calls from the nightmaws grew farther and farther away as Dusk led the way out of the canyon, then directly north, slightly downslope. He kept expecting the screeches to turn and follow.

They did not.

The company fortress was a horridly impressive sight. A work of logs and cannons right at the edge of the water, guarded by an enormous iron-hulled ship. Smoke rose from it, the burning of morning cookfires. A short distance away, what must have been a dead shadow rotted in the sun, its mountainous carcass draped half in the water, half out.

He didn't see his own corpse anywhere, though on the final leg of their trip to the fortress he had seen it several times. Always in a place of immediate danger. Sak's visions had returned to normal.

Dusk turned back to the fortress, which he did not enter. He preferred to remain on the rocky, familiar shore—perhaps twenty feet from the entrance—his wounded arm aching as the company people rushed out through the gate to meet Vathi. Their scouts on the upper walls kept careful watch on Dusk. A trapper was not to be trusted.

Even standing here, some twenty feet from the wide wooden gates into the fort, he could smell how wrong the place was. It was stuffed with the scents of men—sweaty bodies, the smell of oil, and other, newer scents that he recognized from his recent trips to the homeisles. Scents that made him feel like an outsider among his own people.

The company men wore sturdy clothing, trousers like Dusk's but far better tailored, shirts and rugged jackets. Jackets? In Patji's heat? These people bowed to Vathi, showing her more deference than Dusk would have expected. They drew hands from shoulder to shoulder as they started speaking—a symbol of respect. Foolishness. Anyone could make a gesture like that; it didn't mean anything. True respect included far more than a hand waved in the air.

But they did treat her like more than a simple scribe. She was better placed in the company than he'd assumed. Not his problem anymore, regardless.

Vathi looked at him, then back at her people. "We must hurry to the machine," she said to them. "The one from Above. We must turn it off."

Good. She would do her part. Dusk turned to walk away. Should he give words at parting? He'd never felt the need before. But today, it felt . . . wrong not to say something.

He started walking. Words. He had never been good with words.

"Turn it off?" one of the men said from behind. "What do you mean, Lady Vathi?"

"You don't need to feign innocence, Winds," Vathi said. "I know you turned it on in my absence."

"But we didn't."

Dusk paused. What? The man sounded sincere. But then, Dusk was no expert on human emotions. From what he'd seen of people from the home-isles, they could fake emotion as easily as they faked a gesture of respect.

"What *did* you do, then?" Vathi asked them.

"We . . . opened it."

*Oh no . . .*

"Why would you do that?" Vathi asked.

Dusk turned to regard them, but he didn't need to hear the answer. The answer was before him, in the vision of a dead island he'd misinterpreted.

"We figured," the man said, "that we should see if we could puzzle out how the machine worked. Vathi, the insides . . . they're complex beyond what we could have imagined. But there are seeds there. Things we could—"

"No!" Dusk said, rushing toward them.

One of the sentries above planted an arrow at his feet. He lurched to a stop, looking wildly from Vathi up toward the walls. Couldn't they see? The bulge in mud that announced a deathant den. The game trail. The distinctive curl of a cutaway vine. Wasn't it *obvious*?

"It will destroy us," Dusk said. "Don't seek . . . Don't you see . . . ?"

For a moment, they all just stared at him. He had a chance. Words. He needed *words*.

"That machine is deathants!" he said. "A den, a . . . Bah!" How could he explain?

He couldn't. In his anxiety, words fled him, like Aviar fluttering away into the night.

The others finally started moving, pulling Vathi toward the safety of their treasonous fortress.

"You said the corpses are gone," Vathi said as she was ushered through the gates. "We've succeeded. I will see that the machine is not engaged on this trip! I promise you this, Dusk!"

"But," he cried back, "it was never *meant* to be engaged!"

The enormous wooden gates of the fortress creaked closed, and he lost sight of her. Dusk cursed. Why hadn't he been able to explain?

Because he didn't know how to talk. For once in his life, that seemed to matter.

Furious, frustrated, he stalked away from that place and its awful smells. Halfway to the tree line, however, he stopped, then turned. Sak fluttered down, landing on his shoulder and cooing softly.

Questions. Those questions wanted into his brain.

Instead he yelled at the guards. He demanded they return Vathi to him. He even pled.

Nothing happened. They wouldn't speak to him. Finally, he started to feel foolish. He turned back toward the trees, and continued on his way. His assumptions were probably wrong. After all, the corpses *were* gone. Everything could go back to normal.

. . . Normal. Could anything *ever* be normal with that fortress looming behind him? He shook his head, entering the canopy. The dense humidity of Patji's jungle should have calmed him.

Instead it annoyed him. As he started the trek toward another of his safecamps, he was so distracted that he could have been a youth, his first time on Sori. He almost stumbled straight onto a gaping deathant den; he didn't even notice the vision Sak sent. This time, dumb luck saved him as he stubbed his toe on something, looked down, and only then spotted both corpse and crack crawling with motes of yellow.

He growled, then sneered. "Still you try to kill me?" he shouted, looking up at the canopy. "Patji!"

Silence.

"The ones who protect you are the ones you try hardest to kill," Dusk shouted. "Why!"

The words were lost in the jungle. It consumed them.

"You deserve this, Patji," he said. "What is coming to you. You *deserve to be destroyed*!"

He breathed out in gasps, sweating, satisfied at having finally said those things. Perhaps there was a purpose for words. Part of him, as traitorous as Vathi and her company, was *glad* that Patji would fall to their machines.

Of course, then the company itself would fall. To the Ones Above. His entire people. The world itself.

He bowed his head in the shadows of the canopy, sweat dripping down the sides of his face. Then he fell to his knees, heedless of the nest just three strides away.

Sak nuzzled into his hair. Above, in the branches, Kokerlii chirped uncertainly.

"It's a trap, you see," he whispered. "The Ones Above have rules. They can't trade with us until we're advanced enough. Just like a man can't, in good conscience, bargain with a child until they are grown. And so, they have left their machines for us to discover, to prod at and poke. The dead man was a ruse. Vathi was *meant* to have those machines.

"There will be explanations, left as if carelessly, for us to dig into and learn. And at some point in the near future, we will build something like one of their machines. We will have grown more quickly than we should have. We will be childlike still, ignorant, but the laws from Above will let these visitors trade with us. And then, they will take this land for themselves."

That was what he should have said. Protecting Patji was impossible. Protecting the Aviar was impossible. Protecting their entire *world* was impossible. Why hadn't he explained it?

Perhaps because it wouldn't have done any good. As Vathi had said . . . progress would come. If you wanted to call it that.

Dusk had arrived.

Sak left his shoulder, winging away. Dusk looked after her, then cursed. She did not land nearby. Though flying was difficult for her, she fluttered on, disappearing from his sight.

"Sak?" he asked, rising and stumbling after the Aviar. He fought back the way he had come, following Sak's squawks. A few moments later, he lurched out of the jungle.

Vathi stood on the rocks before her fortress.

Dusk hesitated at the brim of the jungle. Vathi was alone, and even the sentries had retreated. Had they cast her out? No. He could see that the gate was cracked, and some people watched from inside.

Sak had landed on Vathi's shoulder down below. Dusk frowned, reaching his hand to the side and letting Kokerlii land on his arm. Then he strode forward, calmly making his way down the rocky shore, until he was standing just before Vathi.

She'd changed into a new dress, though there were still snarls in her hair. She smelled of flowers.

And her eyes were terrified.

He'd traveled the darkness with her. Had faced nightmaws. Had seen her near to death, and she had not looked this worried.

"What?" he asked, finding his voice hoarse.

"We found instructions in the machine," Vathi whispered. "A manual on its workings, left there as if accidentally by someone who worked on it before. The manual is in their language, but the smaller machine I have . . ."

"It translates."

"The manual details how the machine was constructed," Vathi says. "It's so complex I can barely comprehend it, but it seems to explain concepts and ideas, not just give the workings of the machine."

"And are you not happy?" he asked. "You will have your flying machines soon, Vathi. Sooner than anyone could have imagined."

Wordless, she held something up. A single feather—a mating plume. She had kept it.

"Never move without asking yourself, is this too easy?" she whispered. "You said it was a trap as I was pulled away. When we found the manual, I . . . Oh, Dusk. They are planning to do to us what . . . what we are doing to Patji, aren't they?"

Dusk nodded.

"We'll lose it all. We can't fight them. They'll find an excuse, they'll *seize* the Aviar. It makes perfect sense. The Aviar use the worms. We use the Aviar. The Ones Above use us. It's inevitable, isn't it?"

*Yes,* he thought. He opened his mouth to say it, and Sak chirped. He frowned and turned back toward the island. Jutting from the ocean, arrogant. Destructive.

Patji. Father.

And finally, at long last, Dusk understood.

"No," he whispered.

"But—"

He undid his pants pocket, then reached deeply into it, digging around. Finally, he pulled something out. The remnants of a feather, just the shaft now. A mating plume that his uncle had given him, so many years ago, when he'd first fallen into a trap on Sori. He held it up, remembering the speech he'd been given. Like every trapper.

*This is the symbol of your ignorance. Nothing is easy, nothing is simple.*

Vathi held hers. Old and new.

"No, they will not have us," Dusk said. "We will see through their traps, and we will not fall for their tricks. For we have been trained by the Father himself for this very day."

She stared at his feather, then up at him.

"Do you really think that?" she asked. "They are cunning."

"They may be cunning," he said. "But they have not lived on Patji. We will gather the other trappers. We will not let ourselves be taken in."

She nodded hesitantly, and some of the fear seemed to leave her. She turned and waved for those behind her to open the gates to the building. Again, the scents of mankind washed over him.

Vathi looked back, then held out her hand to him. "You will help, then?"

His corpse appeared at her feet, and Sak chirped warningly. Danger. Yes, the path ahead would include much danger.

Dusk took Vathi's hand and stepped into the fortress anyway.

# POSTSCRIPT

The original version of this story had Dusk referring to himself as "Sixth," which was super confusing to readers. I liked it because it was so different, but in the end I relented to the feedback I was getting—because it was the right thing to do. Not only is "Dusk" more important thematically than "Sixth," it's way easier to keep track of in a sentence.

For those who don't know, this story was brainstormed on an episode of Writing Excuses. We did four episodes where we brainstormed together, then one of us took that idea and wrote a story on it. The initial brainstorming session we did for me ended up failing; I just wasn't excited about the story. So we tried again, and this was the result.

This is the only story in the anthology where the world wasn't built into the original Cosmere plan. I did, however, leave myself room in my Cosmere outline for a handful of worlds I hadn't defined yet—as I knew I'd eventually have stories I wanted to tell that didn't fit on a planet with a Shard. Our brainstorming session on air wasn't specifically for a Cosmere story, but as I worked on the outline, I was intrigued by the idea of using symbiosis (in a new way) for a Cosmere Investiture.

I quickly fell in love with the idea, and the resulting story. You'll likely see more from the people of this planet, though there are no plans for another story or novel in the world. If you can't tell from the Alcatraz books and the Horneater culture in the Stormlight Archive, I have a fascination with Polynesian culture. The concept of wayfinding through the lapping of waves is just one of those things that won't leave me alone, and the ability to write about a character out on his own on the ocean—isolated in multiple ways—was intriguing to me. Also, considering how many talkative characters I do in books, it was a pleasure to try something new in someone like Dusk.

This is the farthest forward, timeline-wise, of any of the stories in this collection. So, at the time of Khriss's writing of the introduction to the system, the events of this story haven't actually taken place yet.

If you'd like to read the original brainstorming sessions in print form, along with early drafts of this story, they're available (along with the three stories written by the other hosts of Writing Excuses: Mary Robinette Kowal, Dan Wells, and Howard Tayler) in an anthology called *Shadows Beneath.*

# THE ROSHARAN SYSTEM

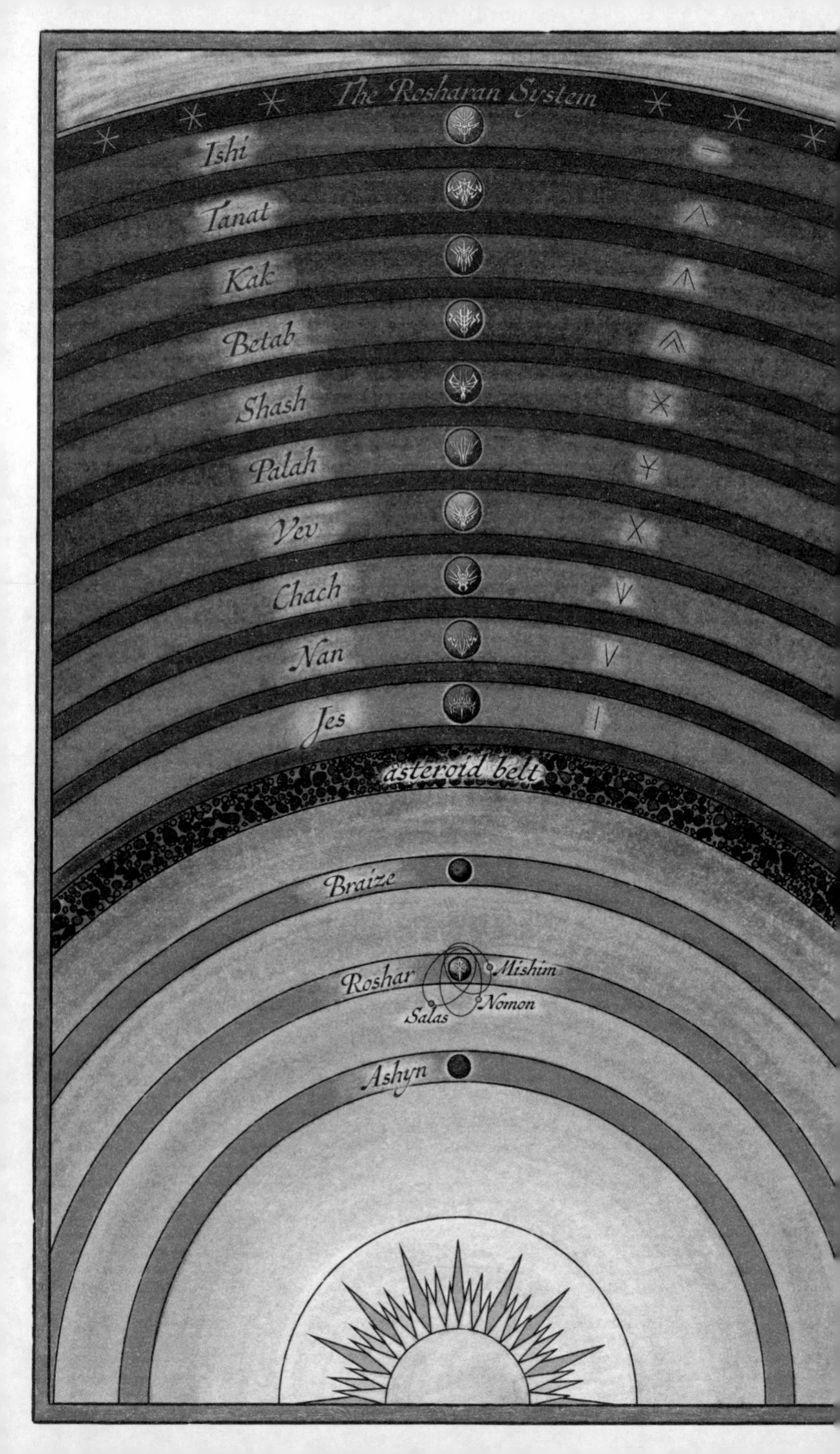

The Rosharan System
Ishi
Tanat
Kak
Betab
Shash
Palah
Vev
Chach
Nan
Jes
asteroid belt
Braize
Roshar
Mishim
Nomon
Salas
Ashyn

# THE ROSHARAN SYSTEM

Roshar (which—characteristic of the dominant confidence of its people—is the name of a planet, a system, *and* the main continent on the planet) is a busy place. As empty as the Scadrian system seems, this one always feels crowded to me. A series of enormous gas giants crowd the outer reaches of the system, though nobody has been able to observe them directly, as their manifestation on Shadesmar is minor.

There are a whopping *three* planets in the habitable zone, all of which are inhabited to one extent or another. There is Ashyn, the burning planet, which suffered a cataclysm long ago. People here live in very small pockets of survivability, including the famous floating cities. Farthest out of the three is Braize, which despite being cold and inhospitable to men is home to an ecosystem of self-aware Splinters. (The local parlance would call them spren.) I believe it's possible some of these are actually Cognitive Shadows, but research here is difficult and dangerous, so I will hold back on theorizing for the moment.

The showpiece of the system is, of course, the middle planet of Roshar itself. At 0.7 cosmere standard in gravitation and 0.9 in size—and possessing a high-oxygen environment—Roshar is home to a diverse and unique ecology containing dramatic megafauna and fascinating symbiotic relationships between creatures (both humanoid and not) and Splinters of Investiture.

The most dramatic of these is the relationship between humans and self-aware spren, which is the basis for the magic of Surgebinding. This magic has strong roots in natural physics, with the spren being personifications of the forces themselves (called Surges locally). Gravitation, the strong axial force, surface tension . . . these things have come alive, as have more abstract notions such as transformation and transportation.

However, this pattern (the bonding of spren to human) is merely an expansion of what already exists in the nature of the planet. Gargantuan crustaceans grow to incredible size without collapsing under their own weight not just through the nature of the planet, but through symbiosis with spren. Certain animals obtain flight through similar means, and there is even a race of equines that—through the spren bond—have adapted to life on the planet and obtained a high enough level of self-awareness to nearly be named a sapient species.

I will not speak on the relationship of Roshar's divergent ecology here, as that is a topic too large to address in a simple survey such as this one. However, travelers to the planet should be made aware of the storms. Life on Roshar has been shaped over millennia by massive, Invested storms, which pose a danger that cannot be overstated.

These storms, by my best guess, predate the arrival of the Shards Honor and Cultivation—as do many of the spren. However, the presence of the Shards molded and transformed the planet's nature to the point that it is difficult to distinguish what is pre-Shattering in origin, and what is a newer development. Surely, many of the spren that now exist on the planet have arisen from the friction between Honor, Cultivation, and Odium.

Odium. Be aware that this system is the current habitation of the Shard of Odium on the Physical and Cognitive Realms. This Shard undoubtedly caused the Splintering of Devotion, Dominion, Honor, and perhaps others throughout the cosmere.

Visitors to Roshar should know that fire will respond unusually because of the high-oxygen environment, which I believe is part of the reason that an alternative light source was developed during the early days of humanoid life on the planet. Be aware that lengths and times mentioned in essays and stories about the world usually use local measurements. A Rosharan year is longer than cosmere standard, and a Rosharan foot is larger than cosmere standard. It is difficult not to feel very small, at times, on this domineering, majestic tempest of a planet.

# EDGEDANCER

This story takes place after and contains spoilers for *Words of Radiance*.

# 1

LIFT prepared to be awesome.

She sprinted across an open field in northern Tashikk, a little more than a week's travel from Azimir. The place was overgrown with brown grass a foot or two high. The occasional trees were tall and twisty, with trunks that looked like they were made of interwoven vines, and branches that pointed upward more than out.

They had some official name, but everyone she knew called them drop-deads because of their springy roots. In a storm, they'd fall over flat and just lie there. Afterward they'd pop back up, like a rude gesture made at the passing winds.

Lift's run startled a group of axehinds who had been grazing nearby; the lean creatures leaped away on four legs with the two front claws pulled in close to the body. Good eating, those beasties. Barely any shell on them. But for once, Lift wasn't in the mood to eat.

She was on the *run*.

"Mistress!" Wyndle, her pet Voidbringer, called. He took the shape of a vine, growing along the ground beside her at superfast speed, matching her pace. He didn't have a face at the moment, but could speak anyway. Unfortunately.

"Mistress," he pled, "can't we please just *go back*?"

Nope.

Lift became awesome. She drew on the stuff inside of her, the stuff that made her glow. She Slicked the soles of her feet with it, and leaped into a skid.

Suddenly, the ground didn't rub against her at all. She slid as if on ice, whipping through the field. Grass startled all around her, curling as it yanked down into stone burrows. That made it bow before her in a wave.

She zipped along, wind pushing back her long black hair, tugging at the loose overshirt she wore atop her tighter brown undershirt, which was tucked into her loose-cuffed trousers.

She slid, and felt free. Just her and the wind. A small windspren, like a white ribbon in the air, started to follow her.

Then she hit a rock.

The stupid rock held firm—it was held in place by little tufts of moss that grew on the ground and stuck to things like stones, holding them down as shelter against the wind. Lift's foot flashed with pain and she tumbled in the air, then hit the stone ground face-first.

Reflexively, she made her face awesome—so she kept right on going, skidding on her cheek until she hit a tree. She stopped there, finally.

The tree slowly fell over, playing dead. It hit the ground with a shivering sound of leaves and branches.

Lift sat up, rubbing her face. She'd cut her foot, but her awesomeness plugged up the hole, healing it plenty quick. Her face didn't even hurt much. When a part of her was awesome, it didn't rub on what it touched, it just kind of . . . glided.

She still felt stupid.

"Mistress," Wyndle said, curling up to her. His vine looked like the type fancy people would grow on their buildings to hide up parts that didn't look rich enough. Except he had bits of crystal growing out of him along the vine's length. They jutted out unexpectedly, like toenails on a face.

When he moved, he didn't wiggle like an eel. He actually grew, leaving a long trail of vines behind him that would soon crystallize and decay into dust. Voidbringers were strange.

He wound around himself in a circle, like rope coiling, and formed a small tower of vines. And then something grew from the top: a face that formed out of vines, leaves, and gemstones. The mouth worked as he spoke.

"Oh, mistress," he said. "Can't we stop playing out here, *please*? We need to get back to Azimir!"

"Go back?" Lift stood up. "We just escaped that place!"

"Escaped! The *palace*? Mistress, you were an honored guest of the emperor! You had everything you wanted, as much food, as much—"

"All lies," she declared, hands on hips. "To keep me from noticin' the truth. They was going to *eat* me."

Wyndle stammered. He wasn't so frightening, for a Voidbringer. He must have been like . . . the Voidbringer all the other ones made fun of for wearing silly hats. The one that would correct all the others, and explain which fork they had to use when they sat down to consume human souls.

"Mistress," Wyndle said. "Humans do *not* eat other humans. You were a guest!"

"Yeah, but *why*? They gave me too much stuff."

"You saved the emperor's life!"

"That should've been good for a few days of freeloading," she said. "I once pulled a guy out of prison, and he gave me five whole days in his den for free, and a nice handkerchief too. *That* was generous. The Azish letting me stay as long as I wanted?" She shook her head. "They wanted something. Only explanation. They was going to starvin' eat me."

"But—"

Lift started running again. The cold stone, perforated by grass burrows, felt good on her toes and feet. No shoes. What good were shoes? In the palace, they'd started offering her heaps of shoes. And nice clothing—big, comfy coats and robes. Clothing you could get lost in. She'd liked wearing something soft for once.

Then they'd started asking. Why not take some lessons, and learn to read? They were grateful for what she'd done for Gawx, who was now Prime Aqasix, a fancy title for their ruler. Because of her service, she could have tutors, they said. She could learn how to wear those clothes properly, learn how to write.

It had started to consume her. If she'd stayed, how long would it have been before she wasn't Lift anymore? How long until she'd have been gobbled up, another girl left in her place? Similar face, but at the same time all new?

She tried using her awesomeness again. In the palace, they had talked about the recovery of ancient powers. Knights Radiant. The binding of Surges, natural forces.

*I will remember those who have been forgotten.*

Lift Slicked herself with power, then skidded across the ground a few feet before tumbling and rolling through the grass.

She pounded her fist on the stones. Stupid ground. Stupid awesomeness. How was she supposed to stay standing, when her feet were slipperier than if they'd been coated in oil? She should just go back to paddling around on her knees. It was so much easier. She could balance that way, and use her hands to steer. Like a little crab, scooting around this way and that.

*They were elegant things of beauty,* Darkness had said. *They could ride the thinnest rope, dance across rooftops, move like a ribbon on the wind. . . .*

Darkness, the shadow of a man who had chased her, had said those things in the palace, speaking of those who had—long ago—used powers like Lift's. Maybe he'd been lying. After all, he'd been preparing to murder her at the time.

Then again, why lie? He'd treated her derisively, as if she were nothing. Worthless.

She set her jaw and stood up. Wyndle was still talking, but she ignored him, instead taking off across the deserted field, running as fast as she could, startling grass. She reached the top of a small hill, then jumped and coated her feet with power.

She started slipping immediately. The air. The air she pushed against when moving was holding her back. Lift hissed, then coated her *entire self* in power.

She sliced through the wind, turning sideways as she skidded down the side of the hill. Air slid off her, as if it couldn't find her. Even the sunlight seemed to melt off her skin. She was between places, here but not. No air, no ground. Just pure motion, so fast that she reached grass before it had time to pull away. It flowed around her, its touch brushed aside by her power.

Her skin started to glow, tendrils of smoky light rising from her. She laughed, reaching the bottom of the small hill. There she leaped some boulders.

And ran face-first into another tree.

The bubble of power around her popped. The tree toppled over—and, for good measure, the two next to it decided to fall as well. Perhaps they thought they were missing out on something.

Wyndle found her grinning like a fool, staring up at the sun, spread out on the tree trunk with her arms interwoven with the branches, a single golden gloryspren—shaped like an orb—circling above her.

"Mistress?" he said. "Oh, mistress. You were *happy* in the palace. I saw it in you!"

She didn't reply.

"And the emperor," Wyndle continued. "He'll miss you! You didn't even tell him you were going!"

"I left him a note."

"A note? You learned to write?"

"Storms, no. I ate his dinner. Right out from under the tray cover while they was preparing to bring it to him. Gawx'll know what that means."

"I find that doubtful, mistress."

She climbed up from the fallen tree and stretched, then blew her hair out of her eyes. Maybe she *could* dance across rooftops, ride on ropes, or . . . what was it? Make wind? Yeah, she could do that one for sure. She hopped off the tree and continued walking through the field.

Unfortunately, her stomach had a few things to say about how much awesomeness she'd used. She ran on food, even more than most folks. She could draw some awesomeness from everything she ate, but once it was gone, she couldn't do anything incredible again until she'd had more to eat.

Her stomach rumbled in complaint. She liked to imagine that it was cussing at her something awful, and she searched through her pockets. She'd run out of the food in her pack—she'd taken a *lot*—this morning. But hadn't she found a sausage in the bottom before tossing the pack?

Oh, right. She'd eaten that while watching those riverspren a few hours ago. She dug in her pockets anyway, but only came out with a handkerchief that she'd used to wrap up a big stack of flatbread before stuffing it in her pack. She shoved part of the handkerchief into her mouth and started chewing.

"Mistress?" Wyndle asked.

"Mie hab crubs onnit," she said around the handkerchief.

"You shouldn't have been Surgebinding so much!" He wound along on the ground beside her, leaving a trail of vines and crystals. "And we *should* have stayed in the palace. Oh, how did this happen to me? I should be gardening right now. I had the most *magnificent* chairs."

"Shars?" Lift asked, pausing.

"Yes, chairs." Wyndle wound up in a coil beside her, forming a face that tilted toward her at an angle off the top of the coil. "While in Shadesmar, I had collected the most magnificent selection of the souls of chairs from your side! I cultivated them, grew them into grand crystals. I had some Winstels, a nice Shober, *quite* the collection of spoonbacks, even a throne or two!"

"Yu gurdened *shars*?"

"Of course I gardened chairs," Wyndle said. His ribbon of vine leaped off the coil and followed her as she started walking again. "What else would I garden?"

"Fwants."

"Plants? Well, we have them in Shadesmar, but I'm no *pedestrian* gardener. I'm an artist! Why, I was planning an entire exhibition of sofas when the Ring chose me for this atrocious duty."

"Smufld gramitch mragnifude."

"Would you take that out of your mouth?" Wyndle snapped.

Lift did so.

Wyndle huffed. How a little vine thing huffed, Lift didn't know. But he did it all the time. "Now, what were you trying to say?"

"Gibberish," Lift said. "I just wanted to see how you'd respond." She stuffed the other side of the handkerchief into her mouth and started sucking on it.

They continued on with a sigh from Wyndle, who muttered about gardening and his pathetic life. He certainly was a strange Voidbringer. Come to think of it, she'd never seen him act the least bit interested in consuming someone's soul. Maybe he was a vegetarian?

They passed through a small forest, really just a corpse of trees, which was a strange term, since she never seemed to find any bodies in them. These weren't even drop-deads; those tended to grow in small patches, but each apart from the others. These had branches that wound around one another as they grew, dense and intertwined to face the highstorms.

That was basically the way to do it, right? Everyone else, they wound their branches together. Braced themselves. But Lift, she was a drop-dead. Don't intertwine, don't get caught up. Go your own way.

Yes, that was definitely how she was. That was why she'd had to leave the palace, obviously. You couldn't live your life getting up and seeing the same things every day. You had to keep moving, otherwise people started to know who you were, and then they started to expect things from you. It was one step from there to being gobbled up.

She stopped right inside the trees, standing on a pathway that someone had cut and kept maintained. She looked backward, northward, toward Azir.

"Is this about what happened to you?" Wyndle asked. "I don't know a lot about humans, but I *believe* it was natural, disconcerting though it might appear. You aren't wounded."

Lift shaded her eyes. The wrong things were changing. She was supposed to stay the same, and the world was supposed to change around her. She'd asked for that, hadn't she?

Had she been lied to?

"Are we . . . going back?" Wyndle asked, hopeful.

"No," Lift said. "Just saying goodbye." Lift shoved her hands in her pockets and turned around before continuing through the trees.

# 2

YEDDAW was one of those cities Lift had always meant to visit. It was in Tashikk, a strange place even compared to Azir. She'd always found everyone here too polite and reserved. They also wore clothing that made them hard to read.

But everyone said that you had to see Yeddaw. It was the closest you could get to seeing Sesemalex Dar—and considering *that* place had been a war zone for basically a billion years, she wasn't likely to ever get there.

Standing with hands on hips, looking down at the city of Yeddaw, she found herself agreeing with what people said. This *was* a sight. The Azish liked to consider themselves grand, but they only plastered bronze or gold or something over all their buildings and pretended that was enough. What good did that do? It just reflected her own face at her, and she'd seen that too often to be impressed by it.

No, *this* was impressive. A majestic city cut *out of the starvin' ground.*

She'd heard some of the fancy scribes in Azir talk about it—they said it was a new city, created only a hunnerd years back by hiring the Imperial Shardblades out of Azir. Those didn't spend much time at war, but were instead used for making mines or cutting up rocks and stuff. Very practical. Like using the royal throne as a stool to reach something on the high shelf.

She really shouldn't have gotten yelled at for that.

Anyway, they'd used those Shardblades here. This had once been a large, flat plain. Her vantage on a hilltop, though, let her make out hundreds of trenches cut in the stone. They interconnected, like a huge maze. Some of the trenches were wider than others, and they made a vague spiral toward the center, where a large moundlike building was the only part of the city that peeked up over the surface of the plain.

Above, in the spaces between trenches, people worked fields. There were virtually no structures up there; everything was down below. People *lived* in those trenches, which seemed to be two or three stories deep. How did they avoid being washed away in highstorms? True, they'd cut large channels leading out from the city—ones nobody seemed to live in, so the water could escape. Still didn't seem safe, but it *was* pretty cool.

She could hide really well in there. That was why she'd come, after all. To hide. Nothing else. No other reason.

The city didn't have walls, but it did have a number of guard towers spaced around it. Her pathway led down from the hills and joined with a larger road, which eventually stopped in a line of people awaiting permission to get into the city.

"How on Roshar did they manage to cut away so much rock!" Wyndle said, forming a pile of vines beside her, a twisting column that took him high enough to be by her waist, face tilted toward the city.

"Shardblades," Lift said.

"Oh. Ooooh. Those." He shifted uncomfortably, vines writhing and twisting about one another with a scrunching sound. "Yes. Those."

She folded her arms. "I should get me one of those, eh?"

Wyndle, strangely, groaned loudly.

"I figure," she explained, "that Darkness has one, right? He fought with one when he was trying to kill me and Gawx. So I ought to find one."

"Yes," Wyndle said, "you should do just that! Let us pop over to the market and pick up a legendary, all-powerful weapon of myth and lore, worth more than many kingdoms! I hear they sell them in bushels, following spring weather in the east."

"Shut it, Voidbringer." She eyed his tangle of a face. "You know something about Shardblades, don't you?"

The vines seemed to wilt.

"You *do.* Out with it. What do you know?"

He shook his vine head.

"Tell me," Lift warned.

"It's forbidden. You must discover it on your own."

"That's what I'm doing. I'm discovering it. From you. Tell me, or I'll *bite* you."

"*What?*"

"I'll bite you," she said. "I'll gnaw on you, Voidbringer. You're a vine, right? I eat plants. Sometimes."

"Even assuming my crystals wouldn't break your teeth," Wyndle said, "my mass would give you no sustenance. It would break down into dust."

"It's not about sustenance. It's about torture."

Wyndle, surprisingly, met her expression with his strange eyes grown from crystals. "Honestly, mistress, I don't think you have it in you."

She growled at him, and he wilted further, but didn't tell her the secret. Well, storms. It was good to see him have a backbone . . . or, well, the plant equivalent, whatever that was. Backbark?

"You're supposed to obey me," she said, shoving her hands in her pockets and heading along the path toward the city. "You ain't following the rules."

"I am indeed," he said with a huff. "You just don't know them. And I'll have you know that I am a gardener, and not a soldier, so I'll *not* have you hitting people with me."

She stopped. "Why would I hit anyone with you?"

He wilted so far, he was practically shriveled.

Lift sighed, then continued on her way, Wyndle following. They merged with the larger road, turning toward the tower that was a gateway into the city.

"So," Wyndle said as they passed a chull cart, "this is where we were going all along? This city cut into the ground?"

Lift nodded.

"You could have told me," Wyndle said. "I've been worried we'd be caught outside in a storm!"

"Why? It ain't raining anymore." The Weeping, oddly, had stopped. Then started again. Then stopped again. It was acting downright strange, like regular weather, rather than the long, long mild highstorm it was supposed to be.

"I don't know," Wyndle said. "Something is wrong, mistress. Something in the world. I can feel it. Did you hear what the Alethi king wrote to the emperor?"

"About a new storm coming?" Lift said. "One that blows the wrong way?"

"Yes."

"The noodles all called that silly."

"Noodles?"

"The people who hang around Gawx, talking to him all the time, telling him what to do and trying to get me to wear a robe."

"The *viziers* of *Azir*. Head clerks of the empire and advisors to the Prime!"

"Yeah. Wavy arms and blubbering features. Noodles. Anyway, they thought that angry guy—"

"—Highprince Dalinar Kholin, de facto king of Alethkar and most powerful warlord in the world right now—"

"—was makin' stuff up."

"Maybe. But don't you feel something? Out there? Building?"

"A distant thunder," Lift whispered, looking westward, past the city, toward the far-off mountains. "Or . . . or the way you feel after someone drops a pan, and you see it falling, and get ready for the clatter it will make when it hits."

"So you do feel it."

"Maybe," Lift said. The chull cart rolled past. Nobody paid any attention to her—they never did. And nobody could see Wyndle but her, because *she* was *special*. "Don't your Voidbringer friends know about this?"

"We're not . . . Lift, we're spren, but my kind—cultivationspren—are not very important. We don't have a kingdom, or even cities, of our own. We only moved to bond with you because the Cryptics and the honorspren and everyone were starting to move. Oh, we've jumped *right* into the sea of glass feet-first, but we barely know what we're doing! Everyone who had any idea of how to accomplish all this died centuries ago!"

He grew along the road beside her as they followed the chull cart, which rattled and shook as it bounced down the roadway.

"Everything is wrong, and nothing makes sense," Wyndle continued. "Bonding to you was supposed to be more difficult than it was, I gather. Memories come to me fuzzily sometimes, but I do remember more and more. I didn't go through the trauma we all thought I'd endure. That might be because of your . . . unique circumstances. But mistress, listen to me when I say something big is coming. This was the wrong time to leave Azir. We were secure there. We'll need security."

"There isn't time to get back."

"No. There probably isn't. At least we have shelter ahead."

"Yeah. Assuming Darkness doesn't kill us."

"Darkness? The Skybreaker who attacked you in the palace and came very close to murdering you?"

"Yeah," Lift said. "He's in the city. Didn't you hear me complaining that I needed a Shardblade?"

"In the city . . . in Yeddaw, where we're *going right now*?"

"Yup. The noodles have people watching for reports of him. A note came in right before we left, saying he'd been spotted in Yeddaw."

"Wait." Wyndle zipped forward, leaving a trail of vines and crystal behind. He grew up the back of the chull cart, curling onto its wood right in front of her. He made a face there, looking at her. "Is *that* why we left all of a sudden? Is *that* why we're here? Did you come *chasing* that monster?"

"Course not," Lift said, hands in her pockets. "That would be stupid."

"Which you are not."

"Nope."

"Then *why* are we *here*?"

"They got these pancakes here," she said, "with things cooked into them. Supposed to be super tasty, and they eat them during the Weeping. Ten varieties. I'm gonna steal one of each."

"You came all this way, leaving behind luxury, to eat some pancakes."

"Really *awesome* pancakes."

"Despite the fact that a deific Shardbearer is here—a man who went to great lengths to try to execute you."

"He wanted to stop me from using my powers," Lift said. "He's been seen other places. The noodles looked into it; they're fascinated by him. Everyone pays attention to that bald guy who collects the heads of kings, but *this* guy has been murdering his way across Roshar too. Little people. Quiet people."

"And we came here why?"

She shrugged. "Seemed like as good a place as any."

He let himself slide off the back of the cart. "As a point of fact, it most expressly is *not* as good a place as any. It is demonstrably worse for—"

"You sure I can't eat you?" she asked. "That would be super convenient. You got lots of extra vines. Maybe I could nibble on a few of those."

"I assure you, mistress, that you would find the experience *thoroughly* unappealing."

She grunted, stomach growling. Hungerspren appeared, like little brown specks with wings, floating around her. That wasn't odd. Many of the folks in line had attracted them.

"I got two powers," Lift said. "I can slide around, awesome, and I can make stuff grow. So I could grow me some plants to eat?"

"It would almost certainly take more energy in Stormlight to grow the plants than the sustenance would provide, as determined by the laws of the universe. And before you say anything, these are laws that even *you* cannot ignore." He paused. "I think. Who knows, when *you're* involved?"

"I'm *special*," Lift said, stopping as they finally reached the line of people waiting to get into the city. "Also, hungry. More hungry than special, right now."

She poked her head out of the line. Several guards stood at the ramp down into the city, along with some scribes wearing the odd Tashikki clothing. It was this *loooong* piece of cloth that they wrapped around themselves, feet to forehead. For being a single sheet, it was really complex: it wound around both legs and arms individually, but also wrapped back around the waist sometimes to create a kind of skirt. Both the men and the women wore the cloths, though not the guards.

They sure were taking their time letting people in. And there sure were a lot of people waiting. Everyone here was Makabaki, with dark eyes and skin—darker than Lift's brownish tan. And a lot of those waiting were families, wearing normal Azish-style clothing. Trousers, dirty skirts, some with patterns. They buzzed with exhaustionspren and hungerspren, enough to be distracting.

She'd have expected mostly merchants, not families, to be waiting here. Who were all these people?

Her stomach growled.

"Mistress?" Wyndle asked.

"Hush," she said. "Too hungry to talk."

"Are you—"

"Hungry? Yes. So shut up."

"But—"

"I bet those guards have food. People always feed guards. They can't properly hit folks on the head if they're starvin'. That's a *fact*."

"Or, to offer a counterproposal, you could simply *buy* some food with the spheres the emperor allotted you."

"Didn't bring them."

"You didn't . . . you didn't *bring the money*?"

"Ditched it when you weren't looking. Can't get robbed if you don't have money. Carrying spheres is just asking for trouble. Besides." She narrowed her eyes, watching the guards. "Only fancy people have money like that. We normal folk, we have to get by some other way."

"So now you're normal."

"Course I am," she said. "It's everyone else that's weird."

Before he could reply, she ducked underneath the chull wagon and started sneaking toward the front of the line.

# 3

TALLEW, you say?" Hauka asked, holding up the tarp covering the suspicious pile of grain. "From Azir?"

"Yes, of course, officer." The man sitting on the front of the wagon squirmed. "Just a humble farmer."

*With no calluses,* Hauka thought. *A humble farmer who can afford fine Liaforan boots and a silk belt.* Hauka took her spear and started shoving it into the grain, blunt end first. She didn't run across any contraband, or any refugees, hidden in the grain. So that was a first.

"I need to get your papers notarized," she said. "Pull your cart over to the side here."

The man grumbled but obeyed, turning his cart and starting to back the chull into the spot beside the guard post. It was one of the only buildings erected here above the city, along with a few towers spaced where they could lob arrows at anyone trying to use the ramps or set up position to siege.

The farmer with the wagon backed his cart in very, very carefully—as they were near the ledge overlooking the city. Immigrant quarter. Rich people didn't enter here, only the ones without papers. Or the ones who hoped to avoid scrutiny.

Hauka rolled up the man's credentials and walked past the guard post. Scents wafted out of that; lunch was being set up, which meant the people in line had an even longer wait ahead of them. An old scribe sat in a seat near the front of the guard post. Nissiqqan liked to be out in the sun.

Hauka bowed to him; Nissiqqan was the deputy scribe of immigration on duty for today. The older man was wrapped head-to-toe in a yellow shiqua, though he'd pulled the face portion down to expose a furrowed face with a cleft chin. They were in home lands, and the need to cover up before Nun Raylisi—the enemy of their god—was minimal. Tashi supposedly protected them here.

Hauka herself wore a breastplate, cap, trousers, and a cloak with her family and studies pattern on them. The locals accepted an Azish like her with ease—Tashikk didn't have much in the way of its own soldiers, and her credentials of achievement were certified by an Azimir vizier. She could have gotten a similar officer's job with the local guard anywhere in the greater Makabaki region, though her credentials *did* make clear she wasn't certified for battlefield command.

"Captain?" Nissiqqan said, adjusting his spectacles and looking at the farmer's credentials as she proffered them. "Is he refusing to pay the tariff?"

"Tariff is fine and in the strongbox," Hauka said. "I'm suspicious though. That man's no farmer."

"Smuggling refugees?"

"Checked in the grain and under the cart," Hauka said, looking over her shoulder. The man was all smiles. "It's new grain. A little overripe, but edible."

"Then the city will be glad to have it."

He was right. The war between Emul and Tukar was heating up. Granted, everyone was always saying that. But things *had* changed over the last few years. That god-king of the Tukari . . . there were all sorts of wild rumors about him.

"That's it!" Hauka said. "Your Grace, I'll bet that man has been in Emul. He's been raiding their fields while all the able-bodied men are fighting the invasion."

Nissiqqan nodded in agreement, rubbing his chin. Then he dug through his folder. "Tax him as a smuggler *and* as a fence. I believe . . . yes, that will work. Triple tariff. I'll earmark the extra tariffs to be diverted to feeding refugees, per referendum three-seventy-one-sha."

"Thanks," Hauka said, relaxing and taking the forms. Say what you would of the strange clothing and religion of the Tashikki, they certainly did know how to draft solid civil ordinances.

"I have spheres for you," Nissiqqan noted. "I know you've been asking for infused ones."

"Really!" Hauka said.

"My cousin had some out in his sphere cage—pure luck that he'd forgotten them—when that unpredicted highstorm blew through."

"Excellent," Hauka said. "I'll trade you for them later." She had some information that Nissiqqan would be very interested in. They used that as currency here in Tashikk, as much as they did spheres.

And storms, some lit spheres would be nice. After the Weeping, most people didn't have any, which could be storming inconvenient—as open flame was forbidden in the city. So she couldn't do any reading at night unless she found some infused spheres.

She walked back to the smuggler, flipping through forms. "We'll need you to pay this tariff," she said, handing him a form. "And then this one too."

"A fencing permit!" the man exclaimed. "And smuggling! This is thievery!"

"Yes, I believe it is. Or was."

"You can't prove such allegations," he said, slapping the forms with his hand.

"Sure," she said. "If I could *prove* that you crossed the border into Emul illegally, robbed the fields of good hardworking people while they were distracted by the fighting, then carted it here without proper permits, I'd simply seize the whole thing." She leaned in. "You're getting off easily. We both know it."

He met her eyes, then looked nervously away and started filling out the forms. Good. No trouble today. She liked it when there was no trouble. It—

Hauka stopped. The tarp on the man's wagon was rustling. Frowning, Hauka whipped it backward, and found a young *girl* neck-deep in the grain. She had light brown skin—like she was Reshi, or maybe Herdazian—and was probably eleven or twelve years old. She grinned at Hauka.

She hadn't been there before.

"This stuff," the girl said in Azish, mouth full of what appeared to be uncooked grain, "tastes terrible. I guess that's why we make stuff out of it first." She swallowed. "Got anything to drink?"

The smuggler stood up on his cart, sputtering and pointing. "She's ruining my goods! She's *swimming* in it! Guard, do something! There's a dirty refugee in my *grain*!"

Great. The paperwork on this was going to be a nightmare. "Out of there, child. Do you have parents?"

"Course I do," the girl said, rolling her eyes. "Everyone's got parents. Mine'r'dead though." She cocked her head. "What's that I smell? That wouldn't be . . . pancakes, would it?"

"Sure," Hauka said, sensing an opportunity. "Sun Day pancakes. You can have one, if you—"

"Thanks!" The girl leaped from the grain, spraying it in all directions, causing the smuggler to cry out. Hauka tried to snatch the child, but somehow the girl wiggled out of her grip. She leaped over Hauka's hands, then bounded forward.

And landed right on Hauka's shoulders.

Hauka grunted at the sudden weight of the girl, who jumped off her shoulders and landed behind her.

Hauka spun about, off-balance.

"Tashi!" the smuggler said. "She stepped on your *storming shoulders*, officer."

"Thank you. Stay here. Don't move." Hauka straightened her cap, then dashed after the child, who brushed past Nissiqqan—causing him to drop his folders—and entered into the guard chamber. Good. There weren't any other ways out of that post. Hauka stumbled up to the doorway, setting aside her spear and taking the club from her belt. She didn't want to hurt the little refugee, but some intimidation wouldn't be out of order.

The girl slid across the wooden floor as if it were covered in oil, passing right under the table where several scribes and two of Hauka's guards were eating. The girl then stood up and knocked the entire thing on its side, startling everyone backward and dumping food to the floor.

"Sorry!" the girl called from the mess. "Didn't mean to do that." Her head popped up from beside the overturned table, and she had a pancake sticking half out of her mouth. "These aren't bad."

Hauka's men leaped to their feet. Hauka lunged past them, trying to reach around the table to grab the refugee. Her fingers brushed the arm of the girl, who wiggled away again. The child pushed against the floor and slid right between Rez's legs.

Hauka lunged again, cornering the girl on the side of the guard chamber.

The girl, in turn, reached up and wiggled through the room's single slotlike window. Hauka gaped. Surely that wasn't big enough for a person, even a small one, to get through so easily. She pressed herself against the wall, looking out the window. She didn't see anything at first; then the girl's head poked down from above—she'd gotten onto the roof somehow.

The girl's dark hair blew in the breeze. "Hey," she said. "What kind of pancake *was* that, anyway? I've gotta eat all ten."

"Get back in here," Hauka said, reaching through to try to grab the girl. "You haven't been processed for immigration."

The girl's head popped back upward, and her footsteps sounded on the roof. Hauka cursed and scrambled out the front, trailed by her two guards. They searched the roof of the small guard post, but saw nothing.

"She's back in here!" one of the scribes called from inside.

A moment later, the girl skidded out along the ground, a pancake in each hand and another in her mouth. She passed the guards and scrambled toward the cart with the smuggler, who had climbed down and was ranting about his grain getting soiled.

Hauka leaped to grab the child—and this time managed to get hold of her leg. Unfortunately, her two guards reached for the girl too, and they tripped, falling in a jumbled mess right on top of Hauka.

She hung on though. Puffing from the weight on her back, Hauka clung tightly to the little girl's leg. She looked up, holding in a groan.

The refugee girl sat on the stone in front of her, head cocked. She stuffed one of the pancakes into her mouth, then reached behind herself, her hand darting toward the hitch where the cart was hooked to its chull. The hitch came undone, the hook popping out as the girl tapped it on the bottom. It didn't resist a bit.

*Oh, storms no.*

"Off me!" Hauka screamed, letting go of the girl and pushing free of the men. The stupid smuggler backed away, confused.

The cart rolled toward the ledge behind, and she doubted the wooden fence would keep it from falling. Hauka leaped for the cart in a burst of energy, seizing it by its side. It dragged her along with it, and she had terrible visions of it plummeting down over the ledge into the city, right on top of the refugees of the immigrant quarter.

The cart, however, slowly lurched to a halt. Puffing, Hauka looked up from where she stood, feet pressed against the stones, holding onto the cart. She didn't dare let go.

The girl was there, on top of the grain again, eating the last pancake. "They really are good."

"Tuk-cake," Hauka said, feeling exhausted. "You eat them for prosperity in the year to come."

"People should eat them all the time then, you know?"

"Maybe."

The girl nodded, then stood to the side and kicked open the tailgate of the cart. In a rush, the grain *slid* out of the cart.

It was the strangest thing she'd ever seen. The pile of grain became like liquid, flowing out of the cart even though the incline was shallow. It . . . well, it *glowed* softly as it flowed out and rained down into the city.

The girl smiled at Hauka.

Then she jumped off after it.

Hauka gaped as the girl fell after the grain. The two other guards finally woke up enough to come help, and grabbed hold of the cart. The smuggler was screaming, angerspren boiling up around him like pools of blood on the ground.

Below, the grain billowed in the air, sending up dust as it poured into the immigrant quarter. It was rather far down, but Hauka was pretty sure she heard shouts of delight and praise as the food blanketed the people there.

Cart secure, Hauka stepped up to the ledge. The girl was nowhere to be seen. Storms. Had she been some kind of spren? Hauka searched again but saw nothing, though there was this strange black dust at her feet. It blew away in the wind.

"Captain?" Rez asked.

"Take over immigration for the next hour, Rez. I need a break."

Storms. How on Roshar was she ever going to explain *this* in a report?

# 4

LIFT wasn't supposed to be able to touch Wyndle. The Voidbringer kept saying things like "I don't have enough presence in this Realm, even with our bond" and "you must be stuck partially in the Cognitive." Gibberish, basically.

Because she *could* touch him. That was very useful at times. Times like when you'd just jumped off a short cliff, and needed something to hold on to. Wyndle yelped in surprise as she leaped, then he immediately shot down the side of the wall, moving faster than she fell. He was finally learning to pay attention.

Lift grabbed ahold of him like a rope, one that she halfway held to as she fell, the vine sliding between her fingers. It wasn't much, but it did help slow her descent. She hit harder than would have been safe for most people. Fortunately, she was awesome.

She extinguished the glow of her awesomeness, then dashed to a small alleyway. People crowded around behind her, praising various Heralds and gods for the gift of the grain. Well, they could speak like that if they wanted, but they all seemed to know the grain hadn't come from a god—not directly—because it was snatched up quicker than a pretty whore in Bavland.

In minutes, all that was left of an entire cartload of grain was a few husks blowing in the wind. Lift settled in the alleyway's mouth, inspecting her surroundings. It was like she'd dropped from noonday straight into dusk. Long shadows everywhere, and things smelled wet.

The buildings were cut right into the stone—doorways, windows, and everything bored out of the rock. They painted the walls these bright colors, often in columns to differentiate one "building" from another. People swarmed all about, chatting and stomping and coughing.

This was the good kind of life. Lift liked being on the move, but she didn't like being alone. Solitary was different from alone. She stood up and started walking, hands in pockets, trying to look in all directions at once. This place was amazing.

"That was quite generous of you, mistress," Wyndle said, growing along beside her. "Dumping that grain, after hearing that the man who had it was a thief."

"That?" Lift said. "I just wanted something soft to land on if you were snoozing."

The people she passed wore a variety of attire. Mostly Azish patterns or Tashikki shiquas. But some were mercenaries, probably either Tukari or Emuli. Others wore rural clothing with a lighter coloring, probably from Alm or Desh. She liked those places. Few people had tried to kill her in Alm or Desh.

Unfortunately, there wasn't much to steal there—unless you liked eating mush, and this strange meat they put in everything. It came from some beast that lived on the mountain slopes, an ugly thing with dirty hair all over it. Lift thought they tasted disgusting, and *she'd* once tried to eat a *roofing tile.*

Anyway, on this street there seemed to be far fewer Tashikki than there were foreigners—but what had they called this above? Immigrant quarter? Well, she probably wouldn't stick out here. She even passed a few Reshi, though most of these were huddled near alleyway shanties, wearing little more than rags.

That was an oddity about this place, for sure. It had shanties. She hadn't seen those since leaving Zawfix, which had them inside of old mines. Most places, if people tried to build homes out of shoddy material . . .

well it would all just get blown away in the first highstorm and leave them sitting on the chamber pot, looking stupid with no walls.

Here, the shanties were confined to smaller roadways, which stuck out like spokes from this larger one, connecting it to the next large road in line. Many of these were so packed with hanging blankets, people, and improvised houses that you couldn't see the opening on the other side.

Oddly though, it was all up on stilts. Even the most rickety of constructions was up four feet or so in the air. Lift stood at the mouth of one alleyway, hands in pockets, and looked down along the larger slot. As she'd noted earlier, each wall of the city was also a set of shops and homes cut right into the rock, painted to separate them from their neighbors. And for all of them, you had to walk up three or four steps cut into the stone to get in.

"It's like the Purelake," she said. "Everything's up high, like nobody wants to touch the ground 'cuz it's got some kind of nasty cough."

"Wise," Wyndle said. "Protection from the storms."

"The waters should still wash this place away," Lift said.

Well, they obviously didn't, or the place wouldn't be here. She continued strolling down the road, passing lines of homes cut into the wall, and strings of other homes smushed between them. Those shanties looked inviting—warm, packed, full of life. She even saw the green, bobbing motes of lifespren floating along among them, something you usually only saw when there were lots of plants. Unfortunately, she knew from experience that sometimes no matter how inviting a place looked, it wouldn't welcome a foreigner urchin.

"So," Wyndle said, crawling along the wall next to her head, leaving a trail of vines behind him. "You have gotten us here, and—remarkably—avoided incarceration. What now?"

"Food," Lift said, her stomach grumbling.

"You just ate!"

"Yeah. Used up all the energy getting away from the starvin' guards though. I'm hungrier than when I started!"

"Oh, Blessed Mother," he said in exasperation. "Why didn't you simply *wait* in *line* then?"

"Wouldn't have gotten any food that way."

"It doesn't matter, since you burned all the food into Stormlight, then jumped off a wall!"

"But I got to eat pancakes!"

They wove around a group of Tashikki women carrying baskets on their arms, yammering about Liaforan handicrafts. Two unconsciously covered their baskets and gripped the handles tight as Lift passed.

"I can't believe this," Wyndle said. "I *cannot* believe this is my existence. I was a gardener! Respected! Now, everywhere I go, people look at us as if we're going to pick their pockets."

"Nothing in their pockets," Lift said, looking over her shoulder. "I don't think shiquas even *have* pockets. Those baskets though . . ."

"Did you know we were considering bonding this nice cobbler man instead of you? A very kindly man who took care of children. I could have lived quietly, helping him, making shoes. I could have done an entire *display* of shoes!"

"And the danger that is coming," Lift said. "From the west? If there really *is* a war?"

"Shoes are important to war," Wyndle said, spitting out a splatter of vines on the wall about him—she wasn't sure what that was supposed to mean. "You think the Radiants are going to fight barefoot? We could have made them shoes, that nice old cobbler and me. Wonderful shoes."

"Sounds boring."

He groaned. "You *are* going to slam me into people, aren't you? I'm going to be a weapon."

"What nonsense are you talking about, Voidbringer?"

"I suppose I need to get you to say the Words, don't I? That's my job? Oh, this is *miserable*."

He often said things like this. You probably had to be messed-up in the brain to be a Voidbringer, so she didn't hold it against him. Instead, she dug in her pocket and brought out a little book. She held it up, flipping through the pages.

"What's that?" Wyndle asked.

"I pinched it from that guard post," she said. "Thought I might be able to sell it or something."

"Let me see that," Wyndle said. He grew down the side of the wall, then up around her leg, twisted around her body, and finally along her arm onto the book. It tickled, the way his main vine shot out tiny creepers that stuck to her skin to keep it in place.

On the page, he spread out other little vines, completely growing over the book and between its pages. "Hmmm. . . ."

Lift leaned back against the wall of the slot as he worked. She didn't feel like she was in a city, she felt like she was in a . . . tunnel that led to one. Sure, the sky was open and bright overhead, but this street felt so isolated. Usually in a city you could see ripples of buildings, towering off away from you. You could hear shouts from several streets over.

Even clogged with people—more people than seemed reasonable—this street felt isolated. A strange little cremling crawled up the wall beside her. Smaller than most, it was black, with a thin carapace and a strip of fuzzy brown on its back that seemed spongy. Cremlings were strange in Tashikk, and they only got stranger the farther west you went. Closer to the mountains, some of the cremlings could even *fly*.

"Hmm, yes," Wyndle said. "Mistress, this book is likely worthless. It's only a logbook of times the guards have been on duty. The captain, for example, records when she leaves each day—ten on the dot, by the wall clock—replaced by the night watch captain. One visit to the Grand Indicium each week for detailed debriefing of weekly events. She's fastidious, but I doubt anyone will be interested in buying her logbook."

"Surely someone will want it. It's a book!"

"Lift, books have value based on what is *in* them."

"I know. Pages."

"I mean what's on the pages."

"Ink?"

"I mean what the ink *says*."

She scratched her head.

"You really should have listened to those writing coaches in Azir."

"So . . . no trading this for food?" Her stomach growled, attracting more hungerspren.

"Not likely."

Stupid book—and stupid people. She grumbled and tossed the book over her shoulder.

It hit a woman carrying a basket of yarn, unfortunately. She yelped.

"You!" a voice shouted.

Lift winced. A man in a guard's uniform was pointing at her through the crowd.

"Did you just assault that woman?" the guard shouted at her.

"Barely!" Lift shouted back.

The guard came stalking toward her.

"Run?" Wyndle asked.

"Run."

She ducked into an alley, prompting further shouts from the guard, who came barreling in after her.

# 5

ROUGHLY a half hour later, Lift lay on a stretched-out tarp atop a shanty, puffing from an extended run. That guard had been *persistent.*

She swung idly on the tarp as a wind blew through the shantied alleyway. Beneath, a family talked about the miracle of an entire cart of grain suddenly being dumped in the slums. A mother, three sons, and a father, all together.

*I will remember those who have been forgotten.* She'd sworn that oath as she'd saved Gawx's life. The right Words, important Words. But what did they mean? What about her mother? Nobody remembered her.

There seemed far too many people out there who were being forgotten. Too many for one girl to remember.

"Lift?" Wyndle asked. He'd made a little tower of vines and leaves that blew in the wind. "Why haven't you ever gone to the Reshi Isles? That's where you're from, right?"

"It's what Mother said."

"So why not go visit and see? You've been halfway across Roshar and back, to hear you talk. But never to your supposed homeland."

She shrugged, staring up at the late-afternoon sky, feeling the wind.

It smelled fresh, compared to the stench of being down in the slots. The city wasn't ripe, but it was thick with contained smells, like animals locked up.

"Do you know why we had to leave Azir?" Lift said softly.

"To chase after that Skybreaker, the one you call Darkness."

"No. We're not doing that."

"Sure."

"We left because people started to know who I am. If you stay in the same place too long, then people start to recognize you. The shop-keepers learn your name. They smile at you when you enter, and already know what to get for you, because they remember what you need."

"That's a bad thing?"

She nodded, still staring at the sky. "It's worse when they think they're your friend. Gawx, the viziers. They make assumptions. They think they know you, then start to expect things of you. Then you have to be the person everyone thinks you are, not the person you actually are."

"And who is the person you actually are, Lift?"

That was the problem, wasn't it? She'd known that once, hadn't she? Or was it just that she'd been young enough not to care?

How did people know? The breeze rocked her perch, and she snug-gled up, remembering her mother's arms, her scent, her warm voice.

The pangs of a growling stomach interrupted her, the needs of the now strangling the wants of the past. She sighed and stood up on the tarp. "Come on," she said. "Let's go find some urchins."

# 6

"GOTTA lunks," the little girl said. She was grimy, with hands that probably hadn't been washed since she'd gotten old enough to pick her own nose. She was missing a lot of teeth. Too many for her age. "The marm, she gotta lunks good."

"Gotta lunks for smalls?"

"Gotta lunks for smalls," the girl said to Lift, nodding. "But gotta snaps too. Biga stone, that one, and eyes is swords. Don't lika smalls, but gotta lunks for them. Real nogginin, that."

"Maybe for outsida cares?" Lift said. "Lika the outsida, they gotta light for her, ifn she given lunks for smalls?"

"Maybe," the girl said. "Maybe that right. But it might be nogginin, but it's wrack too. I say that. Real wrack."

"Thanks," Lift said. "Here." She gave the girl her handkerchief, as promised. In trade for the information.

The girl wrapped it around her head and gave Lift a gap-toothed grin. People liked trading information in Tashikk. It was kind of their thing.

The grimy little girl paused. "That lighta above, the lunks from the sky. I heard loudin about it. That was you, outsida, eh?"

"Yeah."

The girl turned as if to leave, but then reconsidered and put a hand on Lift's arm.

"You," the girl said to Lift. "Outsida?"

"Yeah."

"You listenin'?"

"I'm listenin'."

"People, they don't listen." She smiled at Lift again, then finally scuttled away.

Lift settled back on her haunches in the alleyway across from some communal ovens—a vast, hollowed-out cavern in the wall with huge chimneys cut upward. They burned the rockbud husks from the farms, and anyone could come cook in the central ovens there. They couldn't have fires in their own places. From what Lift had heard, early in the city's life they'd had a fire blaze through the various slums and kill *tons* of people.

In the alleys you didn't see smoke trails, only the occasional pinprick of spherelight. It was supposed to be the Weeping, and most spheres had gone dun. Only those who had spheres out, by luck, during that unexpected highstorm a few days ago would have light.

"Mistress," Wyndle said, "that was the strangest conversation I've *ever* heard, and I once grew an entire garden for some keenspren."

"Seemed normal to me. Just a kid on the street."

"But the way you talked!" Wyndle said.

"What way?"

"With all those odd words and terms. How did you know what to say?"

"It just felt right," Lift said. "Words is words. Anyway, she said that we could get food at the Tashi's Light Orphanage. Same as the other one we talked to."

"Then why haven't we gone there?" Wyndle asked.

"Nobody likes the woman who runs it. They don't trust her; say that she's starvin' mean. That she only gives away food in the first place because she wants to look good for the officials that watch the place."

"To turn your phrase back at you, mistress, food is food."

"Yeah," Lift said. "It's just . . . what's the challenge of eating a lunch someone *gives* you?"

"I'm certain you will survive the indignity, mistress."

Unfortunately, he was right. She was too hungry to produce any awesomeness, which meant being a regular child beggar. She didn't move though, not yet.

*People, they don't listen.* Did Lift listen? She did usually, didn't she? Why did the little urchin girl care, anyway?

Hands in pockets, Lift rose and picked her way through the crowded slot street, dodging the occasional hand that tried to swat or punch her. People here did something strange—they kept their spheres in rows, strung on long strings, even if they put them in pouches. And all the money she saw had holes in the bottoms of the glass spheres, so you could do that. What if you had to count out exact change? Would you unstring the whole starvin' bunch, then string them up again?

At least they used spheres. People farther toward the west, they just used chips of gemstone, sometimes embedded in hunks of glass, sometimes not. Starvin' easy to lose, those were.

People got so mad when she lost spheres. They were strange about money. Far too concerned with something that you couldn't eat—though Lift figured that was probably the point of using spheres instead of something rational, like bags of food. If you actually traded food, everyone would eat up all their money and then where would society be?

The Tashi's Light Orphanage was a corner building, cut into a place where two streets met. The main face pointed onto the large thoroughfare of the immigrant quarter, and was painted bright orange. The other side faced a particularly wide alleyway mouth that had some rows of seats cut into the sides, making a half circle, like some kind of theater—though it was broken in the center for the alleyway. That strung out into the distance, but it didn't look quite as derelict as some others. Some of the shanties even had doors, and the belching that echoed from within the alley sounded almost refined.

She'd been told by the urchins not to approach from the street side, which was for officials and real people. Urchins were to approach from the alleyway side, so Lift neared the stone benches of the little amphitheater—where some old people in shiquas were sitting—and knocked on the door. A section of the stone above it was carved and painted gold and red, though she couldn't read the letters.

A youth pulled open the door. He had a flat, wide face, like Lift had learned to associate with people who weren't born quite the same as other folk. He looked her over, then pointed at the benches. "Sit there," he said. "Food comes later."

"How much later?" Lift said, hands on hips.

"Why? You got *appointments*?" the young man asked, then smiled. "Sit there. Food comes later."

She sighed, but settled down near where the old people were chatting. She got the impression that they were people from farther in the slum who came out here, to the open circle cut into the mouth of the alleyway, where there were steps to sit on and a breeze.

With the sun getting closer to setting, the slots were falling deeper and deeper into shadow. There wouldn't be many spheres to light it up at night; people would probably go to bed earlier than they normally did, as was common during the Weeping. Lift huddled on one of the seats, Wyndle writhing up beside her. She stared at the stupid door to the stupid orphanage, her stupid stomach growling.

"What was wrong with that young man who answered the door?" Wyndle asked.

"Dunno," Lift said. "Some people are just born like that."

She waited on the steps, listening to some Tashikki men from the slums chat and chuckle together. Eventually a figure skulked into the mouth of the alleyway—it seemed to be a woman, wrapped all in dark cloth. Not a true shiqua. Maybe a foreigner trying to wear one, and hide who she was.

The woman sniffled audibly, holding the hand of a large child, maybe ten or eleven years old. She led him to the doorstep of the orphanage, then pulled him into a hug.

The boy stared ahead, sightless, drooling. He had a scar on his head, healed mostly, but still an angry red.

The woman bowed her head, then her back, and slunk away, leaving the boy. He just sat there, staring. Not a baby in a basket; no, that was a children's tale. This was what actually happened at orphanages, in Lift's experience. People left children who were too big to keep caring for, but couldn't take care of themselves or contribute to the family.

"Did she . . . just leave that boy?" Wyndle asked, horrified.

"She's probably got other children," Lift said softly, "she can barely keep fed. She can't spend all her time looking after one like that, not any longer." Lift's heart twisted inside her and she wanted to look away, but couldn't.

Instead, she stood up and walked over toward the boy. Rich people, like the viziers in Azir, had a strange perspective on orphanages. They imagined them full of saintly little children, plucky and good-hearted, eager to work and have a family.

In Lift's experience though, orphanages had far more like this boy. Kids who were tough to care for. Kids who required constant supervision, or who were confused in the head. Or those who could get violent.

She hated how rich people made up this romantic dream of what an orphanage should be like. Perfect, full of sweet smiles and happy singing. Not full of frustration, pain, and confusion.

She sat down next to the boy. She was smaller than he was. "Hey," she said.

He looked to her with glazed eyes. She could see his wound better now. The hair hadn't grown back on the side of his head.

"It's going to be all right," she said, taking his hand in hers.

He didn't reply.

A short time later, the door into the orphanage opened, revealing a shriveled-up weed of a woman. Seriously. She looked like the child of a broom and a particularly determined clump of moss. Her skin drooped off her bones like something you'd hack up after catching crud in the slums, and she had spindly fingers that Lift figured might be twigs she'd glued in place after her real ones fell off.

The woman put hands on hips—amazingly, she didn't break any bones in the motion—and looked the two of them over. "An idiot and an opportunist," she said.

"Hey!" Lift said, scrambling up. "He's not an idiot. He's just hurt."

"I was describing you, child," the woman said, then knelt beside the boy with the hurt head. She clicked her tongue. "Worthless, worthless," she muttered. "I can see through your deception. You won't last long here. Watch and see." She gestured backward, and the young man Lift had seen earlier came out and took the hurt boy by the arm, leading him into the orphanage.

Lift tried to follow, but twigs-for-hands stepped in front of her. "You can have three meals," the woman told her. "You pick when you want them, but after three you're done. Consider yourself lucky I'm willing to give anything to one like you."

"What's that supposed to mean?" Lift demanded.

"That if you don't want rats on your ship, you shouldn't be in the business of feeding them." The woman shook her head, then moved to pull the door shut.

"Wait!" Lift said. "I need somewhere to sleep."

"Then you came to the right place."

"Really?"

"Yes, those benches usually clear out once it gets dark."

"Stone *benches*?" Lift said. "You want me to sleep on stone benches?"

"Oh, don't whine. It's not even raining any longer." The woman shut the door.

Lift sighed, looking toward Wyndle. A moment later, the young man from before opened the door and tossed something out to her—a large baked roll of clemabread, thick and granular, with spicy paste at the center.

"Don't suppose you have a pancake?" Lift asked him. "I've got a goal to eat—"

He shut the door. Lift sighed, but settled down on the stone benches near some old men, and started gobbling it up. It wasn't particularly good, but it was warm and filling. "Storming witch," she muttered.

"Don't judge her too harshly, child," said one of the old men on the benches. He wore a black shiqua, but had pulled back the part that wrapped the face, exposing a grey mustache and eyebrows. He had dark brown skin with a wide smile. "It is difficult to be the one that handles everyone else's problems."

"She doesn't have to be so mean."

"When she isn't, then children congregate here begging for handouts."

"So? Isn't that kind of the *point* of an orphanage?" Lift chewed on the roll. "Sleep on the rock benches? I should go steal her pillow."

"I think you'd find her ready to deal with feisty urchin thieves."

"She ain't never faced *me* before. I'm *awesome.*" She looked down at the rest of her food. Of course, if she used her awesomeness, she'd just end up hungry again.

The man laughed. "They call her the Stump, because she won't be blown by any storm. I don't think you'll get the best of her, little one." He leaned in. "But I have information, if you are interested in a trade."

Tashikki and their secrets. Lift rolled her eyes. "Ain't got nothing left to trade."

"Trade me your time, then. I will tell you how to get on the Stump's good side. Maybe earn yourself a bed. In turn, you answer a question for me. Is this a deal?"

Lift cocked an eyebrow at him. "Sure. Whatever."

"Here is my secret. The Stump has a little . . . hobby. She is in the business of trading spheres. An exchanging business, so to speak. Find someone who wants to trade with her, and she will handsomely reward you."

"Trade spheres?" Lift said. "Money for money? What is the point of that?"

He shrugged. "She works hard to cover it up. So it must be important."

"What a lame secret," Lift said. She popped the last of the roll into her mouth, the clemabread breaking apart easily—it was almost more of a mush.

"Will you still answer my question?"

"Depends on how lame *it* is."

"What body part do you feel that you are most like?" he asked. "Are you the hand, always busy doing work? Are you the mind, giving direction? Do you feel that you are more of a . . . leg, perhaps? Bearing up everyone else, and rarely noticed?"

"Yeah. Lame question."

"No, no. It is of most importance. Each person, they are but a piece of something larger—some grand organism that makes up this city. This is the philosophy I am building, you see."

Lift eyed him. Great. Angry twig running an orphanage; weird old man outside it. She dusted off her hands. "If I'm anything, I'm a nose. 'Cuz I'm filled with all kinds of weird crud, and you never know what's gonna fall out."

"Ah . . . interesting."

"That wasn't meant to be helpful."

"Yes, but it was honest, which is the cornerstone of a good philosophy."

"Yeah. Sure." Lift hopped off the stone benches. "As fun as it was talkin' crazy stuff with you, I got somewhere important to be."

"You do?" Wyndle asked, rising from where he'd been coiled up on the bench beside her.

"Yup," Lift said. "I've got an *appointment*."

# 7

Lift was worried she'd be late. She'd never been good with time.

Now, she could keep the important parts straight. Sun up, sun down. Blah blah. But the divisions beyond that . . . well, she'd never found those to be important. Other people did though, so she hurried through the slot.

"Are you going to find spheres for that woman at the orphanage?" Wyndle said, zipping along the ground beside her, weaving between the legs of people. "Get on her good side?"

"Of course not," Lift said, sniffing. "It's a scam."

"It is?"

"Course it is. She's probably launderin' spheres for criminals, takin' them as 'donations,' then givin' others back. Men'll pay well to clean up their spheres, particularly in places like this, where you got scribes looking over your shoulder all the starvin' time. Course, it might not be *that* scam. She might be guiltin' people into giving her donations of infused spheres, traded for her dun ones. They'll feel sympathetic, because she talks about her poor children. Then she can trade infused spheres to the moneychangers and make a small profit."

"That's *shockingly* unscrupulous, mistress!"

Lift shrugged. "What *else* are you going to do with orphans? Gotta be good for something, right?"

"But profiting off people's emotions?"

"Pity can be a powerful tool. Anytime you can make someone else feel something, you've got power over them."

"I . . . guess?"

"Gotta make sure that never happens to me," Lift said. "It's how you stay strong, see."

She found her way back to the place where she'd entered the slots, then from there poked around until she found the ramp up to the entrance of the city. It was long and shallow, for driving wagons down, if you needed to.

She crawled up it a ways, just enough to get a glimpse at the guard post. There was still a line up there, grown longer than when she'd been in it. Many people were actually making camp on the stones. Some enterprising merchants were selling them food, clean water, and even tents.

*Good luck,* Lift thought. Most of the people in that line looked like they didn't own much besides their own skins, maybe an exotic disease or two. Lift retreated. She wasn't awesome enough to risk another encounter with the guards. Instead she settled down in a small cleft in the rock at the bottom of the ramp, where she watched a blanket merchant pass. He was using a strange little horse—it was shaggy and white, and had horns on its head. Looked like those animals that were terrible to eat out west.

"Mistress," Wyndle said from the stone wall beside her head, "I don't know much about humans, but I do know a bit about plants. You're remarkably similar. You need light, water, and nourishment. And plants have roots. To anchor them, you see, during storms. Otherwise they blow away."

"It's nice to blow away sometimes."

"And when the great storm comes?"

Lift's eyes drifted toward the west. Toward . . . whatever was building there. *A storm that blows the wrong way,* the viziers had said. *It can't be possible. What game are the Alethi playing?*

A few minutes later, the guard captain walked down the ramp. The woman practically dragged her feet, and as soon as she was out of sight of the guard post, she let her shoulders slump. Looked like it had been a rough day. What could have caused that?

Lift huddled down, but the woman didn't so much as look at her. Once the captain passed, Lift climbed to her feet and scuttled after.

Tailing someone through this town proved easy. There weren't nearly as many hidden nooks or branching paths. As Lift had guessed, now that it was getting dark, the streets were clearing. Maybe there would be an upswing in activity once the first moon got high enough, but for now there wasn't enough light.

"Mistress," Wyndle said. "What are we doing?"

"Just thought I'd see where that woman lives."

"But why?"

Unsurprisingly, the captain didn't live too far from her guard post. A few streets inward, likely far enough to be outside the immigrant quarter but close enough for the place to be cheaper by association. It was a large set of rooms carved into the rock wall, marked by a window for each one. Apartments, rather than one single "building." It did look pretty strange—a sheer rock face, broken by a bunch of shutters.

The captain entered, but Lift didn't follow. Instead, she craned her neck upward. Eventually one of the windows near the top shone with spherelight, and the captain pushed open the shutters for some fresh air.

"Hm," Lift said, squinting in the darkness. "Let's head up that wall, Voidbringer."

"Mistress, you could call me by my name."

"I could call you lotsa stuff," Lift said. "Be glad I don't got much of an imagination. Let's go."

Wyndle sighed, but curved up the outside of the captain's tenement. Lift climbed, using his vines as foot- and handholds. This took her up past a number of windows, but only a few of them were lit. One pair of windows on the same side helpfully had a washing line draped between them, and Lift snatched a shiqua. Nice of them to leave it out, up high enough that only she could get to it.

She didn't stop at the captain's window, which Wyndle seemed to find surprising. She went all the way up to the top and eventually climbed out onto a field of treb, a grain that grew in bunches inside hard pods on vines. The farmers here grew them in little slits in the stone, just under a foot wide. The vines would bunch up in there, and grow pods that got wedged so they didn't tumble free in storms.

The farmers were done for the day, leaving piles of weeds to get carried away in the next storm—whenever that came. Lift settled down on the lip of the trench, looking out over the city. It was pinpricked by spheres. Not many, but more than she'd have expected. That made illumination shine up from the slots, like they were cracks in something bright at the center. How must it look when people had more infused spheres? She imagined bright columns of light shining up from the holes.

Below, the captain closed her window and apparently hooded her spheres. Lift yawned. "You don't need sleep, right, Voidbringer?"

"I do not."

"Then keep an eye on that building. Wake me up anytime someone goes into it, or if that captain comes out."

"Could you at least tell me *why* we're spying on a captain of the city watch?"

"What else are we going to do?"

"Anything else?"

"Boring," Lift said, then yawned again. "Wake me up, okay?"

He said something, likely a complaint, but she was already drifting off.

It seemed like only moments before he nudged her awake.

"Mistress?" he said. "Mistress, I find myself in awe of your ingenuity, and your stupidity, both at once."

She yawned, shifting on her stolen shiqua blanket and swatting at some lifespren that were floating around. She hadn't dreamed, thankfully. She hated dreams. They either showed her a life she couldn't have, or a life that terrified her. What was the good of either one?

"Mistress?" Wyndle asked.

She stirred, sitting up. She hadn't realized that she'd picked a spot surrounded by and overgrown with vines, and they'd gotten stuck in her clothing. What was she doing up here again? She ran her hand through her hair, which was snarled and sticking out in all sorts of directions.

Sunlight was peeking up over the horizon, and farmers were already out working again. In fact, now that she'd sat up out of the nest of vines, a few had turned to regard her with baffled looks. It probably wasn't often you found a little Reshi girl sleeping by a cliff in your field. She grinned and waved at them.

"Mistress," Wyndle said. "You told me to warn you if someone went into the building."

Right. She started, remembering what she'd been doing, the fog leaving her mind. "And?" she asked, urgent.

"And Darkness himself, the man who almost killed you in the royal palace, just entered the building below us."

Darkness himself. Lift felt a spike of alarm and gripped the edge of the cliff, barely daring to peek over. She'd wondered if he would come.

"You *did* come to the city chasing him," Wyndle said.

"Pure coincidence," she mumbled.

"No it's not. You showed off your powers to that guard captain, *knowing* that she'd write a report about what she saw. And you knew that would draw Darkness's attention."

"I can't search a whole city for one man; I needed a way to get him to come to me. Didn't expect him to find this place so quickly though. Must have some scribe watching reports."

"But *why*?" Wyndle said, his voice almost a whine. "Why are you looking for him? He's dangerous."

"Obviously."

"Oh, mistress. It's crazy. He—"

"He kills people," she said softly. "The viziers have tracked him. He murders people that don't seem to be connected. The viziers are confused, but I'm not." She took a deep breath. "He's hunting someone in this city, Wyndle. Someone with powers . . . someone like me."

Wyndle trailed off, then slowly let out an "aaahh" of understanding.

"Let's get down to her window," Lift said, ignoring the farmers and climbing over the cliff's edge. It was still dark in the city, which was waking up slowly. She shouldn't be too conspicuous until things got busier.

Wyndle helpfully grew down in front of her, giving her something to cling to. She wasn't completely sure what drove her. Maybe it was the lure of finding someone else like her, someone who could explain what she was and why her life made no sense these days. Or maybe she just didn't like the idea of Darkness stalking someone innocent. Somebody who, like her, hadn't done anything wrong—well, nothing big—except for having powers he thought they shouldn't.

She pressed her ear against the shutters of the captain's room. Within, she distinctly heard *his* voice.

"A young woman," Darkness said. "Herdazian or Reshi."

"Yes, sir," the captain said. "Do you mind? Can I see your papers again?"

"You will find them in order."

"I just . . . special operative of the prince? I've never heard of the title before."

"It is an ancient but rarely used designation," Darkness said. "Explain exactly what this child did."

"I—"

"Explain again. To me."

"Well, she gave us quite the runaround, sir. Slipped into our guard post, knocked over our things, stole some food. The big crime was when she dumped that grain into the city. I'm sure she did it on purpose; the merchant has already filed suit against the city guard for willful neglect of duty."

"His case is weak," Darkness said. "Because he hadn't yet been approved for admittance into the city, he didn't come under your jurisdiction. If anything he needs to file against the highway guard, and classify it as banditry."

"That's what I told him!"

"You are not to be blamed, Captain. You faced a force you cannot understand, and which I am not at liberty to explain. I need details, however, as proof. Did she glow?"

"I . . . well . . ."

"Did she *glow,* Captain."

"Yes. I swear, I am of sound mind. I wasn't simply seeing things, sir. She glowed. And the grain glowed too, faintly."

"And she was slippery to the touch?"

"Slicker than if she had been oiled, sir. I've never felt anything like it."

"As anticipated. Here, sign this."

They made some shuffling noises. Lift clung there, ear to the wall, heart pounding. Darkness had a Shardblade. If he suspected she was out here, he could stab through the wall and cut her clean in half.

"Sir?" the guard captain said. "Could you tell me what's going on here? I feel lost, like a soldier on a battlefield who can't remember which banner is hers."

"It is not material for you to know."

"Um . . . yes, sir."

"Watch for the child. Have others do the same, and report to your superiors if she is discovered. I will hear of it."

"Yes, sir."

Footsteps marked him walking for the door. Before he left, he noted something. "Infused spheres, Captain? You are lucky to have them, these days."

"I traded for them, sir."

"And dun ones in the lantern on the wall."

"They ran out weeks ago, sir. I haven't replaced them. Is this . . . relevant, sir?"

"No. Remember your orders, Captain." He bade her farewell.

The door shut. Lift scrambled up the wall again—trailed by a whimpering Wyndle—and hid there on the top, watching as Darkness stepped out onto the street below. Morning sunlight warmed the back of her neck, and she couldn't keep herself from trembling.

A black and silver uniform. Dark skin, like he was Makabaki, with a pale patch on one cheek: a birthmark shaped like a crescent.

Dead eyes. Eyes that didn't care if they were looking at a man, a chull, or a stone. He tucked some papers into his coat pocket, then pulled on his long-cuffed gloves.

"So we've found him," Wyndle whispered. "Now what?"

"Now?" Lift swallowed. "Now we follow him."

# 8

TAILING Darkness was a far different experience from tailing the captain. For one, it was daylight now. Still early morning, but light enough that Lift had to worry about being spotted. Fortunately, encountering Darkness had completely burned away the fog of sleepiness she'd felt upon awaking.

At first she tried to stay on the tops of the walls, in the gardens above the city. That proved difficult. Though there were some bridges up here crossing over the slots, they weren't nearly as common as she needed. Each time Darkness hit an intersection she had a shiver of fear, worrying he'd turn down a path she couldn't follow without somehow leaping over a huge gap.

Eventually she took the more dangerous route of scrambling down a ladder, then chasing after him within a trench. Fortunately, it seemed that people in here expected some measure of jostling as they moved through the streets. The confines weren't completely cramped—many of the larger streets had plenty of space. But those walls did enhance the feeling of being boxed in.

Lift had lots of practice with this sort of thing, and she kept the tail inconspicuous. She didn't pick any pockets, despite several fine opportunities—people who were practically holding their pouches up, demanding them to be taken. If she hadn't been following Darkness, she might have grabbed a few for old times' sake.

She didn't use her awesomeness, which was running out anyway. She hadn't eaten since last night, and if she didn't use the power, it eventually vanished. Took about half a day; she didn't know why.

She dodged around the figures of farmers heading to work, women carrying water, kids skipping to their lessons—where they'd sit in rows and listen to a teacher while doing some menial task, like sewing, to pay for the education. Suckers.

People gave Darkness lots of space, moving away from him like they would a guy whose backside couldn't help but let everyone know what he'd been eating lately. She smiled at the thought, climbing along the top of some boxes beside a few other urchins. Darkness, though, he wasn't that *normal.* She had trouble imagining him eating, or anything like that.

A shopkeeper chased them down off the boxes, but Lift had gotten a good look at Darkness and was able to scurry after him, Wyndle at her side.

Darkness never paused to consider his route, or to look at the wares of street vendors. He seemed to move too quickly for his own steps, like he was melting from shadow to shadow as he strode. She nearly lost sight of him several times, which was bizarre. She'd always been able to keep track of where people were.

Darkness eventually reached a market where they sure had a lot of fruit on display. Looked like someone had planned a really, really big food fight, but had decided to call it off and were reluctantly selling their ammunition. Lift helped herself to a purple fruit—she didn't know the name—while the shopkeeper was staring, uncomfortably, at Darkness. As people did. It—

"Hey!" the shopkeeper shouted. "Hey, stop!"

Lift spun, tucking her hand behind her back and dropping the fruit—which she kicked with her heel into the crowd. She smiled sweetly.

But the shopkeeper wasn't looking at her. He was looking at a different opportunist, a girl a few years Lift's senior, who had swiped a whole basket of fruit. The young woman bolted the moment she was spotted, leaning down and clinging to the basket. She sprinted deftly through the crowd.

Lift heard herself whimper.

*No. Not that way. Not toward—*

Darkness snatched the young woman from the crowd. He flowed toward her almost as if he were liquid, then seized her by the shoulder with the speed of a snapping rat trap. She struggled, battering against him, though he remained stiff and didn't seem to notice or mind the attack. Still holding to her, he bent and picked up the basket of fruit, then carried it toward the shop, dragging the thief after him.

"Thank you!" the shopkeeper said, taking back the basket and looking over Darkness's uniform. "Um, officer?"

"I am a special deputized operative, granted free jurisdiction throughout the kingdom by the prince," Darkness said, removing a sheet of paper from his coat pocket and holding it up.

The girl grabbed a piece of fruit from the basket and threw it at Darkness, bouncing it off his chest with a splat. He didn't respond to this, and didn't even flinch as she bit his hand. He just tucked away the document he'd been showing the shopkeeper. Then he looked at her.

Lift knew what it was like to meet those cold, glassy eyes. The girl in his grip cringed before him, then seemed to panic, reaching to her belt, yanking out her knife and brandishing it. She tried a desperate swing at Darkness's arm, but he easily slapped the weapon away with his empty hand.

Around them, the crowd had sensed that something was off. Though the rest of the market was busy, this one section grew still. Lift pulled back beside a small, broken cart—built narrow for navigating the slots—where several other urchins were betting on how long it would be before Tiqqa escaped "this time."

As if in response to this, Darkness summoned his Shardblade and rammed it through the struggling girl's chest.

The long blade sank up to its hilt as he pulled her onto it, and she gasped, eyes going wide—then shriveling and burning out, letting twin trails of smoke creep toward the sky.

The shopkeeper screamed, hand to his chest. He dropped the basket of fruit.

Lift squeezed her eyes closed. She heard the corpse drop to the ground, and Darkness's too-calm voice as he said, "Give this form to the market watch, who will dispose of the body and take your statement. Let me witness the time and date . . . here. . . ."

Lift forced her eyes open. The two urchins beside her gaped in horror, mouths wide. One started crying with a disbelieving whine.

Darkness finished filling out the form, then prodded the shopkeeper, forcing the man to witness it as well in pen, and write a short description of what had happened.

That done, Darkness nodded and turned to go. The shopkeeper—fruit spilled at his feet, a stack of boxes and baskets to his side—stared at the corpse, papers held limply in his fingers. Then angerspren boiled up around him, like red pools on the ground.

"Was that *necessary*!" he demanded. "Tashi . . . Tashi above!"

"Tashi doesn't care much for what you do here," Darkness said as he walked away. "In fact, I'd pray that he doesn't reach your city, as I doubt you'd like the consequences. As for the thief, she would have enjoyed imprisonment for her theft. The punishment prescribed for assaulting an officer with a bladed weapon, however, is death."

"But . . . *But that was barbaric!* Couldn't you have just . . . taken off her hand or . . . or . . . something?"

Darkness stopped, then looked back at the shopkeeper, who cringed.

"I have tried that, where the law allows discretion in punishments," Darkness said. "Removing a hand leads to a high rate of recidivism, as the thief is left unable to do most honest work, and therefore must steal. In such a case, I could make crime worse instead of reducing it."

He cocked his head, looking from the shopkeeper to the corpse, as if confused why anyone would be bothered by what he had done. Without further concern for the matter, he turned and continued on his way.

Lift stared, stunned, then—heedless of being seen—forced away her shock and ran to the fallen girl. She grabbed the body by the shoulders and leaned down, breathing out her awesomeness—the light that burned inside her—and imparting it to the dead young woman.

For a moment it seemed to be working. She saw something, a luminescence in the shape of a figure. It vibrated around the corpse, quivering. Then it puffed away, and the body remained on the ground, immobile, eyes burned.

"No . . ." Lift said.

"Too much time passed for this one, mistress," Wyndle said softly. "I'm sorry."

"Gawx was longer."

"Gawx wasn't slain by a Shardblade," Wyndle said. "I . . . I think that humans don't die instantly, most of the time. Oh, my memory. Too many holes, mistress. But I do know that a Shardblade, it is different. Maybe if you'd reached this one right after. Yes, you'd have been able to then. It was just too long. And you don't have enough power, either way."

Lift knelt on the stones, drained. The body didn't even bleed.

"She *did* draw a knife on him," Wyndle said, his voice small.

"She was terrified! She saw his eyes and panicked." She gritted her teeth, then snarled and climbed to her feet. She scrambled over to the shopkeeper, who jumped back as Lift seized two of his fruits and stared him right in the eyes as she took a big, juicy bite of one and chewed.

Then she chased after Darkness.

"Mistress . . ." Wyndle said.

She ignored him. She followed after the heartless creature, the murderer. She managed to find him again—he left an even bigger wake of disturbed people behind him now. She caught sight of him as he left the market, going up a set of steps, then walking through a large archway.

Lift followed carefully, and peeked out into an odd section of the city. They'd carved a large, conical chunk out of the stone here. It was deep a ways, and was filled with water.

It was a really, really big cistern. A cistern as big as several houses, to collect rain from the storms.

"Ah," Wyndle said. "Yes, separated from the rest of the city by a raised rim. Rainwater in the streets will flow outward, rather than toward this cistern, keeping it pure. In fact, it seems that most of the streets have a slope to them, to siphon water outward. Where does it go from there though?"

Whatever. She inspected the big cistern, which did have a neat bridge running across it. The thing was so big that you needed a bridge, and people stood on it to lower buckets on ropes down into the water.

Darkness didn't take the path across the bridge; there was a ledge running around the outside of the cistern also, and there were fewer people on it. He obviously wanted to take the route that involved less jostling.

Lift hesitated at the entrance into the place, fighting with her frustration, her sense of powerlessness. She earned a curse or two as she accidentally blocked traffic.

*Her name was Tiqqa,* Lift thought. *I will remember you, Tiqqa. Because few others will.*

Below, the large cistern pool rippled from the many people drawing water from it. If she followed Darkness around the ledge, she'd be in the open with nobody between them.

Well, he didn't look behind himself very often. She just had to risk it. She took a step along the path.

"Don't!" Wyndle said. "Mistress, stay hidden. He has eyes you cannot see."

Fine. She joined the flow of people moving down the steps. This was the shorter route, but there were a *lot* of people on the bridge. In the bustle, because of her shortness, she lost sight of Darkness.

Sweat prickled on the back of her neck, cold. If she couldn't see him, she felt certain—irrationally—that he was now watching her. She pictured again and again how he'd emerged from the market to grab the thief, a supernatural ease to his movements. Yes, he knew things about people like Lift. He'd spoken of her powers with familiarity.

Lift drew upon her awesomeness. She didn't make herself Slick, but she let the light suffuse her, pep her up. The power felt like it was alive sometimes. The essence of eagerness, a spren. It drove her forward as she dodged and squeezed through the crowd of people on the bridge.

She reached the other side of the bridge, and saw no sign of Darkness on the ledge. Storms. She left through the archway on the other side, slipping back into the city proper and entering a large crossroads.

Shiqua-wrapped Tashikkis passed in front of her, interrupted occasionally by Azish in colorful patterns. This was certainly a better part of town. Light from the rising sun sparkled off painted sections of the walls, here displaying a grand mural of Tashi and the Nine binding the world. Some of the people she passed had parshman slaves, their marbled skin black and red. She hadn't seen many of those here, not as many as in Azir. Maybe she just hadn't been in rich enough sections of the city.

Lots of the buildings here had small trees or ornamental shrubs in front of them. They were bred and cultivated to be lazy, so their leaves didn't pull in despite the near crowds.

*Read those crowds . . .* Lift thought. *The people. Where are the people being strange?*

She scrambled through the crossroads, intuiting the way. Something about how people stood, where they looked. There was a ripple here. The waves of a passing fish, silent but not still.

She turned a corner, and caught a brief glimpse of Darkness striding up a set of stairs beside a row of small trees. He stepped into a building, then shut the door.

Lift crept up beside the building Darkness had entered, her face brushing the leaves of the trees, causing them to pull in. They were lazy, but not so stupid that they wouldn't move if touched.

"What are these 'eyes' you say he has?" she asked as Wyndle wound up beside her. "The ones I can't see."

"He will have a spren," Wyndle said. "Like me. It's likely invisible to you and anyone else but him. Most are, on this side, I think. I don't remember all the rules."

"You sure are dumb some of the time, Voidbringer."

He sighed.

"Don't worry," Lift said. "I'm dumb *most* of the time." She scratched her head. The steps ended at a door. Did she dare open it and slip in? If she was going to learn anything about Darkness and what he was doing in the city, she'd have to do more than find out where he lived.

"Mistress," Wyndle said, "I might be stupid, but I can say with certainty that you're *not* a match for that creature. There are many Words you haven't spoken."

"Course I haven't said those kinds of words," Lift said. "Don't you ever listen to me? I'm a sweet, innocent little girl. I ain't going to talk about bollocks and jiggers and stuff. I'm not *crass*."

Wyndle sighed. "Not *those* kinds of words. Mistress, I—"

"Oh, hush," Lift said, squatting beside the trees lining the front of the building. "We have to get in there and see what he's up to."

"Mistress, please don't get yourself killed. It would be *traumatic*. Why, I think it would take me months and months to get over it!"

"That's faster than I'd get over it." She scratched at her head. She couldn't hang on the side of the building and listen at Darkness, like she had at the guard captain's place. Not in a fancy part of town, and not in the middle of the day.

Besides, she had loftier goals today than just eavesdropping. She had to actually break into this place to do what she needed to do here. But how? It wasn't like these buildings had back doors. They were cut directly into the rock. She could maybe get in one of the front windows, but that sure would be suspicious.

She glanced at the passing crowds. People in cities, they'd notice something like an urchin breaking in through a window. Something that looked like trouble. But other times they'd ignore the most obvious things in front of their own noses.

*Maybe* . . . She did have awesomeness left from that fruit she'd eaten. She eyed a shuttered window about five or six feet up. That would be on the first story of the building, but it was up somewhat high, because everything was built up a ways in this city.

Lift hunkered down and let some of her awesomeness out. The little tree beside her stretched and popped softly. Leaves budded, unfurled, and gave a good morning yawn. Branches reached toward the sky. Lift took her time, filling in the tree's canopy, letting it get large enough to obscure the window. Around her feet, seeds from storm-blown rockbuds puffed up like little hot buns. Vines wrapped around her ankles.

Nobody passing on the street noticed. They'd cuff an urchin for scratching her butt in a suspicious manner, but couldn't be bothered with a miracle. Lift sighed, smiling. The tree would cover her as she broke in through that window, if she moved carefully. She let her awesomeness continue to trickle out, comforting the tree, making it even more lazy. Lifespren popped up, little glowing green motes that bobbed around her.

She waited for a lull in the passing crowds, then hopped up and grabbed a branch, hauling herself into the tree. The tree, drinking of her awesomeness, didn't pull its leaves back in. She felt safe here surrounded by the branches, which smelled rich and heady, like the spices used for broth. Vines wrapped around the tree branches, sprouting leaves, much as Wyndle did.

Unfortunately, her power was almost out. A couple pieces of fruit didn't provide much. She pressed her ear against the window's thick stormshutters, and didn't hear anything from the room beyond. Safe in the tree, she softly rattled the stormshutters with her palms, using the sound to pick out where the latch was.

*See. I can listen.*

But of course, this wasn't the right kind of listening.

The window was latched with some kind of long bar on the other side, probably fitted into slots across the back of the shutters. Fortunately, these stormshutters weren't as tight as those in other towns; they probably didn't need to be, down here safe in the trenches. She let the vines wind around the branches, drinking of her Stormlight, then twist around her arms and squeeze through cracks in the shutters. The vines stretched up the inside of the shutters, pressing up the bar that held the shutters closed, and . . .

And she was in. She used the last of her awesomeness to coat the hinges of the shutters, so they slid against one another without a hint of a sound. She slipped into a boxlike stone room, lifespren pouring in behind her, dancing in the air like glowing whispermill seeds.

"Mistress!" Wyndle said, growing in onto the wall. "Oh, mistress. That was *delightful*! Why don't we forget this entire mess with the Skybreakers, and go . . . why . . . why, go *run a farm*! Yes, a farm. A lovely farm. You could sculpt plants every day, and eat until you were ready to burst! And . . . Mistress?"

Lift padded through the room, noting a rack of swords by the wall, sheathed and deadly. Sparring leathers on the floor near the corner. The smell of oil and sweat. There was no door in the doorway, and she peeked out into a dark hallway, listening.

There was a three-way intersection here. Hallways lined with rooms led to her left and right, and then a longer hallway led straight forward, into darkness. Voices echoed from that direction.

That hallway in front of her cut deeper into the stone, away from windows—and from exits. She glanced right instead, toward the building's entrance. An old man sat in a chair there, near the door, wearing a white and black uniform of the type she'd only seen on Darkness and his men. He was mostly bald, except for a few wisps of hair, and had beady eyes and a pinched face—like a shriveled-up fruit that was trying to pass for human.

He stood up and checked a little window in the door, watching the crowd outside with suspicion. Lift took the opportunity to scuttle into the hallway to her left, where she ducked into the next room over.

This looked more promising. Though it was dim with the stormshutters closed, it seemed like some kind of workroom or den. Lift eased open the shutters for a little light, then did a quick search. Nothing obvious on the shelves full of maps. Nothing on the writing table but some books and a rack of spanreeds. There was a trunk by the wall, but it was locked. She was beginning to despair when she smelled something.

She peeked out of the doorway. That guard had wandered off; she could hear him whistling somewhere, alongside the sound of a stream of liquid in a chamber pot.

Lift slipped farther down the corridor to her left, away from the guard. The next room in line was a bedroom with a door that was cracked open. She slipped in and found a stiff coat hanging on a peg right inside—one with a circular fruit stain on the front. Darkness's jacket for sure.

Below it, sitting on the floor, was a tray with a metal covering—the type fancy people put over plates so they wouldn't have to look at food while it got cold. Underneath, like the emerald treasures of the Tranquiline Halls, Lift found three plates of pancakes.

Darkness's breakfast. Mission accomplished.

She started stuffing her face with a vengeful enthusiasm.

Wyndle made a face from vines beside her. "Mistress? Was this all . . . was this all so you could *steal his food*?"

"Yeph," Lift said, then swallowed. "Course it is." She took another bite. That'd show him.

"Oh. Of course." He sighed deeply. "I suppose this is . . . this is pleasant, then. Yes. No swinging about of innocent spren, stabbing them into people and the like. Just . . . just stealing some food."

"*Darkness's* food." She'd stolen from a palace, and the starvin' emperor of Azir. She'd needed *something* interesting to try next.

It felt good to finally get enough food to fill her stomach. One of the pancakes was salty, with chopped-up vegetables. Another tasted sweet. The third variety was fluffier, almost without any substance to it, though there was some kind of sauce to dip it in. She slurped that down—who had time for dipping?

She ate every scrap, then settled back against the wall, smiling.

"So, we came all this way," Wyndle said, "and tracked the most dangerous man we've ever met, merely so you could steal his breakfast. We didn't come here to do . . . to do anything more, then?"

"Do you want to do something more?"

"Storms, no!" Wyndle said. He twisted his little vine face around, looking toward the hallway. "I mean . . . every moment we spend in here is dangerous."

"Yup."

"We should run. Go found a farm, like I said. Leave him behind, though he's likely tracking someone in this city. Someone like us, someone who can't fight him. Someone he will murder before they even start to grasp their powers . . ."

They sat in the room, empty tray beside them. Lift felt her awesomeness begin to stir within her again.

"So," she asked. "Guess we go spy on them, eh?"

Wyndle whimpered, but—shockingly—nodded.

# 9

JUST try not to die too violently, mistress," Wyndle said as she crept closer to the sounds of people talking. "A nice rap on the head, rather than a disemboweling."

That voice was definitely Darkness. The sound of it gave her chills. When the man had confronted her in the Azish palace, he'd been dispassionate, even as he half apologized for what he was about to do.

"I hear that suffocation is nice," Wyndle said. "Though in such a case, don't look at me as you expire. I'm not sure I could handle it."

*Remember the girl in the market. Steady.*

Storms, her hands were trembling.

"I'm not sure about falling to your death," Wyndle added. "Seems like it might be messy, but at the same time at least there wouldn't be any *stabbing*."

The hallway ended at a large chamber lit by diamonds that gave it a calm, easy light. Not chips, not even spheres. Larger, unset gemstones. Lift crouched by the half-open door, hidden in shadows.

Darkness—wearing a stiff white shirt—paced before two underlings in uniforms in black and white, with swords at their waists. One was a Makabaki man with a round, goofish face. The other was a woman with skin a shade lighter—she looked like she might be Reshi, particularly with that long dark hair she kept in a tight braid. She had a square face, strong shoulders, and *way* too small a nose. Like she'd sold hers off to buy some new shoes, and was using one she'd dug out of the trash as a replacement.

"Your excuses do not befit those who would join our order," Darkness was saying. "If you would earn the trust of your spren, and take the step from initiate to Shardbearer, you must dedicate yourselves. You must prove your worth. Earlier today I followed a lead that each of you missed, and have discovered a second offender in the city."

"Sir!" the Reshi woman said. "I prevented an assault in an alleyway! A man was being accosted by thugs!"

"While this is well," Darkness said, still pacing back and forth in a calm, even stroll, "we must be careful not to be distracted by petty crimes. I realize that it can be difficult to remain focused when confronted by a fracture of the codes that bind society. Remember that greater matters, and greater crimes, must be our primary concern."

"Surgebinders," the woman said.

Surgebinders. People like Lift, people with awesomeness, who could do the impossible. She hadn't been afraid to sneak into a palace, but huddled by that door—looking in at the man she had named Darkness—she found herself terrified.

"But . . ." said the male initiate. "Is it really . . . I mean, shouldn't we *want* them to return, so we won't be the only order of Knights Radiant?"

"Unfortunately, no," Darkness said. "I once thought as you, but Ishar made the truth clear to me. If the bonds between men and spren are reignited, then men will naturally discover the greater power of the oaths. Without Honor to regulate this, there is a small chance that what comes next will allow the Voidbringers to again make the jump between worlds. That would cause a Desolation, and even a small chance that the world will be destroyed is a risk that we cannot take. Absolute fidelity to the mission Ishar gave us—the greater law of protecting Roshar—is required."

"You're wrong," a voice whispered from the darkness. "You may be a god . . . but you're still wrong."

Lift nearly jumped clear out of her own skin. Storms! There was a guy sitting just inside the doorway, *right next to where she was hiding*. She hadn't seen him—she'd been too fixated on Darkness.

He sat on the floor, wearing tattered white clothing. His hair was short, a brown fuzz, as if he'd kept it shaved until recently. He had pale, ghostly skin, and held a long sword in a silvery sheath, pommel resting against his shoulder, length stretching alongside his body and legs. He held his arms draped around the sheath, as if it were a child's toy to hug.

He shifted in his place, and . . . storms, he left a soft white *afterimage* behind him, like you get when staring at a bright gemstone for too long. It faded away in a moment.

"They're already back," he whispered, speaking with a smooth, airy Shin accent. "The Voidbringers have already returned."

"You are mistaken," Darkness said. "The Voidbringers are not back. What you saw on the Shattered Plains are simply remnants from millennia ago. Voidbringers who have been hiding among us all this time."

The man in white looked up, and Lift shied away. His movement left another afterimage that glowed briefly before fading. Storms. White clothing. Strange powers. Shin man with a bald head. Shardblade.

This was the starvin' *Assassin in White*!

"I saw them return," the assassin whispered. "The new storm, the red eyes. You are wrong, Nin-son-God. You are wrong."

"A fluke," Darkness said, his voice firm. "I contacted Ishar, and he assured me it is so. What you saw are a few listeners who remain from the old days, ones free to use the old forms. They summoned a cluster of Voidspren. We've found remnants of them on Roshar before, hiding."

"The storm? The new storm, of red lightning?"

"It means nothing," Darkness said. He did not seem to mind being challenged. He didn't seem to mind anything. His voice was perfectly even. "An oddity, to be sure."

"You're wrong. So wrong . . ."

"The Voidbringers have not returned," Darkness said firmly. "Ishar has promised it, and he will not lie. We must do our duty. You are questioning, Szeth-son-Neturo. This is not good; this is weakness. To question is to accept a descent into inactivity. The only path to sanity and action is to choose a code and to follow it. This is why I came to you in the first place."

Darkness turned, striding past the others. "The minds of men are fragile, their emotions mutable and often unpredictable. The *only* path to Honor is to stick to your chosen code. This was the way of the Knights Radiant, and is the way of the Skybreakers."

The man and woman standing nearby both saluted. The assassin just bowed his head again, closing his eyes, holding to that strange silver-sheathed Shardblade.

"You said that there is a second Surgebinder in the city," the woman said. "We can find—"

"She is mine," Darkness said evenly. "You will continue your mission. Find the one who has been hiding here since we arrived." He narrowed his eyes. "If we don't stop one, others will congregate. They clump together. I have often found them making contact with one another, these last five years, if I leave them alone. They must be drawn to each other."

He turned toward his two initiates; he seemed to ignore the assassin except when spoken to. "Your quarry will make mistakes—they will break the law. The other orders always did consider themselves beyond the reach of the law. Only the Skybreakers ever understood the importance of boundaries. Of picking something external to yourself and using it as a guide. Your minds cannot be trusted. Even my mind—especially my mind—cannot be trusted.

"I have given you enough help. You have my blessing and you have our commission granting us authority to act in this city. You will find the Surgebinder, you will discover their sins, and you will bring them judgment. In the name of all Roshar."

The two saluted again, and the room suddenly darkened. The woman began glowing with a phantom light, and she blushed, looking sheepishly toward Darkness. "I'll find them, sir! I have an investigation in progress."

"I have a lead too," the man said. "I'll have the information by tonight for certain."

"Work together," Darkness said. "This is not a competition. It is a test to measure competence. I'm giving you until sunset, but after that I can wait no longer. Now that others have begun arriving, the risk is too great. At sunset, I will deal with the issue myself."

"Bollocks," Lift whispered. She shook her head, then scuttled back along the hallway, away from the group of people.

"Wait," Wyndle said, following. "Bollocks? I thought you claimed you didn't say words like—"

"They've all got 'em," Lift said. "'Cept the girl, though with that face I can't be certain. Anyway, what I said wasn't crass, 'cuz it was just an *observation.*" She hit the intersection of corridors, and peeked to the left. The old man on watch was dozing. That let Lift slip across, into the room where she'd first entered. She climbed out into the tree, then closed the shutters.

In seconds she'd run around a corner into an alleyway, where she let herself slide down until she was sitting with her back against the stone, her heart pounding. Farther into the alleyway here, a family ate pancakes in a somewhat nice shanty. It had two whole walls.

"Mistress?" Wyndle said.

"I'm hungry," she complained.

"You just ate!"

"That was catching me up for spending so much getting into that starvin' building." She squeezed her eyes closed, containing her worry.

Darkness's voice was so cold.

*But they're like me. They glow like me. They're . . . awesome, like I am? What in Damnation is going on?*

And the Assassin in White. Was he going to go off and kill Gawx?

"Mistress?" Wyndle coiled around her leg. "Oh, mistress. Did you hear what they called him? Nin? That's a name of Nalan, the Herald! That can't be true. They went away, didn't they? Even we have legends about that. If that creature is truly one of them . . . oh, Lift. What are we going to do?"

"I don't know," she whispered. "I don't know. Storms . . . why am I even here?"

"I believe I've been asking that since—"

"Shut it, Voidbringer," she said, forcing herself to roll over and get to her knees. Deeper into the cramped alley, the father of the family reached for a cudgel while the wife tugged the curtain closed on the front of their hovel.

Lift sighed, then went wandering back toward the immigrant quarter.

# 10

WHEN she arrived at the orphanage, Lift finally figured out why it had been set up next to this open space at the mouth of the alleyway. The orphanage caretaker—the Stump, as she'd been called—had opened the doors and let the children out. They played here, in the most boring playground ever. A set of amphitheater steps and some open floor.

The children seemed to love it. They ran up and down the steps, laughing and giggling. Others sat in circles on the ground, playing games with painted pebbles. Laughterspren—like little silver fish that zipped through the air, this way and that—danced in the air some ten feet up, a whole school of the starvin' things.

There were lots of children, younger on average than Lift had assumed. Most, as she had been able to guess, were the kind that were different in the head, or they were missin' an arm or leg. Things like that.

Lift idled near the wide alleyway mouth, near where two blind girls played a game. One would drop rocks of a variety of sizes and shapes, and the other would try to guess which was which, based on how they sounded when they hit the ground. The group of old men and women in shiquas from the day before had again gathered at the back of the half-moon amphitheater seats, chatting and watching the children play.

"I thought you said orphanages were miserable," Wyndle said, coating the wall beside her.

"Everyone gets happy for a little while when you let them go outside," Lift said, watching the Stump. The wizened old lady was scowling as she pulled a cart through the doors toward the amphitheater. More clemabread rolls. Delightful. Those were only *slightly* better than gruel, which was only *slightly* better than cold socks.

Still, Lift joined the others who got in line to accept their roll. When her turn came, the Stump pointed to a spot beside the cart and didn't speak a word to her. Lift stepped aside, lacking the energy to argue.

The Stump made sure every child got a roll, then studied Lift before handing her one of the last two. "Your second meal of three."

"Second!" Lift snapped. "I ain't—"

"You got one last night."

"I didn't ask for it!"

"You ate it." The Stump pushed the cart away, eating the last of the rolls herself.

"Storming witch," Lift muttered, then found a spot on the stone seats. She sat apart from the regular orphans; she didn't want to be talked at.

"Mistress," Wyndle said, climbing the steps to join her. "I don't believe you when you say you left Azir because they were trying to dress you in fancy clothing and teach you to read."

"Is that so," she said, chewing on her roll.

"You liked the clothing, for one thing. And when they tried to give you lessons, you seemed to enjoy the game of always being gone when they came looking. They weren't forcing you into anything; they were merely offering opportunities. The palace was *not* the stifling experience you imply."

"Maybe not for me," she admitted.

It was for Gawx. They expected all *kinds* of things of the new emperor. Lessons, displays. People came to watch him eat every meal. They even got to watch him sleeping. In Azir, the emperor was owned by the people, like a friendly stray axehound that seven different houses fed, all claiming her as their own.

"Maybe," Lift said, "I just didn't want people expecting so much from me. If you get to know people too long, they'll start depending on you."

"Oh, and you can't bear responsibility?"

"Course I can't. I'm a starvin' street urchin."

"One who came here chasing down what *appears* to be one of the Heralds themselves, gone mad and accompanied by an assassin who has murdered *multiple* world monarchs. Yes, I believe that you *must* be avoiding responsibility."

"You giving me lip, Voidbringer?"

"I think so? Honestly, I don't know what that term means, but judging by your tone, I'd say that I'm probably giving you lip. And you probably deserve it."

She grunted in response, chewing on her food. It tasted terrible, as if it had been left out all night.

"Mama always told me to travel," Lift said. "And go places. While I'm young."

"And that's why you left the palace."

"Dunno. Maybe."

"Utter nonsense. Mistress, what is it really? Lift, what do you *want*?"

She looked down at the half-eaten roll in her hand.

"Everything is changing," she said softly. "That's okay. Stuff changes. It's just that, I'm not supposed to. I *asked* not to. She's supposed to give you what you ask."

"The Nightwatcher?" Wyndle asked.

Lift nodded, feeling small, cold. Children played and laughed all around, and for some reason that only made her feel worse. It was obvious to her, though she'd tried ignoring it for years, that she *was* taller than she'd been when she'd first sought out the Old Magic three years ago.

She looked beyond the kids, toward the street passing out front. A group of women bustled past, carrying baskets of yarn. A prim Alethi man strode in the other direction, with straight black hair and an imperious attitude. He was at least a foot taller than anyone else on the street. Workers moved along, cleaning the street, picking up trash.

In the alleyway mouth, the Stump had deposited her cart and was disciplining a child who had started hitting others. At the back of the amphitheater seats, the old men and women laughed together, one pouring cups of tea to pass around.

They all seemed to just . . . know what to do. Cremlings knew to scuttle, plants knew to grow. Everything had its place.

"The only thing I've ever known how to do was hunt food," Lift whispered.

"What's that, mistress?"

It had been hard, at first. Feeding herself. Over time, she'd figured out the tricks. She'd gotten good at it.

But once you weren't hungry all the time, what did you *do*? How did you *know*?

Someone poked at her arm, and she turned to see that a kid had scooted up beside her—a lean boy with his head shaved. He pointed at her half-eaten roll and grunted.

She sighed and gave it to him. He ate eagerly.

"I know you," she said, cocking her head. "You're the one whose mother dropped him off last night."

"Mother," he said, then looked at her. "Mother . . . come back when?"

"Huh. So you *can* talk," Lift said. "Didn't think you could, after all that staring around dumbly last night."

"I . . ." The boy blinked, then looked at her. No drooling. Must be a good day for him. A grand accomplishment. "Mother . . . come back?"

"Probably not," Lift said. "Sorry, kid. They don't come back. What's your name?"

"Mik," the boy said. He looked at her, confused, as if searching—and failing—to figure out who she was. "We . . . friends?"

"Nope," Lift said. "You don't wanna be my friend. My friends end up as emperors." She shivered, then leaned in. "People *pick his nose* for him."

Mik looked at her blankly.

"Yeah. I'm serious. They pick his nose. Like, he's got this woman who does his hair, and I peeked in, and I saw her sticking something up his nose. Like little tweezers she used to grab his boogies or something." Lift shivered. "Being an emperor is real strange."

The Stump dragged over one of the kids who'd been fighting and plopped him on the stone. Then, oddly, she gave him some earmuffs—like it was cold or something. He put them on and closed his eyes.

The Stump paused, looking toward Lift and Mik. "Making plans on how to rob me?"

"What?" Lift said. "No!"

"One more meal," the woman said, holding up a finger. Then she stabbed it toward Mik. "And when you go, take that one. I *know* he's faking."

"Faking?" Lift turned toward Mik, who blinked, dazed, as if trying to follow the conversation. "You're not serious."

"I can see through it when urchins are feigning illness in order to get food," the Stump snapped. "That one's no idiot. He's pretending." She stomped away.

Mik wilted, looking down at his feet. "I miss Mother."

"Yeah," Lift said. "Nice, eh?"

Mik looked at her, frowning.

"We get to remember ours," Lift said, standing. "That's more than most like us get." She patted him on the shoulder.

A short time later, the Stump called that playtime was over. She herded the kids into the orphanage for naps, though many were too old for that. The Stump gave Mik a displeased eye as he entered, but let him in.

Lift remained in her seat on the stone, then smacked her hand at a cremling that had been inching across the step nearby. Starvin' thing dodged, then clicked its chitin legs as if laughing. They sure did have strange cremlings here. Not like the ones she was used to at all. Weird how you could forget you were in a different country until you saw the cremlings.

"Mistress," Wyndle said, "have you decided what we're going to do?"

Decide. Why did she have to decide? She usually just *did* things. She'd taken challenges as they'd arisen, gone places for no reason other than that she hadn't seen them before.

The old people who had been watching the children slowly rose, like ancient trees releasing their branches after a storm. One by one they trailed off until only one remained, wearing a black shiqua with the wrap pulled down to expose a face with a grey mustache.

"Ey," Lift called to him. "You still creepy, old man?"

"I am the man I was made to be," he said back.

Lift grunted, climbing from her spot and strolling over to him. Some of the kids from before had left their pebbles, with painted colors that were rubbing off. A poor kid's imitation of glass marbles. Lift kicked at them.

"How do you know what to do?" she asked the man, her hands shoved in her pockets.

"About what, little one?"

"About *everything*," Lift said. "Who tells you how to decide what to do with your time? Was it your parents who showed you? What's the secret?"

"The secret to what?"

"To being human," Lift said softly.

"That," the man said, chuckling, "I don't think I know. At least not better than you do."

Lift looked at the sky, up along slotlike walls, scraped clean of vegetation but painted a dark green, as if in imitation of it.

"It is strange," the man said. "People get such a small amount of time. So many I've known say it—as soon as you feel you're getting a handle on things, the day is done, the night falls, and the light goes out."

Lift looked at him. Yup. Still creepy. "I guess when you're old and stuff, you get to thinkin' about being dead. Kind of like when a fellow's got to piss, he starts thinkin' about finding a convenient alleyway."

The man chuckled. "Your life may pass, but the organism that is the city will continue on. Little nose."

"I'm *not* a nose," Lift said. "I was being cheeky."

"Nose, cheek. Both are on the face."

Lift rolled her eyes. "That's not what I meant either."

"What are you then? An ear, perhaps?"

"Dunno. Maybe."

"No. Not yet. But close."

"Riiight," Lift said. "And what are you?"

"I change, moment by moment. One moment I am the eyes that inspect so many people in this city. Another moment I am the mouth, to speak the words of philosophy. They spread like a disease—and so at times I *am* the disease. Most diseases live. Did you know that?"

"You're . . . not really talking about what you're talking about, are you?" Lift said.

"I believe that I am."

"Great." Of all the people she'd chosen to ask about how to be a responsible adult, she'd picked the one with vegetable soup in place of brains. She turned to go.

"What will you make for this city, child?" the man asked. "That is part of my question. Do you choose, or are you simply molded by the greater good? And are you, as a city, a district of grand palaces? Or are you a slum, unto yourself?"

"If you could see inside me," Lift said, turning and walking backward so she faced the old man on the steps, "you wouldn't say things like that."

"Because?"

"Because. At least slums know what they was built for." She turned and joined the flow of people on the street.

# 11

I don't think you understand how this is supposed to work," Wyndle said, curling along the wall beside her. "Mistress, you . . . don't seem interested in evolving our relationship."

She shrugged.

"There are Words," Wyndle said. "That's what we call them, at least. They're more . . . ideas. Living ideas, with power. You have to let them into your soul. Let *me* into your soul. You heard those Skybreakers, right? They're looking to take the next step in their training. That's when . . . you know . . . they get a Shardblade. . . ."

He smiled at her, the expression appearing in successive patterns of his growing vines along the wall as they chased her. Each image of the smile was slightly different, grown one after another beside her, like a hundred paintings. They made a smile, and yet none of them *was* the smile. It was, somehow, all of them together. Or perhaps the smile existed in the spaces between the images in the succession.

"There's only one thing I know how to do," Lift said. "And that's steal Darkness's lunch. Like I came to do in the first place."

"And, um, didn't we do that already?"

"Not his food. His lunch." She narrowed her eyes.

"Ah . . ." Wyndle said. "The person he's planning to execute. We're going to snatch them away from him."

Lift strolled along a side street, and ended up passing into a garden: a bowl-like depression in the stone with four exits down different roads. Vines coated the leeward side of the wall, but they slowly gave way to brittels on the other side, shaped like flat plates for protection, but with planty stems that crept out and around the sides and up toward the sunlight.

Wyndle sniffed, crossing to the ground beside her. "Barely any cultivation. Why, this is no garden. Whoever maintains this should be reprimanded."

"I like it," Lift said, lifting her hand toward some lifespren, which bobbed over her fingertips. The garden was crowded with people. Some were coming and going, while others lounged about, and still others begged for chips. She hadn't seen many beggars in the city; likely there were all *kinds* of rules and regulations about when you could do it and how.

She stopped, hands on hips. "People here, in Azir and Tashikk, they *love* to write stuff down."

"Oh, most certainly," Wyndle said, curling around some vines. "Mmm. Yes, mistress, these at least are fruit vines. I suppose that is better; it's not *completely* haphazard."

"And they love information," Lift said. "They love tradin' it with one another, right?"

"Most certainly. That is a distinguishing factor of their cultural identity, as your tutors said in the palace. You weren't there. I went to listen in your place."

"What people write can be important, at least to them," Lift said. "But what would they do with it all when they're done with it? Throw it out? Burn it?"

"Throw it out? Mother's vines! No, no, no. You can't just go throwing things out! They might be useful later on. If it were me, I'd find someplace safe for them, and keep them pristine in case I needed them!"

Lift nodded, folding her arms. They'd have his same attitude. This city, with everyone writing notes and rules, then offering to sell everyone else ideas all the time . . . Well, in some ways this place was like a *whole city* of Wyndles.

Darkness had told his hunters to find someone who was doing strange stuff. Awesome stuff. And in this city they wrote down what kids had for *breakfast.* If somebody had seen something strange, they'd have written it down.

Lift scampered through the garden, brushing vines with her toes and causing them to writhe away. She hopped up onto a bench beside a likely target, an older woman in a brown shiqua, with the head portions pulled up and down to show a middle-aged face wearing makeup and displaying hints of styled hair.

The woman wrinkled her nose immediately, which was unfair. Lift had taken a bath back a week or so in Azir, and it had had soap and everything.

"Shoo," the woman said, waving fingers at her. "I've no money for you. Shoo. Go away."

"Don't want money," Lift said. "I've got a *deal* to make. For information."

"I want nothing from you."

"I can give you nothing," Lift said, relaxing. "I'm good at that. I'll go away, and give you nothing. You just gotta answer a question for me."

Lift hunched there on the bench, not moving. Then she scratched herself on the behind. The woman fussed, looking like she was going to leave, and Lift leaned in.

"You are disobeying beggar regulations," the woman snapped.

"Ain't beggin'. I'm tradin'."

"Fine. What do you want to know?"

"Is there a place," Lift said, "in this city where people stuff all the things they wrote down, to keep them safe?"

The woman frowned, then raised her hand and pointed along a street, which led straight for a distance, toward a moundlike bunker that rose from the center of the city. It was big enough to tower over the rest of the stuff around it, peeking up above the tops of the trenches.

"You mean like the Grand Indicium?" the woman asked.

Lift blinked, then cocked her head.

The woman took the opportunity to flee to a different part of the garden.

"Has that always been there?" Lift asked.

"Um, yes," Wyndle said. "Of course it has."

"Really?" Lift scratched her head. "Huh."

# 12

WYNDLE's vines wove up the side of an alleyway, and Lift climbed, not caring if she drew attention. She hauled herself over the top edge into a field where farmers watched the sky and grumbled. The seasons had gone insane. It was supposed to be raining constantly—a bad time to plant, as the water would wash away the seed paste.

Yet it hadn't rained for days. No storms, no water. Lift walked along, passing farmers who spread paste that would grow to tiny polyps, which would eventually grow to the size of large rocks and fill to bursting with grain. Mash that grain—either by hand or by storm—and it made new paste. Lift had always wondered why she didn't grow polyps inside her stomach after eating, and nobody had ever given her a straight answer.

The confused farmers worked with their shiquas pulled up to their waists. Lift passed, and she tried to listen. To hear.

This was supposed to be their one time of year where they didn't have to work. Sure, they planted some treb to grow in cracks, as it could survive flooding. But they weren't supposed to have to plant lavis, tallew, or clema: much more labor-intensive—but also more profitable—crops to cultivate.

Yet here they were. What if it rained tomorrow, and washed away all this effort? What if it never rained again? The city cisterns, which were glutted with water from the weeks of Weeping, would not last forever. They were so worried, she caught sight of some fearspren—shaped like globs of purple goo—gathering around the mounds upon which the men planted.

As a counterpoint, lifespren broke off from the growing polyps and bobbed over to Lift, trailing in her wake. A swirling, green-glowing dust. Ahead of her, the Grand Indicium rose like the head of a bald man seen peeking above the back of the chair he was sitting in. It was a huge rounded mass of stone.

Everything in the city revolved around this central point. Streets turned in this direction, curling up to it, and as Lift drew close, she could see that an enormous swath of stone had been cut away around the Indicium. The round bunker wasn't much to look at, but it sure did seem secure from the storms.

"Yes, the land *does* slope away from this central point," Wyndle noted. "This focus had to be the highest point of the city anyway—and I guess they figured they'd just accept that, and make the central knob into a fortress."

A fortress for books. People could be so strange. Below, crowds of people—most of them Tashikki—flowed in and out of the building, which had numerous screwlike sloped walkways leading up to it.

Lift settled down on the edge of the wall, feet hanging over. "Kinda looks like the tip of some guy's dangly bits. Like some fellow had such a short sword, everyone felt so sorry for him they said, 'Hey, we'll make a *huge* statue to it, and even though it's tiny, it'll look real big!' "

Wyndle sighed.

"That wasn't crude," Lift noted. "That was being poetic. Ol' Whitehair said you can't be crass, so long as you're talkin' 'bout art. Then you're being elegant. That's why it's okay to hang pictures of naked ladies in a palace."

"Mistress, wasn't this the man who got himself *intentionally* swallowed by a Marabethian greatshell?"

"Yup. Crazy as a box full of drunk minks, that one. I miss him." She liked to pretend he hadn't actually gotten eaten. He'd winked at her as he'd jumped into the greatshell's gaping maw, shocking the crowd.

Wyndle piled around on himself, forming a face—eyes made of crystals, lips formed of a tiny network of vines. "Mistress, what is our plan?"

"Plan?"

He sighed. "We need to get into that building. Are you just going to do whatever strikes you?"

"Obviously."

"Might I offer some suggestions?"

"Long as it doesn't involve sucking someone's soul, Voidbringer."

"I'm not— Look, mistress, that building is an archive. Knowing what I do of this region, the rooms in there will be filled with laws, records, and reports. Thousands upon thousands upon thousands of them."

"Yeah," she said, making a fist. "Among all that, they'll have written down strange stuff for sure!"

"And how, precisely, are we going to find the specific information we want?"

"Easy. You're gonna read it."

". . . Read it."

"Yup. We'll get in there, you'll read their books and stuff, and then we'll decide where strange events were. That will lead us to Darkness's lunch."

". . . Read it *all*."

"Yup."

"Do you have any idea how much information is likely held in that place?" Wyndle said. "There will be hundreds of thousands of reports and ledgers. And to state it explicitly, yes, that's a number more than ten, so you can't count to it."

"I'm not an idiot," she snapped. "I got toes too."

"It's still far more than I can read. I can't sift through all of that information for you. It's impossible. Not going to happen."

She eyed him. "All right. Maybe I can get you *one* soul. Perhaps a tax collector . . . 'cept they ain't human. Would they work? Or would you need, like, three of them to make up one normal person's soul?"

"Mistress! I'm not *bargaining*!"

"Come on. Everyone knows Voidbringers like a good deal. Does it have to be someone important? Or can it be some dumb guy nobody likes?"

"I don't *eat souls,*" Wyndle exclaimed. "I'm not trying to haggle with you! I'm stating facts. I *can't read* all the information in that archive! Why can't you just see that—"

"Oh, calm your tentacles," Lift said, swinging her feet, bouncing her heels against the rock cliff. "I hear you. Can't help but hear you, considering how much you whine."

Behind, the farmers were asking whose daughter she was, and why she wasn't running them water like kids were supposed to. Lift scrunched up her face, thinking. "Can't wait until night and sneak in," she muttered. "Darkness wants the poor person killed by then. 'Sides, I bet those scribes work nights. They feed off ink. Why sleep when you could be writin' up some new law about how many fingers people can use to hold a spoon?

"They know their stuff though. They sell it all over the place. The viziers were always writing to them to get some answer to something. Mostly news around the world." She grinned, then stood up. "You're right. We gotta do this differently."

"Yes indeed."

"We gotta be *smart* about it. *Devious.* Think like a Voidbringer."

"I didn't say—"

"Stop complaining," Lift said. "I'm gonna go steal some important-looking clothes."

# 13

Lift liked soft clothing. These supple Azish coat and robes were the wardrobe equivalent of silky pudding. It was good to remember that life wasn't only about scratchy things. Sometimes it was about soft pillows, fluffy cake. Nice words. Mothers.

The world couldn't be completely bad when it had soft clothes. This outfit was big for her, but that was okay. She liked it loose. She snuggled into the robes, sitting in the chair, crossing her hands in her lap, wearing a cap on her head. The entire costume was marked by bright colors woven in patterns that meant very important things. She was pretty sure of that, because everyone in Azir wouldn't shut up about their patterns.

The scribe was fat. She needed, like, three shiquas to cover her. Either that or a shiqua made for a horse. Lift wouldn't have thought that they'd give scribes so much food. What did they need so much energy for? Pens were really light.

The woman wore spectacles and kept her face covered, despite being in lands that knew Tashi. She tapped her pen against the table. "*You're* from the palace in Azir."

"Yup," Lift said. "Friend of the emperor. I call him Gawx, but they changed his name to something else. Which is okay, because Gawx is kind of a dumb name, and you don't want your emperor to sound dumb." She cocked her head. "Can't stop that if he starts talking though."

On the ground beside her, Wyndle groaned softly.

"Did you know," Lift said, leaning in to the scribe, "that they've got someone who *picks his nose* for him?"

"Young lady, I believe you are wasting my time."

"That's pretty insulting," Lift said, sitting up straight in her seat, "considering how little you people seem to do around here."

It was true. This whole building was full of scribes rushing this way and that, carrying piles of paper to one windowless alcove or another. They even had this spren that hung out here, one Lift had only seen a couple of times. It looked like little ripples in the air, like a raindrop in a pond—only without the rain, and without the pond. Wyndle called them concentrationspren.

Anyway, they had so much starvin' paper in the place that they needed parshmen to cart it about for them! One passed in the hallway outside, a woman carrying a large box of papers. Those would be hauled to one of a billion scribes who sat at tables, surrounded by blinking spanreeds. Wyndle said they were answering inquiries from around the world, passing information.

The scribe with Lift was a slightly more important one. Lift had gotten into the room by doing as Wyndle suggested: not talking. The viziers did that kind of thing too. Nodding, not saying anything. She'd presented the card, where she'd sketched the words that Wyndle had formed for her with vines.

The people at the front had been intimidated enough to lead her through the hallways to this room, which was larger than others—but it still didn't have any windows. The wall had a brownish yellow stain on the white paint though, and you could pretend it was sunlight.

On the other wall was a shelf that held a really long rack of spanreeds. A few Azish tapestries hung at the back. This scribe was some kind of liaison with the government over in Azir.

Once in the room though, Lift had been forced to talk. She couldn't avoid that anymore. She just needed to be persuasive.

"What unfortunate person," the large scribe asked, "did you mug to get that clothing?"

"Like I'd take it off someone while they were *wearing* it," Lift said, rolling her eyes. "Look. Just pull out one of those glowing pens and write to the palace. Then we can get on to the important stuff. My Voidbringer says you got *tons* of papers in here we're gonna have to look through."

The woman stood up. Lift could practically hear her chair breathe a sigh of relief. The woman pointed toward the door dismissively, but at that moment a lesser scribe—spindly, and wearing a yellow shiqua and a strange brown and yellow cap—entered and whispered in the woman's ear.

She looked displeased. The newcomer shrugged awkwardly, then hurried back out. The fat woman turned to eye Lift. "Give me the names of the viziers you know in the palace."

"Well, there's Dalky—she's got a funny nose, like a spigot. And Big A, I can't say his real name. It's got those choking sounds in it. And Daddy Sag-butt, he's not really a vizier. They call him a scion, which is a different kind of important. Oh! And Fat Lips! She's in charge of them. She doesn't really have fat lips, but she hates it when I call her that."

The woman stared at Lift. Then she turned and walked to the door. "Wait here." She stepped outside.

Lift leaned over toward the ground. "How'm I doin'?"

"Terribly," Wyndle said.

"Yeah. I noticed."

"It's almost as if," Wyndle said, "it would have been *useful* to learn how to talk politely, like the viziers kept telling you."

"Blah blah," Lift said, going to the door and listening. Outside, she could faintly hear the scribes talking.

". . . matches the description given by the captain of the immigration watch to search for in the city . . ." one of them said. "She showed up right here! We've sent to the captain, who luckily is here for her debriefing . . ."

"Damnation," Lift whispered, pulling back. "They're on to us, Voidbringer."

"I should never have helped you with this insane idea!"

Lift crossed the room to the racks of spanreeds. They were all labeled. "Get over here and tell me which one we need."

Wyndle grew up the wall and sent vines across the nameplates. "My, my. These are important reeds. Let's see . . . third one over, it will go to the royal palace scribes."

"Great," Lift said, grabbing it and scrambling onto the table. She set it into the right spot on the board—she'd seen this done tons of times—and twisted the ruby on the top of the reed. It was answered immediately; palace scribes weren't often away from their reeds. They'd sooner give up their fingers.

Lift grabbed the spanreed and placed it against the paper. "Uh . . ."

"Oh, for Cultivation's sake," Wyndle said. "You didn't pay attention at all, did you?"

"Nope."

"Tell me what you want to say."

She said it out, and he again made vines grow across the table in the right shapes. Pen gripped in her fist, she copied the words, one stupid letter at a time. It took *forever.* Writing was ridiculous. Couldn't people just talk? Why invent a way where you didn't have to actually see people to tell them what to do?

*This is Lift,* she wrote. *Tell Fat Lips I need her. I'm in trouble. And somebody get Gawx. If he's not having his nose picked right—*

The door opened and Lift yelped, twisting the ruby and scrambling off the table.

Beyond the door was a large gathering of people. Five scribes, including the fat one, and three guards. One was the woman who ran the guard post into the city.

*Storms,* Lift thought. *That was fast.*

She ducked toward them.

"Careful!" the guard shouted. "She's slippery!"

Lift made herself awesome, but the guard shoved the scribes into the room and started pushing the door shut behind her. Lift got between their legs, Slick and sliding easily, but slammed right into the door as it closed.

The guard lunged for her. Lift yelped, coating herself with awesomeness so that when she got grabbed, her wide-sleeved Azish coat came off, leaving her in a robelike skirt with trousers underneath, and then her normal shirts.

She scuttled across the ground, but the room wasn't large. She tried to scramble around the perimeter, but the guard captain was right on her.

"Mistress!" Wyndle cried. "Oh, mistress. Don't get stabbed! Are you listening? Avoid getting hit by anything sharp! Or blunt, actually!"

Lift growled as the other guards slipped in, then quickly shut the door. One prowled around on either side of the room.

She dodged one way, then the other, then punched at the shelf with the spanreeds, causing the scribe to scream as several toppled over.

Lift bolted for the door. The guard captain tackled her, and another piled on top of *her.*

Lift squirmed, making herself awesome, squeezing through their fingers. She just had to—

"Tashi," a scribe whispered. "God of Gods and Binder of the World!" Awespren, like a ring of blue smoke, burst out around her head.

Lift popped out of the grips of the guards, stepping up to stand on one of their backs, which gave her a good view of the desk. The spanreed was writing.

"Took them long enough," she said, then hopped off the guards and sat in the chair.

The guard stood up behind her, cursing.

"Stop, Captain!" the fat scribe said. She looked at the spindly scribe in yellow. "Go get another spanreed to the Azish palace. Get two! We need confirmation."

"For what?" the scribe said, walking to the desk. The guard captain joined them, reading what the pen wrote.

Then, slowly, all three looked up at Lift with wide eyes.

"'To whom it may concern,'" Wyndle read, spreading his vines up onto the table over the paper. "'It is decreed that I—Prime Aqasix Yanagawn the First, emperor of all Makabak—proclaim that the young woman known as Lift is to be shown every courtesy and measure of respect.

"'You will obey her as you would myself, and bill to the imperial account any charges that might be incurred by her . . . foray in your city.

What follows is a description of the woman, and two questions only she can answer, as proof of authentication. But know this—if she is harmed or impeded in any way, you will know imperial wrath.'"

"Thanks, Gawx," Lift said, then looked up at the scribes and guards. "That means you gotta do what I say!"

"And . . . what is it you want?" the fat scribe asked.

"Depends," Lift said. "What were you going to have for lunch today?"

# 14

THREE hours later, Lift sat in the center of the fat scribe's desk, eating pancakes with her hands and wearing the spindly scribe's hat.

A swarm of lesser scribes searched through reports on the ground in front of her, piles of books scattered about like broken crab shells after a fine feast. The fat scribe stood beside the desk, reading to Lift from the spanreed that wrote Gawx's end of their conversation. The woman had finally pulled down her face wrap, and it turned out she was pretty and a lot younger than Lift had assumed.

"'I'm worried, Lift,'" the fat scribe read to her. "'*Everyone* here is worried. There are reports coming in from the west now. Steen and Alm have seen the new storm. It's happening like the Alethi warlord said it would. A storm of red lightning, blowing the wrong direction.'"

The woman looked up at Lift. "He's right about that, um . . ."

"Say it," Lift said.

"Your Pancakefulness."

"Rolls right off the tongue, doesn't it?"

"His Imperial Excellency is correct about the arrival of a strange new storm. We have independent confirmation of that from contacts in

Shinovar and Iri. An enormous storm with red lightning, blowing in from the west."

"And the monsters?" Lift said. "Things with red eyes in the darkness?"

"Everything is in chaos," the scribe said—her name was Ghenna. "We've had trouble getting straight answers. We had some inkling of this, from reports on the east coast when the storm struck there, before blowing into the ocean. Most people thought those reports exaggerated, and that the storm would blow itself out. Now that it has rounded the planet and struck in the west . . . Well, the prince is reportedly preparing a diktat of emergency for the entire country."

Lift looked at Wyndle, who was coiled on the desk beside her. "Voidbringers," he said, voice small. "It's happening. Sweet virtue . . . the Desolations *have* returned. . . ."

Ghenna went back to reading the spanreed from Gawx. "'This is going to be a disaster, Lift. Nobody is ready for a storm that blows the wrong direction. Almost as bad, though, are the Alethi. How do the Alethi know so much about it? Did that warlord of theirs summon it somehow?'" Ghenna lowered the paper.

Lift chewed on her pancake. It was a dense variety, with mashed-up paste in the center that was too sticky and salty. The one beside it was covered in little crunchy seeds. Neither were as good as the other two varieties she'd tried over the last few hours.

"When's it going to hit?" Lift asked.

"The storm? It's hard to judge, but it's slower than a highstorm, by most reports. It might arrive in Azir and Tashikk in three or four hours."

"Write this to Gawx," Lift said around bites of pancake. "'They got good food here. These pancakes, with lots of variety. One has sugar in the center.'"

The scribe hesitated.

"Write it," Lift said. "Or I'll make you call me more silly names."

Ghenna sighed, but complied.

"'Lift,'" she read as the spanreed wrote the next line from Gawx, who undoubtedly had about fifteen viziers and scions standing around telling him what to say, then writing it when he agreed. "'This isn't the time for idle conversation about food.'"

"Sure it is," Lift replied. "We gotta remember. Storm might be coming, but people will still need to eat. The world ends tomorrow, but the day after that, people are going to ask what's for breakfast. That's your job."

"'And what about the stories of something worse?'" he wrote back. "'The Alethi are warning about parshmen, and I'm doing what I can on such short notice. But what of the Voidbringers they say are in the storms?'"

Lift looked at the room packed with scribes. "I'm workin' on that part," she said. As Ghenna wrote it, Lift stood up, wiping her hands on her fancy robes. "Hey, all you smart people. Whatcha found?"

The scribes looked up at her. "Mistress," one said, "we don't have *any* idea what we're even looking for."

"Strange stuff!"

"What kind of 'strange stuff'?" asked the scribe in yellow, the spindly fellow who looked silly and balding without a hat. "Unusual things happen every day in the city! Do you want the report of the man who claims his pig was born with two heads? What about the man who says he saw the shape of Yaezir in the lichen on his wall? The woman who had a premonition her sister would fall, and then she fell?"

"Nah," Lift said. "That's *normal* strange."

"What's abnormal strange, then?" he asked, exasperated.

Lift started glowing. She called upon her awesomeness, so much that it started radiating out of her skin, like she was a starvin' sphere.

Beside her, the seeds on top of her uneaten pancake sprouted, growing long, twisting vines that curled around one another and spat out leaves.

"Somethin' like this," Lift said, then glanced to the side. Great. She'd ruined the pancake.

The scribes stared at her in awe, so she clapped loudly, sending them back to their work. Wyndle sighed, and she knew what he must be thinking. Three hours, and nothing relevant so far. He'd been right—yeah, they wrote stuff down in this city. That was the problem. They wrote it *all* down.

"There's another message from the emperor for you," Ghenna said. "Um, Your Pancake . . . Storms that sounds stupid."

Lift grinned, then looked over at the paper. The words were written in a flowing, elegant hand. Probably Fat Lips.

"'Lift,'" Ghenna read. "'Are you going to come back? We miss you here.'"

"Even Fat Lips?" Lift asked.

"'Vizier Noura misses you too. Lift, this is your home now. You don't need to live on the streets anymore.'"

"What am I supposed to do there, if I do come back?"

"'Anything you want,'" Gawx wrote. "'I promise.'"

That was the problem.

"I don't know what I'm gonna do yet," she said, feeling strangely . . . isolated, despite the roomful of people. "We'll see."

Ghenna eyed her at that. She apparently thought that what the emperor of Azir wanted, he should get—and little Reshi girls shouldn't make a habit of denying him.

The door cracked open, and the guard captain from the city watch peeked in. Lift leaped off the desk, running over to her, then hopping up to see what she was holding. A report. Great. More words.

"What did you find?" Lift said eagerly.

"You are right," the captain said. "One of my colleagues in the quarter's watch has been watching the Tashi's Light Orphanage. The woman who runs it—"

"The Stump," Lift said. "Meanest thing. Eats the bones of children for afternoon snack. Once had a staring contest with a painting and won."

"—is being investigated. She's running some kind of money-laundering scheme, though the details are confusing. She's been seen trading spheres for ones of lesser value, a practice that would end with her bankrupt, if she didn't have another income scheme. The report says she takes money from criminal enterprises as donations, then secretly transfers them to other groups, after taking a cut, to help confuse the trail of spheres. There's more too. In any case, the children are a front to keep attention away from her practices."

"I told you," Lift said, snatching the paper. "You should arrest her and spend all her money on soup. Give me half, for tellin' you where to look, and I won't tell nobody."

The guard raised her eyebrows.

"We can write down that we did it, if you want," Lift said. "That'll make it *official*."

"I'll ignore the suggestions of bribery, coercion, extortion, and state embezzlement," the captain said. "As for the orphanage, I don't have jurisdiction over it, but I assure you my colleagues will be moving against this . . . Stump soon."

"Good enough," Lift said, climbing back up on the desk before her legion of scribes. "So what have you found? Anybody glowing, like they're some stormin' benevolent force for good or some such crem?"

"This is too large a project to spring on us without warning!" the fat scribe complained. "Mistress, this is the sort of research we normally have *months* to work on. Give us three weeks, and we can prepare a detailed report!"

"We ain't got three weeks. We barely got three hours."

It didn't matter. Over the next few hours, she tried cajoling, threatening, dancing, bribing, and—as a last-ditch, crazy option—remaining perfectly quiet and letting them read. As the time slipped away, they found nothing and everything at the same time. There were *tons* of vague oddities in the guard reports: stories of a man surviving a fall from too high, a complaint of strange noises outside a woman's window, spren acting odd every morning outside a woman's house unless she left out a bowl of sugar water. Yet none of them had more than one witness, and in each case the guard had found nothing specifically strange other than hearsay.

Each time a weirdness came up, Lift itched to scramble out the door, squeeze through a window, and go running to find the person involved. Each time, Wyndle cautioned patience. If all these reports were true, then basically every person in the city would have been a Surgebinder. What if she ran off chasing one of the hundred reports that were due to ordinary superstition? She'd spend hours and find nothing.

Which was exactly what she felt like she was doing. She was annoyed, impatient, *and* out of pancakes.

"I'm sorry, mistress," Wyndle said as they rejected a report about a Veden woman who claimed her baby had been "blessed by Tashi Himself to have lighter skin than his father, to make him more comfortable interacting with foreigners."

"I don't think any of these is more likely a sign than the one before. I'm beginning to feel we just need to pick one and hope we get lucky."

Lift hated luck, these days. She was having trouble convincing herself that she hadn't hit an unlucky age of her life, so she'd given up on luck. She'd even traded her lucky sphere for a piece of hog's cheese.

The more she thought of it, the more that *luck* seemed the opposite of being *awesome.* One was something you did; the other was something that happened to you no matter what you did.

Course, that didn't mean luck didn't exist. You either believed in that, or you believed in what those Vorin priests were always saying—that poor people was *chosen* to be poor, on account of them being too dumb to ask the Almighty to make them born with heaps of spheres.

"So what do we do?" Lift said.

"Pick one of these accounts, I guess," Wyndle said. "Any of them. Except maybe that one about the baby. I suspect that the mother might not be honest."

"Ya think?"

Lift looked over the papers spread before her—papers she couldn't read, each detailing a report of some vague curiosity. Storms. Pick the right one and she could save a life, maybe find someone else who could do what she did.

Pick the wrong one, and Darkness or his servants would execute an innocent. Quietly, with nobody to witness their passing or to remember them.

Darkness. She hated him, suddenly. With a seething ferocity that startled even her with its intensity. She didn't think she'd ever actually *hated* anyone before. Him though . . . those cold eyes that seemed to refuse all emotion. She hated him more for the fact that it seemed like he did what he did without a shred of guilt.

"Mistress?" Wyndle asked. "What do you choose?"

"I can't choose," she whispered. "I don't know how."

"Just pick one."

"I can't. I don't make choices, Wyndle."

"Nonsense! You do it every day."

"No. I just . . ." She went where the winds blew. Once you made a decision, you were committed. You were saying you thought this was *right.*

The door to their chamber was flung open. A guard there, one Lift didn't recognize, was sweating and puffing. "Status Five emergency diktat from the prince, to be disseminated through the nation immediately. State of emergency in the city. Storm blowing from the wrong direction, projected to hit within two hours.

"All people are to get off the streets and go to storm bunkers, and parshmen are to be imprisoned or exiled into the storm. He wants the alleys of Yeddaw and slot cities evacuated, and orders government officials to report to their assigned bunkers to do head counts, draft reports, and mediate confusion or evacuation disputes. Find a draft of these orders posted at each muster station, with copies being distributed now."

The scribes in the room looked up from their work, then immediately began packing away books and ledgers.

"Wait!" Lift said as the runner moved on. "What are you doing?"

"You've just gotten overruled, little one," Ghenna said. "Your research will have to be put on hold."

"How long!"

"Until the prince decides to step down our state of emergency," she said, quickly gathering the spanreeds from her shelf and packing them in a padded case.

"But, the emperor!" Lift said, grabbing a note from Gawx and wagging it. "He said to help me!"

"We'll gladly help you to a storm bunker," the guard captain said.

"I need help with this problem! He *ordered* you to obey!"

"We, of course, listen to the emperor," Ghenna said. "We will listen very well."

But not necessarily obey. The viziers had explained this. Azir might *claim* to be an empire, and most of the other countries in the region played along. Just like you might play along with the kid who says he's team captain during a game of rings. As soon as his demands grew too extravagant though, he might find himself talking to an empty alleyway.

The scribes were remarkably efficient. It wasn't too long before they'd ushered Lift into the hallway, burdened her with a handful of reports she couldn't read, then split to run to their various duties. They left her with one junior sub-scribe who couldn't be much older than Lift; her job was to show Lift to a storm bunker.

Lift ditched the girl at the first junction she could, scuttling down a side path as the girl explained the emergency to a bleary-eyed old scholar in a brown shiqua. Lift stripped off her nice Azish clothing and dumped it in a corner, leaving her in trousers, shirt, and unbuttoned overshirt. From there she set off into a less-populated section of the building. In the large corridors, scribes gathered and shouted at one another. She wouldn't have expected such a ruckus from a bunch of dried-up old men and women with ink for blood.

It was dark in here, and Lift found reason to wish she hadn't traded away her lucky sphere. The hallways were marked by rugs with Azish patterns to differentiate them, but that was about it. Periodic sphere lanterns lined the walls, but only every fifth one had an infused sphere in it. Everyone was still starvin' for Stormlight. She spent a good minute holding to one, chewing on its latch and trying to get it undone, but they were locked up tight.

She continued down the hallway, passing room after room, each stuffed with paper—though there weren't as many bookshelves as Lift had expected to find. It wasn't like a library. Instead there were walls full of drawers that you could pull open to find stacks of pages.

The longer she walked the quieter it became, until it was like she was walking through a mausoleum—for trees. She crinkled up the papers in her hand and shoved them in her pocket. There were so many, she couldn't properly get her hand in as well.

"Mistress?" Wyndle said from the floor beside her. "We don't have much time."

"I'm thinkin'," Lift said. Which was a lie. She was trying to *avoid* thinkin'.

"I'm sorry the plan didn't work," Wyndle said.

Lift shrugged. "You don't want to be here anyway. You want to be off gardening."

"Yes, I had the most lovely gallery of boots planned," Wyndle said.

"But I suppose . . . I suppose we can't sit around preparing gardens while the world ends, can we? And if I'd been placed with that nice Iriali, I wouldn't be here, would I? And that Radiant you're trying to save, they'd be as good as dead."

"Probably as good as dead anyway."

"But still . . . still worth trying, right?"

Stupid cheerful Voidbringer. She glanced at him, then pulled out the wads of paper. "These are useless. We gotta start over with a new plan."

"And with much less time. Sunset is coming, along with that storm. What do we do?"

Lift dropped the papers. "Somebody knows where to go. That woman who was talkin' to Darkness, his apprentice, she said she had an investigation going. Sounded confident."

"Huh," Wyndle said. "You don't suppose her investigation involved . . . a bunch of scribes searching records, do you?"

Lift cocked her head.

"That would be the smart thing to do," Wyndle said. "I mean, even *we* came up with it."

Lift grinned, then ran back in the direction she'd come from.

# 15

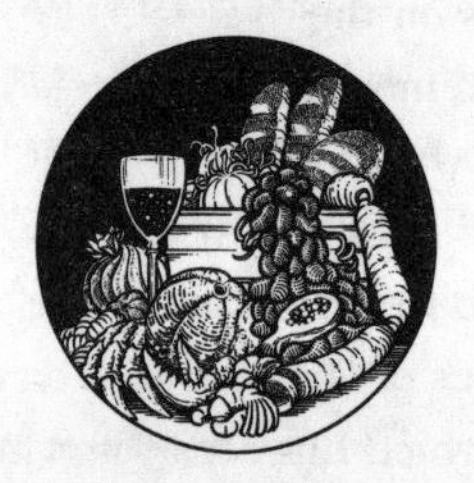

Yes," the fat scribe said, flustered after looking through a book. "It was Bidlel's team, room two-three-two. The woman you describe hired them two weeks ago for an undisclosed project. We take the secrecy of our clients *very* seriously." She sighed, closing the book. "Barring imperial mandate."

"Thanks," Lift said, giving the woman a hug. "Thanksthanksthanks-thanks."

"I wish I knew what all this meant. Storms . . . you'd think I would be the one who got told everything, but half the time I get the sense that even kings are confused by what the world throws at them." She shook her head and looked to Lift, who was still hugging her. "I *am* going to my assigned station now. You'd be wise to seek shelter."

"Surewillgreatbye," Lift said, letting go and dashing out of the room full of ledgers. She scurried through the hallway, directly *away* from the steps down to the Indicium's storm shelter.

Ghenna poked her head out into the hallway. "Bidlel will have already evacuated! The door will be locked." She paused. "Don't break anything!"

"Voidbringer," Lift said, "can you find whatever number she just said?"

"Yes."

"Good. 'Cuz I don't got that many toes."

They hurried through the cavernous Indicium, which was already feeling empty. Only a half hour or so since the diktat—Wyndle was keeping track—and everyone was on their way out. People locked the doors in the advent of a storm, and moved on to safe places. For those with regular homes, those homes would do, but for the poor that meant storm bunkers.

Poor parshmen. There weren't many in the city, not as many as in Azimir, but by the prince's orders they were being gathered and turned out. Left for the storm, which Lift considered hugely unfair.

Nobody listened to her complaints about that though. And Wyndle implied . . . well, they might be turning into Voidbringers. And he would know.

Still didn't seem fair. She wouldn't leave *him* out in a storm. Even if he claimed it probably wouldn't hurt them.

She followed Wyndle's vines as he led her up two floors, then started counting off rows. The floor on this level was of painted wood, and it felt weird to walk on it. Wooden floors. Wouldn't they break and fall through? Wooden buildings always felt so flimsy to her, and she stepped lightly just in case. It—

Lift frowned, then crouched down, looking one way, then the other. What was that?

"Two-Two-One . . ." Wyndle said. "Two-Two-Two . . ."

"Voidbringer!" Lift hissed. "Shut up."

He twisted about, creeping up the wall near her. Lift pressed her back against the wall, then ducked around a corner into a side corridor and pressed her back against that wall instead.

Booted feet thumped on the carpet. "I can't believe you call *that* a lead," a woman's voice said. Lift recognized it as Darkness's trainee. "Weren't you in the guard?"

"Things work differently in Yezier," a man snapped. The other trainee. "Here, everyone is too coy. They should just say what they mean."

"You expect a Tashikki street informant to be *perfectly clear*?"

"Sure. Isn't that his job?"

The two strode past, and thankfully didn't glance down the side hall toward Lift. Storms, those uniforms—with the high boots, stiff Eastern jackets, and large-cuffed gloves—were imposing. They looked like generals on the field.

Lift itched to follow and see where they went. She forced herself to wait.

Sure enough, a few seconds later a quieter figure passed in the hallway. The assassin, clothing tattered, head bowed, with that large sword—it *had* to be some kind of Shardblade—resting on his shoulder.

"I do not know, sword-nimi," he said softly, "I don't trust my own mind any longer." He paused, stopping as if listening to something. "That is not comforting, sword-nimi. No, it is not. . . ."

He trailed after the other two, leaving a faint afterimage glowing in the air. It was almost imperceptible, less pronounced now that he was moving than it had been in Darkness's headquarters.

"Oh, mistress," Wyndle said, curling up to her. "I nearly expired of fright! The way he stopped there in the hallway, I was *sure* he'd seen me somehow!"

At least the hallways were dark, with those sphere lanterns mostly out. Lift nervously slipped into the hallway and followed the group. They stopped at the right door, and one produced a key. Lift had expected them to ransack the place, but of course they wouldn't need to do that—they had legal authority.

Actually, so did she. How bizarre.

Darkness's two apprentices stepped into the room. The Assassin in White remained outside in the hallway. He settled down on the floor across from the doorway, his strange Shardblade across his lap. He sat mostly still, but when he did move, he left that fading afterimage behind.

Lift pulled into the side corridor again, back pressed to the wall. People shouted somewhere distant in the Grand Indecision, calls for people to be orderly.

"I have to get into that room," Lift said. "Somehow."

Wyndle huddled down on the ground, vines tightening around him.

Lift shook her head. "That means getting past the starvin' *assassin* himself. Storms."

"I'll do it," Wyndle whispered.

"Maybe," Lift said, barely paying attention, "I can make some sorta distraction. Send him off chasin' it? But then that would alert the two in the room."

"I'll do it," Wyndle repeated.

Lift cocked her head, registering what he'd said. She glanced down at him. "The distraction?"

"No." Wyndle's vines twisted about one another, tightening into knots. "I'll do it, mistress. I can sneak into the room. I . . . I don't believe their spren will be able to see me."

"You don't know?"

"No."

"Sounds dangerous."

His vines scrunched as they tightened against one another. "You think?"

"Yeah, totally," Lift said, then peeked around the corner. "Something's wrong about that guy in white. Can you get killed, Voidbringer?"

"Destroyed," Wyndle said. "Yes. It's not the same as for a human, but I have . . . seen spren who . . ." He whimpered softly. "Maybe it *is* too dangerous for me."

"Maybe."

Wyndle settled down, coiled about himself.

"I'm going anyway," he whispered.

She nodded. "Just listen, memorize what those two in there say, and get back here quick. If something happens, scream loud as you can."

"Right. Listen and scream. I can listen and scream. I'm good at these things." He made a sound like taking a deep breath, though so far as she knew he didn't need to breathe. Then he shot out into the corridor, a vine laced with crystal that grew along the corner where wall met floor. Little offshoots of green crept off his sides, covering the carpeting.

The assassin didn't look up. Wyndle reached the doorway into the room with the two Skybreaker apprentices. Lift couldn't hear a word of what was being said inside.

Storms, she hated waiting. She'd built her life around not having to wait for anyone or anything. She did what she wanted, when she wanted.

That was the best, right? Everyone should be able to do what they wanted.

Of course if they did that, who would grow food? If the world was full of people like Lift, wouldn't they just leave halfway through planting to go catch lurgs? Nobody would protect the streets, or sit around in meetings. Nobody would learn to write things down, or make kingdoms run. Everyone would scurry about eating each other's food, until it was all gone and the whole heap of them fell over and *died.*

*You knew that,* a part of her said, standing up inside, hands on hips with a defiant attitude. *You knew the truth of the world even when you went and asked not to get older.*

Being young was an excuse. A plausible justification.

She waited, feeling itchy because she couldn't do anything. What were they saying in there? Had they spotted Wyndle? Were they torturing him? Threatening to . . . cut down his gardens or something?

*Listen,* a part of her whispered.

But of course she couldn't hear anything.

She wanted to just rush in there, make faces at them all, then drag them on a chase through the starvin' building. That would be better than sitting here with her thoughts, worrying and condemning herself at the same time.

When you were always busy, you didn't have to think about stuff. Like how most people didn't run off and leave when the whim struck them. Like how your mother had been so warm, and kindly, so ready to take care of everyone. It was incredible that anyone on Roshar should be as good to people as she'd been.

She shouldn't have had to die. Least, she should have had someone half as wonderful as she was to take care of her as she wasted away.

Someone other than Lift, who was selfish, stupid.

And lonely.

She tensed up, then prepared to bolt around the corner. Wyndle, however, finally zipped out into the hallway. He grew along the floor at a frantic pace, then rejoined her—leaving a trail of dust by the wall as his discarded vines crumbled.

Darkness's two apprentices left the room a moment later, and Lift pulled back into the side corridor with Wyndle. In the shadows here, she crouched down against the floor, to avoid standing out against the distant light. The woman and man in uniforms strode past a moment later, and didn't even glance down the hallway. Lift relaxed, fingertips brushing Wyndle's vines.

Then the assassin passed by. He stopped, then looked in her direction, hand resting on his sword hilt.

Lift's breath caught. *Don't become awesome. Don't become awesome!* If she used her powers in these shadows, she'd glow and he'd spot her for sure.

All she could do was crouch there as the assassin narrowed his eyes—strangely shaped, like they were too big or something. He reached to a pouch at his belt, then tossed something small and glowing into the hallway. A sphere.

Lift panicked, uncertain if she should scramble away, grow awesome, or just remain still. Fearspren boiled up around her, lit by the sphere as it rolled near her, and she knew—meeting the assassin's gaze—that he could see her.

He pulled his sword out of the sheath a fraction of an inch. Black smoke poured from the blade, dropping toward the floor and pooling at his feet. Lift felt a sudden, terrible nausea.

The assassin studied her, then snapped the sword into its sheath again. Remarkably, he left, following after the other two, that faint afterimage trailing behind him. He didn't speak a word, and his footfalls on the carpet were almost silent—a faint breeze compared to the clomping of the other two, which Lift could still hear farther down the corridor.

In moments, all three of them had entered the stairwell and were gone.

"Storms!" Lift said, flopping backward on the carpet. "Storming Mother of the World and Father of Storms above! He about made me die of fright."

"I know!" Wyndle said. "Did you hear me not-whimpering?"

"No."

"I was too frightened to even make a sound!"

Lift sat up, then mopped the sweat from her brow. "Wow. Okay, well . . . that was something. What did they talk about?"

"Oh!" Wyndle said, as if he'd forgotten completely about his mission. "Mistress, they had an entire study done! Research for weeks to identify oddities in the city."

"Great! What did they determine?"

"I don't know."

Lift flopped back down.

"They talked over a whole lot of things I didn't understand," Wyndle said. "But mistress, *they* know who the person is! They're heading there right now. To perform an execution." He poked at her with a vine. "So . . . maybe we should follow?"

"Yeah, okay," Lift said. "Guess we can do that. Shouldn't be too hard, right?"

# 16

TURNED out it was *way* hard.

She couldn't get too close, as the hallways had grown eerily empty. And there were tons of branching paths, with little side hallways and rooms everywhere. Mix that with the fact that there weren't many spheres on the walls, and it was a real trick to follow the three.

She did it though. She followed them through the whole starvin' place until they reached some doors out into the city. Lift managed to slip out a window near the doors, falling among some plants beside the stairs outside. She huddled there as the three people she'd been tailing stepped out onto the landing overlooking the city.

Storms, but it felt good to be breathing the open air again, though clouds had moved in front of the setting sun. The whole city felt chilly now. In shadow.

And it was empty.

Before, people had been swarming up and down the steps and ramps into the Grand Indishipium. Now they held only a few last-minute stragglers, and even those were rapidly vanishing as they ducked through doorways, seeking shelter.

The assassin turned eyes toward the west. "The storm is coming," he said.

"All the more reason to be quick," the female apprentice said. She took a sphere from her pocket, then held it up before her and sucked in the light. It streamed into her, and she started to glow with awesomeness.

Then she rose into the air.

She rose into the starvin' air itself!

*They can fly?* Lift thought. *Why in Damnation can't* I *fly?*

Her companion rose up beside her.

"Coming, assassin?" The woman looked down toward the landing and the man wearing white.

"I've danced that storm once before," he whispered. "On the day I died. No."

"You're never going to make it into the order at this rate."

He remained silent. The two floating people eyed each other, then the man shrugged. The two of them rose higher, then shot out across the city, avoiding the inconvenience of traveling through the trenches.

They could *storming* fly.

"You're the one he's hunting for, aren't you?" the assassin said softly.

Lift winced. Then she stood up and peeked over the side of the landing where the assassin stood. He turned and looked at her.

"I ain't nobody," Lift said.

"He kills nobodies."

"And you don't?"

"I kill kings."

"Which is *totally* better."

He narrowed his eyes at her, then squatted down, sheathed sword held across his shoulders, with hands draped forward. "No. It is not. I hear their screams, their demands, whenever I see shadow. They haunt me, scramble for my mind, wishing to claim my sanity. I fear they've already won, that the man to whom you speak can no longer distinguish what is the voice of a mad raving and what is not."

"Oooookay," Lift said. "But you didn't attack me."

"No. The sword likes you."

"Great. I like the sword too." She glanced at the sky. "Um . . . do you know where they're going?"

"The report described a man who has been spotted vanishing by several people in the city. He will turn down an alleyway, then it will be empty when someone else follows. People have claimed to see his face twisting to become the face of another. My companions believe he is what is called a Lightweaver, and so must be stopped."

"Is that legal?"

"Nin has procured an injunction from the prince, forbidding any use of Surgebinding in the country, save that specifically authorized." He studied Lift. "I believe the Herald's experiences with you were what taught him to go straight to the top, rather than dancing about with local authorities."

Lift traced the direction the other two had gone. That sky was darkening further, an ominous sign.

"He really is wrong, isn't he?" Lift said. "That one you say is a Herald. He says the Voidbringers aren't back, but they are."

"The new storm reveals it," the assassin said. "But . . . who am I to say? I am mad. Then again, I think that the Herald is too. It makes me agree that the minds of men cannot be trusted. That we need something greater to follow, to guide. But not my stone . . . What good is seeking a greater law, when that law can be the whims of a man either stupid or ruthless?"

"Oooookay," Lift said. "Um, you can be crazy all you want. It's fine. I like crazy people. It's real funny when they lick walls and eat rocks and stuff. But before you start dancing, could you tell me where those other two are going?"

"You won't be able to outrun them."

"So no harm in telling me, right?"

The assassin smiled, though the emotion didn't seem to reach his eyes. "The man who can vanish, this presumed Lightweaver, is an old philosopher well known in the immigrant quarter. He sits in a small amphitheater most days, talking to any who will listen. It is near—"

"—the Tashi's Light Orphanage. Storms. I shoulda guessed. He's almost as weird as you are."

"Will you fight them, little Radiant?" the assassin asked. "You, alone, against two journeyman Skybreakers? A Herald waiting in the wings?"

She glanced at Wyndle. "I don't know. But I have to go anyway, don't I?"

# 17

LIFT engaged her awesomeness. She dug deeply into the power, summoning strength, speed, and Slickness. Darkness's people didn't seem to care if they were witnessed flying about, so Lift decided she didn't care about being seen either.

She leaped away from the assassin, Slicking her feet, then landed on the flat ramp beside the steps that wound up the outside of the building. She intended to shoot down toward the city, sliding along the side of the steps.

Of course, she lasted about a second before her feet shot out in two different directions and she slammed onto the stones crotch-first. She cringed at the flash of pain, but didn't have time for much more, as she fell into a tumble before dropping right off the side of the tall steps.

She crunched down to the bottom a few moments later, landing in a humiliated heap. Her awesomeness prevented her from getting too hurt, so she ignored Wyndle's cries of worry as he climbed down the wall to her. Instead she twisted about, scrambling up onto her hands and knees. Then she took off running toward the slot that would lead her to the orphanage.

She didn't have time to be bad at this! Normal running wouldn't be fast enough. Her enemies were literally *flying*.

She could see, in her mind's eye, how it should be. The entire city sloped away from this central rise with the Grand Indigestion. She should be able to hit a skid, feet Slick, zipping along the mostly empty street. She should be able to slap her hands against walls she passed, outcroppings, buildings, gaining speed with each push.

She should be like an arrow in flight, pointed, targeted, unchecked.

She could see it. But couldn't *do* it. She threw herself into another skid, but again her feet slipped out from under her. This time they went backward and she fell forward, knocking her face against the stone. She saw a flash of white. When she looked up, the empty street wavered in front of her, but her awesomeness soon healed her.

The shadowed street was a major thoroughfare, but it sat forlorn and empty. People had pulled in awnings and street carts, but had left refuse. Those walls crowded her. Everyone knew to stay out of canyons around a storm, or you'd be swept up in floodwaters. They'd gone and built an entire starvin' city in direct, flagrant violation of that.

Behind her in the distance, the sky rumbled. Before that storm hit, a poor, crazy old man was going to get a visit from two self-righteous assassins. She needed to stop it. She *had* to stop it. She couldn't explain why.

*Okay, Lift. Be calm. You can be awesome. You've always been awesome, and now you've got this extra awesomeness. Go. You can do it.*

She growled and threw herself into a run, then twisted sideways and slid. She *could* and *would*—

This time, she clipped the corner of a wall at an intersection and ended up sprawled on the ground, with feet toward the sky. She knocked her head back against the ground in frustration.

"Mistress?" Wyndle said, curling up to her. "Oh, I do not like the sound of that storm. . . ."

She got up—feeling ashamed and anything *but* awesome—and decided to just run the rest of the way. Her powers did let her run at speed without getting tired, but she could *feel* that it wasn't going to be enough.

It seemed like ages before she stumbled to a stop outside the orphanage, exhaustionspren swirling around her. She'd run out of awesomeness a short time before arriving, and her stomach growled in protest. The amphitheater was empty, of course. Orphanage to her left, built into the solid stones, seats of the little amphitheater in front of her. And beyond it the dark alleyway, wooden shanties and buildings cluttering the view.

The sky had grown dark, though she didn't know whether it was from the advent of dusk or the coming storm.

Deep within the alleyway, Lift heard a low, raw scream of pain. It sent chills up her spine.

Wyndle had been right. The assassin had been right. What was she doing? She couldn't beat two trained and awesome soldiers. She sank down, worn out, right in the middle of the floor of the amphitheater.

"Do we go in?" Wyndle asked from beside her.

"I don't have any power left," Lift whispered. "I used it up running here."

Had that alleyway always felt so . . . deep? With the shadows of the shanties, the draping cloths and jutting planks of wood, the place looked like an extended barricade—with only the narrowest of pathways through. It seemed like an entirely different world from the rest of the city. It was a dark and hidden realm that could exist only in shadows.

She stood up on unsteady feet, then stepped toward the alleyway.

"What are you doing?" a voice shouted.

Lift spun to find the Stump standing in the doorway of the orphanage.

"You're supposed to go to one of the bunkers!" the woman shouted. "Idiot child." She stalked forward and seized Lift by the arm, towing her into the orphanage. "Don't think that just because you're here, I'll take care of you. There's not room for ones like you, and don't give me any pretense about being sick or tired. Everyone's always pretending in order to get at what we have."

Though she said that, she deposited Lift right inside the orphanage, then slammed the large wooden door and threw the bar down. "Be glad I looked out to see who was screaming." She studied Lift, then sighed loudly. "Suppose you'll want some food."

"I have one meal left," Lift said.

"I've half a mind to give it to the other children," the Stump said. "Honestly, after a prank like that. Standing outside screaming? You should have gone to one of the bunkers. If you think that acting forlorn will earn my pity, you are sadly misguided."

She walked off, muttering. The room here, right inside the doors, was large and open, and children sat on mats all round. A single ruby sphere lit them. The children seemed frightened, several holding to one another. One covered his ears and whimpered as thunder sounded outside.

Lift sank down onto an open mat, feeling surreal, out of place. She'd run all the way here, glowing with power, ready to face monsters that flew in the sky. But here . . . here she was just another orphaned urchin.

She closed her eyes, and listened to them.

"I'm frightened. Is the storm going to be long?"

"Why did everyone have to go inside?"

"I miss my mommy."

"What about the gummers in the alley? Will they be all right?"

Their uncertainty thrummed through Lift. She'd been here. After her mother died, she'd been here. She'd been here dozens of times since, in cities all across the land. Places for forgotten children.

She'd sworn an oath to remember people like them. She hadn't *meant* to. It had just kind of happened. Like everything in her life just kind of happened.

"I want control," she whispered.

"Mistress?" Wyndle said.

"Earlier today," she said. "You told me you didn't believe I'd come here for any of the reasons I'd said. You asked me what I wanted."

"I remember."

"I want control," she said, opening her eyes. "Not like a king or anything. I just want to be able to control it, a little. My life. I don't want to get shoved around, by people or by fate or whatever. I just . . . I want it to be me who chooses."

"I know little of the way your world works, mistress," he said, coiling up onto the wall, then making a face that hung out beside her. "But that seems like a reasonable desire."

"Listen to these kids talk. Do you hear them?"

"They're scared of the storm."

"And of the sudden call to hide. And of being alone. So uncertain . . ."

In the other room she could hear the Stump, talking softly to one of her older helpers. "I don't know. It's not the day for a highstorm. I'll put the spheres out up top, just in case. I wish someone would tell us what was happening."

"I don't understand, mistress," Wyndle said. "What is it I'm supposed to get from this observation?"

"Hush, Voidbringer," she said, still listening. Hearing. Then, she paused and opened her eyes. She frowned and stood, crossing the room.

A boy with a scar on his face was talking to one of the other boys. He looked up at Lift. "Hey," he said. "I know you. You saw my mom, right? Did she say when she was coming back?"

What was his name again? "Mik?"

"Yeah," he said. "Look, I don't belong here, right? I don't remember the last few weeks very well, but . . . I mean, I'm not an orphan. I've still got a mom."

It was him, the boy who had been dropped off the night before. *You were drooling then,* Lift thought. *And even at lunch, you were talking like an idiot. Storms. What did I do to you?* She couldn't heal people that were different in the head, or so she'd thought. What was the difference with him? Was it because he had a head wound, and wasn't born this way?

She didn't remember healing him. Storms . . . she said she wanted control, but she didn't even know how to use what she had. Her race to this place proved it.

The Stump strode back in with a large plate and began handing out pancakes to the children. She got to Lift, then handed her two. "This is the last," she said, wagging her finger.

"Thanks," Lift mumbled as the Stump moved on. The pancakes were cold, and unfortunately of a variety she'd already tried—the ones with sweet stuff in the middle. Her favorite. Maybe the Stump wasn't all bad.

*She's a thief and a thug,* Lift reminded herself as she ate, restoring her awesomeness. *She's laundering spheres and using an orphanage as cover.* But maybe even a thief and a thug could do some good along the way.

"I'm so confused," Wyndle said. "Mistress, what are you thinking?"

She looked toward the thick door to the outside. The old man was surely dead by now. Nobody would care; likely nobody would notice. One old man, found dead in an alley after the storm.

But Lift . . . Lift would remember him.

"Come on," she said. She stepped over to the door. When the Stump's back was turned to scold a child, Lift pushed up the bar and slipped outside.

# 18

The hungry sky rumbled above, dark and angry. Lift knew that feeling. Too much time between meals, and looking to eat whatever it could find, never mind the cost.

The storm hadn't fully arrived yet, but from the distant lightning, it seemed that this new storm didn't have a stormwall. Its onset wouldn't be a sudden, majestic event, but instead a creeping advance. It loomed like a thug in an alley, knife out, waiting for prey to wander past.

Lift stepped up to the mouth of the alleyway beside the orphanage, then crept in, passing between shanties that looked far too flimsy to survive highstorms. Even if the city had been built to absolutely minimize winds, there was just so much *junk* in here. A particularly vigorous sneeze could leave half the people in the alley homeless.

They realized it too, as almost everyone here had gone to the storm bunkers. She did catch the odd face peeking suspiciously between rags draped on windows, anticipationspren growing up from the floor beside them like red streamers. They were people too stubborn, or perhaps too crazy, to be bothered. She didn't completely blame them. The government giving sudden, random orders and expecting everyone to hop? That was the sort of thing she usually ignored.

Except they should have seen the sky, heard the thunder. A flash of red lightning lit her surroundings. Today, these people should have listened.

She inched farther into the alleyway, entering a place of undefined shadows. With the clouds overhead—and everyone having taken their spheres away—the place was nearly impenetrable. So silent, the only sound that of the sky. Storms, was the old man actually in here? Maybe he was safe in a bunker somewhere. That scream from earlier could have been something unrelated, right?

*No,* she thought. *No, it wasn't.* She felt another chill run through her. Well, even if the old man was here, how would she find his body?

"Mistress," Wyndle whispered. "Oh, I don't like this place, mistress. Something's wrong."

Everything was wrong; it had been since Darkness had first stalked her. Lift continued on, past shadows that were probably laundry draped along strings between shanties. They looked like twisted, broken bodies in the gloom. Another flash of lightning from the approaching storm didn't help; the red light it cast made the walls and shanties seem painted with blood.

How long *was* this alleyway? She was relieved when, at last, she stumbled over something on the ground. She reached down, feeling at a clothed arm. A body.

*I will remember you,* Lift thought, leaning over and squinting, trying to make out the old man's shape.

"Mistress . . ." Wyndle whimpered. She felt him wrap around her leg and tighten there, like a child clinging to his mother.

What was that? She listened as the silence of the alley gave way to a clicking, scraping sound. It encircled her. And for the first time she noticed that the figure she was poking at didn't seem to be wrapped in a shiqua. The cloth on the arm was too stiff, too thick.

*Mother,* Lift thought, terrified. *What is happening?*

Lightning flashed, granting her a glimpse of the corpse. A woman's face stared upward with sightless eyes. A black and white uniform, painted crimson by the lightning and covered in some kind of silky substance.

Lift gasped and jumped backward, bumping into something behind her—another body. She spun, and the skittering, clicking sounds grew agitated. The next flash of lightning was bright enough for her to make out a body pressed against the wall of the alleyway, tied to part of a shanty, the head rolling to the side. She knew him, just as she knew the woman on the ground.

*Darkness's two minions,* Lift thought. *They're dead.*

"I heard an interesting idea once, while traveling in a land you will never visit."

Lift froze. It was the old man's voice.

"There are a group of people who believe that each day, when they sleep, they die," the old man continued. "They believe that consciousness doesn't continue—that if it is interrupted, a new soul is born when the body awakes."

*Storms, storms, STORMS,* Lift thought, spinning around. The walls seemed to be moving, shifting, sliding like they were covered in oil. She tried shying away from the corpses, but . . . she'd lost where they were. Was that the direction she'd come from, or did that lead deeper into this nightmare of an alleyway?

"This philosophy," the old man's voice said, "certainly has its problems, at least to an outside observer. What of memory, and continuity of culture, family, society? Well, the Omnithi teach that each are things you inherit in the morning from the previous soul that inhabited your body. Certain brain structures imprint memories, to help you live your single day of life as best you can."

"What are you?" Lift whispered, looking around frantically, trying to make sense of the darkness.

"What I find most interesting about these people is how they continue to exist at all," he said. "One would assume chaos would follow if each human sincerely believed that they had only one day to live. I wonder often what it says about you that these people with such dramatic beliefs live lives that are—basically—the same as the rest of you."

*There,* Lift thought, picking him out in the shadows. The shape of a man, though as lightning lit him she could see that he wasn't all there. Chunks were missing from his flesh. His right shoulder ended in a stump, and storms, he was naked, with strange holes in his stomach and thighs. Even one of his eyes was missing. There was no blood though, and in a quick succession of flashes she picked up something climbing his legs. Cremlings.

That was the skittering sound. Thousands upon thousands of cremlings coated the walls, each the size of a finger. Little beasts of chitin and legs clicking away and making that awful buzz.

"The thing about this philosophy is how difficult it is to disprove," the old man said. "How do you know that *you* are the same *you* as yesterday? You would never know if a new soul came to inhabit your body, so long as it had the same memories. But then . . . if it acts the same, and thinks it is you, why would it matter? What is it to be *you,* little Radiant?"

In the flashes of lightning—they were growing more common—she watched one of the cremlings crawl across his face, a bulbous protrusion hanging off its back. The thing crawled *into* the eye hole, and she realized that bulbous part was an eye. Other cremlings swarmed up and began filling in holes, forming the missing arm. Each had a portion on the back that resembled skin. It presented this outward, using its legs to interlock with the many others holding together on the inside of the body.

"To me," he said, "this is all no more than idle theory, as unlike you I do not sleep. At least, not all of me at once."

"What *are* you?" Lift said.

"Just another refugee."

Lift backed away. She didn't care anymore about going back in the direction she had come—so long as she got away from this thing.

"You needn't fear me," the old man said. "Your war is my war, and has been for millennia. Ancient Radiants named me friend and ally before everything went wrong. What wonderful days those were, before the Last Desolation. Days of . . . honor. Now gone, long gone."

"You killed these two people!" Lift hissed.

"In defense of myself." He chuckled. "I suppose that is a lie. They were not capable of killing me, so I can't plead self-defense, any more than a soldier could plead it in murdering a child. But they did ask, in not so many words, for a contest—and I gave it to them."

He stepped toward her, and a flash of lightning revealed him flexing his fingers on his newly formed hand as the thumb—a single cremling, with little spindly legs on the bottom—settled into place, tying itself into the others.

"But you," the thing said, "did not come for a contest, did you? We watch the others. The assassin. The surgeon. The liar. The highprince. But not you. The others all ignore you . . . and that, I hazard to predict, is a mistake."

He took out a sphere, bathing the place in a phantom glow, and smiled at her. She could see the lines crisscrossing his skin where the cremlings had fit themselves together, but they were nearly lost in the wrinkles of an aged body.

This was just the *likeness* of an old man though. A fabrication. Beneath that skin was not blood or muscle. It was hundreds of cremlings, pulling together to form a counterfeit man.

Many, many more of them still scuttled on the walls, now lit by his sphere. Lift could see that she'd somehow made it around the body of the fallen soldier, and was backing into a dead end between two shanties. She looked up. Didn't seem too difficult to climb, now that she had some light.

"If you flee," the thing noted, "he'll kill the one you wanted to save."

"You are just fine, I'm sure."

The monster chuckled. "Those two fools got it wrong. I'm not the one that Nale is chasing; he knows to stay away from me and my kind. No, there's someone else. He stalks them tonight, and *will* complete his task. Nale, madman, Herald of Justice, is not one to leave business unfinished."

Lift hesitated, hands in place on a shanty's eaves, ready to haul herself up and start climbing. The cremlings on the walls—she'd never seen so many at once—scuttled aside, making room for her to pass.

He knew to let her run, if she wanted to. Clever monster.

Nearby, bathed in cool light that seemed bright as a bonfire compared to what she'd stumbled through before, the creature unwrapped a black shiqua. He started winding it around his right arm.

"I like this place," he explained. "Where else would I have the excuse to cover my entire body? I've spent thousands of years breeding my hordelings, and still I can't make them fit together quite *right.* I can pass for human almost as well as a Siah can these days, I'd hazard, but anyone who looks closely finds something off. It's rather frustrating."

"What do you know about Darkness and his plans?" Lift demanded. "And Radiants, and Voidbringers, and *everything*?"

"That's quite the exhaustive list," he said. "And I confess, I am the wrong one to ask. My siblings are more interested in you Radiants. If you ever encounter another of the Sleepless, tell them you've spoken with Arclo. I'm certain it will gain you sympathy."

"That wasn't an answer. Not the kind I wanted."

"I'm not here to answer you, human. I'm here because I'm interested, and you are the source of my curiosity. When one achieves immortality, one must find purpose beyond the struggle to live, as old Axies always said."

"You seem to have found purpose in talkin' a whole bunch," Lift said. "Without being helpful to nobody." She scrambled up on top of the shanty, but didn't go any higher. Wyndle climbed the wall beside her, and the cremlings shied away from him. They could sense him?

"I'm helping with far more than your little personal problem. I'm building a philosophy, one meaningful enough to span ages. You see, child, I can *grow* what I need. Is my mind becoming full? I can breed new hordelings specialized in holding memories. Do I need to sense what is going on in the city? Hordelings with extra eyes, or antennae to taste and hear, can solve that. Given time, I can make for my body nearly anything I need.

"But you . . . you are stuck with only one body. So how do you make it work? I have come to suspect that men in a city are each part of some greater organism they can't see—like the hordelings that make up my kind."

"That's great," Lift said. "But earlier, you said that Darkness was hunting someone *else*? You think he still hasn't killed his prey in the city?"

"Oh, I'm certain he hasn't. He hunts them right now. He will know that his minions have failed."

The storm rumbled above, close. She itched to leave, to find shelter. But . . .

"Tell me," she said. "Who is it?"

The creature smiled. "A secret. And we are in Tashikk, are we not? Shall we trade? You answer me honestly regarding my questions, and I'll give you a hint."

"Why me?" Lift said. "Why not bother someone else with these questions? At another time?"

"Oh, but you're so *interesting.*" He wrapped the shiqua around his waist, then down his leg, then back up it, crossing to the other leg. His cremlings coursed around him. Several climbed up his face, and his eyes crawled out, new ones replacing them so that he went from being dark-eyed to light.

He spoke as he dressed. "You, Lift, are different from anyone else. If each city is a creature, then you are a most special organ. Traveling from place to place, bringing change, transformation. You Knights Radiant . . . I must know how you see yourselves. It will be an important corner of my philosophy."

*I am special,* she thought. *I'm awesome.*

*So why don't I know what to do?*

The secret fear crept out. The creature kept talking his strange speech: about cities, people, and their places. He praised her, but each offhand comment about how special she was made her wince. A storm was almost here, and Darkness was about to murder in the night. All she could do was crouch in the presence of two corpses and a monster made of little squirming pieces.

*Listen, Lift. Are you listening? People, they don't listen anymore.*

"Yes, but how did the city of your birth know to create you?" the creature was saying. "I can breed individual pieces to do as I wish. What bred you? And why was this city able to summon you here now?"

Again that question. *Why are you here?*

"What if I'm *not* special," Lift whispered. "Would that be okay too?"

The creature stopped and looked at her. On the wall, Wyndle whimpered.

"What if I've been lying all along," Lift said. "What if I'm not *strictly* awesome. What if I don't know what to do?"

"Instinct will guide you, I'm sure."

*I feel lost, like a soldier on a battlefield who can't remember which banner is hers,* the guard captain's voice said.

Listening. She was listening, wasn't she?

*Half the time, I get the sense that even kings are confused by the world.* Ghenna the scribe's voice.

Nobody listened anymore.

*I wish someone would tell us what was happening.* The Stump's voice.

"What if you're wrong though?" Lift whispered. "What if 'instinct' doesn't guide us? What if everybody is frightened, and nobody has the answers?"

It was the conclusion that had always been too intimidating to consider. It terrified her.

Did it have to, though? She looked up at the wall, at Wyndle surrounded by cremlings that snapped at him. Her own little Voidbringer.

*Listen.*

Lift hesitated, then patted him. She just . . . she just had to accept it, didn't she?

In a moment, she felt relief akin to her terror. She was in darkness, but well, maybe she'd manage anyway.

Lift stood up. "I left Azir because I was afraid. I came to Tashikk because that's where my starvin' feet took me. But tonight . . . tonight I *decided* to be here."

"What is this nonsense?" Arclo asked. "How does it help my philosophy?"

She cocked her head as a realization struck her, like a jolt of power. *Huh. Fancy that, would you?*

"I . . . didn't heal that boy," she whispered.

"What?"

"The Stump trades spheres for ones of lesser value, probably swapping dun ones for infused ones. She launders money because she *needs the Stormlight;* she probably feeds on it without realizing what she's doing!" Lift looked down at Arclo, grinning. "Don't you see? She takes care of the kids who were born sick, lets them stay. It's because her powers don't know how to heal those. The rest, though, they get better. They do it so suspiciously often that she's started to believe that kids must *come to her faking* to get food. The Stump . . . is a Radiant."

The Sleepless creature met her eyes, then sighed. "We will speak again another time. Like Nale, I am not one to leave tasks unfinished."

He tossed his sphere along the alleyway, and it plinked against stone, rolling back toward the orphanage. Lighting the way for Lift as she jumped down and started running.

# 19

The thunder chased her. Wind howled through the city's slots, windspren zipping past her, as if fleeing the advent of the strange storm. The wind pushed against Lift's back, blowing scraps of paper and refuse around her. She reached the small amphitheater at the mouth of the alley, and hazarded a glance behind her.

She stumbled to a stop, stunned.

The storm *surged* across the sky, a majestic and terrible black thunderhead coursing with red lightning. It was enormous, dominating the entire sky, wicked with flashes of inner light.

Raindrops started to pelt her, and though there was no stormwall, the wind was already growing tempestuous.

Wyndle grew in a circle around her. "Mistress? Mistress, oh, this is bad."

She stepped back, transfixed by the boiling mass of black and red. Lightning sprayed down across the slots, and thunder hit her with so much force, it felt as if she should have been flung backward.

"Mistress!"

"Inside," Lift said, scrambling toward the door into the orphanage. It was so dark, she could barely make out the wall. But as she arrived, she immediately noticed something wrong. The door was open.

Surely they'd closed it after she'd left? She slipped in. The room beyond was black, impenetrable, but feeling at the door told her that the bar had been cut right through. Probably from the outside, and with a weapon that sliced wood cleanly. A Shardblade.

Trembling, Lift felt for the cut portion of the bar on the floor, then managed to fit it into place, holding the door closed. She turned in the room, listening. She could hear the whimpers of the children, choked sobs.

"Mistress," Wyndle whispered. "You can't fight him."

*I know.*

"There are Words that you must speak."

*They won't help.*

Tonight, the Words were the easy part.

It was hard not to adopt the fear of the children around her. Lift found herself trembling, and stopped somewhere in the center of the room. She couldn't creep along, stumbling over other kids, if she wanted to stop Darkness.

Somewhere distant in the multistory orphanage, she heard thumping. Firm, booted feet on the wooden floors of the second story.

Lift drew in her awesomeness, and started to glow. Light rose from her arms like steam from a hot griddle. It wasn't terribly bright, but in that pure-black room it was enough to show her the children she had heard. They grew quiet, watching her with awe.

"Darkness!" Lift shouted. "The one they call Nin, or Nale! Nakku, the Judge! I'm here."

The thumping above stopped. Lift crossed the room, stepping into the next one and looking up a stairwell. "It's me!" she shouted up it. "The one you tried—and failed—to kill in Azir."

The door to the amphitheater rattled as wind shook it, like someone was outside trying to get in. The footfalls started again, and Darkness appeared at the top of the stairs, holding an amethyst sphere in one hand, a glittering Shardblade in the other. The violet light lit his face from below, outlining his chin and cheeks, but leaving his eyes dark.

They seemed hollow, like the sockets of the creature Lift had met outside.

"I am surprised to see you accept judgment," Darkness said. "I had thought you would remain in presumed safety."

"Yeah," Lift called. "You know, the day the Almighty was handin' out brains to folks? I went out for flatbread that day."

"You come here during a highstorm," Darkness said. "You are trapped in here with me, and I know of your crimes in this city."

"But I got back by the time the Almighty was givin' out looks," Lift called. "What kept you?"

The insult appeared to have no effect, though it was one of her favorites. Darkness seemed to flow like smoke as he started down the stairs, footsteps growing softer, uniform rippling in an unseen wind. Storms, but he looked so *official* in that outfit with the long cuffs, the crisp jacket. Like the very incarnation of law.

Lift scrambled to the right, away from the children, deeper into the orphanage's ground floor. She smelled spices in this direction, and let her nose guide her into a dark kitchen.

"Up the wall," she ordered Wyndle, who grew along it beside the doorway. Lift snatched a tuber from the counter, then grabbed on to Wyndle and climbed. She quieted her awesomeness, becoming dark as she reached the place where wall met ceiling, clinging to Wyndle's thin vines.

Darkness entered below, looking right, then left. He didn't look up, so when he stepped forward, Lift dropped behind him.

Darkness immediately spun, whipping that Shardblade around with a single-handed grip. It sheared through the wall of the doorway and passed a finger's width in front of Lift as she threw herself backward.

She hit the floor and burst alight with awesomeness, Slicking her backside so she slid across the floor away from him, eventually colliding with the wall just below the steps. She untangled her limbs and started climbing the steps on all fours.

"You're an insult to the order you would claim," Darkness said, striding after her.

"Sure, probably," Lift called. "Storms, I'm an insult to my own *self* most days."

"Of course you are," Darkness said, reaching the bottom of the steps. "That sentence has no meaning."

She stuck her tongue out at him. A totally *rational* and *reasonable* way to fight a demigod. He didn't seem to mind, but then, he wouldn't. He had a lump of crusty earwax for a heart. So tragic.

The second floor of the orphanage was filled with smaller rooms, to her left. To her right, another flight of steps led farther upward. Lift dashed left, choking down the uncooked longroot, looking for the Stump. Had Darkness gotten to her? Several rooms held bunks for the children. So the Stump didn't make them sleep in that one big room; they'd probably gathered there because of the storm.

"Mistress!" Wyndle said. "Do you have a plan!"

"I can make Stormlight," Lift said, puffing and drawing a little awesomeness as she checked the room across the hall.

"Yes. Baffling, but true."

"He can't. And spheres are rare, 'cuz nobody expected the storm that came in the middle of the Weeping. So . . ."

"Ah . . . Maybe we wear him down!"

"Can't fight him," Lift said. "Seems the best alternative. Might have to sneak down and get more food though." Where *was* the Stump? No sign of her hiding in these rooms, but also no sign of her murdered corpse.

Lift ducked back into the hallway. Darkness dominated the other end, near the steps. He walked slowly toward her, Shardblade held in a strange reverse grip, with the dangerous end pointing out behind him.

Lift quieted her awesomeness and stopped glowing. She needed to run him out, and maybe make him think she was running low, so he wouldn't conserve.

"I am sorry I must do this," Darkness said. "Once I would have welcomed you as a sister."

"No," Lift said. "You're not really sorry, are you? Can you even *feel* something like sorrow?"

He stopped in the hallway, sphere still gripped before him for light. He actually seemed to be considering her question.

Well, time to move then. She couldn't afford to get cornered, and sometimes that meant charging at the guy with a starvin' Shardblade. He set himself in a swordsman's stance as she dashed toward him, then stepped forward to swing.

Lift shoved herself to the side and Slicked herself, dodging his sword and sliding along the ground to his left. She got past him, but something about it felt too easy. Darkness watched her with careful, discerning eyes. He'd expected to miss her, she was sure of it.

He spun and advanced on her again, stepping quickly to prevent her from getting down the steps to the ground floor. This positioned her near the steps going upward. Darkness seemed to want her to go that direction, so she resisted, backing up along the hallway. Unfortunately, there was only one room on this end, the one above the kitchen. She kicked open the door, looking in. The Stump's bedroom, with a dresser and bedding on the floor. No sign of the Stump herself.

Darkness continued to advance. "You are right. It seems I have finally released myself from the last vestiges of guilt I once felt at doing my duty. Honor has suffused me, changed me. It has been a long time coming."

"Great. So you're like . . . some kind of emotionless spren now."

"Hey," Wyndle said. "That's insulting."

"No," Darkness said, unable to hear Wyndle. "I'm merely a man, perfected." He waved toward her with his sphere. "Men need light, child. Alone we are in darkness, our movements random, based on subjective, changeable minds. But light is pure, and does not change based on our daily whims. To feel guilt at following a code with precision is wasted emotion."

"And other emotion isn't, in your opinion?"

"There are many useful emotions."

"Which you totally feel, all the time."

"Of course I do. . . ." He trailed off, and again seemed to be considering what she'd said. He cocked his head.

Lift jumped forward, Slicking herself again. He was guarding the way down, but she needed to slip past him anyway and head back below. Grab some food, keep him moving up and down until he ran out of power. She anticipated him swinging the sword, and as he did, she shoved herself to the side, her entire body Slick except the palm of her hand, for steering.

Darkness dropped his sphere and moved with sudden, unexpected speed, bursting afire with Stormlight. He dropped his Shardblade, which puffed away, and seized a knife from his belt. As Lift passed, he slammed it down and caught her clothing.

Storms! A normal wound, her awesomeness would have healed. If he'd tried to grab her, she'd have been too Slick, and would have wriggled away. But his knife bit into the wood and caught her by the tail of her overshirt, jerking her to a stop. Slicked as she was, she just kind of bounced and slid back toward him.

He put his hand to the side, summoning his Blade again as Lift frantically scrambled to free herself. The knife had sunk in deeply, and he kept one hand on it. Storms, he was strong! Lift bit his arm, to no effect. She struggled to pull off the overshirt, Slicking herself but not it.

His Shardblade appeared, and he raised it. Lift floundered, half blinded by her shirt, which she had halfway up over her head, obscuring most of her view. But she could feel that Blade descending on her—

Something went *smack,* and Darkness grunted.

Lift peeked out and saw the Stump standing on the steps upward, holding a large length of wood. Darkness shook his head, trying to clear it, and the Stump hit him again.

"Leave my kids alone, you monster," she growled at him. Water dripped from her. She'd taken her spheres up to the top of the building, to charge them. Of course that was where she'd been. She'd mentioned it earlier.

She raised the length of wood above her head. Darkness sighed, then swiped with his Blade, cutting her weapon in half. He pulled his dagger from the ground, freeing Lift. *Yes!*

Then he kicked her, sending her sliding down the hallway on her own Slickness, completely out of control.

"No!" Lift said, withdrawing her Slickness and rolling to a stop. Her vision shook as she saw Darkness turn on the Stump and grab her by the throat, then pull her off the steps and throw her to the ground. The old lady *cracked* as she hit, and fell limp, motionless.

He stabbed her then—not with his Blade, but with his *knife.* Why? Why not finish her?

He turned toward Lift, shadowed by the sphere he'd dropped, more a monster in that moment than the Sleepless thing Lift had seen in the alleyway.

"Still alive," he said to Lift. "But bleeding and unconscious." He kicked his sphere away. "She is too new to know how to feed on Stormlight in this state. You I'll have to impale and wait until you are truly dead. This one though, she can just bleed out. It's happening already."

*I can heal her,* Lift thought, desperate.

He knew that. He was baiting her.

She no longer had time to run him out of Stormlight. Pointing the Shardblade toward Lift, he was now truly just a silhouette. Darkness. True Darkness.

"I don't know what to do," Lift said.

"Say the Words," Wyndle said from beside her.

"I've said them, in my heart." But what good would they do?

Too few people listened to anything other than their own thoughts. But what good would listening do her here? All she could hear was the sound of the storm outside, lightning making the stones vibrate.

Thunder.

A new storm.

*I can't defeat him. I've got to change him.*

Listen.

Lift scrambled toward Darkness, summoning all of her remaining awesomeness. Darkness stepped forward, knife in one hand, Shardblade in the other. She got near to him, and again he guarded the steps downward. He obviously expected her either to go that way, or to stop at the Stump's unconscious body and try to heal her.

Lift did neither. She slid past them both, then turned and scrambled up the steps the Stump had come down a short time earlier.

Darkness cursed, swinging for her, but missing. She reached the third floor, and he charged after her. "You're leaving her to die," he warned, giving chase as Lift found a smaller set of steps that led upward. Onto the roof, hopefully. Had to get him to follow . . .

A trapdoor in the ceiling barred her way, but she flung it open. She emerged into Damnation itself.

Terrible winds, broken by that awful red lightning. A horrific tempest of stinging rain. The "rooftop" was just the flat plain above the city, and Lift didn't spot the Stump's sphere cage. The rain was too blinding, the winds too terrible. She stepped from the trapdoor, but had to immediately huddle down, clinging to the rocks. Wyndle formed handholds for her, whimpering, holding her tightly.

Darkness emerged into the storm, rising from the hole in the clifftop. He saw her, then stepped forward, hefting his Shardblade like an axe.

He swung.

Lift screamed. She let go of Wyndle's vines and raised both hands above herself.

Wyndle sighed a long, soft sigh, melting away, transforming into a silvery length of metal.

She met Darkness's descending Blade with her own weapon. Not a sword. Lift didn't know crem about swords. Her weapon was just a silvery rod. It glowed in the darkness, and it blocked Darkness's blow, though his attack left her arms quivering.

*Ow,* Wyndle's voice said in her head.

Rain beat around them, and crimson lightning blasted down behind Darkness, leaving stark afterimages in Lift's eyes.

"You think you can fight me, child?" he growled, holding his Blade against her rod. "I who have lived immortal lives? I who have slain demigods and survived Desolations? I am the Herald of Justice."

"I will listen," Lift shouted, "to those who have been ignored!"

"What?" Darkness demanded.

"I heard what you said, Darkness! You were trying to prevent the Desolation. Look behind you! Deny what you're seeing!"

Lightning broke the air and howls rose in the city. Across the farmlands, the ruby glare revealed a huddled clump of people. A sorry, sad group. The poor parshmen who had been evicted.

The red lightning seemed to linger with them.

Their eyes were glowing.

"No," Nale said. The storm appeared to withdraw, briefly, around his words. "An . . . isolated event. Parshmen who had . . . who had survived with their forms . . ."

"You've failed," Lift shouted. "It's come."

Nale looked up at the thunderheads, rumbling with power, red light ceaselessly roiling within.

In that moment it seemed, strangely, that something within him emerged. It was stupid of her to think that with everything happening—the rain, the winds, the red lightning—she could see a difference in his eyes. But she swore that she could.

He seemed to focus, like a person waking up from a daze. His sword dropped from his fingers and puffed away into mist.

Then he slumped to his knees. "Storms. Jezrien . . . Ishar . . . It is true. I've failed." He bowed his head.

And he started weeping.

Puffing, feeling clammy and pained by the rain, Lift lowered her rod.

"I failed weeks ago," Nale said. "I knew it then. Oh, God. God the Almighty. It has returned!"

"I'm sorry," Lift said.

He looked to her, face lit red by the continuous lightning, tears mixing with the rain.

"You actually are," he said, then felt at his face. "I wasn't always like this. I *am* getting worse, aren't I? It's true."

"I don't know," Lift said. And then, by instinct, she did something she would never have thought possible.

She hugged Darkness.

He clung to her, this monster, this callous thing that had once been a Herald. He clung to her and wept in the storm. Then, with a crash of thunder, he pushed away from her. He stumbled on the slick rock, blown by the winds, then started to glow.

He shot into the dark sky and vanished. Lift heaved herself to her feet, and rushed down to heal the Stump.

# 20

So you don't hafta be a sword," Lift said. She sat on the Stump's dresser, 'cuz the woman didn't have a proper desk for her to claim.

"A sword is traditional," Wyndle said.

"But you don't *hafta* be one."

"Obviously not," he said, sounding offended. "I must be metal. There is . . . a connection between our power, when condensed, and metal. That said, I've heard stories of spren becoming bows. I don't know how they'd make the string. Perhaps the Radiant carried their own string?"

Lift nodded, but she was barely listening. Who cared about bows and swords and stuff? This opened all *kinds* of more interesting possibilities.

"I do wonder what I'd look like as a sword," Wyndle said.

"You went around all day yesterday *complainin'* about me hitting someone with you!"

"I don't want to be a sword that one *swings,* obviously. But there is something stately about a Shardblade, something to be displayed. I would make a fine one, I should think. Very regal."

A knock came at the door downstairs, and Lift perked up. Unfortunately, it didn't sound like the scribe. She heard the Stump talking to someone who had a soft voice. The door closed shortly thereafter, and the Stump climbed the steps and entered Lift's room, carrying a large plate of pancakes.

Lift's stomach growled, and she stood up on the dresser. "Now, those are *your* pancakes, right?"

The Stump, looking as wizened as ever, stopped in place. "What does it matter?"

"It matters a *ton,*" Lift said. "Those aren't for the kids. You was gonna eat those yourself, right?"

"A dozen pancakes."

"Yes."

"Sure," the Stump said, rolling her eyes. "We'll pretend I was going to eat them all myself." She dropped them onto the dresser beside Lift, who started stuffing her face.

The Stump folded her bony arms, glancing over her shoulder.

"Who was at the door?" Lift asked.

"A mother. Come to insist, ashamed, that she wanted her child back."

"No kidding?" Lift said around bites of pancake. "Mik's mom actually came *back* for him?"

"Obviously she knew her son had been faking his illness. It was part of a scam to . . ." The Stump trailed off.

*Huh,* Lift thought. The mom couldn't have known that Mik had been healed—it had only happened yesterday, and the city was a mess following the storm. Fortunately, it wasn't as bad here as it could have been. Storms blowing one way or the other, in Yeddaw it didn't matter.

She was starvin' for information about the rest of the empire though. Seemed everything had gone wrong again, just in a new way this time.

Still, it was nice to hear a little good news. *Mik's mom actually came back. Guess it does happen once in a while.*

"I've been healing the children," the Stump said. She fingered her shiqua, which had been stabbed clean through by Darkness. Though she'd washed it, her blood had stained the cloth. "You're sure about this?"

"Yeah," Lift said around a bite of pancakes. "You should have a weird little thing hanging around you. Not me. Something *weirder.* Like a vine?"

"A spren," the Stump said. "Not like a vine. Like light reflected on a wall from a mirror . . ."

Lift glanced at Wyndle, who clung to the wall nearby. He nodded his vine face.

"Sure, that'll do. Congrats. You're a starvin' Knight Radiant, Stump. You've been feasting on spheres and healing kids. Probably makes up some for treatin' them like old laundry, eh?"

The Stump regarded Lift, who continued to munch on pancakes.

"I would have thought," the Stump said, "that Knights Radiant would be more majestic."

Lift scrunched up her face at the woman, then thrust her hand to the side and summoned Wyndle in the shape of a large, shimmering, silvery fork. A Shardfork, if you would.

She stabbed him into the pancakes, and unfortunately he went all the way through them, through the plate, and poked holes in the Stump's dresser. Still, she managed to pry up a pancake.

Lift took a big bite out of it. "Majestic as Damnation's own gonads," she proclaimed, then wagged Wyndle at the Stump. "That's saying it fancy-style, so my fork don't complain that I'm bein' crass."

The Stump seemed to have trouble coming up with a response to that, other than to stare at Lift with her jaw slack. She was rescued from looking dumb by someone pounding on the door below. One of the Stump's assistants opened it, but the woman herself hastened down the steps as soon as she heard who it was.

Lift dismissed Wyndle. Eating with your hands was way easier than eating with a fork, even a *very nice* fork. He formed back into a vine and curled up on the wall.

A short time later, Ghenna—the fat scribe from the Grand Indifference—stepped in. Judging by the way the Stump practically scraped the ground bowing to the woman, Lift judged that maybe Ghenna was more important than she'd assumed. Bet she didn't have a magic fork though.

"Normally," the scribe said, "I don't frequent such . . . domiciles as this. People usually come to me."

"I can tell," Lift said. "You obviously don't walk about very much."

The scribe sniffed at that, laying a satchel down on the bed. "His Imperial Majesty has been somewhat cross with us for cutting off the communication before. But he is understanding, as he must be, considering recent events."

"How's the empire doing?" Lift said, chewing on a pancake.

"Surviving," the scribe said. "But in chaos. Smaller villages were hit the worst, but although the storm was longer than a highstorm, its winds were not as bad. The worst was the lightning, which struck many who were unlucky enough to be out traveling."

She unpacked her tools: a spanreed board, paper, and pen. "His Imperial Majesty was very pleased that you contacted me, and he has already sent a message asking for the details of your health."

"Tell him I ain't eaten nearly enough pancakes," Lift said. "And I got this strange wart on my toe that keeps growin' back when I cut it off—I think because I heal myself with my awesomeness, which is starvin' inconvenient."

The scribe looked to her, then sighed and read the message that Gawx had sent her. The empire would survive, it said, but would take long to recover—particularly if the storm kept returning. And then there was the issue with the parshmen, which could prove an even greater danger. He didn't want to share state secrets over spanreed. Mostly he wanted to know if she was all right.

She kind of was. The scribe took to writing what Lift had told her, which would be enough to tell Gawx that she was well.

"Also," Lift added as the woman wrote, "I found another Radiant, only she's *real* old, and kinda looks like an underfed crab without no shell." She looked to the Stump, and shrugged in a half apology. Surely she knew. She had mirrors, right?

"But she's actually kind of nice, and takes care of kids, so we should recruit her or something. If we fight Voidbringers, she can stare at them in a real mean way. They'll break down and tell her all about that time when they ate all the cookies and blamed it on Huisi, the girl what can't talk right."

Huisi snored anyway. She deserved it.

The scribe rolled her eyes, but wrote it. Lift nodded, finishing off the last pancake, a type with a real thick, almost mealy texture. "Okay," she proclaimed, standing up. "That's nine. What's the last one? I'm ready."

"The last one?" the Stump asked.

"Ten types of pancakes," Lift said. "It's why I came to this starvin' city. I've had nine now. Where's the last one?"

"The tenth is dedicated to Tashi," the scribe said absently as she wrote. "It is more a thought than a real entity. We bake nine, and leave the last in memory of Him."

"Wait," Lift said. "So there's only *nine*?"

"Yes."

"You all *lied* to me?"

"Not in so much—"

"Damnation! Wyndle, where'd that Skybreaker go? He's got to hear about this." She pointed at the scribe, then at the Stump. "He let you go for that whole money-laundering thing on my insistence. But when he hears you been *lying* about *pancakes,* I might not be able to hold him back."

Both of them stared at her, as if they thought they were innocent. Lift shook her head, then hopped off the dresser. "Excuse me," she said. "I gotta find the Radiant refreshment room. That's a fancy way of saying—"

"Down the stairs," the Stump said. "On the left. Same place it was this morning."

Lift left them, skipping down the stairs. Then she winked at one of the orphans watching in the main room before slipping out the front door, Wyndle on the ground beside her. She took a deep breath of the wet air, still soggy from the Everstorm. Refuse, broken boards, fallen branches, and discarded cloths littered the ground, snarling up at the many steps that jutted into the street.

But the city *had* survived, and people were already at work cleaning up. They'd lived their entire lives in the shadow of highstorms. They had adapted, and would continue to adapt.

Lift smiled, and started off along the street.

"We're leaving, then?" Wyndle asked.

"Yup."

"Just like that. No farewells."

"Nope."

"This is how it's going to be, isn't it? We'll wander into a city, but before there's time to put down roots, we'll be off again?"

"Sure," Lift said. "Though this time, I thought we might wander back to Azimir and the palace."

Wyndle was so stunned he let her pass him by. Then he zipped up to join her, eager as an axehound puppy. "Really? Oh, mistress. *Really?*"

"I figure," she said, "that nobody knows what they're doin' in life, right? So Gawx and the dusty viziers, they need me." She tapped her head. "I got it figured out."

"You've got what figured out?"

"Nothing at all," Lift said, with the utmost confidence.

*But I will listen to those who are ignored,* she thought. *Even people like Darkness, whom I'd rather never have heard. Maybe that will help.*

They wound through the city, then up the ramp, passing the guard captain, who was on duty there dealing with the even *larger* numbers of refugees coming to the city because they'd lost homes to the storm. She saw Lift, and nearly jumped out of her own boots in surprise.

Lift smiled and dug a pancake out of her pocket. This woman had been visited by Darkness because of her. That sort of thing earned you a debt. So she tossed the woman the pancake—which was really more of a pan*ball* at this point—then used the Stormlight she'd gotten from the ones she'd eaten to start healing the wounds of the refugees.

The guard captain watched in silence, holding her pancake, as Lift moved along the line breathing out Stormlight on everyone like she was tryin' to prove her breath didn't stink none.

It was starvin' hard work. But that was what pancakes was for, makin' kids feel better. Once she was done, and out of Stormlight, she tiredly waved and strode onto the plain outside the city.

"That was very benevolent of you," Wyndle said.

Lift shrugged. It didn't seem like it had made much of a difference—just a few people, and all. But they *were* the type that were forgotten and ignored by most.

"A better knight than me might stay," Lift said. "Heal everyone."

"A big project. Perhaps too big."

"And too small, all the same," Lift said, shoving her hands in her pockets, and walked for a time. She couldn't rightly explain it, but she knew that something larger was coming. And she needed to get to Azir.

Wyndle cleared his throat. Lift braced herself to hear him complain about something, like the silliness of walking all the way here from Azimir, only to walk right back two days later.

". . . I was a very *regal* fork, wouldn't you say?" he asked instead.

Lift glanced at him, then grinned and cocked her head. "Y'know, Wyndle. It's strange, but . . . I'm starting to think you might not be a Voidbringer after all."

# POSTSCRIPT

Lift is one of my favorite characters from the Stormlight Archive, despite the fact that she has had very little screen time so far. I'm grooming her for a larger role in the future of the series, but this leaves me with some challenges. By the time Lift becomes a main Stormlight character, she'll have already sworn several of the oaths—and it feels wrong not to show readers the context of her swearing those oaths.

In working on Stormlight Three, I also noticed a small continuity issue. By the time we see him again in that book, the Herald Nale will have accepted that his work of many centuries (watching and making sure the Radiants don't return) is no longer relevant. This is a major shift in who he is and in his goals as an individual—and it felt wrong to have him undergo this realization offscreen.

*Edgedancer*, then, was an opportunity to fix both of these problems—and to give Lift her own showcase.

Part of my love of writing Lift has to do with the way I get to slip character growth and meaningful moments into otherwise odd or silly-sounding phrases. Such as the fact that in the novelette from *Words of Radiance* she says she's been ten for three years (as a joke) can be foreshadowing with a laugh, which then develops into the fact that she actually thinks her aging stopped at ten. (And has good reason to think that.)

This isn't the sort of thing you can do as a writer with most characters.

I also used this story as an opportunity to show off the Tashikki people, who (not having any major viewpoint characters) were likely not going to get any major development in the main series.

The original plan for this novella was for it to be 18,000 words. It ended up at around 40,000. Ah well. That just happens sometimes. (Particularly when you are me.)